RETURN OF THE
CRIMSON GUARD

TOR BOOKS BY IAN C. ESSLEMONT

Night of Knives

Return of the Crimson Guard

RETURN OF THE CRIMSON GUARD

A NOVEL OF THE MALAZAN EMPIRE

Ian C. Esslemont

TOR®

A Tom Doherty Associates Book

New York

RETURN OF THE CRIMSON GUARD

Copyright © 2008 by Ian Cameron Esslemont

Map by Neil Gower

Previously published in the UK in 2008 in a limited edition by PS Publishing
LLP and by Bantam Press, a division of Transworld Publishers.

A Tor Book
Published by Tom Doherty Associates, LLC
175 Fifth Avenue
New York, NY 10010

www.tor-forge.com

Tor® is a registered trademark of Tom Doherty Associates, LLC.

Library of Congress Cataloging-in-Publication Data

Esslemont, Ian C. (Ian Cameron)
     Return of the Crimson Guard : a novel of the Malazan empire / Ian C.
Esslemont.—1st Tor ed.
       p. cm.
     "A Tom Doherty Associates book."
     ISBN 978-0-7653-2370-5 (hc)
     ISBN 978-0-7653-2372-9 (tpb)
     I. Title.
PS3605.S684R48 2010
813'.6—dc22

                                                                   2009039509

First Tor Edition: April 2010

Printed in the United States of America

0 9 8 7 6 5 4 3 2 1

This novel is dedicated to the first Winnipeg gang of the Treherne Room and the second of Rick's Place. For all those afternoons and evenings honing the trade.

With gratitude I acknowledge Peter Crowther, who made this work possible; John Jarrold, who extended a great deal of faith; and Simon Taylor, whose encouragement and welcome meant, and continue to mean, more than he knows.

Thanks also to Bill Hunter and Chris for their early readings.

Gerri, Conor, Ross, and Callum: you give it meaning.

DRAMATIS PERSONAE

IN UNTA
Imperial High Command

Laseen	Empress
High Fist Anand	Commander 4th Malazan Army (Quon Tali)
Havva Gulen	New Imperial High Mage
Korbolo Dom	High Fist and Sword of the Empire
Possum	Master of the Claw (the Imperial assassins)
Mallick Rel	Councillor and Assembly Representative

Unta Harbour Guard

Atelen Tinsmith	Sergeant of squad
Rigit Hands	Corporal of squad
Nait	Squad saboteur
Heuk	A cadre mage
Honey Boy	Soldier
Least	Half-Barghast soldier

Others in Unta

Coil	A Clawleader
Lady Batevari	A Seeress / Fortuneteller from Darujhistan
Oryan	A Seven Cities mage, bodyguard to Mallick Rel
Taya Radok	A dancing girl / assassin from Darujhistan

IN LI HENG
Malazan Army

Harmin Els D'Shil	A captain of the garrison
Gujran	A captain of the garrison
Banath	A sergeant of the garrison
Fallow	A healer of the garrison

Storo Matash's Squad

Storo Matash	Captain of a saboteur company, 3rd Army veteran
Shaky	Ranking saboteur
Hurl	Saboteur
Sunny	Saboteur
Silk	Squad corporal and cadre mage
Jalor	A Seven Cities recruit
Rell	A Genabackan recruit

Civilians in Li Heng

Magistrate Ehrlann	Member of the Ruling Council of Magistrates
Jamaer	Ehrlann's servant
Magistrate Plengyllen	Member of the Ruling Council of Magistrates
Liss	A city mage
Ahl	A city mage (with brothers Thal and Lar)

IN CAWN

Nevall Od' Orr	Chief Factor of Cawn
Groten	Nevall's bodyguard

ON THE SETI PLAINS

Toc the Elder	Seti Warlord and Malazan 'Old Guard'
Wildman	Seti champion, also known as 'the Boar', Sweetgrass
Imotan	Shaman of the Jackal warrior society
Hipal	Shaman of the Ferret warrior society
Captain Moss	Malazan cavalry captain
Redden Brokeleg	Ataman (chieftain) of the Plains Lion Assembly
Ortal	Ataman (chieftain) of the Black Ferret Assembly

ON THE WICKAN FRONTIER
Malazan Army

Rillish Jal Keth	Lieutenant of the Malazan 4th Army
Chord	Company sergeant
Talia	Malazan veteran

Wickans

Clearwater	A Wickan shaman
Nil	A Wickan warlock and veteran of the Seven Cities campaigns
Nether	A Wickan witch and veteran of the Seven Cities campaigns
Mane	A young Wickan warrior
Udep	A Wickan hetman (chieftain)

In the Pit

Ho (Hothalar)	A Li Heng mage
Yathengar 'ul Amal	A Seven Cities priest ('Faladan')
Sessin	Yathengar's bodyguard
Grief	A new prisoner
Treat	A new prisoner
Devaleth	A Korelan sea-witch and new prisoner
Su	A Wickan witch

IN QUON TALI PROVINCE

Ghelel Rhik Tayliin	Duchess, and last surviving member of the Tayliin family line
Amaron	Malazan 'Old Guard', once commander of the Talons
Choss	Malazan 'Old Guard', once High Fist
Marquis Jhardin	Commander of the Marchland Sentries
Prevost Razala	A cavalry captain
Molk	An agent of Amaron's

THE CRIMSON GUARD
Surviving Named Avowed

K'azz D'Avore	Commander, known by various titles

First Company

Skinner	Captain
Mara	Company mage
Gwynn	Company mage
Petal	Company mage
Kalt	Lieutenant
Farese	
Hist	
Shijel	
Black the Lesser	

Second Company

Shimmer	Captain
Cowl	High Mage and Master of Assassins, 'Veils'
Stoop	Siegemaster of the Guard
Smoky	Company mage
Shellarr	'Shell', company mage
Blues	Company mage and swordmaster
Fingers	Company mage
Opal	Company mage
Isha	Company assassin, 'Veil'
Keitil	Company assassin, 'Veil'
Cole	
Treat	
Dim	
Reed	
Amatt	
Sept	
Lazar	
Halfdan	
Lean	
Inese	
Turgal	

Third Company

Tarkhan	Captain and company assassin, 'Veil'
Lor-sinn	Company mage
Sour	Company mage
Toby	Company mage

Balkin   Company mage
Lacy   Company assassin, 'Veil'
Black
Baker
Janeth
Slate
Bower
Lucky

Fourth Company
Cal-Brinn   Captain and company mage
Iron Bars
Jup Alat

Among the First Induction (recruitment)
Sergeant Trench
Corlo
Voss
Ambrose
Palla

Among the Second Induction
Lurgman Parsell, 'Twisty'
Jaris
Pilgrim
Ogilvy
Bakar
Tolt
Meek
Harman
Grere
Geddin
Boll

Among the Third Induction
Stalker
Badlands
Coots
Kyle

OF THE TALIAN LEAGUE

Urko Crust	Commander of Falaran forces, 'Old Guard', also known as 'Shatterer'
V'thell	Commander of Gold Moranth forces
Choss	Commander of Talian forces, 'Old Guard'
Toc the Elder	Seti Warlord, 'Old Guard'
Amaron	Chief of intelligence, 'Old Guard'
Ullen Khadeve	Urko's lieutenant-commander and chief of staff, 'Old Guard'
Bala Jesselt	Cadre mage, 'Old Guard'
Eselen Tonley	A captain of Falaran cavalry
Orlat Kepten	A captain of Talian forces, 'Old Guard'

OTHERS

Liossercal	Ascendant, titled 'Son of Light,' also known as Osserc, Osric
Anomandaris	Ascendant, titled 'Son of Darkness'
Jhest Golanjar	Jacuruku mage
Shen	A warlock
Tayschrenn	Imperial High Mage
D'Ebbin	Malazan commander 4th Army, 'Fist'
Braven Tooth	Malazan Command Master Sergeant
Temp	Malazan Master Sergeant
Blossom	Moranth Gold officer
Tourmaline	Moranth Gold infantry sergeant
Cartharon Crust	Captain of the *Ragstopper*, rumoured 'Old Guard'
Denuth	An Elder, among the Firstborn to Mother Earth
Draconus	An Elder God
Ereko	An ancient wanderer
Greymane	Once a Malazan Fist, now outlawed
Lim Tal	Ex-private guard of Untan noble
Traveller	A wanderer of mixed Dal Hon and Quon descent
Ragman/ Tatterdemalion	A wanderer of the Imperial Warren

This, the first of wars, paroxysmed for time unmeasured. Ever Light thrust yet dissipated, and ever Night retreated yet smothered. Thus the two combatants locked in an ever-widening gyre of eternal creation and destruction. Countless champions of both Houses arose, scoured the face of creation in their potency, only to fall each in turn, their names now lost to memory.

Then, in what some named the ten thousandth turn of the spreading whorl of the two hosts, there came to the shimmering curtain edge of battle one unknown to either House, and he did castigate the combatants.

'Who are you to speak thusly?' demanded he who would come to be known as Draconus.

'One who has moved upon the Void long enough to know this will never end.'

'It is ordained,' answered a champion of Light, Liossercal. 'Ever must one rise, the other fall.'

Disdainful, the newcomer thrust the opponents apart. *'Then agree that this be so and name it done!'*

And so both Houses fell upon the stranger tearing him into countless fragments.

Thus was Shadow born and the first great sundering ended.

Myth Fragment
Compendium Primal, Mantle

PROLOGUE

The Elder Age,
Time unmeasured

THE ERUPTION HAD WOUNDED THE WORLD. DENUTH, A CHILD of the Earth, was first to penetrate the curtains of drifting cinders and so come upon the crater. Steaming water the colour of slate pooled at the centre of a basin leagues across. A slope of naked jagged rock led down to the silent shore. All was still, layered in a snow of ash. Yet a stirring of movement caught his attention and he picked his way to the water's edge to find an entity sembled in a shape akin to his own with two legs and arms, but slashed and gouged by ferocious wounds. Blood was a black crust upon the one and darkened the waters around him.

Gently, Denuth turned the being over only to start, amazed. '*Liossercal!* Father's own first born! Who is it that set upon you?'

A savage smile of blunt canine tusks. 'None. Best ask whom I set upon. Are there no others?'

'None I saw.'

The smile crooked down to a feral scowl. 'All consumed then. Taken by the blast.'

'Blast?' Denuth narrowed his gaze upon the alien power. Yes, alien – for who could possibly fathom the mind of one born with Light's first eruption? 'What exactly has occurred here?'

Wincing, Liossercal shrugged himself from Denuth's support. He sat hunched, arms clasped tight about himself as if to hold his body together. Thick dark blood welled fresh from his deeper lacerations. 'An experiment. An attempt. An assault. Call it what you will.'

'An assault? Upon what? There was naught here but . . ' Denuth's voice died away into the stillness of the ash-choked water. 'Mother

1

Preserve us! An Azath!' Glancing about, he took in the immense crater, attempted to grasp the scale of the calamity. *It has pained us all!* 'You fool! Would you stop at nothing in your questing?'

The pale head rose, amber eyes hot. 'I do as I choose.'

Denuth recoiled. *Indeed. And here then was the quandary. Something must be done about these ancient powers before their antagonisms and limitless ambitions destroy all order once again. Draconus's solution horrifies, yet well now could I almost understand such ... exigencies. After all, was not eternal imprisonment preferable to such potential for destruction?*

Liossercal struggled to his feet, stiff, hissing at his many wounds, and Denuth knew a terrible temptation. Never before had he heard an account of this entity so vulnerable, so weakened. Soletaken, Elient, what were such labels to this power who may have moved through Light before it knew Dark? Yet now he was obviously wounded almost unto expiration. Should he act now? Would ever such a chance come again to anyone?

As if following the chain of the Child of Earth's thoughts, Liossercal smiled, upthrusting canines prominent. 'Do not be tempted, Denuth. Draconus is a fool. His conclusions flawed. Rigidity is not the answer.'

'And what is?'

A pained grimace, fingers gently probed a deep laceration high on one cheek. 'I was exploring alternatives.'

'Explore elsewhere.'

A flash of white rage, quelled. 'Well taken, Child of Earth. He comes, does he not?'

'He does. And he brings his answer with him.'

'I had best go.'

'Indeed.'

Liossercal threw his arms up, his outline blurring, sembling, but he gasped in mid-shift, roared his pain and collapsed to the shore. A dragon shape of silver and gold writhed over the brittle rocks before Denuth who hurriedly backed away. Boulders crashed into the lake as slashed wings laboured. Eventually, unsteady, the enormous bulk arose to snake heavily away. Its long tail hissed a cut through the steaming waters of the crater.

Denuth remained, motionless. Wavelets crossed the limpid water, lapped silently. The snow of cinders limned the dull black basalt of his shoulders and arms. Then steps crunched over the broken rock and he felt a biting cold darkness at his side, as of the emptiness that was said to abide between the stars. Keeping his face averted, Denuth bowed. 'Consort of Dark and Suzerain of Night. Draconus. Greetings.'

'Consort no longer,' came a dry rasping voice. 'And that suzerainty long defied. But I thank you just the same.'

Rigid, Denuth refused to turn to regard the ancient potent being, and the equally alarming darkness he carried at his side. How many had disappeared into that Void, and what horrifying shape would its final forging take? Such extreme measures yet revolted him.

'So,' Draconus breathed. 'The Bastard of Light himself. And weakened. His essence will be a great addition.'

That which Denuth thought of as his soul shivered within him. 'He is not for you.'

A cold regard. Denuth urged himself not to look.

After some time, 'Is this a foretelling – from *Her*?'

'My own small adeptness. I suspect he may one day find that which he seeks.'

'And that is?'

'That which we all seek. Union with the *All*.'

Time passed. Denuth sensed careful consideration within the entity at his side. He heard rough scales that were not of metal catching and scraping as armoured arms crossed. A slow thoughtful exhalation. 'Nonetheless. I will pursue. After all, I offer my own version of union . . . Is that not so?'

Your perversion of it. But Denuth said nothing; he knew he walked a delicate line with this power that could take him should he wish. Only a reluctance to antagonize his parent, Mother to all who come from the Earth, stilled this ancient one's hand. 'Perhaps Anomandaris—' Denuth began.

'Speak not to me of that upstart,' Draconus grated. 'I will bring him to heel soon enough.'

And I hope to be nowhere near when that should come to pass . . .

The power stirred, arms uncrossed. 'Very well, Child of the Earth. I leave you to your – ah, contemplations. A troubling manifestation of existence, this world. All is change and flux. Yet I find in it a strange attraction. Perhaps I shall remain a time here.' Such a prospect made Denuth's stone hands grind as they clenched.

Ultimately, after no further words from either, the soul-numbing cold night gathered, swirling, and Denuth once again found himself alone on the bleak shore. It occurred to him that peace would evade everyone so long as entities such as these strode the face of the world pursuing their ages-old feuds, enmities and uncurbed ambitions. Perhaps once the last has withdrawn to uninterrupted slumber – as so many have, or been slain, or interred – perhaps only then would accord come to those who may walk the lands in such a distant time.

Or perhaps not. Denuth was doubtful. If he had learned anything from observing these struggles it was that new generations arose to slavishly take up the prejudices and goals of the old. A sad premonition of the future. He sat on the shore and crossed his legs – a heap of rock no different from the tumbled broken wreckage surrounding him. This unending strife of all against all wearied him. Why must they contend so? Was it truly no more than pettiness and childish prickliness, as Kilmandaros suggests? He would consider what it might take to end these eternal cycles of violence. And he would consult with Mother. It would, he imagined, take some time to find an answer. Should there be any.

BOOK I

Diaspora's End

CHAPTER I

'The wise say that as vows are sworn, so are they reaped. I have
found this to be true.'

Prince K'azz D'Avore
Founder of the Crimson Guard

The Weeping Plains,
Bael Subcontinent
1165th year of Burn's Sleep
11th year of Empress Laseen's reign
99th year of the Crimson Guard's Vow

ON THE EDGE OF A TILED ROOFTOP, A SMALL TENT HEAVED AND
swayed under the force of the battering wind. It was nothing
more than an oilskin cape propped up by a stick, barely
enough to keep off the worst of the pounding rain. Beneath it sat a
youth squinting into the growing murk of storm and twilight.
Occasionally he glimpsed the ruins of surrounding buildings wrecked
by the siege and, if he looked hard enough, he could just make out
high above the rearing silhouette of the Spur.

What, he wondered, was the point of having a watch if you
couldn't see a damned thing?

The Spur towered alone, hundreds of feet above the plains. Local
legend had it an ancient power raised it when the world was young
– perhaps the warlock, Shen, occupying it now. Kyle knew nothing
of that. He knew only that the Guard had besieged the rock more
than a year ago and still wasn't anywhere near to taking it. What was
more, he knew that from the fortress on its peak Shen could take on
all the company's mage corps and leave them cross-eyed and panting.

He was powerful enough for that. *And when a situation like that comes around*, Stoop had told him, *it's time for us pike-pushers to stick our noses in.*

Stoop – a saboteur, and old enough to know better. He was down in the cellar right now, wielding a pick in his one hand. And he wasn't alone – with him worked the rest of the Ninth Blade alongside a few other men tapped by Sergeant Trench. All of them bashing away at the stone floor with hammers and sledges and picks.

The wind gusted rain into Kyle's face and he shivered. To his mind the stupid thing was that they hadn't told anyone about it. *Don't want anyone stealing our thunder*, Stoop had said grinning like a fool. But then, they'd all grinned like fools when Stalker put the plan to Trench. They trusted his local knowledge being from this side of Seeker's Deep, like Kyle himself. Stalker had been recruited a few years back during the Guard's migration through this region. He knew the local dialects, and was familiar with local lore. That was to be expected from a scout, Kyle knew.

The Guard had bought *him* from a Nabrajan slave column to help guide them across the steppes. But he didn't know these southern tongues. His people raided the Nabrajans more often than they talked to them.

Kyle pulled the front fold of the cloak tighter about himself. He wished he understood the Guard's native tongue, Talian, better too. When Stoop, Trench and Stalker had sat with their heads together, he'd crept close enough to overhear their whispers. Their dialect was difficult to make out, though. He'd had to turn the words over and over before they began to make sense. It seemed Stalker had put together different legends: that of the ancient Ascendant who'd supposedly raised the Spur and started a golden age, and this current 'Reign of Night' with its ruins. Since then he and the others had been underground taking apart the walls and stone floor, Stoop no doubt muttering about his damned *stolen thunder*. Kyle whispered a short prayer to Father Wind, his people's guiding spirit. If this worked he figured they were in for more thunder than they'd like.

Then there was the matter of these 'Old Guard' rivalries and jealousies. He couldn't understand the first of it even though he'd been with the Guard for almost a year now. Guard lore had it his Ninth Blade was one of the storied, established a century before, and first commanded by a legendary figure named Skinner. Stoop put a lot of weight on such legends. He'd hopped from foot to foot in his eagerness to put one over the Guard's mage corps and its covert Veils.

The rain fell hard now, laced by hail. Above, the clouds in the darkening sky tumbled and roiled, but something caught Kyle's eye – movement. Dim shapes ducked through the ceiling of clouds. Winged fiends summoned by Shen on the Spur above. Lightning twisted actinic-bright about them, but they circled in a lazy descent. Kyle peered up as they glided overhead, wings extended and eyes blazing. He prayed to Wind for them to pass on.

Then, as if some invisible blade had eviscerated it, the leading creature burst open from chin to groin. It dissolved into a cloud of inky smoke and its companions shrieked their alarm. As one they bent their wings and turned towards the source of the attack. Kyle muttered another prayer, this one of thanks. Cowl must be on the roster tonight – only the company's premier mage could have launched so strong an assault.

Despite the battle overhead, Kyle yawned and stretched. His wet clothes stuck to his skin and made him shiver. A year ago such a demonstration would have sent him scrambling for cover. It was the worst of his people's stories come to life: fiends in the night, men wielding the powers of a shaman but turned to evil, warlocks. Then, he had cringed beneath broken roofs. Now, after so many months of sorcerous duelling the horror of these exchanges had completely worn away. For half a bell the fireworks kept up – fireworks – something else Kyle hadn't encountered until his conscription into the Guard. Now, as though it was there for his entertainment, he watched a green and pink nimbus wavering atop a building in the merchants' district. The fiends swooped over it, their calls harsh, almost taunting, as they attacked. One by one they disappeared – destroyed, banished or returned of their own accord to the dark sky. Then there was nothing but the hissing rain and the constant low grumble of thunder that made Kyle drowsy.

Footsteps from the tower at the corner of the roof brought him around. Stalker had come up the stairs. His conical helmet made him look taller, elegant even, with the braided silk cord that wrapped it. No cloak this night – instead he wore the Guard's surcoat of dark crimson over a boiled and studded leather hauberk, and his usual knee-high leather moccasins. The man squinted then sniffed at the rain. Beneath his blond moustache his mouth twisted into a lazy half-smile. Stalker's smiles always made Kyle uneasy. Perhaps it was because the man's mouth seemed unaccustomed to them, and his bright hazel eyes never shared them.

'All right,' he announced from the shelter of the stairwell. 'We're set. Everyone's downstairs.'

Kyle let the tented cape fall off his head and clambered over the roof's broken tiles and dark gaps. Stalker had already started down the circular stairway, so Kyle followed. They were halfway down before it occurred to him that when Stalker had smiled, he'd been squinting up at the Spur.

The cellar beneath was no more than a vault-roofed grotto. Armed and armoured men stood shoulder to shoulder. They numbered about thirty. Kyle recognized fewer than half. Steam rose from some, mixing with the sooty smoke of torches and lanterns. The haze made Kyle's eyes water. He rubbed them with the back of his hand and gave a deep cough.

A hole had been smashed through the smoothly set blocks of the floor and through it Kyle saw steps leading down. A drop ran coldly from his hair down his neck and he shivered. Everyone seemed to be waiting. He shifted his wet feet and coughed into his hand. Close by a massive broad-shouldered man was speaking in low tones with Sergeant Trench. Now he turned Kyle's way. With a catch of breath, Kyle recognized the flattened nose, the heavy mouth, the deeply set grey-blue eyes. Lieutenant Greymane. Not one of the true elite of the Guard himself, but the nearest thing to it. The man waved a gauntleted hand to the pit and a spidery fellow in coarse brown robes with wild, kinky black hair led the way down. Smoky, that was his name, Kyle remembered. A mage, an original Avowed – one of the surviving twenty or so men and women in this company who had sworn the Vow of eternal loyalty to the founder of this mercenary company, K'azz D'Avore.

The men filed down. Greymane stepped in followed by Sergeant Trench, Stoop, Meek, Harman, Grere, Pilgrim, Whitey, Ambrose and others Kyle didn't know. He was about to join the line when Stalker touched his arm.

'You and I – we're the rear guard.'

'Great.'

Of course, Kyle reflected, as the Ninth's scouts, the rear was where they ought to be given what lay ahead. They'd been watching the fireworks for too long now and seen the full mage corps of the company scrambling on the defensive. Kyle was happy to leave that confrontation to the heavies up front.

The stairs ended at a long corridor flooded with a foot of stagnant water. Rivulets squirmed down the worked-stone walls. Rats squealed and panicked in the water, and the men cursed and kicked at them. From what Kyle could tell in the gloom, the corridor appeared to be leading them straight to the Spur. He imagined the file of dark figures an assembly of ghosts – phantoms sloshing wearily to a rendezvous with fate.

His thoughts turned to his own youthful night raids. Brothers, sisters and friends banding together against the neighbouring clan's young warriors. Prize-stealing mostly, a test of adulthood, and, he could admit now, there had been little else to do. The Nabrajans had always been encroaching upon his people's lands. Settlements no more than collections of homesteads, but growing. His last raid ended when he and his brothers and sisters encountered something they had no words for: a garrison.

The column stopped abruptly and Kyle ran into the compact, bald-headed man at his front. This man turned and flashed a quick smile. His teeth were uneven but bright in the dark. 'Ogilvy's the name.' His voice was so hoarse as to be almost inaudible. 'The Thirty-Second.'

'Kyle. The Ninth.'

Ogilvy nodded, glanced to Stalker, nodded again. 'We'll have the spook this time. Ol' Grey's gonna get Cowl's goat.'

Cowl. Besides being the company's most feared mage, the Avowed was also second in command under Shimmer and the leader of the Veils, killers of a hardened kind Kyle couldn't have imagined a year before. He had seen those two commanders only from a distance and hoped to keep it that way.

Stalker frowned his scepticism. 'This Greymane better be as good as everyone says.'

Ogilvy chuckled and his eyes lit with a hidden joke. 'A price on his head offered by the Korelans and the Malazans too. Renegade to both, he is. They call him Stonewielder. I hear he's worth a barrelful of black pearls.'

'Why?' Kyle asked.

Ogilvy shrugged his beefy shoulders. 'Betrayed 'em both, didn't he? Hope to find out exactly how one of these days, hey?' He winked to Kyle. 'You two are locals, ain't ya?'

Kyle nodded. Stalker didn't. He didn't move at all.

Ogilvy rubbed a hand over the scars marbling his bald scalp. 'Well, I've been with the Guard some ten years now. Signed on in Genabackis.'

Kyle had heard much of that contract. It was the company's last major one, ending years ago when the Malazan offensive fell to pieces. All the old hands grumbled that the Malazan Empire just wasn't what it used to be. And while the veterans were close-mouthed about their and the Guard's past, Kyle gathered they often opposed these Malazans.

11

'This contract's been a damned strange one,' Ogilvy continued. 'We're just keeping our heads down, hey? While the mage corps practise blowing smoke outta their arses. Not the Guard's style.' He glanced significantly at them. 'Been recruiting to bust a gut, too.'

The column started moving again and Ogilvy sloshed noisily away.

'What was that about?' Kyle asked Stalker as they walked.

'I don't know. This Ogilvy has been with the Guard for a decade and even he's in the dark. I've been doing a lot of listening. This company seems divided against itself – the old against the new.'

The tall lean scout clasped Kyle's arm in a grip sharp as the bite of a hound. They stopped, and the silence seemed to ring in Kyle's ears. 'But I'll tell you this,' he said, leaning close, the shadows swallowing his face, 'there are those in this Crimson Guard who have wandered the land a very long time indeed. They have amassed power and knowledge. And I don't believe they intend to let it go. It's an old story – one I had hoped to have left behind.'

He released Kyle's arm and walked on leaving him alone in the dark and silence of the tunnel. Kyle stood there wondering what to make of all that until the rats became bold and tried to climb his legs.

He found Stalker at a twisted iron gate that must have once spanned the corridor. He was bent low, inspecting it, a tiny nub of candle cupped in one hand.

'What is it?' Kyle whispered.

'A wreck. But more important than what is when. This is recent. The iron is still warm from its mangling. Did you hear anything?'

'I thought maybe something . . . earlier.'

'Yes. As did I.' He squinted ahead to a dim golden lantern's glow where the column's rear was slowly disappearing. He squeezed a small leather pouch at his neck and rubbed it. A habit Kyle had noticed before. 'I have heard talk of this Greymane. They say he's much more than he seems . . .'

Kyle studied the wrenched and bowed frame. The bars were fully half as thick around as his wrist. Was the northerner suggesting that somehow Greymane had thrust it aside? He snorted. Ridiculous!

Stalker's eyes, glowing hazel in the flame, shifted to him. 'Don't be so quick to judge. I've fought many things and seen a lot I still do not believe.'

Kyle wanted to ask about all these other battles but the man appeared troubled. He glanced to Kyle twice, his eyes touched by worry as if he regretted speaking his mind.

In the light of Stalker's candle Kyle could make out a short set of steps rising beyond the gate. It glittered darkly – black basalt, the rock of the Spur. The steps had been worn almost to bowls at their centre. He straightened; his hand seemed to find the grip of his tulwar on its own. Stalker shook out the candle and after a moment Kyle could discern the glow of lantern light ahead.

They met up with Ogilvy who gestured up and gave a whistle of awe. The tunnel opened to a circular chamber cut from the same rock as the steps. More black basalt, the very root-rock of the Spur. The dimensions of the chamber bothered Kyle until he realized it was the base of a hollow circular stairway. Torches flickered where the stairs began, rising to spiral tightly around the inside of the chamber's wall. Squinting up, he saw the column slowly ascending, two men abreast, Smoky and Greymane leading. He stepped out into the centre and looked straight up. Beyond the men, from high above, dark-blue light cascaded down along with a fine mist of rain. The moisture kissed his upturned face. A flash of lightning illuminated a tiny coin-sized disc at the very top of the hollowed-out column of rock. Dizzy and sickened, Kyle leant against one slick, cold wall. Far away the wind howled like a chained dog, punctuated by the occasional drum-roll of thunder.

Without a word, Stalker stepped to the stairs, a hand on the grip of his longsword. His leather moccasins were soundless against the rounded stone ledges. Ogilvy slapped Kyle on his back. 'C'mon, lad. Just a short hike before the night's done, hey?' and he chuckled.

After the twentieth full revolution of the stairs, Kyle studied curving symbols gouged unevenly into the wall at shoulder height. They were part of a running panel that climbed with the stairs. Portions of it showed through where the moss and cobwebs had been brushed aside. It seemed to tell a story but Kyle had never been taught his symbols. He recognized one only: the curling spiral of Wind. His people's totem.

After a time his legs became numb, his breath short. What would be there waiting for them? And more importantly, what did Smoky and Greymane plan to do about it? Just ahead, Ogilvy grunted and exhaled noisily through his flattened nose. The veteran maintained an even pace despite a full mail coif, shirt and skirting that hung rustling and hissing with each step. Kyle's armour, what cast-offs the guard could spare, chafed his neck raw and tore the flesh of his shoulders. His outfit consisted of an oversized hauberk of layered and lacquered horn and bone stripping over quilted undershirts, sleeves of soft leather sewn with steel rings – many of these missing – studded skirting over leather leggings, gloves backed with mail, and a naked iron helmet with a nose guard that was so oversized it nearly rested on his shoulders. Kyle had adjusted its fit by wrapping a rag underneath. The combined weight made the climb torture. Yet one morning a year ago when Stoop had dumped the pieces in his lap he had felt like the richest man in all Bael lands. Not even their tribe's war-leader could have boasted such a collection. Now he felt like the company's beggar fool.

He concentrated on his footing, tried to grimace down the flaring pain of his thighs, chafed shoulders and his blazing lungs. Back among his brothers and cousins he'd been counted one of the strongest runners, able to jog from sun's rise to sun's set. There was no way he'd let this old veteran walk him into the ground.

A shout from above and Kyle stopped. Distant blows sounded together with shouts of alarm. Weapons hissed from sheaths. He leaned out to peer up the inner circular gap but couldn't see what was going on. He turned to speak to Ogilvy but the veteran silenced him with a raised hand. The man's eyes glistened in the dark and he held his blade high. Gone was the joking, bantering mask and in its place was set a cold poised killer, the smiling mouth now tight in a feral grin. It was a chilling transformation.

The column moved again, steel brushing against stone in jerking fits and starts. Three circuits of the stairs brought Kyle to a shallow alcove recessed into the wall. At its base lay the broken remains of an armoured corpse, ages dead. Its desiccated flesh had cured to a leathery dark brown. Kyle stared until Ogilvy pushed him on.

'What in Wind's name was that?' he asked, hushed.

Ogilvy was about to shrug but stopped himself and instead spat out over the open edge. 'A guardian. Revenant. I've heard of 'em.'

Kyle was startled to see that he'd unsheathed his tulwar. He didn't remember doing that. 'Was it . . . dead?'

Ogilvy gave him a long measuring stare. 'It is now. So be quiet, and keep your eyes open. There'll be trouble soon.'

'How do you know?'

'Like fish in a barrel.' He jerked his head to the rear. 'Tripped the alarm, didn't we? He'll be here, or should be. Stay between me and the wall, hey?'

That sounded fine to Kyle and he was about to ask why when a burst of light flashed above blinding him followed by a report that shook the steps. Ogilvy snatched at the ringed leather of his sleeve, pulling him back from the open lip of the stairs. Wind sucked at him as something large rushed past down the central emptiness. A scream broke the silence following the report. Kyle's vision returned in time for him to see a Guardsman plummet by down into darkness – the head and neck a bloody ruin. At his side, Ogilvy fumed.

'He's pullin' us off one by one! Where's Grey?'

Kyle squinted up the hollow column; he could see better now that they were nearly at the top where moonlight and lightning flashes streamed down with the misted rain. A dark shape hovered. The warlock, Shen. Guardsmen swung torches and swords at him. He stood on nothing, erect, wrapped in shifting shadows. His hands were large pale claws. One of those claws reached out for another man but was swatted aside. Shen snarled and gestured. A cerulean flash blazed. A Guardsman crumpled as if gut-stabbed; he tottered outward, fell like a statue rushing past so close his boots almost struck Kyle's upturned face.

Guardsmen howled their rage. Thrown weapons and crossbow bolts glanced from the slim erect figure. He laughed. His gaze shifted to the man next in line. Kyle leaned out as far as he dared, howled his own impotent rage and fear.

'Hood drag you down, you piece of inhuman shit!' Ogilvy bellowed, shaking his fist.

Above, Smoky leaned out to Shen, his hands open, palms out at stomach level. Guardsmen lining the curve of the stairs spun away, raised arms across their faces.

'Heads up!' Ogilvy snapped and pulled Kyle back by his hauberk.

Flames exploded in the hollow tube of the circular staircase. They churned at Kyle like liquid metal. He gulped heated air and covered his face. A kiln thrust itself at him. Flames yammered at his ears, scalded the back of his hands. Then, like a burst of wind, popping his ears, the flames snapped away leaving him gasping for breath. Through the smoke and stink of burnt hair and singed leather he heard Ogilvy croak, 'Togg's teeth, Smoky. Take it down a notch.'

They peered up, searched the smoke for some sign of the warlock. Churning, spinning, the clouds gathered as if drawn by a sucking wind and disappeared leaving an apparently unhurt Shen hovering in the emptiness. The warlock raised his amber gaze to Smoky, reached out a pale clawed hand. Kyle yearned to be up there, to aid Smoky, the only mage accompanying their party. It was clear to him now that they were hopelessly out-classed.

The arm stretched for Smoky. The warlock curled his pale fingers, beckoning. The men close enough swung but to no effect. Then the hulking shape of Greymane appeared, stepping forward from the shadows and he thrust a wide blade straight out. The two-handed sword impaled Shen who gaped, astonished. The warlock's mouth stretched open and he let go an ear-tearing shriek and grasped the sword with both hands. He lurched himself backwards off the blade. Before Greymane could thrust again the warlock shot straight up through the opening.

At Kyle's side, Ogilvy scratched his chin and peered speculatively to the top. 'Well, that wasn't so bad now, was it?' he said with a wink.

Kyle stared, wordless. He shook his head, horrified and relieved. Then he started, remembering. 'Stalker!' Searching the men, Kyle spotted him close to Greymane. They locked gazes then Stalker, his pale eyes bright against the darkness of his face, looked away.

Ogilvy sniffed and sheathed his sword. 'Asked me to keep an eye on you, he did. Back down at the bottom.'

'I don't need anyone to keep an eye on me.'

'Then there's one thing you'll have to learn if you want to stay live in this business,' Ogilvy hawked and spat into the pit. 'And that's accepting help when it's offered 'cause it won't be too often.'

The column moved again and Ogilvy started up the stairs.

They exited from the corner tower of a rectangular walled court. The rain lashed sideways, driven as harshly as sand in a windstorm. The men huddled in groups wherever cover offered. Kyle fought to pull on his leather cape and ran to the waist-high ledge of an over-flowing pond and pressed himself into its slim protection. Cloud-cover smothered the fortress like fog. The wind roared so loud together with the discharge of thunder that men side by side had to shout into each other's ears to be heard. By the almost constant discharge of lightning, Kyle saw that the structure was less a fortress and more of a walled private dwelling. The central courtyard, the walls, the benches, the buildings, were all made from the living black basalt of the Spur. He was astounded by the amount of work that must have gone into the carving.

Only Greymane stood upright, his thick trunk-like legs apart and long grey hair whipping about from under his helmet. He motioned with his gauntleted hands, dividing the men into parties. Kyle wondered what he had done with the two-handed sword he'd used against Shen, for the renegade carried no sheath large enough for it – only a slim longsword now hung at his belt.

Smoky suddenly appeared skittering toward Kyle like a storm-driven crow. His soaked robes clung to his skinny frame. His black hair, slicked by the rain, gave his narrow face the frenzied look of a half-drowned rat.

'You the scout, Kyle?' the mage yelled, his voice hoarse.

Kyle nodded.

A shudder took the mage and he scowled miserably, drew his soaked robes tighter about his neck. The rain ran in rivulets down his face. He pointed to four men near Kyle. These men nodded their acknowledgement. Of them, Kyle knew only one: Geddin, a hulking swordsman Kyle was relieved to have with him.

Smoky leaned his mouth close to Kyle's ear. Even in the rain, soaked through to the bone, the smell of wood smoke and hot metal still unaccountably wafted from the man. He pointed a bony finger to a wall fronted by a long colonnade entirely carved of the dark basalt: the roof, pillars and dark portals that opened to rooms within. 'We check out these rooms. You got point.'

Smoky caught Kyle's reaction to that announcement and he laughed. The laugh transformed into a racking cough.

Kyle drew his tulwar and searched for intervening cover. Point. Great.

'Wait.' Smoky grasped Kyle's weapon hand.

Kyle almost yanked free, but he remembered Ogilvy's words and stopped himself. The mage frowned as he studied the blade. Kyle waited, unsure. Now what was the matter? The rain beat upon his shoulders. The mage's grip was uncomfortably hot. Smoky turned to peer to where Greymane stood with his group. Kyle could see nothing more than a smear of shapes through the slanting curtains of rain. Smoky raised Kyle's sword and arm, his brows rising in an unspoken question. Kyle squinted but could make out nothing of Greymane's face or gestures. The mage grunted, evidently seeing some answer and fished a slim steel needle from his robes. He began scratching at the curved blade. 'Anything you want? Your name? Oponn's favour? Fire, maybe?'

Thinking of his own totem, Kyle answered, 'Wind.'

The needle stopped moving. Rain pattered like sling missiles against Kyle's shoulders. Smoky looked up, his eyes slitted, searching Kyle's face, and then he flashed a conspiratorial grin. 'Saw the histories on the way up too, aye? Good choice.' He etched the spiral of Wind into the blade. Incredibly, the tempered iron melted like wax under Smoky's firm pressure. The sword's grip heated in Kyle's hand.

17

Rain hissed, misting from the blade. The mage released him. What had that been all about? What of Wind? What was it his father used to say . . . '*All are at the mercy of the wind*'?

Kyle looked up to see Smoky, impatient, wave him ahead.

The rooms hollowed out of solid basalt were empty. Kyle kicked aside rotting leaves and the remains of crumbled wood furniture. He felt disappointment but also, ashamedly, relief as well. He felt exposed, helpless. What could *he* do against this warlock? His stomach was a tight acid knot and his limbs shook with uncoiled tension.

Ahead, the wind moaning and a mist of rain betrayed an opening through to the outside. He entered a three-walled room facing out over the edge of the Spur. The lashing wind yanked at him and he steadied himself in the portal. The room held a large wood and rope cage slung beneath a timber boom that appeared able to be swung out over the gulf. Rope led up from the cage to a recess in the roof then descended again at the room's rear where it circled a fat winch barrel as tall as a man.

Smoky peered in over Kyle's shoulder. He patted his back. 'Our way down.'

'Not in this wind,' grumbled one of the men behind Smoky. 'We'll be smashed to pieces.'

Scowling, Smoky turned on the Guardsman – perhaps the only one in the company shorter than him. 'Always with a complaint, hey, Junior?'

A concussion shook the stone beneath their feet, cutting off any further talk. Distant muted reports of rock cracking made Kyle's teeth ache. Smoky recovered his balance, cackled. 'Ol' Grey's fished him out!'

A second bone-rattling explosion kicked at the rock. Kyle swore he felt the entire Spur sway. He steadied himself. The hemp and wood cage rocked, creaking and thumping in its housings. Smoky's grin fell and he wiped water from his face. 'I think.'

'Let's go back,' suggested another Guardsman, one Kyle couldn't name. He'd used the company's native tongue, Talian. 'The Brethren are worried.'

Pulling at his sodden robes, Smoky grunted his assent. Kyle eyed this unknown Guardsman; *brethren*, the man had said. He'd heard the word used before. Something to do with the elite of the Guard, the originals, the Avowed. Or perhaps another word for them, used only among themselves? Kyle continued to study the fellow sidelong: battered scale hauberk, a large shield at his back, sheathed longsword. He could very well be of the Avowed himself – they wore no torcs or rank insignias. You couldn't tell them from any other Guardsman. Stoop had explained it was deliberate: *fear*, the old fellow had said. *No one knows who they're facing. Makes 'em think twice, that does.*

When they returned to the inner chambers, Guardsmen filled the rooms. It appeared to be a pre-arranged rallying point. Through the arched gaps between stone pillars Kyle watched the mercenaries converging on the complex of rooms. Men slipped, fumbling on the rain-slick polished stone. He turned to the short mercenary beside him. 'What's going on, Junior?'

Beneath the lip of his sodden cloth-wrapped helmet, the man's eyes flicked to Kyle, wide with outrage. 'The name's not *Junior*,' he forced through clenched teeth.

Kyle cursed his stupidity and these odd foreign names. 'Sorry. Smoky called you that.'

'*Smoky* can call anyone whatever he damned well pleases. *You* better show more respect . . .'

'Sorry, I—'

Someone yanked on Kyle's hauberk; he spun to find Stoop. The old sapper flashed him a wink, said, 'Let's not bother friend Boll here with our questions. He's not the helpful type.'

Boll's lips stretched even tighter into a straight hound's smile. Inclining his helmet to Stoop, he pushed himself from the wall and edged his way through the crowd of Guardsmen.

'What's going on?' Kyle whispered.

'Not too sure right now,' the old veteran admitted candidly. 'Have to wait to find out. In this business that's how it is most of the time, you know.'

And just what business is that? Kyle almost asked, but the men all suddenly stood to attention, weapons ready. Kyle peered about, confused. What was going on? Why was he always the last to know? It seemed to him that they straightened in unison like puppets on one string. It was as if the veteran Guardsmen shared a silent language or instinct that he lacked. Countless times he'd been sitting in a room watching a card game, or dozing in a barracks, only to see the men snap alert as if catching a drum's sounding. At such times he and the other recent recruits were always the last ready, always bringing up the rear.

This time Kyle spotted everyone's centre of attention as the open portal of the main structure on the far side of the roof garden. The men assembled along the colonnade, levelled cocked crossbows at that door. The front rank knelt and the rear rank stood over them. Kyle himself carried no such weapon as the company was running short.

'Here they come,' Stoop murmured.

Through the sheets of driving rain, Kyle made out a squad of men exiting the portal. Greymane emerged last. All alone he manhandled shut its stone slab of a door. The men jog-trotted across the abutting levels of gardens and patios. They threw themselves behind benches and stone garden planters that now held nothing more than the beaten down stalks of dead brush. These men and women covered the doorway while their companions jogged and skittered to another section of the courtyard. Stalker was among them, his own crossbow held high. Greymane brought up the rear, walking slowly and heavily as if deep in thought. Not once did he look behind. Oddly, wind-lashed mist plumed from the man like a banner.

The men reached the cover of the colonnade. As Greymane emerged from the curtain of rain Kyle saw that a layer of ice covered the man – icicles hung from the skirts of his hanging scaled armour. The Malazan renegade slapped at the ice, sending shards tinkling to the stone floor. Vapour curled from him like smoke. To Kyle's astonishment, no one commented upon this.

Smoky closed to Greymane's side. 'Can't take the cage,' he shouted. 'The wind's too blasted high.'

Greymane nodded wearily. 'The stairs are no good. Shen saw to that.'

The solid stone under Kyle's feet jumped as if kicked. A column cracked, splitting like a dry tree trunk, sending men ducking and flinching aside. Rock dust stung Kyle's nose.

'He's awake,' Greymane said to some unspoken question from Smoky. 'Be here any moment.' He turned to face the main building which was a long and low black bunker without windows or ornamentation. 'Shen woke it before I could stop him, the filthy Warren-leech.' At Greymane's side, Sergeant Trench waved to the men to spread out. They shuffled to both sides, crouching for cover, crossbows trained.

Smoky rubbed his rat-thin moustache while chewing on his lower lip. 'Maybe we ought to get Cowl.'

Greymane's sky-pale eyes flashed, then he rubbed them with a gauntleted hand and sighed. 'No. Not yet.' He crossed his arms. 'Let's see what we've roused.'

Kyle almost spoke then. What was going on? These two seemed to have led everyone into a position without escape. What was wrong with the stairs? Stoop, as if reading his mind, caught his eye and glanced to the back of the rooms. Kyle nodded.

He met Stoop at the last portal offering a view out on the courtyard. Before them, men crouched and leaned behind pillars, crossbows ready. They muttered among themselves in low voices, glanced with tired gauging eyes to Greymane. A few laughs even reached Kyle through the thunder and drumming of rain. He wondered whether half this mercenary business was simply how much indifference you could muster in the face of impending death.

Stoop gave him an encouraging grin, rubbed his hand at a thigh. 'What is it, lad? You look like your favourite horse just dropped down dead.'

Despite himself, Kyle burst out a short laugh. Great Wind preserve him! Was the man insane? 'We're trapped, aren't we? There's no escape and the Mocking Twins alone know what's about to swallow us.'

Stoop's brows rose. He pulled off his boiled leather cap of a helmet and scratched his scalp. 'Damn me for a thick-headed fool. One forgets, you know. Serve with the same men long enough and it gets so you can read their minds.' He felt at his fringe of brush-cut hair, crushed something between his fingernails. His eyes, meeting Kyle's, were so pale as to be almost colourless. 'Sorry, lad. I forgot how green you are. And me the one who swore you in too! A fine state of affairs.' He glanced away, chuckling.

'And?' Kyle prompted.

'Ah! Yes. Well, lad. You see, Shen – the warlock – he's dead now. Greymane finished him. But the thing Cowl and Smoky feared might be up here, is. Shen has been bleeding off its power all this time. Then he woke it when he died. It's powerful, and damned old.'

'What is it?'

'Some kind of powerful mage. A magus. Maybe even an Ascendant of some kind. A master of the Warren of Serc.'

Ascendant – Kyle had heard the name a few times – a man or woman of great power? He knew his own tribal labels for the Warrens. Some of the elders still insisted upon calling them 'The Holds'. But he didn't know the Talian names. 'Serc. What Warren is that?'

'Sky.'

It was as if the very wind howling around Kyle whisked him away into the air, tumbling head over heels while the roaring all around transformed into thunderous laughter. The booming filled his head, drove out all thought. He remembered his father saying that thunder was Wind laughing at the conceit of humans and all their absurd

21

struggles. His vision seemed to narrow into a tiny tunnel as if he were once again peering up the Spur's hollow circular staircase. Blinking and shaking his head, he felt as if he were still spinning.

Stoop was peering away, distracted. 'Have to go, lad.' Without waiting for an answer the old saboteur clapped Kyle on the shoulder and edged his way through the men.

Kyle fell back against a wall, his knees numb. He raised the tulwar to his eyes. Water beaded and ran from the Wind symbol etched into its iron. Could it be? Could this being be one of them? A founder of his people. A blessed Spirit of Wind?

The rain was thinning, and Kyle squinted into the surrounding walls of solid cloud. The Spur seemed to have pierced some other realm – a world of angry slate-dark clouds and remorseless wind. Even as Kyle watched, that wind rose to a gale, scattering the pools of rainwater and driving everyone behind cover. Only Greymane remained standing, legs wide, one scaled arm shielding his face.

The door to the main house burst outward as if propelled by a blast such as those Moranth munitions Kyle had heard described. It exploded into fragments that shot through the air and cracked like crossbow bolts from the pillars and walls. Kyle flinched as a shard clipped his leg. One Guardsman was snatched backwards and fell so stiffly and utterly silent that no one bothered to lower their aim to check his condition.

A man stepped out. Kyle was struck by the immediate impression of solidity, though the fellow was not so wide as Greymane. His hair was thick, bone-white and braided – and lay completely unmoved by the wind. His complexion was as pale as snow. Folded and tasselled wool robes fell in cascading layers from his shoulders to his feet. Not one curl or edge waved. It was as if the man occupied some oasis of stillness within the storm.

His gaze moved with steady deliberation from face to face. When that argent gaze fixed upon Kyle he found that he had to turn away; the eyes seized him like a possession and terrified him by what they seemed to promise. For some reason he felt shame heat his face – as if he were somehow unworthy. The winds eased then, their lashing and howling falling away. The churning dense clouds seemed to withdraw as if gathering strength for one last onslaught.

Into the calm walked Smoky. His sandals slapped the wet stone. The magus – and Kyle held little doubt the being was at least that – watched the little man with apparent amusement. Smoky knelt and did something with his hands over the stone floor. Flames shot out from his hands along the wet rock. The line of fire darted forward very like a snake nosing ever closer to the entity. The magus watched all this with a kind of patient curiosity. His head edged down slightly as his eyes shifted to follow the flame's advance.

Once the line of fire reached close to the magus's sandalled feet, it split into two branches that encircled him. The being's heavy gaze climbed to regard Smoky who flinched beneath its weight. The magus flicked his fingers and the flames burst outwards like shattered glass. Smoky flew backwards as if punched. He slid across the slick stone to lie at Greymane's feet. 'That's something you don't see every day,' Kyle heard the little man gasp. The magus was immobile but Greymane didn't take his eyes from him to acknowledge Smoky. 'We ought to call *him*,' the mage said, pushing himself up.

The magus slowly raised his arms straight outwards from its body as if he were a bird about to take flight. Greymane took a breath to speak but stopped, glancing sharply to one side. Three figures, two men and one woman, all wearing wind-whipped dark cloaks, approached up the colonnaded walk. Three whom Kyle knew for certain had not come with the party. Greymane cursed under his breath. Smoky blew on his hands and kneaded them together.

The Guardsmen edged aside for these three. The lead one Kyle knew for Cowl, hatchet-faced, bearing blue curled tattoos at his chin and a thatching of pearly knife-scars at his neck. His seconds Kyle assumed to be Keitil, a dark-faced plainsman like himself though from a place called Wick. And Isha, a wide solid woman with long, coarse dark hair woven in a single braid. All three were Veils, covert killers – mercenary assassins.

Greymane shot a look to Smoky who shrugged, saying, 'The Brethren must've gone to him.'

'I see you've made some headway,' Cowl called to Greymane.

The renegade hunched his shoulders and bit down any response. He finally ground out, 'I don't want your kind of help.'

Cowl waved a gloved hand. 'Then by all means – bring it to a close either way. If you can.'

Greymane shifted his gaze to the immobile magus. '*Your* solution's always the same. It requires no thought . . .'

'Something's up,' Smoky warned.

The magus had bent his head back to regard the clouds above. He edged his arms up further, straight, hands open, fingers splayed. The thick wool sleeves of his robes fell away revealing the blue swirling tattoos of spirals and waves encircling both arms – from his hands all the way up to his naked shoulders: the assembled symbols of Wind.

'No!' Kyle choked out. A Spirit of Wind! He must be! A Blessed Ancestor – so claim his tribe's teachings. Kyle lurched forward, opened his mouth to call out. A warning? A plea?

But Cowl shouted, '*Get down.*'

The magus stretched his arms high, reached up as if grasping the clouds. His hands clenched into fists then the arms snapped down.

A fusillade of lightning lashed the Spur. The barrage seemed to drive the stone down beneath their feet. Men howled all around, true terror cracking their voices. Kyle fell as the rock kicked back at him. The continuous flashing blinded him. He lay with his arms over his head, shouting wordlessly, begging that it end.

The storm passed. Thunder crashed and grumbled off across the leagues of plains surrounding them. Kyle raised his head, blinking. He felt as if he had been beaten all over by lengths of wood. All around Guardsmen dragged themselves upright, groggy and groaning. Incredibly, Greymane still stood. Kyle wondered whether anything could drive him from his feet – though he was wincing and had his face bent to one shoulder to shield his eyes. Smoky lay motionless on the floor. Stoop was cradling the mage's head and examining his eyes.

The magus had not moved at all; he stood now with his arms crossed.

Kyle crawled to Stoop. 'Will he be all right?'

Stoop cuffed the mage's cheek. 'Think so. He's a tough one.'

Kyle peered around; Cowl and his two followers were gone. 'Where are the Veils?'

'They're on the job.'

Kyle straightened up. 'What do you mean? *On the job?*'

The old saboteur jerked his head to the magus.

'No!' Kyle pushed himself to his feet.

'Lad?' Stoop squinted up. 'What's that, lad?'

'They can't. They mustn't . . .'

Stoop took hold of Kyle's arm. 'The fiend's a menace to everyone. We've had a hand in its rousing so we ought to—'

'No! He hasn't threatened anyone.'

Stoop just shook his head. 'Sorry. That's not the way things work. We can't risk it.'

Kyle pulled away and staggered out to the courtyard.

'Lad!'

As he ran, he could not help flinching with every step. He was certain that at any instant lightning would blast him into charred flesh. But nothing struck. No lightning flashed, nor one crossbow bolt flew – he also feared summary justice from the Guard for his disobedience. There were shouts; the voices garbled through the howling wind. The magus remained as immobile as any one of the other stone statues decorating the court. His heavy-browed head was cocked to one side as if he were listening. Listening for some distant message.

Kyle vaulted benches, crossed mosaics of inlaid white and pink stone. At some point he had drawn his sword – perhaps not the wisest thing to do while charging a magus or possible Ascendant. But he would have to stop to sheathe it, and he couldn't bring himself to throw it away either. Somewhere about lurked Cowl and his two Veils.

'Ancient One!' he shouted into the gusting, lashing wind. '*Look out!*'

The being uncrossed his arms. His crooked smile grew. Cowl appeared then at the man's back: he just stepped out from empty air. Something unseen tripped Kyle, sending him tumbling and sliding along the slick rock. Cowl struck with a blurred lashing of both arms.

Kyle yelled his frustrated rage. The world burst into shards of white light. He spun while an explosion boomed out. The noise echoed and re-echoed, transforming into a terrifying world-shaking laughter that roared on and on while he spun falling and tumbling, terrified that it would never end or that he would at any instant smash to pieces upon rocks.

Distantly, beneath the roaring, he heard a woman say in the Guard's native tongue, 'So, what in Shadow's smile was that?'

A man answered, 'I'm not sure.'

'Did you connect?'

'Yes, surprisingly. Solid. At the end though – strange. Still, he's gone for good. I'm sure.'

The woman spoke again, closer, 'What of this one?'

'He's alive. Looks like the sword took most of the blast.'

A hand, cool and wet, held his chin, edged his head back and forth. The woman asked, 'Can you hear me?'

Kyle couldn't answer. It was as if had lost all contact with his flesh. Slowly, darkness gathered once more: a soft furry dark that smothered his awareness. The woman spoke again but her voice was no more than a murmur. Then silence.

Pain jabbed him awake. A fearsome blazing from his right hand. Blearily, he raised it to his eyes and found it swaddled in rags. He frowned, tried to remember something.

'With us again, hey?' a familiar hoarse voice asked.

He edged his head up, hissed at the bursts of starry pain that throbbed within his skull. Stoop was sitting next to him. They were within one of the rooms carved from black basalt. A guardsman sat propped up against a wall beyond Stoop. Rags wrapped his face where one brown eye stared out, watching him like a beacon burning far off on the plains at night.

Kyle looked away, swallowed to wet his throat. 'What – what happened?'

Stoop shrugged, drew a clay pipe from a pouch at his belt. 'Cowl knifed the magus, or Ascendant, or whatever by the Cult of Tragedy he was. Lightning like the very end of creation like some religions keep jabbering on about came blasting down right then and there and when it stopped only the Veils were left standing. Not a single sign left of the bugger. Burst into ashes. You're damned lucky to be alive. Left your hand crisp as a flame-cooked partridge though.'

Kyle peered at the dressings. Gone? Killed? 'How could that be?'

With his thumb, Stoop tamped rustleaf into the pipe bowl. 'Oh, you don't know Cowl like I do. Ain't nothing alive he can't kill.' Stoop, leaned close. 'I told 'em you was rushing in to do him in yourself. You know – make your name for yourself an' all that. Something like "The Damned Fool with the Flaming Hand". Something like that. If you understand me.'

Kyle snorted a laugh then held his throbbing head and groaned. 'Yeah. I understand. So, now what?'

Stoop clamped the pipe between his teeth. 'So now we wait. The wind's dying. Soon it will be safe enough to take the basket down. Our contract's finished now.'

'Did you succeed?'

Stoop's grey bushy brows drew together. 'Succeed? What're you gettin' at?'

'Stealing your thunder.'

The old saboteur sighed, took his pipe from his mouth and shoved it back into his pouch. 'Now, lad, don't get yourself all in a—'

'You knew some *thing* or some *one* was up here, didn't you? All along?' He pushed himself up to one elbow, tried to get up on a knee. Stoop took him under the arm and pulled him upright. He leaned against the cool reviving wall. He pressed his left hand to his forehead to stop its spinning. 'That's why you came here in the first place, isn't it? Why you took this contract – even though it was a strange one for the Guard?'

Stoop hovered at Kyle's side, ready should he faint. 'Now, no need to get all lathered up. Sure we suspected there was something worth our time up here. Otherwise we would've kept right on going. I'm sorry that you 'n' him were both pledged to Wind.'

Kyle laughed. *Pledged!*

'That's just unfortunate. That's all. Why, us soldiers, we're used to that. Half the men I've killed were sworn to Togg, same as myself. Doesn't mean nothing, lad.'

Kyle shook his head. 'You don't understand.' How could anyone not of his people see that that being must have been a Wind Spirit itself. And they killed it. Yet how could Cowl, a mere mortal, kill a spirit? Surely that was impossible.

'Well, maybe we don't understand. We're just passing through Bael lands after all. 'Struth. But I know there is one thing we understand and you don't.' Stoop pointed to the west. 'The Guard is locked in a duel to the death with a great power, lad. A force that would lay waste to these entire lands to get to us.'

'The Malazans.'

'You've the right of it. Good to see that you've been paying attention. Now, power is power. We knew this warlock, Shen, was no way potent enough to whip up this sort of storm. Why, the entire weather of this subcontinent is affected. Your own plains are dry because of all the rains that are drawn here to run off to the eastern coast. We'd hoped it was something we could use in our war against the damned Malazans. But, as you saw, it was some blasted dreaming magus.'

'Dreaming?'

'Yes. Cowl says that all this – the storm – was summoned up and sustained just by his dreaming. Imagine that, hey?'

Kyle almost threw himself upon Stoop. *You fools! You've slain a God of my people!* But blinding pain hammered within his skull and he rubbed furiously with his one good hand at his forehead.

'You OK, lad?'

Kyle jerked a nod. 'Could use some fresh air.'

Stoop took his arm to help him up the corridor. Outside, beyond the colonnaded walk, Guardsmen were lounging on the benches and planters, talking, resting and oiling weapons and armour. Stoop sat Kyle on the top ledge of a broad set of stairs that led down to a sunken patio, now a fetid pool of rotting leaves and branches. Clouds still enshrouded the Spur's top and would remain for some time yet, Kyle imagined. But the edge was off the storm. Thunder no longer burst overhead or rumbled out over the plains spread out below. High sheet lightning flickered and raced far above, leaping and flashing soundlessly.

It could not be. How could it? It was impossible. Nothing after this, he decided, could ever touch him again. Yet *something* had happened. He studied his wrapped hand. It was numb of any feeling but for a constant nagging ache. They must've put some kind of salve on it. His tulwar, he noted, had been sheathed by some considerate soul. Odd-handed, he drew it. The leather of the grip came away like dry bark in his hand. He brushed away the burnt material leaving the scorch-marked tang naked. The blade, however, remained clean and unmarred. The swirls and curls of Wind seemed to dance down its gleaming length. Turning it over, Kyle paused: the design now ran down both sides of the curved blade. He didn't remember Smoky engraving both sides.

He touched the cold blade to his forehead and invoked a prayer to Wind. He'd have to get it re-gripped. And he'd name it *Tcharka*. Gift of Wind. And he'd never forget what happened here this day.

'Have a rest,' Stoop advised. 'It'll be a while yet.'

Kyle let his head fall back to the stone wall. Through slitted eyes he spotted Stalker crouched against a pillar next to two Guardsmen he didn't know; one extraordinarily hairy and ferociously scarred; the other an older man whose beard was braided and tied off in small tails. Both were nut brown, as burly as bears, and reminded Kyle of the men of the Stone Mountains to the far west of his lands. The scout watched him with his startling bright hazel eyes while murmuring aside to the men. Exhausted, Kyle drowsed in the fitful weak wind.

Near dawn came Kyle's turn in the basket. He and four others stepped in while the wicker, hemp and wood construction hung extended out over empty yawning space. Eight Guardsmen manned the iron arms of the winch. A gusting wind pulled and tossed Kyle's hair as he now carried his helmet under an arm.

'How will they get down?' he asked a man with him in the basket as the crew started edging the winch on its first revolution.

The Guardsman swung a lazy glance up to the men at the winch. A smile of cruellest humour touched his lips. 'Poor bastards. Better them than us. They'll have to come down the ropes.'

The wind rose as the basket descended close to the naked cliffs. It batted at the frail construction and pulled at Kyle's Crimson Guard surcoat. *Us*, the Guardsman had said. Kyle knew now he was one of them yet could never be one with them. He was part of the brotherhood but that same brotherhood had killed something like his God: one of his people's ancestors, progenitors, guides or protectors – perhaps even an avatar of the one great Father Wind himself. He knew now it would be easier for him to use the weapon at his side. To turn flat, unresponsive eyes upon death and killing. To do what must be done. He studied the men suspended with him over what could be their own deaths. Two watched the clouds above, perhaps searching for hints of the coming weather. Another peered down, curious perhaps as to where they might disembark. The last stared ahead at nothing. Their eyes, surrounded by a hatching of wrinkles, appeared flat and empty. These were the ones who could not be touched. Kyle felt drawn to them, sensed now that he shared something of the dead world they inhabited. He watched their sweaty, scarred, boiled-leather faces and felt his own hardening into that mask. He could stare at them now, at anyone dead or alive, and not see them.

CHAPTER II

For generations the poles of the Quon Talian continent stood as the province of Unta in the east and the province of Quon Tali (which gave the land its name) in the west. Each in turn dominated mercantile trade and strove to crush its distant rival while the lesser states, Itko Kan, Cawn, Gris and Dal Hon, danced in a myriad of alliances, trade combines and Troikas marshalled against one or both of these poles. Who could have predicted that these two major capitals would fall to the invader while poorer states would resist for years?

Chronicler Denoshen
South Kan Hermitages

UNDER A BLAZING NOON SUN THE CROWD JOSTLING ITS WAY UP Unta's street of Opals thickened to an immovable clamouring mass. Ahead, the thoroughfare debouched into Reacher's Square where the animal roar of tens of thousands of voices buffeted those straining for entrance. Second-storey balconies facing the street sagged with the weight of more paying spectators than good sense should allow.

For the frustrated citizens caught in the street, advance was impossible. Possum, however, easily slipped his way forward, edging from slim gap to slim gap, passing with a brush here or a well-placed elbow there. Those of his profession were trained to use crowds and this was one reason why he enjoyed them so much. Anonymity, it seemed to him, was assured as one among so many. But it was also his opinion of human nature that with so many people gathered together no one could possibly organize anything.

He stepped out on to the littered bricks of Reacher's Square to find it a heaving sea of citizens of the Empire; for today was execution day. The Empress was dispatching her enemies in as messy and public a manner as possible. All to serve as salutary warnings to those contemplating any such crimes. And of course to entertain her loyal masses. Edging his way around the perimeter of the huge square, Possum kept close to one enclosing wall. He estimated the crowd at some fifty thousand, all peering and straining their attention to the central platform where various minor criminals had already met their ends in beheadings, eviscerations and impalings.

This month's crowd was above average and Possum had no doubt the extra numbers were lured by the star prisoner scheduled to meet his excruciating and bloody end this day: Janul of Gris Province. Mage, once High Fist, who, during the recent times of unrest had named himself Tyrant of Delanss and was only brought to heel by a rather expensive diversion of resources. For this Janul rightly earned the Empress's ire and thus this very public venue for his expiration. Yet it could also be that all these citizens crammed into Reacher's Square – and, Possum could admit, himself as well – wondered that perhaps another reason lay behind this particular execution: that long ago Janul had been of the emperor's select cadre. He was *Old Guard*.

As Possum slipped behind the backs of men and women, someone addressed him. This alone was not unusual as he had through the Warren of Mockra altered his appearance only slightly while dressing as a common labourer. In the jostling crowd all around him people gossiped, yelled their wares and made bets on the fates of the condemned. This voice, however, had spoken from Hood's Paths. Possum straightened, turned and peered about. No one seemed to be paying him any particular attention.

'*Up*,' the voice urged. '*Up here.*'

Possum looked up. The enclosing wall rose featureless, constructed of close-fitted stone blocks mottled by mould and lichen. There, at the very top nearly four man-lengths above, rested small balls resembling some joker of Oponn's idea of battlements: a row of spiked human heads.

He turned away, glanced about – could it be?

'*Yes. Up here.*'

Possum leaned against the wall, his face to the rear of the crowd. 'You can hear me?' he whispered low.

'*I have ears.*'

'That's about all.'

Possum sensed exasperation glowing from the other side of Hood's Paths. '*Fine. Let's have them – get them all over with.*'

'What?'

31

'*The head jokes. I can tell you're just aching to try one. Like, ended up ahead, didn't you?*'

Possum snorted. A few men and women glanced his way. He coughed, hawked up phlegm and spat. The faces turned away.

'Hood forefend! I would never be so insensitive.'

'*Sure. Like I was spiked yesterday.*'

'Why are we talking then? Poor company up there? Cat got their tongues?'

'*I have a message for you.*'

Despite his control, Possum stiffened. Such a message could only be from one source. 'Yes,' he managed, his voice even fainter.

'*They are returning.*'

'Who are?'

'*The death-cheaters. The defiers. All the withholders and arrogators.*'

'Who?'

'*Ah – here comes one now.*'

Possum lurched forward into a ready crouch, weapons slipping into his palms. He scanned the nearest backs. Who? What was this spirit on about? A woman stepped out from the crowd. Short, athletic with dishevelled tightly cropped grey-shot hair, dressed as a servant in a plain shirt and frayed linen trousers, her feet bare and dirty.

His superior, Empress Laseen.

Possum straightened. 'I didn't think you'd come.'

Laseen regarded him through half-lidded eyes. 'Who were you speaking with just now?'

'No one. I was talking to myself.'

'How very boring for you.'

Rage flashed hot across Possum's vision. He exhaled, unclenched his shoulders. *In time. In due time.*

Laseen continued her lazy regard. Always judging, it seemed to Possum. How far could she push? How much does he fear me?

She laughed then, suddenly. 'Poor Urdren. How transparent you are.'

Possum stared, uncertain. Urdren? How could she know his first name? He'd left it behind – along with the corpse of his father.

Laseen turned away. 'She's here. I'm sure of it. Keep an eye out. I'll circulate.'

Possum almost bowed but caught himself in time. Laseen disappeared into the crowd. He returned to leaning against the wall.

'*He told me you wouldn't tell her.*'

'Who told you?'

A sigh from the other side. '*Think about it.*'

'What do you mean, "death-cheaters"?'

'*How do I know? I'm just the messenger boy.*'

'What do you—'

'*Here he is. The main attraction.*'

A sussurant wave of anticipation swept through the crowd, surged to a deafening roar. Possum, at the very rear, could see nothing of the stage. 'Have a good view, do you?'

'*Best seat in the house.*'

In many ways Possum was indifferent to the show; it wasn't why he was here. While he scanned the backs of heads, watching for movement or the blooming of Warren magics, he asked, 'So, what's happening?'

'*Janul's been led out. Looks like he's been worked over already. His hands are tied behind his back, his clothes are torn. Might be doped. We used to do that in the old days before the emperor. But then, I don't recall a Talent ever being up there. How does one manage that anyway?*'

'Otataral dust.'

'*Ah. I see.*'

'What about you? You're obviously a Talent. Weren't you executed?'

'*We up here along this wall are all that's left of the last ruling council of Unta.*'

Possum was impressed. That was long before his time.

'*When Kellanved's fleet took the harbour I fled inland with half the city's treasury. The horses panicked and the blasted carriage toppled over. Broke my neck.*'

The crowd roared, shouting all at once. Fists shook in the air. 'What is it?'

'*They're reading out the charges. A brazier's been set up. Knives are being sharpened. Looks like they're going to cook his entrails right in front of him while keeping him alive as long as possible. Never seen it work.*'

'It will this time.'

'*How so?*'

'A Denul healer will sustain him.'

'*But the Otataral?*'

'Precious little is used. The strain of the opposing forces of the magic-deadening Otataral and the healing magics would kill him, of course – if he lived long enough.'

'*I see. He is being restrained, standing, head forced down to watch. His shirts have been torn away. A cut is being made side to side across his lower abdomen. Another cut, this one vertical down his front. The brazier's being moved closer. Now they're—*'

The crowd thundered a roar that to Possum sounded of commingled disgust, fear, awe and fascination. Yet the mass pressed even closer to the stage, confirming for Possum his opinion of human nature.

'*They've set his viscera on to the hot coals in front of him – he's still standing! – though I cannot say for certain that he is conscious. What is this? A large axe?*'

'They will dismember him now, starting at the hands, cauterizing each cut.'

'*I'll give you this – you Malazans put on better shows than we ever did. A hand is gone. He must be unconscious, supported by the executioner's assistants. No, I see his mouth moving. Here comes another of the defiers.*'

Startled, Possum flinched from the wall, crouching, scanning the backs of the crowd before him. A woman edged into view, faced him. Not a slim athletic figure such as the Empress but a stocky older woman, grey-haired, mouth wrinkled tight and frowning her displeasure. Their target this night: Janul's sister and partner, Janelle.

'You,' she spat. 'The lap-dog. I'd hoped for the lap itself.'

Possum smiled. 'I like to think of myself as a lap-guard-dog.'

'Save your poor wit.' The woman straightened, crossed her arms. 'I know what you want and I'm not going to give it to you.'

Edging one foot forward, Possum scanned her carefully. A dangerous mage, an adept of the D'riss Warren. Together the two siblings had run many dangerous missions for Kellanved. Yet he detected no active magics. What was this?

She hissed a long breath through her clamped teeth. 'Hurry, damn you. I'm losing my nerve.'

Possum darted forward. He hugged her to him, slipped his longest stiletto up through her abdominal cavity. She clung to him with that startled look they always get when cold iron pricks the heart.

'At least you can stab straight,' she gasped huskily into his ear.

Faces nearby turned to them. 'The heat,' Possum said. 'Poor woman.' They turned away. He brought his face close to hers. '*Why?*'

The woman's expression relaxed into a kind of wistfulness. 'There he goes, they will say,' she whispered. 'He took Janelle, they will say

34

. . . but *you'll* know. You'll know what you have always known,' she took a shuddering wet breath, '. . . that you are nothing more than . . . a fraud.'

Possum lowered her to the ground, kneeling over her. *Damn the bitch! This was not how things were supposed to go.* He stepped away from the body, slipped behind bystanders, edged his way slowly to the opening of the street of Opals. As he went he relaxed his limbs, allowed himself to merge with the crowd streaming from the square. Behind him the meat that had been Janul was being chopped to pieces and those pieces thrown into a fire to be burned to ashes. Ashes that would then be tossed into Unta Bay.

He walked as just another of the crowd, jostled, head down. But all the while he wondered at the iron self-control it would take, when all that mattered was lost and there was nothing left, to somehow turn even one's death into a kind of victory. Could he manage the same when his time came? Denying one's killer everything; even the least satisfaction of a professional challenge. He couldn't imagine it. A fool might dismiss the act as despair but he saw it as defiance. And was the difference so fine as to reside in the eye of the beholder?

He recognized the calloused bare dirty feet walking along beside his and straightened from his musings.

Laseen too was quiet. Her hands were clasped behind her back. He imagined she too was thinking of the dead woman – dead compatriot – Possum corrected himself. And thinking of that, how far back together might the three of them have known each other? Something not to forget, he decided.

Glancing about, he noted the bodyguard now walking with them ahead and behind. *A bodyguard selected by me since Pearl's disaster on Malaz took so many.*

After a time Laseen nodded to herself as if ending an internal conversation. She cleared her throat. 'I want you to personally look into a number of recent things that have been troubling me. Domestic disturbances. Reports of strengthened regional voices.'

'And the disappearances in the Imperial Warren . . . ?' He'd heard much talk of this from the Claw ranks.

'No. I'm sending no more into that Abyss.'

'I believe it's haunted. We know almost nothing of it, truth be told.'

'It's always been unreliable. It's these rumours from the provinces that trouble me. Is anyone behind all the troubles? Who? Put as many on it as it takes. I must know who it is.'

Possum gave a slight bow of the head. So, internal dissent. Rising graft and perhaps even feuding within the administrative ranks. An emboldened nationalist voice here. A large border raid there. Old tribal animosities rekindled. And the Imperial Warren becoming increasingly dangerous. Connected? By whom? She is worried. She is wondering. Could it be *them*? After so long? Was it now because she is alone?

Or, Possum considered with an internal sneer, could it simply be plain old boredom on their part?

He stopped because Laseen had slowed and halted. She glanced to him. 'We once were friends you know,' she said, almost reflective. 'That is, I thought we understood each other . . .' She looked away, the crow's feet at the corners of her eyes tight.

So why did she do it? Why did she betray you? Is that what you're wondering? Or, what did they know that you do not?

Laseen's jaw line hardened. 'So. You brought her down. Very good. I didn't think—'

'That I could?'

Laseen blinked. Her lips drew tight and thin. 'That she would go so quietly.'

Possum shrugged. 'I surprised her.'

Her gaze snapped to him, sidelong. Possum refused to acknowledge the attention. Let her imagine what she may. Had she not been *his* right hand? Was he now not *hers*? Let her wonder, and consider.

Without a word the Empress moved on. Possum followed.

Atop a wall of Reacher's Square a spiked skull laughed but no one heard.

* * *

Ereko and Traveller had left behind the mountains and descended south into the vast leagues of evergreen forest when they met the first brigands. Ereko was not surprised when these men treated with Traveller, for though they were robbers and cutthroats he knew they were still men all the same and so craved company and news of the outside world here in their isolated mountain retreats.

They wore rotting pelts, the remains of smoke-cured leather leggings and shirts, and a mishmash of looted armour fittings and weapons. Pickings, so they appeared to Ereko, were painfully thin here along this desolate pass. To his sensitive nose they stank worse than animals. Traveller crouched at their fire to exchange news.

Ereko kept to the rear, erect, arms crossed. Traveller had told him he loomed much more imposing in this manner. He watched the men eye him up and down impressed, he hoped, by his height – at least twice their squat malnourished measure. But he had walked long enough among humans to know their thoughts; in their shared sly looks he could see them considering that anyone, no matter what their astonishing size or kind, falls down if you put enough holes in them.

'Late in the season to be coming down from Juorilan,' said their chief. Grime and grease painted his face nearly black. His beard shone with oil and was shot through with grey. His long black hair was drawn up and tied with a leather thong at the top of his head. 'Does the Council still claim Jasston, and deny passage to Damos Bay to all?'

'That is so,' allowed Traveller.

'And this one here with you,' the chieftain pointed the honed knife he played with in Ereko's direction. 'I have met Thelomen. Even Toblakai. He is not of those. He is far too tall. What is he?'

Traveller glanced back over his shoulder. Ereko saw no humour in the man's dark-blue eyes even though he'd lately been complaining of human ignorance and bigotry. 'Ask him yourself,' he answered. 'He can speak.'

'Yes?' The brigand chief raised his chin to Ereko. 'Well? Who are your people?'

Though Traveller had his back turned, at that particular phrasing of the question Ereko saw him flinch beneath his layered shirts, armour and pelts. Ereko thanked him silently for that gesture of empathy.

'Cousins. Those you name and I. We are something of cousins.'

The bandit chief grunted, placated. He cut a strip of flesh from a boar's thigh skewered over the fire's embers. 'And the Malazans? What of them? The traders say they have been as quiet as stones all summer.'

'That is so. Mare and the Korelans hold them pinned in Fist. There they rot.'

The bandit chief slapped his thigh. 'Good!'

Ereko kept watch on the woods – was this man delaying while his rabble completed an encirclement? But no one moved through the sparse forest of scrawny spruce and short pine over naked granite. The bandit chief had stepped out to meet them with six men – two of whom appeared to be his own sons. They wanted to kill the both of them, Ereko could see that. How often the chief's eyes went to the slim sword strapped on Traveller's back. But Traveller's assured manner gave them pause. That, and Ereko's size and even taller spear.

'I say good because we are all descended here by pure blood from the Crimson Guard. Know you that, friend?'

Traveller nodded.

The bandit chief's voice grew louder. He gestured to the woods around. 'Yes. The Malazans are frightened to come here because the bones of Guardsmen protect these lands. I myself am a descendant of Hap the Elder, a sergeant under Lieutenant Striker. The bones of many Guardsmen litter these northern forests. And there is an ancient legend, you know. A prophecy. A promise that should the Malazans come again the Guardsmen will rise from the dead to destroy them. That is why they have never come back to our lands. They are afraid. We beat them once.'

'That is true,' said Traveller. 'You beat them once.'

'And you, friend? There are many black men among the Malazans and some among the Korelri as well. But you are no Korelri. You speak the Talian tongue well.'

Traveller shrugged beneath his shaggy bear hide cloak. 'I am of Jakata myself. My companion is from farther afield as you can see. I'm travelling south to find a spot to build a ship. My companion here wishes to travel beyond, down to the old North Citadel to take passage east around the Cape.'

The chieftain smiled as if he'd been expecting an answer similar to that. 'It takes much gold to build a ship – or buy any passage. Traders come down this pass each year bearing much wealth for just such a purpose.'

Traveller laughed easily despite this ominous threat. 'Those men are rich traders. They can also afford many guards, can they not? We have no guards for we have no wealth to guard. I will build the ship myself. With my own hands. My friend here plans to work for his passage east. He is of great use at sea.'

The chief joined in Traveller's easy laughter and stuffed more shreds of greasy boar meat into his mouth. 'Of course, of course. Visit the coast by all means. See how you like it.' And he laughed anew.

Traveller handed a drinking skin across the fire and Ereko winced to see it was one of their three of Jourilan brandy. The bandit gulped it down without comment, spilling much from his mouth. He slung it over his shoulder. Ereko groaned silently at that – does Traveller want him to think we're afraid and trying to buy him off?

'I have heard rumours that the Korelri claim the Malazans have formed unholy pacts with the Ice Demons. What think you of that?'

Traveller's answered that he had neither seen nor heard anything to substantiate such a rumour. The two exchanged more news then on the Council of the Chosen, the likelihood of this winter being a harsh one, and, as usual when such shallow and shifting topics as contemporary politics among humans came up, Ereko became bored. The chief's six men in their mismatching of studded leather hauberks, rusting iron helmets and vests of rings sown on to leather watched him unswervingly. Avarice, boredom, fascination and dull angry resentment glittered in their eyes as they glanced between Traveller and him.

The treat dragged on past the mid-day and into the afternoon and still Traveller made no move to break off. Ereko wondered at such uncharacteristic patience. Normally it was Traveller who chafed to be on, who resented any delay or obstruction in his path. Surely he must see that this man sought to delay them – perhaps he had sent for the rest of his men and now waited for their arrival.

Talk then turned to the subject that preoccupied all the inhabitants of the continent to the north: the state of the Shieldwall, the strength of the ranks of the Chosen, and of Korelri readiness to repel the Riders this coming winter season. Speculation all the more anxious and uncertain these last years now that the Malazans had drained off so much of the needed Korelan strength.

Ereko watched the chief closely then for some sign that he knew: that word had reached him through the mouths of traders who had traversed the pass before them this season. Word of two outlanders who have been named deserters from the Wall. Traitors condemned by the Council of the Chosen with all swords and hands raised against them within northern lands. Yet the man's eyes betrayed no such knowledge; they glittered with animal cunning, yes, but appeared empty of the triumph and satisfaction that hidden advantage can bring.

Eventually, much delayed, the rambling exchange ended and the chief groaned and grumbled as he pushed himself to his feet. His followers rose with him. Their hands went to knife-grips and hatchet handles, and their eyes to their chief for any sign or direction. Traveller backed away from the fire. 'Many thanks for your hospitality.'

The chief laughed his exaggerated good humour. 'Yes, yes. Certainly, certainly.' He waved away his followers. 'Good travelling. To the coast. Ha!'

Ereko and Traveller backed away for a short time then returned to their path. Traveller struck a south-west course. They walked in silence, listening. They came to a narrow stream that descended steeply among boulders, foaming and chuckling its way west to the coast, and Traveller followed it.

'I make it to be two,' he said after a time.

'Yes. The youths, I think.'

'They'll wait till night.'

'Yes. How many, do you think?'

'More than the six. That's for certain.'

They pushed through a bracken of fallen trees and dry branches, jumped from rock to rock. 'Why did you not break things off?'

Traveller's nut-brown features drew down into a pained grimace. 'I hoped to show him that we were not afraid to travel alone. To make him think about that, and what that might mean.' He shook his head. 'But the fool did not appear to be the thoughtful kind.'

'Perhaps he knows.'

Traveller glanced to him. 'Then nothing will stop them from coming for us tonight.'

They made camp among a tumble of boulders. Traveller struck a small fire but sat with his back to it. Ereko sat across the fire and sometimes watched the darkness and sometimes watched Traveller. The man sat with his sheathed sword across his lap, waiting, and Ereko wondered again at this man who could show such gentleness and what was called, generally, *humanity* and yet be willing to cut down a handful of ill-armed and untrained rabble, youths included, none of whom could possibly stand a chance against him.

'Let us just keep going,' Ereko urged again across the fire. 'Why stop at all?'

'I'll not watch my back all the way to North Citadel. Any fool can get lucky with a bow.'

Ereko eyed him, perplexed. Yes, that was true; at least in Ereko's own case. Though he aged very slowly, he could still be killed by mundane physical trauma. But what of Traveller? Was he not beyond such concerns? Obviously not. He was yet a man. He lived still. Clearly, he remained wary of that unlooked-for bolt from behind. Perhaps no matter how competent – or miraculously exquisite in Traveller's case – one's skills in personal combat, a random bolt or arrow could always spell the end.

Extending his awareness out through the earth, Ereko could sense them: a handful of men down the slope closer to the stream. They were gathered together, hesitant perhaps because of Traveller's and his refusal to sleep. Would they wait until they did? He prayed not; already the delay was agonizing.

He glanced back across the dim glow of the embers to find that Traveller had already reached the same conclusion. He now lay wrapped in his bear-hide cloak, pretending sleep. Ereko followed suit by easing himself down the rock he leant against and although he did not feel the cold or heat as sharply as humans, he pulled up his own broad cloak of layered pelts and let his head droop.

They waited. From a great distance up the mountains a wolf's howl drifted through the night and Ereko wondered if it was one of the shaggy pack that had shadowed them across the ice wastes north of the mountains. Owls called, and an even more distant booming as of an avalanche or the cracking of an ice field echoed among the mountain slopes.

A three-quarter moon emerged from behind thick clouds and Ereko sensed the men advancing. They had been waiting for better light; he cursed himself for not thinking of it.

Traveller threw himself aside as arrows and a crossbow bolt thudded into his bedding. Ereko had already rolled into shadow and now crouched, waiting. He held his spear reversed for he couldn't set aside his pity, yet.

A surprised scream of fear and pain tore through the cold night air only to be cut off almost instantly and he knew Traveller was now among them. The scream destroyed any pretence to silence or stealth so now shouts sounded all around.

'Where is he?'

'Pullen? You see him?'

Sandals scraped over stone. Fallen branches snapped. A head appeared silhouetted by the silver moonlight. Ereko lashed out with the butt-end of his spear and connected in a meaty yielding thump. Iron rang from stone. A crossbow cracked its release and simultaneous pain knocked the wind from his chest. The blow rocked him and he fell. As he lay he blessed the efficacy of this human mail he'd adopted and damned these human missile weapons; they were a constant plague.

Someone stood over him. Moonlight revealed one of the youths. He lashed out, tripping him, then wrapped a hand over his mouth and pulled him tight. '*Shhh!*' he mouthed and waited, motionless in shadow.

Someone approached the camp. He came to stand next to the fire's dying embers. By the fitful sullen light Ereko saw that it was

Traveller. The red glow – the colour of war – it suited him; he carried his sword in one hand and its narrow length gleamed slick and wet. His cloaks were gone, revealing his tight shirt of supple blackened mail. He crossed to Ereko and touched the tip of his sword to the youth's chest. Blood, black in the dark, ran down to pool over the layered untreated hides. The youth's eyes swelled huge. His breath was hot and panting against Ereko's hand. It felt to him that he held a trembling colt fresh from foaling. 'The others?' Ereko asked.

'One got away.' His eyes did not leave the youth. The sword point pressed down further, broke the surface of the leather.

'No. I forbid it.'

'He'll just come back. He and his friends will shadow us. Wait for their chance. For *vengeance*.'

'No. This I will not allow. He is just a child. A child.'

Traveller's eyes flickered then. The fey spell of battle-fury broke, revealing something beneath, something that made Ereko look away, and the man lurched aside. 'Get him from my sight.'

Ereko whispered, 'Run now. Don't stop.' The youth scrambled away, gulping down air, sobs rising in his breaths.

Traveller threw himself on to his bear-pelt cloak. Ereko lay holding himself silent and still as if some enchantment might shatter should he speak or move. In time, the man slept, his breath steadying. Ereko lay awake listening to the night and sensing the mood of this new land. Expectant, it seemed. He wondered whether pain such as he glimpsed in his companion's eyes could ever be healed. Perhaps never. As he should very well know.

Before the new moon he and Traveller topped a hillock to the view of a forested coast, tidal mudflats and the ocean stretching beyond to the western horizon. Some humans, Ereko knew, called this the Explorer's Sea, for so much of it remained to be discovered. Others named it the White Spires Ocean for the islands of floating ice that menaced its mariners. His own people, the Thel Akai, named it Gal-Eresh: The Ice Dancer. 'What now?' he asked of Traveller.

Crouched on his haunches, the man took a pine twig from his mouth and shrugged. 'We follow the coast. Find a settlement.'

'South, then? We go south?'

'For now.' And he started down the forested slope. Ereko followed, sighing his irritation. Oh, Goddess, why did you speak to me of this most difficult of men? Why did you break your silence of centuries to say to me when he appeared dragged out in chains on to the Stormwall: *this one shall bring your deliverance.*

By that time Ereko had long lost count of his seasons upon the Stormwall. The Korelan winters had come and gone one after the other. The storms unique to the Riders had gathered their ferocity in ice-rafted waves and nimbuses of power that flickered in the night sky as auroras. He came to know that slow stirring of potential just as well as the change of season. The winds would always swing to a steady hard south, south-west pressure that chilled even his bones and left an overnight frost glittering in the morning light on the stone battlements. Snow-flurries blasted the wall during the worst of the storms – and the Riders themselves were never far behind any snow.

Malazan soldiers had been appearing on the wall for some years by then. They came in chains, captured prisoners of war. Their Korelan guards threw them weapons only just before the waves of Riders hit. They acquitted themselves well. The bravest and most cunning turned those weapons upon themselves thereby leaving a portion of the wall unmanned until a replacement could be brought up. Few cowered or wept when the Riders finally appeared cresting waves of ice-skeined ocean to assault the wall, as even some trained Chosen have from time to time. For who could possibly prepare themselves for such a sight as that? A collision of Realms, should certain theurgical scholars be believed. The power-charged impact of alien eldritch sorcery countered purely by brute stubbornness, courage and martial ferocity.

'Who is that?' he had asked of his Korelan guards. They answered easily enough as he had stood the wall for longer than some of them had been alive.

'They say he's a Malazan deserter,' the guards explained. 'Caught on a ship trying to run the blockade. The Mare marines say he fought like a tiger so they set fire to the ship beneath him and pushed off. They say he saw reason then. Jumped ship and swam to them. They handed him over to us to stand the wall.'

He watched them drag the man to an empty slot a few hundred yards down the curving curtain wall. The Korelan guards fixed his ankle fetters to the corroded iron rings set into the granite flagging then freed his arms. Ereko studied his own lengths of ankle chain and listened once again for the Enchantress's soft voice. But she was silent. No further guidance would be his.

He resolved to act as soon as a quiet night presented itself. But such a night never came and within weeks the first of the Riders' storms were upon them and thousands of Korelan soldiery jammed the wall.

They followed the forest's edge south. In the evenings they clambered down to the sand and rock shore to collect shellfish. The first sign of human settlement they met was the fire-blackened and overgrown remains of a fort: a choked trench faced by burned ragged stumps of logs surrounding an open court. The court held a burnt barracks longhouse and the beginnings of a stone and mortar central keep abandoned, or sacked, in mid-construction. They slept wrapped in their pelts in the dry, grass-gnarled court. The fire cast a faint glow upon the vine-shrouded stones of the keep's curving wall.

'They were here,' Traveller announced while leaning back on his pelts, his dark brooding gaze on the ruined tower.

Ereko peered up from his share of the fish they'd found trapped in a tide-pool. 'Who? Who was here?'

'The Crimson Guard. Like the old bandit said. This was their work.'

'When?'

'More than half a century ago.'

'You knew them?'

Across the fire the eyes swung to Ereko and he felt a chill such as no human had ever instilled within him. How was it that this man's gaze carried the weight and aching depth of the ancients? Was he deciding just now whether to kill me for my curiosity? Such desolation there within; the gaze reminded him of doomed Togg whom he met once in another forested land – or the beast some call Fanderay – whom he saw last so long ago.

The eyes dropped. 'Yes. I knew them. This could be Pine Fort, their northernmost outpost on this coast of Stratem. The next settlement would be North Citadel, but that is far to the south and my information is long out of date. I'm hoping to come to a settlement before that.'

'What happened to them?'

'You really do not know the story?'

'Only what the Korelans spoke of. Something about a war in Talian lands to the north.'

'Yes. A decades-long war. A war of conquest waged by Kellanved across the entire continent. And everywhere his armies marched they found ranks of the Guard opposing them. From Kan to Tali, even out upon the Seti plains, mercenary companies of the Crimson Guard unfurled their silver dragon banner against the sceptre of the invading Malazan armies.

'Eventually, after decades, the last of their ancestral holds, the D'Avore family fastness in the Fenn Mountains, fell. The Citadel, it was called. Kellanved brought it down with an earthquake. He killed thousands of his own men.'

Traveller fell silent at that, staring into the fire. For some unknown reason he had now opened up and was talking more than all the months they had been together. Ereko waited a time then prompted quietly, 'I have heard much talk of this emperor. Why did he not use his feared Imass warriors upon the Guard?'

So intent was Traveller upon the fire – reliving old memories? – Ereko believed the man would not answer yet he spoke without stirring. 'Have you heard of K'azz's vow?'

'I heard he swore to oppose the Malazans.'

'That and more. Much more. Eternal opposition enduring until the Empire should fall. It bound them together, those six hundred men and women. Bound them with ties greater than even they suspected, I think. Kellanved ordered the Imass to crush them but the Imass refused.'

This news surprised Ereko. 'Why should they do that?' Few things walking the face of the world in this young age terrified him and this army of the undying was one.

'None know for certain. But I had heard . . .' His voice trailed into a thoughtful silence.

'Yes? What?'

The man scowled, perhaps thinking he had revealed enough. He broke a twig into sections that he then threw upon the embers. 'I heard that the Imass said only that it would be wrong for them to oppose such a vow. Yet I am sure that by now, to all those who swore it, this vow must seem more of a curse.'

Three days later they came upon the first settlement. A squalid fishing village. Traveller had Ereko remain hidden in the woods while he approached alone to dispel their panic. As it was, the appearance of a single man walking out of the forest generated panic enough. Old men and youths came running carrying spears, javelins and bows. Traveller treated with them at the edge of their collection of shacks where a stream braided its way out of the rocks and trees to run in a sheen down the mudflats to the ocean.

He returned alone. 'They're a wary lot. The usual fears. Don't know if I soothed them at all. Let's continue on a way south. Keep an eye out for good trees.'

'Trees? So you *are* building a boat then.'

'Yes. I am.'

'Then what?'

'Then we wait.'

He walked away and Ereko almost laughed at his own surprised flash of frustration. Dealing with this man was almost as irritating as negotiating with that most reclusive of races, the Assail. He shook his head at himself and followed. To think that during all his many years he had prided himself on his patience!

Traveller pushed his way through the dense underbrush, stopping occasionally to point out a possible tree for harvesting and to talk through its merits. Eventually, Ereko joined in his speculations and they exchanged wisdom on the fine art of wood selection for the construction of a sturdy, yet flexible, ocean-going craft.

Ereko decided that Traveller knew a fair bit on the subject, for a human.

* * *

In the aftermath of the Nabrajan contract payment arrived in the form of war material of weapons and armour, treated hides, iron ingots and pack animals. The mercantile houses, traditional slave-traders, were also happy to pay in slaves, which Shimmer was also happy to accept. The Guard marched east, downriver, through rolling farmed plains to the coast. On the trading road to the coastal city of Kurzan, the existence of which had only been a rumour to Kyle's people, Shimmer ordered the slaves assembled in a muddy field.

Dressed in bright mail from her neck to her calves, her helmet under an arm, and her long black hair blowing free in the wind, she faced them. 'We in the Guard do not accept slavery. Therefore, you will all be released.'

Stunned silence met the announcement. Even fellow tribesmen and women stared a cringing wary disbelief. Kyle was ashamed.

'Those of you who wish to take up arms and join the Guard of your own free will please go to the standard for examination and induction. The rest of you will be free to go.'

And so through that day the line of men and women wishing induction into the ranks of the Guard ran its course. Those too old or infirm were rejected to rejoin their fellows awaiting their release. Eventually, as dusk came, all those who voluntarily chose to join and were found acceptable were marched away.

Needless to say, those remaining were not released. They were re-bound into their linked manacles and led away. They hardly moaned. So beaten down were they that perhaps they imagined the whole exercise a sham solely meant to single out the strong and young to be sold elsewhere. And perhaps, in its own way, that's exactly what it was.

The army, nearly seven thousand souls strong, wound its way east skirting the River Thin. After two weeks the Guard camped on the coast south of Kurzan, overlooking the Anari Narrows where ships rested at anchor in its sheltered, calm waters. Northward, Kyle could just make out the grey and tan towers of the city harbour defences.

'Ships!' Stoop announced, slapping him on the back. 'Ships,' he repeated, savouring the word.

'Ships,' Kyle echoed, having only heard them described. He did not relish having to enter the belly of one. It seemed unnatural.

'Now what?'

'We camp. Train. Wait.'

'What's happening?'

Stoop adjusted his leather cap of a helmet, scratched his grey fringe of bristles. 'Negotiations, Kyle. Shimmer's negotiating in the city to hire ships.' The old saboteur pinched something between his nails, grimaced. 'Tell me, lad. How do you feel about swimming?'

'It's not natural for people to go into water.'

'Well, now's a fine time for you to learn.'

Over the next week Kyle joined some forty male and female recruits being forcefully dunked in the muddy water of one of the broader channels of the River Thin's delta. Veteran Guardsmen enforced the lessons and swung truncheons to quiet all rebellion. Kyle sometimes saw Stoop sitting on the shore, smoking his pipe and shouting his encouragement.

From the first day of practice Kyle witnessed another duty of the Guardsmen keeping a close eye upon them when a shout went up and crossbow bolts hissed into the dark water. Immediately, the surface foamed and a great long beast thrashed and writhed, snapping its jaws and lashing its scaled tail. All the swimmers flailed for the shore. After the beast sank below the surface those same soldiers used truncheons to beat the recruits back into the water. Three youths refused entirely, were beaten unconscious and dragged away.

For his part, Kyle decided not to go meekly. When a Guardsman came to force him into the muddy channel he surprised her, a female veteran from Genabackis named Jaris. Together they tumbled down

47

the slick mud slope into the water. From the shore and the shallows the mercenaries laughed and hooted while Kyle and Jaris thrashed in the murky water. He was lucky and managed to get behind her, hook his elbow under her chin, and he thought he might just force her to take his place as a swimmer. While he strained to push her head down below the water, something sharp and cold pricked his crotch. He jerked, strained to climb higher on his toes.

'That's right, boy,' laughed Jaris. 'There's another biter in the water and it's after your little fish.' The point pricked Kyle's crotch again. 'What'll it be? You want to get bit?'

Kyle released her and she backed away through the waist-deep water. She raised a particularly wicked-looking dagger. 'Smart choice. And a stupid move, lad. There's others who would've knifed you just for gettin' them wet.'

Eventually, Kyle was selected as part of a troop and was given floats of tarred inflated skins to hang on to and paddle around for hours at a time in the river. Guardsmen kept watch on shore and in the tall grasses of the marsh.

The second role of the many Guards Kyle discovered on the eighth day when shouts went up from the shore of a mud island out in the channel and mercenaries came running from all around. They splashed through the murky shallows, dived into the tall stands of grasses. Kyle and the other swimmers stopped to watch.

A boy in a ragged tunic appeared, flushed from the grasses and cattails. He ran down the clay shore of the channel island, barefoot, wild-eyed. A Guardsman jumped from the cover of the grasses and tackled the youth into the water. Both disappeared beneath the brown surface. Kyle swam for them as fast as he could.

The mercenary surfaced, dragged a limp shape to the shore. Kyle arrived to see the thick red of heart's blood smearing the mud and the youth's chest. The Guardsman was the short veteran, Boll, whom Stoop had warned him to stay clear of. Despite this, Kyle charged in sloshing through the shallow water. He raised the boy's head – a bare youth – and dead.

'What did you have to kill him for?'

The veteran ignored Kyle, began cleaning and re-oiling his knife blade.

'He's just a kid. Why did you?'

'Shut up. Orders. No spying allowed.'

'Spying?' Kyle couldn't believe what he was hearing. '*Spying?*

Maybe he was just watching. Maybe he was just curious. Who wouldn't be?'

'You watch your mouth. I don't play nice like that Genabackan cow, Jaris.'

Kyle almost jumped the squat knifeman – from some place called Ehrlitan, he'd heard – but Boll still held his blade while Kyle held only his ridiculous goatskin bladder. He raised the bladder. 'You and this thing are a lot alike, Boll. You're both puffed up.' Kyle pried at a tarred seam of the bladder until the air farted out in a stream. 'And you both make a lot of loud noise.'

Boll slapped the bladder from Kyle's hands. 'Don't ride me. This ain't a game.'

Other Guardsmen arrived then and waved Kyle away. He went to find a replacement bladder. The mercenaries dragged the body into the thick stands of marsh grasses.

*

The next week Kyle was kicked awake in the middle of the night. He squinted into the blackness of a moonless night barely able to make out someone standing over him.

'Get up. Assemble at the beach. Double-time.'

It was Trench, his sergeant. 'Aye, aye.'

He collected his armour and equipment by the dim glow of a fire's embers then stumbled down to the beach to find a mixture of recruits and veteran Guardsmen assembled in knots. Trench, wearing only pantaloons and a vest of leather, shook all of his equipment from his hands.

'Won't be needing that.'

Trench moved on to the other recruits. Stalker appeared at Kyle's side, knelt with him to sort through his gear.

'Take the knife,' he whispered. 'Keep it at your neck.' He examined Kyle's mishmash of armour. 'Wear the leather alone – no padding – and the skirting's OK. Go barefoot.'

'What's going on?'

'We're swimming out to the ships. I hear negotiations have gone sour.'

Kyle pulled on his leathers. 'Gone sour? Looks like this has been in the works for some time.'

'An option. Shimmer seems cunning. I'll give her that.'

Squinting out over the water, Kyle could see nothing. The Narrows were calm and smooth, not a breath of air stirred, but it was as dark as the inside of a cave. 'I can't see a damned thing.'

'Don't you worry. There'll be plenty of light.'

Kyle hefted his tulwar – more than a stone's weight of iron.

'Don't take it,' Stalker said.

'I want to take it.'

'Then at least get rid of the blasted sheath. Hang it on a strap over your neck. If it looks like you can't make it – cut it loose.'

'I'll never part with this.'

A spasm of irritation crossed Stalker's brow. 'Dark Hunter take you! It's your burial.'

The tall scout stormed away. Kyle found the bladders in baskets. Men and women were strapping them to their chests. He hung the freshly re-gripped tulwar by a leather strap at its hilts and ran the strap under one shoulder and up around his neck. Mercenaries pushed out past him into the placid, nearly motionless surf.

'Where are we going?' Kyle asked them.

'Quiet,' someone hissed.

'Hood take your tongue.'

Kyle bit back a retort. He joined the ranks of almost naked men and women pushing out into the water.

The water was cold, terrifyingly so. Kyle felt his toes and fingers already tingling. What use might he be when he eventually reached a ship, too numb to swing a weapon? Had anyone thought of that?

He pulled up short as the water reached his waist. He turned to speak to someone – anyone – but was pushed on.

'Let's go.'

'Ain't got much time.'

'Time till what?' he hissed.

A hand like a shovel took him by his hauberk and pushed him along. He spun to see the wide shape of Greymane in the dark. Kyle had never seen him without his mail and banded armour, and out of it the man was, if anything, even more impressive. His chest was massive, covered in a pelt of grey hair plastered down by water. Black hair covered his thick arms.

'Swim to the fourth ship,' he rumbled to Kyle, and shook him by his hauberk.

'Fourth?'

'The fourth most distant, lad.'

'Oh, right. Yes. What about the cold?'

The renegade blinked, puzzled. 'What cold?'

Wind preserve him! 'What ship are you heading to?'

'Ship? Treach's teeth, I'm not going.'

'You're not?'

'No. Water 'n' me – we don't get along.'

The renegade pushed Kyle on before he could wonder whether he was being serious or not. He swam, kicked with his legs in a steady rhythm as he had been taught. He hugged the bladder to his chest, but didn't squeeze it, kept his arms and legs as loose as possible, conserving his strength. Soon he was surrounded by shapeless night. The stars shone overhead and from all around, reflecting from the bay's eerily still surface. Men kicked and splashed. Curses and gasps sounded from all sides. Squinting ahead, Kyle could see no sign of ships, the first let alone the fourth.

He kicked and kicked. The cold seeped up his legs and arms in a gathering numbness. He wondered if he was swimming in circles; how would he know? How could any of them know? Yet he lacked the strength to call out. His teeth chattered and his shoulders cramped.

From the middle distance shouting reached him. A cry for help, a plea. A recruit: the voice was a youth's. He had panicked, or was cramped. Splashing sounded followed by a sharp gasp, then, terrifyingly, a long silence. Kyle stopped kicking. He floated, listening to the night. Gods all around! What kind of a brotherhood had he entered into? Did they . . . could they have killed one of their own?

Someone bumped him and he flinched, the bladder almost slipped from his grasp like a greased pig and he nearly screamed, *No!*

'Get a move on.'

Kyle didn't know the voice, though he recognized the accent: north Genabackan. 'Can't see a damned thing,' he gasped.

'Never mind. Keep moving. Keep warm.'

Kyle couldn't argue with that. The dark form swam past. Kyle kicked himself into motion and tried to keep the Guardsman in sight.

The cold took his legs. At least that was how it felt; the water's frigid grasp had somehow cut him off at the waist. He still kicked but he could no longer feel his legs. His arms were likewise numb wrappings clasped around the bladder at his chest. The sword's weight pulling on his left threatened to swamp him. His teeth chattered continuously and so loudly he was sure he would be next to be pushed under the surface.

'Close now,' someone whispered behind. Kyle could only grunt an acknowledgement. 'Right,' the voice warned.

'The fourth ship?' he stammered.

'Hood kiss that. It's a ship ain't it? Take it! Sharpish, turn. There, reach up.'

Kyle raised his numb arm, found slimy cold timbers. 'How . . . ?'

'A rope ladder ahead.'

He bumped his way forward and managed to entangle his arm in the ladder and slowly, laboriously, dragged himself up the first few wood rungs. Hands from above heaved him up the rest of the way and he lay on the warm deck gasping. 'There's another – help him.'

The dark shape peered down over the side. 'There's no one there,' and the man padded off silent.

The ship had already been taken. Kyle warmed himself at coals simmering in an iron brazier at mid-deck. Two Guardsmen hurried about, clearing the ship's deck. 'We're leaving now?' Kyle asked of one.

This one paused, eyed him up and down. 'A new hand, hey?'

'Yes.'

'Who swore you in?'

'Stoop.'

This fellow nodded, impressed by the name. Kyle wondered what could possibly be impressive about the broken-down one-handed saboteur.

'Know ships?'

'No.'

'Then you are now officially a marine. Scrounge armour and weapons – especially missile weapons. Ready for blockade.'

'Blockade?'

'Aye. We'll need all their ships.'

Kyle forced down a laugh of disbelief. 'But that's an entire city!'

The Guardsman's smile shone bright in the dark. 'Just their best ships then.' The smile disappeared. 'Below, collect equipment.'

'Yes sir.'

Kyle expected blood-spattered slaughter belowdecks and so descended the set of steep stairs slowly. But what he found disturbed him in a far worse way; all the holds and bunk-lined ways he explored he found completely empty. Not one person, dead or alive. Where was everyone? What had happened? He could find no arms or armour anywhere.

The rattling of metal sounded from sternward. Kyle readied his tulwar and edged forward. The narrow corridor ended at a room cramped by benches and tables. An open door led further to the stern. The noise of metal rattling continued. Kyle peeked in to see the back of a man, barefoot, in a wet shirt and trousers, struggling with a closed and chained cabinet door.

'Wait a moment,' the man said in Talian without turning around.

Kyle wondered how he could have possibly known he was here. The noise of the vessel's rocking and creaking had covered his approach, he was sure.

'Aye.'

More rattling, then the chains fell from the door. 'Ha!' The man pulled open the metal-bolted and barred door. Kyle glimpsed racks of spears and bows and swords within.

'Help me bring these up.'

'Where is everyone? The crew, I mean.'

The Guardsman began unlocking the racks. Kyle now saw that he carried an immense ring of keys. 'Merchants,' the man sighed. 'They want weapons locked away yet they expect to be protected at all times.' His thick black hair, hacked short, shone like wet fur and the lines of his face appeared ready to creep up into a constant grin. 'The crew? Just a skeleton watch. Some fought, some dived overboard.'

'What's the plan?'

The man stopped short, gave an exaggerated frown then returned to his grin. 'The plan? Ah, you're a new hand. Capture the ships.'

'Right. Capture ships.'

Thunder rolled over and through the vessel, a burst from the middle distance. Kyle frowned, puzzled – it was a clear night. The Guardsman's grin turned eager. 'It's started. Let's go.' He collected an armful of weapons.

A faint orange glow flickered over the deck. Flames now engulfed the Kurzan waterfront. While Kyle watched, a fresh burst of yellow and white flame rocked one harbour tower. It hunched, then, with an awful slow grace, toppled sideways, flattening as it went. More thunder rolled up the inlet.

'Something's got Smoky all in a froth,' murmured the Guardsman.

'What about the ships?'

'Naw. Don't worry about them. Cowl would murder him.'

'They're on their way!' someone shouted from the bows.

The Guardsman laughed. 'You see? All they needed was a little encouragement.'

'And just what do we do when they get here?' Kyle asked.

Surprised, the mercenary looked to Kyle. 'Sorry. I keep forgetting. It's hard for us old-timers. My name is Cole. You?'

'Kyle. Are you – Avowed?'

'Yes.' Cole gestured to two others with him. 'I'll hold the deck. You two flank me. You,' he pointed to Kyle, 'can you use a bow?'

'Yes.'

'Good. Get up on the foredeck with the man there – follow his orders.'

'Aye, aye.' Kyle gathered all the arrow sheaths he could hold.

The man at the raised bow deck was pale, skinny and obviously freezing cold as he stood in a soaked linen shirt and hide trousers hugging himself and stamping his feet.

'You an archer?' the Guardsman asked Kyle in accented Talian.

'I can shoot.'

'OK. Try out those. Find one you like.'

Kyle strung one bow, took a test shot out into the darkness. Weak, he judged, but true. 'What's the plan?'

'I'll pick out targets. You hit them.'

'OK.' To get a better feel for the bow, Kyle shot more arrows into the dark.

'You a local recruit?' the man asked.

'Yes. Kyle. You?'

'Parsell, Lurgman Parsell. Genabackis.' Distracted, the man peered out over the dark waves of the inlet glimmering with reflected flames. 'Less than one league now,' he called to mid-ship.

'I mark them,' Cole answered.

Kyle squinted out over the calm waters. He could barely discern dark shapes approaching, pale lines at their bows, let alone any possible target. How was he to hit anything? 'Ah, there's a problem. I can't see a thing.'

'You can't—' Lurgman sighed, pulled a leather pouch from under his shirt, took out a slip of oiled cloth. 'There might be enough left on this, try it.'

'What do I do with it?'

'You rub it over your eyes. Open, mind you – they have to be open.'

'Doesn't that hurt?'

'Like a rasp.'

Kyle studied the parchment, dubious. 'Do I have to?'

The thump of distant crossbows and catapults echoed across the inlet. Incendiaries shot high up into the night, arced to reveal scores of vessels bearing down upon them.

'No choice now.'

Kyle opened one eye wide and pressed the cloth to it then flinched, snarling and cursing as acid ate at his eye. 'Wind take you! Gods, man! Gods!'

'The other one – quick.'

Cole roared, 'Get rid of those two war-galleys! We don't want them.'

'Aye, aye.'

Blinking, eyes watering, Kyle straightened to a near monochrome half-light of blindingly bright flames, searing stars in the night sky, and a clear vision of ships, all under oar, making slow progress towards them. Distantly, the clash of battle sounded as ship met ship.

Lurgman was grunting and hissing his effort, eyes shut, hands held out before him, and the hair on Kyle's neck and arms tingled as he realized he stood with a mage, possibly another Avowed.

'Are they in range?' Lurgman ground through clenched teeth.

The nearest vessels, two broad-bellied cargo ships, had been attempting to pass to either side of their ship. Both had lost all headway and rocked as if rudderless. The decks of both swarmed with soldiers. Kyle was surprised to see how all their oars were warped and curled – utterly useless.

'Now, yes.'

Arrows pelted down and Kyle hunched low for cover behind the gunwale. Lurgman didn't move. 'Stand up. We won't get hit.' Then he flinched as if slapped. ''Ware a mage!' he bellowed.

At that moment a ball of actinic-bright energy burst alight on deck. It spun about randomly, striking a mast with a flash then ricocheting to a barrel that it consumed in a deafening eruption.

'Bring that man down!' Cole bellowed, outraged.

'Aye,' Lurgman answered. He scanned the ships.

Grapnels struck the gunwales. The cargo ships drew closer, one to either side. Beyond, two long and low war-galleys foundered in the relatively calm waters, sinking for no reason Kyle could see. Soldiers jammed the decks. They wrestled frantically with their armour. Some fell overboard to disappear instantly. For the first time Kyle felt safe in his thin leathers.

'There!' Lurgman shouted, catching Kyle's arm. 'The stern. The old fellow in the dark hat like a hood. Gold at his neck.' Kyle spotted him, sighted and loosed. The arrow hung in the dark as if suspended then took the throat of a man at the mage's side. His gaze darted to Kyle, narrowed to luminous slits. His hands rose, gestured. Gold and jewellery glittered at the fingers.

''Ware your back,' someone called behind Kyle who spun to see a darkening and swirling like oil-smoke at the far side of the bow deck.

'Lurgman!' he warned.

The mage turned and gaped. 'Hood's curse! Cole! A summoning!'

Kyle snapped a glimpse to the deck to see Cole and his two flankers encircled by a sea of Kurzan soldiery.

The mage pushed Kyle forward. 'Buy me time. Time!'

A scaled and clawed foot emerged from the Warren portal. A long face, scaled olive-green like that of an insect, peered out. Kyle pressed the blade of his tulwar to his lips. *Wind save me!* He edged forward, hunched to receive heavy blows.

The demon, or sending, or whatever it was, reached out as if to simply grasp Kyle in one taloned hand and so he swung. The tulwar severed the forearm sending the hand spinning out overboard. The fiend shrieked. A hot stream of ichor gushed over Kyle who jerked back, stung, blinking to clear his eyes.

Kurzan soldiers appeared at the stairs up from the mid-deck, took in the battle scene at the upper deck, and flinched away.

The fiend grasped the end of his forearm. Smoke fumed from the wound. It withdrew its hand revealing a hardened, cauterized stump. Its jaws moved, crackling and snapping, and somehow Kyle understood the words: '*Who are you to have done this?*'

'Just a soldier,' he answered because he himself had no idea what had just happened.

Arrows stormed down around the vessel, deflected somehow. Flames spread across the waves engulfing a ship as it rammed the vessel next to Kyle's. The fiend straightened. '*I was not forewarned that one of your stature awaited. But, so be it. Let us test our mettle, you and I.*'

Then, and Kyle could only understand it this way, the fiend melted. Its scaled keratin or bone skeleton, or armour, melted and ran, buckling and twisting. It fell to its knees and before its skull collapsed like heated wax Kyle thought he saw horror and astonishment in its black eyes.

Kyle retreated to the ship's side, saw Lurgman slumped, one arm hooked over the gunwale. He helped the mage up. 'How did you do that?' he whispered, awed.

'I could very well ask you the same question,' the mage anwered, his voice ragged. Blood ran from his nose and blotched his eyes carmine. Those eyes narrowed and Lurgman turned to glare out over the water. Kyle looked – men now supported the Kurzan mage. His hat was gone, his bald head shining.

'So, it's going to be the hard way is it?' Lurgman growled beneath his breath. 'Can you throw better than you shoot?'

'From this distance, yes.'

'Then throw this.' The mage passed Kyle a small ball like a

slingstone. Kyle hefted it, nodded. He aimed, reached back and threw. The stone landed, unseen, somewhere near the mage. While Kyle watched, the men at the stern deck suddenly clutched at their faces. Their mouths gaped into dark ovals. Their eyes bulged. Clawed fingers gouged into flesh and all crowding the stern of the vessel fell. The mage toppled among them. Kyle turned away, feeling his stomach rising into his throat. Lurgman eased himself down to sit with his back to the ship's side.

Queasy, his limbs quivering with unspent energy, Kyle threw himself down beside the man. 'So this is the way you Avowed finish your arguments.'

'Avowed? Me? Gods no. I'm not in *their* rank. Anyway, I'm from Genabackis. No Avowed are from Genabackis.'

Kurzan soldiers edged warily up the stairs. Lurgman raised a menacing hand to them and they flinched away. 'No, I was just a healer in Cat when the Malazans invaded. A Bone Mage we're called back there. Was a damned good one too. I healed breaks, straightened bones, cleaned infections. So, as you saw, I'm really not much of a battle mage.'

'Could've fooled me.'

The clash of steel and thump and rattle of armour subsided below.

Lurgman eyed Kyle sidelong. 'What of you? What's the story on that blade?'

Kyle shrugged. 'Smoky inscribed it, if that's what you mean.'

Cole appeared at the top of one stairway; his tunic hung in bloody shreds about his waist. Shallow cuts crisscrossed his arms and chest. Sweat ran from his soaked hair. He peered around the bow, frowned his surprise. 'I thought a demon ate you two.'

'We got lucky,' said Lurgman.

'Well, get down here, Twisty. My flankers need healing and more ships are coming.' He thumped back down the stairs.

Kyle helped Lurgman to his feet. 'Twisty?'

The mage's mouth curled wryly. 'Twisty. They insist on calling me Twisty.'

*   *   *

At night in a barren stone valley a man sat wrapped in a thick cloak next to a roaring bonfire. The firelight flickered against surrounding stone cliffs. He sat listening to the distant roar of ocean surf, tossed sticks into the blaze. Presently, a whirring noise echoed about the valley and the man stood, squinted into the night sky.

A winged insect much like a giant dragonfly descended to land amid the brush and rock to one side. An armoured figure slowly and stiffly dismounted.

Cloak cast aside, the man approached. His arms hung at his sides, long and thick and knotted with muscle. His sun-browned and aged face wrinkled in pleasure. Grinning, he called, 'You're late, Hunchell. But it does my heart good to see you again.'

The flames reflected gold from the figure's armour. 'My father, Hunchell, is too old for such long flights now, Shatterer. But he sends his continued loyalty and regards. I am first son, V'thell.'

'Welcome to my humble island.' The two clasped forearms.

'Will this then be our marshalling point?'

'Yes. The island is secure. It will serve as one of our depots and staging grounds.'

'I understand.' The Gold Moranth, come by all the distance from far northern Genabackis, regarded the man for a time in silence, the chitinous visor of his full helm unreadable.

'Go ahead, ask it,' the man ground out.

'Very well. Why do you pursue this course? You risk – shattering – it all.'

'We can't stand idly by any longer, V'thell. Everything's slipping away bit by bit. Everything we struggled to raise. She doesn't understand how the machine we built must run.'

'Yet she had a hand in that building.'

The man's mouth clenched into a hard line. 'Yeah, that's true. I didn't say it was easy.' He waved the topic aside. 'But what about the Silver. Are they with us?'

'Yes. We can count on a flight of Silver quorl. Some Green are with us as well. The Black and the Red . . . well, we shall see. As for the Blue – they tender transport contracts with everyone. I suspect it is they who will come out ahead after all this.'

'Ain't that always the way. Will you rest here?'

'No, I must go immediately.'

'Well, give my regards to your father. Tell him to begin moving matériel. Contract all the Blue vessels you can.'

V'thell inclined his armoured head. 'Very well.'

The man watched as the Gold Moranth remounted. The wings of the insect quorl became a blur. He ducked his head against the dust and thrown sand, watched the creature rise and disappear into the night. After a time another figure emerged from the darkness. He wore a long dark cloak and hood.

'Can we trust them?'

The man named Shatterer by the Moranth barked a laugh at that. 'Yeah, so long as there remains a chance we might win. Then they will renegotiate. What of you?'

'*My* loyalty? Or my news?'

Shatterer smiled thinly.

'There are rumours of the return of the Crimson Guard.'

A derisive snort. 'Every year you hear that. Especially with bad times. I wouldn't give that any weight.'

The cloaked man's hood rose, yet the absolute darkness within was unchanged. 'Have you considered the possibility that they might actually return? There are, after all, names among them that echo like nightmares.'

'There are nightmare names among us too.'

'When you say us – whom do you mean? Dassem is gone. Kellanved and Dancer are gone. Who remains to face them?'

'We've always beaten them.'

'In the past, yes.'

Shatterer rubbed the back of his neck. 'If you're lookin' for a sure thing you've come to the wrong place. You toss your bones and the Twins decide.'

'I'm not one to leave anything to chance.'

'Everything's a chance. But if you haven't learned that by now then I suppose you never will.'

'Why should I, when I leave nothing to chance?'

'Anything else?'

'No. I am convinced of this Moranth connection. I will report appropriately.'

'Then do so.'

The cloaked figure inclined its head. 'We will remain in touch through the usual channels.'

'Yeah. Those.'

The man – or woman – strolled away into the night.

Shatterer watched the flames for a time, sighed, cracked his knuckles. Dealing with traitors always set his teeth on edge. Especially a Claw traitor. But then, he now fell within that same category as well. He remembered the first contacts with the Moranth and how he had crushed the torso armour of one in a bear hug. They insisted on that ridiculous name after that. Easier if they'd just call him Crust, or Urko.

The traitor Claw's worries returned to him and he recalled the image of Skinner striding across ravaged battlefields, shrugging off the worst anyone could throw at him and killing, killing. He shuddered. Hood help her should he show up again. But no, all analysis said she would simply send the entirety of the Claw lists at them until only the regulars remained. It might take hundreds but eventually superior numbers would tell.

In any case, they would act regardless. It was cruel and hard but they meant to win and this was their best chance this generation. In a way he felt sorry for her; she was caught in a nightmare of her own making – Abyss, she might even thank them for it. Yet he knew in the end she would accept it. Laseen understood exigencies. She'd always understood those.

* * *

'It won't stand.'

'Sure it will.'

'No – not enough support on the right. It'll give on that side and bring the whole thing down.'

'No, it won't. We packed it tight. There's enough counter-strain.'

The two Malazan marines, a man and a woman, sat on a heap of bricks outside Li Heng's east-facing Dawn Gate. They studied the towering outer arch of the massive gatehouse. To the north and south stretched the curtain walls of Li Heng's legendary ten man-heights of near-invincible defences.

A robed man edged his way out of the gate – a shadowed entrance broad enough to swallow four chariots side by side. He peered about, a hand shading his gaze, and spotted the two. He turned and bellowed something that the acoustics of the long tunnel echoed and magnified into an unintelligible roar. Another man came running out, raced up to the first and extended an umbrella over him. This one straightened his robes, adjusted his wide sleeves, and approached. The second kept pace, umbrella high.

'You there – you two! Where is your commander?'

The two eyed one another. The woman, wearing a mangled leather cap, touched a finger to it. 'Magistrate Ehrlann. What brings you out to the construction project you're in charge of? Bad news, I'd wager.'

Ehrlann dabbed a white silk handkerchief to his face, smiled thinly. 'Your disrespect has long been noted, you, ah, engineers. Criminal conviction, I think, will see a due improvement in manners.'

'Did you hear that, Sunny?' said the woman. 'We're engineers. But how are we gonna keep your walls built for you if you take us to court?'

'In chains, I imagine,' smiled the magistrate. 'Your commander?'

'Working.'

Ehrlann waved flies away. 'Drunk, you mean. Jamaer! Switch!'

'Switch what?' asked Sunny.

'Not you fools.'

With his free hand the umbrella-holder extended a stick tied at one end with a tuft of bhederin hair. Ehrlann took it and waved it before his face. 'Don't bother yourselves. I see him now.'

Ehrlann marched off, stumbling over the loose tumbled brick and rock. Jamaer followed, umbrella held high.

The two eyed one another. 'Should we go along?' asked the female saboteur and she adjusted the leather cap on her hacked-short brown hair.

'Storo might kill him. That'd look bad when we're in court.'

'You're right.'

They followed.

Ehrlann had stopped at an awning made from a military cloak roped from the side of a towering block of limestone half-buried in the ground. A man was straightening out from under it, weaving, coughing, wiping his hands down the front of his stained loose jerkin.

The two engineers saluted crisply. 'Captain Storo, sir!'

Storo shot them a dark look, swallowed and grimaced at what he tasted. 'That's sergeant. What is it now, Ehrlann?'

'I have come to demand the opening of Dawn Gate, sir. Demand it. Our builders tell us that restorations are long complete. They say the structure is now sound and that commercial access is long overdue.'

Storo scratched his sallow stubbled cheeks, shaded his eyes from the sun. 'Would those be the same builders the Fist ordered you to fire for turning a blind eye to the wall's dismantling?'

'Mere nuisance pilfering over the years carried out by these undesirables.' The magistrate waved his switch to the squatter camp spread out from both sides of the east road.

Storo squinted at the camp. 'They live in tents, Ehrlann.'

'Nevertheless, you can delay no longer. Work here is done. Your contract is over. Finished. If we must, the court will report to High Fist Anand that we no longer require the services of his military engineers and that the defences of Li Heng have been returned to their ancient bright glory.'

Sunlight shone on Ehrlann and he winced, snapping, 'Higher, you fool!'

Jamaer raised the umbrella higher.

'You can report all you like.' Storo said. He crouched to retrieve a helmet from under the awning, pulled it on. 'But the only report Anand will listen to is mine.'

Ehrlann dabbed at the sweat beading his face, took hold of the robes at his front. 'Do not force the Court of Magistrates to bring formal charges, commander.'

Storo's gaze narrowed. 'Such as?'

'There have been unfortunate assaults upon citizens, commander. Harassment of officials in the course of their duties.'

Storo snorted. 'If I were you, Ehrlann, I would not try to arrest any of my men. Jalor, for one, is a tribesman from Seven Cities. He wouldn't take to it. And Rell –' Storo shook his head. 'I'd hate to think of what he'd do. In any case, Fist Rheena wouldn't honour any of your civil writs.'

'Yes. She would. The city garrison is not behind you, commander.'

'Meaning you've bought them.'

'Commander! I object to that language!'

'Don't bother, Ehrlann. Hurl, Sunny . . . what's your opinion on the gate fortress, the tunnel, the arches?'

'Good for fifty years,' said Hurl.

'It will fall – sooner than later,' said Sunny.

'There you go,' Storo told Ehrlann.

The magistrate waved the switch before his face, eyed Storo. 'Meaning . . . ?'

'Meaning you have your gate. Open it to traffic tomorrow.'

The magistrate beamed, threw his arms wide as if he would embrace Storo. 'Excellent, commander. I knew you would listen. All finished then. I must admit it has been an education dealing with you veterans – we do not see too many here in the interior. Tell me, just what was the name of those barbarian lands you conquered all to the glory of the Empress? Gangabaka? Bena-gagan?'

'Genabackis,' Storo sighed. 'And we're not finished. Not yet.'

Ehrlann frowned warily. 'I'm sorry, commander?'

'That hill over there,' Storo lifted his chin to the north.

'Yes? Executioner's Hill?'

'I want to take one man's height—'

'Two,' said Hurl.

'Two man-heights off it.'

The switch stopped moving. 'You are joking, commander.' Ehrlann pointed the switch. '*That* is where we execute our criminals. *That* is where city justice is enacted. It is an ancient city tradition. You cannot interfere with that. It is simply impossible.'

'It's not ancient tradition.'

'Claims whom?'

'My mage, Silk. He says it only goes back seventy years and that's good enough for me. In any case, you can strangle your starving poor elsewhere, Ehrlann. After you provide the labour to lower the profile of that hill we'll start on the moat.'

'The moat? A moat? Where is that, pray?'

'Right where you're standing.' Storo picked up his weapon belt and dusty hauberk. 'Good day, magistrate. Hurl, Sunny. I need a drink.'

Magistrate Ehrlann watched the veterans head to Dawn Gate. He peered down to the loose dirt, broken brick and trampled rubbish at his feet. Sunlight struck the top of his head and he flinched.

'Jamaer! Umbrella!'

* * *

The fat man in ocean-blue robes walked Unta's street of Dragons deck readers, Wax Witches and Warren Seers – Diviner's Row – with the patient air of a beachcomber searching a deserted shore for lost treasure. Yet Diviner's Row was far from deserted. As the Imperial capital, Unta was the lodestone, the vortex, drawing to it all manner of *talent* – legitimate or not. Mages, practitioners of the various Warrens, but also that class of lesser 'talents', such as readers of the Dragons deck, soothsayers, fortune-tellers of all kinds, be they scholiasts of entrails or diviners of the patterns glimpsed in smoke, read in cracked burnt bone or spelled by tossed sticks.

Divination was the current Imperial fashion. As the day cooled and the blue sky darkened to purple, the Row seethed with crowds from all stations of life, each seeking a hint of – or protection against – Twin Oponn's capricious turns: the Lad's push, or the Lady's pull. Amid the jostling evening crowd charm-sellers touted the vitality of their clattering relics, icons and amulets. Stallkeepers hectored passersby.

'Your fortune this night, gracious one!'

'Chart the influences of the Many Realms upon your Path!'

'The Mysteries of Ascension revealed, noble sir.'

'A great many enemies oppose you.' The plump man in blue robes froze. He peered down at a dirty street-urchin just shorter than he. 'You risk all,' the youth continued, his eyes squeezed shut, 'but for a prize beyond your imaginings.' The man's brows climbed his seamed forehead and his thick lips tightened, then he threw back his head and guffawed. His laughter revealed teeth stained a fading green that rendered them dingy and ill-looking.

'Of course!' he agreed. 'But of course! The future you have right. A great talent is yours, lad.' He mussed the youth's greasy hair then handed him a coin. Waving to the nearest stallkeeper, he called, 'A great future I foretell for that bold one!' then he continued on, leaving a confused foreteller of Dead Poliel's visitations squinting into the crowd.

Hawkers of Dragons decks thrust their wares at the man. He turned a tolerant eye upon all. The merits of each ancient velvet-wrapped stack of cards he queried until finally purchasing one at a greatly reduced sum due to sudden misfortune within the family that had held it for generations.

Passing a stall offering relics, invested jewellery and stacks of charms, he paused and returned. The man beside the cart straightened from his stool, noted the fat, expensively-robed man's gaze fixed upon a sheath of necklaces. He smiled knowingly. 'Yes. You have a discriminating eye, noble sir.' The vendor took down the knotted necklaces, offered them to the man who flinched away. 'Note the links, sir, chains in miniature. And the pendants! Guaranteed slivers of bone from the very remains of the poor victims of that fiend Coltaine's death march.' The fat man's eyes seemed to bulge in their sockets. He swallowed with difficulty. 'My Lord is familiar with that sad episode?'

Mastering himself, Mallick Rel found his voice, croaked, 'Yes.'

'A most disgraceful tragedy, was it not?'

Mallick straightened his shoulders. His lips drew back from his stained teeth. 'Yes. An awful failure. Hauntings of it ever return to me like waves.'

'Thank the wisdom of the Empress in her call for all Quon to rise against the traitorous Wickans.'

'Yes. Thank her.'

'Then my Lord must have this relic – may we all learn from what it carries.'

Bowing, the vendor missed Mallick's eyes, deep within their pockets of fat, dart to him with a strange intensity. 'Yes,' he said. 'A lesson ever to be heeded.' Then he smiled beatifically. 'Of course I shall purchase your excellent relic – and is that a charm to deflect Hood's eternal hunger I see next to it?'

*

As the evening darkened into night and moths and bats came out, servants lit lanterns outside the shops of the more enduring fortune-tellers and deck-readers. Mallick entered the premises of one Lady Batevari. A recent arrival in the capital herself, Lady Batevari had, in a short space of time, established a formidable reputation as a most profound sensitive to the hints and future patterns to be glimpsed within the controlling influences of the Warrens. Known throughout the streets as the High Priestess of the Queen of Dreams, her official position within the cult remained uncertain since she and the Grand Temple on God's Round determinedly ignored each other. Some dismissed her as a charlatan, citing her claim to be from Darujhistan where no one who had ever been there could remember hearing her name mentioned. Others named her the true practitioner of the cult and pointed to her record of undeniably accurate prophecies and predictions. Both sides of the debate noted Mallick Rel's devotion as proof positive of their position.

Unaware of the debate, or perhaps keenly aware, Mallick entered the foyer. He was met by a servant dressed in the traditional leggings and tunic of a resident of Pale in northern Genabackis – for it had become fashionable for wealthy households to hire such emigrants and refugees from the Imperial conquests to serve as foot-men, guards and maids in waiting. Mallick handed the man his ocean-blue travelling robes and the man bowed, waving an arm to the parlour.

At the portal, Mallick froze, wincing. A phantasmagoric assemblage of furniture, textiles and artwork from all the provinces of the Empire and beyond assaulted him. It was as if a cyclone such as those that occasionally struck his Falaran homeland had torn through the main Bazaar of Aren and he now viewed the resultant carnage. Entering, he sneered at a Falaran rug – cheap tourist tat, sniffed at a Barghast totem – an obvious fake, and grimaced at the clashing colours of a Letherii board-painting – a copy unfortunate in its accuracy.

A frail old woman's voice quavered from the portal, 'Is that you, young Mallick?'

He turned to a grey-haired, stick-limbed old woman shorter even than he. A slip of a girl, Taya, in white dancing robes steadied the old woman at one arm. Mallick bowed reverently. 'M'Lady.'

Taya steered Lady Batevari to the plushest chair and arranged herself on the carpeted floor beside, feet tucked under the robes that pooled around her. Her kohl-ringed eyes sparkled impishly up at Mallick from above her transparent dancer's veil. The footman entered carrying a tray of sweetmeats and drinks in tall crystal glasses. Mallick and Lady Batevari each took a glass.

'The turmoil among the ranks of these so-called gods continues, Mallick,' Batevari announced with clear relish. 'And it is, of course, reflected here with appropriate turmoil in our mundane Realm.'

Mallick beamed his agreement. 'Most certainly,' he murmured.

She straightened, hands clenching like claws at the armrests. 'They scurry like rats caught in a house aflame!'

Mallick choked into his drink. *Gods, it was a wonder the woman's clients hadn't all thrown themselves into Unta Bay.* Coughing, he shouted, 'Yes. Certainly!'

Lady Batevari fell back into her chair. She emptied her glass in one long swallow. Taya gave Mallick a dramatic wink. 'So, Hero of the crushing of the Seven Cities rebellion,' the old woman intoned, her black eyes now slitted, 'what can this poor vessel offer you? You, who have so far to go – and you will go far, Mallick. Very far indeed, as I have said many times . . .'

'M'Lady is too kind.'

'That was not a *prediction*,' she sneered. 'It is the *truth*. I have *seen* it.'

Mallick exchanged quick glances with Taya who rolled her eyes heavenward. 'I am reassured,' he answered, struggling to keep his naturally soft voice loud.

'Should you be?' Mallick fought a glare. 'In any case,' she continued, perhaps not noticing, 'we were talking of the so-called gods.' The woman stared off into the distance, silent for a long time.

Mallick examined her wrinkled face, her eyes almost lost in their puckered crow's-feet. Not more of her insufferable posing?

'I see a mighty clash of wills closing upon us sooner than anyone imagines,' she crooned, dreamily. 'I see schemes within schemes and a scurrying hither and thither! I see the New colliding against the Old and a Usurpation! Order inverted! And as the Houses collapse the powers turn upon one another like the rats they are. Brother 'gainst sister. They all eye the injured but he is not the weakest. No, yet his time will come. The ones who seem the strongest are . . . Too long have they stood unchallenged! One hides in the dark while they all contend . . . Yet does he see his Path truly – if at all? The darkest – he—' She gasped, coughing and hacking into a fist. 'His Doom is so close at hand! As for the brightest . . . He is ever the most exposed while She who watches will miss her chance and the beasts arise to chase one last chance to survive this coming translation. So the Pantheon shall perish. And from the ashes will arise . . . will arise . . .'

Mallick, staring, drink forgotten despite his utter scepticism, raised a brow, 'Yes? What?'

Lady Batevari blinked her sunken eyes. 'Yes? What indeed?' She held up her empty glass, frowned at it. 'Hernon! More refreshments!'

Mallick pushed down an impulse to throttle the crone. Sometimes he, who should know better than anyone, sometimes even he wondered . . . he glanced to Taya. Her gaze on the old woman appeared uncharacteristically troubled.

'Your presentiments and prophecies astonish me as always,' he announced while Hernon, the servant, refilled the Lady's glass. She merely smiled loftily. 'Your predictions regarding the Crimson Guard, for example,' he said, watching Hernon leave the room. 'They are definitely close now. Much closer than any know. As you foresaw. And a firm hand will be needed to forestall them . . .'

Draining her glass of wine in one long draught, Lady Batevari murmured dreamily, 'As I foresaw . . . And now,' she announced, struggling to rise while Taya hurried to help her. 'I will leave you two to speak in private.' A clawed hand swung to Mallick. 'For I know your true motives for coming here to my humble home in exile, Mallick, Scourge of the Rebellion.'

Standing as well, Mallick put on a stiff smile. He and Taya shared a quick anxious glance. 'Yes? You do?'

'Yes, of course I do!'

Leaning close, she leered. 'You would steal this young flower from my side, you rake! My companion who has been my only solace through my long exile from civilization at sweet Darujhistan.' She raised a hand in mock surrender. 'But who am I to stand between youth and passion!'

Bowing, Mallick waved aside any such intentions. 'Never, m'Lady.'

'So you say, Confounder of the Seven Cities Insurrection. But do not despair.' Lady Batevari winked broadly. 'She may yet yield. Do not abandon the siege.' Taya lowered her face, covering her mouth.

Stifling her laughter, Mallick knew, feeling, oddly, a flash of irritation.

'And so I am off to my quarters – to meditate upon the Ineffable. Hernon! Come!'

The footman returned and escorted Lady Batevari from the parlour. Mallick bowed and Taya curtsied. From the hall she called, 'Remember, child, Hernon shall be just within should our guest forget himself and in the heat of passion press his suit too forcefully.'

Taya covered her mouth again – this time failing to completely mask a giggle. Mallick reflected with surprise on his spasm of anger. If only he knew for certain – senility or malicious insult? He poured himself another glass of the local Untan white.

Taya threw herself into the chair, laughing into both hands.

Mallick waited until certain the old hag was gone. He swirled the wine, noting the dregs gyring like a mist at the bottom. 'Were not I so sure the waters shallow,' he breathed, 'profound depths I would sometime suspect.'

Smiling wickedly, Taya curled her legs beneath her. 'It's her job to appear profound, Mallick. And she really is rather good – wouldn't you say?'

Mallick sipped the wine. Too dry for his liking. 'And this speech? These current prophetic mouthings?'

'Her most recent line.' Taya rearranged the wispy dancer's scarves to expose her long arms. 'Nothing too daring, when you think about it, what with Fener's fall, Trake's rise, eager new Houses in the Deck and swarms of new cards. Rather conventional, really.'

'Yet a certain elegance haunts . . .'

Taya pulled back her long black hair, knotted it through itself. 'If there is any elegance, Mallick, dear,' she smiled, 'it is all due to you.'

Mallick bowed.

'So. The Crimson Guard.' Taya stroked her fingers over the chair's padded rests. 'I heard much of them in Darujhistan, of course. How I wish we had seen them there. They are coming?'

Mallick pursed his lips, thought about sitting opposite the girl, then decided against it. He paced while pretending to examine the artwork, cleared his throat. 'Like the tide, they are close and cannot be forestalled. Their vow — it drags them ever onward. As always, their greatest strength and greatest weakness. And so standing idly by I do not see them.'

Taya's gaze flicked to Mallick. 'Standing idly by during what?'

'Why, during the current times of trouble, of course,' he smiled blandly.

Affecting a pout, Taya blew an errant strand of hair from her face. 'I do not like it when you hold out, Mallick. But never mind. I too have my sources, and I listen in on every one of the old bat's consultations. You would be surprised who comes to see her – then again, I suppose you wouldn't – and no one has such information. Do not tell me you have a source within the Guard.'

Mallick smiled as if at the quaintness of the suggestion and shook his head. 'No, child. If you knew anything about the Guard such a thought would never occur. It is an impossibility.'

The girl shrugged. 'Any organization can be penetrated. Especially a mercenary one.'

Mallick halted, faced Taya directly. 'I must impress upon you the profoundness of your error. Do not think of the Guard as mercenaries. Think of them more as a military *order*.'

Exhaling, Taya looked skyward. 'Gods, not like the ones out of Elingarth. *So* dreary.' She stretched, raising her arms over her head. The thin fabric fell even more, revealing pale, muscular shoulders. 'So, why the visit today, Mallick? Who is it now?'

Mallick watched the girl arc her back, stretching further, thrusting her high small breasts against the translucent cloth. *Mock me also, would you, girl? I need your unmatched skills, child, but like the depths, I ever remember.* Clearing his throat, Mallick topped up his glass and sat. 'Assemblyman Imry, speaking for the Kan Confederacy, must step down. I suggest illness, personal, or in the family . . .'

'Do not presume, Mallick, to tell me how to do my work. I do not tell you how to manoeuvre behind the Assembly.'

Mallick allowed his voice to diminish almost to nothing. 'But you do, cherished.'

She giggled. 'A woman's prerogative, Mallick.'

He raised the glass, acknowledging such.

'So, Councillor Imry . . . This will take a while.'

'Soon.'

'*A while*,' Taya repeated, the sudden iron in her voice surprising from such a slip of a girl.

Mallick raised a placating hand. 'Please, love. Listen. Time for subtlety and slyness is fast dissipating. Waters are rising and all indications tell it will soon be time to push our modest ship on to the current of events.'

Taya leaned back, plucked at the feather-like white cloth draped over one thigh. 'I see. Very well. But it may be very messy. There may be . . . questions.'

Mallick set aside his glass, stood. 'Such questions swept aside by the coming storm. Now, I shall leave you to your work.'

'Am I to begin tonight, then? Dressed as I am?' She spread her arms wide.

Mallick eyed her indifferently. 'If you think it best. I would never presume to instruct you how to pursue your work.'

Taya's slapped the plush cloth of the armrests. 'Damn you, Mallick, to the Chained One's own anguish. I don't know why I put up with you.'

He bowed. 'Perhaps because together we have chance of achieving mutual ambitions.'

Taya waved him away. 'Yes. Perhaps. Why, in the last month alone I have frustrated two assassination attempts against you.' She peered up at him from under lowered eyelids. 'You must be gaining influence.'

Mallick hesitated, unsure. *A mere reminder, or veiled threat?* He decided to bow again – discretion, ever discretion. He had in her, after all, an extraordinary asset. A talent undetected by anyone in the capital. 'You are too kind. And remember, mention the Guard to the old woman again. And the firm hand needed. She must speak of it more often now.'

Taya nodded without interest. 'Yes, Mallick. As ever.'

Outside, Mallick pulled his robes tight against the cooling evening air and pursed his fleshy lips. How dispiriting it was to have to stoop to cajoling and unctuous flattery to gain his way. Still, it had proved a worthy investment. No one, not even Laseen and her Claws who used to have this city tied in silk ribbons, could suspect who it was that had so successfully secreted herself within striking distance of the Imperial Palace. It was only his own *peculiar* talents that revealed her to him. Taya Radok of Darujhistan. Daughter of Vorcan Radok herself, premier assassin of that city. Trained by her own mother in the arts of covert death since before she could walk. Come to Unta to exact revenge against the Empire that slew her mother. And what a delicious vengeance together they would inflict – though not the sort the child might have in mind.

Stepping down into the loud, lantern-lit street, thoughts of assassins and eliminations turned Mallick's mind to his own safety. He glanced about, searching for his own minder but realized that of course he would never catch a glimpse of the man. He sensed him, however, nearby. Another of the orphans he seemed to have a talent for collecting: an old tattooed mage, long imprisoned in the gaol of Aren – how easy to effect his escape and gain his loyalty. And how valuable the man's – how shall he put it – *unconventional* talents have proven.

Slipping into the tide of citizens and servants crowding Diviner's Way, Mallick allowed himself a tight satisfied grin. Only two, dearest Taya? He had lost count of the number of sorcerous assaults Oryan had deflected with the strange Elder magic of his Warren delvings. Taya and Oryan: two powerful servants, of a kind. And of course, Mael, his God – and something else as well. It was almost as if the fates had woven the pattern for him to trace all the way to . . .

Mallick stopped suddenly, almost tripping himself and those next to him within the flow of bodies. He thought of the old woman's rantings. The Gods meddling? *Him?* No. It couldn't be. None would dare. He was his own man. No one led him.

A hand hard and knotted with arthritis took his elbow, eyes as dark and flat as wet stones close at his side studying him – Oryan. Mallick shook him off. It could not be. He would have a word with Mael. Soon.

* *. *

The first inkling Ghelel had of trouble was when the family fencing-master, Quinn, raised his dagger hand for a pause. She took the opportunity to squeeze her side where the pain of exertion threatened to double her over. 'Why stop?' she panted, breathless. 'You had me there.'

Ignoring her, the old man crossed to the closed doors of the stable and used the point of his parrying blade to open one a slit.

'What is it? Father come to frown at you again for training me?' The stamp of many hooves reached her and she straightened, rolling one shoulder, wincing. 'Who is it? The Adal family early from Tali? I should change.'

'Quiet – m'Lady.'

She sheathed her parrying gauche and slim longsword, pushed back the long black hair pasted to her face. The front of her laced leather jerkin was dark with sweat. She picked up a rag to wipe her face. How properly horrified they would be to see her all dishevelled like this. But then, in the final count, her reputation didn't really matter; she was only a ward of the Sellaths, not blood-related. She dropped the rag when raised voices sounded from the main house. Shouts? 'What is it, Quinn?'

He turned from the main doors. Dust curled in the narrow shaft of light streaming into the stables. The horses nickered behind Ghelel, uneasy. He hadn't sheathed either his narrow Kanian fencing longsword or his parrying weapon. Beneath the man's mop of grey-shot hair his gaze darted about the stable, still ignoring her.

A crash of wood being kicked, hooves stamping, a clash of metal – swordplay! She started for the doors. Through the gap she glimpsed soldiers of the Malazan garrison. Damned Malazans! What could they want here? She took breath to yell but Quinn dropped his dagger and slapped a hand to her mouth.

71

How dare the man! What was this? Was he in league with them? She fought to force an elbow beneath his chin.

Somehow he twisted her around, lifted her at the waist and began backing down the length of the stable. All the while he was murmuring, 'Quiet lass, m'Lady. Quiet now.'

Kidnapping! Was this all some kind of Malazan plot? But why her? What could they possibly want with her? Struggling, she managed to free a hand and drew her dagger. The man did something at her elbow – a pinch or thrust of his thumb – and the blade fell from her numb hand. *How did he do that?* He snapped up the blade and kept going.

He carried her to a stall, gently shushed the mare within, then kicked aside the straw and manure. Both her wrists in one hand he began feeling about the wood slats of the floor. 'We have to hide,' he whispered. 'Hide from them. Do you understand?'

'*Hide?* We have to help! Are you some kind of coward?'

He winced at her tone. 'Lower your voice, Burn curse you! Or I'll use this on you.' He raised her dagger, pommel first.

'I don't have to hide. I'm not important.'

The sturdy blade of the gauche caught at an edge. A hidden trapdoor, no wider than a man's shoulders, swung up. 'Yes you are.'

Ghelel stared, bewildered. *What?* In that instant Quinn pushed her headfirst into the darkness.

She landed face down into piled damp rags that stank of rot. 'Aw, Gods! Hood take you, you blasted oaf! Help! Anyone!'

Darkness as the trapdoor shut, a thump of Quinn jumping down. 'Yell again and I'll knock you out,' he hissed, his voice low. 'Your choice.'

'Knock me out? Neither of us can see a thing!'

'Your eyes will adjust.'

Silence, her own breath panting. 'What's going on?'

'Shhh . . .' The gentle slide of metal on leather and wood as he raised his longsword.

She could make out faint streams of light now slanting down from between the slats. 'Are you going to . . . murder me?'

'No, but I'll stick whoever opens that trap.'

'What's going on?'

'Looks like the local Fist is rounding up hostages from all the first families.'

'Hostages! Why?'

She could just make out the pale oval of his face studying her. 'Not been paying attention to things, hey?' He shrugged. 'Well, why should you have, I suppose . . .'

'What do you mean?'

'Insurrection. Secession. Call it what you will. The Talian noble houses never accepted Kellanved's rule – certainly not Laseen's.'

'My father . . .'

'Stepfather.'

'Yes, I'm a ward! But he might as well be my father! Is he safe? What about Jhem? Little Darian?'

'They may all have been taken.'

Ghelel threw herself at the ladder she could now just see. He pulled her down. She punched and kicked him while he held her to him. As he had to the mare above, he made soft shushing noises. Eventually she relaxed in his arms. 'Quiet now, m'Lady,' he whispered. 'Or they'll take you too.'

'I'm not important.'

'Yes you are.'

'What—'

He put his finger to her mouth. She stilled. Listening, she kept her body motionless, but relaxed, not straining, worked to remain conscious of her breath which she kept deep, not shallowing – techniques Quinn himself had taught her.

A step above. A booted foot pressing down on straw. The scratching of a blade on wood. Quinn raised his longsword. He held her dagger out to her, which she took.

A pause of silence then boots retreating, distant muted talk. Quinn relaxed. 'We'll wait for night,' he breathed. She felt awful about it but she nodded.

A nudge woke Ghelel to absolute darkness and she started, panicked. 'Shhh,' someone said from the dark and, remembering, she relaxed.

'Gods, it's dark.'

'Yes. Let's have a peek.'

She listened to him carefully ascending the ladder, push at the trapdoor. Starlight streamed down. Ghelel checked her sheathed weapons, adjusted her leather jerkin and trousers. Quinn stepped up out of sight. A moment later his hand appeared waving her up.

Someone had ransacked the stable but most of the horses remained. The double doors hung open. A light shone from the kitchens of the main house. Ghelel strained to listen but heard only the wind brushing through trees. It was more quiet this night at the country house than she could ever remember. Quinn signalled that he would go ahead for a look. She nodded.

Weapons ready, Quinn edged up to one door, leaned out. He was still for a long moment, then he gave a disdainful snort. 'I can smell you,' he called to the night.

Movement from all around: a scrape of gravel, a creak of leather armour. 'Send the girl out,' someone called, 'Quinn, or whatever your name really is. She's all we want. Walk out right now and keep walking.'

'I'll just go get her,' and he hopped back inside, ducking. Crossbow bolts slammed into the timbers of the door, sending it swinging.

'Cease fire, damn your hairless crotches! He's only one man!'

Hunched, Quinn took her arm, nodded to the rear. They retreated as far back as was possible. 'Now what?' she whispered.

'If this fellow knows what he's doing this could get very ugly very quick. We'll have to make a run for it – out the back.'

Something crashed just inside the front of the barn then three flaming brands arced through the doors. Blue flames spread like animals darting across the straw-littered floor. 'Damn,' said Quinn, 'he knows what he's doing.' He clenched Ghelel's arm. 'Whatever you do, do *not* stop! Keep going, cut and run! Into the woods, yes?'

'Yes.'

'Good. Now, we dive out then come up running.'

He kicked open the rear door, waited an instant, then dived out, rolling. Ghelel followed without a thought as if this was just another exercise in all the years she'd spent training in swordplay and riding – there'd been little else for her to do as a mere ward. Something sang through the air above her, thudding into wood. Ahead, Quinn exchanged blows with two Malazan soldiers. Then he was off again even though the two men still stood. Coming abreast of them Ghelel raised her weapons but neither paid her any attention. One had a hand clenched to his neck where blood jetted between his fingers; the other was looking down and holding his chest as if pressing in his breath. Ghelel ran past them.

Shouts sounded behind. Boots stamped the ground. Quinn was making for the closest arm of woods, avoiding the nearby vineyards. Whistling announced crossbow fire. Distantly, horses' hooves slammed the ground. Ghelel cursed; there was no way they could outrun mounted pursuit. What had Quinn been thinking? But then, there was no way they could have remained within.

Further missiles whipped the air nearby. She put them out of her mind, concentrated on running. All that remained ahead was the moonlit swath of a turned field then the cover of dense woods would be theirs. Ahead, Quinn gestured to the right: horsemen racing the treeline, all in Malazan greys. Fanderay take them! They'd been so *close*.

Quinn kept glancing back, 'Keep going!'

Ghelel put everything she could into her speed but the soft uneven earth clung to her boots. The horsemen cut ahead of them. They turned their mounts side to side, swords bright in the cold light. Quinn made directly for the nearest. The man's fearlessness almost brought a shout of admiration from Ghelel. He sloughed the man's swing then did something to the horse that made it rear, shrieking. The man fell, tumbling sideways. Quinn ignored him to turn to the next. Ghelel reached their line. The nearest Malazan had already dismounted. He thrust as if she would obligingly impale herself but she stopped short, avoiding the jab, then spun putting everything she had into a thrust of the gauche. The blade caught him full in the stomach, was held by the mail. Perhaps only an inch of blade entered him. Yet she'd been trained to expect this – more importantly the man had just had the breath knocked from him. She knelt then straightened thrusting up with the short blade to feel it enter upwards behind his chin. It locked there so tightly the man's convulsion tore it from her hand. She turned away to check the next threat, thinking, *Burn forgive me – I have killed a man.*

Quinn was engaging two opponents, the rest were closing.

'Run, damn you!' he yelled.

'*No.*' She thrust at the nearest; he parried, declined to counterattack. *Damn them! They're holding us up.* Hooves shook the ground from behind. She turned: a calvaryman, leaning sideways, blade raised. She thrust hers up crossways. The blow smashed her arm, her hilts slammed high on her chest and she was down.

Yelling came dimly through her ringing ears; rearing horses kicked up mud around her. Her breath steamed in the cold night air. She climbed to her feet, weaving, blinking. Quinn still stood, dodging, parrying blows from above. She bent to retrieve her longsword from the churned mud. Another horse reared, shrieking, stumbled backwards into the brush and Quinn thrust her after it. She fell, clawing at the struggling animal. Its rider was pinned beneath; she ignored him. Quinn forced her on. Together they fell into the thick brush. Branches slashed her face, cutting her cheeks, tore at her hair. She pushed forward.

They burst out into low brush and the thick entangled branches of young pines. Quinn took her arm and suddenly she found she had to support him. Longsword still in her grip, she held him up. Bright blood smeared his left side where his shirt hung open, sliced. He smiled blearily at her, his grey hair wet with sweat. 'Gave them a good run we did. Proud of you.'

'Shh, now. We'll be all right.'

'No, no. You go on. Leave me. Run.'

'No.'

He raised his hilt to her, saluting. 'Proud of you. You did well, Ghelel Rhik Tayliin. A pleasure to serve.'

Hooves pounded the treeline, shouts for the crossbowmen. 'We're not done yet.' What did he mean, Tayliin? The only Tayliins she knew of had ruled during the last Hegemony. Kellanved and Dancer had the last of them slain when they took Tali.

They heard more horses thundering up the slope of the field. Quinn urged her on. Just pushing her away made him fall to his knees. She couldn't leave him like that and put an arm around him to raise him up. 'Apologies,' he mumbled.

'What did you mean, Tayliin?'

The old man just smiled, his face as pale as sun-bleached cloth. Shouts snapped her head around – angry yelling – the clash of weaponry. What in the name of the Queen of Mysteries was going on out there? Why hadn't they come for them?

Silence but for the thumping of hooves and horses' nickering.

'Hello within! Are you there, Quinn?' someone bellowed from the field.

The weaponmaster raised a finger to his lips, gave Ghelel a wink.

'It's me, damn you! You know my voice!'

Quinn struggled to sheathe his longsword. Ghelel helped him.

'Very well!' came a vexed call. 'It's me, Amaron!'

Quinn smiled. 'What are you doing here!' he called back and winced in pain. He finished, softer, 'Haven't you heard of delegating?'

'Yes, yes. Came as quick as I could. Come on down, will you.'

Quinn waved her forward. 'It's safe, m'Lady. Amaron was my commander.'

'Your commander?'

'In the, ah, military. I served under him.' He tried to walk but stumbled. She held him up. 'My thanks – apologies.'

'Here.' Arm around him, Ghelel guided him forward.

'Thank you. Not the impression I wish to give.'

'Togg can take that.'

'You curse like a marine now, m'Lady. I despair.'

'Sorry.'

'Do not apologize. Offer sarcasm.'

'Always teaching, hey?'

'Touché.'

They pushed their way through to stumble out on to the field and into a unit of some thirty cavalry, the horses' breath clouding the night air. Almost all Quinn's weight now rested on Ghelel's arm. Dismounted soldiers immediately took him from her. Calls sounded for a healer. They laid him on a horse blanket.

'Who of you is Amaron?' she asked.

'I.' A man dismounted, his boots thumping to the mud. He was a giant of a fellow, Napan, in blackened unadorned mail beneath dark-green riding cloaks.

'He's lost a lot of blood.'

'He's in good hands.'

'What of the Sellaths? Can you take me to them?'

Amaron rested his gauntleted hands at his waist, studied her. He dropped his gaze. 'I'm sorry – Ghelel. They've been taken. Fist Kal'il will no doubt be using them, and others, as guarantors of safe passage.'

'Safe passage?'

'Out of Tali. By ship, probably. The capital is now under the control of a troika of Talian noble families.'

Ghelel glanced about at the men; none wore Malazan greys. Amaron himself wore no insignia or sigil at all. In fact the calvarymen wore dark blue – the old Talian colours. 'Who commands?'

'Choss. General Choss has been granted military command.'

'Not the same Choss who was High Fist for a time?'

'Yes, the same.'

'I thought he was dead.'

'That was the general idea.'

Ghelel found herself studying this man; Quinn had called him his old commander. 'What of you? May I ask what you do?'

A shrug. 'Whatever needs be done. You could say I'm in charge of intelligence gathering.'

Un-huh. 'Well, thank you, Amaron, for our deliverance.' He bowed. 'But may I accompany Quinn?'

'Certainly. We'll take him to the manor house, yes? There we can have a private conversation.'

Yes, a private conversation about certain ravings of a delirious wounded man perhaps? Until she knew whether Quinn should have revealed what he had she would play the innocent. Right now she wasn't certain how much she trusted this fellow. Quinn clearly did but the man felt cold to her, oddly detached. Quinn's condition didn't seem to affect him at all. She needed the weaponmaster conscious and well. Startled, she realized that he was possibly the last remaining link to her old life. She hurried to follow the soldiers carrying him down to the house. Their way was lit by the stables now sending tall flames high into the night sky.

* * *

Twelve days after descending from the mountains they reached the squalid village Traveller named Canton's Landing – no more than a collection of straw-roofed huts next to a slumped moat and ancient burned-down palisade overlooking the tidal flats of the Explorer's Sea.

'We must wait here?' Ereko asked.

He nodded, his guarded, lined brown face revealing nothing.

Ereko sighed. *Enchantress give me the patience to endure.*

It was close to evening and they claimed an abandoned hut. Ereko attempted to stretch his cramped arms and legs and failed. Human dwellings simply did not agree with him. He'd always been better off sleeping under the stars. A villager, an old woman, came hobbling up with a basket under one arm. 'A meal approaches,' he told Traveller. 'I wish they wouldn't. From the look of them they need the food more than us.'

'They are afraid of us and it's all that they have to offer. I also believe they want us to do something for them.'

Grinning a mouth empty of teeth, bowing, the old woman set out bowls of fish mush and hard-baked bread.

'Send your headman,' Traveller said to her in Talian. 'We would speak with him.'

'The headman is dead. His nephew will speak with you. I will send him tomorrow.'

Later, while Traveller slept, Ereko stared out over the embers of the fire to the phosphor-glow of the waves rolling in to the strand. He saw another sea in his thoughts, a far angrier and savage sea, this one iron-grey and heaving with cliff-tall breakers. That last season the Riders had arrived early at the Stormwall. The section of curtain wall he faced remained quiet as the Riders no longer challenged him. Indeed, these last few years his time upon the wall had actually been boring. Of course this pleased his Korelan captors no end; one more portion of the wall they need not worry about.

Ereko had watched the distant figure as he was chained as all were at the ankle. Watched as he'd been lowered to his station, a narrow stone ledge, without commotion or resistance. The man sat unperturbed as the ice-skeined waves smashed the wall and the spray obscured him. Many pointed as Riders surfaced far out in the strait. Some screamed, begged for release. His man remained sitting and the whisper of a fearful suspicion touched Ereko: might this fellow be one of those brave enough to refrain from defending their piece of the wall, sacrificing themselves to contribute in a small way to the enormous structure's erosion?

A file of the Riders closed, distant dark shapes upon the waves. The otherworldly cold that accompanied them gripped even Ereko's limbs. Frost limned the leathers of his sleeves and trousers. Ice thickened over the stones making the footing slick and treacherous. As the Riders neared, the Korelan Chosen tossed down weapons to those lost souls lowest and most exposed.

He was relieved when his man stood, sword in hand. The waves breasted ever higher. Their foaming crests entirely submerged some defenders. He watched closely now; the first rank would strike soon. Arrows and bolts shot from above arced down among the broaching Riders. Ice-jagged lances couched at hips, they rolled forward mounted upon what seemed half wave, half ice-sculpted horse. Armour of ice-scales glittered opalescent and emerald among the whitecaps.

Spray obscured the first strike. When the waters pulled back his man still stood. Up and down the curtain wall men clashed against wave-born Riders. Most failed, of course, for what mere man or woman could oppose such eldritch alien sorcery? Auroras played like waves themselves across the night sky. The lights of another world, or so claimed the Korelri.

In the pause between ranks of attacking Riders the waters withdrew revealing most stations empty or supporting fallen prisoners hanging by their ankle fetters like grotesque fruit. Korelri Chosen descended on ropes to clear away the dead. New prisoners were lowered, arms flailing. These the Chosen did not bother securing by the ankles.

His man remained. He'd sat again, not out of bravado, Ereko realized, but for warmth as he hugged his legs to his chest.

The Chosen used knots that pulled in a certain way released their burden and in this fashion the prisoners were stranded at their landings. Some grabbed hold of the ropes in a futile effort to regain the heights but archers shot these and the lesson was not lost on the others.

The surf of the strait regathered its power. The Riders who had been circling far out swung landward once again. And so it would go for days on end until the storm blew itself out. Then would come a week or two of relative calm when the wall faced mere mundane weather. During this time the incomprehensible presence deep within the strait regenerated its strength.

That night the second wave came swiftly. As it closed, a Malazan prisoner of war farther along the curving wall bellowed a challenge or prayer and launched himself from his landing. A Korelri Chosen was swiftly lowered to take his place. The crest struck, shuddering the stone of the Stormwall as if the force of an entire sea were launching itself against the land.

When the waters and ice slabs sloughed away from the scarred stone, his man remained. Another, a fellow Malazan prisoner by his rags, was shouting to him, calling, one arm out entreating. His man saluted him and the fellow straightened and gravely responded in kind.

As the storm continued through the night Ereko's man was the only original left within his line of sight. Prisoners continued to be lowered from above – the Korelri considered it a favour to offer these men and women the chance to regain their dignity by falling in defence of the wall. The prisoners obviously held other opinions.

Slowly, almost imperceptibly, the pattern of Rider attacks at this section of wall changed. Pressure eased along the curtain as the Riders circled and withdrew. Korelri Chosen gathered above, watching, pointing excitedly. Ereko peered out to sea: darker smears had emerged from the depths, the Wandwielders, Stormrider mages. He raised himself higher; rarely did he see these beings. Night-black ice was their armour, forged perhaps within the lightless utter depths of the sea. They carried rods and wands of precious stone and crystal, olivine, garnet and serpentine, with which they lashed the wall with summoned power and shattering cold during the most hard-pressed and ferocious assaults.

The Riders circled out amid the whitecaps; one approached, headed directly for the man the Enchantress had pointed out to Ereko as being the instrument of his deliverance. The Rider closed, rearing as his wave crested and smashed upon the wall. When the spume and mist cleared his man still stood and the Rider was gone.

A bloodthirsty, triumphant cheer went up among the Korelri Chosen gathered above. It seemed to Ereko to shake the wall just as ferociously as the waves themselves.

His man peered up for a time, then pointedly turned his back.

Another single Rider rolled forward, lance raised. Ereko was horrified to see his man toss his sword aside to stand unarmed, waiting. The Rider pulled up short, lance couched. It rose and fell with the waves and it seemed to Ereko that the two spoke. Then the Rider leaned to one side and withdrew.

Far out, the Wandwielders lowered their staves of glittering crystal and all withdrew to the right and left of this course of the broad Stormwall curtain. For this section of wall, the attack was over.

The Korelri Chosen left Ereko's man chained to his landing. That night Ereko yanked open the corroded fetter at his ankle, climbed the wall, descended to the fellow's station, tore the fetter from him and carried him numb with cold up and over the wall. He swam the warmer inner Crack Narrows behind the wall with him held high at his shoulder. He reached the abandoned shores of what the Korelri name Remnant Isle before dawn touched the uppermost pennants of the wall's watchtowers.

Within the shelter of boulders he sat and waited for sunrise. The man lay insensate, almost dead from exposure. Yet he was undoubtely much more than a man. Ereko's sight, while nowhere as penetrating as that of his ancestors, told him that. And then there was the attention of his Enchantress, whom some now named the Queen of Dreams. The fellow was fit, certainly. But not overly broad or large, which so many mistakenly equate with prowess in combat. No, it was more an aura about him – even in repose. A great burden and a great danger. Not in the mere physical sense. Rather, a spirituality. Potential. Great potential to create. Or to destroy. And there the danger.

After the sun warmed the fellow sufficiently he wakened and Ereko greeted him. 'My name is Ereko.'

'Traveller.' He peered around at the weed-encrusted rocks of the shore. 'Why have you done this?'

'I have been planning my own escape for some time. Yet I knew I would have a much better chance were I not alone. Your performance yesterday convinced me that with you my chances would be much greater.'

The man laughed. 'It looks like I wasn't much help.'

'Do not be fooled. We are far from free. We are in the centre of the Korelan subcontinent. The Korelri Chosen have no doubt alerted everyone to hunt for us. We have far to go yet.'

He nodded at that; accepting the story or merely disinclined to pursue it. Ereko could not be certain. 'And who are you? You are no Jaghut – you are taller. You are not Toblakai either, nor Trell. But there is something of them about you.'

81

'We called ourselves "The People" – *Thel Akai*.'

Traveller stared, confused. 'Tarthinoe . . . or Thelomen, you mean?'

'No, Thel Akai. Those you name are descendants of my people.'

'Their ancestor? But that is impossible. I have never heard of your kind.'

'All have been gone for ages – save myself. That is, I have met no others.'

'I am sorry.'

'Thank you.'

'And I am sorry for something else as well.'

'What is that?'

'I must return to the wall. They have my sword.'

Ereko took a long deep breath. *Enchantress, how could you have done this to me?* 'I see. Then it seems I must unrescue you.'

The next morning at Canton's Landing they marked trees for the ship. At noon they returned to the hut to find an old man crouched there in the shade awaiting them. This was the nephew? The man nodded and smiled and nodded and smiled, stopping only when Traveller knelt beside him and rested a reassuring hand on his arm.

'You have suffered a tragedy here,' he said, startling the man.

'Yes, honoured sir. We are afflicted. Death from the seas. Slavers and raiders. Again and again they come. Soon there will be none of us left.'

'Move inland,' Ereko suggested.

The old man's smile was gap-toothed. 'We are fisher folk here. We know of no other way of life.'

'We are very sorry but we cannot—' Ereko began, but Traveller raised a hand.

'Do you have any possessions from these raiders? Weapons? Armour?'

The old man nodded eagerly. 'Yes, yes . . . old gear can be found here and there.'

'Show us.'

Mystified, Ereko accompanied Traveller and the old man as they patrolled the strand. They picked up a piece of corroded metal here, a fragment of broken stone there. Traveller knelt to pull a length of sun-bleached wood from the sand; the broken handle of a war club. A tassel of some sort hung from its grip. He rubbed the ragged feathers and dried leather in his fingers then stood.

'I will help you,' he said, and he brushed his hands clean.

Ereko stared, astonished. *What unforeseen turn does the Lady send now?*

'Yes, yes,' the old man repeated. 'Yes. Thank you, honoured sir. We can never—'

'Help us build our boat.'

'Yes. Of course. Whatever you need.'

As they walked Traveller asked over the loud susurrus of the waves, 'You are expecting them soon, aren't you?'

The old man flinched, startled again. 'Yes. Soon. They come this season. The grey raiders from the sea.'

*   *   *

A patrol of Malazan regulars posted to the Wickan frontier spotted the smoke in the distance and altered their route to investigate. They found a burnt camp of the Crow Clan. The Wickan dead lay where they had fallen. The patrol sergeant, Chord, took in the Crow bodies: elders wrapped in prayer blankets, three obvious cripples and an assortment of youths. He studied the trampled wreckage of pennants, flag-staves, a covered cart and painted yurts. All hinted at some sort of a Wickan religious pilgrimage or ceremonial procession. Seated around a roaring fire, a gang of invaders, more of the tide of self-styled 'settlers', feasted on slaughtered Crow horses in front of bound Wickan captives. As they gorged themselves on horseflesh they ignored the regulars.

'Ran out of supplies on your long march, hey?' Chord called to the closest man.

This one smiled, continued to eat. A felt blanket flew back and a man straightened from one squat dwelling, cinching up his pants. Chord glimpsed a small pale figure curling beneath blankets.

'Greetings, brother Malazans,' this one called.

'We ain't your brothers.'

'Well, thank you for coming by, but we're safe now from these barbarians.'

'*You're* safe.'

'They attacked us.'

'You invaded their lands.'

'*Malazan* lands, as the Empress has reminded us all. In any case, they refused to sell even one of their horses – and us starving!'

'Wickans regard their horses like members of their own family. They'd no more sell one of them than their own son or daughter.'

'We offered fair price. They refused us out of plain obstinacy.'

Chord leaned to one side, spat a brown stream of rustleaf juice. 'So you helped yourself.'

The man gestured his confusion. 'We set down a fair price in coin and took the worst of the herd. Lame, useless to anyone. And they attacked! All of them. Children! Crones! Like rabid beasts they are. Less than human.'

The sergeant looked to the bound youths, pushed a handful of leaves into his mouth. 'And these?'

'Ours. Captives of war. We'll sell them.'

'Hey? What's that you say? Captives of *war*?'

'Aye. A war of cleansing. These Wickan riff-raff have squatted on the plains long enough. All this good land uncultivated. Wasted.'

Adjusting his crossbow, the sergeant pressed a hand to his side, fingers splayed. As one, the men of the patrol levelled their crossbows on the gang of settlers.

The men gaped, strips of flesh in their hands. Their spokesman paused but then calmly resumed straightening his clothes. 'What's this? We've broken no laws. The Empress has promised this land to all who would come to farmstead. Put up your weapons and go.'

'We will, once we've taken what's ours.'

'Yours? What's that?'

'Just so happens I'm also a student of Imperial law, an' those laws say that any captives of war are the property of the Throne. An' as a duly sanctioned representative of the Throne I will now take possession of the captives.'

'You'll *what*? Whoever heard of such a law!'

'I have, an' that's good enough. Now stand aside.'

A skinny shape exploded from the tent, a waif in an oversized torn shirt. She yelled a torrent of Wickan at the sergeant, who cocked a brow. 'Well, well. Seems everyone's a damned lawyer these days.'

'What's she on about?' the spokesman asked.

'This lass here has invoked Wickan law 'gainst you. A blood cleansing.'

'What in the name of Burn does that mean?'

'Knives. Usually to the death.'

The man gaped at Chord. 'What? *Her*?'

The men at the bonfire slowly climbed to their feet. 'Cover them, Junior,' Chord said aside.

'Aye.' The patrol spread out, crossbows still levelled.

'You can't be serious. You're listening to this Wickan brat?'

'I am.'

'She's just a child!'

The sergeant stilled, his eyes hard on the spokesman. 'Seein' as she's old enough for you to rape, maybe she's old enough to hold you accountable for it, don't you think?'

The man eased back into a fighting stance, shrugging. He drew a knife from his belt sheath. 'Fine. I'll just have to kill her too.'

Chord tossed the girl his own knife. She took it, screamed a Wickan curse and leapt.

It was over even more swiftly than Chord had assumed. In the end he had to pull the girl off the hacked body. The patrol lined up the youths and marched them off to the fort. As they went the men swore that word of this would spread and that they'd see the fort burnt to the ground. Part of Chord hoped they'd try; the other part worried that maybe he'd just bought his lieutenant more trouble than their garrison of one undersized company could handle.

＊　＊　＊

Kyle lay in his bunk on board the *Kestral*, his eyes clenched closed. Seasick, his stomach roiling, he tensed his body against the juddering of the ship as it rolled alarmingly once more. Nearly a month at sea, their last landfall along the west coast of Bael lands, and now for these last five days the *Kestral* had ridden the leading edge of a storm driving them north-west – a direction the superstitious sailors would not even look.

The tag-end of his dream eluded his efforts to grasp it and he groaned, giving in to wakefulness. For the fleetest moment the sweet scent of perfume had seemed to tease his nose and the soft warmth of a hand seemed to linger at his brow. But now he was still in his bunk aboard the *Kestral*, weeks at sea and the Gods alone knew how close to, or how far from, its destination: Stratem. The adopted homeland of the Crimson Guard.

A land that meant nothing to Kyle.

Tarred wood shivered and creaked two hand-widths from his nose. Beaded condensation edged down the curved wall of planking to further soak the clammy burlap and straw padding he lay upon. The wood shivered visibly, pounded by the storm that threatened to shake the vessel into wreckage. His eyes watered in the smoke of rustleaf and D'bayang poppy that drifted in layers in the narrow companionway. The stink of old vomit, oil, sweat and stagnant sea-water all combined to make his stomach clench even tighter. Below him, Guardsmen talked, gambled and studied the Dragons deck.

He rolled on to his side. The curved plainsman's knife that he kept on a thong around his neck gouged into his shoulder. Blocking the narrow passage, the men were gathered in a knot around a small wood board on which the Dragon cards lay arranged. Slate was the Talent for this reading – everyone agreed Slate was one of the most accurate in the Guard.

Stoop's grizzled face appeared; he'd climbed the four berths to Kyle's topmost slot. He hooked the stump of his elbow over the cot's lip and winked, motioning down to the reading.

'Slate's angry as Hood. Says the Queen of the House of Life dominates. Says that's damned odd and the reading's about as useful as a D'rek priest in a whorehouse.'

Kyle sighed and lay back on his berth. 'Hood's bones, it's just a bunch of cards.' Since joining the Guard he'd been confronted by more superstitions and gods than he'd ever imagined could exist, let alone keep straight or even believe.

Stoop scratched his grimed fingers through his patchy beard. 'Lot more'n that,' he said, mostly to himself.

'Try again,' someone urged Slate.

'Can't,' he answered. 'Once a day.'

The thin, painted wood cards clicked as Slate gathered them together.

'Try anyway.'

'Bad luck.'

'You mean maybe we'd see through your horseshit?'

'I mean I could bring all kinds a trouble down on our heads.'

From the corner of his eye, Kyle saw Stoop nod seriously at that. Once a day, not near a shrine or sanctified ground, burial grounds or a recent battle. Kyle couldn't believe all the folklore and ritual that surrounded the deck. The cards were supposed to reveal the future but how could they if you couldn't use them half the time? He thought that too convenient for whoever sold the damned things.

Bored, weak and nauseous from the constant roll and bucking of the ship, he shut his eyes against the smoke and tried to seek out that dream once more. It eluded him; he attempted to doze again.

The door of the companionway crashed open allowing a rush of water down the stairs and a gust of frigid damp air that pulled at the lanterns. Everyone cursed the man coming down the stairs. It was one of the hired Kurzan sailors. His bare feet slapped the boards and his woollen shirt dripped sea-water on to the planks. Beneath black hair, plastered down by rain and spray, his bearded face was pale.

'The captain wants you all on deck, armed,' he announced in

Nabrajan, and stood aside. Everyone pulled on what leathers or gambesons they had; most metal armour had been greased in animal fat and stowed against rusting. Besides, it was more a danger than protection at sea. They asked questions of the sailor but he would say no more, only make signs against evil at his chest while his eyes, resigned and haunted, avoided them all. Kyle dressed in his gambeson shirt. He pulled on the leather cap he wore beneath his helmet and cinched his weapon belt as everyone lined up. They climbed the stairs passing the sailor, who shivered and wouldn't raise his eyes.

On deck, Kyle found a guide-rope and covered his eyes from the spray. He took in the reefed sails and the white-capped, churning seas. Men pointed, shouting, their words torn away by the wind. Kyle followed their gazes and couldn't believe what he saw: among the waves and blowing spume moved human figures. What appeared to be armour upon them gleamed sapphire and rainbow opalescent. They seemed to ride the waves. White foam flew about them. While he watched, some of the waves curled into horse-like shapes and dived, carrying their riders with them only to broach the rough waters further along. The armour shone like frost and they carried jagged-edged lances.

Kyle searched the horizons. Of the Guard's fleet of twenty ships, he could only see the *Wanderer*. The nearest mercenary, Tolt, gripped Kyle's arm, shouted, 'Stormriders! We've blown into the Cut! We don't have a chance!'

Kyle's immediate reaction was one of awe and numb fear. Two months ago, near the beginning of the journey, Stoop had explained something of the strange convoluted archipelago and continents that the Crimson Guard called home. Quon Tali, and to the north, Falar. To the south, Korel. A deep ocean trench of unpredictable storms and contrary currents, Stoop explained, separated Quon Tali from Korel, or Fist, as it was sometimes known. The Stormriders had claimed this passage for as long as anyone could recall. Twice the Malazans had tried to push through to reach Korel, and twice the Riders sank the fleets. They allowed none to trespass and warred continuously with the Korelans over the coastline of their lands.

Kyle went to the gunwale. Through the spray he could make out a number of Riders circling the ship. While he watched, incredulous, the ones nearest the *Kestral* saluted the vessel with upraised lances and submerged. More surged abreast of his vessel. One broached the waters close by and seemed to be watching him. But as the tall helm hid the being's eyes, Kyle couldn't be sure. On impulse he drew his tulwar and raised it straight up before his face, saluting the Rider. The alien entity straightened and raised his lance, its barbed point flashing cruelly. Kyle laughed his palpable relief and sheathed his sword. Tolt was right, it seemed to him – if it had come to a fight they wouldn't have stood a chance.

'That Rider saluted you.'

Kyle turned. There stood Greymane, the only person fully armoured in banded iron, his legs planted wide apart, yet steadying himself at a guide-rope. Kyle remembered the Malazan renegade's words at Kurzan: 'water 'n' me, we don't get along.' The veteran's eyes held a calculation Kyle had never seen before. 'Or he was saluting you.'

A tight sardonic smile reached the man's sky-pale eyes. 'No. I told them to cut that out long ago.'

Kyle turned away; this was not what he wanted to hear from this strange Malazan turncoat. Jokes! This renegade had torn something irreplacable from him – something that drove him to his own vow – but not one in sympathy to the Guard's. He gripped the gunwale. It was numbing cold, yet any change from the rank enclosed quarters below was welcome for a time. They were packed tight on all the ships. Every Guardsman squeezed shoulder to shoulder. 'You've been through here before, haven't you?' Kyle asked, facing the slate-grey sea. He watched the Riders circling, submerging one by one. A few mercenaries remained on deck, their faces hardened now that panic had passed. He reminded himself some of these men had witnessed wonders far greater than this.

For some time Greymane didn't answer, but Kyle could feel him there, close. He heard the man's layered banding grating at his shoulders and arms as he shifted his stance with the lurching of the ship. 'Aye. Many times. I grew up on Geni – an island south of Quon. My father fished the Cut. Saw them many times I did, as a boy. Before my father went out and never came back. Taken by them, some said. I swore off the sea then. Joined the army.'

The renegade paused and Kyle could imagine him offering a rueful grin – fat lot of good that choice had done! But Kyle refused to look. This man had taken all that was precious from him. Murdered a guiding spirit of his people! He did not want to hear this.

'Command thought my familiarity with the Cut would be an asset for the Korel invasion,' Greymane continued. 'And for a time they were right. But as the years passed the stalemate drove me to try something no one had ever tried . . .'

The last of the Riders disappeared in swirls of pale emerald froth.

Kyle shivered. Despite himself, he turned. 'What? What did you do?'

The renegade was frowning, his pale gaze fixed on the waters. He wiped the spray from his face then made a gesture as if throwing something away. 'Well, let's just say it lit a fire under the Korelri like nothing else ever before and got me arrested by command. I made a mistake – misjudged the situation – and a lot of people got killed that didn't have to.'

'I'm sorry.'

'Yeah, so was I. But I accept it. Now I'm just plain fed up.' A crooked smile, the eyes bright as the ice that clings to the mountain-tops in the north of Kyle's homeland. Or these Riders' own glimmering armour.

Kyle's face grew hot despite the frigid wind, and he turned away. This was not what he wanted: an opening up, confessions. Not from this man. A man of the company he had vowed to . . . *Damn him for this!*

'Well, better go below. Gotta re-oil everything thanks to these blasted Riders.'

Kyle said nothing, not trusting himself to speak. When he glanced back he was alone.

* * *

Evening darkened; the low overcast horizon to the west glowed deep pink and orange. The water lost its chop, the troughs shallowing and the wind dropping. The *Kestral* and the *Wanderer*, just visible as a smear to the north, were swinging over to a southward heading. Despite the wind that drove knives of ice across Kyle's back, he remained on deck. The closed rankness below churned his stomach. To the stern the glow of a pipe revealed the old saboteur Stoop sitting wrapped in a blanket. Kyle made his way sternward hand over hand by ratlines to stand next to him.

Stoop examined the pipe, tamped the bowl with his thumb, pushed it back into his mouth. 'You can relax, lad. Be more at ease. You're home now.'

'Home?'

'Certainly! You're of the Guard now, son.'

'Am I?'

'Aye. Swore you in m'self.'

'What about you? Where's your home?'

An impatient snort. 'The soldier's home is his or her company, lad. You should know that by now. Sure, there's always gonna be longing an' drippy honey memories of the places we've left behind but what happens to us when we go back to those places, hey?' The old saboteur didn't wait for an answer, 'We find out something we don't want to know – that they ain't home no more. No one there recognizes us no more. We don't fit in. No one understands. An' after a while you realize that you made a mistake. You can't go back.'

The saboteur sighed, pulled the horse-blanket tighter. 'No, those of us who take to soldiering, our home is the Guard, or the brigade, or whichever. That's our true home. An' there's those who'd sneer at what I'm sayin' and dismiss it all as maudlin, sayin' they'd heard it all before so many times – but that don't change the truth of it for us, do it?'

Kyle couldn't help smiling at the saboteur's pet conviction – how they're all brothers and sisters in the Guard. 'No. I suppose not.' He looked down at the old veteran, his veined red eyes, grey-shot ragged beard, seamed sun-burnished face. 'You've been with the Guard for a long time then?'

A broad smile. 'I've seen about a hundred and sixty years of battle. All of them under this Duke and his father and grandfather afore him.'

Kyle stared, unable to breathe. 'You're *Avowed*?'

'Aye.' He drew hard on the pipe. 'You should've been there, lad. Some six hundred swords were raised that evening under a clear sky, and six hundred voices spoke as one. We vowed eternal loyalty and servitude to our Duke so long as he should live and the Empire stand. And he still lives, somewhere.' The saboteur examined his pipe, pushed it back into the corner of his mouth. 'The Duke, now he was a man to follow. We stopped them for a time, you know. The only ones that ever did. Skinner fought Dassem, the Sword of the Empire, to a standstill. But it broke us. We were tired, so tired. And the Duke disappeared soon after that. So we divided into companies and went our separate ways.'

'And now the wandering's over,' Kyle said, his voice tight, and he felt a searing anger burning in his chest. 'Then why? Why the contracts? Why come to Bael lands?' *Why . . . Spur?*

Stoop sighed. 'Aye. The Diaspora's ended. We're going back to reclaim our land. We weren't just wandering though. We searched everywhere – for the Duke. We didn't find him. But maybe one of the other companies . . . I don't know.'

They remained side by side in silence for a time. Kurzan sailors clambered around them, raising sail. The embers of Stoop's pipe died. The saboteur roused himself, stood. 'I don't know about you but I'm freezing my arse out here.' He pulled the blanket higher and went below.

Kyle stayed for a while longer on the deck, watching the waves without really seeing them. His thoughts kept returning to Stoop's words that day on the Spur, '*We knew* someone *was up here . . .*'

The next day the storm broke and the *Kestral* made better time. Word came down from the deck that contact had been lost with all but the *Wanderer*. Talk went around of wrecks, the Riders and sea monsters, and Slate offered to read Kyle's future from the Dragons deck.

Kyle lay in his berth, sick from the storm-cursed crossing. He was a tribesman, for Hood's sake! What was he doing in a damned ship? Earlier in the voyage he'd laughed at the fat mercenary and his readings but now he welcomed any distraction, no matter how ridiculous. Slate was pleased, he'd done all the other men more times than he could count. Kyle was his last chance for something new.

'The Field, or Realm, as some call it, can be divided into four parts,' Slate began, brushing off the square of wood. Kyle knelt opposite him on one knee. A lantern hung above swinging wildly as the ship bucked and heaved. The fat Guardsman wore a felt shirt, its lacing open at the front revealing numerous scars and a thick mat of black hair. He took out the cards. These were tied by white silk ribbon and wrapped in black leather. Kyle knew that the corporal carried them in a thin wood box rolled into his blanket. Claimed they'd been in his family for generations.

Slate searched through the deck. 'Right now I'm using what we call the "short deck". These four cards, the Houses, rule the Field.' He held them up, one after the other. 'Light, Dark, Life and Death.' He then held up one other. 'But when I was young this new House appeared: Shadow.' He laid the five cards down and began taking out others as he explained them. 'Each of the four old Houses possess their High Attendants: King, Queen, Knight or Champion, and Low Attendants, or Servants. In some they're known as Herald, Magi, Soldier, Seamstress, Mason and Wife an' such. Shadow has its own attendant cards: King, Queen, Knight, Assassin – some say Rope – Priest or Magi, and Hound. In some spreads the Houses each have assigned quarters, or directions, where their influence is greatest. Shadow has no such allocation. It can appear anywhere at any time.'

'There are also these six cards.' Slate sorted through them. 'These serve no House: Oponn, signifying chance or odds; Obelisk, meaning the past or future; and these four: Crown, Sceptre, Orb and Throne.'

'And the rest?' Kyle asked, looking at the cards still in Slate's hands.

The mercenary grimaced. 'These are new additions – they go with a house that appeared just recently. New powers, striving influences, these come and go all the time . . . don't know if these'll last any longer.' He laid down a card very different from the others. Like those of Shadow House, it differed in manufacture – the rest were obviously a set, cut after the same pattern, painted by the same hand. The Shadow cards were cut from slightly thicker wood, but smoothed now from much handling. Their faces were smoky dark, black almost, hinting at vague shapes and movement. This new card wasn't even squared like the others. Ragged-edged, its plain un-finished wood face bore a design that had obviously been scored there by a knife-blade. It was of a hut or a shack, some sort of shabby dwelling, and it struck Kyle as a kind of mockery of what Slate had named the others, *Houses*.

'This new presence is called the House of Chains,' Slate continued. 'So far, it supports these Attendants: King, Consort, Reaver, Knight, The Seven, Cripple, Leper and Fool.'

While Slate talked Kyle eyed the card signifying the King of House of Chains. Like its House card, it was of an unfinished wood. Gouged on its face – perhaps by Slate's amateur hand – was a high-backed heavy seat, a throne. Drying, the wood of the card had shrunk, cracking from top to bottom through the solid, imposing chair. Compared to the richly varnished and detailed deck, these additions struck Kyle as ridiculous. Yet he could not deny that the clumsy image held a certain strange menace. The splitting wood was blood-red beneath its bleached surface, giving the appearance of streams of blood running down the surface of the throne. Somehow, Kyle would have felt much more at ease had the throne been occupied; at least then he would know where its occupant was. The face of the card appeared to shift and blur in the swinging lantern light; its uneven grain suggested to Kyle blowing dust, such as over the dune fields one can encounter on the steppes. The throne appeared closer now, dominating much more of the face. No, it was as if he or it were moving together, drawing closer, the dunes blurred by speed.

A hand interposed itself, turned over the card. Kyle pulled his gaze up to Slate's close, gleaming face, the man's eyes hooded. A chilling sweat was clammy on his back and arms and he felt strangely dizzy.

'Ain't good, starin' like that,' Slate said, his voice low and tight.

He appeared to want to say more, but collected the cards instead, looking down at them. 'Maybe we'll give this a try later.' The Talent's thick hands shook as he tucked the cards away.

Kyle went to his berth, clutched his sword and stared at the beads of moisture running down the tarred wood. He pulled the blade a handbreadth from its wood and leather sheath and rubbed at the symbols etched in its iron. Their depth, cut as if the tempered blade were wax, always surprised him. He breathed a short prayer to the Wind King, prayed trying to believe that somehow he was close and watching over him. But could that magus, or Ascendant, have been the one? It was too outrageous. His world had been turned upside down and with every month he saw how naive and impossible was the vow he swore upon the iron of this blade to somehow avenge what had occurred atop that jutting finger of stone.

That night he tried to dream of a woman's hand and a fountain that no doubt held the sweetest water he had ever tasted. If he succeeded, he couldn't remember.

*   *   *

Nait Simal 'Ap Url, of the Untan harbour guard, sat in the warm afternoon light watching yet another wallowing merchantman loaded with the collected loot of an empire lumber its way from the wharf pulled along by oared launches. *Stinking rats*. He leaned forward to spit a red stream of kaff juice into the oily waves beneath the piers. *Fat rats*. They must smell something – not the Imperial rot we regular vermin smell all around – no, their noses must quiver after other scents shifting in the wind. The stink of influence; the perfume of power. Nait smiled, his lips a red smear. He liked that one. *The perfume of power*. The musk of money? He frowned. Well, no, maybe not that one.

But where could they expect safe refuge if not here in the capital? Malaz? He chuckled, almost gagged on the wad of leaves tucked into one cheek. Hood no! Maybe a small anchorage somewheres, an isolated bay. Out of the way. Maybe buy protection from the fortified harbours of Nap or Kartool . . .

Leaning back, he banged on the wall of the harbour guard shack. 'Sarge?'

'What?'

'I was thinkin'—'

'How many times I gotta tell you not to do that, son. Bad for your health.'

'I was just thinkin' that maybe we oughta charge an exit fee. You know, like a departure tax. Somethin' fancy like that. There's a whole flock o' sheep skippin' out unsheared.'

'You think those merchant houses aren't paid up already? You want a visit from the Claw?'

'The Claw? What've they got to do with anything? We got our thing goin' as do others. Everyone gets a piece of the pie, no one gets hurt. Always been that way.'

'Some folks want to run the bakery,' his sergeant said so low Nait barely caught it.

The gold afternoon light warming Nait was occluded. Squinting, he made out a pair of polished black leather boots that climbed all the way up to wide hips, ending under the canted weaponbelt and broad heavy bosom of the corporal of the guard, Hands.

'You're chewin' that outland filth again, Nait,' she said.

'Yes, ma'am.'

'That's "*sir*" to you, skinny.'

'Yes – *sir*.'

'Spit it out.'

'Aw, Hands—'

'*Sir!*'

'It cost me my last—'

'I don't give a dead rat to Hood what you choose to waste your money on. You're on duty.'

'That's right,' came Sergeant Tinsmith's voice.

Scowling, Nait leaned forward opening his mouth wide and pushed out the wad with his tongue. It landed on the grey slats of the pier with a spray of red spit that dappled Hands' boots.

'Damn you to Fener!'

Nait wiped his sleeve across his mouth. 'Sorry – *sir*.'

Hands reached up to straighten the braid of auburn hair tucked down the back of her scaled hauberk. Raising her chin to the shack she said, low, 'We'll talk later, soldier.'

As she walked away Nait blew a kiss.

'Like I said, soldier,' said his sergeant, 'bad for your health.'

'I'm not scared of her.'

'You should be.'

Bending down again, Nait picked up the wet lump and shoved it back into his mouth. Ha! He could take her. Maybe that's what she's been holding out for all this time – for him to show her who was the boss. Nait smiled again. Then he frowned, puzzled. What the Abyss had that been? He peered out over the edge of the slats. Little pads, like leaves, floating out on the waves. Some appeared to hold copper coins, twists of ribbon, rice, fruit and the stubs of candles, a few still burning. They bobbed along together like some kind of flotilla. It was more of those damned offerings to that ruddy sea god cult. He'd been seeing more of that lately. He spat out a stream, upending a swath of the pads. Ha! Stupid superstitions for fearful times. He could understand such things out in the backwaters of Nap or Geni, but here in Unta? People were supposed to be sophisticated here. He shook his head. What was civilization coming to?

*　*　*

Fist Genist D'Irdrel of Cawn took one glance at Fort Saran and despaired. A four-year stint in this sore on the hind of a mule? Why couldn't command have been moved to the settlement of Seti? Pitiable though it may be. He wiped the sweat-caked sleeve of his grey Malazan jupon once more across his face. Squinting against the glare of the sun, he studied the burnt umber of the low rolling grassland hills, the clumps of faded greenery here and there in cut streams and slumps. But what most caught his attention was the surprisingly large number of Seti camps, collections of their felt and hide tents, gathered around the fort in slums of cookfires, corralled horses and mongrel dogs. By the Gods, he vowed, someone back at staff headquarters was going to pay for this insult.

'Not so bad if you squint real hard,' the man riding behind remarked.

Genist swung in his saddle, glared. 'You said something, *Captain*?'

The captain, newly transferred to the 15th Horse, shrugged in a way that annoyed Genist. In fact, everything about the man annoyed Genist. The man had only been with the regiment for a few weeks yet almost immediately the sergeants deferred to him – he'd seen how when he gave orders their eyes shifted edge-wise to this captain, Moss, he called himself, for confirmation. Yet there was also something about his sharp eyes, worn gloves and the equally worn sheaths of the two ivory-gripped sabres at his sides that blunted Genist's usual treatment of his subordinates.

Behind them, the double-ranked column of two thousand Malazan cavalry waited silent under the beating sun.

'Sign the advance,' Genist snarled to the signaller.

Captain Moss cleared his throat.

'*What now?*' Genist hissed.

'The scouts haven't returned from the fort, Commander.'

'Well, what of it? There it is! The fort! What do we need scouts for, by Hood's own eyes!'

'It's not regulation.'

'Regulation!' Genist blinked, lowered his voice. 'We're not at the front, you damned fool. This is the centre of the continent.' Genist took a low breath, turned on the signaller. 'The advance.'

As they rode, for once Captain Moss said nothing. The man's slowly learning his place, Genist decided. In the distance, cresting the hillocks, groups of mounted Seti cavalry raised plumes of dust into the still hot air. *Gods*, Genist groaned inwardly. Two years among these half-breed barbarians. What might the whores look like? Probably not a decent one in the whole plains. He squinted at the nearest horsemen – grey fur standard. Wolf soldiers. He scanned the hills, searching. There, to the rear, a white fur standard. Jackal soldiers – the legendary aristocracy of the warrior societies, sworn to the terror of the plains, Ryllandaras, the white jackal. An ancient power of the same blood, so legend went, as the First Heroes themselves. Treach, now Trake, the newly risen god of battle, among them.

Ahead, the tall double doors of Fort Saran opened. The officer of the gate saluted Genist, who nodded his acknowledgement. Within, the central marshalling grounds lay empty. A stone tower stood a squat and broad three storeys at the fort's north palisade wall. Thank the Lady for that, Genist allowed. A delegation awaited before it.

'Order the assembly,' he told the signaller, and urged his mount forward. To his irritation, Moss accompanied him. 'I do not see Fist Darlat.' Behind them, the cavalry formed up ranks on the grounds.

'Never met her,' said Moss.

Instead of Fist Darlat, all that awaited Genist and formal transfer of command was a motley gang of scruffy officers in faded, worn surcoats. Surely they could not be serious! True, Saran was only a fort, but command here was putative Malazan military governor of the entire Seti plains! A region as large as Dal Hon itself to the south. Was this some kind of calculated insult?

Genist pulled up his mount before the gathered officers, examined them for some sign of who was in charge, but failed. He saw no rank insignia or emblems, nothing to distinguish one from the other. They looked alike in their tanned, wind-raw faces and worn equipage. Veterans, one and all. Why here, in the middle of nowhere? Had they been recently rotated in from Seven Cities? As some of his staff suggested Moss may have been? Damn them for staring like that! How dare they?

'Who commands here? Where is Fist Darlat?'

'Fist Darlat is indisposed,' said the eldest of the lot, standing on the extreme left.

Whoever this man was, he had seen many years of hard service. His hacked-short hair stood tufted in all directions. Burn wounding, perhaps. It was sun-bleached pale and grey-shot. His eyes were mere slits in a seamed, wind-scoured face. A black Seti-style recurve bow stood tall at his back.

'And who are you?'

'Name's Toc. Toc the Elder.'

After a moment of silence, Genist burst out laughing. 'Surely you are joking. Not *the* Toc the Elder, certainly.'

'Only one I know of.'

Genist glanced to the assembled officers – none were laughing. None, in fact, were smiling. Even Moss now suddenly wore the hardest face Genist had ever seen on the man. 'But this is fantastic, unheard of. I thought, that is, everyone assumed . . . you were dead.'

'Good.' The man stepped up and stroked the neck of Genist's mount. 'Fist Genist Urdrel – might I borrow your horse for a few moments?'

Genist gaped at the man. 'I'm sorry? You'd like to *what*? Why?'

Captain Moss quickly dismounted. 'Take mine, sir.'

Toc turned away from Genist. 'Name, soldier?'

'Moss. Captain Moss.'

'Well, thank you, Captain Moss, for the use of your horse.' Toc the Elder mounted, nodded to the assembled officers and cantered out to the marshalling grounds.

Two of the officers closed on Genist and pulled the reins from his hands. Genist reached for his sword.

'Wouldn't do that,' Moss murmured from his side. 'We're rather outnumbered.'

Genist glared down at him. 'I have two thousand—'

'Do you? We'll see.'

'What by Beru's beard do you mean by that?'

Moss lifted his chin to the grounds behind Genist who turned to stare.

Toc the Elder now walked his mount back and forth before the marshalled ranks. 'Any veterans among you?' he shouted in a voice that carried all the way to Genist. 'Any old-timers from the campaigns? Sergeants? Bannermen? Do you know me? Do you recognize me? Who am I? Shout it out!'

Genist heard responses called but couldn't make out the words. A general mutter swelled among the ranks. Heads turned to exchange words.

'Do you know me?' Toc shouted. 'I was flank commander under Dassem at Valan when Tali fell! I scoured Nom Purge! I brought the Seti into the fold!'

Genist's blood ran cold as he began to consider the possibility that this man could indeed be Toc himself, not some opportunist outlaw trying to exploit the name. Hood's breath! Toc the Elder, the greatest cavalry commander the Empire ever produced! Abyss, there was no Imperial cavalry before this man. Then the man's words brought a shiver to Genist; he recalled who it was that had negotiated the Seti tribal treaties and whom columns of thousands of Seti lancers had followed from these plains across Quon, even into Falar, and he turned, dreading what he might see, to the open fort gates. There, astride their mounts, five tribal elders watched, white furs at their shoulders, lances tufted by fetishes of white fur.

Gods Below! What may be unleashed here?

A call rose from the ranks, gathered cadence to a mounting chant. 'Toc the Elder! Toc the Elder!' Blades hissed from sheaths and waved in salute to the sky. '*Toc the Elder!*'

Even Moss, standing beside Genist's mount, thumb brushing his lips, breathed musingly, 'Toc the Elder . . .'

CHAPTER III

And so Trake ascends.
Who can say what influence this casts upon his brothers and
  sisters?
First Heroes All. Shall they too ascend? Is now the time of savage
  uncivilized gods?
Brutal gods for a depressingly brutal age?

Tol Geth, Aesthete
Darujhistan

THE ROD AND SCEPTRE STOOD WITHIN THE SOUTH QUARTER OF
the Outer Round of Li Heng. This address means nothing to
those new to the city, but to any long-time resident it spelled
one thing and one thing only: poverty. For Li Heng was a city of
Rounds, or nested circular precincts. At its centre was set the Inner
Focus, containing at its hub the Palace, and within the Palace, at its
cynosure, the City Temple – once sanctified to the Protectress – and
now, under Malazan administration, re-sanctified to the full
pantheon of Quon Talian Gods, Heroes and Guardian Spirits.
Surrounding the Inner Focus lay the Greater Intermediate Round,
home to the ancient aristocrat families of Li Heng, the wealthier
merchant houses and the government officials. Next came the Lesser
Intermediate, wider yet. Here, the majority of city commerce was
pursued, for Li Heng stood at the centre of Quon Tali, halfway
between coasts astride the main trade artery connecting Unta with
distant Tali province to the far west, and trade was the city's
lifeblood. Encircling the Lesser Intermediate was the Outer Round,
the fourth and widest. Here stood the crowded tenements of the
labourers, the manufactures, the animal corrals and the ghettoes of
Seti tribals and other outsiders.

As to what might reside outside its legendary walls – it is telling that within the particular merchant cant of Li Heng there was not even a word for that. Banished, then, to the Outer Precinct, the Rod and Sceptre could not even claim the distinction of proximity to one of the two main gates of the city: the eastward-facing Gate of the Dawn and the westward-facing Gate of the Dusk. No, the inn rested within sight of the far less distinguished or profitable southward-facing Gate of the Mountains. At least, its owner and patrons could congratulate themselves, it was nowhere near the wretched northward-facing Gate of the Plains.

The Rod and Sceptre was also by tradition a martial establishment. In the golden days – before the murder of the Blessed Protectress and the yoke of Malazan occupation – the inn hosted merchant bodyguards and elements of the Protectress's own City Guard. Now, the inn quartered caravan guards and housed Malazan soldiery.

The Malazan contingent currently billeted was of the Malazan Marines, 7th Army, 4th Division, a field-assembled provisional saboteur squad, the 11th, currently attached to the 4th Army Central Command, under Fist Rheena, military governor of Li Heng.

The commander of the 11th saboteurs, field-promoted, was Captain Storo Matash, a Falaran native, of the island of Strike. Currently, Captain Storo was sitting at a table, drinking steadily while listening to a ranking saboteur, Shaky.

'No sense pursuin' it, Captain. No sense at all. Can't be done, no way, never.' Then Shaky raised both hands. 'Well – maybe it could be done – if you worked real hard on it. Maybe then.'

'That's Sergeant, Corporal.'

'Right, Cap'n.'

Storo sighed, rubbed a palm over his brush-cut bristling hair. He looked to his two other saboteurs. 'What have you two to say for yourselves? Hurl?'

Hurl screwed up her eyes, thinking. 'With the full resources of the city behind us we could have it done in a year.'

'Sunny?'

Sunny grimaced, tossed back the contents of his mug, coughed and wiped his mouth. 'Useless project. No point. Wasn't a moat to begin with anyway.'

Storo glanced around the gloom of the low-roofed common room of the Rod and Sceptre. 'The locals all say it was moat. Very proud of their ancient moat, these Hengans.'

Sunny snorted his scorn. 'Weren't no moat.'

'Then what was it?'

Sunny was called Sunny because of the awfulness of his smiles, which were less like smiles than agonized, toothy glowers. He gave one of these strained leers. 'Firstly, sure you got your Idryn River cutting right through the city, but it's a muddy river comin' a long way through a dry plain. Too uncertain to fill a moat – and would only silt it up anyway. Secondly, hey, Hurl – what's the easiest way to raise the walls?'

Hurl winked, and her smiled was much more pleasant. 'Lower the ground.'

'There you go. It was a ditch. A big-ass ditch. Not a pleasant moonlit froggy pool. A dusty rubbish-strewn bung-hole full of dead dogs 'n' shit.'

'OK! I get it.' Storo signalled to the landlord's wife, Estal, for another round. 'You don't have to elaborate.'

Sunny frowned. 'Weren't elaborating. Me 'n' Hurl and Shaky, we sank a pit to the bottom of the ditch. That's what we found down there. Dead dogs 'n' shit.'

While Estal thumped down a flagon of ale, Storo eyed his crew of saboteurs. He hadn't decided whether to be angered or relieved by the relentless maintenance of the games and habits that had seen them though years of combat in north Genabackis. If he shut his eyes, it was almost as if he were back in the campaigns and Sunny and Hurl were playing Stones with the Mott defenders, shouting their moves out to the night. He rubbed his forehead with a thumb and forefinger, took a long deep drink of the cheap Hengan ale. 'So. We drop the moat – the ditch.'

Shaky shook his head. 'No way. Ah, that is, maybe not. Hurl's got an idea.'

Hugging herself, Hurl leaned towards the table, lowered her voice. 'Sinking that pit.' She stopped herself, glanced around the room. Perplexed, Storo followed her gaze: the place was empty but for a few drunken caravan guards, and Estal. Hurl leaned forward once again. 'The ditch is just a big dump fulla wood and litter and rags and has all kinds a gaps. Holes. I say we fill it. But not with water. What say you, Cap'n?'

Sunny smiled his ghastly smile.

Four flagons of ale later, while Shaky, Hurl and Sunny sat playing cards and Storo drank, three Malazan soldiers entered the common room. Two sat at an empty table midway between the door and Storo's table. The third, an officer, stalked up to the table and opened his arms wide. 'Look who's here.' He turned to his companions. 'It is him. Just like Rheena said. Ol' Sergeant Storo back from Genabackis.'

Shaky, Hurl and Sunny did not look from their cards. Storo squinted blearily up at the man. 'Do I know you?'

The officer used his boot to hook a chair from the table, sat. The pommels of twin duelling swords thrust forward under his armpits. His black hair hung curled in tight thin rat-tails tied off by bright twists of cloth; these he pushed back from his wide, tanned face. 'No. Haven't had the pleasure. Allow me to introduce myself. Harmin, Captain Harmin Els D'Shil, of Fist Rheena's staff.' He inclined his head in the ghost of a bow.

Shaky, Hurl and Sunny glanced sidelong. Storo grunted his recognition. 'What can I do for you?'

Harmin's smile was as smooth as Sunny's was gnarled yet they seemed eerily akin. 'Well, imagine my surprise – nay, my dismay – to learn that the hero of the north Genabackis campaigns had returned only to be digging dirt and piling rocks like a convicted criminal.'

Shaky, Hurl and Sunny lowered their cards. Storo growled, 'Hero?' He yanked Sunny's hand from the pouch at his side. 'What do you mean, *hero*?'

The bright focus of Harmin's smile shifted to Sunny. 'Surely your men have no doubt heard the story many times by now, yes?' The smile returned like a bared blade to Storo. 'How your Sergeant Storo here slew an Avowed of the Crimson Guard?'

Hurl blew her hair from her sweaty grimed forehead, brought her arms down under the table to rest her hands near her belted knives. 'Yeah. We'd heard. An' that's *Captain*, now, ah . . . Captain.'

Harmin inclined his head to Hurl. 'I didn't believe it myself when I first heard it, of course. I thought it one of those wild stories you hear of from the front.' He crossed his arms, leaving his hands near the pommels of his swords. His smile on Storo revealed even more teeth. 'You know the sort . . . lies woven by fame hounds . . .'

Sunny lurched up from his chair only to be pulled down by Storo. Harmin, who had not moved, bestowed his smile once more on Sunny. Storo thumped his elbows to the table, rested his chin in his hands. 'But you found out it was true.'

Nodding, Harmin slowly uncrossed his arms. He took the cup from in front of Shaky, sniffed at it and set it down untasted. 'Yes. Needless to say I was astonished. But Fist Rheena assures me of its veracity.'

'So you have come to get a look at me and to hear how it happened.'

'Yes, that. And to deliver a message.' He raised a hand. 'But please, do not misunderstand. My interest is not merely that of the common dumb gawping foot soldier. I have something of a connection to the Guard. As you can tell from my family name. The D'Avore family are – were – cousins of mine.'

Storo topped up his cup and sat back with a long-suffering sigh. 'All right. I'll tell you all about it.' Shaky, Hurl and Sunny all shot their commander surprised looks. Shaky quickly dumped out his own cup on to the straw-heaped floor then refilled it. Storo took a long drink, cleared his throat.

'It was just outside Owndos, during the siege. My squad was assigned the objective of a tower overlooking the sea of that same name. Take it, or, failing that, destroy it to deny it to the warlord Brood. We were lucky 'cause we still had our cadre battle mage, Silk – who's still with me now.' Storo raised his voice. 'Ain't that so, Silk?'

Harmin glanced around and jerked, startled. A slim, pale man now sat at the next table. He wore a fine dark silk shirt, vest, and trousers now faded and worn. He offered a mocking smile to Harmin who returned it through clenched teeth.

Storo took another drink. 'Silk scouted the tower, reported a sizeable enemy contingent occupied it: Free City soldiers, Barghast tribals and local townsmen militia. Seemed it offered a strategic view of surrounding forest and Owndos coastline. In any case, we weren't concerned about the locals. We even had Barghast allies of our own – those boys will fight anyone, anywhere. No, the Lad's push of things was that the tower was commanded by four of the Crimson Guard. Now, that was a pause. You know the old official policy – don't engage the Guard unless you outnumber them five to one. We didn't. So that night I sent in Silk and the boys to mine the tower. The next morning a patrol went out led by three of the Guard. That suited us. We sat pretty till they were long gone then we charged the compound. The plan was to hit fast and hard an' drive them back into the tower then blow it. Sure enough, things sailed along fine. Once most of the defenders retreated to the tower, we blew it. The whole thing went up, came crashing down in a great blast of stone and dust. The remaining Free City soldiers an' Barghast were just stupefied and we chased them off easily enough.

'But then the fourth Guard came staggering out of the fire and wreckage – seemed she was an Avowed. She must've been on an upper floor when the blast went off so she didn't get the worst of it. But dropping a four-floor stone tower on her was slowing her down some in any case. She wasn't walking so good – maybe a broken hip – and one arm was all mangled. Our Barghast circled her and thrust her full of javelins and spears. Must've been near ten spears pinning her down on the ground but she was still squirmin', pulling them out, one by one. That impressed the Barghast no end. Their shamaness called off her boys. Yelled something about *spirits* and *pacts* and made it clear they weren't gonna have anything more to do with the Avowed. By this time she was sittin' up. Only the javelins through her legs were holding her down.'

Storo took a drink, raised and lowered his beefy shoulders. 'So it was up to me. I charged in and though all she had with her was a knife I nearly got my leg sliced off for my trouble. I went down. She went back to tuggin' at the javelins. Time was passing, so I limped over to the side of her bad arm and got a few good two-handed licks in. These slowed her down some even more and I was able to tag her head a few times. After that I could really step in and I managed to chop away until her head came away from her neck. And so she died.

'Later someone told me her name: Sarafa Lenesh.'

While Storo talked Harmin's smile had melted away into an expression of disgust. He let out a low hissed breath. 'So, you attacked a wounded woman. Cut her head off while she was pinned down.'

Storo nodded. 'That's about the bare bones of it.'

Harmin seemed at a loss for words; he shook his head in mute denial. 'You are a barbarian. You destroyed something irreplaceable. Unique in all the world.'

'They're the goddamned enemy,' Sunny growled.

Harmin found his smile once more. He stood. 'Thank you for the story, Storo. Though it does you no credit.'

'The message?' Storo asked, and took a drink.

His eyes thinning to slits, Harmin pulled a slip of folded paper from his belt. He tossed it on to the table. 'Fist Rheena requested I deliver this. It arrived through Imperial administrative channels.' The smile quirked up. 'Perhaps it's a notice of retirement. One can always hope.' After a shallow bow, he turned from the table. The two who had entered with him stood. Just short of the entrance, he paused as he caught sight of two men sitting to either side of the door. Both he knew by sight as the muscle of Storo's under-strength command: Jalor, a Seven Cities tribesman, bearing a tightly trimmed and oiled beard that did little to disguise the scars crisscrossing his dark face; and a fellow named Rell, from Genabackis, slouched in his chair, his

104

greasy black hair hanging down over his face. These two Harmin couldn't be bothered to smile at, and chose to ignore. They returned the favour.

Once Harmin left, Jalor and Rell crossed to the squad's table. Silk caught Storo's eye, glanced significantly to the door.

Storo frowned a negative. 'Let them go.' He sat rubbing his fingers over the folded slip.

'Do you think he read it?' Shaky asked.

'A' course,' said Sunny.

Hurl blew the hair from her brow. 'Why'd Rheena send *him* of all the garrison?'

'She probably sent someone else,' offered Silk, 'but he stepped in.'

Storo grunted his agreement. He opened the paper, stared for a very long time then crumpled it in his hand. He took a drink. His command exchanged glances. Sunny nudged Silk who shifted uncomfortably then finally asked, 'So. What did it say?'

Storo did not answer. He offered the slip to Shaky who took it and smoothed it out. He read aloud: ' "Storo Matash, we regret to inform you that the *Graven Heart* sank in a storm off Gull Rocks."' Shaky looked up. 'Did you know someone on board?'

'No. It's code. An old smuggler's code shared by Strike, and Malaz, and Nap, and a few other isles. It's an offer of a meeting from a man I knew when I was young. A friend of my father. A man I'd thought dead a long time ago.'

Sometime later that night Hurl offered to the table, 'Hey, that guy, Harmin, I think from now on we should call him *Smiley*.'

* * *

The ruins of the shore temple were half-submerged in the waters west of Unta Bay. Its broken columns stood in the waves as mere barnacle-encrusted humps. Though an easy day's ride from Unta, this shore was a deserted stretch of rearing cliff-sides home to no more than water-birds and sea otters. A short fat man in a dark ocean-blue cloak carefully picked his way down the treacherous turning footpath that traced a way to the base of the cliff.

Reaching the rocky shore, he dabbed the sheen of sweat from his wide face then pulled a folding camp stool of wood and leather from under his cloak and sat with a weary sigh just short of the misting sea-spray.

Fanning himself, the man addressed the surf: 'Come now! This coyness achieves nothing.'

Though the waves had been pounding the tumbled rocks at the base of the cliff, the surf stilled, subsiding. The water seemed almost to withdraw. The man cocked his head as if listening to the splashing as one might a voice. And a voice spoke, though few else living would have understood it. 'You compelled, Mallick?' came the response sounding from the gurgle and murmur of the waves.

Mallick Rel wiped spots of spray from his cloak. 'Indeed. What news of the mercenaries?'

'Their ships converge.'

'And upon those ships – there are Avowed, yes?'

'Yes. I sense their presence. What will you do, Mallick, when they come for you?'

'They will not live long enough.'

A chuckled response, 'Perhaps it is you who will not live long enough.'

'I have my guardians, and you have no idea what they are capable of.'

'You are transparent to me, Mallick. It is you who has no idea of what your guardians are capable. I know this for should you have the slightest inkling you would have come begging for deliverance.'

'Kellanved had his army of undead, the Imass.'

'A common misconception – they never died. They were . . . preserved. Regardless, even they would not tolerate either them – or you.'

'Fortunately, these Imass are no threat to anyone any longer.'

The voice of splashing and whispering water was silent for a time, then came a wondering 'How brief the memory of humans.'

Mallick gave a languid wave. 'Yes, yes. In any case, we were discussing the mercenaries. Do not attempt to deflect me.'

'Of the Guard, their end has not yet been foreseen.'

'Do not lie to your High Priest, Mael. It is only through the rituals of Jhistal that you yet have a presence here in the world.'

The water stilled, smoothing to glass. A bulge rose swelling to a broad pillar of water. It wavered, fighting to lean forward towards the seated man, then burst in a great rushing crash. 'And so the bindings hold,' came the voice again. 'Rituals so awful, Mallick, even Kellanved was revolted. Regrettable that some of you escaped.'

The man's thick lips drew down in mock pain. 'Struck to the core, I am. How can you name your own worship revolting? Shall more innocents have their innards splashed out upon you? Or do you resist?'

'None of your acts are of my choosing, Mallick. You and your cult pursued your own interests. Not mine.'

'As is true for all worship. But enough theology, diverting though it may be. When the mercenary ships head for Quon you must rush their passage. They must make Quon with all speed. Do you understand?'

'Yes.'

'And speed the ships of the secessionists.'

'You would have me hurry their progress as well?'

'Yes.'

More chuckling echoed among the rocks. 'Mallick – you disgust and amaze me. I wonder who of them will get your head first.'

'I am not dismayed. It is a sure sign of success when everyone wants your head.'

* * *

The captain of her Royal Bodyguard woke the Primogenatrix at midnight. 'T'enet sends word. The wards of the fourth ring are falling.'

Timmel Orosenn, the Primogenatrix of Umryg, rose naked and waved her servants to her. 'I felt nothing.'

'T'enet says they are eroding this last barrier physically.'

'Physically?' Timmel turned while her servants dressed her. 'Physically? Is that possible?'

'T'enet seems to think so.'

A servant wrapped Timmel's hair in a silk scarf and raised a veil across her face. 'Immanent, I assume?'

'Yes, Primogenatrix.'

'Then let us see.'

Her bodyguard escorted the Primogenatrix's carriage inland to the valley of the burial caverns. Her column passed through the massed ranks of the army, bumped down and up earthworks of ancient defensive lines, up to the front rank of the gathered Circlet of Umryg thaumaturgs who bowed as she arrived. One limped forward, aided by a cane of twisted ivory. He bowed again.

'Primogenatrix. We believe that this night before dawn the fourth ring shall fall.'

'T'enet.' From the extra height of her carriage Timmel peered ahead to where thrown torches lit the bare dead earth before the granite monoliths blocking the cavern's entrance. She probed with her senses and felt the ward's weakening like a weave of cloth

107

stretched ever further by a fist. Soon it would tear. Then it would snap.

She stepped down. Bowing again, T'enet invited her to the tent atop a small hillock overlooking the cavern opening. The Primogenatrix's bodyguard surrounded the entire party.

'Why here?' the Primogenatrix asked as they walked. 'Why not dig out elsewhere in the caves? They must know we are here waiting for them.'

'No doubt, your highness. We chose wisely, it seems. Like our ancestors who explored them so long ago, these demons have reached the same decision: the caverns, vast through they may be, offer no other exit.'

'Why erode the ward physically?'

'Two prime potentials, your highness. One: their practitioners are spent or dead. Two: the practitioners are hoarding their strength against the moment of escape.'

'Which of these do you favour?'

'The second, your highness.'

Beneath the tent's awning, the Primogenatrix assumed her seat in a backless leather chair facing the distant entrance. The thaumaturgs of the Circlet arranged themselves before her. Ahead of her position, the group dipped, sloping down to rank after rank of serried Umryg soldiery, wide empty oil traps awaiting the touch of flame, pit traps floored by spikes, and buried nets woven of iron wire.

The Primogenatrix motioned for T'enet who edged his bald head to her, both hands firm at the cane planted before him. 'You and I alone survive from the entombing, T'enet. So many died in that war. I acquiesced to your council then. Yet here we are once again. It is as if nothing has changed. We may well succeed again, re-establish all the wardings, rebuild all the barriers. Yet something speaks to me that we would be doing our descendants no favours in that. Indeed, they may well curse us for it.'

'I understand, Primogenatrix. Your concern does you credit. No doubt, however, they are much reduced after their imprisonment. Perhaps we will manage to destroy them this time.'

Timmel said nothing. She remembered what it took just to entomb these twenty remaining foreign horrors her sister had hired – *summoned* many said now – to aid her in her bid to usurp the throne. It had taken her island kingdom decades to recover from that destruction. That, and the warriors' dark-red uniforms, had given birth to their name: the Blood Demons.

*

As the night progressed the migraine pain of her strongest warding fraying and releasing like a taut rope snapping tore a gasp from Timmel. T'enet steadied her with a wave of his own power. She nodded to him. 'Now.'

T'enet stamped his cane to the ground and a great belling note rang within the valley. Shouts sounded from commanders. A low rustling as of distant rain muttered as the soldiery readied themselves. The pools of oil dug before the entrance flamed alight. Siege catapults and springalds mounted on stands ratcheted taut.

The Primogenatrix stood, gathered her power to her. The Circlet wove its ritual of containment.

They waited. Dust fell from the face of the granite blocks, each the size of a bull, as if the heap had received some sharp blow from within. Men within the ranks shouted their alarm.

Flame-lit, the face of the barrier shifted, tilted outwards as if levered from within.

Great Ancestor, Timmel swore. She had not anticipated this.

The blocks thundered outwards into the pool of burning oil sending a great wave and showers of flame among the front ranks who shrank back amid screams. Storms of arrows and crossbow quarrels shot into the dark within the cave to no effect Timmel could see.

Then, a bloom of muted power within followed by movement. A grey wall broaching the dark. Dust? Smoke? Timmel looked to T'enet. 'What sorcery is this?'

'Not sorcery . . .' The bald mage paused, watching while the grey wall edged ever forward. Arrows and bolts bounced from its face. 'Tactics, your highness. Such battle formations are hinted at in foreign sources. Interlocking shields.'

'They carried no such shields when we forced them in there, T'enet.'

'No, your highness. These appear to have been carved from stone.'

Hurled grenadoes of oil burst into flames upon the dome of shields. A massive scorpion bolt, three feet of iron, cannoned from the angled face without so much as a quaver.

Timmel's eyes narrowed. Hardened, sorcerously, from within. Very well. So it will be a fight after all. 'Circlet Master! Slow them down.'

'Indeed.' T'enet nodded to his companions. The Circlet brought its will to bear upon the shuffling dome.

Timmel did her best to ignore the screams and clash of battle – the amazed and fear-tinged shouts as the dome broached the first moat of burning oil only to continue on. She reached out her senses to touch this strange foreign presence. First she noted great strength in the mysteries of the earth. That would be difficult to overcome in a direct assault. Timmel's senses next brushed up against a diamond-like lattice of investiture that left her stunned. Years in the manufacture. Such mastery! She would have given anything to speak with the author of such work. It was beyond her. And beneath all, a dark swirling of Shadow mysteries that troubled her. Whence this influence? Not within the shield-dome, now climbing the slope leading up to the first rank of men. Yet striving potently . . . from where?

Timmel's gaze shot to the gaping cavern entrance, dark, open . . . ignored. *Gods of the Elder Ice*. She threw herself aside yet not quickly enough to avoid a stabbing flame of pain that skittered along her scapula to slide in straightening up into her right armpit. She fell on her back, right arm clasped to her side, stared up at an apparition. A walking corpse it seemed to her. Ghostly pale, female, in tattered rags of crimson cloth wrapped at her loins, eyes wild, hair white, matted and as long as her waist.

Looking down at her, the demon woman spoke something in her tongue before disappearing. Timmel recognized none of her words save one that shocked her utterly, *Jaghut*.

Her bodyguard arrived, glaring, weapons bared. Timmel struggled to her feet. The superior strength and resilience of her line that also brought her potent talents saw her through the shock and pain of her wound.

T'enet, she glimpsed over the heads of the shorter of her bodyguards, was not so lucky. He lay sprawled face down. The Circlet was too committed to their ritual to spare him any attention.

'Your wounds—'

Timmel waved aside the captain of her bodyguard. 'The battle?'

The officer bowed to her. Timmel searched for his name . . . Regar Y'linn.

'Brief me, Regar.'

The man bowed again. 'The shield formation makes progress. The second line of defences has been breached. Commander Fanell has been assassinated.'

Timmel cast her senses about the valley, searched for any hint of the Shadow mysteries. Nothing. Gone to ground. 'Direction?'

Regar frowned his uncertainty. 'I'm sorry, Primogenatrix?'

'Direction of the shield-dome?'

'Ah! South-east, towards the river.'

Timmel nodded to herself. Yes, just as before. Down slope, to water. Ever to water. T'enet had strenuously opposed her before and against her better judgment she had acceded to his council. Now she would do things her way. 'Have the ranks thinned to the south-east, commander. Then report back.'

Regar hesitated.

'Commander?'

'As you order, Primogenatrix.'

Timmel sat heavily in her chair. 'Circlet?'

'Yes, Primogenatrix,' the voice of every thaumaturg, slowly and emotionlessly, responded.

Timmel threw off the shivering terror their shared awarenesses clawed at her. 'Ease off your efforts.'

'Yes, Primogenatrix.'

She rested. Her blood dripped from the tips of her numb fingers then ceased as her family lineage's healing abilities knitted the wound. The clash of battle receded as the shield-dome edged ever farther away. *That word, that forbidden word.* So, all has not been forgotten out there in the wider world. Ancient truths remain alive somewhere. One place too many for her and her kind.

Footsteps approaching roused her. She raised her head to see Regar. 'Yes?'

'They are following the course of the river.'

'Downstream?'

'Yes.'

Timmel felt a tension slip away that had held her rigid in her chair the entire night. High above, dawn now touched the inland mountain peaks gold and pink. 'Send a rider to the city, Regar. Have a ship – our sturdiest – waiting at the mouth of the river. Unmanned. Anchored.'

'I'm sorry, Primogenatrix?'

Timmel straightened in her chair, bringing her almost eye to eye with the soldier. 'Did you hear me, Commander?'

'Yes.'

'Do so. Immediately.'

Regar saluted, turned smartly and hurried off.

'Circlet?'

'Yes, Primogenatrix?'

'Harry them, Circlet. Ride them all the way. Let them know. Let them know they're not wanted here.' *Yes, go. Go with all our curses. You invaders. You Crimson Guardsmen.*

'Yes, Primogenatrix.'

*   *   *

111

Kital E'sh Oll, newly initiated as full Claw under Commander Urs, straightened from the mummified corpse to scan the layered rock walls of the surrounding canyon here in the Imperial Warren. It seemed eerie to him, the way the smoothly sculpted stone resembled water frozen in mid-fall. How could this be the work of wind alone? Yet things did not always work the same from Realm to Realm.

The remains at his feet were not that old. A few months at most. Scavengers had disturbed the site obscuring any hint of the means of death – and just what those scavengers might be, here in the *seemingly* lifeless Imperial Warren, was yet another mystery of this place likely never to be solved.

Whoever this had been in life, all indications were that he had been a Malazan Claw. Yet another vital message, and messenger, lost. Kital examined the surrounding dust-laden rock. Who was intercepting Imperial traffic? One of the unknown local denizens? Hood knew they were legion – demons, revenants, spirits lingering from the Warren's cursed past. Yet all these threats were nothing new. Everyone agreed the Warren was haunted. No one walked its paths for longer than absolutely necessary. Why should it suddenly have become so much more perilous?

A faint scratching brought his attention around. A man – or what appeared to be a man – now crouched on a ledge of rock behind. Dust-hued rags of what might have once been rich clothes hung from him and his hair was a tangled white matting. Kital drew his long-knives. 'You are . . . ?' The man stood – tallish, Kital noted, with a good reach, though emaciated.

'Surprised,' the stranger answered alike in Talian.

'Surprised? How so?' Kital glanced about for any others. The man's bearing was unnerving; could he really be alone?

The stranger jumped down, bringing himself almost within striking range. 'That you keep coming.'

Despite himself, Kital gave ground to the apparition. Rumours of the Warren's hidden past whispered in his ears. Who, or what, was this? What was it talking about? *Coming?* 'What do you mean?'

The figure looked down at the half-buried corpse now at his sandalled feet. 'I mean when will that toad you call your master ever learn.'

'Toad? I serve the Empress!'

'So you think, lad. So you think.' He stretched out his arms. 'Come. I am unarmed. I will make it quick.'

Kital took in the long thin limbs, the dusky hue of the man's skin beneath the ash-laden dust. Stories whispered beneath breaths in the

Claw training halls and dormitories stirred in his memories. 'Who *are* you?'

The man assumed a ready stance, hands open. 'Good question. I have been many men. I was one for some time, then another, and then another, though that last one was a lie. Now, out here for so long alone, I have begun to wonder myself . . . and I have decided to become the man I could have been and to test myself against the only one who is my peer. *That* is my goal. For the meantime, I have no name.'

Kital stared. Deranged. The fellow was completely deranged. But then, becoming lost here in the Imperial Warren would do that to anyone.

'You should have attacked me by now, young initiate. While I so obligingly talked.'

'My mission is to gather intelligence.'

The madman hung his head for a moment. 'I understand. You are following your protocols. Well done, Initiate. Well done. A pity.' He exhaled a long slow breath. 'You would have been a great asset to the ranks. Now I regret what I must do—'

The man sprang upon him. Parrying, Kital yielded ground. The fool was unarmed! Yet every cut and strike Kital directed at him touched no skin. Knuckles struck his elbow and a long-knife flew from numbed fingers. A blow to his head disoriented him then pain erupted at his chest as his breath was driven from him as if he'd been kicked by a horse. He lay staring up at the dull, slate-hued sky, unable to inhale, his chest aflame. The stranger's face occluded the sky.

'I am sorry,' Kital heard him say through the roaring in his ears.

The face so close – *those eyes!* – Kital guessed the name and mouthed it. The man nodded, placed his hands on either side of Kital's head, hands so warm, and twisted.

Alone once more, flanked by corpses, one fresh, one old, the man straightened. He stood for a time, head cocked, listening, perhaps only to the dreary wind. The shifting of dry soil brought his attention to the older of the two bodies. That corpse's ravaged fingers of tattered sinew and bone now spasmed in the dust. The man edged away, his hands at his sides twitching. The bare broken ribs rose. Air whistled into the cadaver's torn cavities. It lurched up, its desiccated skin creaking like the leather it had become. Gaping eye sockets regarded the man.

Uncertain whether to leap on the body or away, the man offered, warily, 'Whom am I addressing?'

'Not the prior occupant.'

'Hood's messenger, then?'

A laugh no more than air whistling. 'A message. But not from him.'

'Who then?'

The corpse jerked its arms, which swung loose from frayed ligaments. 'Look closely, fool in rags. You see the inevitable. Flesh imperfect. The spirit failing. All is for naught.' Again the whistling laugh. 'Come, you are not one to delude yourself like the rest of the common herd. Why pretend? Everything human is flawed and pre-ordained to failure.'

Grimacing his disgust, the man eased his stance. 'As you can see, my limbs are all whole. You're wasting your time.'

A chuckle dry as ashes. 'Now you *are* deluding yourself. Or attempting to deceive me. Surely you above all are aware of the unimportance – the plain cultivated artifice — of all outward appearances.'

The man eyed the ridges above for movement. Was he being delayed? Were agents on the way? What lay behind the Chained One's contact, here, now?

'I assure you we are quite alone. We have all the time in the world to discuss our mutual interests.'

He regarded the cadaver. 'You can assure that – *here*?'

A convulsive laugh raised a cloud of dust from the body. 'Oh, yes. Most surely. Through the influence of one of my representatives. Which brings me to my point. You, sir, are most qualified to join my House. If the positions as currently revealed do not interest you, then perhaps a new one could be forged. A new card called into creation for you and you alone. Imagine that. Is that not a singular achievement?'

'It's been done.'

Stillness from the corpse, which the man interpreted as icy irritation. 'Do not be so impetuous. It ill befits you. Come. Be reasonable. Surely you do not imagine you will survive the forces now arraying themselves against the Throne – and more. Do not throw yourself away needlessly.'

'Tell me more of these forces.'

A gnawed digit reduced to one knuckle rose to shake a negative. 'Now, now. We have not yet struck a bargain. Nor does it appear we shall.' The arm fell and the carious grin widened. 'A pity. For while you refuse to see wisdom, I've no doubt *he* shall . . .' The corpse laughed its desiccated heaving whistle and with a snarl the man kicked it down. It fell clattering into pieces as the presence animating it withdrew.

The figure in rags stood for a time, silent, listening to that anaemic wind. No, he decided. No one would rob him of his satisfaction – not even the Chained One himself. But *he* would be no more likely to accept either, would he? No, he knew him too well. They were too much alike. Neither would accept any diversion until the final deed was done, the final knife driven home. And the beauty of all this waiting was that eventually, ultimately, the bastard Cowl would have to come to him.

* * *

When Traveller and a few villagers went out to search the highlands for a mast tree, Ereko left the hut at mid-morning. He would have preferred going while the man slept but he was reluctant to pursue a reading at night; only a fool would tempt fate so. The house, a sod-roofed fisherman's dwelling, stood near the edge of the strand's modest lip. A sturdy skiff was pulled up at the shore, a man repairing its side. An old woman sat at the hut's door mending a coat. She looked up at him without fear, the first sign he had of what was to come.

'I was told a Talent lives here.'

The old woman nodded and set aside her mending. She held out a clawed hand. Ereko set a silver piece into her hardened palm.

She showed no surprise, merely tucked the coin into her wide skirt at the waist. This he should have taken as the second sign.

'Hrath!' she called, her voice harsh and clipped, like a sea bird's. 'Hrath!'

A young boy whom he had noticed earlier playing among the black algae-skirted rocks at the headland ran up to them. The old woman took his hand. 'The cards, Hrath,' she said, and pushed him inside.

Ereko noticed immediately the marks of a Talent on the smooth face of the boy. He appeared to be about ten, prepubescent for a certainty – another strong sign. He wondered for how long the entwined strings of fate had woven for this encounter. It had been a long time since he had last dared a reading. For him, more than others, they tended to be messy. For Traveller, they would be deadly.

Stooping, Ereko sat cross-legged on the packed dirt floor of the hut. The old woman now tended a fire at the back of the one room while the boy smoothed the bared dirt of the floor. He stretched the cards out for inspection. Ereko noted their damp chill, another strong sign.

The boy held the deck calmly for a moment then began placing them in a cross design that divided the patch of earth into quarters. An old arrangement. Ereko had been told it was a field not popular in the cities. That it favoured the influence of the Houses too much, so the Talents there complained. When the boy began speaking his voice startled Ereko, so full of assurance and experience it was.

'The Queen of Life is high,' the boy began, as most true Talents do for him. 'Protection, I think. You are favoured. I see House of Death; it is also concerned. How they ever dog each other! Shadow is present, growing over time. The Sceptre close to the Knight of Death reversed . . . Betrayal. By whom? But no, that is the past. It regards another and intrudes. I see multiple convergences and revenge, but all bitter. Obelisk is close – it travels with you, both a blessing and a burden. Kallor, the High King, twisted inversion of all rulership, stands opposite . . .'

Ereko was startled. How could this boy know that? Then he chided himself. If a true Talent, the boy knew more than he now spoke even if his poor deck had no cards of the new house.

'I . . . that is,' something struggled on the face of the boy. 'So many wrestle here, drawn by the one close to you! I see the ancient past threatening to prove a future preordained. I see fear promising blindness to opportunities – as ever, self-interest threatens to prevent natural fulfilment. For you: only one card remains. Tell him, tell the Soldier of Light – fear none but the Chained.' These last words rushed out, stopping abruptly as the boy drew one last card that he held up before his face, silenced by its appearance. 'No,' he breathed. '*It cannot be* . . .' He pitched forward, scattering the cards.

The old woman came and picked up the insensate boy and carried him to a pallet. She crooned over him, caressed his gleaming face. Lying face-up on the beaten earth was the last card: King of Night – the most ill-omened of all stations and attributes. Ereko left without a word. It was as he'd suspected, the fates were done with him; scarcely any of the reading regarded him. He was close now – one card could only mean one remaining path for his future. As he walked back to the keel lain on its rollers and set with its ribs, he wondered: who was the Soldier of Light? And King of Night? That card had always carried symbolic meaning only. How could it have become active? What could it mean? Were they related? And what, if anything, had it all to do with him or Traveller?

The clanging of the iron bar suspended over the mine-head roused Ho from his mid-afternoon doze. Wincing at joints stiff and swollen, he swung his feet down from the sleeping ledge and fumbled about for his tunic and leggings. New arrivals. Surprising, that. Shipments of prisoners to the Otataral mines had thinned to a trickle these last few years. Seemed Laseen was at last running out of enemies. He snorted: not too bloody likely.

Though decades had passed since he'd been the Pit's unofficial mayor and inmate spokesman to the Warder – and who was the damned Warder these days anyway? – Ho still felt obliged to put in a showing at the welcoming ceremony.

He nodded to familiar faces as he tramped the twisting narrow tunnels – shafts themselves once – each following a promising vein of Otataral. Most of those he met returned his nod; it was a small world down here among those exiled for life in these poisonous mines. Poison indeed, for Otataral is anathema to Warren manipulation and magery, and they were all of them down here mages. Each condemned by the emperor, or the Empress in her turn. And Ho had been among the first.

Mine-head was the ragged base of an open cylinder hacked from the rock, about forty paces in diameter and more than twenty man-heights deep. Harsh blue sky glared above, traced by wisps of cloud. A wood platform, cantilevered out over the opening and suspended from rope, was noisily creaking its way up. It was drawn and lowered from above by oxen and a winch at the surface.

The new arrivals stood in a ragged line, four men and one female. The man at one end carried the look of a scholar, emaciated, bearded, blinking at his surroundings in stunned disbelief. The woman was older and dumpy, her mouth tight with disgust. The next man shared her sour disapproval, though tinged with apprehension. All three were older individuals and all three conformed to the norm of those consigned to the Pit: all Talents who have garnered the displeasure of the Throne. The remaining two stood slightly apart, however; their appearance sent alarm bells ringing through Ho's thoughts. Younger, fit men, scarred and tanned – one even carrying the faint blue skin hue of the island of Nap. Battle mages, army cadre possibly. Veterans no doubt. The community would not like this.

The current mayor of the Pit, a Seven Cities mage named

Yathengar, swept up before the arrivals, his long robes tattered and rust-stained in Otataral dust. He leaned on a staff trimmed down from a shoring timber.

'Greetings, newcomers,' he said in Talian. 'We speak the Malazan tongue down here as a common language between us Seven Cities natives, Genabackans, Falarans and others. Perversely,' he added, sliding a glance to Ho, 'there are precious few Malazans left down here.'

Ho gave the man a thin smile – ex-Faladan of Ehrlitan. *Never did forgive us for that. Never did explain why he failed to die defending his city-god, either.* Ho watched the newcomers take in the tall bearded patriarch, how their gazes lingered on the stains of his robes. Yath noted the fascination as well; one hand, knotted, dark as the stave's wood, brushed at the cloth.

'Oh yes, newcomers. It cannot be avoided. It is in the air you are breathing now. The water you will drink, the food you will eat. Your hair, every wrinkle.'

'Queen protect me,' breathed the scholar at the far end, appalled.

Yath turned on him. 'No, she won't.'

'So what now?' the woman demanded in strongly accented Talian. 'You beat us? Search us for valuables? Are we newcomers to be slaves to you thug survivors down here?'

Yath gave a bow of his head. 'Good points. No, no. No rule of violence here – unlike Skullcap – or Unta, for that matter. We are all scholars and mages here, educated men and women. We have a council. Food is distributed evenly. The sick are cared for—'

'Sounds like paradise.' This from the tall veteran cadre mage at the opposite end.

The wood of the stave creaked in Yath's hands. He paced to stand before the two. 'You three,' he said to the others, 'can go.'

Members of the welcoming committee took these three aside to be assigned quarters, receive food bowls and such. Ho remained. Yath held his stave lengthwise across his front, silent until distance from the other newcomers allowed some privacy. The two remained motionless as well, waiting without discussion between them. Companions, Ho decided. Very unusual. Counter to prison procedure, in fact.

'Do not think that because we are learned men and women down here we will be helpless before you,' said Yath, his voice low. 'There are exiles here who do not need the Warrens to kill.'

'Those stains,' said the shorter of the two, the Napan, 'we'd heard the Pit was all mined out.'

Ho swore he could hear Yath's teeth grinding. 'A few live veins remain,' he allowed.

'And let me guess,' continued the Napan. 'Everyone gets a turn.'

Straightening, Yath stamped the stave to the sandy ground. He thrust his face forward, his long grey beard bristling. 'And do you refuse?'

The muscles around the Napan cadre mage's mouth bunched. He examined his hands. 'No.'

Yath slowly nodded. 'Good. Your names then?'

'Grief,' gave the Napan.

'Treat,' said the tall one.

'Very well. Go and get quarters assigned.'

Ho watched the two leave, guided by old exiles. He'd keep an eye on them; why send two obvious fighting men down here among all us fossils? To dig up information, Ho answered himself. Yath's gaze followed the two as well. Ho translated the man's glower: more damned Malazans.

* * *

Amaron was waiting for her at the bottom of the stairs beneath the old Tayliin fortress. *My family's ancestral keep. My keep.* Ghelel still had trouble believing it. Yet all agreed. She was the third generation in hiding of the old Tayliin family. The clan that hundreds of years ago had extended Quon Talian hegemony across the continent. The troika that had taken power invoked her name; General Choss had been granted command – *in her name.* Yet she had no illusions: still a puppet. A figurehead needed to lend the veneer of legitimacy to their insurrection. That was all. Yet strings go both ways and even a puppet, should it gather enough strength to itself, can reverse the pull. Or even cut the strings if need be. In any event, she certainly intended to find the full extent of their slack.

Such as now; demanding to see the captive she'd heard languished within her keep. A true Claw captured by Amaron's counter-intelligence. A Claw such as those who slew her family so long ago. All great aunts, uncles, nephews and nieces; all except her grandfather, then a boy, who escaped. She had to meet this murderer. Had to see who it was, *what it was,* she faced.

The tall and, Ghelel could now see, rather wide around the middle Amaron bowed. 'M'Lady. I am against this. It's an unnecessary danger.'

'Surely the Claw didn't get himself captured on the chance of getting to me.'

119

'That is not my suggestion. A tiger, though captured, is still a danger.'

'Perhaps instead you could reassign Quinn to me.'

In the dark the man's deep-blue Napan face was almost unreadable. He shook his head. 'No, m'Lady. He has duties elsewhere. His work with you is done.'

'Then at least assign someone other than this Molk fellow. He is completely inappropriate.'

A low rumbling chuckle. 'I assure you he is completely appropriate.'

Ghelel allowed herself a sigh of exasperation. 'If this is your idea of negotiation, Amaron, I am not impressed.'

'I am greatly saddened, m'Lady.'

'Let's see him.'

'Please, m'Lady, reconsider. He will only take the opportunity to lie and undermine your trust and confidence.'

'I understand, Amaron.'

The man was silent, thinking. His presence before her in the dark gave her the impression of a wall of stone; many she'd met in the fortress were in awe of Choss's reputation and were elated to have a military commander of such standing. But those same people were also obviously wary, if not fearful, of this man. Amaron let out a long hard breath. 'Very well. Do *not* approach him, yes?'

'Yes.'

He turned, walked up the dark stone corridor. She followed wondering whether she'd just won a victory of a sort, or had just expended vital goodwill on a useless whim. Amaron unlocked a door and preceeded her into the surprisingly large chamber within. A man sat fettered to a chair at the room's centre.

'Ghelel Rhik Tayliin!' the fellow announced once Amaron stood aside. 'Pleasure to meet you.'

Ghelel strove to suppress a shudder – of fear or disgust – she didn't know. Or the cold: the room was damp and chilly. She took a slow step forward. 'So you know my name. What is *your* name?'

The man shrugged, or made a show of it to reveal that his wrists were secured behind his back. 'What matter names? For example, Claw or Talon? All the same, hey, Amaron?'

Ghelel slid her gaze between the two. 'What do you mean by that?'

'M'Lady . . .' Amaron began.

'I mean that Laseen instituted the Claws, yes, but who was in charge of Dancer's own killers, the Talons, way back then? Hmm?'

Ghelel settled her attention on Amaron. 'So you are a murderer as well.'

The big man rested his hands at his belt. 'I prefer the term political agent.'

'There you are,' the Claw said. 'You have picked up the very knives that wiped out – or very nearly wiped out – your own family.'

'We had nothing to do with those killings.'

'So you say, Amaron . . . So you say.'

Ghelel again glanced from one to the other, shocked. Why had Amaron allowed her to interview this man knowing what he would no doubt reveal? Was this some sort of a test? But why bother? She suddenly found she could not draw breath; the cell felt as if it had slammed shut upon her. She backed away to the door, searching blindly behind her for the jamb. 'I will not allow such things,' she managed, her voice hardly audible to her.

The Claw arched a brow. 'Not even for those who deserve it? Laseen, perhaps? Be assured, Tayliin, that list, once begun, will grow long and long . . .'

'Never.'

'So be it. You will fail then. And all those soldiers who will die for your cause will have died in vain.'

Ghelel felt as if the man had stabbed her then and there. 'What are you doing?' She wiped wetness from her eyes.

'Educating you,' he said. But his eyes were on Amaron and the smile that had been playing about his mouth was gone. It seemed to Ghelel that the man was now uncertain of something. *He's wondering why Amaron is letting him talk!* Yes, she had been wondering as well. She drew strength from the man's doubt.

'Yes? To what end?'

The Claw laughed his derision. 'You stupid child! Can't you see you'll end up exactly like her? You say you hate Laseen yet to succeed in the path you have chosen you must pick up the tools of power – the very tools you pretend to scorn!'

Amaron cleared his throat. 'That's enough, I think. M'Lady . . . ?'

'Yes.' Ghelel pulled a hand across her face. Yes, more than enough. She turned and left the cell. The Claw did not call after her. Amaron locked the cell and followed. At the stairs, she stopped and stood waiting, hugging herself. He stopped as well and studied her with what she thought a dispassionate evaluative gaze.

'Why did you allow that? Why not have him killed?'

A slow thoughtful shrug. 'You would have heard this accusation eventually. Better directly now than whisperings later when you might wonder if I had tried to cover it up. This way there is a chance – a small chance – that you might come to trust me.'

Right now she could hardly trust herself to speak. 'You play a dangerous game, Amaron,' she managed, her voice dry and hoarse. He was a solid shape in the darkness, silent for a time.

'That is the only kind worth playing.'

Ghelel studied the man, his aged, lined dark face that had seen, what, a century of service? Yes, she could see how the old ogre must've liked this one. 'No killings in my name, Amaron. That I will not allow.' He frowned, considering.

'Hard to guarantee. But I will promise this – I'll ask first.'

Ghelel hugged herself even more tightly, as if afraid of what might happen should she let go. 'Yes. You can ask. But I swear. Not the way it used to be. It will not be like that.'

Amaron nodded. And as Ghelel climbed the stairs, still hugging herself, it seemed to her that in the man's slow assent she read the surety on his part that, eventually, things would slide that way – if only through their own accumulating weight. *Please Burn and Fanderay preserve her from that! Please preserve her!*

*   *   *

The night of the meeting, Hurl watched Storo push himself from his seat in the Rod and Sceptre after the gongs of the wandering street watch rang the half-night call. The squad had all cleared out long before then. No sense hanging around exactly where anyone watching would want you to be. She and Sunny had a corner across the way, eyeing the Cap'n as he wandered – well, swayed, really – drunk as a Dal Hon trader up the street. They followed far back.

Sunny and me, we're army sappers, she reflected. What in Hood's name do we know about following people and bein' sneaky 'n' all? Truth is – nothing. Zilch. But then we're not supposed to be *successful*. We're the stalking horse. Leastways, that was how Silk explained it once. We're here because the people watching expect someone to be here, and so here we are. Simple. Ha. Truth is, she wouldn't be here at all if it weren't for the fact that Sunny was the meanest saboteur in a fight any of them knew and she's the only one he'll listen to.

Sunny tapped Hurl on the arm, motioned ahead; the Captain was heading west around the main curve of the Outer Round to the Idryn River. They slowed their pace to keep the distance. The Round wasn't nearly as quiet or deserted as Hurl imagined it would be at this hour. This section of the way was a run-down night market. Torches burned at stalls and at the open doors of inns and taverns. Benches and stools spilled out across the cobbles holding the most resilient drunks while she and Sunny stepped over the less hardy. Whores called from fires at tall iron braziers. Their ages looked to Hurl to vary directly with their distance from the light. Some shops appeared to never close: a blacksmith hammered on into the night. The lonesome ringing reminded Hurl of her youth in Cawn, her own father downstairs hunched over, tapping at his smithing. A sound that ached of sadness and waste to her. A lifetime of sweat and scrimping wiped away by a noble who refused his debts, leaving her family imprisoned. Joining up or whoring had been the only two legal choices left for her – that was, if she didn't want to starve.

They passed a Seti horse-minder standing watch with his sons over his charges all roped together while a pack of the mongrel Seti dogs roamed the Round snarling at everyone. In the chaos it seemed a miracle to Hurl that they didn't lose the Captain, but the man was making no effort to hide.

All around them in the dark she imagined a constant dance of positions and vantages. Silk was out there in the night, maybe overhead on the domed rooftops these Heng architects seemed to favour. Jalor and Rell were also following, but on a far lower profile – Jalor because that son of the Seven Cities could move like a cat, while Rell, well, that guy was just amazing – none of the squad could figure out why he was wasting his time with them. Storo had tried to promote him more times than Hurl could recall but he wasn't having it. The young fellow would just look away all shamefaced whenever the subject of promotion or commendation came up. As for Shaky, Hurl suspected the bastard had just plain slunk off on everyone like he always did.

Now, Hurl knew the Captain was on his way to meet a crew he'd warned them was the ruthless gang of pirates he'd started out with long ago. A gang he said was outlawed by the Empress. Were they watching to see whether Storo had reported the contact to Fist Rheena? Hurl's back itched trying this alley-work. This was Silk's trade, not hers.

'They're gonna try to turn him,' she whispered to Sunny as the Captain angled on to the main way to the riverfront warehouses. Sunny grunted his assent. 'Will he, do you think?'

'Will he what?' Sunny growled.

'Turn.'

Sunny pulled Hurl to a plaster wall. 'Put it this way,' he said, smiling his toothy leer, and he opened the cloak he wore over his armour. Pockets and bags held sharpers, cussors, smokers, crackers and burners – their entire treasure hoard, piled up over the years.

She gaped. 'Dammitall! When did you dig them up?'

'Right after you turned your back.' He closed the cloak. 'That's your problem, Hurl. You're too trusting.' He grinned again. 'Need me to take care of you.'

Hurl thought of her own two measly sharpers. 'Well, hand some over!'

He pushed himself from the wall. 'Cap'n's gettin' too far ahead . . .'

Clamping down hard on her urge to cuff the bastard, she followed with hands tight and hot on the grip of the crossbow she carried flat under her cloak. Grisan scum! How dare he! Then she slowed, thinking, *He'd taken all of it?* Truthfully? What a hole that would make. Maybe take out an entire fortress . . .

Ahead, the Captain yanked open a slim door to a gable-roofed warehouse and disappeared inside. A faint glow of lantern-light shone from its barred windows. Sunny edged his way down a side alley. Hurl followed, her back itching worse than ever: wouldn't whoever was waiting inside have sentinels on the roof armed with bows? Swordsmen posted in the alley? Sunny didn't hesitate, but then he never did. Even on the battlefield. He waved her to a narrow side-door, rolled his eyes. It was secured by a bronze lock-plate bolted to planks with an iron padlock. Solid enough for everyday. Whoever was inside might even feel confident of its strength. But against a trained Malazan engineer armed with Moranth alchemicals it was a joke. Hurl took out her tools.

While she worked Hurl thought again of her father. He'd been a smith. A whitesmith specializing in acid etching. She'd been his unofficial apprentice all her youth – unofficial because of course no girl could apprentice. Never mind she was ten times better at the work than her doltish brothers. At least, she thought, he'd given her that much – if only that. She brought those skills with her when she signed up and the Malazans shipped her fast as they could to the engineering academy. There the instructors introduced her to Moranth alchemy and it was love at first smell.

The most dilute mixture Hurl could manage on the spot did the job. She gave Sunny the nod and he levered a knife-blade into the wood surrounding the lock-plate. It gave like wet leather. He had to fight a bit at the end to open the door as the planks were thick and the acid barely weakened the innermost finger's breadth. All the while Hurl covered the alley with her crossbow, wondering why they weren't yet full of arrows. This wasn't how she'd be guarding some kind of secret meet.

Sunny hissed to wave her in. She pulled the door closed behind them. They were in a thin passage between crates and barrels piled almost as high as the ceiling. The light was a weak wash of distant lanterns and starlight from high barred windows. Glaring, Sunny raised his knife. Pitting and staining marred the iron blade. She shrugged, mouthed, 'Shoulda used an old one.'

Sunny took breath to snarl something but Hurl motioned to the maze of passages ahead and that silenced him. Grumbling far beneath his breath, he took the lead. Hurl smiled – just the way she wanted him for a fight, feeling ornery.

Voices murmured ahead from the dark. They edged closer. Hurl's back was on fire now. No way they should have been able to get this close. They must be walking into an ambush. She was about to signal Sunny when he stopped before a turn in the passage. He pointed up. Hurl studied the stacked crates – *possible*. It looked possible. She let her crossbow hang from the strap around her neck and one shoulder. She unpinned and dropped her cloak. A twist and the weapon hung at her back. Sunny covered her while she heaved herself up to the first slim ledge.

The climb itself was easy but she took it slowly, trying to be as quiet as she could. As it was, she was sure everyone in the blasted echoing warehouse heard her. At the top she lay flat, surprised that no one had been there to greet her with a thrust in the face. Where was everyone? Had they called it off?

While Sunny climbed Hurl unslung the crossbow and exchanged the bolt for one set with a sharper at its head. Reaching the top, Sunny crouched, drew his twinned long-knives. The crates rocked and creaked alarmingly beneath them. He lifted his chin to the centre of the long barn-like building and carefully made his way forward. Hurl followed, crouched as low as she could. The rafters loomed from the dark just above. They stank of tar and dust and bat droppings and trailed cobwebs that caught at Hurl's shoulders. Talking echoed from below much more clearly now; she could make out the odd word, recognize Storo's voice. Sunny lay down at the cliff-edge of their long rectangular island of stacked goods. Hurl lay beside him, peeked over the wooden lip.

In a central cleared square of bare beaten earth the Captain was leaning on a barrel and facing two men and a woman. No one Hurl knew. To her they looked seasoned, especially a silver-haired Dal

Honese fellow as broad across the beam as they come. 'Captain now, is it?' the big Dal Hon was saying. And he whistled. 'My, my. Coming up in the world, are we?'

The Captain was just looking down, giving his half-smile, and rubbing his hand over his nearly bald head the way Hurl knew he did when he was dismissing what you're saying but didn't want you to know it.

'I would have seen you a commander, Storo. You know that. A Fist even. We reward talent. That's *our* way. If your father hadn't gone down off Genabaris he'd be standing here right now saying the same thing.'

'*She* has talent,' the Captain said, still looking down. The three strangers exchanged glances. The woman signed something to the Dal Hon fellow. Looking closer Hurl saw that though slim and sword-straight, she was an older gal herself. This crew was what in Imperial service everyone referred to as *Old Hands* and the little hairs on Hurl's arms prickled at the thought of just what they might be facing here. And what of the Captain? He knew this crew. Just what had *he* been hiding all this time?

The Dal Honese hooked his meaty hands under his arms, sighed. 'Look, Storo. We need to know tonight. Now. For old times' sake we've gone out of our way here. But all that only goes so far. We want you – could really use you – but we need to know.'

The Captain pulled a hand down his face to rub his unshaven jowls, grimaced. He shrugged. 'I think you know the answer already, Orlat . . .'

Orlat! Familiar, thought Hurl. She just couldn't place it. In any case, Orlat was nodding. He looked genuinely regretful himself. 'Yeah. I know. I was just hoping you'd come to your senses. I'm sorry it has to be this way . . .'

'So am I, Orlat. So am I.'

The man and woman with Orlat disappeared. *Hood take it! Old cadre mages!* Six swordsmen entered the square to take Orlat's side, hardened veterans every one of them. Rell stepped out of the dark to take the Captain's side. Neither Storo nor Orlat moved a muscle. *Six veterans! This could give Rell a run for his money.*

Then the needle point of a knife touched Hurl's back and she flinched. 'Turn around real slow,' someone said from behind. Hurl hung her head – *the Lady's Pull!* She rolled on to her back. A little runt of a guy dressed all in dark colours knelt over both her and Sunny. Twin long blackened poniard blades hovered a finger's breadth over their vitals. 'Now,' this guy said, and his lips pulled back over grey rotting teeth, 'you got just one chance to give the right answer to the question—'

And darkness opened up, swallowing him. And he disappeared. Hurl looked to Sunny, blinked. 'Well, I guess we'll never know what the right answer was.' Silk floated up from within the crates. 'Where'd he go?' Sunny asked him.

Silk smiled and winked. 'Elsewhere.'

'What's the plan?' Hurl whispered.

'Living through the night. The exits are all sealed. Open a way out to the riverside. We'll keep them occupied.'

'The *riverside*? Why there?' But Silk was already sinking from view. *I'm busy*, he mouthed and was gone. Sunny crawled to another edge, waved Hurl over. She threw herself down next to him. 'This is bad. Real bad.'

'Yeah. We'll be dead any minute for sure.'

'Wonderful.'

He motioned to the stacked crates and barrels across the narrow passage. 'Have to jump it.'

'*What?*' But the fool was already backing up. 'Listen, let's talk about this—' Sunny kicked himself into a run and the crates swayed beneath them. As he took long strides to gather speed Hurl suddenly remembered just what he carried snug in the pockets of his cloak and vest and bags. A vision of the entire warehouse and surrounding buildings disappearing in an eruption of light froze her. *Sweet Twins, no!* She flinched away.

A crack sounded as Sunny jumped – the release of a crossbow – then a crash of him lying dead flat on his back on the crates that rocked, creaking and scraping against one another. Swords rang from the dark below followed by a gasp and panting and Hurl knew that couldn't be Rell because he never made a sound when he fought, ever. She peeked down to see Rell holding off four remaining soldiers while the Captain was drawing his sword. Orlat's gaze was narrow as he watched Rell's form. 'No sense making this any harder than it has to be,' he told Storo, though he sounded less sure of himself.

'That's what I was thinking,' answered the Captain.

Hurl backed up and ran for the gap. The crossbow on her back slammed her down as her feet hit the crates and that sent her face-first into the unfinished wood, knocking the breath from her. The side of her face scraped raw. Finding her breath again, she touched her cheek and came away with blood. She sat up to see Sunny holding his leg from which a quarrel jutted. *Shit.*

'That was not a nice trick your friend pulled,' a familiar voice called from across the way. It was Runty the Knifer, back from who-knew-where. He jumped the gap with ease, came down standing. The crates rocked beneath them all like a lazy sea swell. 'But I got friends too. Now, where was I? Oh yeah,' he raised his knives. 'Killing you two.'

'Shut the Hood up,' Sunny snarled, tossing something at the fellow's feet that went off with an ear-splitting bang. Though she recognized it as a smoker, Hurl flinched. Black impenetrable clouds engulfed them, blinding and choking. She was sure that whatever the Moranth put in those was not meant to be inhaled. Sunny took her shoulder, yanked her to the edge of the crates. They hung for an instant at the lip, held on to break the distance, then they fell. Sunny roared as his weight hit his wounded leg. They both lay winded on the beaten earth.

The fellow landed lithely as a cat next to them. Flat on her stomach, Hurl groaned her disgust. He waggled a blade and shrugged. 'Nothing personal, you understand. Just business.'

'Well, you missed *your* chance,' said Sunny smiling nastily as he glanced up the alley.

Runty cursed, twisting, but a thrown knife took him in the side. He went down, rolled, and dived from sight around a corner. Jalor came jogging up, the gold rings at his fingers bright. He grinned but blood smeared his teeth and was running from his mouth down over his trimmed beard. The dark robes he wore over his armour were slashed. He drew another knife to replace the one he'd thrown and kept his beatific grin. 'It is good to kill Malazans again!'

Hurl helped Sunny to his feet. 'Just don't make a habit of it.'

He frowned. 'Why?' then added, 'Didn't Silk give you two a job to do?'

'Yeah,' said Sunny. 'Gotta blow us all up.'

Jalor shrugged. 'As I've said – I should have died a long time ago.'

Sunny grumbled under his breath, 'Just do us a favour and do it tomorrow.' Jalor grinned and offered Hurl a wink. He set off after Runty.

Hurl tried to take Sunny's arm but he shook her off. 'Fine. Be that way.'

'What do you think,' he panted as he limped, his voice taut with pain, 'a cracker?'

'Yeah. That should overkill it nicely.'

The passage opened on to an open square of beaten earth that ended at a wide sliding door. Hurl held Sunny's arm to halt him.

Silk had said the exits were sealed; what had he meant by that? 'What are you waiting for?' Sunny hissed.

'Silk warned us off the doors.'

He pulled his arm free. 'Just blast it and let's go!'

While Hurl watched, shadows on the panels shifted and stretched. They seemed to drip on to the ground then they snaked out like wet black ink reaching towards them. *Shit again.*

Flinching back, Sunny almost knocked her down.

Light blazed across the square in a cutting curtain of blinding white. Blinking away the after-images Hurl saw the shadows on the door writhing as if in pain. In the darkness of an alley across the way she glimpsed the slim older woman who had stood with Orlat. She was examining the door as well. Then she turned her lazy gaze to them. 'Your friend is good,' she called, 'but we'll corner him.' She frowned. 'Ule should've finished with you two already.'

Without aiming Hurl lifted the crossbow from under her arm and fired. It wasn't bang-on, but it was close. She was sure the blast caught the woman before she entered her Warren. As it was, she at least blew up two barrels damn good. Sunny offered her a reluctant nod. 'Nice one.'

They ran to the wall as far from the loading dock as possible. 'I'll take that,' said Sunny, holding out a cracker. They exchanged. Sunny covered her while she studied the wall and kicked at its base: solid hand-shaved planks sunk far into beaten earth. Tricky. The cracker could obliterate any section above but it would need a solid foundation to direct the blast. She drew her shortest blade and started hacking at the dry packed earth. While she worked she saw Sunny set down the crossbow and unwrap a cussor. He caught her watching him. 'I'm tired of playing around.'

'Might as well chuck it against the wall now.'

'That'd be a waste.'

Hurl had to agree. The cracker was bad enough, but a cussor used against a wall of timbers was enough to make any sapper cry. Used against any one particular enemy who has pissed you off mightily, well, that was pretty much a tradition in the corps started by Hedge. Sword-play and stamping feet echoed up the alley behind. She hurriedly set the cracker, kicked the earth down around it. 'Have to do.'

'Now,' came Sunny's tight warning.

She risked a glance: Storo and Rell were shuffling in a fighting retreat against a pressing gang of swordsmen. She let two drops of undiluted acid fall on to the dirt packed over the cracker, then, jumping up, took Sunny's arm to help him run aside and yelled the standard sapper warning: 'Munitions!'

They dived. The eruption was like twin hammers slamming into her head from either side. Shredded timber tumbled down all around. Though Sunny and she were insanely close they were still in one piece because the whole point behind crackers was to direct the main force of the blast in one direction – up the wall in this case. Lying there, shaking off the effect of the explosion, she found that instinctively she'd thrown herself on top of Sunny to protect what he carried, and that he was curled on to his side facing away from the impact, despite the quarrel sticking out of his leg. The risks they were taking with their ordnance appalled her.

An arm yanked her, marched her to the smoking gap – Rell. Somehow the Genabackan swordsman retained his grip of both weapons while hooking one arm around her. Wet gore covered both blades and splashed his leathers. None, she was sure, was his. He urged her on through the jagged hole.

The riverside wharf-front was dark. Watch torches lit the Idryn's far shore. Dirt gave way to the wood planks of the wharf and docks. Storo pushed Sunny through to Hurl then he and Rell covered the smoking gap in the warehouse wall. Planking from the roof fell all around. 'Where to?' she yelled.

'The river!' Storo answered.

Hurl staggered backwards with Sunny who fought to remain. 'We'll cover them,' she told him and he subsided. A shout sounded – a Seven Cities war challenge – and Jalor erupted from the blasted section at a dead run. Men poured out after him. Arrows nicked the ground all around, fired from the roof.

While Hurl hobbled with Sunny a familiar thump sounded from the docks and she grinned, tracing an imaginary path through the night sky to the roof behind and was rewarded by the crack of a sharper clearing the archers from one side of the roof. 'Shaky has us covered!' she laughed. Sunny's look told her she'd sounded a touch panicked.

Storo, Rell and Jalor fought a tight retreat. Pot-shots from Shaky cleared any group that pressed too close. Hurl found him crouched behind cover next to a moored river launch. 'Get in,' he snarled and reached for her crossbow. Hurl let Sunny down and raised the weapon herself.

From the wharf-walk Hurl saw that things were finally getting ugly. Some kind of summoning stepped out of a Warren. She imagined you'd call it a demon, or monster, all scales and jagged horns. In any case, it sure wasn't one of theirs. It turned on the

Captain and closed ground. Rell actually looked ready to take it on but Storo pulled him back, bellowing, 'Silk!'

Hurl held her breath, but nothing happened. Usually when the Captain called that loud for their cadre mage, smoke, flame and lightning and you name it came flying. But now nothing. A nagging thought surfaced; had the old gal and her buddy finally managed to corner him?

A whistle brought Hurl's attention around: Sunny on the launch. He held up a cussor then tossed it. She practically fired her crossbow in her panic to empty her hands. She let the cussor strike her chest and closed her arms around it then lay down to take the weight from her sagging knees. *Gods!* Cussor tossing! No matter that it took more than a shock to set them off – the imagination did wonders.

Shaky was looking down at her. 'They're too close anyway.' Arrows pattered around like rain. A bestial roar rattled the dock, echoing from the wharf-walk. Hurl peered over the piled cargo.

The demon was sinking. At least that was how it looked. The beast was up to its scaled waist in dirt and flailing madly. Everyone had stopped to watch, fascinated, the way Hurl had seen the fighting on battlefields halt when a particularly impressive piece of magery was in the process of going horribly awry. It sank to its chest, its neck, then, roaring what sounded like panic, disappeared but for its spasming arms. Those arms remained standing from the streaming dirt like two malformed plants, jerking and clawing.

'Hood's bones!' Shaky breathed. 'What a way to go.'

'Shoot, dammit!' Sunny called from the launch. 'Shoot!'

Hurl took aim and fired at the firmer parts of the warehouse roof where the archers had edged forward once more. Shaky dropped one into the closest knot of Orlat's men. That broke the spell. Men dived for cover. The rest of the squad made the dock. Hurl and Shaky fired last warning shots as the launch unmoored then everyone jumped for it. The archers peppered the boat as they drifted away into the dark. Rell and Sunny rowed while everyone else ducked for cover.

Shaky relieved Sunny who eased himself down next to Jalor who lay, eyes shut, breathing wetly. He looked to have taken a beating. The launch rocked alarmingly, dipping at the bow, and there was Silk, his trademark dark silks smoking and tattered. His long blond hair plastered his head, soaked in sweat. He let himself slump on to a thwart and leaned back, breathing in deep lungfuls of the cool river air.

So, they'd all made it. But what now? Hurl eyed the Captain. He was looking ahead, downriver, his gaze thoughtful. Would he send

Silk by Warren to Fist Rheena? Surely now he had to let her know that a gang of pirates were in the city recruiting. She cleared her throat. The Captain nodded, grimacing. 'Yes, Hurl . . . What now?'

'Tell Rheena. She's been square.'

He rubbed an unshaven cheek, wincing at Hurl's words. 'Yeah. Well, that's the problem. That just makes this all the harder.'

'What?'

'She's dead,' said Silk.

Storo nodded sourly.

'What do you mean?'

'He means,' continued Silk, 'that there's been a coup tonight in the city. Rheena is surely dead. We're all alone.'

'C'mon, a coup? That's ridiculous. The Claws would crush it.' But Sunny, Hurl noticed, wasn't sneering. Holding his leg, he looked personally affronted by the news. She bent to that wound, tore the trousers for a better look.

'Not if they're too busy elsewhere,' said Storo.

'Where?' Hurl took hold of the quarrel shaft, held Sunny's eyes. Rell eased over to take hold of his shoulders. He gave a sharp nod, gasped, 'Do it.'

Hurl leaned her weight on to the shaft, bore on to it until the head burst through the other side of the thigh. Sunny thrashed in Rell's grip, snarled through his teeth clamped in his permanent leer. She eased off. He lay limp, his face glistening in a cold sweat. She unrolled her kit and set to work.

'Orlat and I had a chat,' continued Storo. 'From what he hinted at I got the idea that the Seti were rising, as was Tali, and others of the old kingdoms. An organized insurrection. Laseen's been bleeding the garrisons dry for years now to fuel those overseas wars of hers. There's hardly more than a division between here and Unta. And most of those probably turned.'

'Turned to who?' Hurl glanced to the Captain. He was looking away, over the river to the torches and golden lanterns gleaming over the domes of the city.

'Did you recognize the name Orlat?' he asked.

'Sounded familiar.' Everyone, Hurl noted, was watching the Captain now. Even Sunny, who'd come to.

'Orlat Kepten. Was captain of the *Spear* long ago. I was his first mate.'

Kepten! Yes, Fat Kepten. How could she have not made the connection? But he'd been a captain in Urko's fleet. That meant . . . *You served with Urko?*

132

Looking embarrassed, Storo rubbed again at his jowls. 'Yeah. There at the end. My father served much longer. He was one of the first Falarans to join up – even before the invasions.'

While Storo was speaking, Silk had taken the stern and now directed them to the north shore. Storo turned to him. 'What's this?'

'My arrangements,' Silk answered. He studied the maze of docks and jetties cluttering the shore like a mess of snaggled teeth. They slid under one sagging dock and Silk grabbed hold of a timber and they waited, silent. Waves licked at the glistening slimed wood of the old posts. Rell cleaned his blades in the water then ran an oiled cloth over them and sheathed them. Once again, Hurl saw, the youth had escaped any injury. In all the years campaigning together she'd yet to see him cut. There was something unnatural about that. She turned to Jalor's wounds.

'That's all right, Hurl. Help should be coming,' Silk told her gently.

'You're just full of arrangements this night, ain't ya?' Sunny challenged, watching the mage through slit eyes. Silk answered with an enigmatic smile of his own – one that Hurl had seen turn many a girl's head.

'What do you mean?' asked Shaky.

'I mean Silk here showed a lot more tricks tonight than ever before. Those two mages must've been damn good but he kept both busy. How does a plain squad mage manage that? And these arrangements . . . he knew something was up for tonight.'

Shaky was watching Sunny; Hurl saw his eyes bugging out the way they did when he was scared. 'What're you sayin?'

Sunny's smile was a death's-head. 'I'm sayin' maybe we don't need to tell Rheena anything because maybe Laseen already knows. What say you, Silk? Gonna fess up?'

Shaky gaped at Silk. 'You a Claw, Silk?'

'Quiet,' Storo said. 'We've enough to worry about.'

Silk raised a hand. 'It's all right, Captain. I'll talk. Truth is, I happen to be from Heng. I grew up here. This is home turf for me. I pull more out of myself here than anywhere.'

An old woman's crow of a laugh sounded from above. 'Bicker, bicker. I smell sour defeat!'

Silk pushed his fingers through his hair, sighing. 'Down here, Liss.'

Hard heels clacked and clattered above. Rell and Storo eased the launch to a floating dock. Two youths, no more than ragged street urchins, helped an old woman down the short ladder to the dock. She took hold of the gunwales of the launch with hands all gnarled and disfigured with arthritis and in a very unladylike manner swung a leg over the side. Grinning a dark wide mouth full of rotten stumps she squatted over Jalor, cackling at what she saw. Hurl backed away because the old hag stank of rotting fish.

'Greetings, Loyalists,' she said, laughing.

Loyalists? Hurl wondered. What did the old crow mean by that?

'Morning,' answered Storo.

'Ah, the great Slayer of Avowed. Captain Matash himself!' She squinted at him, snorted. 'You don't look like much.'

'Liss . . .' Silk whispered, warning.

'Yes, yes.' She took hold of Jalor's head, twisted it side to side while he grunted his pain. 'Ah! Courage and resilience here. Good. He will live.' She turned on Sunny who flinched from her swollen hands. Those hands darted out to his leg. 'Ah! Stubbornness here. Good. He will walk again.' One of those hands then snapped to Hurl's upper arm and clenched there, squeezing the bone; Hurl winced at the woman's strength. The fetid stink of a muddy river bank at low-water assaulted her and she turned her head away. Seeing that, the old woman cackled. Hurl didn't find it funny at all. 'Greetings, Builder. I am pleased to meet you.' *Builder? She must mean engineer.*

The old woman faced Rell next. He sat motionless, his limbs tense, almost quivering, looking up through his long tangled hair. She pulled her hands from him at the last moment and a long breath hissed from her. Turning away she inclined her head, mouthing something beneath her breath. It seemed to Hurl there was certainly significance to the woman's actions but for the life of her she had no idea what it might be.

The youths helped the old woman out of the launch. From the dock she reached down to flick a tear in Silk's shirt. 'All faded now,' she chuckled. 'What's become of us, hmm?'

'The Twins turn, Liss,' Silk murmured with an affectionate smile.

'Hunh! They do, do they? Well, they're taking their own sweet time about it.'

'Many thanks,' Silk said softly and he pushed off.

As they drifted away Hurl heard her call after them, 'Protectress Bless you!'

They drifted downriver, east with the sluggish current. Soon the next broad curve of the Idryn would bring them to the first of the River Gates, the huge iron grills sunk from bridges that served as extensions of the curtain walls surrounding the city. Jalor suddenly lurched upright, nearly swamping them. He glared about as if still in the fight then eased back under Shaky and Rell's grip.

'How's the leg?' Storo asked Sunny.

'Fine,' he grunted, sour.

'Good. 'Cause you're going to need it.'

Sunny's smile slid back to its usual sneer. 'Why?'

'Because we're headed to the Palace.'

Everyone gabbled at once. The Captain raised a hand for silence. 'We've no choice. We have to act now before they firm up control. Before everyone salutes *them* tomorrow.'

Shaky goggled at Storo. 'What? Us against the whole garrison?'

Storo waved that aside. 'There's only a handful of officers behind any coup. Them plus some outside muscle. Can't be more than that. The soldiers are just waiting it out. They'll take their orders from whoever's around tomorrow at the dawn mustering.'

'What about Orlat and his crew?' asked Sunny.

'They have to stay behind the scenes for now. Can't show themselves. But we'll have to keep an eye out.'

Hurl caught Sunny's gaze. 'For sure Smiley's one of 'em.'

Sunny showed even more teeth. Then he frowned. 'Don't matter, do it? We'll never make it to the Palace. There's two River Gates 'tween us 'n' them.'

'No, there isn't,' said Silk from the bow. He gestured ahead.

Sure enough, as they'd drifted along, helped by Rell and Shaky's rowing, the bend of the Idryn brought the hulking barrier into view and in the faint light of torches and lanterns Hurl saw that the centre river portcullis was raised. She skewered Silk with a glare. 'How did you know?'

He smiled back. 'Don't you see, Hurl? They raised it themselves to bring in their own men. Now it's our way in too.'

She wouldn't let go of Silk's gaze. 'Too convenient, Silk.'

He gave his most charming smile – the one that she'd seen never fail on any female. Any except her. 'As you've seen, Hurl. I still have a few old friends here. They jammed the gates for me.'

Sunny snorted his scorn. Hurl sat back, now convinced. Sunny had it half right: more than he seems, yes. But no Claw. No, maybe *more* than that. Yet the Captain trusted him as his second in command, and that was good enough for her.

'What's the plan?' asked Shaky while he sorted through his remaining crossbow quarrels.

Storo was watching the dark shore, his gaze tight. 'Silk here will get us into the Palace. We have to establish control of what used to be the old Protectress's Throne room, the City Temple. From there, we work our way out to the garrison's marshalling grounds. We want to be there when the sergeants come out to test which way the wind's blowing.'

Sunny sneered at Silk. 'What'ya going to do, Silk? Bring us in by Warren? The *Imperial* Warren maybe?'

The mage brushed dirt from his torn vest of dark green silk. He needn't have bothered, it was long past salvaging. 'For your information, Sunny, no one can enter or exit the City Temple by Warren.' He gave the condescending smile that Hurl knew drove Sunny insane. 'We'll take the secret entrance.'

Silk's secret entrance turned out to be a fetid sewer tunnel hardly above the sullen waves of the Idryn. Shaky took one whiff of the damp fumes limping from the brick archway and rocked the boat in his effort to flinch away. 'Aw, Gods! Give us a break, Silk! You can't mean it . . .'

'Don't be so dainty,' Silk purred. 'Remember, you're a sapper, right?'

'Don't rub it in,' Hurl grumbled beneath her breath.

'Let's just go,' Sunny announced, and he nearly swamped the boat as he set one boot on to the slimed bricks. One by one, they carefully stepped out on to the ledge. Hurl hissed her disgust as to steady herself she couldn't help but touch the soft wet walls. Storo ordered Jalor to let the boat slip away. Great, Hurl thought. Now there was no going back. The stench was a physical thing jabbing its furry fingers down her throat, gagging her. Silk lit a hooded lantern and moved to lead the way but Rell stepped in front of him, both swords out, to take point.

'What're we goin' to do?' Sunny said, 'Pull ourselves up through a privy hole and say, *Hello*!'

'A reverse birth for you, eh, Sunny?' called Shaky – from the rear.

Sunny just smiled, his teeth bright in the gloom.

'For your information, yes, something just like that,' said Silk from up front with Rell.

'You just had to ask,' Hurl whispered to Sunny.

'Quiet.' This from the Captain behind.

Stooped, wincing at the stench, they sloshed along, slipping and skidding on the centuries' accumulation of the city's ruling elite's excrement. How fitting! Hurl imagined floors above, in a dark alcove, some magistrate extending his withered arse out over her head and wrinkling up his monkey face in effort to deposit . . . suddenly dizzy she almost heaved and had to lean against the slimy wall. Storo steadied her. 'You OK?'

'I can't do this.'

'Just a bit further. Bear down on it.'

'*Please!* Cap'n!'

'Sorry.'

Ahead, a yell of mingled anger and disgust from Sunny echoed through the tunnel. They groped into a broad underground chamber, dome-roofed, lit by the lantern carried by Silk. Sunny stood knee deep in the pool of filth filling its floor. Everyone else kept to the shallows at its edges. 'Poliel's rotting tits!' he snarled. 'I can't believe the mage led us to this!' He pointed a long-knife to the far side. There, the flow of excrement dribbled from a sculpture twice Hurl's height – that of a closed snouted dog's maw. As Hurl's vision adjusted she could make out more detail: long pointed ears, slanted canine eyes. An entire carved hound's head, down here! In the dark! What could be the reason for that?

But the nose was too long, the head too narrow. All of a sudden she recognized it: a jackal. Ryllandaras. The White Jackal of Winter. Quon's Curse. The man-jackal First Hero who rampaged for centuries across these central plains rendering them all but impassable but for the intercession of the tribes who worshipped him – the Old Seti.

Silk pushed his way forward through the sluggish wash until he touched the gigantic head. He turned to them. 'Who recognizes this?'

'Ryllandaras,' Hurl supplied.

He nodded, pleased. 'Yes, I thought you might know, Hurl. Though none of you has ever seen him. Gone from these plains for near a century now. Great was the hatred of this city for their ancient enemy, the man-jackal of the grasslands. As you can see.'

'We all know the stories,' Sunny sneered. 'Until the emperor, or Dancer, slew him. Get on with it.'

'That's *one* version of things . . . in any case, this is an entrance. A very old one. One dating back far before the current Empire when Heng was an independent city state, and the third most powerful one on the continent. Back then Ryllandaras and the Seti tribes were the eternal enemy, ever washing up against its walls . . .'

The mage was silent for a time, regarding the faeces-smeared titanic statue. He shook his head as if reliving old memories. Hurl shot a questioning look to Storo but the Captain frowned a negative. *Not now.*

Silk edged himself up a forelimb, leaned forward up beside the head and whispered something into one tall stone ear. One word. After a moment the stones groaned, grated, clots of muck and excrement showered down. The pointed teeth scraped as they parted. The maw reared open.

'Hood's balls!' said Shaky. 'I ain't goin' in there!'

'Then wait out here alone in the dark,' Storo suggested.

Rell had already ducked within. He returned, gesturing them on. 'There is a raised walk.'

Along the walkway Hurl manoeuvred next to Silk. 'You've shown too much of your hand,' she said in an undertone.

'This night it's all or nothing.'

'You were a city mage back then, weren't you? When Kellanved came.' The man was silent for a time. Perhaps he thought it too obvious for comment. Well, if the piece won't give in one place, try another, as her old Da used to say. 'What is this place?'

'A final bolt-hole retreat. It leads from the City Temple.'

'But it wasn't used.'

'No. She wouldn't flee. We . . . everyone, should've known she'd never abandon her city.'

The hairs on the back of Hurl's neck and arms prickled. Her. *Shalmanat*. Protectress of Li Heng for millennia. Some said since its first founding as a caravan crossroads. Slain by Kellanved – or Dancer, to be precise. Her gaze slid sideways to the slim mage with his long blond hair and tattered silks – always an object of mockery and scorn among the troops. Just who was he? And why was he here, in Li Heng, at this moment in time? 'This is no accident,' she said as she thought it, then damned the short connection between her thoughts and her mouth. He said nothing. 'You, finding yourself here for this coup I mean. You knew.'

He flashed his most winning smile, the warm yet teasingly distant, slightly impish expression that captured camp followers and serving girls. It only raised Hurl's ire. 'Don't try that on me. You knew.'

'I only knew *something* was coming, Hurl. That's all. A change in the day's light.'

And that had brought him here? She considered the hidden implications of that claim. Bluster? Bluff? Or what if it was true? What influence could he have had on their, admittedly unusual, posting? Did he actually mean to imply that he . . .

Hurl stopped walking. Silk carried on. The Captain urged her forward with one big hand at her back. *He'd* brought *her* in. That is, she remembered him asking what she thought of Storo and the next thing she knew she was somehow transferred to this squad. He'd even brought in Rell. She remembered him taking the Captain to see this swordsman he'd come across in the Malyntaeas gaol. Shortly after that new recruit Rell was in the squad. By all the Gods above and below – had Silk somehow been *recruiting*? All with an eye to this evening, this eventuality? No. That was too outrageous. Just who was he?

The stone-flagged walkway ended at a locked iron door that Silk opened, and that in turn led to a hall and a stone circular stairway. He stopped them here then pushed back his hair and tied it with a faded strip of silk. 'Ready yourselves,' he whispered. 'The door above opens on to the City Temple. There's no way of knowing who's within, or how many.' He looked to Storo, who cleared his throat.

'Right. So, saboteurs – put away the crossbows.'

'Bullshit,' said Shaky. 'From my dead hands maybe.'

Storo eyed him. 'Don't tempt me . . . Crossbows away. Each of you ready a satchel of sharpers and smokers and such – all we've got. This is gonna be room to room. Me 'n' Jalor will be up front. OK? OK.'

Shaky and Hurl pillaged Sunny's hoard even as he squirmed and snarled and tried to snatch it all back. Storo unslung his two-handed cutlass while Jalor tightened the strap of his domed helmet then drew his long-knives. Rell unsheathed each of his two odd slim longswords, single-edged, slightly curved, and then threw the sheaths away into the dark. That gesture dried Hurl's mouth.

As they climbed the stairs, Silk leading, Hurl hooked the crossbow on her belt and used her foot to cock it, then left it hanging from its shoulder-strap. They got to the door, or what Silk indicated was the door: it looked like just another length of wall to Hurl. Using battle signs Storo ordered an initial charge followed by a halt during which he and the heavies would defend while the saboteurs cleared the room. Everyone signed their understanding.

Silk did something there at the wall and a door appeared. He stepped through then aside. Storo, Rell and Jalor followed in as silently as they could but for the soft jangling of armour. Hurl came in next. She blinked in the brightness. Squinting, one hand holding a sharper shading her eyes, she saw an empty room.

It struck her that she didn't know what people imagined when someone said *Throne room*, but what came to her mind were images of large raised thrones occupied by a dried-up man or woman, simpering concubines, monkey-faced ministers eyeing the slave boys, and eunuch clerks eyeing the silverware. In any case, the room was empty, domed and circular. It was also very clean and very white and bright – though no source of light was visible.

So this was it. The Cynosure of Heng. Hurl was disappointed but also strangely impressed. The Inner Focus. The City Temple at last. Where was everyone?

Silk gestured opposite to a set of nearly indistinguishable double doors. The Captain signed the advance and they crossed the chamber.

As they came to the middle they found that in fact the chamber was not empty. Dead centre they reached a small seat. Nothing more than a leather-saddled folding camp stool with wooden armrests. Everyone except Rell stopped to stare down at it. No one spoke a word. Was this the Throne of Li Heng? Hurl didn't know what to think – it was too strange. Yet as he was looking down, Silk's face held that sadness, that mysterious yearning, that so drew the serving wenches. Of them all Rell had kept his eyes on the doors. The Captain signed to move on.

Hurl came alongside Silk. 'I don't see any lamps or smell smoke. How's this place lit?'

That smile. 'Just the fading afterglow of the glory that was, Hurl.'

'Quiet.' The Captain.

Jalor pulled open the doors revealing the backs of four guards who turned, amazed. Rell lunged, his blades flashing, and the four were down before they could unsheathe their weapons.

Everyone stared, just as stunned. 'I thought you had some kinda code,' Shaky said to Rell. 'Ain't that against your code, them being unarmed 'n' all?'

'They were armed,' answered Rell without even turning. 'They were just slow.'

They now faced a long hallway ending at another, much taller, set of double doors. Small portals opened on to the hall down its length. 'Don't like this,' grumbled Shaky.

Silk pointed to the doors opposite. 'That is the only entrance to these temple quarters.'

'Down the hall, double-time,' ordered Storo.

They charged. Civilians gaped from archways. One tall bearded fellow bellowed something – they ignored him. Just as they reached the doors they opened at the hands of the old gal herself at the head of a column of some fifteen men, soldiers obviously, though none wore Malazan livery.

'Get them!' she managed before Rell's blades pierced the air where she'd been an instant before. The men snarled and drew. Rell almost threw himself upon them but was muscled back by the Captain with a growled 'Not . . . *yet*.'

Silk had already disappeared. Jalor and the Captain crossed blades with the front of the column. Rell moved to cover the rear. Sunny raised a fist, shouting, ''Ware!' The men went ashen-faced and flinched – definitely veterans. Sunny threw and ducked, as did everyone. The sharper cracked just past the threshold in the midst of the column. The detonation threw bodies to the walls in a flash of sprayed gore. Jalor and the Captain finished off the stunned survivors.

'What is the meaning of this slaughter!'

Hurl turned; it was the bearded old fellow. He wore long dark robes of some rich cloth Hurl knew she'd probably never even touched in her life and came marching up to Rell who stopped him with one glistening wet sword point. The man should thank all the Gods that he was unarmed.

Storo crossed to him. He touched the rim of his helmet. 'Magistrate Plengyllen. What can I do for you?'

'Do! *Do!*' the man spluttered. 'These are sacred precincts! Holy grounds! How dare you pollute—'

'There's been a coup,' Storo cut in. 'Fist Rheena has been murdered.'

The magistrate subsided at that. He straightened his robes. 'Yes. I was informed that assassins . . .' His voice trailed away and his eyes bulged. He pointed. 'You! Burn protect us!' He backed away, arms raised, then fled through a portal shouting, 'Guards! Assassins! Murder!'

'Should I shut him up?' asked Sunny.

Storo waved him off, sighing, 'Never mind.'

'Reinforcements!' Shaky called from the double doors.

They pushed their way through the halls of the City Temple. Hurl reflected that Fat Kepten had come with a lot more men than the Captain had thought; that or that Storo had underbid, not wanting them to back out right from the start. In any case, Kepten's men – plain hireswords or true-believing soldiers out of uniform – kept coming. Though the garrison did keep out of it, as the Captain had said they would. Whenever crossbowmen massed at a corner or doorway Shaky and Hurl rousted them with munitions. The squad made it plain that whenever Kepten's crew resorted to missile-fire they'd return in kind, and theirs blew up. They took the hint. Hurl wasn't sure why they hadn't come with any alchemicals of their own, but they did have the mages. Ropes of flame would lash out only to be snuffed by Silk. Some kind of shadow thing took a bite out of the

141

Captain only to disappear in a flash of blinding pure white light. Hurl's old friend Runty even appeared in their midst, knifed three including her, and brought down Jalor only to be thrust through the back by Rell. Shaky took a knife in the side and dropped a sharper closer to himself than the enemy. The Captain took the brunt of that. Hurl thought it a shame; the Captain been doing damn fine until then.

After kicking aside the bodies blocking the outer doors, only the Captain, Hurl, Sunny and Rell remained standing. And only Rell was in any shape to fight. All through the night Hurl had wondered why the Captain had constantly shouldered the Genabackan youth to rear guard. Now she saw the light. Canny Captain. Reserves. Rell was by far the best fighter of them all and he was fresh. The poor lad fairly vibrated with the need to slay.

Weaving, the Captain leaned against the stout oak doors and wiped an arm across his glistening face. Hurl sheathed her long-knife and opened her satchel: two left. She looked to Sunny who held up one finger then tried to smile; he could only muster a grimace.

The Captain pushed open the outer doors. In a brightening pink light, past white marble stairs, on stone flags surrounding the broad empty marshalling grounds, stood Fat Kepten and some fifty men. The men, Hurl noted, standing far apart. The sight took the strength from her legs and she nearly sat right then and there.

Storo straightened, his jaws working against the pain, and he pushed his helmet back to point to Kepten. 'It's nearly dawn, Orlat. The garrison's watching. They know me. They don't know you from a mule's arse. Maybe you should pack it all in and go back to fishing.'

Kepten gave a low laugh. 'Like I said, Storo. We really could've used you. Too bad. You have no idea who you are up against. As you can see – I brought the whole crew. Tell you what. One last chance. You lay down your weapons right now and you'll have safe passage. Right now. You've done yourself proud, I have to say. But it's over now. Time to walk away – no shame in that.'

Hurl looked to the Captain. Would he accept? Surely they were finished now; how could they beat more than they'd faced so far? They'd had a damned good run. In truth, they got farther than she'd thought possible. Then she blinked away the sweat and salt stinging her eyes. Damn this mind-numbing exhaustion! These pirates would cut them down the minute the weapons left their hands! Surely the Captain must know that.

Storo hawked up a mouthful of phlegm and spat. 'No, Orlat. It's you that's got no idea who you're facing.' The Cap'n nodded to Rell. 'Your turn. We'll guard your back. Hold the door, lad.'

The swordsman's eyes were practically shining. His voice thick with emotion he barely managed, 'You have no idea the gift you have given me . . .'

'Take it easy, lad. I plan on living through this.'

The youth ducked his head, murmuring, 'I plan on nothing.'

'Yeah, whatever,' snarled Sunny. 'Here they come.'

With a roar, the first of the squads charged.

True to his promise, Rell held the door. Hurl was astonished by his form, speed and, most of all, his ruthless surgical efficiency. He seemed to have been trained exactly how to cut for maximum disabling or plain maiming power. Men fell gushing blood from severed thigh arteries, inner arms slashed, necks slit, disembowelled and eviscerated like fish. Hurl found it terrifying to watch; it was more a slaughter than a fight. Blood painted the bright white marble steps black. She wondered if it would ever be scrubbed away. Sunny merely stepped in now and then when some wounded fool tried to crawl closer for a jab.

All the while she stood behind Rell, a cussor raised in one hand, with a look in her eye that she hoped promised utter annihilation the moment Rell should fall. She liked to think that put a bit of hesitation into their limbs.

In any case, the siege ended with a furious yell from Orlat. The men backed off and Hurl did a quick head-count. Twenty-nine men still standing. Rell had put out of action or outright slain over twenty-one men. Astounding. She glanced back to see the Captain down, slumped along the wall, head sunk to his chest. Damn. Loss of blood. All those holes Shaky's sharper had punched in him. Orlat, she could see now, was far beyond banter. He gestured angrily and the remaining men spread out.

'This has gone too far, Storo,' he called. 'Should've backed down when I gave you the chance.' He nodded to some unseen presence and his two mages appeared at his sides, the old gal and her near twin, a rail-thin old guy with grey brush-cut hair. They snapped their arms down and both burst into flames.

Hood's grin.

'Take 'em!' Sunny yelled, throwing his last sharper. Both mages thrust their arms forward as if repelling something and Hurl felt the heat wash over her even from that distance – the breath of a kiln glowing yellow. The sharper burst in the air long before reaching the mages.

143

The cussor even felt warm in Hurl's hands. *Togg's shit!* She thrust the munition back into the satchel then backed off to slide it far down the hall as gently as she could. She returned to find Sunny and Rell arguing.

'Leave me,' Rell was saying.

Sunny had him by the jerkin. 'No. We gotta retreat. Jump them inside on the sly.'

'I have my charge. Go if you wish.'

All the while the heat was devastating. The mages advanced side by side, twin pyres, ropes of flame chaining between them. The Warren of Thyr unleashed like Hurl had never seen or heard of. Some kind of ritual battle magery. The metal fittings of her armour made her wince when they touched her flesh. The hairs on her arms were crisping.

'We have to retreat,' she shouted to Rell. 'Don't be a fool! They've won this round.'

But the damned fool would not budge.

'Fine!' Sunny snarled and he backed off, shading his face from the heat. Hurl threw one last begging look to Rell who shook his head, then to her shame she too was driven back by the excruciating heat. *And where was Silk!*

They dragged the Captain with them up the hall. The mages had advanced into view. The blood pooled at the threshold and stairs boiled, steaming, then crisped, flaking into ash that flew driven into Hurl's eyes. The corpses abandoned before the entrance burst into flames. The unfettered power of the Warren drove seared flesh into the air like smoke. Greasy soot coated Hurl's face and arms. She gagged worse than she ever had in the sewer. Through the haze she saw Rell still held the doorway, swords raised. Smoke streamed from his smouldering hair. Somehow, he hadn't even shifted from his ready stance. How was such inhuman discipline possible?

'No,' came a voice from Hurl's side. She turned, arm shielding her face, and there was Silk. The man's eyes blazed a rage she had never seen upon him. '*Not again.*' The searing incandescent heat suddenly diminished to an uncomfortable glow. The mage advanced into the storm. Hurl pulled herself along in his wake.

Silk reached the threshold and took it from Rell whom he eased backwards to Hurl. 'You have done more than we could have hoped and more,' he told the swordsman. Rell was like an ember in Hurl's arms as she dragged him back. Crisp skin sloughed from his arms where she held him.

Silk now faced the twin pillars of flame that had halted, perhaps uncertain. '*You would dare unleash such flames upon this threshold!*' His outrage pierced the furnace roar. '*Bastard practitioners of a degenerate Warren! Thyr! Retarded child of incestuous union! You provoke me now to teach you the blind shortcomings of your sad ignorance! Behold now, for the last instant of your consciousness, the true wellspring of power of which yours is but a corrupted rivulet!*'

Silk threw his arms wide and Hurl gaped. Of all the Forgotten Gods! Had the man lost his mind?

'*I summon you!*' His words shook the stones beneath Hurl's feet. She winced at their power. '*Come! You who have been gone so long! Grant us a glimpse of that which has gone out from the World! Show us how it was when Light first cleaved Night! Bless us with a vision of Pure Undiluted Light, Kurald Liosan!*'

Nothing happened. Hurl, recovering, almost cursed the man. Orlat, she saw far beyond, had cocked his head as if reaching the same conclusion as her: poor guy, the pressure was just too much.

Then something struck Hurl from behind. Not a fist or a club, but a wall. It was like falling backwards into water only it was the water that was rushing up to hit her. Then nothing. Silence. Whiteness. The physical presence of light like a sea of blinding radiance. Silk in silhouette like a shadow eroding. The two mages and Orlat and his men, black paper cutouts shredding and wisping away like dust in a wind of Light.

Then gone. Dawn coming like darkness, so pale and weak was it. The ceiling dim above her. A face, close. Bearded. Malazan greys. A voice near but sounding so far away. 'Bring healers.'

CHAPTER IV

See the mourning exile sitting by the lake. His cloak is ragged, his stomach cramped. Does he cry for fallen friends, for tankards never to be raised again to the long rafters? Where are his companions, his brothers and benchmates? All stiff and staring in fields they lie. Their spears are broken, their swords blunt. Oh, where shall he go, this lone exile? Shall he cross the water? What is to become of him? What if he were you?

Lament of the Lonely Traveller
Anonymous (attributed by some to Fisher Tel Kath)

TWELVE DAYS AFTER THE STORM, THE *KESTRAL* AND THE *Wanderer* dropped anchor at a length of uninhabited shoreline of the Sea of Chimes. At Shimmer's orders, the Nabrajan captains had kept clear of all coastline where possible, yet what lengths of shore Kyle had glimpsed appeared far from promising: grey and black tumbled rocks skirted by twisted and stunted trees, distant dusty-grey rounded hillocks, and forests of thin black-limbed evergreens. Glimpses of a level plateau of some sort broken up by copses of trees.

That dawn Kyle had watch. In the calm, almost glass-like bay, he sat cross-legged on the raised cargo hatch at mid-deck, needle in hand, attempting to mend the padded quilted shirt he wore beneath his hauberk.

'A sailor'd do a better job of that.'

Kyle looked up. It was Greymane, standing at the gunwale. He hadn't heard a thing. How could a man so big be so quiet? He returned to his sewing. 'Have to learn some time.'

'True enough.'

Kyle kept his head down. Why was the renegade talking to him? The man was practically an Avowed – had even fought against them

146

in the past, so he'd heard. The Malazan cleared his throat. 'Kyle, is it?'

'Yes.'

'I've been meaning to have a word about the Spur. I understand you're a Bael native – that the Ascendant, or whatever he was, we found up there meant something to you, and maybe your people . . .'

Kyle looked up from his sewing. 'Yes?'

'Well,' the man frowned at the deck, 'I suppose I want to apologize for that. I didn't intend for things to go the way they went.' He looked out over the water, to the dark treed shore a stone's throw distant, crossed his arms. 'Things just have a way of taking on a life of their own . . .'

Kyle watched, wondering if perhaps he'd been forgotten. For the man was now obviously thinking of other things.

After standing silent for a time the Malazan said, 'You know they call me a renegade.'

Kyle looked up from his sewing once more. 'Yes.'

'Ever wondered why?'

Kyle shrugged. 'No. It means nothing to me.'

The man laughed. 'Good. Then I'll tell you. I'm a renegade because I tried to make peace, Kyle. Strike an accord. For that I enraged the Korelans and was denounced by Malazan command. Me 'n' a handful of others.' The big man glanced to Kyle, his pale ice-blue eyes bright in the gathering dawn. 'And do you know why of all of them I alone survived the hunt that followed?'

'No.'

'Because I ran the farthest of all of them. Was the most thorough coward of the lot.'

Kyle's fists clenched his undershirt. This was not what he wanted to hear. Apologies! Confessions! Damn the man. He, a coward? What could he mean by such a ridiculous claim? 'Perhaps I'm not the one you should be talking to . . .'

'No. You're the one. Perhaps the only one. Because you're not from around here, Kyle. No one from around here would understand.'

The renegade pushed himself from the gunwale, walked off, his sandalled feet silent on the deck. Kyle watched him go. Understand? He didn't understand any of it.

The next morning Kyle saw Shimmer for the first time in months; apparently she'd been locked away in the only private cabin for what seemed the entire crossing. A sailor told him that she appeared suddenly that dawn, startling the captain as had no other event during the voyage. Later, word came for the Ninth squad to assemble.

They stood at attention, some having come across from the *Wanderer*. Shimmer examined them and they in turn examined her. At first Kyle hardly recognized her. Gone was all her usual garb of war and so startling was the transformation he could well appreciate the captain's reaction. Her hair was unbounded by her usual bright steel domed helmet and hung midnight-black and shimmering to the small of her back. The next thing Kyle noted was her height – she barely reached his chin. He'd always held an impression of her as taller. Her eyes, however, remained the same. Black under narrow slanted lids, they matched the blue-Napan cast of her face. And they held that slow reserved light that had seen just about all they possibly could, and wouldn't be surprised by anything more. Instead of her glittering coat of fine mail that reached her ankles and her long whipsword sheathed at her back, she now wore only a short-sleeved soft leather jacket and loose pantaloons.

'Just north up the coast stands Fortress Haven,' she began, 'one of the first of our settlements here in Stratem. There, Lieutenant Skinner pledged he would return and await us. The Ninth Blade will go secretly without alarming any Malazan forces or spies that may be present, and contact him.'

While Shimmer spoke, her hands moved restlessly, brushing at her waist or searching for the scabbard that would've rested at her back. Kyle didn't know her well enough to read her moods, but she appeared nervous and rushed.

'We have no idea if he still lives, or even if Malazan forces occupy Haven. You'll find that out also. But if you do reach him, all the Guard forces will immediately reunite under his command as agreed at the beginning of the Diaspora. Understood?'

'Aye, Commander.'

They gathered their equipment, rolled and belted armour, weapons and one pack each, then climbed down the rope ladder to the waiting launch. The sergeant, the Falari exile Trench, two hulking ex-Free City swordsmen, Meek and Harman, a Barghast half-breed, Grere, the Genabackan Free City mage just attached to the blade, Twisty, and the Bael natives Stalker and Kyle.

Just before they pushed off Stoop came one-handed down a rope ladder to join them. 'Thought I'd have a look,' he told Kyle, grinning, and he took the tiller next to Trench. Everyone else manned oars. They followed the shore north. Stalker next to Kyle at an oar examined the forested shore. 'Uninhabited,' he judged.

'How can you tell?'

'All old growth. No logging, no trails.'

'You know such woods?'

The scout pursed his lips, nodded.

'Quiet,' Trench ordered.

Late in the afternoon they rounded a rocky headland revealing a forested bay and the huts of a modest village. The towers of a grey stone fortress thrust high above the treetops overlooked the settlement. A set of rotting canted docks stretched out from the shore beneath.

'Back oars,' Trench ordered.

Hidden behind the headland, they pulled the launch up out of the water and camouflaged it as best they could. While the light held, they moved inland. Stalker, Grere and Kyle spread out to scout. All he saw that afternoon was virgin land, forest stretching inland free of any sign of habitation.

After dusk Trench ordered camp set; they would scout the village at dawn. In the light of a small fire he unrolled a tattered vellum map of Stratem. The squad, all but Stalker who stood watch, crowded around. Kyle sensed their hushed anticipation. Meek and Harman exchanged hungry grins. Theirs were the most clear-cut duties of the squad, and the hardest. They were simply expected to stand and fight until they or the attackers were all dead. The squad was in the field again, except this time it was Guard lands, a war more theirs than any before. During the passage Kyle had heard constant talk of the rewards waiting: fiefs, land for each. Titles. Everything a fighting man desired – if they won.

Trench pointed a blunt finger to the unsettled western shore of the inland Sea of Chimes. 'We're here.' Then he pointed to a string of fortresses built by the Guard to keep watch over their southern shores. Exile stood over the extreme east; Thick at the straits leading into the Sea of Chimes; Iron Citadel over the sands to the south-west; and North Bastion over the far west.

'But they ignored them,' said Stoop.

No one asked, 'Who?'

'It was a three-pronged attack,' Stoop said. 'In the middle of the coasts, east, west and south. Forty thousand men. We were vastly outnumbered. They hadn't forgotten the years we opposed them on Quon Tali. They meant to wipe us out. Things were pretty confused then, the Duke disappearing, lines of communication cut, forces encircled. Skinner fought Dassem to a standstill but the effort broke us. The Diaspora was ordered to preserve the Guard for the future.' Stoop grinned, winking. 'And now we're comin' back with ten times the men we left with – not counting what the other companies have assembled. We may find that the Guard now numbers more than thirty thousand.'

Kyle examined the map. A cordillera labelled the Aurgatt Range crossed the extreme north. 'Korel is north of this?' he asked of Stoop.

'Yes. Korel lands. Stratem is the name of the southern lands of this continent. Korel is the northern; then some islands and the south shore of Quon Tali. Took the Malazans long to get here 'cause of the strait, the Sea of Storms. It separates us from them. The Korelri fight demons out of the strait – Riders, they call them. The current is eroding Korel lands. An unfriendly lot. The Empire's welcome to them.'

Kyle tried to imagine the line that their voyage must have taken. As far as he could figure they came from the south-east. There was no way they should have gone anywhere near the Sea of Storms. He stood, said to Trench, 'I'll relieve Stalker.' The sergeant nodded, his eyes on the map.

He walked a ways into the woods and shook a branch. A few minutes later Stalker appeared. They squatted together; Kyle scratched at the damp earth with a twig. The land looked rich: full of resources. During their short march they'd passed only one hint of human activity: an abandoned logging camp. Low, wooded hills appeared to lie ahead, cut by clear streams and thick with wildlife sign. So far the appearance that it wasn't permanently occupied carried.

'What did you see on the *Wanderer*?' Kyle asked, thinking if there was any time to put aside pretences, it was now. He waited, tense for the tall man's reply.

Stalker let out a long breath, pulled off his helmet. 'I listened and watched mostly. Shimmer won't answer a direct question and is suspicious of anyone who asks. What I can piece together is that these Riders were waiting for us. They allowed our two ships through but the rest were scattered. How this was arranged I have no idea.'

The man kneaded a pouch hanging from his neck, a habit of his when thinking. Kyle waited. He realized he shouldn't be surprised there were rivalries among the Avowed. Now that they'd reached the homeland, everything was bound to come to a head.

'I figure the other ships were delayed because Greymane and Shimmer wanted to get here before Cowl and his Veils. From what I picked up this Skinner is one nasty fellow. The only remaining Avowed who can put Cowl in his place. We were sent because the Ninth is Skinner's old command. Seems those who know are afraid the man might be around the bend – the Ninth is the only squad he might listen to.'

Kyle could only shake his head. Far worse than he'd imagined.

The scout stood, grunting. 'A word to the wise: if you come across this Skinner fellow, don't let him near you.' He disappeared into the woods.

*   *   *

Mallick's servants notified him of midnight vistors then saw them to the banquet hall. They offered the representatives of the Untan noble houses drinks and cold meats while letting them know that the master was dressing. Mallick was in fact already dressed but he waited, rearranging the folds of his robes. Timing, he knew, was everything in conspiracy.

Eventually, Mallick nodded to his servants, waved off his body-guards and threw open the double doors of his banquet chamber. The men straightened at his entrance. Dim lamplight flickered at the chamber's centre. 'And to what do I owe this honour?' he asked as he crossed to a table crowded by carafes. He poured a small glass of golden almond liqueur.

'You know,' growled one, a grey-haired elder wrapped in a burgundy cloak.

Mallick swallowed slowly, nodding. 'The generalities, yes, Quall. But not the specifics.'

Quall's answer, a dark 'I wonder', was lost beneath an outbreak of clamour from the others. Mallick raised a hand for quiet.

'Please, please. Illata, would you speak?'

Illata helped himself to a tall glass of red wine. His cloak fell open, revealing that he wore a boiled leather cuirass studded with iron. 'It has happened as you predicted, Mallick. Imry has withdrawn from the Assembly.'

Mallick lowered his gaze to this glass. 'His actions remain his own, of course. Though it weakens our cause greatly. Was any explanation offered?'

'Sickness in the family,' sneered Illata. 'But—'

'I have a source in his household,' interrupted another, 'and that source overheard talk of a visitor in the night and threats to the family.'

151

'And you think . . .'

Illata tossed back his wine. 'Dammit, man, isn't it obvious. The Claws! She goes too far!'

'Illata!' This from several of the men.

A raised bare arm from Quall brought silence. 'Regardless of who – ' he eyed Mallick '– or how . . . we need men and matériel to guard our lands. If we cannot push emergency measures through the Assembly to gain them then we are forced to act independently.'

'The emperor forbade all private armies,' Mallick observed, setting down his empty glass.

'Nonetheless, Grisan nobles are massing on our eastern border. Our intelligence has it they command a "bodyguard" of over four thousand men. And she has done *nothing*.'

'We need the Imperial Arsenal,' said Illata. 'And we are prepared to take it.'

'Much we have speculated on this in our confidence, of course, yet—'

'No more talk,' cut in Illata. 'The plan is in motion. We will hold the arsenal by dawn.'

Mallick regarded the tense gleaming faces arrayed before him. 'I see. And I, like a goat to the slaughter, shall be the one you would push forward?' His sibilant voice fell even further, 'Are you all still so terrified?'

'Your, ah, *influence*, is known. You will speak for us. We mean no disloyalty. We merely wish to defend our own. All costs to Imperial coffers will be redeemed.'

'Very well. I shall humbly bow before her as spokesman and beg our case. There may be complications though, you understand. The arsenal is guarded.'

Illata swept his cloak over his shoulder. 'We understand. It is to be regretted, yet it is unavoidable.'

Mallick gave the slightest of bows. 'Then the chaff is cast upon the waters. We each have our assigned fates. Let us go see what the currents may bring.'

After the men had left the chamber a woman in a dark plain tunic and leggings entered by a side-door. 'Your orders?' she asked. Mallick refilled his glass then turned. At the woman's chest the small silver sigil of a bird's foot grasping a pearl glimmered in the lamp-light; Mallick studied that one bright point of light.

'Send word to all the – well, the glove has become the hand now, has it not? Send word to our Hands. Corrupt officials will be attempting to steal munitions from the arsenal this night. Assassinate them all, enslave their families and confiscate all assets and possessions to the Throne. All in the name of the Empress, of course.'

'And the Empress?'

'The matter is too small to concern her.'

The woman inclined her head. 'So it shall be.' At the door, she turned. 'Strange that none of us visited Imry on any night. What make you of that, Mallick?'

The priest's thick lips turned down as he examined the liquid gold in his glass. 'Laseen must still have her loyal followers among the Claw, Coil. They must be rooted out.'

'Yes. We have our suspicions.'

Mallick's gaze rose, his round face bright in the lantern light. 'Oh? Who?'

'Possum, among others.'

Smiling, Mallick set the glass down. 'Ah, yes. Possum. Your superior now that Pearl is gone. *He* remains.'

The woman stood motionless while the lanterns sputtered and flickered at the centre of the room. Finally, she allowed herself a stiff half bow. 'So be it – for the time.' Yet she did not leave; Mallick pushed his hands into the sash across his wide stomach. '*Yes*, Coil?'

'It occurs to us, Mallick, that with this night you will be in control of the Imperial Assembly. You perforce command the Claw. Therefore, there are those among us who wonder – when will you . . . act?'

'Past failures in Seven Cities and elsewhere have impressed upon me the harsh lesson of patience, Coil. Instruction I, more than any, ought to have appreciated long ago. But, as you say, I command already. Why then act at all?'

'*She* would not show such restraint.'

He waved Coil away. 'Her chance missed. Now none remain. Go!'

* * *

In the doldrums of the Southern Rust Sea, a slave galley, the *Ardent*, came across a sodden raft. The galley's master, Hesalt, ordered the lashed fragments brought alongside. A sailor searched among the sprawled bodies.

'How many live?' Hesalt called down.

The sailor straightened and even from far to the bow Hesalt could see the wonder on his upturned face. 'The God of the Deep's mercy. Every one! Eleven living souls!'

The Twins smiled upon them, whoever they are, Hesalt reflected. But he considered himself lucky as well – eleven warm bodies for the shackles. 'Give them water and food then throw them below.'

'Aye, Master.'

The nine men and two women, whoever they were, recovered with amazing speed. One, a burly scarred fellow – a veteran obviously – even pulled himself upright when a sailor came with a ladle of sweet water. 'I demand to see the captain,' he rasped in a passable north Genabackan dialect of the East Coast.

'The captain is nothing to you now, friend,' whispered the sailor. 'You live, but the price is your freedom.'

The man knew to take only a small sip to wet his throat. 'Tell your captain I demand that he set sail for Stratem at once.'

Those nearby laughed. The sailor took in the castaway's cracked and oozing skin, burnt almost black across his shoulders. How many weeks marooned under this pitiless sun! Amazing the fellow was even conscious. No wonder he was delirious. 'Lay back, heal. Thank Oponn for your life.'

'What is your name, sailor?'

'Jemain.'

'You are a compassionate man, Jemain. Therefore, I warn you – stand aside.'

Something in the man's eyes quelled Jemain's laugh. The castaway pushed himself to his feet, staggered but, with a groan, righted himself. 'See to my men,' he croaked.

The crew watched amused while the castaway made his laborious way to the stern. There, he stopped and stood swaying before the gaze of an old man at the tiller flanked by guards in leather armour who watched him, arms crossed, mouths downturned. 'Who is the captain of this slave-scow?' he asked of the old man.

'That would be Master Hesalt of the Southern Confederacies.'

'That's enough from you,' said one of the guards. 'Turn around or we'll whip the burnt flesh off your back.'

'How many guards does he travel with?'

Brows rising, the tillerman replied, 'Eight.'

The guards pulled truncheons from their belts – no edged weapons that might damage the merchandise. The first to swing had his head grasped in both of the castaway's hands and twisted until a wet noise announced the neck breaking. The second guard beat the man about his shoulders, tearing the burnt skin and raising a sluggish flow of dark blood. But the man ignored the blows until he managed to grasp one forearm, which he twisted, snapping. Then he drove his fingers up under the guard's chin to crush his throat. The guard fell to the deck gagging and thrashing.

All this the tillerman watched without shifting his stance. 'There's six more,' he observed, laconically.

'Think they'll surrender?' the castaway gasped, drawing in great shuddering breaths.

'Don't think that's likely.'

'I fear you're right.'

The yells brought the remaining six stamping up the deck. They surrounded the man, beat him down to the blood-slick timbers. Yet somehow he would not stop struggling. One by one he dragged the guards down. He bashed heads to the decking, throttled necks, clawed eyes from sockets, until the last one flinched away, his face pale with superstitious dread.

'Back off!' shouted a new voice.

The man pulled himself to his feet. Blood ran from him, his skin hung in cracked ribbons down his back and shoulders. Master Hesalt stood covering him with a levelled crossbow. 'Who *are* you?' he asked.

The man felt about in his mouth, pulled out a bloodied tooth. 'My name wouldn't mean a damn thing to you. You going to shoot that, or not?'

'I thought I would do you the courtesy first.'

'Well, to the Abyss with courtesy. Just shoot.'

Hesalt paused. *What a price such a fighting man would bring! What a shame to have to kill him like a rabid dog. Still, he had earned death many times over and the hired crew were watching . . .* He fired. The quarrel took the man low in the chest throwing him back against the gunwale where he slumped. Hesalt lowered the crossbow. *What a loss! Still, if the other ten were anything like this one he might yet squeeze some profit from this debacle.*

A low groan brought the slave master's attention around. Incredibly, impossibly, the man was now struggling to rise. An arm grasped the side, pulled, and he stood, quarrel jutting obscenely from his chest. Hesalt backed away, his throat tightening in horror. What magery was this? Did some God favour this man?

'It never,' the castaway ground out, 'gets any easier.' Ignoring the quarrel, he addressed Hesalt. 'Now, yield this ship to me and no more need be hurt. What say you?'

The slave master could only stare. He'd heard stories of such horrors . . . But he'd never believed . . .

The castaway lurched a step closer. 'Speak, man! For once act to save lives!'

'I . . . That is . . . Who? *What* . . . are you?'

Snarling, the man grasped Hesalt by the front of his shirts and yanked him to the gunwale. 'Too late.' In one swing he lifted the slave master and tossed him, screaming, over the side. He turned to face the stunned sailors. 'I am Bars. Iron Bars. I claim this vessel in the name of the Crimson Guard. Tillerman!'

'Aye?'

Make southwest round the Cape for Stratem.'

'Aye, Captain. Sou'west.'

'Jemain!'

The sailor straightened, dread stealing the breath from him. 'Aye?'

'You are first mate.'

Jemain wiped the cold sweat from his face, swallowed. 'Aye, sir. Your orders?'

A cough took the man and he grimaced at the agony of the convulsion. One hand a claw on the gunwale, he pushed back his shoulders. 'Get my men conscious. The slaves can row for their freedom.'

'Aye, aye, sir.'

'Now help me get this damned thing from my chest.'

* * *

From the top of the frontier fort Lieutenant Rillish watched the mob of would-be settlers, squatters and plain shiftless land-rush opportunists surrounding his command grow each day. By the fifth they must have judged their sprawling strength great enough because they sent an envoy to discuss terms. At the Lieutenant's side his sergeant spat a great stream of brown juice from the rustleaf jammed into a cheek and raised his crossbow.

'Skewer the bastards?'

'No, not yet. Let's see who's taken charge of that mess out there.'

They waited, watching, while a gang of twenty approached the gate.

'Close enough,' Rillish yelled down.

'This is parley!' a man in a bearskin cloak answered. 'Come and talk.'

'I do not negotiate with bandits.'

'Bandits!' The men laughed. 'You should get out more often, Lieutenant. Haven't you heard? But then no, you wouldn't have, would you? No messenger has come in – how long has it been now – almost a month?'

So, there it is. This man is more than he seems, or speaks for someone who is. Rillish decided to cut to the heart. 'Your terms?'

The man waved the matter aside and Rillish caught a clutter of rings at his fingers. His thick black hair was greased as was his beard. 'Simplicity itself. You and your men, the entire garrison, are free to go. March away west. You are of course welcome to keep your weapons.'

Rillish rested his hands upon the sharpened tips of the palisade. Yes, free to go. Free to walk away . . . He turned to the fort compound. There, filling the dirt square, sitting and standing, faces peering back up at him, waited more than a hundred Wickan elders and children. He returned his gaze to the envoy and the mob of would-be besiegers beyond. Sour bile rose in his mouth like iron from a stomach thrust. *Damn these scum to Hood's darkest path.*

'Come now, Lieutenant, surely you must see your situation is untenable. You are surrounded, without hope of succour. Low on provisions and without water. Come, Lieutenant, throw your own life away if you must, but think of your men.'

His sergeant spat over the wall. 'Skewer the bastard *now*?'

Rillish raised a hand to stay his sergeant. 'Who do you speak for?'

The envoy's smile convinced Rillish that his probe had worked. The man pointed off to the low hills of the Wickan territory. 'How does North Unta sound to you?'

Rillish considered ordering his sergeant to skewer the bastard. Damned Untan Great Families – they'd feuded with the Wickans for generations. Now they saw their chance.

And he was in the way.

To his sergeant Rillish asked aside, 'You are certain you saw no soldiers out there?'

'None. Adventurers, opportunists, squatters, shiftless frontier malingerers. Nothing but filth.'

Rillish drew off his helmet, wiped the sweat from his forehead. Hot here on the plains. Not like down south. Or like Korel. It'd been damned cold all those years in Korel. He cinched tight the helmet. 'Pack up your mob and decamp and I promise you we will not pursue.'

The envoy stared, frowning, as if the lieutenant had gibbered in some foreign language. Then he rallied, flushed. 'Aren't you aware of your situation, you ox-brained foot soldier? You haven't even enough men to properly defend your walls!'

157

'And you haven't the belly for a siege.'

Raising his voice, the envoy addressed the entire fort: 'You fools! This man has just thrown away your lives!'

'*Now* I'm gonna skewer the bastard.'

'Is the parley over then?' Rillish called. 'Because if it is, my sergeant here would very much like to shoot you.'

The envoy's jaws worked as he swallowed the rest of his words. 'We are done,' he spat and turned his back to march away.

'What now, sir?' the sergeant, Chord, asked beneath his breath.

'Quarter rations immediately. Confiscate all water. Double the watch. They'll probably try to rush us tonight.'

'Aye-aye, sir. Pardon me for saying so, sir, but this garrison's green, sir. Not like the old command.'

'No new command is ever like the old one, Chord.'

'Yes, sir. That's true as rain, sir.'

'We could use some of that.'

'Use some of what, sir?'

'Rain.'

'That's true, sir.'

Rillish looked out over the fort enclosure. The faces of the Wickan elders and children he'd managed to shelter turned up to him. Their eyes watched him, but not with worry, or with pleading, just watchful, patient. 'A quiet posting until retirement, they said, Chord. A well-earned rest. I should've stayed in that chaos-hole of Korel.'

'May the Gods answer you, sir.'

Rillish strode to the stairs. 'Well, on second thought, let's hope they don't, Chord.'

*　　*　　*

They were trimming and setting the boat's planking when ships breasted the south headlands following the shore north. Shouts from the villagers took Ereko's attention from overseeing the adzing. At his side Traveller set down his axe. 'Locals?' Ereko asked, though he felt certain they were not.

Traveller shaded his eyes. 'Far from it.'

Ereko studied the vessels' low beam, their simple square sail configuration. 'They are daring seamen.'

'They have come a very far way.'

'You know them, then.'

'Yes.'

In that 'yes' rode the strongest emotion Ereko had yet to hear revealed by his companion. Curiosity grew within him to meet these people who had somehow managed to stir within Traveller what could only be called plain human hate. The headman's nephew came running from the huts, pointing out to sea. 'They come! It is they! The grey raiders from the sea!' His people came following in a wave; mothers running with their skirts gathered in one hand, children yanked along in the other.

'Yes.'

The nephew swallowed to still his panting. 'What . . . What do we do?'

'Run away. All of you. Run into the forest. Don't stop.'

'What of you?'

'I'll meet them.'

'But – if we all hide – perhaps they will pass us by.'

'I don't want them to.'

The headman gaped at Traveller as if he'd just promised to commit suicide. He backed away, his gaze troubled, then sad, and finally he turned and jogged off.

Traveller crossed to where he'd left his weapon. He shook it from its sheath. 'You too,' he said. 'You need not involve yourself.'

Ereko joined him as he started down to the strand. 'No, I will come. I should mark these people so that I would know to avoid them in the future.'

Traveller deigned not to answer that, though he did glance side-long. Out in the bay the ship's prows had turned to shore. Either they had seen them or they intended to land in any case.

'Your armour?'

'There's no time.'

Of course he showed no fear but Ereko was worried. Warriors who inspired such dread were obviously no fools. They would bring their bows to bear upon them, if they had such. On the way down he retrieved his spear. 'Two ships,' he mused as they reached the strand.

The ghost of a smile teased Traveller's lips. 'Very well. The right or the left?'

Ereko eyed the two tall-prowed, narrow vessels. Both decks seethed with figures. 'The right, I think.'

The raiders had jumped down into the surf and were pushing their way up on to shore when Ereko understood the reason behind the villager's dread. *The grey raiders from the sea.* To him, nothing more than one more race of alien invaders. Tiste Edur. Children of

Shadow. As they closed where the surf licked the black shingle Ereko dredged up what Edur he'd picked up over the ages. 'Welcome.'

The lead figure, this detachment's war leader probably, gestured a halt and looked Ereko up and down. 'Name yourself.'

Like his men he wore furs over leather armour decorated by tufts of hair, twists of ribbon and smears of orange and umber pigments. His long hair was braided and greased. He bore a spear, sword and knife – Ereko saw no missile weapons. But his relief at that ended when a woman, no more than a girl really, appeared at the ship's high prow. One of their witch women. The long tatters of the cloths, shawls and scarves wrapped about her flickered in the weak wind.

'Stand aside, Ancient One,' she called.

The war leader glanced to her. 'Perhaps we should invite this one to accompany us.'

'Not him. He is no warrior.'

A clash of weapons carried over the heaving of the surf. The dark eyes of the warriors now fixed glittering upon the far vessel.

'Slay him and go,' the war leader commanded.

'Hold!' This from the girl. 'Strike him not! He is sacrosanct.'

The leader spun to the girl. '*Claims who?*'

'I!'

'Warleader . . .' This from one of the Edur.

'*Yes!*'

A nod in the direction of the other vessel. He turned to where all the warriors stared and Ereko watched a sickly paling of this Edur's grey hue. The sounds of battle, Ereko noted, had ended some moments ago. A wave and the warriors charged past. Their leader called up to the girl, '*That* one I hope you will allow us to slay.'

But the young witch woman was deaf to his jibe. She too had seen Traveller, and so too had she seen all that moves inexorably with him. Her body was frozen, yet a war had broken out upon her face as it twisted, appalled, stunned, fascinated and horrified. The war leader had run to engage Traveller. Ereko, however, chose to watch the battle betrayed on this young girl's face as one faith held as immutable truth met the incarnation of another.

Which would win?

So far, of all the spiritual crises he'd witnessed in those open to them, Traveller – or rather that which travels with him – had won.

A slight wash in the surf and Traveller stood beside him. His shirt was slashed and dappled in lashes of blood. Rising in clouds from his stained chamois trousers blood stained the water around him. The girl stared down at them, her face frozen in a rictus that pained

160

Ereko to see, then, with a howl, she threw herself backwards from sight.

'What of the ships?' Ereko asked. They both knew they could not use them; they hadn't the crew.

'We'll have to burn them.' ·

'A shame, that. They are of interesting construction. We can salvage some of the wood, I hope? It would speed our efforts considerably.'

'Very well. But nothing distinctive.'

He turned away and Ereko followed him up out of the surf. So many questions pressed themselves upon him but their peculiar partnership did not permit anything approaching explanations. For his own reasons Traveller wished it that way. But then, so too did Ereko.

A shrill call from the water, 'Revealed One!'

It was the girl. She stood in the surf, supporting herself against the ship's bow. The tatters of cloths and scarves she wore hung from her like draped seaweed. While they watched she dragged herself up the black gravel of the shingle.

'Please! I beg your guidance!'

'What is she saying?' Traveller asked.

'Ahh, you do not know Edur. I will translate. She wishes guidance.' Ereko lowered his voice. 'Should she be allowed to live? She is a witness. There may be reprisals.'

'Some things must be witnessed.'

Traveller's response staggered Ereko. Even he, of another kind and immortal, glimpsed in those words the faintest hint of what this man might be bringing forth upon the world and he was awestruck by its implications. After a time he indicated the girl now prone on the wet stones before them. 'What should I tell her?'

'If it is guidance she wishes tell her that I cannot give her anything she does not already have.'

Ereko translated, 'What you seek lies within.'

She howled, disconsolate. Her fingers clawed through the stones. 'I have nothing. Everything was a lie! I – my life – all is bereft of meaning! I am empty!'

'Tell her to spread the word of what she has seen.'

Ereko thought about Traveller's words. 'What is your name, child?'

She wiped her eyes savagely. 'Sorrow.'

Ancient Mother! Now it was Ereko's turn to stare until, mis-understanding his silence, the girl hung her head. He had to clear his throat before he could find his voice. 'Sorrow, go forth into the world. Bring word of what has been revealed.'

At his words the length of her body convulsed as if struck. She raised her face and deep within her dark eyes Ereko saw flames kindled. Those flames rose to a shining that brought tears streaming down her cheeks. She climbed to her feet. Her mouth tightened to a bloodless slash and she knelt on one knee. 'I will return to my people and all the ancient lies will be cast down. I will bring this new truth to them.'

Ereko translated for Traveller.

He was staggered. 'No. They'd just kill her out of hand. Tell her to go north. She might have a chance up there.'

Ereko translated, 'Your people are not yet ready for the truth, Sorrow. It would destroy them as it nearly did you. Their time will yet come. He bids you travel north as a pilgrim. There you may find fertile ground.'

She straightened, though her eyes now remained downcast. He studied her: such a young malnourished thing! Is this part of the foundation upon which Traveller would set his message? And there were marks upon her, invisible to others, but which he could sense. Monstrous cruelties were there burnt upon her spirit. This one has spilt much blood. But then, who else would possibly dare to carry such a burden as the one Traveller lays upon these converts?

'Tell her to go – I cannot stand to see her trembling.'

'The one who has given up his name, his past, all that he once was, to bring his message to the world, blesses you, and bids you go.'

'*My Lord!*'

The girl's gaze was averted as if from a glaring light. She could not see how her actions, her words, tormented Traveller. 'Go,' Ereko repeated. 'Go.'

She backed away, weeping, a hand at her mouth, the other wiping her eyes. She was beyond words, stricken. Transformed. Annealed by the flames that burn within these mortals' spirits that so erupt in Traveller's presence. Like handfuls of mineral powders tossed upon a fire.

They watched her retreat until she clambered up a cliff of tumbled rocks and disappeared from sight.

'Perhaps we should burn these ships before the villagers loot them,' Traveller said into the long silence.

'I want the wood.'

He let out a long sigh. 'Very well. I'll forbid any looting.'

Ereko turned to him. 'Forgive me, Traveller, but I must ask. What is it they sense? The ones like this.' He was startled to see that Traveller too was trembling. Perhaps it was the chill wind. The man had swung his gaze out to sea, squinting now into the shards of sunlight flashing there among the waves.

'I really do not know. They see what they must see. I didn't lie when I said it was already there within them. It was always there. I believe that I merely show them the Path. They must choose to walk it.'

'And where does this new Path of yours lead?'

His answering smile was full of self-mockery. 'I do not know. I am still walking it. Though I will say this one thing – it leads to a meeting and a choice. A confrontation that I cannot see beyond.'

He left Ereko standing motionless in thought upon the wave-washed shingle. More had been revealed than Ereko had ever expected, or dared ask. Yet it all remained a closed mystery to him. Among his kind they were born of Mother Earth, their flesh remained of the Earth, and when they faltered so they returned to Her embrace. Things, it seemed, were far simpler back then.

* * *

Stalker, Grere and Kyle scouted the settlement the next dawn. Empty rotting huts and grass-choked lanes. The hulks of sunken boats in the weeds of the shore. Long abandoned it was. Yet Kyle could not shake a feeling of unease. The gaping doorways seemed to mock him. Unseen figures seemed to watch from among fallen rafters. His back prickled as if hidden bows were trained upon him. After a quick search they returned to the blade waiting in the woods. 'Abandoned,' Stalker announced. Kyle nodded his agreement.

'Visited now and then,' added Grere. 'Fishermen, hunters, 'n' such.'

'Did you enter the fortress?' Trench asked.

They shook their heads.

'Good. Don't for now.' He stood. 'Let's move in. Stalker, Grere, point. Stoop, with me. Kyle, Twisty, rear.'

The blade spent the day kicking through the falling-down huts and storehouses. Trench appropriated the least collapsed house as the base. He dragged the only usable chair into the shade just inside the gaping front opening and sat facing the bay.

Kyle looked to the hamlet's rear where an overgrown path led into dense brush and on, presumably, to the cliff and fortress above.

'Why not camp down in the woods, out of sight?' Stalker asked.

Sitting on the steps, Stoop answered, ''Cause we want to make contact.'

Trench pulled a pouch from his waist, pushed a pinch of leaf and white powder into one cheek. 'That's right. Keep watch. Someone comes, grab 'em.'

'Aye.'

That night Kyle stood watch with Twisty. They kept no fires. Kyle stood in the dark close to shore, watching the moonlight shimmer from the bay's calm water. It was cool and he wondered how hard a winter this region drew. While he tried to make himself as still as the night he heard someone approaching slowly and stealthily from his rear; listening, he believed he identified the man making the noise. 'You're supposed to be watching the woods.'

Twisty pulled up short, surprised. 'Damn. How'd you know it was me?'

'You told me you were from a city – no woodsman would make that much noise.'

Twisty grimaced his disbelief. 'Is that really true?'

'No. I've never even been in a city. Seen one from a distance though.'

Twisty unrolled a wool cloak he carried over a shoulder and pulled it tight about himself. 'You're down here at the shore, I've come down from the woods. I think we both felt it last night and this night too.'

'Felt what?'

'The spirits.'

'Spirits?'

'Yes.' Twisty's bony shoulders shook as he shivered. 'The land's lousy with them.'

Kyle squinted up to the dark tree line. 'It feels empty to me.'

'Maybe they're the reason why it's empty.'

'Maybe. I'm not sure what I feel.'

'No? Really? They're interested in you.'

Kyle couldn't suppress a flinch of recognition. 'How do you know this?'

'My Warren is Denul. I sense these things.'

Now that it had been named, Kyle shook off the feeling he'd sensed since setting foot in this land – the feeling of being watched. He turned to the bay. 'Warrens,' he ground out. 'I don't understand your Warrens. How do they work? On the steppes we just worshipped the land and the rain and—' Kyle stopped.

'Yes?' Twisty prompted.

'And the wind. We worshipped Father Wind.'

Twisty blew out a long thoughtful breath. 'The Warrens . . . Good question. Hardly anyone actually knows. They're not ours after all. In your lands, do you have brotherhoods, groups of men or women?'

'Yes. We have warrior societies. Most young men join if they can. The Tall Grass, The Red Earth. The women have theirs.'

'Well, you might think of the Warrens that way. Each one has its own way of doing things. Its own secret words, symbols, and rituals. That's all there is to it. Sadly puerile, really.'

Still facing away, Kyle whispered, 'But gods?'

Kyle snorted. 'Just powerful spirits to my mind. Beings who have more power than others – nothing more. But you don't have to believe me. I'm something of a cynic on the matter.'

Kyle turned to eye the mage. 'Just power – is that the only difference?'

'Yes. There should be more but it's not something any of them seem willing to accept.'

'What's that?'

'The connection.'

The next day a small boat entered the bay. An old man rowed it. He tied it up at the least decrepit dock. The men of the blade watched from cover. 'Alive,' Trench whispered, raising a warning finger to Grere who bared his teeth in answer. Stalker, Kyle and Grere spread out among the empty huts.

Kyle allowed the old man to walk past his hiding place then stepped out on to the overgrown lane behind. The man had been whistling but stopped now that Grere suddenly faced him. He shot a glimpse to his rear, saw Kyle and his shoulders slumped. He drew a long-knife from his waist and dropped it. Grere waved him up the hill with a flick of his hand.

'Thought you were ghosts,' the man said to Trench in what Kyle heard as oddly accented Talian.

'Ghosts?' Grere answered, sneering. 'We're flesh and blood.'

'Funny that.'

'Why's that funny?'

'That's what they say too.'

Grere clouted the man across his face and Kyle fought down an urge to do the same to the Barghast tribesman. 'What settlement is north of here, old man?' Trench asked.

'Thikton.'

'How many men and women there?'

'A lot. Many hundreds.'

'How long have the Malazans run the place?'

The old man peered at them all. 'Malazans? Ain't no Malazans here. Just traders, if that's what you mean.'

'No? Then who runs the place?'

The old man scratched his head. 'Well, no one, I s'pose. We just mind our own business.'

Trench's mouth hardened. 'You sayin' there's no ruler? No authority?'

'Oh, well. There's the factor upriver at Quillon. I s'pose you could say he runs things.'

'The factor? A trader?'

'Yes.'

'What if you were attacked? Pirates or raiders?'

The old man nodded eagerly. 'Oh, yes. That used to happen all the time. Korelan raiders from up north. Even invaders from Mare landed south of here.'

'And? What happened?'

The old man swallowed, hunched his shoulders. 'Ah. Well. The ghosts, y'see. They run them all off.'

Trench raised a gauntleted hand to cuff the man but turned away in disgust. 'This is useless.'

'Kill him?' Grere asked.

'Kill him? You Genabackan recruits are a bloodthirsty lot.'

'I think we can manage one fisherman,' Stoop drawled.

'I'll keep watch on him,' said Kyle.

'So will I,' Twisty added.

Trench waved to take the old man away. 'Fine. He goes missing, I'll take the skin off your backs.'

That night Kyle sat on the steps with Stoop who smoked his pipe. High broken clouds moved raggedly across the face of the moon. A weak wind stirred the limbs of the birch and spruce. 'What of the ship?' Kyle asked.

'They'll wait while we scout out this town upriver.'

'Then what?'

'Well, we'll see, won't we? If there's no Malazan garrisons like the man says, then we'll just move right in.'

'But this isn't Quon Tali.'

'No.' Stoop took the pipe from his mouth, knocked the embers in a shower of sparks to the wet ground and gave Kyle a wink. 'But we're real close now, lad. We just have to reach out, and it's ours.'

Somehow Kyle didn't think it would be so easy.

Stoop slipped the pipe into a pocket. 'I'm off for sleep. These old bones don't take to cold bivouacs no more. Did you know that not one of these roofs don't leak?'

'Try the one across the way.'

The old saboteur eyed the canted, sunken-roofed ruin. 'Thanks a lot.'

Kyle sat for a time in the dark. These last few nights he'd hardly slept at all. That feeling of being watched that Twisty blamed on spirits wouldn't leave him. Sometimes he thought he'd heard voices whispering in the night. He even felt as if he'd heard his name called once or twice.

A walk might do him good. Too little action recently; too much waiting. First the agonizing ocean crossing and now this strange non-event of an arrival. Where was everyone? It was an unnerving land. As his feet took him on to a forest path he realized that, for all its foreignness, it was also eerily familiar. He'd felt something just like this land's haunted presence when his clan had ventured on to the northernmost high plateau of their territory. His uncle had gestured to the misty lowlands north of them saying that there they never ventured: those were Assail lands. Just studying them from the distance Kyle had sensed their eerie alienness.

When his feet brushed cut stones, he stopped. A set of stairs overgrown by vines and layered in moss led up to the clifftop fortress, Haven. More of a tower, really, than a full-sized fort. Since it was plain by now that there was no one but his blade around, he decided to climb.

The steps brought him to a dark humid tunnel that opened on to a central court. Saplings had pushed up through the flags and vines gripped the mottled walls. Kyle studied the grounds and it was clear that no one ever came up here. He crossed to another set of stairs along one wall that led up to the battlements. On his way the pale smear of aged ivory caught his eye and he knelt. A skull grinned up at him, helmet fused to it with age and green verdigris. Nearby lay a corroded sword overgrown by moss. Small animals had foraged the carcass, but no larger beasts. Not even humans had scavenged here it seemed, unless swords and armour used to be as common as weeds. No, this soldier still lay where he fell, arms and all. Question was: which army? Was this a fallen brother? Or one of those Malazans? There was no telling now; time and the gnawing teeth of scavengers had rendered them akin.

Straightening from the remains, Kyle wondered at the meanderings of his strange thoughts. Never before had he given a body a second thought. Was this lofty perspective taught by travel? He started up the stairs. Halfway, he paused as the steps ahead seemed to shimmer in the tatters of moonlight. Empty night appeared to be gliding down towards him, engulfing the steps one by one in some dark tide. Then the clouds passed and the shadows dispersed. Kyle felt at the stairs and his hand came away dust dry. An omen? But of what?

From the battlements ragged moonlight painted the Sea of Chimes a mottled blue and silver. Not one light was visible along all the shore. Was this the land the Guard had fled so long ago? Where was everyone? He leant against the gritty stones and let the evening breeze cool him. It was surprisingly quiet but for the wind hissing through the trees and the flutter of night insects. But standing there Kyle slowly became aware of another noise – that hushed whispering called from the night once again and he slowly turned. The patchy shadows of the derelict courtyard seemed to flicker and shift. He thought he could almost see shapes within them – was this why no one was supposed to come up here? Some kind of haunting? He wished Trench had been more plain about the dangers. He wondered if he was now stuck up there all night. It might just be the murmuring of the surf far below, but he imagined he could almost hear a multitude of soft voices down there.

A fresh wind brushed his cheek, this one crossways to the seabreeze. It was hot and thick and smelled not of the sea but of some other place. From a corner turret came a whirlwind of leaves and with them something iridescent in the moonlight. Puzzled, he knelt. A scattering of gold and pink flower petals. Soft and fresh. The wind out of the turret picked up and the stink of rot filled Kyle's nostrils. He backed away. The whispering from the courtyard rose to an eager susurration louder than the wind through the trees then abruptly cut off as if swept away.

A heavy step sounded from the turret, the stamp of iron on stone. Kyle's hand went to his tulwar. Another heavy step and a figure emerged. Layered iron armour that glittered darkly in the silver light encased it head to toe. A tall closed helm accented the man's great height and his hands in articulated gauntlets rested on the grip of a greatsword belted at his waist. Kyle dreaded that he faced one of those nightmares from his people's legends, a Jhag. It waved an arm, seeming to dismiss him.

'The ships await, brother,' it announced in Talian. 'Go now. Kellanved and his lackeys are close. We are agreed on the Diaspora.'

Wonder clenched Kyle's throat. His hand was slick on his tulwar that seemed oddly warm to his touch.

The helm turned and regarded him more closely. Kyle now saw that flower petals dusted the man's surcoat, which was of a dark, almost black, shimmering cloth.

'Go! Dancer has taken too many of our mages, though Cowl made him pay for it. We can counter Tayschrenn no longer. Flee while you may. I will delay them.'

Still Kyle could not move. Was this an apparition? A ghost reliving its last moments in the moonlight? Perhaps its skull was the one below.

The figure seemed to have found its doubts as well for its gauntleted hands returned to the long grip of its sword. 'Who are you, brother? Name yourself. What blade?'

Kyle struggled to find his voice. 'Kyle,' he managed, weakly. 'The Ninth.'

'You lie!' The sword sprang from its sheath.

'Skinner!' someone shouted and Kyle spun to see Stoop at the stairs. 'Skinner! Damn, you're a sight for these old eyes.' Stoop stepped past Kyle while at the same time pushing him away. 'Welcome back. You gave me 'n' the lad here quite the start.'

The helmed head inclined ever so slightly. 'Stoop . . . You are here? Shimmer's command has already departed.'

Stoop gave a loud exaggerated laugh. 'Why, we've returned, man. We're back. Near a century's passed an' we're back.'

The apparition, if it was indeed this Skinner that Kyle had heard so much of, stilled for a time, sword raised to strike. 'Returned? But . . . Malazan columns in the forest . . .'

'Gone, man. Long gone. Just us Guardsmen now.'

A hand went to the helm. 'Yes, of course. I too escaped. Yet, returning, it is as if . . .' Skinner sheathed his blade.

Kyle was relieved to see that sword safely put away. The glimpse he had of it made him recoil. The blade had been mottled black in corrosion and something told him that its slightest touch would be unhealthy.

'Yes,' Skinner continued, his voice firming. 'Now we will crush them.' He raised a gauntleted hand, clenching a fist, iron grating upon iron. 'The last time I nearly had Kellanved but for Dassem's intervention and now I am returned far more than I was then.'

'That so?' said Stoop. 'Thought you looked . . . different.'

A laugh from Skinner. 'Different? More than you imagine, Stoop.'

The old saboteur gestured to the surcoat whose heraldry was too dark to make out in this light. 'And these colours?'

'Heraldry of our Patron, Queen Ardata.'

'Never heard of her. You been with her all this time?'

'She has been very generous to us.'

'Us? How many of our brothers and sisters do you speak for, Skinner?'

The Guard champion shifted to look out over the court. Kyle had noted that the whispering had returned. Its rustling was driving him to distraction; weren't these two bothered?

'I speak for over fifty Avowed and of regular recruits, many thousands.'

The whispering was stilled as if swept away by the wind. Stoop took Kyle's arm. 'You can go back to camp. Get some sleep.'

'Shall I report to Trench? What of the *Kestral*?'

'They know, lad. They know. Word's bein' spread.'

*   *   *

The Imperial Council was convened in new quarters: one of the oldest of Imperial holdings in the capital city – the ancient castle of the old Untan city state overlooking the broad arc of the harbour. Possum, first to arrive in what proved to be a bare stone-walled room, tried to puzzle out the hidden message in this sudden new venue of Laseen's rulership. Was it a subtle reminder for the council of the traditional Untan ruling family, eradicated by Kellanved, Dancer, and, he constantly struggled to keep in mind, Laseen herself? A table only, no chairs, no food or wine in evidence – a calculated insult? But why bother? The council and Laseen were hardly on speaking terms; each treated the other as irrelevant.

It was, he reflected, dragging a gloved finger through the dust layering the thick embrasure of the single window, a damned inefficient way to run an empire. Through his control of the Assembly Mallick held the treasury and the government bureaucracy. Meanwhile, as Sword of the Empire, Korbolo Dom commanded the military. That is, what remained of it. Tayschrenn's continued unsettling silence and Quick Ben's desertion to follow Tavore left command of the Imperial Mage Cadre to the completely unknown Havva Gulen – once Archiveress of Imperial Records. A librarian. Gods above and below, Possum brushed the dust from his hands, the new Imperial High Mage was an ex-librarian. The old emperor, who some say ascended to godhood after his death, must be falling off his throne laughing.

The heavy door rattled open and in strode High Fist Anand, commander of the Malazan 4th Army, its domestic defence forces, which by Possum's intelligence sources now mustered less than twenty thousand men all told. The old commander stopped short at the threshold of the empty room. His white brows rose in silent comment. Possum shrugged.

Pursing his lips as if to say 'well, well', Anand crossed to the table, began sifting through the maps provided.

Possum rocked back and forth on his heels. And what of the Claw? *He* followed Laseen's command, for now. Yet knives were being sharpened all down the hierarchy. It was just a question of where they would be pointed.

The door opened once more and in came the tall and broad figure of Havva Gulen wrapped in dark robes. Again Possum gauged first reactions. A pause of rapid blinking followed by a wide sly smile. Possum gave a nod in welcome, thinking that he just might come to like this new High Mage – despite her matted unwashed hair and ink-spotted robes.

'Chilly in here,' she offered with a mock shudder.

He smiled. 'Palpably.'

'It's the wind off the straits,' Anand said without looking up.

Havva and Possum shared a wry look. 'Of course,' she said. 'Looks like the wind is changing.'

The door banged open. Possum watched surprise, consternation and finally anger darken the blue-Napan features of the Sword of the Empire, Korbolo Dom. 'What is the meaning of this?' Possum shrugged. Havva studied Korbolo the way a scholar might examine a curious specimen. Anand did not even bother to look up from the map table. 'Look at this!' Korbolo waved a hand about the room. 'This is an insult!'

'Rather appropriate, I should think,' said Possum.

Korbolo turned on him. 'You! Why are you even here? You are irrelevant.'

Possum opened his mouth to make the obvious reply when Havva cut in, 'Perhaps we all are, Sword of the Empire. Have you considered that?'

'What are you going on about, woman?'

She glanced about the bare walls. 'In the old days, when a councillor to the King or any high military officer was called to a meeting only to find himself delivered to an empty prison-like room

171

. . . well, the conclusion would be inescapable, don't you think?' She put a fat, ink-stained finger to her mouth. 'Shall we perhaps try the door? Does it even open from the inside, do you think?'

Korbolo stared at the High Mage, his eyes bulging. Possum could not hold back a laugh. The door rattled and everyone glanced to it; Mallick stood in the threshold, blinking. 'Nothing important missed, I trust?'

'Nothing important,' said Possum, 'just us talking.'

Smiling, Mallick rubbed his pale hands together. 'Good.' He shut the door, peered about the room. 'How very severe. Proper war footing, yes? I see we have quorum. Let us begin. High Fist Anand, the Assembly asks me to humbly convey their concerns. How go domestic preparations?'

Anand looked up, frowning. 'Assembly? What Assembly? What can it possibly consist of now? You and your dog?'

Mallick's bland smile on his round moon-like face did not waver. 'Assurances, commander. We have maintained full membership throughout traitorous desertions. Brave new representatives have consented to sit. All provisional, of course, until peace and order restored.'

'And how much did that cost,' Anand muttered into his maps. Sighing, he shrugged his high thin shoulders. 'It is going as well as can be hoped given how hamstrung we are. We've lost most of our resources across the continent. Entire regiments have fallen back to their roots and come out as Itko Kanese or Grisan. Ugly rumours of ethnic slaughters accompany those reports. Armouries have been confiscated; ships impounded. The shortage of competent mages means communication by the old ways of road and sea. It's a damned mess.'

'And what would you advise?'

Korbolo cut in, 'You forget yourself, Mallick. As First Sword I determine strategy.'

Mallick merely raised a placating hand. A hand like a blind fish drawn up from the depths, thought Possum, suppressing a shudder. 'Merely canvassing for opinions. We are here to discuss, after all. Indulgence please. High Fist Anand?'

The glower that knuckled Korbolo's face told Possum that the First Sword was seriously wondering just how much longer to indulge Mallick.

Anand frowned, his white brows drawing down to almost hide his eyes. 'We can't be certain of any territory, therefore we must consolidate. Secure from the centre outward.'

'Excellent. And you, Sword of the Empire? Your opinion?'

Korbolo scowled, almost pouting. 'I disagree. We must move with all speed.'

Mallick folded his hands across his paunch. 'So. Opposing strategies. Perhaps this is good in that relative merits may be examined.'

Possum could not take his eyes from the fat little man. He'd done it again – taken charge. How did he do it? Was it some weakness in their collective character, or strength of a trait in him? Again Possum felt unnerved by the little man's presence, as if Mallick were something other, something less, or more, than what he appeared. It reminded Possum of a similar situation from long ago. One he could not quite place.

The door opened once again. All straightened, turning. Laseen entered. She wore her signature plain slippers, straight trousers and green silk tunic. No symbol of rank or standing upon her – it had long ago occurred to Possum that this lack was not an affectation; the woman simply did not need them to let anyone know who she was. It was in her eyes, her posture: sovereignty. She was shorter than Possum but he always had the impression she was looking down at him. The deepened lines bracketing her thin mouth told him she was not pleased.

A curt nod acknowledged their obeisance. 'You have had a chance to talk?'

'Yes,' said Mallick. 'We were just—'

'A brief, if you please, High Fist Anand,' Laseen cut through Mallick.

Mallick's mouth snapped shut like a fish. Beneath his short greying beard, Anand gave his first smile. 'A pleasure, Your Highness. I was merely awaiting your arrival. Our sources, such as they are, agree that an army is marching in all haste from Tali. It is gathering forces as it moves east. It seems this insurgent Duchess Ghelel is quite certain of her control. Enough to accompany the army, in any case—'

'A Duchess,' snorted Korbolo. 'How absurd!'

Possum shot a glance to the Empress whose mouth tightened even further. Havva, he saw, grinned openly. 'Or those who control *her*,' Korbolo continued, unaware.

Again a shrug like an ungainly seabird adjusting its wings. 'Irrelevant to me. I deal with certainties. Also,' Anand's gaze moved to Possum, 'not my department.'

Possum declined to respond. Anand cleared his throat. 'A

173

rendezvous is no doubt planned with the Seti who have come out strong in favour of independence.' The old commander waved a hand dismissively. 'Some kind of traditionalist movement, I understand. A generation too late, I'd say. In any case, they've dug up a competent warlord who has taken control of the plains and effectively severed all communications. He's cut the continent in half, whoever he is.'

'Their goal?' Laseen prompted.

Korbolo Dom could contain himself no longer. 'Their *goal*? Destroy us, of course! Empress, with all due respect, I suggest you leave such matters to your military commanders. We will settle strategy.'

'First Sword!' Laseen snapped, almost cutting the air between them. 'You are here to advise. And I must remind you that since you possess the title of First Sword of the Empire, you thus command only in the field. Dassem himself deferred to others in matters of strategy.'

Yes, Possum reflected, and should the intelligences he had received be true, among those commanders would be the very names now assembled against them.

Laseen returned to Anand. 'High Fist?'

'Their goal is the same as ours. Consolidation, step by step. Once they take Li Heng then they will threaten Cawn. Then the Kanese will join them for fear of being left behind and having no presence behind the new throne. From there it's a quick march on good roads to us.'

Into the silence following that Laseen asked, 'Our options?'

'We have only two. We can await them here and hope to break them, or meet them in the field and hope to break them there.'

'Thank you, High Fist. First Sword, your assessment?'

Korbolo bared his clenched teeth. 'To say that we have only two courses of action, to stay or to march, is too much of an oversimplification to be of any use at all! Of course that is true. Any fool can see this.'

Havva smiled her ironic agreement while Anand merely raised a brow.

'What would be your advice?'

'We must move, Empress. Your pardon, but this slow *deliberation* is seen by all as hesitation and weakness.'

'Thank you, First Sword. Havva, your evaluation?'

The Empire's new High Mage steepled her fingers at her broad chest. 'Empress, if there is any consolation to be gained from the thinning of our mage corps, it is that this sad state extends to our enemies as well. My compatriots and I are of the opinion that no mage of any stature can be fielded by them. Regrettably, they can say the same of us. That is, unless . . .'

Laseen's lips tightened white. '*He* is not to be counted on.'

'I thought not. As do they, apparently, else they would not be proceeding. So, I shall strive to do my best. An option, though – perhaps a few of the cadre mages from our overseas holdings . . .'

'No.'

'No?' This from Korbolo. 'Why not? They are ours to command. If these nationalists have few mages as Havva claims, then should we not strengthen ourselves in this very regard? Strike them where they are weak. And on the subject – where is the Imperial Navy? Where is Admiral Nok? Why does he not simply land in Quon harbour, take the city?'

It seemed to Possum that Laseen met this outburst with amazing equanimity. She clasped her hands behind her back, as if mistrusting what she might be tempted to do. She cocked her head to Anand without taking her hooded gaze from Korbolo Dom. 'Why would that be, High Fist?'

'Because this Duchess would simply turn around, retake her city, and we'd be back to square one.'

'Then Admiral Nok should—'

'Enough!'

Possum flinched at the snap in that command. Korbolo, however, did not bother to disguise his seething frustration.

'We are on our own, Sword of the Empire,' Laseen said, her tone final. 'My commands to Nok cannot be countered. I have given over to him maintenance of our overseas holdings. He is fully committed with the logistics of supply, troop transport, relief and reinforcement. Expect no succour. We must win back the continent, or be destroyed in the attempt.'

Throughout, Possum noted, Mallick had remained silent, pudgy hands clasped at his stomach, eyes downcast, his thick lips slightly pursed as if in thought. Now he raised his gaze, opened his hands. 'Your orders, then, Empress?'

'For now, as our military hierarchy suggests – gather forces. I want Unta province back under our control. I want those nobles back in the capital with their forces.' Her gaze swung to Possum. 'Clawmaster, take family members hostage to ensure cooperation, starting tonight.'

Possum smiled his acknowledgement.

'In one sense time is now on our side. Theirs is an uneasy alliance of new rulers jealous of their independence. If we can hold out long enough it will unravel. We will do all we can to help that process along. Havva, Possum, send out missives to all your contacts arguing that Tali intends to reassert its old hegemony. Make overtures to Dal Hon. Send messages to the Bloorian nobles that the Gris have been promised their lands. Begin a campaign of mutual suspicion and disinformation that will leave them unable to recognize the truth.'

The High Mage and the Clawmaster bowed.

'And Clawmaster,' Laseen continued, 'general intelligence?'

Possum shrugged dismissively. 'The streets are awash in rumours, of course. But nothing worthy of following. One persistent story does seem to be gathering strength despite its improbability. There's talk of the Crimson Guard's return.'

Anand barked a laugh. 'Every year they're supposed to show up. Those old tales resurface any time morale is low. They're like a dose of the clap. We never seem able to shake them off entirely.'

Laseen smiled thinly. 'Then let us hope they do oblige us, High Fist. It will give us a chance to finally rid ourselves of them.'

'You're so certain?' This from Havva.

'Yes. They'd be fools to come back, and K'azz was no fool.'

Possum noted Mallick watching Laseen more intently than during the entire meeting. The fat man's lips drew down in thought and he lowered his gaze.

'This council has ended. You are dismissed.'

'As the Empress commands,' all responded, even Korbolo.

Laseen caught Possum's eye. 'A word, Clawmaster.'

Possum held back while the others withdrew. Now his time had come. He could delay no longer. What would it be? Denial? Rage? He had to admit to a certain curiosity, even if he feared the clichéd killing of the messenger. The door closed and he and the Empress were alone. She went to the single window, stood facing out, hands clasped at her back.

'Your silence tells me all I need to know, Possum.' She glanced back, sidelong. 'You stand distant, close by the door. Am I that terrifying a tyrant?'

For the life of him, Possum did not know how to respond. Topper, now he would not have had any reservations. How familiar Topper had been with her! Or Pearl . . . he'd have some glib line. Ever ready with the facile patter that man had been. Like oral flatulence. But not Possum. His expertise was lying low. Now he was being called to creep out into the light. How bright the glare!

'Names, Clawmaster.'

Possum cleared his throat, tried to speak, found his mouth too dry. He wondered distantly at this: fear for himself? Or pity for the pain he must convey? 'Amaron,' he managed. 'Toc the Elder, Choss and . . . Urko.'

'So – Toc. He is this Seti warlord, is he not?'

'Yes.'

'Yet Anand does not know.'

'No. Very few are aware – bad for morale, yes?'

Silence. A back so tense Possum imagined it incapable of flexing. Watching her standing there all alone taking this news of the betrayal of so many old companions, Possum settled on pity.

'Leave me,' she said, her voice still under ruthless control.

Possum bowed and exited pulling the door tight behind him. To the guards outside he said, 'The Empress does not wish to be disturbed.'

*   *   *

On board Urko's flagship, the Genabackan barque *Keth's Loss*, Ullen watched the latest wave of Moranth Silver quorls, exhausted, come scudding in low over the waves to set down ever so daintily on shore. Made of spun glass, the giant dragonfly-like monsters seemed to him. Yet surprisingly sturdy. Each carried two riders, a handler and passenger, plus one small box – one exceedingly precious box. The riders dismounted and unloaded the quorl. The passenger, a Moranth Gold warrior, would assemble for transport in one of the ten contracted Moranth Blue galleys while the handler would take his mount to rest and eat. So elegant, Ullen reflected, the flying creatures with their four tissue-thin wings and long segmented tails. Until you see them eat. The damned monsters ate live prey.

A messenger presented papers for his inspection – objections regarding space for water requisition. Ullen scrawled 'Maximum!' and handed back the orders then returned to studying the foreigners. Forty more Gold warriors for Urko's grand alliance of the disaffected. Some two thousand of them now. And the last wave of recruitment, too. Word had come from Quon; events were far ahead of schedule. The fleet had to move now or risk becoming a footnote.

Further out to sea, beyond the anchorage, swift scout vessels already scoured the sea-lanes southward, securing the route of the hundred-vessel convoy that would sail this very night.

'Watching our Genabackan allies, aren't you?' came a woman's rich contralto. Ullen turned. Dominating the mid-deck beneath a

177

shading canopy sat Urko's new mage cadre leader, the ample, midnight-hued Dal Honese witch, Bala Jesselt.

Ullen allowed himself a guarded nod. 'Yes.'

'Can we trust them, hmm? Why are they with us, yes? What are their goals?'

'Yes? What are they? You are the mage.'

Bala shrugged her thick shoulders, fanned her face. 'Well, who can say? Their minds work in strange ways.'

'Strong allies for now though.'

'Yes . . . for now.'

Ullen chose to overlook the opening – Bala was notorious for her innuendo and constant scheming for self-advancement. Her un-bridled ambition had had her eliminated from the cadre long ago. No doubt Urko believed he could keep her in check, but Ullen wondered. Further messages arrived. Bala continued fanning her glistening sweaty face while Ullen answered each. 'What of you?' she asked as he struggled with the final order of sailing.

'I'm sorry?'

'Once Adjutant to Choss, now a mere staff-chief. A demotion, yes?'

Ullen returned the orders. He gave the new mage cadre leader his best smile. 'I think of it as more of a sideways move.'

She sighed her disappointment, flicked her fan. 'I suppose one must make the best of what little one can manage.'

'Speaking of what little one can manage – what word from Li Heng or Dal Hon?'

The fan snapped shut. 'Do not mock me! All of you should be grateful for my presence! If it were not for me shielding this fleet Admiral Nok would have sunk the lot of you.'

'Nok is wholly preoccupied by the Seven Cities pacification. He is wise enough to keep to one war at a time.'

Bala's laugh shook her wide bosom. 'What could you know of the mind of a commander as great as he?'

Ullen almost explained that he was Choss's adjutant and that Choss had been Nok's protégé, but he realized the effort would be lost on one such as this. He gratefully accepted the distraction of a Gold Moranth messenger arrived by launch. 'Yes?'

'Commander V'thell once again asks to be informed of our destination.'

'Inform V'thell that for reasons of security no one but Urko knows our destination. Not even I know. Word will be given once the fleet is at sea.'

178

'Very well. What of storms scattering the fleet?'

'We will communicate by flag, lantern and,' he nodded to Bala, 'mage. What of your quorls?'

'All the quorls will be returned. They hate the water.'

'A shame that.'

The messenger bowed and climbed down the side to the waiting launch. Idly, Ullen wondered if a Moranth in all his armour would sink just as swiftly as any normal armoured man, and whether they were insane not to bow in any way to the altered circumstances of travel at sea.

A half-bell later he decided, reluctantly, that now was as good a time as any. He called to a flagman, 'Signal for the larger vessels, the Blues, and the dromonds, to begin exiting the anchorage.' The Dal Hon witch now had her sleepy-eyed attention on the captain's cabin containing Urko. The man was probably staying in there solely to avoid her. 'What can you do to speed our passage?' he asked her. 'Events are moving faster than we.'

'I? I am no Chem priestess. And the Warren of Mael is a mystery to me, thank Thesorma.'

Ullen rubbed his eyes. Why have the Gods cursed him so? 'Do you know anyone who can be of help? Any of our associates or sympathizers?'

The fan slid open and resumed fluttering. 'I will make inquiries.'

'Thank you.'

As the day's light faded Ullen kept in communication with the fleet through the flag signalmen for as long as he could. Lanterns appeared more and more often, flashing their coded responses. All the while Bala's fan fluttered as a blur. Sometimes she seemed to whisper into it while at other times she wafted its wind over the side of her face. Ullen shaded his gaze to take in the distant huge Blue transports far out to sea. Impatient, that Gold commander, V'thell.

At one point Bala jerked as if pinched, biting back a gasp, and Ullen swung on her. 'Yes?'

The fan resumed its blurred flashing. The puffed lazy eyes slid to the darkening horizon. 'Strange scents from Stratem. Something there. Something very powerful. I smell it; even this far across the world.'

Stratem? Who gave a damn about Stratem? 'Any word on who could help us with the crossing?'

She nodded. 'A hint. A sympathizer in Unta. His representatives are open to the possibility. I think they want gold or political influence in return.'

179

'Tell them that if they speed our passage they will get whatever they ask for.'

The Dal Hon witch appeared doubtful; she pursed her full lips. 'I shall. But a dangerous promise. Who knows what they might ask for?'

'I don't care if they ask for Hood himself. We've dawdled here assembling long enough. We must move.'

'Very well. I will negotiate with this mage of Ruse.'

* * *

The refugees came streaming into Heng like drips of blood leaking down from the Seti plains. Atop the wall next to the Northern Plains Gate, the Gate of Doleful Regards, Captain Storo Matash, now Interim-Fist of the Malazan Garrison, watched the dusty knots of men, women and families while a sour ulcerous pain ate at his stomach. More mouths to feed. More souls to house. More voices to complain. And more potential traitors to watch. How many among this latest train of displaced settlers and traders were Seti agents and spies? Too many, no doubt. As if that new tribal warlord they've got out there needed any more spies in this leaking tub of a city.

A scrape of boots on stone and Silk stood next to him. 'You should still be in bed recuperating,' the mage told him.

'I have no reason to complain. How's Rell doing?'

Silk grimaced in sympathetic pain. 'Recovering. It's a miracle he's alive at all, let alone healing. I've requisitioned and pressed every skilled healer in the city into helping out. But even if he does recover completely there's nothing to be done for the scarring. The man lost most of the skin of his arms and face. High Denul can do only so much. For all that, though, he actually doesn't seem to mind. He's even practising to keep limber as he heals.' Silk raised his hands in wonderment. 'Simply amazing.'

'Well, you move my bed up here and I'll lie down in it. In any case,' Storo eyed the pale, sunken-eyed mage, 'you look worse off than me.'

Silk shrugged, leant his weight against the stone crenellations. 'Up all night with the saboteurs, helping to hide their work. They're making miracles all up and down the walls. Shaky's actually working. I don't think I've ever seen him work before.'

'You too. Back in Genabackis, I always had the feeling you had one hand behind your back. That you weren't committed.'

A dry wind off the prairie tousled the mage's long blond hair. He pushed it back from his face. 'Not my battle. This is.'

'You proved that last week. Going to finally tell me what you did? I was out of it by then. Sunny claims the sun shone out of your arse and you farted everyone away.'

Silk could not keep a grin away. 'Colourful. And not too inaccurate. No, all I did was summon the power of the old city temple and it responded with one last glow of its old reflected glory. That's all.'

'And I'm Dessembrae the Lord of Tragedy.'

The mage shaded his gaze and studied the plain and distant dun-brown hills along the horizon. Storo shifted his own hard stare to share the view. 'All right,' he sighed. 'There's the real worry.' He rubbed his chest beneath his shirts, grimaced his pain. 'Truth is I'm blind, Silk. I've no idea what's going on out there. Don't know how many men they have. Even where they are. There might be fifty thousand Seti tribesmen just over those damned hills and I haven't the faintest idea of it. Or at Unta. What's going on at the capital? Are reinforcements on their way? How much support can I expect?' He spat over the wall. 'It's a mess. A Hood-spawned bitch's-whelp of a mess.'

The mage gave a slow shrug of commiseration. 'I'm sorry. I wish I could be more of a help. But that sort of scrying and communication over great distances is not my forte.'

'Well, who in Utter Night can help? Isn't there another battle mage in the city? Have they found the garrison cadre mages yet?'

'No. One was thought to have joined Orlat. The other disappeared that night, fled or killed by them. That leaves me.' Silk paused; his gaze flicked to Storo. 'There is one other who could be of help – if you'd accept.'

'Who? Gods, I hope you don't mean that hag you got to help us before.'

'Her name is Liss, Captain.'

'Ah. Sorry, Silk.' Wincing, Storo squeezed his side, drew an experimental breath. 'How can she help?'

Silk raised his chin to the distant undulations of the Seti prairie. 'She knows them, Fist. Knows them well. She was once one of their shamanesses – a Seer. I gather that they're actually rather frightened of her.'

'So am I.'

A voice called from far along the wall, 'Sergeant Storo!' Silk and Storo turned. Magistrate Ehrlann approached, the servant at his side struggling to keep him within the shade of a wide umbrella.

'*Sergeant?*' Silk replied. 'This man is senior officer of this Malazan command—'

Storo raised a hand to quiet Silk.

'Yes, yes. All very well,' allowed Ehrlann, waving negligently. 'However, a ruling body recognized by the Throne really cannot afford to acknowledge a field-promotion until it is approved by military high command.'

'And just when might that be?' Silk asked, not even bothering to lighten his tone.

'Why, when the paperwork comes through, of course,' Ehrlann smiled.

Silk pointed to the prairie. 'You do understand that the Imperial Warren is now closed to all. That no mage dare risk travelling any of the Warrens now that civil war is upon us. That the Kingdom of Cawn lies between us and Unta and that it has arisen in rebellion against the Imperial Throne!'

Magistrate Ehrlann frowned. 'Well, then, it may take some time for the paperwork to reach us here.'

Storo clamped a hand on Silk's shoulder and squeezed hard. 'Quite right, magistrate. The City High Court should call an emergency meeting to discuss its course of action. You must settle the positioning of troops, the strategy of the defences, the organization of the civilian population. You must commission a detailed inventory of all logistical necessities and the requisition of the funds to purchase them. And all that is just a beginning.'

Magistrate Ehrlann blinked at Storo, quite stunned. 'Of course . . . well . . . the process has already begun in special committee—'

'Then you'd best get back in case they decide on some idiotic course of action in your absence.'

Ehrlann smiled thinly. 'Thank you. Yes.' He snapped his fingers. 'Come, Jamaer.' The magistrate swung to the stairs.

Storo watched them go then turned away to rest his forearms on the battlements once more. 'Gods, they'll be talking until the Last Night is upon us.' He addressed Silk. 'Until that time comes, what do you suggest?'

'I intend to find us some allies.'

'Good. Please do. As many as possible.'

'And Liss?'

Storo nodded his assent. 'Tell her to keep those Seti shamans as far away as she can.'

Silk's smile was tight with suppressed pleasure. 'Oh, she'll enjoy that a great deal, I'm sure.' He bowed and went to the stairs. At the top he paused. 'Fist, may I ask, just what is our defence strategy in any case?'

'Our defence strategy? An odd one. Kill as many of the Seti bastards as is humanly possible.'

* * *

Ho was releaved to find that the newcomers to the Pit intended to keep a low profile. Thinking it over for a time, however, he realized that this worried him just as much. The two were acting less like the potential tyrants he feared, but more like the suspected spies he feared even more. Yet it all seemed too preposterous; an insignificant detail no doubt buried among the chaos and smoke of the uprising: why did Pit not rise in rebellion? Even after guards were pulled away to help pacify Skullcap, Pit remained a model of quiet. Why should this be? What could over a hundred mages, warlocks, seers, thaumaturgs and assorted *talents* possibly be up to? Not a thing, certainly, sir. No, nothing at all.

A council meeting would have been called to settle upon a course of action but the problem was the two would be sure to hear every word of the screaming matches yammering down the tunnels. And so Yath and his people kept watch; especially that eerie shadow of his, Sessin.

On his way to the minehead, Ho scratched the patches of dry raw skin on his arms and legs that so cursed all inhabitants of the Pit. They all had more than enough to keep themselves busy in any case. There was the question of what to do with Iffin; just two weeks ago the fellow was walking down a tunnel when he meets Sulp 'Ul – a man he'd worked beside peaceably enough for nearly ten years – when suddenly Iffin reaches over and jabs a sharpened stick through Sulp's throat. Sulp dies choking on his own blood. We confine Iffin to a barred cave and question him. Turns out it was a family vendetta from the old Cawn–Itko Kan border wars from before the Empire. And Iffin wasn't even old enough to remember those days!

Hopping to scratch one ankle, Ho had to shake his head. He'd thought those old rivalries and hatreds had all gone the way of the Jaghut. But now, with rumours arriving of nations seceding from the Empire – Quon, Dal Hon, Gris – and every week the list seeming to grow longer, old, long-quiescent hatreds and rivalries were now raising their noses and sniffing the wind. All the old festering slights that only the heel of the emperor manged to quell. Ho could only dread what was to come if the continent returned to its old destructive ways of shifting alliances and the never-ending feud for dominance.

At the great round of the mine-head he spotted the two newcomers silently staring upwards at the circle of clear blue sky overhead. Or so it seemed to any casual observer – to Ho it looked more like they were studying the crumbling, rotten stone of the walls searching for a way up. He came up behind them. 'Those walls won't support the weight of a man.'

The one who gave his name as Grief slowly turned his head to give Ho a long hard stare. 'Looks that way.'

'If I were you I wouldn't waste my time trying to scare up an escape plan. Escape attempts only bring reprisals for the rest of us.'

The one named Treat turned around fully. 'You warnin' us? Gonna turn us in?'

The Napan, Grief, briefly rested a hand on the arm of Treat who eased back a step. So, not equals. This Grief – what a ridiculous name to give! – seemed to outrank his companion. Ho shook his head. 'No. You'll notice there's no one to turn you in to. I'm just asking that you try to keep the welfare of everyone here in mind.'

A broad secretive smile lifted Grief's lips and he bowed his assent to Ho. 'Good idea. We'll try to do just that.' He patted his companion on the arm and they walked off leaving Ho to watch them go, wondering, what did the fellow mean by that – if anything?

Turning away, Ho walked straight into the lean but dense form of Sessin. The tanned Seven Cities native glowered down at him. 'What did he say?' he demanded in thickly accented Talian.

'Nothing significant.' Ho scratched at his scalp. Gods, here he was answering to the man as if he were an Official Inquisitor. 'Listen, do you do this all day? Just follow them around? Aren't they suspicious?'

The scowl edged into a sneer. 'Where would they go?'

OK. The man had a point there. So, they know, he knows, and they know he knows.

'Yath has judged. If they find out anything we will kill them.'

Yath has judged that, has he? Well, he'd have to have a word with the man about that. As for killing those two, something told Ho they could take a whole lot of killing.

* * *

While Traveller slept inside the hut Ereko sat cross-legged in the doorway watching the Moon, strangely mottled as of late, reflecting from the surf. The violent predations of these Edur and Traveller's extreme response had stirred dusty memories in him; ones he'd hoped were buried for ever. Memories that still wrenched after millennia. Memories of ancient vows and the violence of further extreme solutions. Vows of absolute extermination levelled against a people, and answering vows of vengeance. Could a similar cycle of destruction be born out of this new exchange? How similar the ages remain despite the passage of aeons. How disheartening!

Brooding upon what had he worked so hard to put behind him for ever, Ereko saw ghosts. For an instant he thought them his own – phantom memories of friends and family long gone – but these were human. Since descending the mountains he'd glimpsed them some nights in the woods. Pallid shadows. Always they lingered nearby, drawn to them – to Traveller certainly – but unwilling or unable to approach. Perhaps Traveller could not see them; he'd yet to remark upon them.

Perhaps it was the blood still wet upon the sands and the presence of alien spirits now wandering these shores, but this night they assembled out among the sighing grasses beyond the glow of the driftwood fire in numbers far greater than any Ereko had yet glimpsed. A troop of opalescent shades. Soldiers in damaged armour revealing ghastly death-wounds. One held a ragged banner that hung limp from a cross-piece: the snake-like twisting of a shimmering bright dragon against a dark field.

More and more congregated. A spectral host. A great battle must have ravaged this coast some time in history. Somehow, Traveller's presence seemed to call to them. Their empty spirits lusted for his essence. Eyes like torn openings into unending desolation fixed past Ereko into the dark of the hut. Clawed hands reached . . .

Ereko waved them away with the back of a hand. He whispered, 'Be gone spirits! Trouble not the living with your old hatreds.' Sleep, rest, wait. Be patient. Wait long enough and your time will come. Was he not living proof?

The spectres dispersed. Some sank into the earth, others drifted away. One remained, however. The standard-bearer. Tall he must've been in life, for a human. He closed upon Ereko. A horrific wound had carried away half his skull. The empty pits of his eyes fixed upon him.

'My name is Surat,' came his words, achingly faint – such potent yearning to cross an unbridgeable distance. Great must have been this one's power in life. 'They come,' he intoned.

'Who comes?'

'The Diaspora ends. The Guard returns. The appointed time has come to us.' He pointed to the hut. 'This one shall be destroyed.'

'What is he to you now?'

Silence, a coldness that bit even at Ereko. 'Malazan.'

'Whatever he once was he has given all that up now. He is Malazan no longer. Now, I do not even know what he is.'

The empty pits regarded Ereko and he believed he saw in their depths utter uninterest. 'The Vow remains.'

A strange emotion stirred in Ereko's stomach then, roused the hairs upon his neck and forearms. It took him a time to recognize it, so long had it been. Anger. Fury at the plain uselessness of hatreds carried beyond life. Who were these Crimson Guardsmen to awaken such an emotion within him? 'Then you are fools! Put aside your old rivalries, your precious feuds. But you cannot. . . . You dare not release your desperate grip. Without them you would be nothing . . . They are all you have left. Not even Death awaits you now.'

Ghost hands shifted on the haft of the lifeless banner. '*He* waits for you. He is close now. Closer than you think.'

'There are few walking the world today whom I fear.' Ereko's words were trite but he was intrigued and, he must admit, tense with a new emotion, a touch of dread.

'Such a one you will meet.'

The tension drained from him in a gust of exhalation. Nothing new. No revelations. No darkness dispelled. 'That meeting was foretold before humans walked these lands, Surat. You have nothing of interest to me.'

He waved the spectre away. It sank, reluctantly, into the windswept grasses. As it disappeared it raised a hand, accusing: 'That one leads you to Him.'

Ereko nodded. 'That was the promise made long ago.'

*   *   *

Late in the evening, leaning his chair back against the shack of the Untan harbour guard, Nait banged a knuckle on the clapboard slats.

'What is it?' Sergeant Tinsmith grumbled.

'Ship just tied up. Looks like that tub, the Rag-what's it. The *Ragstopper*?'

'The *Ragstopper* sank. Could be his new one, the *Ragstopper*.'

Chair legs thumped to the dock. 'New? You gotta be kidding me.'

'All his new ships are old. He buys them new old. He says he likes them worn in; says they know what to do then.'

Nait shifted the bird's bone he chewed from one side of his

mouth to the other. 'Well, this one looks like it knows what to do, an' that's sink.'

Sergeant Tinsmith came to the open doorway. His white moustache hung to either side of his turned-down mouth. Deep fissures framed the mouth, lancing beneath narrowed brown eyes. 'All right then,' he sighed. 'Let's have a look. Get the boys rousted.'

Jogging, Nait crossed to a row of waterfront three-storey buildings housing poor merchants, flophouses, inns and a Custom House. The building he headed to featured a tall wooden figurehead cut from a man-o'-war and subsequently vandalized by countless knives and fists until all semblance of its original build, paint and gilt were gone. All that remained were two clawed feet, perhaps of some demon or fantastic bird. This tavern, The Figurehead, the harbour guard had adopted as their billet. He found a band of the guard sitting around a table engrossed in a game of troughs. Corporal Hands had just thrown. Nait took the bird legbone from his mouth. 'The old man says to get your gear.' Hands snatched up the knucklebone dice. Yells burst from around the table.

'Hey! That was a six,' said Honey Boy. 'Make the move.'

Hands slipped the dice into a pouch. 'You heard the man – get your gear.'

The biggest man at the table, a Barghast warrior, straightened to his feet, banging the table in the process and sending the counters dancing. Yells of fresh outrage. A shaggy black bhederin cloak hung at his shoulders making them almost as wide as a horse. Twists of cloth and totems swung and clattered in his matted hair. 'You count that throw or I'll use your head.'

'No fighting, Least,' said Hands.

Least frowned. 'Why?'

'Because I might get hurt.' Hands picked up her weaponbelt from the back of her chair. 'What's it about?' she asked Nait.

'How the fuck should I know?'

'Hey! What'd I tell you about that swearing. No swearing.'

Nait walked away. 'Hood on his bone throne! Who the fuck cares?'

Outside Nait stood studying the moonlit forest of masts crowding the harbour. A lot of traffic, even for this time of the season. War was always good for business. He hoped the harbourmaster was keeping his books in good order; their cut had better be up to date. The majority of the company on duty that night came shuffling out, pulling on their guard surcoats and rearranging belts and hauberks.

Hands led the way up the dock to Tinsmith who waited, a leather vest over his shirt, long-knives at his waist.

'Let's go.'

They walked down the pier to the newly berthed ship. It looked worse the closer they got. Nait wondered if it was the original *Ragstopper* drawn up from the bottom of whatever sea it was that took it. 'Cap'n!' Tinsmith called up to the apparently empty deck. A rat waddled along the gunwale.

'Maybe that's him,' suggested Honey Boy.

'No, he's a bigger one,' said Tinsmith, sounding tired by the whole thing.

A head popped up into view from the stern. Wild greasy hair framed a pale smear of a face, eyes bulging. 'What in the Twins' name do you want?'

'Harbour guard. You carrying any contraband?'

The man straightened, lurched to the gunwale, clenched the stained wood in a white-knuckled grip. 'Contraband? Contraband! I wish we were! Tons of it! D'bayang poppy! Moranth blood liquor! White nectar! Barrels of it! Anything! But no! I'll tell you what we're carrying – Nothing! Not a stitch! The full bounteous mercy of Hood we have in our hold! No! Off we go sailing from port to port – empty! It's a crime I'm telling you! A crime!'

Least tapped a blunt finger to his temple. Honey Boy nodded. 'Back home among your people someone like that would be sacred or something, right?'

'No. Back home we'd just kick the shit out of him.'

'What in the infinite Abyss is all the yellin'?' An old man, his face the pale blue cast of a Napan, came to the gunwale. He was wincing, scratching at a halo of white hair standing in all directions, and wore a white patchy beard to match.

''Evening, Cap'n,' said Tinsmith.

'Eh? Who's that?' The man caught sight of Tinsmith, winced anew. 'Oh, it's *you*.' He waved to the squad. 'Why the army? There's no need for all this between us old friends.'

'These days I'm in charge of the peace down here along the water-front, Cap'n. Passing strange you showing up here and now. There's those who'd like to know.'

The captain dragged his fingers through his beard. His tongue worked around his mouth like it was hunting down a bad taste. 'But you wouldn't do that to an old comrade, now would you?'

'No, I wouldn't. Unless there was trouble. Don't like trouble.'

The captain brightened. 'No trouble at all, Smithy. No trouble at

all. Just come to do some salvage work here in the harbour. Gettin'
a little low on funds these days, I am.'

'Because the blasted hold is empty, that's why!' the sailor
screamed. 'You damned senile—'

A wooden belaying pin ricocheted from the sailor's head; he disappeared behind the gunwale. The captain lowered his arm. 'Quiet,
Tillin. Won't have no insolence on board the *Ragstopper*.'

Sergeant Tinsmith gave a long slow shake of his head. 'Haven't
changed a bit I see, Cartharon.'

Captain Cartharon's smile was savage. 'Caught *you* a few times,
hey, Smithy? I never miss.'

On the way back to the Figurehead, Hands asked Tinsmith, 'What
did that crazy old guy mean, he was after salvage in the harbour?'

Tinsmith traced a finger over his moustache. 'Salvage. There's
more cargo 'n' ships sunk in this bay than anyone can guess and that
old guy had a hand in the sinking of most of it. Maybe just for such
an eventuality. Anyways, we'll keep a close eye on him. And
Hands . . .'

'Yes, sir?'

'That name stays with us in the company.'

'Yes, sir. Why? Might someone recognize it?'

At the door to the guardhouse the old sergeant stopped. He
watched his corporal for a time, an unreadable expression on his
long dour face. 'Double the watch, corporal. I'll be inside. I need a
drink.'

'Yes, sir.'

* * *

More than just Kyle were relieved when it became clear that Skinner
intended to keep to the ruins that had once been Fortress Haven. But
it did make life hard for Kyle for a number of days as second
and third investiture men – all those recruited into the Guard since
the original Vow – kept coming around asking what the man
was like. 'Pretty damned scary' was the answer they liked the
best. Skinner had brought through a few of his Avowed. Names
the Guardsmen whispered around the campfires in tones of awe:
a Kartoolan master swordsman named Shijel, and a Napan
named Black the Lesser. He'd also brought over his own personal
bodyguard of Avowed mages, Mara, Gwynn and Petal, all of whom,
Stoop said, now stayed busy masking everyone's presence from

any sorcerous probings. Shimmer once came ashore and climbed the stairs into the ruins for a meet. Kyle wondered if was just him, but when she'd come back down she'd looked shaken.

Another ship had arrived. A foreign vessel storm-battered and listing, its masts shattered. Rumour was the twelve Avowed it held had rowed night and day across half the world. Coming ashore they'd looked the part – emaciated, exhausted, dressed in rags. But the second and third investiture men were jubilant. Apparently the number of Avowed now with the Guard had passed seventy. The men were of the opinion that nothing would stop them now. Kyle couldn't help reflecting that while he knew the Avowed were the nastiest news around, why did it look like they always had their arses kicked?

The days passed in a numbing round of training and practice. New recruits had to be integrated into the Guard. More local recruits came trickling in from the upriver settlements, small villages and homesteads, all eager to join – if only for the chance to get away from their lives here – but numbering far fewer than Kyle thought Shimmer and other of the Avowed had expected.

Two weeks after Skinner's arrival, word came that the other ships of the crossing from Bael were now close after having stopped for repairs and that not one had been lost in the storms. It seemed that the sea was inclined to be kind to the Guard. That night in the squad's shared hut Stoop woke Kyle when he jerked upright from his blankets cursing as if burned. 'What is it?' Kyle whispered.

'Nothing,' he answered, surprised to see Kyle awake. 'Get back to sleep.'

Kyle lay down but kept one eye open. Stoop dressed hurredly, then stamped out into the night. After debating things for a time Kyle finally threw himself out after him. He was bored, frankly, and Stalker had warned him to keep an eye out for anything unusual.

He found that he'd waited too long; Stoop was out of sight. The old saboteur had been heading into the woods though. Kyle snuck along, easily evading one picket. He was surprised, and a little disappointed, to find that while these Guardsmen might be hardened professional soldiers, woodsmen or scouts they certainly weren't. Lying still on the cold damp moss he stilled his breath and listened – after his hearing adjusted to the night sounds he heard voices murmuring deeper into the woods. Staying low, he edged ahead.

As it turned out he needn't have worried about sneaking up: a full-blown argument between three Avowed was raging in a clearing of tall weeds. Stoop was there, with Skinner and, the hairs on Kyle's forearms rose in a tingle, Cowl. What was he doing here? Last he'd heard that man should be days from shore.

'I don't like the way talk here's going, Cowl,' Stoop was saying. 'We have to keep up the search for the Duke.'

'That's always been your priority, Stoop,' Cowl answered, sounding dismissive. 'What about you, Skinner? What's your opinion on the matter?'

'There is no need. The Dolmans remain.'

'No *need*?' Stoop echoed outraged. 'What in Hood's grin does that mean? Dolmans? What're you two dancing around here like a couple o' Talian whores?'

'Dancing around?' asked Cowl. 'Why nothing, Stoop. There can't be anything hidden between us old campaigners, now can there?'

'Then why bar all our brothers and sisters from this meet? Even the Brethren?'

The Guard's High Mage and Master Assassin eyed Stoop in silence. He clasped his hands behind his back. Skinner, for his part, hadn't moved the entire time Kyle had been watching; the man stood with his arms crossed, feet planted firmly wide apart, as still as a statue of iron. 'This is a command discussion between myself and Skinner,' Cowl finally said.

'Don't pull that shit with me,' Stoop answered. 'I was siegemaster to K'azz and his father afore him. Strickly speaking *I* out-rank *you*.'

Kyle was amazed; siegemaster to the Guard? He wished he'd paid more attention when the old man had held forth on various topics the way he always seemed to.

Cowl now paced the clearing, a gloved hand brushing at the dark tattoos down his chin. 'Yes, now that you bring that up, that does remain a problem for us. What to do about it, hmm, Stoop?'

The old saboteur eyed Cowl, puzzled. 'What're you gettin' at?'

The mage's pacing had brought him to a point where Skinner now stood to Stoop's rear. Kyle saw it even as it happened. The huge commander moved with astonishing speed; he drew and thrust in one move, his blade bursting through Stoop's chest. Kyle gasped as if that very blade had pierced him.

The mage's gaze snapped to the brush disguising Kyle's hiding place. 'Finish Stoop,' he snarled. 'I'll deal with this one.'

Kyle could only stare, stunned, utterly immobile. *What was going on?* He knew he should run, but how could he possibly escape the Guard's premier mage and assassin? Stoop broke the spell by lashing out and slapping his hand to Cowl's wrist.

'Takes more than that to kill an Avowed, Cowl,' he ground out through clenched teeth. 'Or have you fogotten?'

Skinner tore his blade free. Stoop grunted but held on. 'Run lad! I've got a good grip o' this snake.'

'*Finish him!*' Cowl bellowed to Skinner.

Kyle ran. In the clearing behind, Skinner raised his blade.

Not far from the clearing a huge figure rose from the darkness to take Kyle's arm. His heart jumping to his throat, Kyle moved to draw his weapon – the man's hand shifted to push the blade down in its sheath. 'What's the fright, lad?' the figure asked.

Kyle saw it was Greymane, Ogilvy, the Genabackan veteran, with him and he struggled to find the words. 'Back in the woods – Skinner killed Stoop! He and Cowl!'

Greymane's gaze flicked to Ogilvy. 'We heard nothing.'

'They're coming . . . please!'

Greymane rubbed a finger along his flattened broken nose in thought. A nod of his head gave Kyle permission to pass. 'I'll see about this. You go on now.'

Kyle ran, not pausing to thank the man. He struck south through the gloom of the woods, avoiding any trail, trusting to the broken moonlight to guide his path. At times he thought he glimpsed figures moving through the dense forest around him. At other times magery flashed in the distances, killing his night vision, and echoing distant thunder. He had no idea why Cowl nor any of the other Guard mages had not yet found him. There must be some explanation. But for now he had no time to think about such things. Now, all that concerned him was when to end this diversion south to strike west into the interior, and how long could he keep this punishing pace given the weeks spent crammed in that ship? He also tried not to think about just how many Guardsmen and Avowed might be at this moment on his trail.

Kyle had grown up running; for days on end he'd jogged after game across the plains of his youth. He'd run from and chased the raiding parties of neighbouring tribes. That sinewy endurance saw him through now, as it was not until the night of the third day of alternating dog-trotting and running that his numb legs collapsed under him and he was too exhausted even to push himself up. He slept where he fell.

While Kyle's body may have been drained beyond all exhaustion, his mind was not. Strange, otherwordly dreams possessed him. Images and colours swirled before his mind's eye. He dreamed the darkness that filled his vision assaulted him; he fought it with a power that drove it back yet entities emerged from within to attack. He and they fought with all manner of limbs, talons, claws and teeth. They wrapped themselves around each other squeezing and tearing. Shapes blended, melded, in a ferocious roiling battle in a dark sky that seemed to have no end or beginning. The enormity of the confrontation numbed him; he could not grasp it. He seemed to float for a time, insensate.

Then, in his dreams it was as if Stoop was still alive: the old saboteur came and knelt at his side. 'Time to wake up, lad,' he said. 'The enemy's coming. T'ain't safe. This is my last warning, I'm sorry. That snake Cowl's sent me off. But I promise I'll try to make it back. Now, wake up – *they've found you.*'

Coughing, groaning, Kyle forced open his eyes and he awoke wincing, surprised that he was still alive, the sun high. He was not alone; a Dal Hon woman stood to one side, hands hidden in the folds of her robes that she wore bunched over one shoulder. Her kinky black hair hung in thick strands that covered her shoulders like foam. Mara, one of Skinner's Avowed mages.

A smile quirked up her full lips. 'So, now that you are rested we can have a conversation, can we not, little rabbit? Such as who you truly work for, yes?'

Kyle was too weak to care; he hadn't eaten in three days. 'Work for? What in Father Sky do you mean?'

'I mean that you have eluded the combined efforts of over twelve mages to locate you and we are now very intrigued – who could possibly be so potent? What power has taken enough of an interest in the Guard to plant a spy among us, hmm? Tell me now, little rabbit, for you surely will later. Who do you work for?'

Kyle gaped up at the woman. '*Spy?* I'm no spy.'

Frowning, Mara drew her hands from the folds of her robes. 'Very well. I find interrogations distasteful, but you leave me no choice. I—'

She broke off, turning to where a crash of undergrowth preceded the arrival of a man who leant against a tree, gasping in air, his leather vest dark with sweat, twigs in his wild grizzled hair. One of the two fellows always hanging out with Stalker, Badlands. 'Damn,' he breathed, 'but you can run, lad.'

Mara lowered her hands. 'You were supposed to have tracked him down by now.'

Hands on his knees he bared his teeth. 'Guess I'm gettin' old.'

'Where is—'

'Here.'

Both Mara and Kyle flinched, surprised to see Stalker crouched opposite from where Badlands had crashed in with so much noise.

'And here.'

Mara turned; the other fellow, Coots, now leaned against a tree behind her. Her mouth tightened. She adjusted the robes at her shoulder. 'Better late then never, I imagine. Perhaps now we could return him alive for questioning.'

'Questions regarding what?' Stalker asked, straightening.

'What power has extended his – *or her* – protection over him. Who is spying upon us.'

'Not questions 'bout why he killed Stoop?'

'*I did not*—' Kyle began but Badlands motioned for his silence.

The Avowed mage paused, the tip of her tongue emerged to touch her upper lip. She turned in place, eyeing the three men surrounding her. 'Of course . . . that as well . . . is of great concern to us . . .'

Coots and Badlands leapt, drawing knives in the air. Mara gestured, yelling, to disappear into darkness as the men landed in a tangle where she'd stood. They helped each other to their feet.

'Suspicious bitch,' Stalker spat into the long silence that followed the echoes of the Warren closing.

Kyle gaped anew from man to man. *What in the name of all these foreign Gods was going on?*

'They'll be back,' said Coots.

'In force,' from Badlands.

'No more questions neither,' finished Stalker.

Badlands and Coots nodded and took off running into the forest. Stalker pulled Kyle to his feet. 'Let's go.'

'Wait! What's—'

The scout yanked Kyle onward. 'Move.'

Kyle wrenched his arm free. '*What's going on, damn you!*'

Stalker grimaced his irritation. 'They'll be comin' back, Kyle. Maybe Cowl himself. We have to move, now.'

'While we go then.'

A curt nod and the scout headed out, following Badlands and Coots. 'I didn't kill Stoop,' Kyle began, pushing aside branches and jumping fallen trunks.

'That's their story,' answered Stalker. 'You killed him 'n' ran.'

'Who'd believe that?'

A shrug from the scout as he trotted along. 'Don't matter. That

194

renegade, Greymane, he doesn't seem convinced. But it's official. What can they do?'

'What about you three? Why attack Mara? What's it to you?'

The tall scout held up a hand for a halt, crouched behind cover, peering behind them. Kyle joined him. They listened, trying to dampen their breathing. After a moment Stalker straightened. He yanked the pin from the breast of his leathers: the silver dragon sigil of the Crimson Guard. He tossed it aside. 'Me 'n' the boys, we never really were cut out for this mercenary business. We don't think much of fighting for money or power. We fight for other things.'

Kyle realized that he still wore his sigil. Somehow, he could not bring himself to throw it away. 'So what now?'

Stalker shrugged. 'Get the Abyss away from here. Clear some land.' He offered a one-sided smile. 'Raise chickens. C'mon, my brothers won't wait for ever.'

'Brothers?'

'Brothers, cousins, call it what you will. We're all descended from one big family. The Lost. That's us. Welcome to the family.' The scout cuffed Kyle on his back and jogged off.

Lost. Well, that's just great. Wonderful! Not only was he a renegade, disbanded and hunted. He was now lost too, by adoption. Shaking his head at the strange rightness of it all he set off as well, hurrying to catch up. Before them stretched league after league of boreal forest. The western reach of the Stratem subcontinent.

CHAPTER V

Past Quon hegemonies never held;
occupations cannot quell unrest,
indeed, even benign ones foster it.
Must this lesson be learned every generation?
Sadly, some things never do change.

Historian Heboric

BEFORE THE SERVANT COULD ANNOUNCE HIM, HIGH FIST KORBOLO
Dom, Sword of the Empire, stormed into Mallick's residence,
throwing down his gloves and travelling cloak. 'It's happened
again! Another of the damned coward nobles has fled the capital,
taken his guard with him – over four hundred horse!'

Silence answered his pronouncement. 'Mallick!' he roared. 'Damn
you! Don't tell me you've run off too!'

'Baron Nira's concern for his lands and crops is well known to
me,' came Mallick's disembodied voice from further within. Korbolo
followed the voice to find the man soaking in the broad shallow pool
at the centre of his quarters, a towel over his shoulders. Mallick
raised a goblet. 'Wine?'

Biting back his rage, Korbolo fought the urge to slap the glass from
the man's hand. *Damn him! Was he insane? Things are slipping
beyond their control and he's bathing!* Sensing another presence he
glanced aside to see the withered old manservant Mallick had brought
with him from Seven Cities, Oryan. He dismissed the man from his
thoughts. 'While you splash in your pool the Assembly is dissolving.
Representatives are fleeing! Even those you put on it! Soon there will
be nothing left to rule, Hood take it, even if we could.'

Mallick sipped the wine. 'Dissolving – how appropriate. My
friend, you are a poet.'

196

Korbolo stared down at the repulsive squat figure at his feet. The strong urge took hold of him to push the man's head beneath the waters, to throttle this monstrous lurking curse that had so taken over his life. But then, for all he knew, that could prove impossible; this creature seemed born of a swamp. 'Meanwhile,' he continued, struggling to regain his thoughts, 'neither you nor she do a thing. Kingdoms continue to rise in revolt against the Imperial Throne and we do *nothing*!'

Mallick sighed. 'But my dear High Fist, First Sword. That is precisely what we have been encouraging them to do.'

Korbolo ground his teeth – mockery! One day this toad would push him too far. 'Riot and dissent against *her*, yes. But *secession*? This is chaos. Nothing less than civil war. It is out of everyone's control!'

Mallick's bulging eyes blinked up at him. 'Again you amaze me, First Sword. Pure poetry – chaos and loss of control. Amazing.' He sipped his wine. 'In the first place it is not a *civil* war, it is devolution to the rather monotonous old-fashioned warfare of a century ago. City state 'gainst city state. Neighbour versus neighbour. I understand that is something of a tradition here on Quon.'

'Yes, before the emperor.'

'Exactly. Before the strong hand of the emperor . . .'

Korbolo stood motionless, breathless, as the implications of Mallick's hints blossomed. And who would the populace accept at the head of the legions restoring peace and order to their smoking, war-ravaged countryside? Surely not this bloated travesty of a man. No, not *him*. He let out a long shuddering breath, swallowed to wet his suddenly tight throat. 'Very well, Mallick. However, this does not explain your or *her* utter inaction.'

'But, High Fist, just what would you have her *do*?'

'March! We have, what, some eight thousand regulars here in the capital? We should march on Gris or Bloor before they ally against us.'

'And leave Unta undefended?'

'Against who? There is no one to threaten her.'

'Not at the moment. But should we leave . . . perhaps our friend Nira and his brother nobles who are so, ah, *coerced* in their support, might put their resources together and decide they could do a better job of defending Imperial interests, hmm, Korbolo?'

The High Fist saw it then – deadlock. Three jackals circling a wounded bhederin. Who dared strike first and risk attack from the rear? Yet how could any of the three walk away to leave such a prize for any other? Laseen, who ruled in name only? Or he and Mallick who ruled in fact? Or the nobles and Assemblymen who also may?

Yet, the thought troubled Korbolo, the beast was dying while they chased one another. Perhaps it didn't matter to this creature Mallick, for whom a dead beast would serve just the same. But it certainly mattered to him. It must then be his duty to be sure to act before Mallick allowed things to degenerate too far. The High Fist nodded to himself, yes, that obviously was to be his responsibility. He looked down; Mallick was watching him expectantly. 'Yes?'

'Is that all, High Fist?'

'Yes, Mallick. That is all.'

'Very good. Then we are in agreement?'

'Yes. Full agreement.'

'Excellent.' Mallick finished his wine.

Korbolo turned away from the sight of the man's nauseating pallid flesh. He straightened his shirt. 'You presume much, priest. Too often in the past you've promised everything but delivered nothing. The rebellion of Seven Cities – failure. Laseen's fall in Malaz city – failure. If you fail this time you will not live to promise anew. Do I make myself clear?'

'You do, First Sword of the Empire.'

Korbolo loosened his fists, forced himself to breathe out. How did the man manage to make even that title an insult? 'When I wish to speak to you again I will summon you, Mallick.'

As he went to collect his cloak he heard the man's soft voice responding, 'So you command, Sword of the Empire.'

Some time later Mallick set his goblet on the marble border of his pool. Oryan padded silently forward to collect it. He stood over Mallick for a time, looking to the door. 'Yes, Oryan?'

'Why is that man still alive, master?'

'I have always found it convenient to keep someone around upon whom everything can be blamed. Also, armour gives me hives.'

The old man sneered his disgust. 'Any fool can wave a sword and order men to their deaths.'

'As all of these military commanders prove again and again. Yes, Oryan. But this one is our fool.'

* * *

The morning of the second week of siege Lieutenant Rillish stood staring into a polished copper-fronted shield attempting to dry-shave himself. His hand shook so abominably it was his third attempt. He told himself it must be from having just stood command through the entire night; at least he hoped that was the case. A knock at his barracks door allowed him an excuse to abandon the effort. 'Yes?'

'Sergeant, sir.'

'It's not the Hood-damned south wall again, is it?'

'No, sir. Not that,' Sergeant Chord called through the door. 'Given up on that they have sir, as a bad job.'

'Then pray what is it, Sergeant?'

'It's the elders, sir. Another delegation. Like a word.'

Again? Hadn't he made it plain enough? Rillish eased himself down into a camp stool. He massaged his thigh where a leaf-bladed spearhead had slid straight in. 'Very well, Sergeant, let them in.'

The door opened and in shuffled five Wickan elders of those trapped with them within the fort. Rillish knew the names of two, the hetman, Udep, and a shaman held in high regard, Clearwater. It struck him how beaten down they looked. Eyes downcast, shoulders slumped. Trousers of tattered cloth and torn thin leather. Even their amulets and wristlets of beaten copper looked tarnished and cheap. These were the feared warriors the Empire could not tame? But then, a Wickan without a horse was a sad sight no matter the circumstances; and these were the worst.

'Pardon, Commander,' Udep began, 'we would speak again.'

'Yes, hetman. You are aways welcome. And you, shaman.'

The grey-haired shaggy mage managed a jerked nod. It seemed to Rillish that the man was dead on his feet: hands twitching with exhaustion, face pale as if drained of blood. A haunted look in his sunken eyes. Was the man expending himself sending curses out among the besiegers? If so, he'd heard nothing of it. He'd have to question Chord.

'We again ask that we be allowed the dignity of defending that which is ours.'

'We've been through this before, hetman. Malazan soldiery will defend this installation.'

The man's scarred hands clenched and unclenched on his belt as if at the throat of an enemy. 'What is it you wish, Malazan? Would you have us beg?'

'*Beg?*'

Barked Wickan from the three old women with Udep made the man wince. He took a great shuddering breath. 'My pardon, Commander. That was unworthy. Even now you spill your own blood in defence in our land.' The hetman looked down.

Rillish saw that his leg wound had re-opened. The packed dirt under his chair was damp with blood. He took hold of his leg. One of the old women said something that sounded suspiciously like *idiot* and slapped his hands aside. She began rebinding the wound.

'You need every hand you can get, Commander,' continued Udep.

'We've been over that already.'

'At least we would die fighting.'

'Don't be impatient. There's every chance of it yet.'

The hetman crossed his arms, hugging himself. He seemed to be struggling with something; he and Clearwater exchanged tight glances. 'You leave us very little choice. We still have our pride.'

Rillish knew the elders had been cooking something up in the main stone building he'd moved them and the children to. So far he'd not interfered. He raised a finger. 'No attacks. Not until the last soldier falls. This is still a Malazan military possession. Understood?'

The shaman Clearwater opened his mouth to address Rillish, but Udep cut him off with a curt command. They turned to go. Rillish touched the arm of the aged Wickan grandmother who had rebound his leg. She turned back, her gaze narrowed, wary.

'My thanks.'

A smile of bright white teeth melted decades from the squat woman and dazzled Rillish. At the door the hetman paused. 'Commander, when you lose the walls you will be falling back to us at the main building, yes?'

For a moment Rillish thought about disputing whether they would ever lose control of the walls but because it was so obvious to the both of them he decided against insulting the man with empty assurances. Instead, he allowed a curt nod.

Udep answered in kind and left. Sergeant Chord stuck his head in. 'Movement in their camp, sir. Looks like new arrivals.'

'*More* of them, Sergeant?'

The man grinned. 'Don't matter. We've iron enough for all.'

Rillish stood, wincing. He belted on his twinned Untan duelling swords. 'Let's hope it's not someone who knows what he's doing.'

'No, sir. Baron Horse's-Ass still looks to be in charge.'

'Well thank Trake for small blessings, hey, Sergeant? Let's have a look.'

*   *   *

He thought of himself as Ragman now. A knotted bundle of used up bits and pieces whose original cut had long since been lost. Walking the seeming endless plains of ash and fields of broken rock that was the Imperial Warren the man stopped suddenly, examined the tattered remains of his once fine clothes and nodded, satisfied. Yes, inside and out; so it should be. Allowing himself to fall forward he twisted the move into a series of cartwheels and spinning high kicks. Tatterdemalion, he named himself as he ran through his impromptu pattern. Harlequin. Clown. He froze, crouched, arms outstretched. No – he must not lose hold of the one thread that could lead him back. Though they were coming far less often now; perhaps they'd learned their lesson.

Movement above in the unchanging lead sky drove him to cover behind a large boulder. Dark shapes moving across the sky, far off, ponderously huge. *So, not just wild reports and stories from sources of . . .* questionable *. . . veracity.* Telling himself they were too distant and that he was no doubt too insignificant, he stood and set off at a jog, following.

The ground steadily broke into shallow gullies and high buttes surrounded by erosional slopes and gravel fans. Skittering down one such slope he stopped just short of a jutting spine of basalt. His Warren-sensitivity told him someone was near, hiding, watchful. After catching his breath he called, 'You can come out.'

A figure detatched itself from the shadows of one jagged black spire. It climbed down, lithe and quick. Ragman caught his breath – one of them yet not. Different by her style. Much more colourful, individual. Similar, yet not regimented in her moves. She stopped before him, a safe distance off. Dark eyes regarded him through a slit between veil and headscarf. 'And you are?' she asked.

'Impressed.'

A glance toward the spires. 'They are that. Like a peek?'

'Very much so.'

'After you.'

He gave a courtier's bow and climbed the spine to a gap between spires. Beyond, across a plain of twisting gullies and dunes five titanic geometric shapes hovered. Beneath them the winds blew constantly, billowing outwards in dust clouds that reached high overhead. What were they up to? Could anyone guess? He climbed back down.

The woman joined him. 'An invasion, you think?'

'Or the landlords come to fumigate.'

The dark eyes widened. 'What do you mean?'

'I mean that one must abandon one's self-centred blinders. Not everything relates back to us.'

The woman stepped away, eased into a ready stance. 'Who are you?'

'A lost fragment of bureaucratic oversight.'

More questions obviously occurred to the woman but she clamped down on them. 'Well, as intriguing as all this is . . .'

'You must report it.'

She nodded. He bowed his agreement, but instead of straightening he rolled forward, sweeping. The woman cartwheeled aside. They stood, facing one another, he astonished, she calculating in her narrowed glance. He did not bother to hide his delight. 'Wonderfully done! It has been a long time since I've seen *his* style.'

The woman – girl, he corrected himself – gave an elegant bow. 'You recognize it! My father taught me. And you not ought to have revealed your familiarity . . .'

'It will not matter . . . shortly.'

She bowed again. 'Apologies. Must be off.' Shadows threaded up from the dirt to spin about her like a whirlwind. His surprise lasted only an instant; he thrust out both arms and lances of darkness struck the girl throwing her backwards. She lay gasping for air, her ribs shattered, lungs punctured.

He crossed to stand over her.

Still conscious she stared up, her gaze accusing. 'Kurald Galain!' she gasped.

He knelt on his haunches next to her. 'I am sorry.'

'You! But we thought you . . . you were no . . .'

'Yes. I know. I am so very sorry. More sorry because I would not have sent someone like you. For, as you see, I've come myself.' He rested a hand on her shoulder. Unconscious. Still, her heart beat. There was yet a chance . . .

He gestured and a pool of utter darkness emerged from beneath the girl like liquid night. She sank into it, disappearing as if into a well of ink. A small enough gesture . . . but he felt that he owed her at least that. A pity that it is always the best who are sent.

He should've anticipated that.

* * *

Five days' continuous favourable winds driving the fleet south-west was good luck enough to draw Urko from his cabin to endure the company of his High Mage, Bala Jesselt. Ullen steadied himself next to his commander, noting how the man remained rock solid no matter the shock of each swell or shudder of a fall into a deepening trough. Yet every league gained seemed to deepen furrows at the old admiral's brows.

'Unexpected reach and influence this new ally possesses, yes?' said Bala from mid-deck. Ullen glanced back to her; somehow, the woman's voice, pitched no higher than usual, penetrated the howling winds and crashing seas. An eerie calm also surrounded the giant woman, no spray or winds touching her layered robes, or her intricately bunched hair.

'The latest count?' Urko growled.

'None missing. The transports are still falling behind, though.'

'Have the lead elements drop sail. Hold back, if necessary. No sense arriving without the damned army.'

'Yes, sir. If I may, Admiral . . .'

'Yes?'

'Our speed – does this not change our plans? Will we not arrive ahead of schedule?'

Scowling, Urko eyed Bala. 'Anything new from Choss?'

The Dal Hon mage edged her head side to side, her fan flickering so swiftly as to be invisible. 'Nothing, dear Urko. A word perhaps, to my resource – congratulations? He has earned as much surely.'

'That or my fist in his face. I'll decide which once all this is over and done. Until then, nothing. Understood?'

Bala gave an exaggerated huff that shook her broad bosom. She muttered under her breath, 'All my efforts . . .'

Ullen could only shake his head. Here they were running ahead of typhoon winds threatening to swat them from the face of the sea, shouting to be heard, and she's fanning herself, able to communicate her faintest complaints. 'Will they be there, in Cawn, to rendezvous?' he called to Urko.

The admiral shook his head; spray glistened on his scar-mottled mostly bald pate. 'No. At this rate, we'll beat them. Mind you, making the Horn could be touch 'n' go. No matter, when we arrive in the harbour those Cawnese'll come around. Always able to tell which way the wind's blowing, them.' And he laughed then for the first time in months. 'Get it? Wind blowin'? Ha!'

Ullen smiled, relieved to see his commander in a lightened mood. Yet he could not keep his gaze from returning to the glistening dark face of their High Mage. She sat where she always had, at centre deck, where she'd first positioned herself, and, thinking on it, Ullen could not call to mind a single time when she could not be found there. She even took her meals there, and slept sitting up, her fan shimmering and hissing through the night like a giant insect. He had to admit to being impressed – she reminded him of their old powerful cadre mages, A'Karonys or Nightchill.

Her eyes rose then, capturing his – huge brown pools, and she smiled as if guessing his thoughts. 'They don't know you have me,' she said, or seemed to say; he could not be sure. 'They think this will be a contest of hedge-wizards and wax-witches. But I am of the old school, friend Ullen. I was taken in by Kellanved – and expelled by Tayschrenn. And for that I will teach him regret.'

The fan seemed to snap then with a slash that Ullen could almost feel above the storm driving them on. He glanced to Urko but the commander seemed oblivious to the exchange. *Keep her in check* – Urko had expressed every confidence he could keep the woman in check. Yet even now she hinted at larger ambitions and her own motives, playing her games undeterred by, or contemptuous of, his presence. What sort of a viper had they taken into their midst – a viper even too traitorous and unreliable for the emperor and his kind?

All the while the fan hummed, almost invisible, shimmering, and Ullen wondered, was it this ally of a priest of a sea cult helping them along, or were they all merely at the mercy of a flickering fan?

*　*　*

From the profound dark of a tunnel opening off the Pit, Ho sat watching the slightly lesser dark of the shadowed half of the large circular mine-head. He started, jerking, as yet again his chin touched his chest and he glared about wondering what he'd missed. But all remained quiet. Everyone seemed asleep, including, for all he knew, the two newcomers; the spies he'd last seen entering those shadows and now sat waiting just as he was. Waiting for what? Some sign among the stars? The right moment for a midnight escape attempt? Ho tried to identify their figures amidst the monochrome dark, but failed. No movement. He chided himself; maybe they just couldn't sleep in the caves; maybe they simply longed for a touch of the slight breeze that sometimes made its way down here when conditions were just right. Yeah, and maybe they were worshippers of the cult of Elder Dark.

Something then – movement? Someone standing there in the dark? The pale oval of a face upturned? Ho leaned forward, straining. A call sounded, an owl's warning call. From his friends? Or above? Hard to say. A flash in the moonlight streaming down into the open mine-head. Something small falling. His friends stepped out into the light; one, Grief, stooped, picked up the thing, examined it. They talked but Ho couldn't hear any of it.

As they retreated into the shadows Ho could not contain himself any longer. He marched out to confront them. Damn them and their schemes! Don't they know everyone here lives only at the sufferance of their captors above? That the slightest provocation could mean shortened rations, perhaps death for the more sickly among them?

When he reached them they were waiting for him, the object, whatever it was, nowhere in evidence. He glared. The one who gave his name as Grief eyed him back, unperturbed. 'You're up late, Ho.'

'Cut it out. What're you two up to?'

Grief sighed, glanced to Treat who shrugged. 'Nothing that concerns you.'

'You're wrong there, brother. Everything to do with this place concerns me. We're all one big family down here.'

'Somehow I knew you were going to say that. Listen, if it'll help any, what we're up to is no threat at all. In fact, it could prove just the opposite.'

'And I'm supposed to trust you on that, am I?'

Grief lifted his arms in a helpless shrug. 'I guess that's about the meat of it.'

'Not good enough.'

'Yeah. I know. So, what now? Gonna denounce us to your ruling committee?'

Ho decided that now would be as good a time as any to test his estimate of the character of these two strangers. He raised his chin to indicate the surface. 'Maybe I'll have to let the guards know – what do you think of that?'

The two men went still. For an instant Ho feared he'd overplayed his hand; that his reading of these two was wrong – after all, they truly did seem to be all alone right now. A body found in the morning, who would be the wiser? A big risk; but then, what kind of a test would it be otherwise? Grief crossed his arms. 'No, I think we aren't going to do anything at all, because if you really were going to tell them the last thing you would do is let us know.'

Damn him. 'OK. So I'm not about to run to the Malazans. But I need to know what you two are doing. What you're up to.'

Grief slowly edged his head from side to side; he seemed genuinely regretful. 'Sorry, old man. We can't say a thing – yet. But what I can ask is: where is our faithful watchdog right now? One of your happy family members, I believe. Sessin. Where's he? Maybe he decided it convenient to leave you alone with us, eh, Ho?'

Ho had more to say but the two walked off leaving him fuming with unspent words. In the shadows his sandalled feet stepped on something and he knelt, feeling about. He came up with the shredded remains of a piece of driftwood.

* * *

Walking the plains surrounding Li Heng was a dangerous undertaking now with the Seti riding at will. Worse so, since Silk was headed the wrong direction: that is, away from the city. The young Seti of the various soldier societies, the Wolf, Dog, Ferret and Jackal, were happy to chivvy any refugees or fleeing traders *into* the city. But for anyone to attempt to leave was another matter altogether. The arrow-tufted bodies of those who tried to run south to Itko Kan lands, or downriver to Cawn, were left to rot within sight of the city walls as object lessons to all.

Silk kept to the lowest-lying of the prairie draws and sunken creekbeds as he headed west, parallel, more or less, with the Idryn. His goal was visible ahead as the source of the thick smoke of green wood and the stink of unwashed bodies and unburied excrement. A refugee camp of the most wretched and sick, those turned away from the city gates and judged too abject to be a worthy of a lancing or an arrow from the Seti warriors.

Faces turned to watch him pass as he walked the rutted trampled mud of the camp. Old men and women sat in the entrances of tents of hide. Children squatted in the mud peering up at him with open mouths. They did not even have the energy to beg. He stopped before one child whom he thought to be ten or so. 'I'm looking for some Elders, child. Two or three who are always together. Heard of them?'

The child merely stared with liquid brown eyes; she was so dark he suspected mixed Dal Honese blood. One arm hung twisted and stick-thin, some old injury or illness. Sudden compassion for the child caught the breath in Silk's chest. He allowed himself the gesture of tousling her hair despite the crawling vermin. A woman ran up, snatched the child's good hand. 'What do you want? Go away! If the Seti see us talking with you they'll cut our throats!'

'I'm looking—'

'You're looking for the Hooded One, that's what you're doing!' She dragged the child off. Lurching behind the woman the child glanced back; smiling shyly she raised her crippled arm to point to the river. Silk answered with a sign of the Blessing of the Protectress.

He found the three of them sitting in a line along the muddy shore of the Idryn, fishing. 'Catch anything?'

None moved. 'Same as what you're gonna catch,' said one.

'Which is . . .' said the second.

'Nothing,' finished the third.

Sighing, Silk peered about and spotted a young willow with a passable amount of shade. He crouched on his haunches beneath, took out a silk handkerchief and wiped his face. This was *not* going to be easy. 'We're going to defend the city—'

'Wrong. What you're . . .'

'Gonna do . . .'

'Is lose.'

Silk forced open the fist he'd closed on his handkerchief, pushed it back into his shirt pocket. 'Look. All that was a long time ago, OK? I'm sorry. We did what we thought was right at the time.'

'You . . .'

'Talkin' . . .'

'To us?'

Old simmering grudges flared within Silk. 'Hood take you! She would've lost anyway! There was no way Kellanved would've kept his word! They wiped out all the other local cults! Or made them their own. The same thing would've happened here.'

'Sounds like . . .'

'You're askin' us . . .'

'To trust you?'

Silk stared at their hunched backs. Their bloody stiff backs, all of them. 'Liss is with me. Together we're going to give it everything we have. This is our best chance in the last century. You know that. Even you can sense it.' Their heads edged side to side as they shared glances.

'Been that long?'

'A damned century?'

'And I haven't caught a damned fish yet?'

Silk straightened and pushed his way out from under the willow. 'You know where I'll be. The way's open to you now should you choose. With or without you we're going all the way with this.' When Silk looked up from straightening his shirt and vest he saw that he'd been speaking to no one; the three were gone, sticks and all. *Smartarses.*

At noon of that same day Hurl sat uncomfortably on her horse as part of the official Hengan emissary to delegates of the Seti tribal high council, or 'Urpan-Yelgan', as it was known. She, Sunny and Liss constituted the representatives of High Fist Storo. Or, as the Hengan Magistrates insisted: 'Provisional military commander of Li Heng, and Interim governor of the central provinces.' Or, as Storo described himself, 'everyone's favourite arrow-butt'.

For her part, Hurl thought it far beyond her duty simply to be mounted on a horse. To her mind if there was anything more evil than Jhags on the face of the earth, it was horses. She rode hers with one hand on the reins and the other on her knife – just in case. The day before a rider had approached under a white flag to request a meet. Storo had out and out refused. 'I've got nothing to say to them,' he'd complained. Hurl had been stupid enough to say, 'Someone has to go.' So, sure enough, she had to go.

Thankfully, the city magistrates thought it beneath their dignity to meet. As Magistrate Ehrlann put it, 'I wouldn't know whom to address: them, their horses or their dogs.'

Now, Hurl sat uncomfortable and suspicious on her evil horse next to Sunny on his mount amid a veritable host of the malevolent beasts in the form of the 17th Mounted Hengan Horse. Mounted Horse? What a doubly iniquitous conceit!

The meet would take place on the summit of a hillock within sight of the city walls. Ahead, in the distance, lances tufted with white jackal fur could just be made out marking the spot. As they drew close Hurl motioned for the cavalry captain to hold back; she, Sunny and Liss would go on alone. Hurl kneed her mount onward – forward fiend! It cooperated, content perhaps for the moment to lull her suspicions. Sweat ran down from her helmet though the day was cool. A helmet! She couldn't remember the last time she actually wore a damned helmet. Sunny and Liss moved to flank her as the 'official' representative. Three mounted figures became visible climbing the opposite gentle slope, three men, two obvious shamans in their furred regalia, long tufted lances, headdresses and full draping fur cloaks. The lead man was harder to place; a soldier, that much was obvious, and foreign, non-Seti. He wore a plain ringed leather hauberk over a quilted undershirt, a battered blackened helmet under one arm. Dominating his figure though, stood the length of a Seti double recurve bow jutting up from a saddle sheath yet reaching fully as tall as he. His grey hair was brush-cut and barely visible over a balding scalp tanned nut-brown. A grey goatee framed a thin mouth that drew down his long face. He nodded to Hurl, who responded in kind.

'Whom am I addressing?' he asked in unaccented Hengan.

'Hurl, representative of Fist Storo Matash, military commander of Li Heng.'

The man's colourless brows rose. 'Fist, is it? Not endorsed, I should think.'

'You are?'

'I am Warlord of the Seti tribes. They have seen fit to place their confidence in me.' He indicated the bearded shaman in jackal furs. 'This is Imotan.' He motioned to the shaman in ferret furs. 'Hipal.'

Hurl motioned to her flankers. 'Sunny. Liss.'

At the name Liss the jackal shaman started. Beneath his tall furred hat his craggy brows drew down. 'Liss? Liss in truth?'

Liss let out a throaty laugh and slapped a wide thigh. 'He knows the story! I am flattered. Yes that was me, the seductive dancing girl – lithesome Liss! I've never forgotten the vows of your predecessor all those years ago. "Come to me, Liss," he begged. "Let me be your first! I will love you forever!"'

The shaman's eyes bulged further and further with every word from Liss. His face darkened almost blood-red. 'Quiet, woman!' he spluttered. 'Will you shut up!' He glared about as if the hilltop were crowded. 'Have you no honour? No modesty?'

'Honour? Modesty? But that was the last thing he ever wanted from me.' She leant aside to Hurl and whispered in mock soft-voice: 'How he begged me to throw aside all modesty, *then*! And he certainly didn't want my mouth closed, *then*.'

'Do tell,' Hurl managed, torn between horror and falling off her horse from stifling her laughter. At her other side Sunny's evil grin was as wide as Hurl had ever seen it.

'I, ah, take it the two of you require no introduction,' the warlord offered – showing astounding tact, Hurl thought.

'None at all,' Liss answered before anyone could speak again. 'Let me tell you a story. Long ago I was a young Seeress of the White Sand tribe, the youngest and most gifted in ages. And I was a Sun Dancer, too. Perhaps that was when I caught the eye of a certain youth selected to become a shaman of the feared man-jackal? So long ago, wasn't it, Imotan? But at that time I was too young for wooing and marked as sacred as well, a spirit vessel. But what is that to those who think themselves entitled to anything, eh? What did your predecessor long ago care that by seducing me he destroyed my potential as Sun Dancer? I, who called the sun back to the plains at the year's turn, who interceded for the blessing of rain? Never mind the evil of rape that marked my body and my spirit! Do you remember the vow I swore when it was *I* who was thrown from the tribe, not *he*? Do you not know the story, Imotan . . . ?'

Both shamans now gaped at the old woman. 'Surely,' Hipal sneered, 'you are not standing by that wild claim! Vessel of Baya-Gul! Patroness to Seers and guide of our Sun Mysteries?'

'I am she.'

Imotan waved to his warlord. 'I do not know who this poor deluded old woman is, Warlord. Ignore her ravings. There is a story among our people of such a young woman named Liss from long ago and this may even be she, but all that has nothing to do with our business here today.'

The warlord's frown told Hurl that he was not so certain. 'What is this vow?'

'It is nothing, Warlord. Just a legend this witch attempts to exploit.'

'I have heard the name Liss before. But not this vow.'

'Warlord, she is only trying to—'

'The vow!'

Hipal bared his sharp teeth, dismissed Liss with a wave. 'The legend is that the original Liss was exiled as a seductress and disturber of tribal accord. Upon leaving she vowed that the Seti people would wander lost for ever without knowing their true path and that they would never find it again until they welcomed her back into their hearth circles. And,' Hipal spat, 'until they begged for her forgiveness.'

Both shamans eyed Liss as if ready to strike her that very moment. Imotan's hands were white upon his reins. 'Some,' he ground out, 'name that Liss's Vow. Others, however, call it Liss's Curse.'

The warlord nodded his understanding. The leather of his saddle creaked as he leaned forward to rest an elbow on the high pommel. 'So, the story circulated will be that this uprising is just one more wrong path. One more errant turn doomed to fail.'

Liss blew Imotan a kiss.

The warlord offered Hurl a short bow. 'I see. My compliments to your commander, Hurl. I am sorry to say that I suspect we will be seeing much more of each other. Until then,' and he gave the old Malazan salute instituted by the emperor, an open hand to the chest. The two shamans merely yanked their mounts around without a word.

Leaving the hilltop, Hurl caught sight of a knot of outlanders among the Seti escort, and among them sat the slim straight figure of Captain Harmin Els D'Shil. The man sent them an ironic salute. Hurl nudged Sunny. 'Look, there's our old friend, Smiley.'

Sunny waved, leering. 'He's mine.'

D'Shil offered a courtier's horseback bow.

The ride the rest of the way back was quiet. Hurl concentrated on not giving her mount one chance for mischief. She had a boatload of questions for Liss, of course, should she dare. First, though, she'd have to run all she'd just heard past Silk.

'So what did you think of our warlord?' Liss asked of Hurl.

'I'm impressed – unfortunately. I was hoping for someone less competent-seeming.'

Liss nodded her agreement, her broad mouth widening in a smile. 'They said he had something of Dassem about him, and they're right. I've seen both.'

Hurl eyed the old woman. 'Who does?'

'Why, Toc the Elder, of course. Congratulations! Few come away from any meeting with him in such good form.' Reaching over she slapped Hurl's thigh. 'You did well, lass.'

Hurl could only share a wondering look with Sunny. *Gods Above!* Toc the Elder. They were going to get handed their own asses. Then, all she could think of was her commander. Poor Storo! To stand opposite Toc! He was gonna take this hard. They might not see him sober till the Wolf Soldiers battered down the doors of the last tavern in the city.

They rode in silence until just short of the closed North Gate of the Plains. Hurl had returned to keeping an eye on her mount just in case it thought she'd forgotten all about its horse-evil, when Sunny cleared his throat.

'Liss,' said Sunny, and Hurl knew he was about to ask what she was dying to ask but dared not broach. He was always one to dive straight in. 'You're not really this whatsit, this Baya-Gul thing, are you?'

The old woman just smiled at Sunny. Aside, to Hurl, she said, 'Here's a tip, lass. Things only have the power people are willing to give them.'

Hurl frowned over that. Sunny snorted, 'What a crock of shit.'

Liss just kept smiling. 'That's because you don't believe.'

*   *   *

The evening of their sixth day of flight Kyle sat with a thick patch of thorn bush behind him while he ate a raw fish and a handful of mushrooms that the brothers had scavenged during the day's run. Stalker drank from a skin they'd filled at the stream. Their best meal in days. For his part, Kyle hadn't contributed a thing; it was all he

211

could do just to keep up. And these fellows were running and scavenging food all at the same time! He shook his head. He'd always prided himself on his endurance and running prowess, but these three put him to shame. Who were they anyway? Brothers, or close cousins, perhaps. But who were they in truth?

He picked scales from his mouth and stretched his burning legs to stop them from seizing, then he turned his thoughts to the real question plaguing him. Why were they still alive? If these Crimson Guard Avowed were so fearsome why hadn't they caught them already? Or simply murdered them one night as easily as he, Kyle, might swat insects?

Stalker tossed Kyle the waterskin which he caught in one hand. 'How you feelin'?'

'Worn out. You fellows set an awful pace.'

The scout grunted. 'Well, you let me know how you're holdin' up. I'll rein in the boys even more if need be.'

Even more? By the Ancestors, Kyle knew that only the best runners of his tribe could have accomplished what they had managed in the last five days. Still, and he relaxed back to flexing his legs, what did distance matter when those hunting had access to the Warrens? He watched while the rangy, sandy-haired scout examined the bottom of one moccasin. 'What does it matter? If they really wanted us, they could have us.'

'True enough. And they did want you those first few days. But like Mara said, you had protection. Anyway, by now I figure they're long gone.'

The fish slipped from Kyle's grasp. 'Gone? You mean they've left? Where?'

'Quon, o' course. The invasion. They were organizing the departure when me 'n' the boys volunteered to track you down.' The scout gave his wolfish smile. 'Sorry to be the one to give you the bad news, lad, but I guess you're just not that important, hey?'

Kyle gaped, appalled. 'Then why in the Dark Hunter's name have we been killing ourselves running halfway across Stratem!'

'Well. Better safe than sorry, eh?'

'I don't blasted believe it!' Kyle fought to open the waterskin.

'Hey now! Don't be upset. Things are looking up. Remember I said you had protection, right?'

'Yes – what was that about?'

Stalker raised his chin aside. 'Well, let's see if they're willing to talk now.'

Badlands came pushing through branches and brush. With him

was an old woman, squat and bandylegged, her face the hue of ironwood. She wore pale leathers decorated with fur edging, feather tufts and shells. The soft jangling of the shells accompanied her walk and Kyle did not wonder how she could move silent through the woods for he recognized her – his own tribe had its shamans, male and female, healers, priests and even warleaders. He stood to meet her.

Badlands nodded to Stalker. 'This is Janbahashur – as least, that's the best I can manage.' To her he said, 'Stalker, Kyle.'

They bowed. Her smile was wide and showed large white teeth. Kyle was struck by the broad ridges above her deep brown eyes. It was as if she was watching them from within a cave. 'Thank you for your protection,' he said.

She laughed. 'We only helped a little,' she said in Talian. 'You did most.' Kyle was deeply puzzled by that but he bowed just the same. 'You travel west,' she said. 'We will help.'

Badlands and Stalker exchanged glances. 'How so?' the scout asked. It seemed to Kyle that Stalker had wanted to ask another question, *why?* but that good manners stopped him.

'We shall open a way. You cross through. Travel west.'

'A Warren?'

Janbahashur raised her brows, smiling. 'A way, a path, call it what you will.'

Neither of the soldiers spoke, obviously reluctant. Kyle wondered if it was up to him to say something. He decided not to be so well-mannered. 'Why? Why help us – me?'

The old woman's eyes glittered with hidden knowledge and humour. 'You could say it was whispered to us in the wind.'

Wind. There it was. Kyle stared, daring the woman to say more, but her gaze remained calm and steady and he was forced to look away. 'Very well. We'll go.'

Stalker nodded at Kyle's acceptance. 'OK. When and where?'

'Not here. Follow me. It is not far.'

As they walked Janbahashur fell into step next to Kyle. Her soft hide moccasins made no sound as she stepped over fallen branches and patches of moss. She directed them upslope and soon bare lichen-stained rock mounded around them. Dead fallen oak and spruce made the going slow.

'Your people are like us, I think,' she said to Kyle. 'You live on the land, yes?'

'Yes. And we worship it, and the sun, the rain – and wind.'

She smiled again. 'Yes. Wind. Many people worship it. To some it

213

is merely a route to power – a tool to be used. But to us it is life.' She breathed in expansively, exhaled in a gust. 'Every living thing takes it in. Even the trees. It is part of all of us, intermingling. For us it is really a symbol for that most unknowable of things, the life essence.'

'I see – I think.'

She laughed. 'There is no need to understand.' She gestured ahead. 'Here we are. Up here.'

They climbed a rising dome of striated bedrock. Lichen painted it orange and red amid its dark green and zigzag of quartz veins. The peak overlooked virgin forest for as far as Kyle could see. Other than this magnificent view, the dome was empty. A few small round stones dotted it here and there, in what might be drawn as a large circle.

Kyle looked around, caught Stalker's eye, gestured a question. The scout nodded reassuringly.

'One of your friends is watching my people, as should be,' said Janbahashur. 'They watch him in turn. That is good. To do otherwise would be foolish and we do not wish to waste our time on the foolish. Call him up.'

Stalker signed something to Badlands who jogged down the slope.

'It is ready,' Janbahashur said, pointing to the centre of the broad circle. Kyle saw nothing, just empty rock. She smiled at his puzzlement. 'Look more closely. Take your time.'

Shading his eyes from the setting sun, Kyle squinted at the smooth expanse. At first he still saw nothing, then he noticed a slight shimmering of the ground and air around the centre of the circle, as if dust was blowing. While he watched, patches of dust and sand stirred to life on the rock, swirled faster and faster, blurring, then were sucked away to disappear as if by an invisible wind. Listening carefully, he could just make out a loud hissing as of a waterfall heard from far away.

He looked to Janbahashur. 'What is it?'

'As you said, a path of Wind.'

'Like nothing I've ever seen,' said Stalker. 'But I'm new to these Warrens. What I've seen were more like tears, gaps and holes.'

Janbahashur dismissed such things with a wave. 'Faugh. Brute force. Abusing the fabric of things. We use no such painful means. We merely bend the natural ways, concentrate and redirect forces. If you wish to get the stone from a fruit you can throw it to the ground and step on it, or, you can slowly and gently pull where the fruit would halve until it parts on its own.'

Coots and Badlands joined them. Janbahashur waved them on, impatient. 'Go on. Quickly. Do not pause. A few paces, I should think. Go.'

214

Stalker signed something and Badlands gave an out-thrust fist and stepped forward. The gesture had something of the look of a salute to Kyle, but one he'd never seen before. Knees bent in a fighting crouch, arms akimbo, Badlands advanced on the blurred patch of air. As he came close he reached out an arm. Janbahashur, at Kyle's side, hissed her alarm. At that instant Badlands simply disappeared. It was hard to say, but Kyle had the impression that he'd been yanked forward with immense power, as if by a giant or a god. The old woman let out a relieved breath. 'Good. Now, you too. Go.'

Stalker started forward as did Kyle but the old woman caught Kyle's arm. 'A word, young warrior.' Stalker paused as well. His hair, the tag-ends of his shirts, the leather ties, all snapped and strained toward the apex. He was saying something but Kyle could not hear a word of it. While he watched the scout strained forward as if against a storm of wind but was losing ground as his moccasined feet slipped and shuffled backwards on the ridged rock. He must have given up the fight for in the next moment he was gone, snatched into the blur of hissing dust and sand.

Coots now stood at Kyle's side, a hand on one long-knife at his belt. 'He's not goin' last,' he said to Janbahashur.

'I did not mean to alarm. Just a warning. Do not stop on the path. Do not turn or delay. It would be deadly for you. And do not part with your weapons, yes?'

Kyle could not stop his hand from going to the grip of his tulwar. 'I never do.'

'Good, good. Now go.'

Kyle bowed his thanks and climbed the last of the slope. As he closed upon the apex of the dome his steps became lighter, the going easier. As if he was actually descending. Then, something like a hand thrust itself into his back, not slapping, but accelerating so hard it forced the breath from his lungs. The surroundings blurred into a green smear. A waterfall crash detonated upon his ears, then diminished in volume – either that or he was losing his hearing. Most alarming was his footing: whatever it was he stood upon was soft and yielding like thick water, a blur of sluicing pale mud or clay. Kyle couldn't make any sense of it. He had no idea where he was or where he was headed. He also seemed to be all alone.

Or perhaps not. Shapes skimmed through the blurring flow parallel with him. Sleek, streamlined, like fish they were but much larger than he. Knowing he shouldn't, Kyle couldn't help but reach out to one. His fingers broke the surface of the shifing flow as if he'd dipped them over the side of a boat. He had the feeling that all he had to do was jump overboard to find himself in a whole new world. One of the shapes nuzzled over as if in response to his gesture. Closer, Kyle had the impression of a stranger, far more alien creature – what had Stoop called the ugly things? – squid.

He thought that perhaps he'd tempted the Twins enough and pulled his hand back. Now, just how was he supposed to get out?

Something slapped through the barrier surrounding him and lashed itself around his arm. He screamed in searing pain as he was yanked backwards off his feet with the popping of his shoulder. He drew and slashed almost without thought. A distant keening, the braking snapping away, and Kyle felt himself spinning, his arm numb and lashing about. Then impact, loose gravel sushing beneath him and he lay panting.

A stream gurgled beside him the whole time; in this manner Kyle knew he'd not lost consciousness. He lay immobile mainly to rest and to delay any discovery of just how seriously he may be injured. Eventually, as the day dimmed, he had to accept that the demands of his flesh were still enough to force him on; especially a full bladder and an empty stomach. Slowly, painfully, he drew his good arm through the gravel to lever himself up into a sitting position. His other arm hung useless, numb, though the shoulder ached as if a fiend had sunk its teeth into it.

Taking a deep breath, he leaned on his hand to push himself upright. A flight of birds launched themselves from a nearby tree, startled, no doubt, by his resurrection. He was on a stranded gravel shore in the midst of a braided stream. Clear water ran west around him, shallow but swift. Trees taller than any he'd ever seen reared around him, blocking out the surroundings. Night was coming, and the air was chill. He started walking west.

The stream meandered, cutting deeply into its floodplain at times, but ever turned westward. Kyle kept to the open sandbars and gravel. Finally, ravenous, he cut a poplar branch and waded out to mid-stream. There he stood still in the dim light, lance raised. A flicker in the water; a curve of shadow. He threw. A miss.

Eventually, he sloshed to shore with an impaled fish. One-handed, he gathered dry fallen wood and brittle grass in the dark, stuck a flint pressing his knife under a knee until the grass lit. He cleaned the fish sloppily then angled it over the flames, and sat back.

Eating, he tossed branches on to the roaring fire. The night deepened.

Eventually a voice growled out of the dark, 'The lad could be hurt. Knocked out. Bleeding.'

Kyle glanced over his shoulder. 'Evening, Coots.'

'Wounded, maybe,' Coots knelt to his haunches and warmed his hands at the fire. 'In Gods know what trouble.'

Kyle pointed to his shoulder. 'I hurt my arm.'

'The three of us runnin' all over all through the night an' you're sittin' here stuffing your face.'

'Comes around, doesn't it?'

'What happened?'

'Something grabbed my arm. I think it's broke.'

'Hunh.'

'Where are we?'

'Got any more o' that fish?'

'There's more in the stream.'

'Hunh. Funny guy. You're turnin' into a funny guy.'

'So where are we?'

Coots yawned, rubbed a hand across his face, lay down and stretched his legs out. 'Close to the western coast. You can see it from any highland.'

'What then?'

'Don't know. Steal a fishing boat, I s'pose. Maybe head to Korel. Take a look at this Stormwall everyone's goin' on about.'

* * *

Ghelel Rhik Tayliin allowed her fury to grow steadily in the pit of her stomach. This last revelation of the dispersal of the army assembled in her name was too much. Now that they had reached the Seti plains a simple direct forced march east was all that was required. Any fool could see that. But this latest news – to divide the army! Insane! The worst error of any bumbling lackwit. Her own readings of the military arts were plain on that topic. Never, ever, do that.

The grey mud of the churned-up shore of the Idryn sucked at her boots as she made her way to the command tent raised next to the assembled wagons and carts of the army's supply. Matériel never stopped moving, with more arriving even as she pushed her way through the maze of crates, piled sacks and penned animals. The ten swordsmen of her guard followed a stone's throw behind despite her direct orders to remain at the wagon. Her *Royal Palanquin* – Hood take it!

Beyond the ragged borders of the entrepôt, Seti tribesmen rode back and forth, whistling and lashing lengths of braided leather, driving lines of cattle and oxen east. East? Away from the carts? She gaped at the spectacle.

To make things worse the Talian and half-breed Seti drovers nudged each other and grinned her way – the mud-splattered Duchess! Ghelel gathered up the ends of her long white surcoat emblazoned with the winged lion of her family crest, made sure her helmet wrapped in white silk cord rested firmly and evenly on her head, then raised her chin defiantly.

The drovers looked away. She almost congratulated herself on that small victory when she caught sight of her bodyguard slogging up protectively close. Glaring at her guard – who seemed not to notice the attention as they scanned the surroundings – she started off again, wincing as she pulled each boot from the stiff sucking mud. May the Gods forgive her: hand-tooled Rhivi leather imported from Darujhistan. From Darujhistan! Why had they dressed her in such finery? As she neared the tent, laughter and raised voices snapped her gaze around. There, in the mud and shallows of the river, bare-chested men used mattocks and iron bars on wagons. Bashing and levering them apart. Demolishing them! Trake take them! They were destroying the wagons. What in the name of the Abyss was going on in this madhouse?

'Stay here!' she told her guard then tossed open the tent flap. Amaron stood at a camp table assembled from boards over two barrels; behind it sat General Choss, booted feet up on a stool, a towel draped over his face. Neither moved. 'What is the meaning of this insanity!'

Amaron turned, raised a quizzical brow. Again, Ghelel was impressed by his height. Now, however, long into his sorcerously-maintained senescence, the belt across the expanse of his armoured belly seemed embarrassingly taut.

'Which insanity might that be – my Lady?'

Ghelel could never shake the feeling that the two men were laughing at her. But she ploughed on, determined to defend her prerogatives. 'Dividing the forces, firstly.'

Amaron glanced to his commander. 'Ah.'

Sitting up, Choss pulled the towel from his face then rested his hands among the scraps of paper littering the table. The man reminded Ghelel of a lion, a scarred, battle-hardened veteran of countless scrapes, wiry with a bushy tangled head of curly hair and beard. Choss cleared his throat. 'That was settled last night, Duchess. We saw no need to wake you.'

'My presence is requisite at all command meetings.'

'Ah, well, you see. In the field things don't really hold to any regularly scheduled meetings or such. We have to move quickly.'

'Then come and get me, dammit!'

Choss's gaze went to Amaron and he smiled faintly. 'Very well. But please remember – you supported relinquishing command of forces to me and I do not have the time to explain every decision.'

'You seem to have the time now.'

'Flanked you,' said an amused Amaron.

Sighing, Choss poured out a glass of wine from a decanter on the table. He raised it to Ghelel who shook her head. He sat back. 'Very well. So what is it you want explained?'

'I have heard that you are leaving some ten thousand men here south of Tali. Gods, man, that's more than a fifth of the entire force! We need every man for the march east! Heng, you say, may have come out against us, or is at least making a bid for independence. We must intimidate Itko Kan and Cawn. We may face pitched battles in Bloor and, finally, Unta. The very capital! Why weaken ourselves before we even meet the enemy?'

Choss moved to speak but a wave of lowing from the throats of countless oxen and cattle overtook them together with the high-pitched whistles and yipping of Seti horsemen. The tent shook with the rumbling of the hooves.

'What is going on!' Ghelel yelled through the din.

'The Seti are driving most of our animals east.'

'Why!'

Choss raised his voice, 'Duchess, the resistance of Heng has upset our timetable. We must get there quickly, before Laseen reaches the city with forces loyal to her. If she can stop us there our movement will lose its momentum. Commanders and provinces will begin drifting back to her. That will be the end of us.'

'But you assured me Laseen has barricaded herself in the capital!'

The two men exchanged glances once more. As the press of cattle passed, the noise fell. 'Yes, Duchess. However, her agents may make an offer to the Kanese. A privileged position in a new co-dominion rule . . . who knows? They might be bribed into extending their protection to Heng. Then we would be facing two opponents. We must get there before any such arrangement can be effected.'

Ghelel pointed to the shore. 'So tell me, how does leaving men here manage that!'

Choss downed his wine, set the glass carefully on the table.

'Duchess. The old Itko Kan confederacy is not the only principality we must worry about. South of the Idryn is Dal Hon—'

'Who have sent assurances of neutrality.'

'*Officially*, yes. However, we have drained Quon Tali of every hale man and fit woman able to hold a spear. We dare not leave it *completely* defenceless. The Dal Hon Council of Elders might decide to dig out their old treaties with Heng and march on Tali. *That's* why we're leaving ten thousand men between them and Tali.'

'They wouldn't dishonour themselves after assuring us—'

'*Dishonour!*' Choss's hand slapping down on the table smashed the glass flat. 'Honour? Glory? All that horseshit those moon-eyed minstrels sing on about – none of that matters here in the field! Here, a man or woman can have personal honour, yes. But no commander or state can afford it. The price is too high. Annihilation of all those who follow you. I intend to win, Duchess. That's the school I was trained in. Winning! Plenty of time afterwards to rewrite the history to make yourself look good.' He raised his hand and gathered up a handful of reports to wipe the blood away. 'Right now we're makin' rafts. And with the help of our few hamlet mages and some Seti shamans we'll barge down the Idryn as if Hood himself was after our behinds.'

'I'll get a healer,' said Amaron.

'Not yet,' Choss called after him. 'No, now I think is a good time to let Ghelel know our plans for her.' He grinned as he wrapped a cloth around his hand.

Ghelel actually felt the short hairs of her neck bristling. 'Oh yes, do please inform me. Perhaps it involves a royal barge and a hundred slaves rowing?'

Amaron smiled – the first real smile Ghelel could recall from him. 'Don't worry, m'Lady. The dress and the wagon and the bodyguard are all for show.' He hooked his hands once more at his taut belt. 'We have only one real mage worth the name, Lass. That's a joke compared to how things used to be. Our one advantage with you is that no one, absolutely no one, can reliably identify you. We're keeping watch on your old stepfamily, of course, but outside of them there's only a handful who can be used by any mage to get a handle on you – such as Quinn. Thus, the façade of the palanquin,' he pointed to her white surcoat, 'and the costume. We plan for you to slip away from all that during the river trip. A new identity has been pulled together for you.'

She eyed the two men – so obviously pleased with themselves. Schemers. She saw it now. These men loved schemes. Who else could have endured to rise as part of the old emperor's staff? 'A new identity. I see. Pray tell as what . . . ?'

'An officer,' Amaron replied. 'A cavalry leader. Prevost, I believe, is the old rank. In the Marchland Sentries.'

'The Marchland Sentries! Under the Marquis Jhardin? They're all veterans – the raiding is constant on the Nom Purge frontier. They'll never accept me.'

'They accept new recruits all the time. And the Marquis does command.'

'What does he know?'

'Only what he needs to know. I leave the rest up to your discretion. I suggest something close to the truth of your upbringing. Such as being of a minor noble family that spent its last coin purchasing your commission.'

She nodded reluctantly – anything was better than the damned painted carriage and this ridiculous costume. 'When?'

'Molk will have all the details. He will be posing as your servant.'

Ghelel raised a hand. 'I'm sorry. Did you say *servant*?'

Amaron nodded, serious. 'Oh yes.'

'Not like I've been hearing about? All these adjuncts and aides and seconds in the Talian forces?'

Choss and Amaron exchanged wry glances. 'Oh, yes, Duchess. The Talian army has elected to follow the old ways of doing things. Pre-Malazan. Any self-respecting officer must have a servant, even two, or three: a groom for his or her mounts, an aide-de-camp or adjutant for his or her daily duties, even an attendant to go with them into battle. You being poor can only afford one.'

Queen of Mysteries, no. The man's slouched, he stinks and he's wall-eyed to boot. 'No, not him. Anyone but *him*!'

Amaron's grin did not waver; he was obviously very pleased with his arrangements. 'Oh yes, m'Lady. He's perfect.'

*   *   *

In the light of the flames from the burning west palisade wall Lieutenant Rillish could make out figures struggling atop the east. He stood behind the piled sacks and lumber of a last redoubt abutting the stone barracks at the centre of the fort. Already the wounded filled the barracks. The Wickans, Sergeant Chord had informed him, had withdrawn to the large dugout storage vault beneath. Somehow this intelligence disheartened him. But he did not have the energy to think about it; instead, it took all he could muster

221

to stay erect. A javelin lanced out of the dark from the north wall and he threw up both swords to deflect it. The parry staggered him. The two guards Chord had posted with him steadied his back, their large shields raised. Arrows followed, thumping into the shields' layered wood, leather, and copper sheeting. Damn them, they had the advantage now. Rillish gestured for Sergeant Chord.

The sergeant came jogging across the no-man's-land of the central mustering grounds, whisked by arrows and tossed flaming brands.

'Not much longer now,' he bellowed over the inferno of the tarred east timbers, the clashing of swords and the roar of the besiegers. His idiot grin of delight in battle was fixed at his bearded mouth.

Rillish shouted: 'Send the word. Torch the rest and withdraw.'

'Aye, aye.'

Rillish tapped the guards. 'Remain here. Everyone holds to cover the retreat.'

The marine guards saluted. 'Aye, sir.' They rested their shields against the piled timbers, took up their crossbows. Rillish backed away, limping and bent, for the barracks door, and it occurred to him that with men like that he could win any battle – provided he had enough.

Within, in the gloom, the stink of rotting flesh and old blood made him wince and press a hand to his face. His vision slowly adjusted, revealing a madman's image of Hood's realm. Blood and fluids glistened on the timbered floor, draining from a pile beside that door that slowly resolved itself into a heap of naked amputated arms and legs. Men sat hunched at the slit windows, bows and crossbows raised – those with two able arms. The rest supported them, holding pikes and arrow sheaths. A man struggled one-handed to crank his crossbow. Appalled, Rillish took it from him and wound it. 'Fessel?' he bellowed. 'Where are you, man! What is the meaning of this?'

'Healer's dead, sir,' said the crossbowman.

'Dead?'

'Aye.'

'What happened?'

'Old Fessel refused to use his Denul all night, sir. He was cryin' an mumblin' and then he just fell dead. His heart, sir. Seemed to just give out.'

'What was it – was he sick?'

'Don't know. He was bawlin' like a baby at the end there, sayin', "Please stop. No. You have to stop. Soliel's Mercy, please no," while he was fixin' us up best he could. Strangest thing, sir.'

'The Wickans?'

'Downstairs, sir. Quiet as mice.'

'Very good.'

Rillish crossed to the open trap door and dark earthen passage leading down flagged in flat river stones – a construction someone had put a lot of effort into since he'd last seen the subterranean vault. 'Udep? Trake himself is on his way! This is it, man!'

Darkness. The flickering of what might be a single torch somewhere in a far corner of the cellar. Staring down into that dark a shapeless dread tightened the lieutenant's throat. The stink of old blood seemed even stronger here. He thought of the hetman's and the shaman's strange manner during their last meeting. How Udep seemed to be attempting to warn him of something – Clearwater's bruised, almost crazed gaze.

No. *They couldn't have.* Their own children. Yet was not slavery a worse fate for any Wickan? He backed away from the dirt passage and the horror that it promised. Perhaps they were all to meet their end this night – they in their way, and he and his command in theirs.

'They're fallin' back, sir!' someone called from a slit window.

'Yes.' The lieutenant shook himself, cursed the fools beneath his feet. Damn them! Too impatient to meet Hood, they were. There's hundreds without more than happy to lend a hand for that. Why not go down with your iron warm? Rillish took a deep breath, 'Aye! Cover them. Show them how a soldier fights!'

'For the Fourth!' a woman shouted.

'For the Empire!' Rillish countered.

A great shout went up from the men and women lining the walls, 'The Empire!'

A thunderous roar and a blinding gout of flames announced the eruption of the flammables gathered at the base of the remaining palisade walls. For moments the screams of the besiegers stranded upon them rose even above that conflagration. The churning gold light illuminated the passage and in its bright glare Rillish forced himself to descend.

At the bottom his boots sank into yielding damp earth. Kneeling, he felt about with one gloved hand and brought up a fistful of the loam. He squeezed and the flame-light revealed a dark stream dripping from his fingers – earth soaked in blood.

What inhuman will . . . He wiped his gloved hand on the wall then yanked his hand away. Warm. The dirt walls fairly radiated a strange heat. The fires? As his vision adjusted he made out the low shapes of legs lying straight out from either side forming a kind of

223

aisle leading straight to the opposite wall where the lone torch cast a fading light on a single figure, waiting.

Rillish walked the aisle. To either side lay the elders, heart thrust, every one. No sign of any child, nor of any struggle. Their slack features appeared calm, resigned. His boots slipped and sucked in the soaked, mud-slick earth. A strange humid warmth assaulted him while an impenetrable darkness seemed to hover just beyond the torch and motionless figure.

Drawing close, he recognized the shaman, Clearwater, sunk to his knees. Horribly, two spears supported him, thrust downward through his back and crossed beneath his chest, impaling him on his knees. Blood ran drying in rivulets down the wood hafts, pooling beneath him.

Incredibly, the shaman's head rose, sending Rillish backwards, gripping his swords. 'Greetings, Malazan,' the apparition breathed, wetly.

Rillish could not speak. Above, boots stamped the timber floor, shouts for relief for the bulwark beyond the door sounded. Should they yield that, he knew, the end would not be far behind. He found his voice. 'Clearwater – what have you done?'

The shaman's smile was ferocious, and victorious. He glanced to the eerie darkness past the torchlight. 'Forbidden one fight, we found another. And succeeded, though the cost was dear. Go now, bring your men. A way has been bought.'

'What do you mean? Bought? What kind of bargain is *this*?'

A shudder took the shaman and his torso slipped a hand's width down the shafts. The man spoke through lips drained pale. 'An escape, fool. Life for our children and your men. This site was holy once. To our ancestors. Blood called, just as it always did. But hungry! So hungry . . . there were barely enough of us. Now go, send your men. I hold the way.'

'A way where?'

A clipped laugh cut off by an agonized grunt. 'Not far. Go.'

Rillish ran to the stairs, his boots slipping and sliding. He roared up the passage, 'Send Sergeant Chord down here!'

In the end he managed to evacuate thirty-two men and women of his command before the building's burning roof forced him into the passage. His last act was to help those wounded who volunteered to carry out the ones who couldn't walk. Bent over, his leg stabbing with pain, he could wait no longer. A soldier rearguard steadied him on the stairs. Together, they pulled shut the trapdoor against the furnace roar of the barracks.

224

'Sergeant Chord?'

'First through, sir,' she said.

'Very good. Our turn now.'

'Yes, sir. After you, sir.'

'No. I'll go last.'

The woman smiled – dark, Talian or part Dal Hon, her mailed shoulders as broad as any man's. 'Not the sergeant's orders, beggin' your pardon.'

A glow licked its way between the thick timbers of the trapdoor. They backed away, hunched. 'No time for that, soldier. After you.'

A salute. 'Aye, sir.'

At the darkness, the soldier drew her shortsword, readied the wide shield from her back. 'Good luck, soldier,' Rillish said.

'Aye. Hood spare me,' she spat, muttered a short prayer, then launched herself forward, disappearing.

Rillish turned to the now still form of Clearwater; the shaman's head was sunk to his chest, his greasy hair obscuring his face. He knelt beside him. 'Clearwater? Can you hear me? I don't know what to say. . . Thank you. Thank you for my men.'

'Thank not for a fair bargain,' came a hoarse whisper. 'Honour it.'

Rillish straightened, 'Yes.' He faced the darkness, a hand on the grip of one Untan duelling sword, stepped forward . . .

. . . And walked into a forest – tall conifers, birdsong, sunlight shafting down through boughs, movement between the thick trunks, a kind of large deer? – then one more step and into cool night. Hands steadied him, Chord and the female soldier. He looked up and was reassured to see familiar constellations: the Twins, the Wolf, the broad Path of Light. 'Where are we?'

'Just west of the fort, seems,' supplied Chord. 'You can see the flames from the hilltop.'

Rillish peered about, getting his bearings. They were in a deep gully, a dry river bed. Around them was – no one. 'Where is everyone? The children?'

'Headed off north-west already, sir. Couldn't stop them. Said they had directions from Clearwater. I sent the men with them.'

'Very well, Sergeant.'

'Shall we go?' East, a pale orange glow backlit a hill. Rillish watched it for a time. 'Care to take one last look, sir?'

Wincing, Rillish squeezed his leg and brushed the night flies from his face. 'No, Sergeant. It's all right. We best go.'

'Yes, sir. There's our guide.' Chord gestured up the gully where the dim figure of a Wickan girl stood waving them on impatiently.

The female soldier slipped her shield to her back, offered an arm. Rillish accepted.

* * *

The weather of the Western Explorer's Sea had proven remarkably calm these last few days. The morning of the sixth day Shimmer took her usual place next to Jhep, her tillerman on the *Wanderer*. She wore only her long linen undershirt and pantaloons but the cold dawn wind did not chill her. A sailor brought her hot tea that she sipped, her eyes fixed on the waters far ahead on the north horizon. There an emerald nimbus grew, wavering like the lights one sometimes saw in the night sky. *Cowl's ritual*. It made her uneasy, this relying on Ruse's uncharacteristic, how had the High Mage put it, *compliance*. Shimmer's instincts told her to mistrust any such pose – for pose it surely must be. Especially when an Elder is involved. And this demonic rush to reach Quon . . . There was no need as far as she could see; and every reason for the opposite. Again, especially with unfinished business left behind.

She looked to the *Gedrand*, the captured Kurzan three-tiered warship Skinner had taken as his flag vessel. Despite the incalculable advantage his presence brought to their Vow, Shimmer could not help wishing he had never returned. Simply catching sight of him now made her wince – where was the man she'd known? Who was this impostor? Her sources told her they'd yet to see him outside his armour. Reportedly, he slept sitting up, fully accoutred. And that armour; she had never seen anything like it. What was that dark patina that covered it with a crystal-like glitter? Skinner did not hide that his patron, Ardata of Jacuruku, had gifted it to him. She was some sort of witch queen, perhaps an Ascendant herself of those alien lands. And he made no secret they had been close. Lovers? Shimmer felt the cold wind and she wrapped her arms about herself. The Vow still drove him; of that she was sure. Yet what other, lesser, vows might he have sworn during all those years away? She dashed the cold tea over the side.

'Send for Smoky,' she called to a guardsman.

'Aye.'

Shortly afterwards the mage came working his way sternward, hand over hand along the gunwale, his face sickly pale. Shimmer could not help but smile. Never one to find his sea-legs was Smoky. 'No further word from the investigation?' she asked as he came close.

'No, Commander.' The mage's face was milky beneath his greasy tangled locks. His eyes narrowed ahead where a greenish curtain of light now climbed from the waves.

Her sergeants brought Shimmer her armour. She raised her arms for them to slip the quilted aketon over her head, followed by her mail shirt that they shook to hang down to her calves, slit back and front. 'You have questioned the Brethren?'

'Yes. They maintain they saw nothing that night. Indeed, they even claim that nothing happened – because they did not see it.'

'And Stoop has not appeared among them?'

'No. No sign of him.'

'Have they been suborned?'

The question startled Smoky. His glance to Shimmer was alarmed. He answered, thoughtfully, 'I don't think that possible . . .'

'Then we are left with this youth as an enemy agent. A spy with powerful allies.'

'Yes. His escape would suggest such a conclusion.'

Shimmer took her helmet and sword and waved the soldiers away. 'Unless those searching were not trying so very hard.'

The mage's hairless brows rose. 'I had not considered that. It points in, ah, *unhealthy* directions.'

She pulled on her helmet, swung closed the lower face guard. 'Greymane suggested it.'

. Smoky's gaze flicked to the broad back of the man at the bow. 'I see . . . Yes, that makes sense. Close to the matter, but not Vowed, and thus not sharing our blindnesses. It would take an outsider, wouldn't it? Thank you, Commander.'

'The Brethren fully back Skinner, of course.'

'They never stopped demanding it. A strike against Quon.'

'Exactly. Their priorities are not necessarily ours.'

'True. Yet perhaps *suborned* is too strong.' Smoky pushed his wind-blown hair from his face. 'Perhaps seduced, or swayed?'

Shimmer belted on her whipsword, adjusted its weight at her hips. 'Perhaps. Now, shouldn't you be lending your strength to the ritual?'

'Gods, no. I'm just a minor battle mage of Telas – though I admit to some glimpses into Elder Thryllan in moments of inspiration. Not conducive, you imagine, to current shared efforts on the bridling of Ruse.'

'If you say so, mage.' Again, how she wished she had kept Blues and his blade close! But theirs was a desperate gamble they'd decided worth the throw. It was too late for regret. And what of Cal-Brinn? What had happened to his command? His opinion on these ritual magics she would accede to.

227

'Shimmer . . .'

'Yes?'

'Be careful.'

A nod. 'I could say the same to you.'

Snorting, Smoky headed to the bow.

The glow strengthened through the morning, thickening into a wavering curtain of green and deep violet accompanied by a constant thunder ahead. As Cowl and the other Avowed mages readied themselves for just the right moment the partition, or portal, whatever it was, paced them, maintaining its distance some hundred cables before them. The sea that emerged from beneath reached them emerald with foaming bubbles as if churned by energies and, more troubling, flecked by driftwood and litter such as that which gathers along any shore. At mid-deck, the Kurzani first mate bellowed orders: sails were being lowered, men were securing matériel. Shimmer recognized preparations for a coming gale.

What did that screen disguise? Shimmer had heard the ususal legends and stories of whirlpools and ship-shredding storms that awaited any fool impudent enough, or desperate enough, to try Mael's realm. But all such tales came down to them from long ago and might be just no more than that – imaginings. Truth told, no one knew what awaited them; not any of their twelve mages, Avowed or not, nor any of their sailors, for none had ever heard again from anyone who had actually dared.

Why this unholy hurry? Why this quick thrust for Quon – just three vessels darting ahead of the fleet – the *Wanderer*, *Gedrand* and *Kestral*? They carried the majority of the Avowed, yes. But what could Skinner hope to accomplish with a mere two thousand men?

Flags waved from the sides of the neighbouring *Gedrand*. At the bow, Smoky's arms were raised as he communicated with his fellow mages. *Any moment now.* Shimmer wrapped one arm around the stern-mast. Ahead, the gate had stopped its backward sweep and now awaited them, fathoms tall. It resembled an enormous waterfall, appearing from empty air. Shimmer was assaulted by the disorienting impression that the gate that awaited them was in fact the surface of the sea and it was they who were racing uncontrollably down a chute to their destruction. *Togg, Oponn, Burn and Fanderay protect us. But Hood . . . look on you who can never have us!*

As the bow pierced the barrier Shimmer had one last impression of Smoky, arms raised as if to fend off some vision of ruin, Greymane, the Malazan renegade, knees bent in a ready stance, one arm stretched tight, a rope twisted around it, then the roaring – no, hissing, seething, gate was upon them and she was blinded . . .

A shuddering crash – an arm-wrenching blow threw Shimmer down as if hammered. The screech of wood cracking, the heavy slow creak of an enormous weight slamming into the deck – a split mast – and men shrieking. Water splashing and washing sullenly, turgid, followed by silence leaving only the groan of wounded. Shimmer pulled herself to her feet, rubbed her shoulder where she had collided with the mast.

'Man overboard!' came a shout.

'*Man overboard!*' a distant echo sounded. Shimmer looked to port, where the *Gedrand* wallowed, one mast split a third from the top and tangled among its rigging.

'The *Kestral*?' she called across.

A voice responded, faint, 'Here also!'

Yes. Wherever *here* was. 'Smoky!'

'Overboard,' a Guardsman answered.

Shimmer went to the side. Men and women foundered splashing on a surface of wreckage and pale driftwood. So dense was the debris that the ropes thrown to them hardly even got wet. Shimmer spotted the kinky-haired mage clinging to a log. Something about the waters and the horizon was strange but she didn't have the time to give over to that just then. 'Captain!' The Kurzani captain and the first mate came to her. 'Report.'

'Seams sprung,' said the first mate, pulling at his full black beard. 'Taking on water.'

'Can you re-caulk?'

A resigned shrug. 'Have to try.'

'Very well. Take all you need for pumping and bailing. Dismissed.' Shimmer went to help the old tillerman, Jhep, to his feet. He seemed to have taken a blow from the broad wood handle. 'Send the mage to me!' she shouted as loud as she could.

'Aye, aye, sir,' someone responded from the deck.

She sat the man next to the tiller, which stood motionless though no one controlled it. Frowning, Shimmer rested a hand upon it, feeling for any sensation of motion or pull. Nothing. They were dead in the water. *Not what she was expecting.*

'Commander.'

Water dripping to the deck planking next to Shimmer announced Smoky's presence. Shimmer studied the tillerman's eyes: both looking forward, pupils matching. She knew what to look for, the danger signs; years in the battlefield would teach anyone the basic treatment of wounded. 'Take over here, Smoky.'

'Yes, Commander. Have you seen?'

'Seen what? I've been busy.'

Smoky waved an arm in a broad sweep all around. The mage was looking off to the distance. His gaze seemed stricken. 'Well,' he said, his voice tight. 'Better take a look.'

Shimmer straightened and went to the side. Glancing out she stopped, her hands frozen at the shoulders of her mail coat. What she had taken to be distant islands – the source of the driftwood and jetsam – were not. Ships surrounded them, or rather they rested in the midst of a sea of motionless vessels stretching from horizon to horizon.

Complete silence oppressed Shimmer with its weight. A sea of ghost ships. Most of those nearby appeared to be galleys, though more distant vessels looked to be far larger, tiered sailing vessels. One such leagues out among the grey timber expanse must be enormous to stand so tall. All the crew on deck, she now saw, lined the sides motionless, staring. Some kind of enchantment? But no, probably the sight alone sufficed. 'Smoky,' she managed. 'What is this?'

'You're asking me?'

'The Shoals,' said a voice in Kurzan, lifeless and flat.

Shimmer turned. It was Jhep, his eyes dead of emotion. 'The Shoals? Explain.'

A weak shrug. 'Legend. Old myth. Place where the god of the sea sends those he curses. Or those who trespass against him. Maybe this is where all those who try to use Ruse end up, hey? No wonder we heard nothing.' And he laughed, coughing.

The blow to the head – must be. The alternative . . . Gods! No wonder there had been no resistance; you were always welcome to enter. But exiting, well, there was none.

'There must be another explanation. Currents . . . a backwater . . .'

'There's no current,' said Smoky.

'Well – any ship would sink in time.'

'No. No sinking in this sea.'

Exasperated, Shimmer faced Smoky. 'Explain yourself, Hood take you!'

Grinning, the Cawn mage touched a finger to his tongue. 'Salt. The saltiest sea I've ever tasted. Nothing can sink here. Even I floated and I can't swim.'

Shimmer threw herself to the gunwale, gripped it in both hands.

Damn Mael! Damn these fool mages whose arrogance had brought them to such an end. Damn Cowl! How Hood must be laughing now; he need not trouble himself to take them away – they had just up and taken themselves!

Thinking of that, she allowed herself a fey grin, sharing the amusement. The poetic justice of it! She drew off her helmet. It all supported a private conviction of hers; that there existed a persistent balance in creation that in the end somehow always asserted itself. Usually in the manner least anticipated by everyone involved.

She turned to Smoky. 'What now, mage?' She waved to the horizon-spanning fields of marooned vessels. 'You might burn an awful conflagration here to teach Mael a lesson, hey?'

But the wild-haired mage, resembling a drowned rat in his sodden robes already drying leaving a rime of salt flakes, was peering aside, pensive. 'Something's up with the *Kestral*.'

Shimmer spun. Through the jumbled rigging of the *Gedrand* she could make out the tall masts of the *Kestral*. Flags waved from the tallest. 'Captain! Smoky!'

'Aye.'

She sensed Smoky at her side, questing, but he shrugged. *Nothing*. The captain was called up from below. He arrived drying his hands, soaked to his waist. He studied the signals. 'Get a man up high!'

Sailors scrambled up the rigging.

Atop the main-mast a sailor scanned the horizons, gestured a direction. 'Light! A glow far off. Like the magery.'

'What bearing!' the captain bellowed.

Arms held out wide in hopeless ignorance.

Yes. What bearing? Shimmer glanced about the pale, almost colourless sky, the monotonous horizon all around. *Who can say in such a place as this?*

'Show direction!' the captain called. 'Pilot – mark it.' The Kurzani mate squinted up at the sailor, turned and raised a bronze disk to an eye that he peered through – slit with thin needle-fine holes Shimmer knew from studying it. He nodded to the captain. 'Marked.'

The captain clapped his hands together. 'Very good, Pilot. Men!' he roared. 'Lower launches! Ready oarsmen!'

'Aye!'

Shimmer began unbuckling her belt. She looked to the *Gedrand*; they too had reached the same decision as sailors clambered over the launches readying them. *So, becalmed we must oar to the gate – if that is what the glow promises.* She imagined what a trial must await them. Rowing through a millennia of debris! Pushing rotting vessels from their path. Who knew how long it would take. But they were Avowed. They would win their way through . . . eventually. No task could daunt them; what was time to them? It was a perspective natural to Shimmer now, but one she knew others, mortals, could not possibly understand or share. She suspected it made the Avowed something of an alien kind apart.

She peered back to the swath of wreckage the entrance of their three vessels had cut. So, Mael. You strand us here then dangle escape in the distance. Why? To what purpose?

A lesson perhaps, yes? Pass through, Avowed. But do not return. *This* awaits. Now go. And I won't make it easy either.

* * *

Reaching the coast, they turned south, keeping to the screening cover of the treeline. Badlands and Coots scouted and hunted game while Stalker walked with Kyle who fumed, feeling useless, his swordarm in a sling. Now that the pressing rush to flee for his life had passed, the plains youth had begun to wonder now about his circumstances and these worried him. In fact, they struck him as damned mysterious. What had the Avowed mage, and the shaman meant about his having some sort of protection? Who could that be? Or what? And, though he did not want to be ungrateful, why were these three men taking such trouble to help him? Their desertion seemed real; but why now and with him? But could this not have been their best chance? Four do stand a better chance than three. And Stalker did say the Guard were quitting the land for Quon in any case . . .

Kyle stopped. Stalker continued on for a moment then stopped himself, resting a hand on the bole of a pine. 'What is it?'

Shrugging, Kyle adjusted the folds of his sling. 'I was just wondering – you said the Guard were leaving when you volunteered to track me down. But how then did they plan for you to link up with them?'

Stalker pushed up his helmet, wiped the sweat from his brow. 'Only now you've worked your way through to that? I thought it would be obvious . . .' The scout took out a waterskin, squeezed a stream into his mouth. He offered it to Kyle who shook his head. He waved to the sea shimmering in the west. 'We'd bring you to the coast, take a small boat and sail for Quon.'

'Not funny, Stalker.'

The scout brushed droplets from his moustache, smiled, then looked around for a place to sit. He selected a moss-covered rock.

'Apologies.' He pulled off his helmet and rubbed his sweat-slick hair. 'Don't worry, lad. Just a joke.' He invited Kyle to sit. 'Naw. We've left the Guard for sure. No future in it.'

Kyle sat. 'What do you mean?'

'No chance for advancement, hey? And they're crippled anyway. Doomed to rot unless something big happens to shake them up.'

'The Avowed don't strike me as rotting. They're strong.'

The scout waved that aside. 'Not what I mean. I mean they're blind to the present. Stuck in the past.' He rubbed the pouch hanging from his neck. 'It's as if they're walking backwards into the future – you know what I mean?'

How much Kyle understood must have shown on his face for the scout took a deep breath and tried again. 'You asked about Badlands and Coots. Well, we *are* related. Some might call them my cousins, distant cousins. *You* might say brothers. We're all of the Lost back where we come from. Well, back there, it's just the same. Stuck in the past. We left because we'd had enough of it. Imagine our disgust when we found more of the same in the Guard.'

Kyle nodded. 'I see – I think.'

A thin, wintry smile. 'Never mind. Let's see what we got left to eat.'

They sat in the shade of tall cedars, chewed on smoked rabbit then ate wild berries of a kind unknown to either of them. Kyle thought maybe it was the berries that had been giving him the runs. While he sat letting the cool breeze dry his back and hair, Coots lumbered up.

'Ain't disturbing your Hood-damned dinner party, am I?'

'Nope,' said Stalker. 'Have some berries?'

'No. They twist up my guts awful.'

'Is that why you're here,' said Stalker, 'to tell us all about your digestion?'

Coots pushed a hand through his curly grey hair. 'Since you asked, my digestion's been the shits since you dragged us on this Poliel-damned expedition. It's a damned disgrace.' He winked to Kyle. 'This fellow's got the organizational skills of a squirrel in a cyclone.'

'That your digestion acting up, Coots?'

'No. You'll know it when *that* happens.'

'So what's the news then?'

Coots knelt to his haunches. The plain leather vest he wore made his arms look enormous while leather bands strapped them above and below the elbow. He took up a handful of branches that he broke in his wide blunt hands. 'We've found a pitiful little fishing village on the coast. As rundown as you can imagine. But they've got a sweet-looking new boat just sitting there ready to be pushed down the strand. It's like a damned gift from the Gods.'

'And that's what worries you.'

'Yeah. Makes me all queasy – but maybe that's just my innards clenching.'

'OK. We'll keep watch for a while. You and Badlands first.'

'Aye, aye.'

To Kyle, 'We'll wait here, hey? Then we'll steal our boat.'

'OK. But, I have to warn you, I don't know a thing about sailing 'n' such.'

Stalker and Coots exchanged amused glances. 'That's OK,' said Stalker. ''Cause neither do we.'

BOOK II

The Eternal Return

These stories of one-time Trell or Thelomen occupation of our lands are utterly false. There never have been, nor are there any, systematic eliminations or nefarious schemes to eradicate any race. All these rumours are the inventions of our enemies intended to stain us. I ask you, if such peoples once lived here, where are they? Where have they gone? What has become of their works?

Paulus of Rool
Continent of Fist

CHAPTER I

After the mêlée
All is quiet –
Just me
And the Eel.

Uligen of Darujhistan

FAR DOWN BELOW HURL'S BOOTS THE RIVER IDRYN HISSED AS IT parted around the iron bars of Heng's Outer River Gate. She squinted east, downstream, into the dead of the moonless night and held her crossbow tight, balanced on the stone crenellations of the bridge.

'See anything?' asked Shaky from her side.

''Course not. Bloody dark as the inside of your head, isn't it?'

'Just askin'.'

Hurl bit down hard on her anger – Shaky wasn't the cause of it. 'Sorry. No, I can't see a Lady-damned thing.'

'Here they come.' This from Sunny in the dark. Hurl peered down the arc of the bridge's walkway. Figures closed, not one torch or lantern among them: Storo, magistrates Ehrlann and Plengyllen, Sergeant, now Captain, Gujran – turns out the man's a Genabackan from Greydog – and a squad of garrison regulars.

'Again,' Ehrlann was telling Storo in a fierce strained whisper, 'we, the Council, stand against this decision. It that not so, Plengyllen?'

The tall bearded magistrate nodded his ponderous agreement. 'We consider it ill-advised.'

Storo simply threw his arms over the crenel. 'Quiet?' he asked Hurl.

'Until now.'

'They're going of their own free will,' Storo said, louder.

'You could have forbidden it.'

'As you could have.'

The paunchy magistrate held up his hands. 'We have no power to force anyone to do anything. We are not the coercive arm of governance.'

'How convenient for you.'

'That sounds sour, Sergeant – Captain. Ah, my apologies . . . Fist. Why be sour now that you have achieved that for which no doubt you always longed – a command of your own, yes?'

'I didn't ask for it.'

'Yet here you are.'

'Just doing my duty.'

'Oh yes – *that.*'

Seeing Storo's hands tighten into fists, Hurl hastily cut in, 'Where's Jalor, 'n' Rell, and Silk?'

'Out with a squad of Gujran's best on the south shore.'

'The Council was not informed of any sortie!' burst out Plengyllen, outraged.

'That's because I preferred it remain a secret.'

'How dare—'

'Are they ready?' Storo asked Captain Gujran.

'Ready, sir.'

'Raise it.'

Gujran drew his shortsword, held it high. A deep rumbling shook the stone arch. Behind them, the top of the gate ratcheted upwards. Hurl squinted to scour the ghostly shades of trees lining the shores. If the Seti youngbloods weren't out there now, they'd be there soon. Beneath her feet the first of the flotilla of rafts and boats nosed silently out carrying those refugees who had agitated to be allowed to flee the city. Hurl wished them Oponn's favour, but personally she considered their chances slim to nil.

'Ten to one says none make it through,' said Sunny from the dark.

'Shut the Abyss up!' grated Hurl. Noise brought her attention around. A sibilance such as that of many voices speaking, subdued. Movement atop the eastern walls. The populace of Heng gathering to watch. Damn the Lady! This was supposed to be secret – which meant they were probably selling Trake-damned tickets. How could any mass flight such as this have been kept secret?

'Any takers?'

'No one's going to take you up on that, Sunny!'

'Yeah, I'm in,' said Shaky.

'Me too,' said Gujran.

Hurl glared. 'How can you two . . .'

'Movement in the south,' said Storo.

Everyone looked. Hurl slitted her eyes till they hurt, straining to see beyond the silhouettes of the trees to where the hillsides rose into the distance. There, swift movement of lighter greys: Seti horsemen sweeping like clouds across the hills.

'They're using the old Pilgrim Bridge. The road to Kan,' said Magistrate Ehrlann. 'Why didn't you demolish that bridge?' he demanded of Storo. 'I told you to demolish it.'

Storo sighed. 'The Seti can ford the Idryn wherever they want. They don't need any Burn-blasted bridge.'

'So?'

'So, others are coming. Forces that may need the bridge.'

'Forces? What forces could you possibly mean?' demanded Magistrate Plengyllen.

'I don't know right now. We'll see who gets here first.'

'Oh come,' Plengyllen scoffed, 'how could you know *anyone* is coming?'

'Someone is.'

'But how could you know this?'

'*Because Toc and Laseen both know goddamned horses can't climb walls!*'

'They're gettin' away,' called Shaky, his voice rising to a near squeak.

Everyone turned to the river. Jammed with refugees and citizens convinced of Heng's immediate ruin in flame and slaughter, the convoy of small boats and rafts had poled and oared their way beyond bowshot of the city walls. Now, Hurl knew, came the most dangerous time. Now was when any ambush would be sprung. Out past any hope of intervention on the part of the city defenders. Everyone watched, silent, breath held, as the vessels disappeared into the dark. Don't bunch up, she urged. Stay apart. Quiet.

The night remained still. The stars shone bright and hard. Light's Path arched as a smear of paleness across the dark vault. Hurl allowed herself a small hope that perhaps, perhaps, some of the train would escape. Misguided fools though they may be. She stiffened at a hiss from Sunny. 'What is it?'

'Through the trees . . .'

Orange lights now blinked in the far distance under cover of the trees lining the river's edge, north and south. 'Shit . . .'

'Yeah. That's a shitter all right.'

Shortly, a single arrow trailing yellow flames arched high into the night sky. It fell into the river to be snuffed out but it had done its job. Hurl hugged herself, knowing what would follow. Despite her dread she was unable to look away as a storm of flaming arrows sped up into the sky only to descend, like a cloud of falling stars, straight down over the water. Most winked out yet some remained, slammed into wood, marking the helpless vessels for more. Hurl thought, or imagined, she could just make out the panicked cries of the women and children refugees – the fools! How could they imagine they'd be allowed passage? Better, from the Seti point of view, to keep everyone bottled up behind the walls. Down on the streets food was already short.

'Why do you do nothing?' Ehrlann demanded of Storo. 'You must do *something* . . .'

'There's nothing I can do,' Storo ground out, his voice rigid with control. 'I told them this would happen but they went anyway.'

'And that absolves you?'

Storo spun on the magistrate. '*I know it damn well does not!*'

Sunny stepped between the two men. He faced Storo but said to Ehrlann, 'Get out of here before I do what should be done to you.'

Ehrlann drew himself up straight, flicked his bhederin-hair switch across his shoulders. 'Very well. I will go. But know this, Captain, with this debacle this night you have lost all the confidence of the council. Know that. Plengyllen?'

The magistrates marched off down the bridge. Storo signalled Captain Gujran to him.

'Yes, sir?'

'Have your men out this night at key points. There'll probably be riots. Some may even try the gates.'

'Yes, sir.'

Saluting, the captain gestured to his detachment and marched off. Storo turned away only to face east and in the firelight playing across his features Hurl saw the pain of a man facing potential failure. A constant barrage of flame arrows now flew. The pitiful rafts and small boats burned brightly like some kind of grisly offerings as they bumped downstream with the lazy current. The glowing procession reminded Hurl of the Festival of Lights, when the citizenry of Cawn send their offerings in thanks and propitiation out upon the waters – fleets of candles and tiny lamps glimmering like stars in the night. And so to what God or Gods was *this* offering of blood and suffering? To Trake alone, she feared. And Hood of course. Always Hood.

Tossed rocks clattered from the arch and Hurl ducked. The

citizenry of Heng now yelled their outrage. Their curses and screams mingled into an unintelligible roar. The corpse of a dead dog flew through the night sky, struck the stone arch and fell spinning into the river. Stones and offal flew, but no vegetables, these, even rotten ones, being too valuable to toss. It looked to Hurl that none of the venom was directed out against the besieging Seti – all was directed at them atop the Outer River Gate.

* * *

Ho told himself it wasn't spying or probing or prying; he was just being considerate, bringing a small selection of a recent delivery of apples. A rare enough treat worthy of sharing. That's all. Nothing more. He walked the narrow winding slits that served as tunnels here in this, one of the most isolated and distant of the galleries. Ways so narrow at times even he, an emaciated Hengan, had to slide along sideways.

As he neared the hollowed out cave he'd been told the two had moved into, he heard voices and stopped. He was sure he didn't mean to eavesdrop. He told himself he'd stopped out of mere good manners, to clear his throat, or to call ahead that he was coming. But he heard talk and so he listened.

'Still nothing from them?' That was Treat, the tall one.

'I told you, nothing.'

'Not even Fingers?'

'No! Nothing! OK? There's nothing I can do.'

'But I thought you lot had it all worked out that the Brethren shouldn't give a damn about the Otataral.'

A loud exasperated sigh. 'That's right, Treat. We worked all that out. So who knows? Maybe there's another problem.'

'I say we just go. This is a waste of time. We're late now as it is. Say, maybe it's this pack of squirrelly mages. They'd be enough to keep *me* away.'

So not a mage. How was that arranged?

'These squirrelly mages are up to something. Something they think important.'

Could they know? Yath would surely kill them if he suspected.

'So what we'll do is . . .'

The blackened point of a wooden spear thrust itself at Ho who flinched back completely startled, dropping his basket.

Treat faced him. 'It's Ho.'

'Come on in, Ho,' called Grief.

241

After collecting the apples, Ho stepped forward, rounded a curve, and found himself in the men's quarters, stark as it might be. Grief sat on a ledge carved from the naked rock and strewn with rags, whittling with the smallest blade Ho had ever seen. Treat stood next to the entrance, spear still levelled. Ho slowly reached out to touch the point. 'Fire-hardened.'

One edge of Treat's mouth quirked up. 'Right you are. Took me forever to whittle the damned thing. Won't tell anyone, will you?'

Ho shared the smile. 'No, of course not.'

'What can we do for you, Ho?' asked Grief, not looking up from his whittling.

He held out the basket. 'Apples. A rare delivery care of the Malazans.'

'Our thanks.'

Treat reached forward, took the basket, all the while keeping the point of the spear level. Ho watched the weapon – the first he'd seen in, well, longer than he'd care to think about. It occurred to him that Yath and Sessin had no weapons. That he knew of, in any case. He wet his lips and thought about what to say while the spear remained motionless upon him.

'Yes?'

'On behalf of the community I ask again that you not attempt to escape. It will bring reprisals. They'll cut off all food deliveries. They've done it before.'

Grief stopped whittling, hung his hands. 'And I ask again, Ho . . . What are you mages up to here anyway? What's keeping you here?'

Ho wet his lips, found he could not hold Grief's gaze. He looked away. Grief sighed his disappointment. 'Tell you what, Ho. I'll make me an educated guess. How about that?' Without waiting for any reply he continued, 'You lot are investigating the Otataral, aren't you? Researching how it deadens magic. Maybe experimenting with it. You've taken this opportunity to organize a damned academy on how the stuff works and maybe even how to circumvent it. Am I far from the truth?'

Ho stared at Grief. *Definitely more than what he seemed.* The man was closer – and yet so much further – from the truth than he could possibly imagine. Better by far, though, for him and for them, that he suspect it was the Otataral they were investigating. And so Ho nodded. 'Something like that, yes.'

'OK. Now, since we're sharing our innermost secrets and such, I'll let you in on our secret. We can get out of here any time we wish. Believe me, we can. And we can arrange it so that all of you accompany us. What do you say to that?'

The fellow must be mad. The only way that could be managed would be by Warren, which was clearly impossible. Yet Ho studied the fellow's Napan-blue features, his open expectant look and quirked brow; clearly the fellow believed what he was saying. But for the life of him Ho could not see how it could be done. He shook his head. 'I'm sorry, but most of the inmates here would refuse to leave. The – research – is too important to be abandoned. Believe me, it is.'

Grief almost threw the short wand, or baton, he was whittling. 'Damn it to damned Fener! What is the matter with you people? Don't you want a chance to strike back against the Malazans?'

'Certainly there are many here who would jump at the chance for revenge – if they can win free of the contamination – which I am not sure is possible now that we have been eating and breathing the dust for so long.'

'In its raw unrefined form, yes . . .'

Ho waved that aside. 'I know the arguments. All academic, in any case.'

Grief appeared ready to say more then decided against it. He dismissed Ho. 'Thanks for the fruit. Think on the offer. It may be your only chance to get out of this place before you die.'

Ho bowed his head in acknowledgment, stepped away. Returning to the main tunnels, he tried to make sense of what he'd learned. Could these two really escape whenever they wished? Even get everyone out as they promised? Seemed utterly fantastic. Why would they do such a thing? Who were they to them? And that word he'd overheard, *Brethren.* He'd heard it before, he was sure. Somewhere and in some strange context. He'd have to think about it.

For the near future, though, he would have to work on keeping Yath and Sessin away. They mustn't suspect that these two had ideas that fell uncomfortably close to the truth of just what their community had discovered buried so far down within the Otataral-bearing formations.

*   *   *

Ghelel found the raft trip down the Idryn not nearly the ordeal she feared. In fact, it proved rather pleasant, what with the non-appearance of Molk. After the third day she relaxed into her role of pampered sightseer, served by her maid-in-waiting – only *one* servant? she'd chided Amaron – in a tent on her own river barge.

She spent the days watching the treed shore pass, the distant rolling hills of the Seti plain, grassed but dotted with copses of trees. Seti outriders escorted the convoy from the north shore, yelling and yipping as they thundered past. Among them swooped the fetishes and pennants of the various soldier societies: wolf, dog, plains lion and jackal.

It seemed to her that, as promised by Choss, the fleet moved with preternatural speed. A foaming wake actually curled from the bow of her barge. She had not spent much time around water, but even she knew that was unnatural. On the rafts around her Talian and allied soldiery talked and laughed. Fires burned in upturned shields and metal braziers to cook meals as the convoy did not once pull in to stop, even at night. Through the day soldiers, male and female, stripped down to linen tunics and loincloths and dived in, splashing and washing, and, hidden away on a few sheltered raft-sides, held on tight and made love in the warm water.

On the seventh day they reached the falls. The great legendary falls of the Idryn. Broke Earth Falls. Ghelel had never been to it before. Soldiers and boatmen manoeuvred her raft to the shore and a tent was raised. For the meantime she continued to play along with her role as figurehead of the 'Talian League'. She spent the day and night heavily guarded, but with a view of the falls and the equally amazing spectacle of the great convoy of rafts being unloaded, disassembled and carted down the trader road around the falls to be reassembled downstream. A masterpiece of logistical and administrative organization to which she supposed they owed Choss's decades of experience.

In the morning she was carried by palanquin down to her awaiting raft for the rest of the river trip, which she understood to be the matter of only a few more days.

The second evening on the river after that she was beginning to worry. She understood that they were supposed to leave the flotilla before they reached Heng; and Heng was close now. Very close. What had happened to this fellow Molk? Had he deserted? Part of her was glad to be rid of him. Another part was concerned; the man knew too much. When she entered her tent that night she found him sitting in her folding camp chair, his legs out before him.

'I'll thank you to ask permission to enter next time.'

'That would work against sneakin' about, m'Lady.' He leaned aside to spit but she jabbed a finger—

'No! Don't you dare!'

Mouth full, the man searched helplessly about. He picked up a crystal goblet and discharged a stream of dark red saliva that curled viscid in its depths. He set it back on to the table.

'Gods, man!' She picked up the goblet by the stem, opened the tent flap, and tossed it out into the dark.

He scratched his tangled black hair. 'Well, one way to clean the tableware, I suppose. Surprised you have any left.'

'What do you want?'

He fingered the white silk tablecloth. 'Thought you'd be pleased. Time to slip away.' He raised his arms to gesture about the tent. 'You *do* want to leave all this behind, don't you?'

'Well, yes. I do. Just not with you.'

He stood, sighing. 'Well, life's just one vile chore after another, isn't it? Least that's what *I* think.'

Ghelel eyed the rumpled greasy fellow. What was that supposed to mean? She looked him up and down again – he seemed dressed appropriately in his dirty quilted jacket, mud-spattered trousers and sandals. But what of her white dress? Not what Amaron had in mind, surely. She waved to her clothes. 'Do I go out as this?'

The man appeared ready to give one response but caught himself, swallowing and grimacing. 'No, m'Lady. Strip.'

'I'm sorry?'

'Strip down to your royal undies.'

She was still for a good few minutes, almost asked, *what for?* but managed to quell that – no sense giving the man any more openings. 'Where's Heroul?'

'She's keepin' watch.'

'I need her help.'

'Nope. What she don't know she can't tell.'

'Fine.' Ghelel took a knife from the table, reached behind to her back and slit the lacing. His face flat, Molk turned away to open one of the broad wood travelling chests.

'Looking for the silverware?'

Rummaging, he didn't answer. Ghelel stripped down to a silk shirt and shorts.

'Here we go!' Molk pulled a heavy canvas bag from deep within the chest.

'What's that?'

'Your gear. Armour, weapons 'n' suchlike.'

'I see. Won't that sink?'

Molk hefted the bag. 'Yeah. We'll have a moment or two.'

'We?'

He gave her a sideways, wall-eyed look. 'Can't you swim?'

'No.'

'Sweet Hood on his Bony Horse! I was told you were raised a regular tomboy 'n' such.'

'Well, had I known I'd be jumping off rafts I'd have corrected the deficit!'

Wincing, Molk raised a hand. 'OK, OK! Quiet, please, your ladyship. OK. I'll manage.'

'Fine.'

'Now, we just slip off the back, right? Think you can manage that?'

'I can't swim at all.'

Shoulders slumping even further in his slouch, Molk rolled his eyes to the tent ceiling. 'Gods. I'll find something for you to hold on to. OK?'

'If you don't want me to drown, you'll have to.'

'I'll find *something*,' he grumbled as he pulled the bag to the rear of the tent.

Spluttering, flailing, Ghelel attempted to contain the panic that had risen to clench her chest like the hand of a possessing demon the instant she let go of the barge. Never had she known such helplessness and fear. She gripped the broad upturned pot so tightly to her she was afraid she might shatter it. The wake of the barge sent her spinning; the dark shores bobbed in her vision in a sickening way. *Just hold on to this*, Molk had told her, *and the next raft will come to you. Grab hold!*

She almost laughed aloud thinking of the chance of her releasing one hand from the only thing keeping her alive. *Where was the man, Hood take him!* Taken straight to the bottom? Thinking of the bottom brought to mind images of the gigantic whiskered fish, chodren they're called, larger than any man, which the soldiers had been pulling from the Idryn. Ate anything that moved, she'd heard.

The panic was rising near to the point where she could call out for help any moment. She kicked frantically to try to turn around. Or was she already turned around? Who could tell amid the darkness, the splashing grey-green waves? Something loomed, large and, from her vantage up to her chin in the river, impossibly tall above her: the cut timbers of a raft as they emerged from the dark. *Come to her? It was about to plough over her!*

As the timbers neared, Ghelel threw up one hand to grab hold. She banged her head, her body and legs being sucked under. The object that had supported her across the gap of open river was pulled away and run over, tumbling – an upturned chamberpot. *Ha! Very funny, Molk.*

She held for a time, washed by the churning waves, gathered her strength. After this she managed to pull herself up then sat, trailed her legs in water that felt warm now that the cold night air brushed her. Eventually, her breathing returned to normal. Movement, and a dripping wet Molk sat next to her and pulled the bag on to his lap. 'Have a good dip, Captain?'

Ghelel blinked at the man. Captain? 'Oh, yes. *Thank you*, Molk.' Lower, she murmured, 'I was almost killed. And that's Captain Alil.'

'Alil? Very good, Captain.' He sliced the rope sealing the bag. 'Let's see what we've got here for you.'

The lack of personal space among the regulars was the first thing that struck Ghelel. That and the stink. Sitting on piled sacks, she was jammed shoulder to shoulder with Talian soldiery. One fellow even fell against her asleep until Molk straight-armed him down to the sodden logs; all much to the amusement of his squadmates. It was very confusing for Ghelel: these men and women were this fellow's friends yet they found it humorous when some stranger dumped him into the drink.

And the language! If she heard one more time how much some fellow was looking forward to catching some Hengan snatch she'd scream. The farting, belching and spitting were all rather much as well. Every time she almost threw herself to her feet to abandon the whole thing she'd catch Molk's watchful amused gaze and she'd subside: there was no way she'd give the man the satisfaction.

As it was she stayed awake the entire night and did not know what fed her tense muscles and the sharp sensory images from her surroundings: a soldier lighting a pipe from a lantern, a couple, a man and a woman, making out with only a plain camp blanket over their shoulders, a fight stopped by friends pulling the two men apart, the moon reflected bright silver from the rippling surface of the river. Was it excitement at doing what she'd always dreamed, or was it a plain and simple fear coming from the certainty that somewhere knives were being readied for her? She couldn't tell. In any case, she took some satisfaction from the knowledge that Molk also spent a sleepless night; every time she glanced to the man she'd found him watching the surroundings, his eyes scanning, watchful, glittering in the dark.

She pulled at the hauberk of overlapping metal scales over leather, not the best fit. Her sword though – her old one! How did they get hold of it? She almost pulled off the helmet but remembered Molk's comment: *the best place to carry that is on your damned head.*

247

The pre-dawn yellow and pink light gathered over the eastern horizon. It brought a strange optical illusion. A mountain rising all alone on the relatively flat plain. Ghelel squinted into the glow. She caught Molk's eye, gestured ahead. 'What's that?'

Again, that amused knowing look. 'Li Heng.'

'But that's impossible. Those walls must be enormous!'

Wincing, Molk glanced around. Ghelel followed his gaze; soldiers nearby glared. Evidently she'd stuck her foot in it. He sidled closer, lowered his voice. 'Yes. Strongest fortified city on the continent. Those walls have never been breached. Haven't you studied your histories?'

'*Yes!*'

'Well then, you know they were built to keep out more than just humans.'

Something in Ghelel shuddered. Of course! How could they possibly hope to succeed! Those walls were raised against the ancient enemy of the central plains, the rampaging demon – some said God – the man-jackal, brother of Treach, Ryllandaras, the man-eater. And they had never been overcome. Many say they would even have held against Kellanved's continent-sweeping armies. That is, without his dreaded undying T'lan Imass warriors. With their help Dancer assassinated the city's titular Goddess, the Protectress. *Assassinated.* Ghelel held Molk's gaze to let him know she understood his message. He nodded his slow acknowledgement.

Towards midday it was their raft's turn to unload. Ghelel grabbed for a handhold as it bumped up against its neighbours. Poles banged wood, soldiers cursed. The sun glared down with a heat and weight exhausting to her; it was never this hot on the coast. Downriver, the walls of Heng loomed like a distant layered plateau.

'How will we find the Sentries?' she asked Molk.

By way of answer Molk turned to a nearby soldier. 'The Marchland Sentries?' he asked.

'How the Abyss should I know?' the woman snorted.

Surprising Ghelel, Molk simply shrugged. He invited Ghelel to try. She crossed to the woman. 'The Sentries?' she asked loudly.

'I said—' the woman turned, her gaze flicked to the silver gorget at Ghelel's neck. She straightened. 'Sorry, sir. The quartermaster on shore, perhaps, sir.'

'Thank you, soldier.'

'Yes, sir.'

Molk gave Ghelel a small secretive nod. The gorget also worked wonders in getting them ashore. Ghelel merely stepped forward and everyone slipped from her path. Molk picked up a set of saddle-bags that at some time in the night he'd switched for the bag.

Ghelel decided that she might come to like being an officer. Amid the chaos of the rafts and barges being unloaded she merely had to catch a soldier's eye, ask, 'The quartermaster?' and be pointed on her way. By the time she neared the quartermaster's tent she found she was staring down everyone she met.

The tent possessed a floor of lain boards. Ghelel stamped the mud from the tall leather boots – the last item out of Molk's miraculous bag – and entered. Molk waited outside. Within, a man sat studying a slate in his hands amid piled crates and sacks that reached the tent's tall ceiling. Ghelel cleared her throat.

'Yes, sir?' the man replied without looking up.

Well. So much for the talisman of rank. 'The Marchland Sentries?'

'Never heard of them.'

'I didn't ask whether you'd heard of them – I asked to locate them.'

'Don't know where they are. Sorry, sir.'

'Well, then, pray tell who might?'

He looked up, blinked at her bleary-eyed, like a mole. 'Try the Day Officer, Captain Leen.'

'Thank you, soldier.'

The man returned his attention to the slate, scratched at it with a small nubbin of chalk. Ghelel sighed, counted to ten, then asked the damned question. 'And *where* might I find this Captain Leen?'

The man slowly looked up again and said in a carefully neutral tone, 'I would try the command tent . . . sir.'

Ghelel was clenching her jaws so tight she could not respond. With a fierce nod she turned and stamped from the tent. Outside she sucked in long deep breaths of the hot prairie air. 'Where,' she said aloud, 'is the command tent?'

'My guess would be that big one up on the hill,' Molk offered from behind.

'Thank you *so* much.'

'Here to serve, Captain.'

She started up the shallow rise of trampled brown grass.

'I'd say you're doing pretty good so far,' Molk said as they walked.

'Well, I haven't stabbed anyone yet.'

That got a laugh.

Guards at the wide entrance of opened flaps nodded Ghelel in. Molk waited outside. She was met by a young man at a table cluttered with reports who stood, bowing. 'Lieutenant Tahl, aide to Captain Leen. Sorry about the mess – we'll soon be moving to a new location closer to the city. May I be of service?'

'Yes. I'm looking for the Marchland Sentries. Where are they bivouacked?'

Tahl's brows rose and he quickly looked her up and down.

'Yes?'

'Ah! Sorry, it's just that I was unaware they were due . . . a replacement.'

'A replacement?'

'Yes. Well, something of a cock-up you being here. Wrong shore. You should've disembarked to the south.' And he opened his arms, shrugging.

'Silly me.'

He smiled stiffly, sat. 'Good luck, sir. You should find them in a village to the south.'

'Thank you.'

Walking back down the hill she let out a long hard sigh. 'What are they doing here anyway?'

'Special assignment,' Molk replied. 'They were sent in early. They're doing scouting and, ah, intelligence gathering.'

She caught her step but kept walking. 'Thought so.' *Amaron, the scheming rat!* 'Let me guess – they're working for Amaron.'

Molk rubbed the stubble on his chin. 'They're doing their job – guarding a frontier.'

She turned on Molk. 'Burn take it! Amaron's touch will make that the first place anyone will look for me, dammitall!'

He glanced around, motioned for her to lower her voice. 'No they won't. In the first place no one knows what I just told you. And secondly, as far as anyone knows you're still on that barge right now and will soon be disembarking into your wagon to be taken to the Seti camp.'

'Really? You've got someone playing me?'

'Of course! Gods, woman . . . honestly. Sometimes I wonder.'

'I'm new to all this.'

'That's for sure.'

She commandeered a small riverboat to take them across the river while a hundred yards downstream the broad royal barge wallowed in reed-choked shallows and the heavy wagon driven down to meet it looked to be sunk in the mud. On board the barge dozens of men pushed on poles while drovers cracked their whips over the pitiful lowing oxen. Molk sat at the bow of the punt, watching. 'Too bad we missed all the speeches,' he said.

Ghelel sat next to him, lowered her voice. 'This is stupid, me arriving at the unit the same day the barge arrives here at Heng. Shouldn't I have come ahead or something?'

Molk shrugged. 'Down south they've got no idea what's happening here. And I don't think they much care either.'

'Someone will piece it together.'

He sighed. 'They'll all piece something or other together – that's how they are in the unit. The important thing is that if they accept you, they'll defend you.'

She turned to study the man. 'What do you mean *if they accept me . . .?*'

'Don't worry. Just, ah, don't give any silly orders and you'll be fine.'

'I've never given an order in all my life!'

'Really? I find that difficult to believe.'

Ghelel let that pass. 'How am I supposed to know what's silly and what's not?'

He pulled a hand through his tangle of unruly black hair. 'Well, don't give any then.'

'None? But I'm supposed to command!'

The nose of the boat stuck into the mud of the shore. Molk jumped down. 'Our thanks,' he called to the fellow who'd paddled them across.

'Yes, thanks,' Ghelel called.

Throwing the saddle-bags across one shoulder, Molk immediately climbed the steep embankment. He pulled himself up by tree roots and handholds of brush. Ghelel followed. Past the screen of trees, she emerged once more on to the prairie of thick stiff grass. The sharp blades slashed at her mailed sleeves and leather greaves, hissed in the wind. Eastward, past the curve of the Idryn, the walls of Heng reared through a haze of smoke from the countless fires within. Ghelel took the opportunity to study the walls; they appeared to run in three ranks, the outermost the lowest, each rank increasing in height as one moved inward, so that even if one were to capture the outermost defences, one would still be subject to fire from further in. The gates too, she'd heard, ran in staggered openings around the circumferences of the various encircling walls – there was no straight run into the heart of the city. She was no student of siegecraft, but the prospect of investing this city seemed a chancy thing. What if they exhausted themselves taking Heng and had nothing left for Unta?

Couldn't they have simply ignored it? Let the Seti continue to isolate it? She had all these questions for Choss and Amaron after they'd gotten rid of her. How convenient for *them*. She hurried to catch up to Molk. 'Is this it?' she called.

He stopped. 'What?'

She waved hungry wasps from her face. 'Is this it? No escort or mounts or directions – just the two of us wandering across a blasted plain that goes on for thousands of leagues?'

The man made a show of turning full circle to peer in all directions. 'Seems so.' He started off again.

She threw her arms in the air. 'This is ridiculous!'

'Why?' he called back.

'Because . . .' She refused to move another step, watched him walk away. 'Because we'll get lost!'

He turned around, walking backwards. 'No, we won't. I know exactly where I'm headed.'

'Oh? Where's that?'

Molk pointed over his shoulder. 'That way.'

Ghelel glared about the open expanse of wind-swept grasslands – if only to find some sort of alternative, any at all. Completely alone, it seemed the only thing she could do was jog after the crazed fool whom Amaron, in his senile idiocy, had actually set to guard her.

'They say Burn sleeps beneath us,' Molk was saying while Ghelel had been thinking of her youth, the dinners at Sellath House in Quon. What she had then taken as such selfless generosity – raising her as a ward from some distantly related family – seemed poisoned by what she now knew. Damn these noble families and their ambitions; not only had they stolen her future, they'd twisted her past as well.

'Have you heard that?' Molk asked.

'Heard what?' she said absently.

'That Burn sleeps beneath us.'

'She sleeps beneath all of us,' she recited, bored.

'No, I mean right here, beneath the Seti Plains. That's the local legend.'

'No, I hadn't heard that. No doubt every tribe and community has similar myths. All of them equally true.'

Molk stopped short, gestured aside. 'If you don't mind, Captain, I'd like to have a moment in the brush there. Call of nature.'

'What? All of sudden you're all shy? What happened to the cursing, spitting lout I'd come to know? You're all just show after all, hey?' She crossed her arms, waiting.

Molk had ducked into the brush. Invisible, he answered: 'No female officer would allow that kind of behaviour from her servant. Don't you think?'

Ghelel threw her arms wide once more. 'Gods, man! Who in the Abyss is going to know! We're in the middle of an empty wasteland if you haven't noticed.'

Molk appeared, doing up the tie of his trousers. 'You know, that's a false assumption.'

'What is?'

He shouldered the bags. 'That the land of others is a wasteland. Just because they don't use the land in a way familiar to you doesn't make it useless or wasted.'

Ghelel started off. 'I don't know what in Hood's name you're talking about.'

'Obviously. For instance – this is prairie lion pasturage we're trespassing on right now.'

She laughed her scorn. 'How in the Abyss would you know that?'

'Didn't see the markers? I thought they were rather obvious. Anyway, it takes a lot more land to raise animals to support a family than it does tilled land. To a society such as ours based on tillage any open pasture's gonna look like wasteland. And I shouldn't say *open* either – that's misleading. Grazing rights are very carefully controlled and apportioned, you can be sure of that.'

Ghelel just rolled her eyes. 'Why are you going on about all this horseshit?'

Molk nodded. 'Good point. I just thought you might want to know a few things about the Seti riders who've been shadowing us since we left the river.'

Ghelel spun, scanned the shadow-swept hillsides. 'I don't see anything.'

'They're good at what they do.'

'Pardon me for saying this, but as I heard the soldiers say – you're shitting me.'

'Now who's the foul-mouthed lout?'

'I'd rather be a foul-mouthed lout than a gullible fool.'

'You said it.'

Though fuming, Ghelel walked on in silence. Perhaps she should just keep going south – walk away from all this. Clearly the only thing this fool could accomplish was get her killed. Didn't he realize this was serious? Still, at least no one was going to find her out here in the middle of nowhere! That was for certain. She stopped, drew off her scaled gauntlets, tucked them into her belt. 'Did you at least bring water?'

'Of course.' Kneeling, he rummaged in the bags, pulled out a waterskin.

'Thank you,' she allowed, grudgingly. She took a deep pull then gagged, spitting. 'Gods! What's this?'

'River water, laced with a distillation of juniper berries. Makes it healthy.'

'Distilled juniper berry? That's strong stuff.'

'I find it has a calming effect.'

She tossed the skin back. 'You can keep it. So, what happens tonight?'

Molk, who was drinking at the moment, gagged and spluttered out his own mouthful.

'Touch too much distillate?'

Coughing, he wiped his mouth. 'Ah, the Captain should be more careful with her language in the future, I think.'

She eyed the hunched, goggle-eyed hireling – what did Amaron possibly see in this fellow? 'I have no idea what you are talking about.'

'More's the pity – well, I've brought food, blankets. We'll bivouac under the stars this one night. That is, if we have any say in the matter . . .'

'Any say?'

He raised his chin to indicate behind her. 'Our friends – they've made up their minds about us.'

Ghelel spun. Five horsemen were lazily angling in upon them, single-file. Where in Hood's Paths had *they* come from? Grey and brown fur pennants dangled from their lances. Recurved bows stood tall at their backs. They rode on thin leather saddles, no more than blankets, with thin leather strap stirrups and reins.

'Wolf Soldiers,' Molk said.

'Like I give a damn.'

The Seti encircled them while one kneed his mount closer.

'Greetings, friend,' Molk called loudly in the Hengan dialect.

'Trespassers are no friends of ours,' answered the spokesman in kind – a young warrior, his kinky black hair tied in a multitude of tails, a leather jerkin painted in umber and yellow streaks and swirls, the dusting of a moustache at his lip.

'Trespassers?' Molk laughed. 'No, friend. We are Talian – allies.'

The youth frowned, considering. He pointed north. 'Last I saw, Heng was that way.'

Molk laughed again. 'Yes, yes. We're meeting our squadmates in a village south of here.'

'We've burned down all the villages. Killed all the men and . . .' he bared his teeth to Ghelel, 'raped all the women. There's no one alive to the south. That was the last of our fun. Now, we just ride in circles around Heng while they squat in their city. It's dull. Our only fun is riding down Hengans who flee the city.'

'Ah, well, we're Talians. We're wearing blue, as you see.'

The youth nodded. 'Oh yes, you wear blue. But it strikes me, there must be blue cloth in Heng.'

Ghelel had had enough of this adolescent baiting, 'Look here, you Hood-cursed—'

Molk clenched her arm. 'My employer wishes to remind you that your warlord is an ally of our commander, Choss.'

With a squeeze of his knees the warrior began backing his mount. 'The warlord, it seems to me,' he said, 'is very far away.' With a touch of the reins the mount turned aside and the five wheeled, galloping off.

Ghelel watched them go. Damned thugs! She faced Molk. 'Now what?'

He adjusted the saddlebags at his shoulder. 'Well, *seems to me*, they mean to have themselves some fun. Let's move.'

Twilight gathered while they jogged through the tall grass. A whoop or the thump of hooves from the dark announced their pursuers. Occasionally an arrow would slash the grasses next to her and Ghelel would clench her teeth, *Bastards*. Molk, jogging ahead of her, suddenly disappeared. At first she thought it a trick of the late afternoon light but after a few more steps it became clear that the man was gone. Had an arrow from the ingrate ambushing Seti taken him? She involuntarily slowed, wondering, should she throw herself down? Hide? But to what end? They'd just trample her. Walking, her next step kept descending and she found herself falling forward tumbling head over toes and she managed one yell before slamming down on to stone bottom-first. 'Ow!'

'How expressive.'

Wincing, she leaned aside to rub her buttocks. 'What in the Abyss?'

'Just my thought as well.'

'I'm sure. What's this?' She gestured to the flat shadowed road running low between twin rows of tall grasses.

Molk, his head cocked listening to the night, whispered, 'The Imperial road to Dal Hon. Thank the Malazan engineers for it.'

'Quon Talian, you mean,' Ghelel countered. 'The only thing *that* island produces is pirates – not engineers.'

'It produced the will to employ them.'

'Which?'

'Both.'

Sighing her irritation, Ghelel rearranged her armour and belts. 'Now what? On this road the Seti would run us down in an instant.'

'True. And that wouldn't be much fun.'

'No, it wouldn't!'

'I was talking about them.'

'I was talking about both of us.'

Molk grinned crookedly, winked. 'Now you've got the hang of it.' He raised his chin to the north-east, up the road. 'This way . . . there should be a hostelry close by, if memory serves.' He started off and Ghelel followed.

'The Seti said they burned everything down.'

'I'm willing to bet they didn't burn this one down.'

'Why?'

'Well, as the youth said, the warlord is far away . . . Anyway, you'll see.'

Twilight deepened, transforming the road into a slash of darkness. Ghelel thought she heard the movement of something large through the grasses parallel to the road. After a long hike a curve in the flagged way revealed the burnt remains of a building. It resolved into the piled stones of a foundation supporting standing blackened timbers. A field of knee-high weeds surrounded the sacked structure. Ghelel stopped short, set her hands to her belt. Molk stopped beside her. 'Oh,' he said, and scratched his chin.

She was about to loose upon the incompetent fool the full torrent of the day's frustration when a man straightened from beside the road. He was almost indistinguishable in the dark, wearing blackened studded leather armour. He held a cocked crossbow and a long curved sabre hung at his side. A wide black moustache completely hid his mouth. 'Who in cursed Fener's own entrails are you?' he demanded in the Talian dialect.

Molk nodded to the man. 'You're of the Sentries?'

'Who's askin'?'

Molk gestured to Ghelel. 'May I introduce Prevost Alil – a new officer.'

The man looked her up and down. 'Really?'

Ghelel opened her mouth to answer that but the man raised a hand for silence. 'Just a minute,' he said, and walked out on to the road. He faced the darkness, listening, then raised his chin. '*Cut it out!*'

A moment later a horse leapt through the grass and thumped to the road, snorting and stamping. Its rider, the same Seti youth, twisted the reins around one hand, grinning his delight at them as the animal pranced in circles.

'Toven,' the man greeted him.

'Just having some fun,' and he directed the wide grin to Ghelel.

The soldier waved him off. 'Yeah, well. Fun's over.'

Toven raised himself high on his mount and offered a bow. A kick and the mount reared and leapt up, pushing its way through the thick stands of grasses.

Grinning bastard. Ghelel watched the Sentry while he took the bolt from his crossbow and snapped the trigger. He swung the heavy weapon up on to his shoulder. 'And who're you?' he asked Molk.

Molk bowed. 'The Prevost's servant.'

'Oh-ho . . . So, you're the Lady's servant, are you? C'mon. This way.'

'And what is your name, soldier?' Ghelel demanded.

'Shepherd,' he said over his shoulder. 'Sergeant Shepherd.'

They walked a good way into the night, the sergeant content to be silent, Ghelel determined not to ask him a blasted thing, and Molk apparently enjoying the cool night air. Eventually, Ghelel smelled smoke from cookfires, caught snatches of wind-carried conversation. The glow of fires and lanterns brightened the night ahead. 'And just what are your numbers currently, sergeant?'

The man turned his head to eye her and Ghelel wondered if she'd made a mistake but worked to keep all such doubt from her face. She cocked a brow. He shrugged. 'Well, at a guess we number about five hundred now. About four hundred medium cavalry and a hundred mounted heavies.'

Ghelel shot a hard look to Molk who appeared oblivious, peering into the darkness, whistling softly to himself. The road opened up on both sides to trampled fields dotted by tents and horse corrals. Shepherd escorted them through two pickets. Ahead, lights blazed from the windows of a three-storey brick building fronting a square of outbuildings including a large stable. Soldiers, men and women, came and went, laughing and talking, many drinking from leather tankards. Across the front of the house was the legend 'House of Pleasant Welcome'.

Ghelel stopped short. 'A brothel? A Poliel-damned brothel?'

Molk coughed into his fist, head lowered. Shepherd winced as if only now becoming aware of the fact. 'Ah, yes, Ma'am – that is,

Prevost, sir. It's our temporary headquarters. The troopers are only allowed in off-duty.'

'I see. And is this where you're taking me?'

'Taking you to the Marquis, Prevost. He's inside.'

'Off duty, is he?'

Another coughing fit took Molk. Obviously happy to pass this one on to his superior officer, Sergeant Shepherd waved an 'after-you' to the door. Inside, Ghelel winced at the sudden light. The main floor was crowded with tables. Soldiers ate and drank, laughing. The heat brought a sudden sweat to her; it also brought a wave of drowsiness. Her knees suddenly felt weak. No one, it seemed, paid them the least attention. Shepherd led the way to a table next to an open window where a man sat smoking a pipe, talking to a seated female soldier. The man was older, heavyset with short grey hair. He wore a leather vest over a linen shirt. The woman was slim, her brown hair hacked short. The scar of a sword cut drew her lips down into a permanent frown. Sergeant Shepherd leaned close and spoke into the man's ear. He nodded and stood. The tables nearby quieted. The man eyed Ghelel expectantly. She stared back then suddenly remembered and snapped a salute. The man slowly answered the salute. 'Marquis Jhardin at your service, Prevost.' He indicated the woman, 'Prevost Razala. She commands the heavies.'

Ghelel bowed to the Marquis.

'I would offer you a room but I imagine you wouldn't want to stay here.'

'In that you are quite correct.'

'Sergeant, ready quarters for the Prevost. No doubt you would like to freshen up after your journey. Afterwards we could see to the briefing.'

'My thanks, Marquis.'

'Commander will do.'

Sergeant Shepherd saluted and hurried out. Jhardin came out from the table and invited Ghelel to follow him. Lieutenant Razala bowed, 'Welcome,' she said, her voice hoarse – perhaps from the wound.

All eyes now followed as the two made their way through the tables. Ghelel thought their gazes held reserve mixed with open contempt. Molk followed at a distance. On the steps she asked, 'You have been here for some time, Commander?'

He nodded, knocked the embers from his pipe. 'Yes. We were sent ahead by Choss.' He indicated a turn to a row of tents.

'And you knew I was coming?' He sent a questioning look. 'One hardly would put a sergeant on picket duty.' He smiled ruefully.

'Yes. Word was sent.'

Ghelel did not have to ask how. The Warrens. So. She eyed the fellow as he walked along, nodding to salutes from soldiers, salutes which she again belatedly remembered to acknowledge. It seemed to her that he was far too accepting, far too relaxed for an experienced commander who had just been saddled with a young, inexperienced, officer – and female to boot. He must know who she was; or had been directly ordered by Choss or Amaron to watch over her. In either case, she wasn't going to call him on it. Not yet.

Ahead, Sergeant Shepherd waited at a tent. 'Your quarters, Prevost.'

'Thank you.'

Jhardin indicated Molk. 'Send your man when you're ready.'

Ghelel nodded her agreement. Cursing herself, she belatedly saluted once more. The Marquis answered; an easy smile seemed to tell her that he did not set much by such formalities. She was startled as Molk opened the tent flap for her, then ducked within after. The long tent was divided into a general purpose room in front furnished with folding camp stools and a table set with an assortment of fruits, cheeses, bread and decanters of wine. The rear was her private sleeping chamber. Molk dropped the saddlebags and went straight to the table. 'I am famished.'

'Hood-damned nannies,' Ghelel said, keeping her voice low.

He turned, his mouth full of bread. 'What?'

'This fighting force. Babysitters. Choss or Amaron has turned them into nothing more than babysitters. They must hate me for it.'

'I think the word you're looking for is "bodyguard".'

'*Bodyguard?* Five hundred veteran men and women?'

Molk poured himself a glass of wine. 'Think of it as a measure of your importance to our commander.'

Ghelel took the glass from him, downed it in one gulp. 'It's a waste of fighting power. This force is needed at the siege.'

'Five hundred would make no difference in any siege, believe me.'

She glared but could resist the scent of the fresh food no longer and she turned to the cold meats. 'How much do they know?'

'Jhardin certainly knows a lot. Razala less.'

'How open should I be with them?'

'That's up to you.'

She sat heavily in a stool, stretched her legs out before her. It didn't strike her at all as odd when Molk knelt and pulled off her boots. She hadn't slept a wink the night before and had alternately walked and jogged all the day through. She'd never been so drained.

'I'm wrung out, Molk. I don't think I can face them tonight.'

'First thing in the morning then,' he said, standing. 'I'll let them know.'

* * *

Feeling the need for distraction from the monotony of the long voyage, Bars took a spot at a sweep. He pulled gently at first, testing the limits of his chest wound. The deep ones always healed the slowest. As he pulled he was barely aware of the awed, even frightened, glances his fellow oarsmen cast his way. He was busy trying to avoid thinking of what was to come. But their return, their *eventual* return, made that impossible. *Failure.* How it galled him – it burned in his chest even worse than the wound. Even more humiliating, he must deliver news of the probable annihilation of the 4th Company of the Guard. And worst of all, he was worried: would further men then be sent to investigate that end? Cal's last instructions argued flat against that. And Bars agreed. The Guard had lost enough resources to that unforgiving Abyss in Assail. Corlo appeared at his side, tapped him on the shoulder. 'Jemain wants you.'

Grunting, Bars relinquished the oar. 'Keep pulling, men,' he said, trying out his South Genabackan Confederacy vocabulary, 'we'll get out of this eventually,'

'Aye, Captain.'

On the way aft Corlo leaned close. 'How's the chest?'

'Hurts like Hood's own pincers. It always hurts just as much, don't it.'

'You're only spared the dying part.'

'Not even that.' Bars watched as Corlo's round face pulled down. 'Don't worry, we'll get there.'

Corlo gave his wry assent.

Jemain waited at the stern, peering into the dense fog that had enveloped the ship more than a week ago. 'You'll go blind if you keep that up,' Bars called to him.

'Shhh,' he hissed. 'Please.'

'What is it?'

'Something's out there.'

'Un-huh . . .'

'Yes. I think so. Someone becalmed. Just like us. But shadowing us.'

'Really? Corlo?'

'I've quested. *Someone.* Can't do any better than that.'

260

'Un-huh. So? What can we do about it? Maybe they just hope we know where we're going.'

Jemain's face glistened, sweaty and pale; he was clearly unhappy with what he was about to suggest. 'We should stop oars, listen. Perhaps we'll lose them.'

'Or not.'

Jemain shrugged his agreement.

'What's our position?'

'North. Far north of where we want to be.'

Bars turned to Corlo. 'Anything from the Brethren?'

'Whispers. They are, ah, agitated. Hints of movement. Continued movement.'

'Hunh. Very well, Jemain. Orders by word of mouth only. Corlo, you and Lamb take the bow. I'll hold the stern. Stop oars. Arm everyone willing.'

'Aye, Captain.'

Soon, the oars stilled, slid gently into their ports. Bars pulled on the largest set of leather armour available. With hand signals he dispersed his eight remaining regular Guardsmen. He signalled for missile fire first. The men readied what bows and crossbows they'd dug up from the holds and neglected innards of the trader scow. Sailors and oarsmen took the deck as well, indifferently armed.

Jemain followed Bars to the port side; both squinted into the thick creamy curtains of fog. 'Where do you think we are?' Bars whispered.

'Perhaps near the middle of Menigal Waters.'

'Hmph. Reacher's Ocean, maybe.'

Jemain pointed. 'There.'

Bars strained to see, then he caught it – movement. A low dark shape slowly closing on them, coming in at an angle. A single row of sweeps, open-decked. A war-galley, lateen-rigged, the sail reefed now in the dead air. Bars searched the waters at the bow for any hint of a ram but saw no wake or frothing. Strange that, usually a war-galley would have a ram. Shields lined the sides of the vessel. He raised his arm to signal firing the first volley. Oddly, however, no similar volley flew up to meet them now that they could see each other.

Then Jemain lurched back from the side as if struck by an arrow. He snatched Bars' raised arm. Bars searched the man's stricken face, '*What is it?*'

'Don't fire,' he managed, his voice strangled. 'Please. No firing.'

Scanning the decks of the war-galley, Bars could see no movement – he relented. 'Very well.' He signalled a switch to hand-to-hand weaponry. 'Why?'

The Genabackan first mate appeared terrified beyond words. He could only point. 'The shields – don't you *see* . . . ?'

'Gods, what is it, man?' What Bars saw now was what he had taken for shields appeared to be that, but oddly shaped, each painted to resemble a mask. The first mate was no longer listening; he glared about as if seeking escape. The man actually appeared to be considering jumping overboard. Bars grabbed a handful of his ratty sailor's jerkin, bodily lifted him by his front and shook him. '*Who is this?*'

'There are legends but no one's ever actually *seen* . . .'

'Who? Hood curse you . . .'

'It's a *Seguleh* vessel,' he gasped.

Bars dropped him. 'The Seguleh? Who in Togg's tits are they?'

'You don't know?'

'No.' To his men Bars signalled a stand-by. 'Tell me.'

'You must order your men to drop their weapons. Quickly. All weapons. Please.'

Bars stared at the man. 'Really?'

'Yes. Allow me to speak to the crew.'

Feeling almost like laughing, Bars waved for Jemain to go ahead. Meanwhile, the vessel was taking its time manoeuvring to come aside as if this were a rendezvous arranged long ago. Slim straight figures stood motionless, calm and silent. They *were* behaving as if they fully expected to simply come aboard, Bars reflected. Like they were conducting some kind of damned harbour inspection or something.

Jemain called down to the deck where the sailors watched, their faces tense. 'It *is* a Seguleh vessel! Yes, that's right! Drop your weapons and you won't be hurt.'

To Bars' amazement, as one, the sailors and even the freed slaves and oarsmen complied. Jemain dropped his own small sailor's knife. Bars caught Corlo watching from the bow. He raised his shoulders in a question. The mage cocked his head, thinking, then signed agreement.

Bars sighed his utter disbelief. Gods! The things they have to go through to make it back to Stratem. 'OK, lads. Drop them – but keep 'em close. Just in case.' He watched while reluctantly, one by one, his men set down their weapons. All but one who stared back, defiant. The vessel bumped up against theirs. Tossed grapnels took hold at the rail. A few trailed rope ladders. 'Dammit, Tillin! I ordered you to drop them!'

'What's come over you, Bars? I'm not gonna just surrender—'

'Damn you to Hood! I didn't order anyone to *surrender*! I just ordered you to drop your weapons. Now!'

His face dark with fury, Tillin threw his sword to the deck.

'And the other,' called Bars. 'The sticker.'

Tillin pulled a long-knife from the rear of his belt, threw it down.

A rope ladder jerked, straining. Bars took hold of the railing; he had to admit he was damned curious to see who it was that put the fear of Night into these Genabackans. A masked face appeared at the side. Jup grunted his surprise. Well, what d'you know. Just like the shields promised. Then in one swift fluid motion the man was on deck, erect, hands at a broad waist sash where two swords hung, thrust through. Bars grunted again: *damned fast these fellows, whoever they were.* Seven more joined the man, all medium-height, whip-lean in light leather armour and cloth trousers, and, surprisingly, barefoot. All wore intricately painted masks.

The appearance of each of the masked fellows drew a whimper from Jemain. Finally, with the last, he clenched the shoulder of Bars' leather hauberk as if to keep from fainting. 'There's eight of them! *Eight!*'

'I can count,' Bars grumbled. He motioned to the deck of the galley. 'There's still more on the ship.'

The sailors remained motionless, allowing the intruders to wander at will; the Guardsmen took their cue from that. The Seguleh walked about the deck, opening casks, poking into piled equipment. 'What's going on . . .' Bars asked of Jemain.

'I'm not sure. I think—'

A blur of motion, one foot thumping the deck, then a man falling. Bars ran to the mid-deck, pushed aside sailors. There lay Tillin, face up. Bars knelt, felt for a pulse. The man was dead. Bars faced the nearest Seguleh, 'What's the meaning of this!'

'He was armed,' another Seguleh called from across the deck in the dialect of the South Confederacies. The one facing Bars slowly turned his back – pointedly, Bars thought – and walked away.

Bars blinked his surprise. Jemain, who had also come, turned the body over. A sheathed long-knife remained tucked at his belt. He snorted. He'd forgotten Tillin always carried two. He looked up, but the Seguleh who'd spoken had moved. 'Where'd he go?'

'I'm not sure I can find him,' Jemain said.

'Just ask!'

Jemain's laugh sounded a touch crazed. 'No. You don't understand. The one who spoke is the only one who will. He's actually *forced* to speak to us because he's the lowest ranked here. It is shameful for him to have to.'

'Well, find him!'

Jemain raised his hands helplessly. 'I'll try, but I can't read their masks.'

Read their masks? What was the man on about? Bars scanned the deck. Six. Two had gone below. Hood take them – *what had he just done to his men?* Lamb, he saw, had not moved from where he'd dropped his swords. Bars gave him a *wait*. Lamb responded with '*extreme impatience*'. Bars caught Corlo's eye, nodded. Corlo edged his hands up to his shirt-front, took a deep breath, then froze. A gleaming sword-blade had appeared at his neck.

'Who speaks for this vessel?' called out the Seguleh who'd spoken before.

Bars pushed his way forward. 'I do.'

'You have a mage among you. Either he refrains from his arts or he will be slain. Is this clear?'

'Yeah – That is, yes, that's clear.' Bars closed upon the spokesman until he stood face to face, or mask. He studied the mask in a furious effort to memorize the identity. For now he understood Jemain's comment: everything was there on the mask for all to see – provided you could understand the signs. Dark vermillion curls, he noted, low on the cheeks.

The spokesman turned away to face other Seguleh. Some subtle signs or body language was exchanged between them – neither said a word. The spokesman returned his attention to Bars. 'We require your stores of food and drinkable water,' he said in his curious high voice. 'You will provide the labour to move the requisite cargo. Further, our oarsmen are tired. We will take the strongest among you to replace them.'

Bars just stared at the mask, the dark-brown eyes almost hidden within. '*You'll do what?*'

The mask tilted fractionally to one side. 'Our instructions are not clear? Perhaps we should speak to another? One capable of understanding?'

Jemain appeared at Bars' side. 'Yes, honoured sir. We understand. We will comply.' With an effort, he pulled a disbelieving Bars aside. 'We have no choice now,' he whispered. 'At least they'll let us live.'

'To die!' Bars snarled, glaring, but he needn't have made the effort. The spokesman now ignored him as thoroughly as if he'd disappeared. Furious, Bars snapped a hand around Jemain's throat. 'I got my men into this and I will get them *out*! Give me an option, anything . . . *something.*'

The first mate pulled at Bars' fingers, his eyes bulging. 'There is only one thing,' he gasped, 'but it will just get you killed!'

Bars released him. 'What? Name it.'

Falling to his knees, Jemain panted to regain his breath. 'Challenge the spokesman.'

Bars grunted his understanding; something had told him it would come down to that. 'How?'

'Pick up a weapon – but you must keep your eyes on the spokesman! Do not look at anyone else. *He* is the one you are challenging.'

'Right.' Bars cast about the deck for the nearest weapon, found a straight Free City sword and a sturdy sailor's dirk. These he picked up, then, keeping his head down, turned to the Seguleh spokesman. Everyone, he noted from the edges of his vision, had gone quite still. One Seguleh happened to stand in the way. As Bars approached this one drew a weapon, touched it to Bars' chest. Head resolutely held down, Bars paused, then pushed on. He watched the blade's keen edge slice a gash in his leather hauberk as he edged past. Moving with deliberate care, he approached the spokesman and stopped before the man, who had gone immobile. He raised his gaze, travelling up the leather hauberk, the neckscarf, to his mask and the eyes behind. The instant their gazes met the mask inclined minutely – acceptance?

As quick as a hunting cat the man stepped back, his bare foot lightly touching the deck, and hurtled forward attacking. Bars immediately gave ground parrying frantically. The attacks came so swift and unrelenting there was no time to think, no time to plan. He retreated fully half the length of the vessel before he succeeded in wrenching a fraction of a second for a counter-attack to find his own footing and forestall the man's advance. He was appalled; no one had ever done such a thing to him before.

But his relief did not last long. Parrying an elegant series of ripostes overextended him and he saw it even as it came: a thrust high in the thigh. He twisted just in time for the blade to fail its flensing withdrawal. An unfamiliar chill of cold dread took Bars, something he thought Assail had squeezed entirely out of him. This man was not simply trying for a kill – he was choosing his targets! That had been a precise attempt at the femoral artery. If he did not do something right away he would be cut to pieces. All he could think of was his friend Jup's laughter – Iron Bars, finally beaten by some masked jackass!

Less than six of his heartbeats had passed.

Yet while the attacks came as swiftly as Blues'– the Guard's preeminent finesse swordsman – they lacked power. More like surgical touches than blows. Having gathered himself – and he suspected few ever remained alive long enough to do so – he leaned in using all his fury to counter-attack with full strength. Batting aside one blade he surprised the man and got inside to rake the dirk across the forearm. The man's other blade sliced his face in a disengaging move but Bars bore on regardless, backhanding the dirk to the hilt through the man's light leather armour just above the heart. The power of the thrust threw the Seguleh backwards off his feet but even as he fell he flicked his other blade up to kiss Bars' neck. It sawed deep under his chin. Bars lurched away, bellowing his pain.

He fell to his knees, wet warmth pulsed between his fingers. A hand clasped tightly over his. 'Let me see. Let me see.' Corlo. Bars relaxed. A cloth wrapped his neck. 'OK,' Corlo said. 'It's OK. You'll live.'

Panting, Bars choked, could not speak.

Corlo took his arm and he straightened, weaving. He saw Jemain staring at him, incredulous. He waved him close. He tried to speak, failed. He glanced down to see how his front glistened in a red wash. 'Now what?' he croaked to Jemain.

Swallowing, the first mate remained motionless. 'They said it could never be done . . .' he breathed, awed.

'It almost wasn't,' Bars said, speaking as softly as he could.

Jemain motioned to another Seguleh who was now bent over the dead spokesman. *Hood on his dead horse. Not another one! Do I have to duel every last blasted one?*

This Seguleh straightened, faced Bars. 'What is your name that we may enter it among the Agatii.'

'The *Agatii*?'

'The Thousand,' the Seguleh said.

Bars could only stare. There's a *thousand* of these swordsmen? 'Bars. Iron Bars, Fourth Company, Second Blade, Avowed of the Crimson Guard.'

All remaining Seguleh turned to stare. Bars returned the glances then remembered Jemain's warning and looked away. The one Seguleh who had kept the most apart from everyone, standing far at the bow, walked back to face him. His mask was far less decorated than the others, marked by just a few lines. But of course Bars could not make any sense of its design. Then he again recalled Jemain's words and he quickly pulled his gaze from the man's face. 'Word of you Avowed have reached us,' this one said. 'Why did you not identify yourself before?'

Bars shrugged. 'I saw no reason to.'

The Seguleh seemed to understand such reasoning. 'You are a stranger to our ways, so I will be plain. I challenge you.'

'*Don't accept!*' Jemain blurted.

Bars gently touched the wet dressing at his neck, wiped his forearm across his mouth to come away with a slick of drying blood from the gash down his face. The pain of his pierced leg was a roar in his ears. It twitched, hardly able to support him. 'I, ah, respectfully decline,' he murmured, his voice a gurgle.

The Seguleh inclined his mask fractionally. 'Another time, then.' He glanced to his men and as one they moved to the ship's side. 'We go now.'

Bars stared again. *Gods, these people. They were constantly wrong-footing him.* 'Wait. Where are you going? What're you doing out here? Twin's Turning, man. Why're you even talking to me now?'

As the others carried the dead spokesman to the side, their leader, so Bars assumed, faced him again. 'You have standing now. I am named Oru. I am now your, how is it . . . *Yovenai* . . .'

'Patron, or commander – something like teacher, too,' Jemain supplied.

Oru did not dispute Jemain's translation.

Bars gestured to the dead Seguleh. 'And his name?'

'Leal. Her name was Leal.'

'Her? *Her!*'

'Yes.'

Gods Below. He'd no idea. But he would remember her name; he'd rarely come so close to being overborne. Oru had jumped down lithely to the galley. Bars leaned over the side. Holding his neck he croaked, 'What are you doing out here? Why are you just going like this?'

'You are of the Agatii. You have your mission. We have ours. We search for something . . . something that was stolen from us long ago.'

'Well . . . may the Gods go with you.'

'Not with us,' Oru replied flatly.

Crewmen pushed off with poles. As the oars were readied, Bars did a quick head-count and came up with fifteen. *Burn's Mercy, fifteen of them.* Then the fog swallowed the vessel leaving only the echoes of wood banging wood and the splash of water.

Turning from the side Bars found Jemain studying him once more. 'What?'

'I would never have believed it.'

'Yeah. Well, the Lady favoured me.'

'The Seguleh don't believe in luck.'

'There you go. Now, let's get to rowing. You give the orders, first mate. I can hardly speak.'

'Aye, Captain. And Captain . . . ?'

'Yes?'

'I tried to get a good look at Oru's mask. If I'm right, he's ranked among the top twenty.'

* * *

On the second day of their flight from the fallen Border Fort, Rillish awoke to find five Wickan children staring down at him with the runny noses and direct unfiltered curiosity of youths. Rillish sat up on his elbows and stared back. The children did not blink.

'Yes? Are you going to help me up, or not?' The gruelling demands of their escape had worsened Rillish's leg wound. Yesterday soldiers took turns carrying him. His dressings stank and were stained yellow-green.

'No,' said the eldest, their guide, a girl who might just be into puberty.

'No?' Rillish gave a thoughtful frown. 'Then you're planning to put me out of my misery they way you do your wounded.'

The girl's disdain was total. 'A townsman lie. We do no such thing.'

'No,' Rillish echoed. It occurred to him that he was now being studied by what passed for the ruling council of the band of youths he'd rescued – the five eldest. 'May I ask your name?'

'Mane,' said the girl. A sheathed, antler-handled long-knife stood tall from the rope of woven horsehair that served as the belt holding the girl's rags together – all of which amounted to nothing more than a frayed blanket pulled over her head. The blade would have been laughable had the girl's face not carried the tempered edge to match it. It also occurred to Rillish that he knew that blade.

'Then may I ask the purpose of this council meeting?'

'This is not one of your townsman *council meetings*,' the girl sneered. 'This is a command meeting. I command.'

'You command? No, I think I—'

'Think as you like. Here on the plains if you wish to live you'll do as *I* say . . .'

'Mane, I command the soldiers who guard you and who rescued you and your—'

'Rescued *us*?' the girl barked. 'No, Malazan. From where I stand *we* rescued *you* . . .'

It occurred to Rillish that he was arguing with a ten-year-old girl; and that the girl was right. He glanced up to study the shading branches of their copse of trees. 'Very well. So, I will do you the courtesy of assuming all this is leading somewhere . . .'

'Good. He said you would.'

'Who?'

A grimace of self-castigation. 'Never mind. The point is that we've decided you will ride in a travois from now on.'

'A travois. How kind of you.'

'It's not kindness. You're slowing us down.'

I see. The party already burdened by one – a young boy, no more than a toddler, wrapped in blankets and doted on by the children. 'I'll get my men—'

'Your men will not pull it. They are needed to fight. Three of our strongest boys will pull it.'

'Now wait a minute—'

Mane waved him silent. 'It has been decided.' She and the four youths abruptly walked off.

Well. He'd just been dismissed by a gang of brats. 'Sergeant Chord!'

A touch at his shoulder woke him to a golden afternoon light. Sergeant Chord was there jog-trotting beside the travois. The tall grass shushed as it parted to either side and Rillish had the dislocating impression of being drawn through shallow water. 'Lieutenant, sir?'

'Yes, Sergeant?'

'Trouble ahead, sir. Small band of armed settlers. The scouts say we have to take them. Strong chance they'll spot us.'

For some reason Rillish found it difficult to speak. 'Scouts, Sergeant?'

A blush. 'Ah, the lads and lasses, sir.'

Their movement slowed, halted. Sergeant Chord crouched low. Rillish squinted at him, trying to focus; there was something wrong with his vision. 'Very well, Sergeant. Surround the party, a volley, then move in. None must escape.'

'Yes, sir. That's just what she ordered as well.'

'She, Sergeant?'

Another blush. 'Mane, sir.'

'Isn't that your knife at her belt?'

'It is, sir.'

'Doesn't that have some kind of significance here among the Wickans?'

His sergeant was looking away, distracted. 'Ah, yes, it does, sir. Didn't know at the time. Have to go now, sir.'

'Very well, Sergeant,' but the man was already gone. He felt a vague sort of annoyance but already wasn't certain why. Behind him, the other travois sat disguised in the tall grass, its band of carriers kneeling all around it, anxious. Rillish had the distinct impression the older youths, boys and girls, were *guarding* the travois. While he watched, youths appeared as if by magic from the grass, talked with the toddler on the travois, then sped away. It appeared as if they were relaying information and receiving orders from the child. He chuckled at the image. The hand of one of his youthful carriers rocked his shoulder. 'Quiet, Malazan,' the boy said.

Quiet! How dare he! Rillish struggled to sit up; he would show him the proper use of respect. A lance of lightning shot up his leg. The pain blackened his vision to tunnels, roared in his ears like a landslide, and he felt nothing more.

'Lieutenant, sir? Lieutenant!'

Someone was calling him. He was on board a troop transport north-east of Fist in a rainstorm. Giant swells rocked the awkward tub. He felt like a flea holding on to a rabid dog. The captain was yelling, pointing starboard. Out of the dark sped a long Mare war-galley, black-hulled, riding down upon them like Hood's own wrath. Its ram shot a curl of spray taller than the sleek galley's own freeboard.

'Hard starboard!' the captain roared.

Rillish scanned the deck jammed full of standing Malazan regulars – reinforcements on the way to the stranded 6th. He spotted a sergeant bellowing at his men to form ranks. 'Ready crossbows!' he shouted down.

'Aye, sir!' the sergeant called.

Before he could turn back, the Mare war-galley struck. The stern-castle deck punched up to smack the breath from him. Men screamed, wood tore with a crunching slow grinding. A split mast struck the deck.

Entangled beneath fallen rigging, Rillish simply bellowed, 'Fire! Fire at will!'

'Aye, sir!' came the answering yell. Rillish imagined the punishment of rank after rank of Malazan crossbowmen firing down into the low open galley. He hacked his way free, one eye blinded by blood streaming from a head cut. 'Where's the cadre mage, damn her!'

'Dead, sir,' someone called from the dark.

The deck canted to larboard as a swell lifted the two vessels. With an anguished grinding of wood they parted. The ram emerged, gashed and raining pulverized timbers. The war-galley back-oared. Hood take this Mare blockade! The only allies of the Korelri worth a damn. He wondered if one out of any five Malazan ships made it through. The vessel disappeared into the dark, satisfied it had accomplished its mission; Rillish was inclined to agree. The transport refused to right itself, riding the swells and troughs like a dead thing. He picked his way through the ruins of the stern-castle, found the sergeant. 'What do you think?' he asked.

The sergeant grimaced, spat. 'I'm thinking the water's damned cold.'

'I agree. Have the men drop their gear. We'll have to swim for shore or hope another of the convoy is nearby.'

'Aye aye, sir.'

'Lieutenant? Sir?'

Rillish opened his eyes. It was night. The stars were out, but they were behaving oddly, they had tails that swept behind them whenever he looked about. Sergeant Chord was peering down at him. He felt hot, slick with sweat. He tried to speak but couldn't part his lips.

'You've taken a fever, sir. Infection.'

Rillish tore his lips apart. 'I was thinking of the day we met, Chord.'

'That so, sir? A bad day, that one. Lost a lot of good men and women.'

A young Wickan boy appeared alongside Chord. Mane was there as well. 'This lad,' Chord said, 'is a Talent – touched with Denul, so Mane says. He's gonna have a look.' The boy ducked his head shyly.

Just a child! 'No.'

'No, sir?'

'No. Too young. No training. Dangerous.'

Chord and Mane exchanged looks; Chord gave a told-you-so shrug.

'It's been ordered,' Mane said.

'Who?'

Mane glanced to the other travois, bit her lip. 'Ordered. That's all. We're going ahead.'

'No, I—'

Chord took hold of him. Other hands grasped his shoulders, arms and legs. Folded leather was forced into his mouth. Rillish strained, fighting, panted and yelled through the bit. The youth touched his leg and closed his eyes. Darkness took him.

He awoke alone in a grass-bordered clearing under the stars exactly like the one he'd last seen. In fact, so similar was it all that Rillish suspected that perhaps Chord and the others had simply decided it most expedient to abandon him. He found he could raise his head. He saw the youth sitting cross-legged opposite a dead campfire, head bowed. 'Hello?'

'Don't bother yourself, outlander,' growled a low voice from the grasses. 'He won't answer.'

Rillish scanned the wall of rippling brown blades. 'Who's there?'

Harsh laughter all around. 'Not for you, *outlander*. You shouldn't wander lost, you know. Even here.'

He felt at his sides for a blade, found none. Harsh panted laughter again. 'What's going on?'

'We're deciding . . .'

Shapes swept past the wall of grass – long and lithe. 'Deciding . . . what?'

'How to kill you.'

The shapes froze; all hints of movement stopped. Even the air seemed to still. Something shook the ground of the clearing, huge and rippling slow. Rillish was reminded of the times he'd felt the ground shake. Burn's Pain, some called it.

'*Enough* . . .'

The shapes fled.

A presence entered the clearing – at least that was all Rillish's senses could discern. He could not directly see it; his eyes seemed incapable of processing what they saw. A moving blind spot was all he could make out. The rich scent of fresh-turned earth enveloped him, warm and moist. He was reminded of his youth helping the labourers on his family orchards. The presence went to the boy, seemed to envelop him.

'*Such innocence.*' The aching desolation within the voice wrenched Rillish, brought tears to his eyes. '*Must it be punished?*' The entity turned its attention upon him and Rillish found he had to look away. He could not face this thing; it was too much.

'Rillish Jal Keth,' the thing spoke, and the profound weight of a grief behind the voice was heartbreaking. 'In these young times my ways are named old and harsh, I know. But even yet they hold efficacy. Guidance was requested and guidance shall be given. My children needs must now take a step into that other world from which you come. I ask that you help guide that step.'

'You . . . *ask*?'

'Subservience and obedience can be coerced. Understanding and acceptance cannot.'

Rillish struggled to find his voice. 'I understand – that is, I don't understand. I—'

'It is not expected that you do so. All that is expected is that you strive to do so.'

'But how will I know—'

The presence withdrew. '*Enough* . . .'

Rillish awoke to a slanting late afternoon light. The female soldier who had helped him escape the fort was holding a cool wet cloth to his face as she walked along beside the travois. He gave her a smile that she returned, then she jogged off. *Wait*, he tried to call, *what's your name?* Shortly afterwards Sergeant Chord appeared at his side. 'Sergeant,' he managed to whisper.

'Yes, sir.'

'The boy. Where's the boy?'

Chord held a rigid grin of encouragement. 'Never you mind anything. You just rest now, sir.'

'*Sergeant!*' But he was gone.

The next morning Rillish could sit up. He asked for water and food. The most difficult thing to endure was his own smell; he'd shat himself in the night. He asked for Sergeant Chord and waited. It seemed the sergeant was reluctant to come. Eventually, he appeared. Rillish now saw that the man had a good start on a beard and his surcoat of grey was tattered and dirt-smeared. He appeared to be sporting a few new cuts and gashes as well. Rillish imagined he must look worse, he certainly smelled far worse. 'I need to get cleaned up. Is there water enough for that?'

The sergeant seemed relieved. 'Yes, sir.'

Mane came walking up; she now wore settler's gear of soft leather armour over an oversized tunic, trousers and even boots.

'The boy?' Rillish demanded. 'The healer?'

Sergeant Chord lips clenched and he looked away, squinting.

'Dead,' Mane said with her habitual glower. 'He died saving you. Though why I do not know, you being a cursed Malazan. That's a lot of Wickan blood spilled saving you . . .'

'That's enough,' Chord murmured.

Rillish let his gaze fall. She was right, and had a right to her anger. But he had not asked to be healed. He looked up. 'You said something. Something about orders. What did you mean?'

Mane bared her teeth in defiance. 'Not for you, Malazan.'

Her answer chilled Rillish.

He found he could walk part of the next day. The boys with his travois followed along with the other at the centre of their ragged column of some seventy children – a good third of whom were always out ranging far beyond the column at any given time – and the thirty regulars who walked in a van, a rearguard and side-pickets. The more Rillish studied the other travois and the twelve youths who constantly surrounded it, the more he saw it as the true heart of their band. Who was this child to inspire such devotion? The self-styled guards interposed themselves whenever he tried to approach. The youth ignored him, wrapped in horse blankets, his eyes shut most of the time. The scion of some important chieftain's family, Rillish had come to suppose.

Walking just behind the van, he paused to draw off his helmet and wipe his face. Damn this heat! The sun seemed to glare from every blade of grass. Insects hummed around him, flew at his eyes. He was a mass of welts, his lips were cracked and sunburnt and his shit had the consistency of soup. From a satchel he pulled out a balled cloth, unfolded it and eyed the dark matter within. Food, was it? It looked more like dried bhederin shit to him. He tried to tear a bite from an edge and after gnawing for a time managed to pull away a sliver. He waved Sergeant Chord to him.

Sweat stained the flapping remains of the sergeant's grey surcoat. Two crow feathers fluttered at the man's helmet. Studying them, Rillish raised a brow. Chord winced, ducking. 'In case we get separated from the column, sir. Safe passage 'n' all, so I'm told.'

'I see.' Rillish lifted his chin to the west where hazy brown hills humped the horizon. 'Our destination?'

'Yes, sir. The Golden Hills. Some kind of sacred lands for the Wickans, sir.'

'So Mane is reasonably confident on finding other refugees there.'

'Yes, sir.'

'Very good. And . . . well done, Sergeant.'

'Thank you, sir.' Chord saluted, went off.

Sighing, Rillish drew his helmet on again, began walking. That being the case, he now had to give thought to what to do once he'd discharged his responsibilities. Return his command to his regional superior in Unta? Face summary court-martial, execution? Would Fist D'Ebbin be satisfied with just his head, or would he imprison the men as mutineers? He could always appeal to High Fist Anand; the man had a reputation for fairness. Perhaps he should disband his command and return alone. Or not at all. Presumed dead would be the official conclusion. He thought of his family estate hard up by the Gris border; the sweetgourds should be ripening now.

The images of his fever-induced hallucinations returned to him and he snorted at the ridiculous self-aggrandizement of it. His command at Korel had been decimated, his command here at the Wickan frontier had been decimated; it would seem to be best for all if he just threw down his helmet. Yet the face of Tajin would not go away. Tajin had been the boy's name. He could not shut his eyes without seeing Tajin.

Later that afternoon outrunners came scrambling in from the south. They threw themselves down next to the boy's travois. Mane ran up and a fierce argument raged over the seated child until Mane ducked her head with a curt bow. Chord had come to Rillish's side. 'Riders closing from the south,' he said aside.

'Not Wickan, I gather.'

'Lad, no.'

Mane ran up to Rillish, a hand tight on the grip of her long-knife. She stopped before him, but her face was turned away, glaring back to the travois. 'I have been ordered – that is, we are to place ourselves under your command.' She would not raise her gaze.

'Have they spotted us yet?'

'We don't believe so.'

Rillish cast about, pointed to the nearest hillock. 'Retreat to that hill. Lie low, maybe they'll miss us.'

'As you order.' She passed on low commands.

Chord raised a hand, signing to the men and women regulars. Everyone jogged for the rise.

A dry wash cut the rear of the rise allowing for no approach, but eliminating any retreat as well. The regulars crouched in the grass in a double arc around the base. Rillish knelt with a relief of six near the top next to the travois. The guard of youths surrounded the boy; the rest had spread themselves out. Everyone waited, silent, while the pounding of horses' hooves closed upon them. Riders stormed past, pell-mell; armed citizenry without uniform or order, a kind of self-authorized militia. Some eighty men. Their route brought them curving past the rise and on, north-west. It pleased Rillish to see a paucity of bows and crossbows at their backs. He gestured a runner to him. 'Give them time,' he whispered. The girl scrambled down among the grasses on all fours.

Rillish waited, listening. The dull drone of insects and the hiss of the lazy afternoon breeze through the grass returned. The sun was nearing the uneven western horizon – the reason behind the *Golden* hills? Then a return of hooves. Two mounted figures, heads lowered, studying the ground as they walked their mounts south. Both Wickan in their torn deer-hide shirts, long matted black hair.

'Renegade scouts,' Mane hissed, suddenly at Rillish's side.

The two straightened, galvanized; they'd realized they were being watched. Rillish knew he'd now lost all his options. 'Fire!'

Crossbow bolts and arrows whipped from the grass like angry insects. One scout fell, thrown backwards by the blows of four missiles. The other had rolled from his mount. Figures rose from the grasses around the man, threw themselves upon him. A quick high yell; silence. One mount, hit by several crossbow bolts reared its pain, squealing, then fell kicking. *Damn.* The other stood motionless until a youth rose next to it to send it running with a slap at its flank.

The ground thrummed with the return of the main column, but slower, cantering. They rounded the rise bunched up, the van conferring, their words lost in the din. Closing, they spotted the fallen mount. They milled their confusion, peered about at the surrounding hillsides. Men dismounted. *Shit.* 'Fire at will!' Rillish yelled.

A volley of missiles took down mounted and dismounted alike. The rest spurred their horses up the hill, swords flashing from their sheaths.

Rillish's command rose from the grasses to meet them. They slashed mounts, engaged riders. A Wickan girl pulled herself up on to the back of a mount behind one fellow and sank her knife into him then rolled off taking him with her. Most of the invader militia fared better, however, slashing down with their longer weapons, raking the youths from their sides, advancing. Rillish pulled out his twinned Untan duelling swords and raced down the slope.

He engaged the nearest, parrying the down-stroke, thrust the groin, and allowed the man to pass; he'd be faint with shock and blood loss in moments. Another attempted to ride him down but he threw himself aside, rolling. Regaining his feet he turned, expecting to be trampled, but the rider was preoccupied; he was swiping at his face bellowing his frustration. Yells that turned to pain, even terror. The sword flew from his grip, his hands pressed themselves to his face. A dark cloud of insects surrounded the man. Screaming, he fell from the mount that raced off, unnerved. Rillish crossed to the flailing and gurgling figure in the grasses. All about the hillside the men were falling, clutching at themselves, screaming their pain and blood-chilling horror.

The figure at Rillish's feet stilled. A cloud of insects spiralled from it, dispersing. In their wake was revealed the glistening pink and white curve of fresh bone where the man's face had been. Like an explosion, a mass of chiggers, wasps and deer flies as large as roaches vomited up from between the corpse's gaping teeth like an exhalation of pestilence. Rillish flinched away and puked up the thin contents of his own stomach.

Coughing, wiping his mouth, he straightened to see new riders closing upon them. A column of Wickan cavalry. They encircled the base of the rise. Two riders launched themselves from their tall painted mounts to run up the hill. Both wore black crow-feather capes, both also youths themselves. Rillish cleaned his swords on the grasses then slowly made his way up to the travois. His thigh ached as if broken.

Atop the rise he found the two riders had thrown themselves down at the side of the travois and were both kissing the boy, squeezing his hand, holding his chin, studying his face in wonder, babbling in Wickan. Tears streamed down their faces unnoticed.

Chord came to Rillish's side. 'Trake's Wonder, sir,' he breathed, awed. 'Do you know who those two *are*?'

'Aye, Sergeant. I know.'

'There'll be blood and Hood's own butcher's bill to pay on the frontier now, I think.'

'Yes, Sergeant. I think you're right.' Rillish sat, pulled off his helmet and wiped the sweat from his face. He took a mouthful of water, swished it around his mouth.

Eventually, as the evening gathered, the two – twins, a young man and a young woman – came to stand before Rillish. He roused himself to stand as well, bowed an acknowledgment that the two waved aside.

'We owe you more than we can repay, Lieutenant,' the boy said.

'Just doing my duty.'

'In truth?' the girl said sharply, her eyes dark and glittering like a crow's own. '*Counter* to your duty it would seem.'

'My duty to the Empire.'

The two shared a glance, an unspoken communication. 'Our thanks in any case,' the boy said, and he turned to go. 'We will escort you to the Golden Hills.'

Rillish almost spoke a reflexive, *yes sir*. He watched them go while they spoke to Mane and the others who crowded around, touching them reverently and pulling at their leathers. Grown now into gangly long-limbed adolescents but with the weathered faces and distant evaluative gaze of seasoned veterans who have come through Hood's own trials – Nil and Nether. Living legends of the Seven Cities campaign. Possibly the most dangerous mages alive on the continent, and angry, damned angry it seemed to him. And rightfully so, too.

* * *

Kyle awoke to a light kick of his heel. Keeping himself still he glanced over to see Stalker silently wave him up. Awkward, he pushed himself up by his off-hand, his right wrapped tight in a sling. The night was bright, the mottled moon low and glowing. Unaccountably, Kyle thought of ancient legends from the youth of his people when multiple moons of many sizes and hues painted the nights in multicoloured shadow. Even this one had been discoloured as of late. And the nights have been lit by far more falling stars than when he was a child. He glanced to the glittering arc of stars demarking Father's Cast where his people's Skyfather first tossed the handful of bright dirt that would be Creation. As glowing and dense as ever despite his fears.

Stalker brought his head close. 'We have a problem.' In answer to Kyle's querying look he motioned to Coots waiting at the dark tree-edge.

As Kyle approached, Coots adjusted his armoured hauberk of iron rings sewn to leather and checked his sheathed long-knives. His mouth was his habitual sour grimace behind his thickening moustache and beard. 'We've spotted the boat's owner. He's a Togg-damned giant of a fellow. Bigger than any I ever heard of. Bigger'n any Thelomen.'

A shiver of dread ran through Kyle; giants, Jhogen, were creatures from the nightmares of his people. 'A Jhogen?'

'What's that? Jhogen?' Comprehension dawned on Coots with a quiet humourless smile. 'No. Not one of them.'

'I heard talk in the Guard about giants who live in Stratem. In the East. Toblakai.'

Coots grunted. 'No, not like them.'

'The bigger they are, the slower,' Stalker said, urging them on.

'That from personal experience, there, Stalk?' asked Coots, arching a brow. Stalker signed for silence. Making his way through the

278

woods, Kyle wanted to ask Coots more of this giant but the time for that had passed. They moved silent through the trees, reached tended fields cut from the forest edge that led down to a loosely scattered collection of huts and pens that in turn straggled down to a strand of black rock and the grey choppy waters of the White Sea beyond. A biting landward wind stole through Kyle's armour, quilted padding and linen shirts. He pulled his cloak tighter. The gusts seemed to carry the sharpness of the ice that had given birth to it somewhere far out past the western horizon.

Hunched, Coots jogged down between the open ground of the fields. Kyle scanned the scattered huts; not one fire or lamp showed, though white tendrils climbed from some roof smoke-holes. Stalker followed, Kyle brought up the rear. Amid the huts Badlands emerged from behind a stick-pen holding goats. The four of them jogged down to the dark strand where the boat rested slightly aslant, bright against the black water-worn gravel, its single mast tall and gracefully slim.

Badlands pressed a shoulder to the raised stern, feet scraping amid the rocks. He pushed again, gasping. 'Lad take it! Here's a complication.'

'Keep watch,' Stalker told Kyle. The three bent their shoulders to the boat. They strained, breathing in sharp gasps. Their sandalled feet dug into the gravel. Keening loudly, the boat scraped forward a hand's breadth on its log bedding.

Glancing away from their efforts, Kyle was shocked to see two men already approaching. One stunned him by his size, nearly twice the height of a normal man, carrying a spear fully half again as tall as him. The man at the side of this giant of a being, Jhogen or not, was somehow not in the least diminished. Dark, muscular, he moved with an easy grace that captured Kyle's attention. 'Here they come,' he murmured, aside. The three cousins straightened from their efforts. The boat had moved a bare arm's span.

As the two closed, Kyle found that he did not feel fear so much as an unaccountable chagrin and embarrassment – as if he were a common thief caught in the act – which, he reflected, was pretty much the truth of it. 'You surprise me,' the man said in Talian, motioning to the boat. 'I didn't think anyone but my friend here could move it.'

'Yeah, well, we're just full of surprises,' Stalker ground out, a hand close to his sword.

The man's bright gaze moved to Kyle. 'Young for the Crimson Guard, aren't you?'

Kyle glanced down; he still wore his sigil. 'We quit.'

One dark brow rose. 'Really? I did not think that possible.'

Through this exchange the giant stood straight, arms crossed, though a smile played at his mouth. His startling golden eyes held something like wonder as his gaze roved about them.

'We need your boat,' Stalker said.

'If the Guard is after you, no wonder,' the man observed dryly.

'How much do you want for it?' Kyle asked, surprising himself.

'It's not for sale.' The man's eyes were flat though his mouth quirked up in a half-smile. 'But it is for hire.'

Stalker grunted something that sounded like a long curse of all the meddling Gods.

'Where are you headed?' the giant fellow asked in flowing musical Talian. His voice was taut, expectant, almost febrile in its intensity. It was a question Kyle had been giving much thought of late. Where could he possibly head in all the open world? Back to home, Bael lands? Or off to a new land, this Genabackis of which he heard so much among the Guard? But in the end he did not need to wonder; one place, one name, haunted him since overheard accidentally while he hid in the woods. A locale, and a possible mission as well. He addressed the two, 'Have either of you heard of the "Dolmans"?'

Their reaction startled Kyle. To the man the name clearly meant nothing; his gaze remained flat, though it shifted to his companion. The giant flinched as if gut-punched. A shiver took him like the swaying of a tree trunk and he expended a hissed breath in a long murmuring supplication. 'Yes,' he managed, his voice thick with emotion. 'I know it well. The Dolmans of Tien. It is of my homeland, Jacuruku.'

'What fee, then, to take us there?' asked Stalker, his gaze narrow on Kyle.

The man had already half-turned away. He said over his shoulder, 'You've just paid it. We'll get our supplies then we will leave immediately.'

Though clearly unhappy, Stalker nodded. 'What's your name?'

'Traveller. This is Ereko.'

Stalker gave their names. Ereko inclined his head in greetings. 'Well met, comrades,' he said grinning now, having regained his composure. 'We sail shortly into the maw of the Ice Dancer. It is a sea I know well, and judging from this frigid wind, it is readying itself for us.' The two walked back up the strand.

While Stalker eyed Kyle, Badlands let out a long thankful breath. 'Payment might still have to be made . . .'

'Don't know if I'm looking forward to that scrap,' said Coots.

Stalker refused to release Kyle. 'The Dolmans . . . that the place Skinner mentioned?'

'Yes.'

'And his contact. It was in Jacuruku, wasn't it?'

'Yes.'

'And now this Thelomen fellow, or whatever he is, says he's of Jacuruku.'

'Yeah.'

Stalker spun away, disgusted. 'Dark Lady, someone's meddling here. I don't like it. Too overt. There's going to be trouble. Pushback. I know it.'

'What do you mean?'

He rubbed his hands on the planks of the boat. 'A slapping down. A dispersal. Lad,' he said, turning back, 'the Gods are just scheming children. One is attempting to build a castle in the sand here. Soon the others will see this, or they have seen it. They'll come and kick it down.'

'Why?'

'Because they can't let the schemes of others succeed, Kyle. They each of them only want their *own* to succeed.'

'I don't know if I agree with that.'

The tall scout shrugged. 'Agree or not, that is how it is. In any case, seems we're still working for the Guard after all.'

'One direction is as good as any other,' said Coots with a dismissive wave.

'Except home,' said Badlands, hawking up a great throatful of phlegm and spitting on to the rocks.

Coots nodded. 'Yeah. That *would* be the worst.'

Traveller and Ereko returned quite quickly. Kyle had to kick the cousins awake; they'd lain down on their cloaks and gone right to sleep. The two tossed their bundles in then Traveller waved everyone to the boat. One-armed, Kyle had barely touched the overlapping planks of the sides when the boat took off sliding down the logs; Ereko had merely leant his shoulder to the stern and it fairly flew down the strand. It gave a nerve-grating screech of wood-against-wood then charged prow-first into the grey water. Ereko had continued on with it and now stood in what for him was waist-deep water; Kyle, short himself, suspected it would come up near his shoulders. Traveller pointed to a row of sealed earthenware pots. 'Those hold sweet-water. Get them aboard.'

Stalker didn't move, but after an 'Aye, Captain' from Coots the brothers bent to the task.

'Those bundles of charcoal,' Traveller told Kyle, indicating a ready-made pile.

'Aye,' Kyle responded without thought. Eventually, Stalker lent a hand to the loading of wrapped dried fish and roots.

Ereko had manoeuvred the boat closer to shore. They climbed aboard, getting wet only to the knees. Ereko pushed off then pulled himself in over the gunwale. He took the side-tiller while Traveller sat at the high prow.

'Raise sail,' Ereko called. The brothers set to, pulling on ropes. A patchwork square sail rose, luffed full in the strong wind. Ereko steered them north, parallel to the shore and slightly seaward. Already a false dawn brightened the east. They'd worked all night preparing the craft.

Kyle sat close to the stern, wrapped himself in his cloak. 'What's the boat's name?' he asked the giant.

'We call her the *Kite*,' he answered with an easy and pleased smile. 'Let's hope she flies just as swift, hey?'

Kyle could only nod his uncertain agreement. Why must they hurry? Were they afraid the Guard might give chase? Or, more likely, the fellow had his own reasons for speed. The one who'd given his name as Traveller – what an odd choice! – had installed himself at the very prow, looking ahead past the tall spit. Stalker, Badlands and Coots sat amidships, wrapped themselves in cloaks, and promptly went to sleep. Kyle tried to sleep but found that while he was exhausted by the night's work, he was too excited. He was on his way – but to what? Would it prove to be the meeting or the discovery he hoped? But it was too late now for second thoughts. It seemed to him that the splash of the *Kite*'s prow into the water had set a tumble of events into motion that could not be stopped. Not by men nor even these meddling Gods who may have – foolishly! – interfered. They had set off on a chosen path. One path among many that like any in hindsight becomes *Fated*. And their destination, their future, awaited them.

CHAPTER II

The wise learn more from their enemies than fools learn from their friends.

Attribution Unknown
(Possibly Gothos)

'OBELISK HIGH, DEATHSLAYER CLOSE, CROWN INVERTED, THE Apocalyptic!'

Arm raised to throw, Nait stared at Heuk, the company cadre mage. 'So? What the fuck is that supposed to mean?'

The old man blinked sallow bloodshot eyes and fell back into his seat. He gestured to the cards. 'It means something's happening.'

At the company table, Least let go a great farting noise. Nait kept his hand high, shaking the bone dice. 'Something's always happening somewhere, you daft codger!'

'Swearing,' Corporal Hands warned, 'and throw the damned dice.'

'Fine!' Nait shook the dice in Hands' broad sweaty face. 'You want me to throw, I'll throw!' He threw; the dice bounced from the box, disappeared among the sawdust, straw and warped boards of the Figurehead Inn's floor.

'Aw, you dumb bumpkin!' said Honey Boy.

'Shithead.'

'Swearing!'

'Look, you better find them,' said Honey Boy, 'they're made from my grandmother's own knucklebones.'

'Then she can bloody well find them.'

Hands, Honey Boy and Least all stared. Nait threw up his arms. 'Fine! I'll look.' He got on his hands and knees between the crowded tables. 'Can't find shit down here anyway.'

'I did,' Least said, serious.

Nait searched the floor, deciding to look more for dropped coins

283

than anything else. The door banged open and a man stopped in the threshold blocking the bright light of midday. '*It's the end of the world*,' he bellowed into the common room. Conversation and the thumping of pewter tankards stopped. Everyone turned to squint at the man, his eyes wide, hair dishevelled, fine velvet jacket askew and wrenched. '*Hood's Gates have opened and the dead of all the Abyss are vomiting up upon us!*'

Nait, straightening, banged the back of his head on the table. 'What in Hood's ass?'

'*Flee! Run!*' and, taking his own advice, the man ran.

Nait looked to Hands who looked to Honey Boy. A few patrons peered out the oiled and stretched hides that served as blurry windows. The light shining in the door did have a strange greenish cast to it – like that of an approaching storm front. A number of blurred figures, no more than wavering shadows, ran past the windows like fleeing ghosts. Shrugging, most patrons returned to talking – now discussing even stranger things they'd seen; the day a two-headed cat haunted the streets of Unta and the whole quarter was turned upside down so that the cursed thing could be caught and drowned in a trough; or that night not so long ago when a falling god – perhaps Fener himself – turned the night into day.

Yet Nait thought he heard distant yells of alarm and wonder from the open door. Sighing, Hands pushed herself up from the table and stretched her arms, straining the broad front lacings of her linen shirt. Looking up from the table, Least whimpered and Honey Boy sank his head into his hands. Hands glared, 'Oh, c'mon!' She drew on her padded vest and hauberk, took her belt and sword from the back of the chair. Nait pocketed his coins from the table, pushed the birdbone toothpick into the corner of his mouth. He eyed them at the table. 'Well? C'mon, you limpdicks.'

Watching Hands go, Least rumbled sadly, 'Not so limp now.'

Honey Boy slapped the Barghast on the back of his bhederin cloak. 'Wasn't that swearing? I'm sure he swore.'

Nait just spat. *One of these days, Hands, I'll pull those big ol' boots off you.*

Outside the sky over Unta Bay flickered with a strange aura. It reminded Nait of the lights that play over the Straits that some say presage the arrival of the Stormriders; not that he'd ever seen any of those demons himself, being from far inland. The glow was receding or dying away even as he watched, leaving behind the normal midday blue vault laced with high thin clouds.

Honey Boy grunted, pointing to the mouth of the harbour. Two ships had entered, both alarmingly low in the water. One's masts hung shattered, the other listed. Sweeps propelled them, but raggedly, all of them unaccountably short, many broken to stubs. Both vessels seemed to glow as if painted white. The squad headed for the wharf.

Commerce on this reach of the mercantile berthings had stuttered to a halt. Bales and sacks lay abandoned. As they ambled past, labourers gingerly straightened from cover. Sailors watched from the rails of merchantmen. One raised a warding gesture against evil. 'It's the drowned returned – as at the end of times!'

'Damned few of them,' Honey Boy opined.

They came abreast of the guard shack and Nait stepped in, 'Hey, Sarge, did you—'

Sergeant Tinsmith and another stood at one window. The other wore the rags of a dock rat but stood straight with arms folded, a hand at his chin as he peered out. 'Who in the Queen's privates is this?' Nait said.

'Manners,' Sergeant Tinsmith ground out. 'This is a guest.'

'What do you think?' the fellow asked the sergeant.

Tinsmith stroked his grey moustache. 'One of them has a Genabackan cut but the other,' he shook his head, 'I've never seen the like. What's left of it, anyway. No flagging.'

'No, none.'

While they watched, the listing one of the vessels came abreast of an anchored Kanese merchantman. The crew of the sinking vessel swarmed over the sides on to the merchantman. Shortly thereafter, that vessel raised anchor, lowered sweeps and headed for the wharf. The abandoned vessel promptly sank in its wake.

'Damned brazen,' the dock rat observed.

'Get the full company down here, Honey Boy,' Tinsmith shouted outside.

'Aye, sir.'

'They're in an awful hurry to get themselves arrested,' said Nait.

The dock rat regarded him for a moment with hard, amused eyes. 'We'll see.'

The vessels reached the head of the wharf. Figures climbed down, all armed and armoured, though also bizarrely pale as if white-washed, or ghosts. A thought struck Nait and he laughed aloud. Tinsmith raised a brow. 'I was just thinking, sir. It's the sorriest-ass invasion fleet I've ever seen.' Both men regarded him in silence. 'Just a thought.'

The dock rat returned to the window. 'There's something . . .' he began, then fell silent. He jerked backwards a step as if struck. '*Hood no!*' He gestured and Nait felt the prickling sensation of Warren energies gathering. The hairs of his nape tickled and a wind blew about the hut, raising clouds of dust. Nait covered his eyes. A blow sounded, meaty and final, followed by a gurgle. Nait threw himself into a corner, knife out before him. The wind dispersed. He found himself looking up at the long slim legs of a woman who would have been beautiful if she wasn't covered in filth. Her white hair was matted into tangled locks. A crust of white scale limned her bare muscular arms. A tattered shirt and shorts hung in rags limp on her frame. She had Tinsmith up against one wall, an elbow under his neck, knife to his chin. Hands filled the doorway, two dirks out. Tinsmith waved her down.

'Water . . .' the woman croaked through lips swollen and bloodied. Tinsmith glanced aside to a pail. The woman let him fall, grasped the pail and upended it over her head. Hands cocked a questioning look to Tinsmith who waved *wait*.

The woman spluttered and gasped, swallowing. Panting, she turned to them. 'Order your men to stand aside, sergeant, and they won't be harmed. Our argument isn't with you.' Tinsmith rubbed his neck and slowly nodded his agreement. 'Very wise, sergeant.' She gestured and the wind rose again, raising dust and sand and Nait glanced away, shielding his eyes. When he looked back, she was gone.

'Who the Abyss was that?' Hands demanded.

Tinsmith crouched at the side of the dock rat, felt at his neck. The man looked to have been slain by a single thrust. The sergeant returned to the window. 'So they're back,' he said as if thinking aloud.

'Who?' said Hands.

'The Crimson Guard.'

Nait barked a sneering laugh. 'A name to frighten children!'

'Pass the word, Corporal. No hostilities. Fight only if attacked.'

Hands frowned her disapproval, her thick dark brows knotting. But she nodded and withdrew.

'And Corporal!'

'Aye?'

'Put everyone to work readying the chains.'

'Aye, sir.'

His back to Nait, Tinsmith said, 'That was Isha. Lieutenant of Cowl.'

Nait opened his mouth to laugh again but the name Cowl silenced him. Cowl, truly? But he'd been the long-time rival of . . . Dancer. And Dancer was . . . gone . . . as was Kellanved. And Dassem. In fact, no one was left. None who could oppose them. Nait dropped his gaze to his knife; he sheathed it. *As the sergeant says, no hostilities.*

Mallick Rell was reclined on a divan enjoying a lunch of Talian grapes and a Seven Cities recipe for spiced roast lamb when a servant entered. 'The streets are seething with news, sir,' the servant offered, his voice low.

'Oh, yes? And this news contains specifics?'

The servant paused, coughed into a fist. 'Well, sir. They say the Crimson Guard has returned.'

Mallick chewed a pinch of lamb meat, savouring it. 'You interrupt my meal to tell me this? A rumour I myself started?'

'Ah, no. Sir. I understand they're here now. In the harbour.'

Mallick gagged on the meat, spat it to the marble floor. '*What?*'

'That is what some are saying, sir. Reliably.'

Sitting up, Mallick wiped his face, waved the cloth at the servant. 'Get out. *Now*.'

The servant bowed.

'I said get out of my sight!'

The servant hurried out. Mallick gulped a glass of wine, straightened his robes. 'Oryan!'

A shimmer of heat-rippled air and the old man appeared. He bowed. 'Yes?'

'The Crimson Guard are here, Oryan?'

The Seven Cities mage blinked his black stone eyes. 'Some entities of great potential have entered the harbour, yes.'

'*Some entities* . . .' Mallick reached out as if to strangle the old man. He let his arms fall. 'That is the Guard.'

'So you say, Master.'

Mallick's voice was a snake hiss, 'Yes.' He snatched up a crystal carafe of red wine, pressed the cold vessel to his brow, sighing. 'Gods deliver me . . . At least Korbolo isn't in the city.'

The old man snorted his scorn. 'How unfortunate for him.'

'Now, now. So, what steps have you been taking?'

'I have been raising wards, strengthening protections . . .'

The carafe slammed cracking to the marble table. '*What?*'

'Strengthening—'

'No!'

Oryan blinked anew. 'I'm sorry, Master?'

'No, you fool! You'll only pique Cowl's interest. Drop them. Drop them all then hide.'

The mage's wrinkled face puckered in consternation. 'I'm sorry . . .'

'Hide, Oryan. That's your only hope. Now go.'

Visibly struggling with his commands, the old man bowed, arms crossed. The air sighed, shifting, and he was gone. For a moment Mallick thought he could detect a sharp spice scent in the air in the man's passing, but it drifted away before he could identify it. He raised the carafe to pour himself another glass but he found it empty, the blood-red wine pooled on the marble flagging; he threw the carafe aside. The fools! They weren't supposed to come *here*. What could they hope to – Mallick clasped his hands in front of his face as if praying. Of course! 'Sennit. Sennit!'

A far door opened, the servant reappeared. 'Yes, sir?'

'Ready my carriage. I will travel to the Palace.'

'Sir?'

'The Palace, man! The Palace! We have important guests.'

* * *

Shimmer set her mailed feet on the stone wharf and paused to offer up a prayer of gratitude to any of the Gods who had had a hand in their deliverance from Mael's Shoals of the Forgotten. Gods! What a trial. Mael, you have made your point! A third of their force lost to thirst, exhaustion, sickness and those monstrous eels. And how long had it taken to bull their way through the maze of becalmed rotting vessels – some still manned by crews driven insane by their torment? Months? A year? Who knew? Time did not run parallel from Realm to Realm or even Warren to Warren. And that the least of the dangers of daring such short-cuts.

Yet against all odds they had returned. Once more the Guard faced its true opponent – the entity they had vowed to see negated. The Imperium. She waved Smoky to her. 'Activity?'

The mage rubbed the crust of salt and blood from his lips. 'Negligible,' he croaked. 'But *he* is here.'

He. The mage who overturned all the comparisons of numbers and strategies. Tayschrenn, their old nemesis. Shimmer adjusted the hang of her mail coat; damned loose, she'd lost a lot of weight. She drank a long pull from a skin of water scavenged from the merchantman they'd taken. 'He's Cowl's worry. It's the Palace for us.'

'Cowl might not be up to it.'

'Then Skinner will be.'

Smoky picked at the salt-sores on his forehead, frowned in thought. 'True.'

'Blades form up!' Shimmer called, and she started up the wharf. Greymane came to her side.

'I'll take possession of some better vessels, and await your return, if you don't mind?'

Shimmer eyed the renegade. Ah! Ex-Malazan, of course. 'Our *return* you say?'

The man's glacial-blue eyes shared the humour. 'If necessary, of course.'

'Very well. You have command.'

Greymane bowed, waved for a sergeant.

It had been over half a century since Shimmer had last seen Unta. It looked bigger, more prosperous, as befitted the adopted Imperial capital. Stone jetties and a curved sea-wall of fitted blocks now rose where wood and tossed rubbish once served. Many more towers punched high into the air over the sprawling streets, including those of the tallest, the Palace.

They formed into column at the mouth of a main thoroughfare leading to Reacher's Square and the government precincts beyond. She and Skinner led; he ordered the silver dragon banner unfurled. As they marched Shimmer watched the gazes of the citizens who jammed the storefronts and stalls lining the sides of the thoroughfare. She searched their faces hoping to see eager friendliness, even welcome, fearing that she would instead meet hostility and resentment. Yet what she found troubled her even more: open perplexity and confusion. Some even pointed and laughed. One woman called out to ask whether they'd come from Seven Cities. Had none of them any idea who they were? Smoky, at her side, muttered, 'It's like the goddamned carnival's hit town and we're it.'

'Perhaps we have outlived ourselves . . .' And she felt dismay close even more tightly upon her, for the capital was a much larger city than she remembered. The populace lining the street numbered perhaps more than a hundred thousand and it seemed to her that, should they be roused, they could tear them limb from limb. 'Cowl?' she asked of Smoky.

'Dancing with the Claws. Right now they're holding off. Seems they're curious too.'

Shimmer eyed the armoured back of Skinner who had strode ahead with the standard-bearer, Lazar. 'As am I, Smoky. As am I.'

Guards bowed and opened every sealed door he met, locks clicked and yielded, and wards parted like thinnest cloth before his questings, until Cowl found himself before the final barrier between himself and the innermost sanctum of Tayschrenn's quarters. He reached out to the door then hesitated; why should he have been invited onward? Was it a trap? Yet his every sense told him the High Mage awaited within – he and none other. Alone. As it should be; he and Tay, duelling once again.

He pushed the door open with a blow that sent it banging from the wall. A bare empty room, lit by open windows, and at its centre wards carved into the very stone of the marble floor and filled with poured and hardened gold and silver filigree in concentric circles surrounding a bowed, cross-legged man, long scraggly hair fallen forward over his face.

'Greetings, Tay.'

The seated figure did not raise his head. 'You should not have come, Cowl,' the man intoned in a rough voice. 'Yet I knew you could not have stayed away.'

'Getting all mystical in your old age, I see.' Cowl walked the edge of the craven wards – these he could pass but they would send him to wherever it was Tayschrenn had taken himself off to, and all indications were it was a place he would not wish to be. While Cowl paced the circle Tayschrenn failed to respond, so, impatient with the man's theatrics – some things *never* change – Cowl said directly, 'Will you stand aside?'

'If you mean, shall I intervene? The answer is no, I shall not.'

Cowl did not bother keeping a smile of victory from his face. 'Wise move, Tay. All alone now, you would fall to my knives.'

The head rose, greasy lank hair shifting to reveal a haggard strained face, eyes sunken, fevered. 'Wise?' the unnerving figure demanded. 'Do you know the final attainment of absolute power, Cowl?'

'The final what of what?'

'Powerlessness, Cowl. Absolute power diffuses into powerlessness.'

Cowl stepped away from the warded figure. 'Is this some kind of elaborate self-justification for cowardice?'

Tayschrenn continued as if Cowl hadn't spoken, 'I have stretched myself further than I have ever dared before probing onward ahead into the possibilities of what might come. I have glimpsed things that both terrify and exult. Can you answer this puzzle, Cowl? How can both of these things be?'

Despite his dismissal of this Hermetic side of Warren manipulation, Cowl found himself responding by rote, 'Because the future holds everything.'

'Exactly, Cowl. I see that it is possible that you are in fact worthy of the title High Mage. And so, the question then follows, what course of action should I take in the present? Which steps might lead to all that which terrifies, which steps might lead to all that which exults? The answer is of course that I cannot know for certain. Thus I am held back from all choice. Total awareness, my friend, results in paralysis.' The head sank once more, as if dismissing Cowl, indeed as if dismissing all physical reality.

Cowl relaxed, let his hands fall from the crossed baldrics and belts beneath his cloak. He had weapons invested and aspected that might just reach the man, but what he'd found here was no threat to anyone. It was now clear to him that the twisted Gnostic innards of theurgy had claimed the mind of the most promising mage of his generation.

He turned and left the chamber.

Once Cowl exited the room light shimmered next to the open door revealing a woman with short black hair in ash-hued tunic and trousers and carrying a long slim stave. This she planted with a sharp blow upon the marble flags. 'He should never have been allowed to get this close.'

'I am beyond his physical reach,' Tayschrenn answered mildly.

'Yet he is also a formidable mage, so I understand.'

'In certain narrow and sharp applications, yes.'

The woman swung the stave across her shoulders, draped her arms over it. 'And now?'

'They will see that nothing can be decided here. It all lies upon Heng's walls, as before. And they will go.'

'Before?'

Tayschrenn nodded, his eyes closed. 'Yes. When the Protectress fell to Kellanved and Dancer everyone realized that no one was safe from them – all proceeded logically from that.'

The woman stood still for some time, head cocked as if listening. Tayschrenn's head sank lower, his breathing shallowed to imperceptibility. She stepped to the open door. 'Do not involve yourself,' announced the motionless Tayschrenn.

The woman froze, mouthed a silent curse. She set the stave against the wall. 'Just going to keep an eye on things.' She waited a time for an answer but none came. She cursed again and left.

Leaning against a street-side stall, Possum watched the ragged, exhausted column of Crimson Guardsmen enter the tall bronze doors of the Palace precincts. He didn't know whether to laugh or cry; was this it then? The much vaunted Guard? Had the stories over the years so grown in the telling? And what of Cowl? Had he survived?

A Hand-commander stopped at his side. One of the second echelon, vice-commanders. Coil was her name. 'Anand wishes to know if he can count on us cooperating with the barricades.'

Possum leaned forward blocking one nostril to blow his nose to the street. 'Yes. Seed the crowds. Tell everyone to keep their distance.'

'Very good.' Still, the woman did not move. She watched the outer gates swinging ponderously shut.

'Yes, Coil?'

'Hard to believe, yes?'

Irritated by the familiarity, Possum demanded, 'What? That they returned? Or the condition in which they did? Or the chances that they should pick this time to show up?'

Coil did not turn to her head to glance to him. 'Chance? I don't believe in it. And I don't take them.'

Which is why, Coil, you'll never stand where I am. 'You have your orders.'

Coil glanced to him with her half-lidded hard eyes. 'And these orders – from the Empress?'

The Hand-commander's tone quickened Possum's pulse. By the Queen's Mysteries, was she challenging his authority? 'Immaterial. You've just heard them from me.'

Smiling, Coil inclined her head in the shallowest of bows, and sauntered away. Possum watched her go. Why so bold? No need to advertise what everyone in the ranks understands – that all those beneath you think they can do a better job, and are ever watchful for opportunities to demonstrate such by ousting said superior.

Blowing his nose once more, Possum dismissed Coil from his mind. She'd been merely angling for news of the Empress. No need to tell her he'd searched the Palace earlier and found no sign of her; sensibly, she'd run off. No point being disappointed about it. What could she be expected to do against some fifty Avowed and seven hundred Guardsmen? Bravely face them only to be captured? Reduced thereafter to a hostage or mere bargaining chip? What would be the sense in that? No, to Possum's way of thinking she'd done the wise thing. Let the Guard blunder like clod-footed fools through the Palace. What did they expect? To just sit on the throne and be obeyed? No, this whole episode was the shabby and frankly rather embarrassing final chapter to what had once been a noble career. Possum wiped his nose. Yes, thinking about it, he realized that he was quite disappointed by the whole thing and more than a little resentful that they'd bothered showing up at all; they'd ruined the legend for him and for everyone.

*   *   *

For her part, Shimmer saw the humour. She, Skinner and a handful of Avowed marching through the inner precincts, the majority of the force left behind in the marshalling grounds. What could they hope to accomplish, or more precisely, what did Cowl or Skinner have in mind? Surely Laseen would have fled by now, or carried on the ancient solution and taken poison – one could always hope. Perhaps they would end up joining the queue of petitioners hoping for their turn before the August Personage.

But no. Skinner did not stop on his relentless march to the Throne room. Functionaries and clerks pressed themselves against walls and gaped as they strode through colonnaded approaches, seating halls, and long reception chambers. All guards were notable by their absence – almost as if they'd been pulled for service elsewhere – and the *where* of that troubled Shimmer.

The final tall set of double doors crashed open under Skinner's armoured forearm and they faced the long sable carpet leading up to an empty throne. The throne of Malaz, assembled from bones. A not so subtle reminder of the true power behind it, the T'lan Imass. A cold grim seat, it seemed to Shimmer. Skinner set his gauntleted hands to his belt and nodded his head within his tall helm, as if confirming to himself what he'd been expecting all along.

'Empty,' Shimmer said, mostly because someone had to.

'Almost,' Skinner corrected, pointing aside.

A short chubby man in rich blue and green robes bowed where he waited next to a pillar. He gestured to a table holding carafes of clear water. 'Refresh yourselves please, honoured ones. I see that your passage has been a particularly desiccating one.'

Skinner turned away, dismissing him. 'Poison is useless against us.'

The man bowed again. 'As I know. Which is why I would never make such an ill-advised attempt.'

Shimmer drew off her helmet, tucked it under one arm. 'You are?'

'Mallick Rel. Duly elected spokesman for the Assembly of regional governors and representatives.' He smiled unctuously, bobbing his head.

Shimmer helped herself to the water, drank deeply and found it wonderfully refreshing. 'Come to take the measure of your new masters?'

The man's lips drew back in a thin smile, revealing sickly green teeth. 'If the Gods should will it so . . .'

It seemed to Shimmer that this man was not nearly as nervous as he should be. Skinner had turned at the man's words and now regarded him. 'Perhaps I should kill you,' he said, his voice bland.

The man's eyes fluttered as he blinked his confusion. 'But wasn't the water cool and fresh?'

Shimmer laughed. 'It was that. My thanks.'

'Excellent. A job well done is its own reward.'

Now it was Shimmer's turn to stare, uncertain. This man's game was deep – was he angling to maintain his position, or was that actually . . . mockery?

But Skinner waved curt dismissal. 'Leave us.'

The man bowed and backed out. Lazar pulled the doors shut.

'This whole thing is a mistake, Skinner,' Smoky said – for the tenth time. 'And that guy was the oddest of it.' Shimmer had to agree. Why had he elected to be here to meet them? What was his purpose?

Skinner faced them. 'Yes, enough of this foolish charade. Laseen has fled. What we have shown here is that no one dares face us. Shimmer, take the command back to the ships to withdraw down the coast to the west and link up with the rest of the forces when they arrive. Cowl and I will join you later.'

Shimmer bowed. 'You are going on alone?'

'Yes. There is are some . . . options . . . Cowl and I wish to look into.'

Shimmer bowed again. 'As you order.' She gestured Smoky behind her, faced Lazar, Black the Lesser, Shijel and Kalt. 'Form up and have a care.'

They'd left behind the inner halls and were close to the marshalling grounds when the first ambush took them. A concerted toss of Moranth munitions blew Kalt into fragments. Withering volleys from crossbows and bows kept them pinned until Smoky drove the soldiers back with a liquid wall of flame that billowed down the hall. Shimmer stepped out among the still burning tapestries and furniture, waved the smoke aside, squinting ahead. She pointed Lazar back to get Skinner even though she was certain he was gone – if he'd been around he would have come. Smoky raised a hand for silence. 'The Brethren clamour. Listen.'

The muted, distant murmur of battle; her command was under attack.

* * *

Possum strode beneath the fluttering awnings of Collunus Bourse, the second largest of the covered exchanges specializing in imported goods. Deserted, now, in the chaos and rioting of this evening. His guards flanked him and Claw runners came and went reporting developments among the splintered broadening front that, he had to admit, was rapidly gyring beyond his grip. Down narrow passing ways he glimpsed black smoke pluming from the worst of the engagements: burning barricades, the flames of which had surged out of control swallowing defenders, attackers and bystanders alike. Runners reported that the Guard had been held up in its efforts to push through to the harbour. Elements of the 4th had even managed to separate small bands of Guardsmen. He was on his way to one such engagement now, a chance to actually continue with the plan thrown together when the Guard entered the city – to take them out piece by piece.

A runner arrived from the engagement. 'They have them pinned down in a tenement.' He gestured to an alley.

Possum did not try to answer for now they had entered the clamour of the battle zone. Malazan regulars came and went, hustling equipment to the engagement: flammables, shields, sheaths of arrows and crossbow bolts. The disassembled components of a harbour siege weapon came dragged by. Possum thought that a damned good idea. But the regulars were few, vastly outnumbered by the Untan citizen volunteer militia that had arisen to the challenge with a will and a fury no one, certainly not Possum, had anticipated. He couldn't help reflecting with a dose of his old cynicism that it mustn't have hurt that the Claw had spread the offer of ten thousand Imperial gold discs for the head of each Avowed.

The runner led them to a sunken rear entrance then stairs up to a trap and the roof. Here, an individual Claw awaited them, the local Hand-commander. Scrabbling forward, they looked across and down at the target. Below them the militia kept up a ruthless barrage of crossbow fire into the front of the tenement. To Possum's experienced eye what the barrage lacked in accuracy it more than made up for in enthusiasm. Yet while the heads of the Guardsmen were being kept down, it was obvious no one on either side was eager for a rush. A standoff. But one that could break either way, depending on how it played out.

'How many?'

'A few – less than ten. Maybe a blade.'

Possum took the opportunity to look out over the city. The sky was taking on an orange glow, tinted by the flames; the afternoon was giving way to evening. Smoke plumes rose like a handful of tossed markers announcing a ragged line that ran practically half way across the city. Things would soon devolve far beyond any chance of intervention from him. Decisions would fall to the individual judgment of Hand-commanders, so he might as well enter the fray. 'How many munitions do you have access to?' he asked the commander.

'Munitions?'

'Yes.'

The man, his face marred by a severe youthful dose of the pox, glanced sidelong to the runner and Possum's own guards. 'Shouldn't we wait before trying something like that?'

'Wait?

'Yes.'

'Wait for what? For Gods or Ascendants to appear in the bloody streets? We don't have to wait for anything! I'm the Lady-damned Clawmaster!'

The man hunched beneath Possum's tirade, exchanged glances with his runner as if blaming each other. Once again Possum found himself disheartened by the state of the organization since its gutting on Malaz Isle. Kellanved's Revenge, some called that night, evoking the stories that this newly arisen Shadowthrone was in fact the old emperor. It was said that in revenge for past slights, his assassination not the least of them, Kellanved had sent the curse of his own Shadow Queen upon them to harrow the ranks. And what a harrowing that night had been!

Luckily, Possum had then been elsewhere engaged. Now, this night, he almost demoted this Hand-commander on the spot but decided against it; no sense doing what the upcoming fight might accomplish all on its own. 'Spread the word below. *We're* taking over here. We'll open with a volley of whatever munitions you can pull together then close to finish up the survivors.' He indicated the roof opposite. 'Let's come down from above.'

'As you order,' barked the Hand-commander, all obedience now. *Far too late for that, friend.*

They reached the roof together, Possum with his guards and the commander's Hand of five. Eljin, the man had given his name as. Another Hand now kept watch from the ground where the fusillade of crossbow fire had diminished. Possum hoped the mercenaries wouldn't get too suspicious. He signed for the attack – before the Guard decided to rush the damned street in the lull.

Eljin pumped his fist over the lip of the roof then threw himself down. 'Incoming!' The entire Hand lay flat on the steeply sloped tiled roof. A moment later the ancient wooden three-storey tenement jumped beneath Possum's body, tossing him into the air. A Claw screamed as he tumbled down the roof, tiles clattering around him. The building settled with a screeching pained groan like a ship wallowing. Smoke and dust shot up the open roof trap. Possum pushed himself to his feet and stood spread-legged for balance. 'Go, go, go!'

They charged down the stairs. Carnage greeted them; the building hadn't been emptied. Its inhabitants crammed the stairwell, screaming, clambering over one another in a tumble. Flames now flickered below at the first floor and Eljin, to his credit leading the way, found himself facing a tide of panicked citizenry determined to climb the stairs to escape the fire.

He dealt with this barrier through the simple expediency of kicking down those foremost and pushing over the railing anyone too slow to cooperate. All the while he bellowed, 'Down! Get down!'

Possum almost cried his frustration. Time. They were recovering! *Get out of the way, you stupid bhederin!* Then the wood stairway sagged beneath them, timbers splintering and bursting like small secondary explosions. This cleared the way. Like a herd checked by an immovable obstacle, it turned as one mind and reversed course. Eljin helped them on with the pommels of his knives. After the citizens had fled they found a large open space cleared by the explosions. A number of the interior walls had been swept away. The stairwell hung canted behind them, a hundred years of dust sifting down from it.

The Hand spread out among the wreckage. Possum walked to the front. Small fires flickered amid the fallen walls and splintered furniture. *Gone.* The delay had ruined their attack. He checked the street; had they bulled out the front?

A wet blow, like that of a butcher's strike, snapped his attention around. Eljin stared his stunned surprise at a blade now hung caught in his chest having swept down from behind through his collarbone and upper ribs severing his torso almost in two halves. *So much for the man's demotion.* The armoured giant behind Eljin raised a mailed foot to push the standing corpse from his blade. All around Guardsmen erupted from the wreckage engaging Claws and Possum could only stare stunned like Eljin. *They'd laid their own blasted trap!*

As the first echoes of battle hidden far inland reached them, and plumes of smoke rose shortly thereafter over the city, Nait watched the Guardsman commanding the force at the harbour order a withdrawal. They climbed aboard their two commandeered vessels and oared out to the bay where they dropped anchor, waiting. From the wharf side Nait waved every obscene gesture he knew until Hands cuffed him. 'Why'd they go?' she asked Tinsmith. 'Abandon their friends?'

Tinsmith merely spat into the water. 'Don't have enough men to secure the harbour. They're safe from the mob out there.'

'But not them,' Nait said, pointing to the top of the harbour curtain wall. There catapults and mangonels glowed in the light of torches held by their busy attendants. 'Gonna be a pheasant shoot for them,' he chuckled gleefully.

'Don't know about that,' Honey Boy objected, 'don't think I've ever seen them actually shoot one of those rusted things.'

Tinsmith did not look impressed either. 'Let's leave them to their job. Now it's time for us to do ours.'

Nait adjusted the bird-bone toothpick at the corner of his mouth, his eyes narrowing. 'What do you mean?'

'Secure the harbour, of course. We are the harbour guard.'

Hands pulled her gauntlets from her belt. 'About bloody time.'

Least frowned his agreement. Nait could only stare from grim face to grim face. 'Are you all crazy? I know there's only one of them left on the wharf but do you know what he must be?'

'He's a Trake-cursed invader!' said Hands.

He's probably from Unta, Nait silently rejoined.

Tinsmith walked up to the single Guardsman left behind at the foot of the stone wharf. As he got close the man turned to him, his eyes hidden within the helm's closed visor. Whoever he was, he wore a thick scaled hauberk and mailed leggings, and bore a broad shield on his back. His surcoat had originally no doubt been deep crimson but now dried salt scale had turned it white. Close, Tinsmith opened his hands to show he meant no harm.

'You are the sergeant of the Harbour Guard,' the man said.

'Yes. Sergeant Tinsmith. And you?'

'Black.'

Tinsmith nodded a cautious hello. 'Well, Black. Hostilities have been declared. Looks like we're gonna have to do our job.'

'You do yours and I'll do mine.'

Tinsmith nodded again and backed away. A third up the length of the wharf he gestured a signal and ten of the harbour guard rose with crossbows readied. The instant they fired the Avowed leapt behind piled cargo. Having fired, these first ten knelt and a second rank straightened. 'Hold fire!' Tinsmith ordered.

He eyed the piled sacks and barrels now feathered by bolts. Had the Avowed retreated or was he manoeuvring for another approach? Yet no clear path existed, Tinsmith had made sure of that. The man stood suddenly, shield raised, and charged.

'Fire!'

The Avowed dived for new cover but not before bolts slammed into his shield. 'Next rank,' Tinsmith ordered. The first rank straightened once again, crossbows levelled. The Avowed had closed about six paces.

'Now?' Nait asked of Tinsmith where he crouched on his knees behind cover, a heavy sledge in his hands.

'Not yet.'

The Avowed rose again. With an angry swipe he broke the bolts from his shield. He advanced despite a bolt that ran straight through one thigh. 'Fire!'

This time the Avowed did not bother ducking. Bolts slammed into his shield, rocking him backwards. One tore through his right calf, sending him to one knee.

'Next rank,' Tinsmith ordered.

'He's gotta be there by now!' Nait pleaded.

'Almost.'

The next rank stood but three had not yet finished cocking their weapons. This volley, rushed, most wide, did not slow the Avowed. 'Now,' Tinsmith judged. Nait swept up the sledge and slammed it down on the iron pin jammed between chain links at his feet. Nothing happened. 'I said *now*,' Tinsmith repeated.

'She's as tight as a ten-year-old's—'

'Watch it!' snarled Hands next to Tinsmith, sword ready.

Tinsmith was eyeing the closing Avowed. 'Now would be a good time.'

Nait pulled down the sledge with a frantic, urgent swing. The head banged from the pin, which shot from the links like a bolt itself, so great was the pressure upon it. 'She's away!' Nait yelled.

The harbour guard threw themselves down. Chain links rattled, snarling against stone. The Avowed paused, uncertain. Then in an explosion of heaped cargo, a length of chain came sweeping across the width of the wharf, tossing barrels, tearing sacks, splintering timbers, until it came to snatch away the Avowed as it he were a doll and sweep him aside into the water.

Nait ran to the stone ledge of the wharf, danced from foot to foot. 'Ha! We got you! Ha! Not so big now, hey?' Tinsmith came to his side followed by Heuk. All three peered down into the churned, dirty green waves. 'Ha! He's dead.'

Heuk shook his head. 'Not necessarily. Might still be alive. It's a real debate – I'd like to stay to see.'

'Can't.' Tinsmith gestured to the two Guard ships, 'they saw it all. So maybe we should go join the fight.'

Nait lost his smile. 'Oh, right. Yeah. Maybe so.'

Tinsmith signed the guard to form up.

* * *

The mute shuffling and grunts of continued fighting prodded Possum to crack open an eye. The noises came from out back; everyone inside was quite obviously dead. He rose silently to his feet and as he did so the mortal slash that laid open his entrails disappeared leaving behind a much shallower, albeit deep enough, cut. Bodies strewed the blown-out first storey, Claws and Guardsmen alike. Wincing, Possum clenched an arm across his slashed abdomen and surveyed the carnage. He and the seven Claws had managed to take down the five Guard – all but one, an Avowed, who then finished off the two remaining Claw and Possum himself, or thought he had.

Yet the fighting continued. Stiff with pain, Possum crossed carefully to a window looking out on the rubbish-strewn enclosure behind the tenement. There the Avowed duelled a single Claw. Possum stared. *Run, you damned fool!* Who was this idiot? He'd not authorized any lone hunters this night. The man, woman, Possum corrected himself, had elected to face the Avowed barehanded. Possum could not understand it, the highest, most exacting of the disciplines taught at the Claw crèches and the Academy, yes, but against an armoured opponent wielding a longsword? Granted, the Avowed moved rather awkwardly having been thrust through the back and front scores of times by Possum and his own guards before managing to cut them all down, but still: bare hands against iron mail?

The Claw, wrapped all over in black cloth strips, including her head, leaving only a slit for her eyes, circled the Avowed, probing, shifting her stance. He waited, sword raised, his other arm hanging useless having been shattered in the explosion. Possum decided that though she might be the stupidest of his ranks she deserved help if only for, well . . . sheer brainless audacity. He calmed himself to summon his Warren.

A cold knife blade bit his neck. He froze. From behind, a head nestled its weight on his left shoulder. A woman's low voice breathed hot and damp into his ear, 'Let's see what she's got.' Despite the blazing pain of his abdomen Possum felt a shiver of hunger to know the possessor of such a voice.

The flickering glow of burning city blocks lit the enclosure and painted the night sky orange. Distant screams and the murmur of battle marked the front where the Guard inexorably bulled its way back to the harbour. The Claw continued her circling dance while the Avowed clumsily tracked her, one lumbering step after another. So swiftly that Possum missed it, one foot lashed in to swipe the side of the Avowed's helmet, the sword swung after, and the armoured giant righted himself, shaking his head. *Fool! What did that accomplish? You'll only break the bones of your foot.* Another kick, this one connecting square in the chest, rocking the Avowed backwards – again, another slow swing. The woman at his shoulder snorted her impatience and Possum had to agree; what was the point in this wasted time and effort?

Yet useless punishment was not the Claw's purpose, as became clear to Possum in an instant as another kick brought another swing, but this time the arm was trapped, locked and the Claw's own elbow pushed in and the mailed arm snapped backwards with an audible wet popping. The Claw sprang away. The woman at Possum's shoulder grunted her appreciation of the move. The sword had fallen from the numb grip and now the Avowed struggled with his shattered arm to reach a dirk sheathed at his belt. The Claw launched herself upon him, legs twisting around his torso. Hands jabbed straight over the Avowed's vision slit, fisted, thumbs extended to disappear entirely within.

The Avowed bellowed his excruciating pain – the first sound Possum recalled hearing from him. The Claw sprang free once more, faced the blinded, crippled giant. He sank to his knees. He appeared to say something which was lost in the din of the surrounding battle;

she answered. He lowered his helmeted head. The Claw spun, leg lashing out to take the man low on the neck beneath the lip of the helmet, snapping the head sickeningly aside. The Avowed toppled to his side.

Possum could not believe what he'd just seen; how was this possible? *Hood preserve him! Who was this woman?* None he knew of in the ranks. The one holding the blade to his throat snarled something in a language unknown to Possum and withdrew. He spun but she was gone. *So quick!* A mage as well; and damned good.

Turning back, he caught the one wrapped in black swathings staring right at him. He took a breath to call but she ran, disappearing into another tenement. He cradled his front with a gasp; that sudden breath hadn't been a good idea. When he looked up again another lone Claw had entered the garbage-strewn enclosure. This one wore grey cloth, her short black hair uncovered. *Great Fanderay! Yet another one! And another female to boot! Where were they all coming from?* The Claw knelt to examine the fallen Avowed. Possum limped to the shattered rear door.

By the time he reached the Guardsman this third mystery woman was of course gone. He shuffled to the fallen Avowed. A hand at the man's broken neck assured him that the man was indeed dead – asphyxiation, Possum assumed, from feeling his crushed larynx.

He straightened from the corpse. Intriguing mysteries, yes, but all would have to wait. He studied the glow of flames brightening the night sky, black smoke billowing from nearby. Time to reassert some measure of control – if possible. And find a healer too. He probed the slit across his front gummed with drying blood, and grimaced; yes, definitely the closest he'd yet come to the end of his career. A wave and an opening to darkness appeared. Possum stepped through delicately.

*　*　*

Coming up the Way of Opals, Nait and the harbour guard met a wagon headed the opposite way. A tarp covered its contents and the drover was afoot, pulling on the tack of the two harnessed oxen. His face glistened with sweat and his eyes were wide with terror as he nodded to Sergeant Tinsmith. Up the road fires looked to be gathering Strength in the fine tailoring district. 'How goes things?' Sergeant Tinsmith called to the man.

'Very good, sir. Very good. Just trying to save some possessions from the fires.' He pulled two-handed on the yoke, muttered feverishly to the oxen.

'I meant with the battle,' Tinsmith said.

Men and women came running down the street carrying bundles and baskets. A crying child was being dragged along by her shirt-front. The man blinked at Tinsmith. 'Oh, that! Have no idea. Sorry. You'll have to reach the Gemcutters' Bourse for that.'

'The gemcutters?' said Nait. 'They're fighting *there*? Sergeant, please, we've to get a piece of *that*.'

The man clenched both hands in his hair and he stared pleadingly at the oxen. 'There's some kind of riot in the district. Something about protection fees. Move, you great anuses!'

Tinsmith raised an eyebrow. 'I'm sorry . . . ?'

The man yanked on his hair so hard it was as if he was attempting to raise himself from the ground. 'Not *you* – them! Why won't you move? Please! Come *on*.'

'Maybe we can help,' offered Hands.

Tinsmith glared at her. To the man, 'Good luck.'

'I'll fucking kill you!' the man yelled at the oxen.

Honey Boy tapped a finger to the side of his head. Least nodded, the fetishes tied in his hair jangling. As they moved up the Way of Opals the stream of refugees grew so congested they had to push to make any headway. It occurred to Nait that toe-to-toe fighting was not why he'd signed up with the harbour guard, but it looked like that was exactly where the sergeant was taking him unless he could think of something quick. It also occurred to him that he'd seen that fellow before. And recently too. He pushed his way to Tinsmith's side. 'Something strange about that fellow and his wagon, sir.'

'That there certainly was.'

'I mean, he was probably on his way to the harbour, don't you think?'

Tinsmith slowed. 'What tells you that, Nait?'

'Just a hunch.'

Tinsmith shook his head. 'Not good enough, Nait.' He waved a go-ahead to a glaring Hands.

'I've seen that scraggle-haired fellow before, sir,' Nait called.

'Where was that?' Tinsmith called back.

'On board the *Ragstopper*.'

Sergeant Tinsmith stopped. He turned to Nait. 'You sure?'

'My nose tells me so.' He tapped the side of it.

Hands sneered. 'He just doesn't want a sword shoved up it.'

A comment similar in kind occurred to Nait but Tinsmith waved for silence. He stroked his grey moustache. 'OK. Let's check it out.'

He raised his voice, 'Load crossbows! Spread out!' Hands signalled a reverse.

They found the wagon not too far down the way from where they'd left it. The drover ignored them, yanking on the harnessing. He was weeping. Tinsmith walked up, followed by Hands, Nait and Least.

'You with the *Ragstopper*?' Tinsmith called out.

The man jumped as if stabbed. He spun, dragged a sleeve across his face. 'What? Why? Who're you?'

'Sergeant Tinsmith, harbour guard. Are you with the *Ragstopper*? Is that cargo?'

The man wrung his hands. 'What's that? Cargo? No, of course not.' He climbed up on to the seat, took up a whip. 'Now, I have to go. Goodbye!'

'Oughtn't we . . .' began Hands. Tinsmith waved for her to wait.

The man cracked the whip over the oxen. 'Go! Run! Move!'

Tinsmith, Hands and Nait watched him. Nait moved his toothpick from one side of his mouth to the other. 'What'cha got back there, friend?'

He stared at them, then threw down the whip. 'Nothing! Just some supplies.' He clambered up on to the load of tarped boxes. 'You have no right to stop me. This isn't the harbour. Go away!'

Tinsmith sighed, looked up and down the street, watched the citizenry streaming past on their way to the waterfront to escape what might burgeon into a firestorm. 'Looks to me like this wagon represents a blockage in a public thoroughfare. Therefore, by the power invested in me as a public servant and enforcer of civil writs, it lies within my authorization to have this conveyance seized and impounded.'

On his hands and knees on top of the piled boxes, the fellow stared down at them. '*What?*'

'Least, Honey Boy, get this wagon off the main road.'

'Yes, sir,' said Least. He waved Honey Boy to him and the two yanked the oxen by their nose rings into the mouth of an alley. The man threw himself flat, hugging the tarp.

'No! You mustn't! You don't understand – it's mine! Mine!'

'Keep your invoice?' Nait asked with an evil grin.

The fellow rolled off the back. His hands went to his hair, yanked furiously, then flew out wide. He ran down the street, waving his arms, shrieking, 'Noooooo!'

Nait and Tinsmith watched him go. 'Oughtn't we . . .' said Hands. Tinsmith just waved the thought aside. He turned to the wagon.

'All right, let's take a look.' They untied the tarp, threw it up, lowered the gate. Boxes. Identical boxes of dark wood piled four deep in six rows. Nait examined the latches of the nearest. There didn't appear to be a lock plate or a keyhole. He pulled out his knife. 'How do you open these things?' He jammed the point of his knife into the wood.

Tinsmith suddenly knocked the knife flying from his hands. Nait glared at his sergeant. 'What?'

'Blame *my* nose,' Tinsmith said. 'Now stand back. I seem to remember seeing boxes like these back in my old days with the marines in Genabackis.' He stood up on the lowered gate and gingerly felt at the twin latches of one of the top rear boxes. These gave easily. Kneeling, his face close, he lifted the lid a finger's width. Nothing happened. He stared inside for a time, motionless.

'Sergeant?' Hands asked.

Tinsmith cleared his throat. 'Corporal, how close would you say those fires are now?'

'A few blocks – getting closer.'

He closed the box, jumped down. 'Back up the oxen. Get 'em moving. Now.'

'They ain't interested,' complained Least.

'Use your knives.'

Honey Boy blew out a breath and raised his brows as if to say, 'my goodness'.

Nait followed Tinsmith out on to the street. 'What's in the boxes?' His sergeant ignored him, peering up and down the thoroughfare.

'Corporal Hands,' he ordered, 'send men to confiscate and ready a launch large enough for this load.'

'Aye, aye, sir.'

'Is it gold?'

'Least, organize a perimeter of men around the wagon. Don't let anyone on to it.'

'Aye, sir.'

'Is it maybe the Imperial jewels looted from the twelve continents?'

Sergeant Tinsmith snatched the front of Nait's jerkin, lifted him on to his toes. Face to face, he growled, 'I'm going to actually tell you, Nait. But only because I know that if I don't you're going to stick your ugly face into one of them and kill us all. So, what's inside?' He lowered his voice and his eyes held a fey look that Nait had never seen in his sergeant before. 'There's enough Moranth munitions in that wagon to turn the city's entire waterfront into dust and smoke. All of it sealed with the mark of the Imperial Arsenal.'

'No shit?' Nait managed, pulling at Tinsmith's fist.

'But what *really* worries me, Nait, is the fact that someone's pillaging the Arsenal. And sooner or later, that someone's going to make a mistake – and when that happens I plan to be as far away as possible.'

* * *

Shimmer glared out the window of the Black Nacht tavern to the fires that seemed to have spontaneously sprung to life all over the city. Crossbow bolts slammed intermittently into half-closed shutters and bounced from the stone wall with sharp metallic *tings*. Turning, she crooked a finger to Smoky. The mage opened his arms helplessly. 'Don't look at me. Honest. I'm just playing support here. It's the citizens. They're looting and rioting to cover their looting. Honest.'

She crossed her arms. 'I hope so because we do not want to test Tayschrenn's forbearance.'

'Really!'

'Fine.' She faced the two blades that remained with her. 'We've made a mistake, let them pin us down. Their numbers are just growing out there. We have to keep moving.' Her glance fell to the sturdy tavern tables, their hand-adzed timbers fully four fingers thick; she studied the doors – of similar construction. She looked to Voss, a blade saboteur. He nodded and a broad smile gathered at his mouth.

Mantlets was one name Shimmer knew for them. Rattels, elsewhere, pavises as well. In practice they could take many shapes, depending upon the purposes one had in mind and the material available. Large movable shields usually built during sieges to defend attacking crossbowmen, bowmen or sappers. Voss supervised the construction of as many as they could pull together. Held side by side in a tight circle Shimmer would move her command inside a turtle – just like the one the remnants of the 3rd Company reported using to escape their imprisonment.

Yells and the crash of wood in the distance marked another element advancing – Shimmer watched down a side street while hundreds of armed citizens, this Untan volunteer militia, ran to cover the shifting action. Gods, everyone in the city had a crossbow and armfuls of bolts. It was as if they'd kicked a hornet's nest and now couldn't extricate their foot from it. Voss came to her side. 'How many?' she asked.

'Enough – better than none.'

'Are we ready?'

'Could use more time. Do the job right, you know. But they're gathering out there, aren't they.'

'Yes. We have no time. Pull the door and let's go.'

Voss saluted, the single fist to the chest. 'Aye, sir.'

The sturdy front door was yanked from its hinges. Bolts stormed through the opening like driven rain. Everyone had already taken cover. Two mantlets were brought up side by side then edged out one after the other to cover the opening in a 'V' shape. Shimmer waved up the next pair. Crossbow bolts slammed into the shields in a steady driven rhythm like hail. A tossed lit lantern smashed against the wall spraying burning oil. The Guardsmen flinched, but continued on. At her side Smoky pointed, mouthed, '*See!*'

Eventually a full turtle of hefted tall shields now protected her command. Snipers in the taller buildings would still have line of sight down within, but it was the best they could throw together. The tavern's front door served as the final rear mantlet closing all egress. Shimmer peeked ahead through a gap in the timbers. Tossed torches, lamps and lanterns now punished them. The ferocity of the attack amazed her; it was as if the citizens were determined to burn down their own city to get them. Voss had everyone who could carrying water and had doused everyone as they exited, but the flames still inflicted casualties. It was an ugly way to go – Shimmer would prefer anything quicker.

'Left,' she called, directing them to a narrower alley. Before them a ragged mob of armed citizen militia struggled to simultaneously fire their crossbows and retreat. It proved too much for them and they melted away in a general panic of falling bodies and dropped weapons. As they passed over the spot the Guardsmen helped themselves to the weapons. Yet the punishment from the rear was intense; the occasional bolt found an opening and men fell.

'Return fire!' Voss was yelling in the rear.

'Smoky!' Shimmer called.

'On it.'

Flames roared up behind the turtle of jostled mantlets, cutting off the alley.

'How long?' she asked.

'Not long.'

They emerged on to a major north-south avenue lined by vendors' stalls fronting three-storey brick merchants' shops. Fleeing citizenry thronged its centre, flowing south to the waterfront. Bands of armed militia crossed the flow, shifting to new hot spots. All of the citizens stopped, stared at the emerging turtle and fled screaming.

'Left again,' Shimmer called.

Bumping and banging, the ungainly beast lurched left. Through the gap Shimmer could now see down the long slow descent of the avenue to ship masts lit by the glow of the widespread flames. 'I see the harbour!' she called. A cheer went up within the turtle. The staccato impacts of bolts picked up now that their pursuers had poured into the avenue and flowed to surround them once again. A lantern tossed from a third-storey window burst among them splashing burning oil everywhere.

'Hold tight!' Shimmer yelled over the screams as men and women clawed at themselves and rolled to the cobbles. 'Douse them! Cloaks!' Abandoned, a mantlet table-top fell and a storm of bolts lashed into the exposed interior. 'Tighten up!'

A bolt slammed into Shimmer's side, knocking her to her knees. 'Close up!' she gasped, righting herself.

'They're rushing us,' a Guardsman warned.

'Ready weapons! Keep moving!' Shimmer took a long-knife from the belt of the Guardsman supporting the mantlet before her.

'Prepare to repel boarders!' some wit called out.

A spear thrust between mantlets, its leaf-shaped blade skittering from Shimmer's armour. She dropped the long-knife, took hold of the spear and yanked it from its bearer. Holding it up tall to reverse it, she then pushed it out, impaling the man. 'My thanks!'

She thrust to keep the militia back from the mantlets, called again and again, 'Keep moving!' At every breath the bolt in her side sent a sheet of agony through her that darkened her vision.

Then the hand of a God knocked everyone flat.

A great wall of air punched the breath from Shimmer's chest. Dust, smoke and debris stormed over them, obliterating all visibility as if the entire city were being carried out to sea. A moment later all the roof tiles suddenly leapt from the buildings to fly like birds off in a wind of smoke and ash. More crashed down all about like rain. The ground shuddered, bouncing them. She squinted through the dust to see an enormous billowing cloud swelling over the city. It was lit from within by lurid bursts of flame, bloating, climbing, taller it seemed than any mountain. Across the way a three-storey brick building was obliterated by a solid stone block the size of a small boat smashing down into it.

The wall of thunder slowly faded. Small pieces of burning debris fell about like intermittent rain. Carefully, amazed by the mere fact of her continued life, Shimmer pushed herself upright. She weaved, clutched at her side where the bolt emerged obscenely. Without

daring to stop to think about what she meant to do, she took hold
with all her strength and yanked it out. The white-hot resistance of
her own flesh drove her to her knees again. All about, men and
women, citizens and Guardsmen, were standing, peering about
amazed. A pale white ash began to fall from the swelling churning
cloud. It drifted thickly like tattered feathers and covered everything
as if in a layer of down. 'The harbour,' Shimmer croaked and kicked
the nearest Guard. 'Smoky!'

'Aye . . .' A ghost-like shape beneath a blanket of ash stirred to life,
sat up.

'What in Hood's Own Shade was that?'

Dark eyes in a white mask blinked to life. He stood, shook his
kinky hair raising a cloud of dust. 'I think that was maybe the
greatest natural explosion ever yet set off by humans.'

'I've never seen anything like it.'

'No. Nor will we ever again, I expect.'

'*Gods on earth*,' she breathed amazed. 'We better get out of here
before these Untan fools decide we did it. They'll tear us limb from
limb.'

Smoky glanced around at the ash-cloaked figures dazedly stirring
to life and wandering aimlessly: a city of ghosts awakening. He
blinked owlishly. 'I expect you're right . . .'

'Move out, Guardsmen!'

*   *   *

Greymane did not witness the actual explosion. He'd been looking
away, scanning for activity among the anchored Malazan man-o-
wars, when the light suddenly changed – a great white flash threw
his shadow across the deck and punched shouts of amazement and
alarm from the men on the vessel. When he turned to look the light
was gone. In its place rose an immense cloud of smoke that swelled
even as he watched, billowing and burgeoning over the city. All
across the waterfront great knots of birds scattered, wheeling their
panic. While Greymane stared a wave seemed to pass over the city,
bursting tiled rooftops, toppling spires, racing outward from the
blast until it reached the waterfront. He had a moment to yell, 'Brace
yourselves!' as it jumped the intervening water of the harbour,
frothing the calm surface as it charged. Then it struck the vessel,
tearing away half-lowered sails like paper and batting the ship like a
toy. The thunderclap was so loud it deadened Greymane's ears, leaving
him insensible of any sounds; men's mouths moved and equipment

fell but no sound reached him. His first thought was: *so ends the Guard. Obliterated by Laseen in one titanic explosion*. But the blast seemed to have originated much farther inland from the fires marking the fighting. He'd have to make sure.

He righted a man, waved to the wharf and the sweeps. Then the ship shuddered again. He spun; men pointed to the deck – there gaped a smoking hole that hadn't existed a moment ago. *Burn's Mercy – and how many leagues away was that explosion?* A moment later a sailor came up from below carrying a pot. It held a piece of rock still hot to the touch. A shard of scorched building stone. Greymane waved the staring men to the sweeps. There must be some survivors, but he feared the worst.

They passed only one other vessel underway – an old scow merchantman, alarmingly low in the water, sails hanging in shreds, deck a mess of tossed gear, with its wiry, grey-haired Napan captain bellowing scalding invective at his scrambling crew. Greymane was surprised by the name gouged in the rotting wood of the bow; he didn't think anyone would've dared use the name *Ragstopper* after the career of its predecessor, pirate admiral, lieutenant of Laseen then known as Surly, and brother of Urko – Cartharon Crust.

But the mystery of the *Ragstopper* had to wait, for crewmen pointed to the wharf, shouting their amazement. There, massed like an army of shades, waited the surviving Guardsmen. Even as the ship closed more came marching down thoroughfares, surrounded by citizens, weapons held ready, though none attacked. Rather, an unofficial truce seemed to have been agreed upon – perhaps so long as it was obvious that the Guard wanted nothing more than to get away, and the citizens were more than happy to prod them along. All appeared shocked numb by the monumental explosion, while the unearthly white ash that rained down rendered all alike: uniformly pale ghosts, and everyone uniformly eerily silent.

Greymane supervised the loading of the survivors and there found Shimmer, carried on a tabletop serving as a litter, attended by Avowed mages Smoky, Lor-sinn and Shell. 'Take us west,' she gasped, pale with lost blood, long hair sweat-matted to her face.

'Skinner?'

She waved him on. 'He'll find us.'

The last Guardsman to step from the stone wharf was an Avowed named Black. Water dripped from him as he stood scanning the gathering crowd of Untan citizenry that edged ever closer, yelling obscenities. A few pieces of broken litter flew.

'We have to go!' Greymane shouted.

Reluctantly, limping, the man abandoned the wharf. Rocks, broken tiles, offal and vegetables now pelted down upon them as the crowd roared, some even jeering their scorn. Greymane ordered double-time on the sweeps, called to Black, 'What is it?'

'Nothing. You didn't happen – *there the bastards are!*' Pointing, the Avowed threw himself to the railing, almost falling out of the ship.

There, low in the water under a pier, a small crew in a launch waved farewell. Greymane recognized the harbour guard. One of them, a skinny pox-faced fellow, stood and bared his arse to them until the heavyset woman in armour next to him kicked him into the water. The crowd howled their appreciation.

'I swear to Hood I'll find you!' Black was yelling as the open water grew between them. 'I swear!'

When the ship came alongside the harbour mole they found it lined by fist-waving youths. The Guard oared from the harbour accompanied by distant taunts and thrown trash. At the side of the trailing vessel Greymane watched the gesturing youths. His thoughts turned to the Guard and its vow. How could they hope to free a citizenry from their rulers when they so obviously did not wish to be freed? The Guard seemed to have outlived its relevance. Though it did seem from the intelligence they'd gleaned so far that elsewhere the move to end Imperial rule had come very far indeed. From Shimmer's orders to go west he assumed the Avowed intended to link up with that movement. Yet he was troubled. His experience with political power told him that no vacuum would long endure. With what, he wondered, did this secessionist movement – or the Avowed for that matter – intend to replace Imperial rule?

* * *

The next day, escorted by a guard of fifty Malazan regulars, Empress Laseen surveyed the damage of the eruption of the Imperial Arsenal. She picked her way through the still smoking scoured bare dirt of the blast crater, greater than a stone's throw across, where once the Arsenal and surrounding buildings had stood. Havva Gulen paced at her side. 'Could have been worse,' the mage said, hands clasped at the front of her broad stomach.

Laseen shook her head. 'I'm thinking that it should have been much worse.'

'Oh?'

The Empress continued on ahead of the High Mage, kicked at the pulverized ground. 'It was impressive, yes. But more of the city should've been destroyed. The Arsenal couldn't have been half-full.'

'Really? The Guard, you think?'

'Possibly. This whole incident could've been nothing more than a raid to collect munitions – or to simply deplete ours.'

'Alarming strategic thinking on their part, if that be the case.'

'Yes. And no sign of K'azz?'

'No. Skinner seemed to be in charge.'

Laseen took up a handful of the blackened, burnt soil, sifted it through her fingers. 'Skinner. Not known for his subtlety.'

'No. However,' and Havva paused, as if unsure whether to continue.

Facing away, Laseen asked, tiredly, 'Yes?'

'They say Greymane was seen with them at the harbour.'

'Greymane?' She straightened. 'Really? Greymane . . .' She scanned the wreckage but her mind was obviously far away. She nodded to herself.

'Yes,' Havva said. 'The one place he must've thought himself safe from everyone.' She gave a deep belly-laugh. 'Imagine his dismay to find the Guard actually returning! Now he might face his own officers—'

Laseen regarded her silently then glanced away.

Havva decided she'd said quite enough. Further intelligence would have to wait, perhaps for ever. *Oh, my Empress! You are alone; the walls you have raised have driven all from your side. Was it arrogance? Contempt? Failure to understand anything beyond your own drive to rule? Yet you say nothing and so we who could help you cannot know for certain. And there is too much to lose in that uncertainty. Now you stand apart. All alone but perhaps for poor blind Possum. Perhaps that is the cruel logic of your silence. Laseen, if I chose this private moment together to tell you all I know perhaps we would have a chance – a slim chance – of victory against the conspiracy that has closed itself around us. I have been doing all I can. But I dare not speak openly. I dare not take the chance. I am ashamed and so sorry, my Empress. I too have failed you. All because my time in the Archives was not wasted. I know the name Jhistal. And I fear I do not have the power to oppose it.*

The ranks of surrounding guard parted to admit the spear-slim form of High Fist Anand followed by a waddling, sweaty Mallick Rel fanning himself and grimacing at the stink of stale smouldering fires and burnt flesh. A white cloth encircled his head. 'Congratulations, Empress! A great victory!' the councilman called.

312

'Victory?' Laseen repeated flatly. 'A few hundred of the Crimson Guard visit us for less than a day and half the capital is blown up and burnt to the ground?'

'An invasion grandly repulsed!'

'They left because they saw there was nothing here for them,' Havva said.

Anand shook his head. 'I have to admit that it was the volunteer citizen militia that drove them off.' He sounded as if he were still surprised by the fact. 'And for that I apologize, Empress. I hadn't thought them a force worth considering before. They have no formal command structure or professional officer corps.'

'A mere mob,' Mallick sneered.

'Mobs rule urban warfare,' Anand said. 'Bring enough numbers to bear from all directions and you smother any opponent.'

'Apology accepted, High Fist,' Laseen said, cutting through the confrontation. 'Their numbers?'

'My officers in the streets put their numbers as high as ten thousand. And climbing – more are joining every day. There are lines outside their headquarters.'

'And just where are these vaunted headquarters, High Fist?' Mallick inquired mildly, his round face gleaming.

Anand paused, reluctant to answer, then reconsidered, stating boldly, 'neighbourhood taverns.'

'Faugh! Rabble who would melt at the first clash of iron. Empress, such forces are useless. The First Sword would have nothing to do with these undisciplined amateurs.'

'To their great relief, no doubt,' Anand observed. 'In any case, they themselves recognize their shortcomings and they've put out a call for retired regular and marine officers to join them. I understand a ship full of retired sergeants and officers just put in from Malaz Isle. Old Braven Tooth himself among them.'

'Braven Tooth!' Laseen repeated, amazed. 'I thought he was dead.'

'So did everyone.' Anand's smile held rueful affection. 'Seems he sank his decades of back-pay and pension into some kind of Denul ritual that turned him into an oak stump.'

'Unnecessarily,' Laseen remarked, facing aside.

Mallick sucked his stained teeth loudly. 'All very well. However, it would take months to hammer such a force into an army. Time we do not have.'

'What happened to your head?' Havva asked him.

'What?'

Havva gestured to the cloth. 'Your head.'

Mallick's hands flew to the wrap, straightened it. 'The blast. A lamp fell on me.'

Pity that was all. 'Wounded in defence of the city. How noble.'

Mallick's gaze narrowed to slits. 'And where were you, Havva Gulen? Cowering in the Archive's sub-basement, sharpened quill raised?'

Always closer than you know, Mallick Rel.

'I agree with your estimate of our time, Mallick,' Laseen said. 'When is the First Sword expected?'

'Later today,' Anand supplied.

'When he returns, inform him that we will be departing from Unta with all haste. Close the harbour, Anand. Confiscate every vessel. We sail with every available man and woman.'

Anand bowed. 'Very good, Empress.'

'We?' Mallick asked, arched.

'Not you, Spokesman for the Assembly. Will you remain here in Unta, overseeing the rebuilding and the defence of the capital?'

Mallick's brows rose and he bowed. 'It would be my honour, of course. I will report daily on the progress.'

'That will be difficult, Mallick, because I will be leading the army.'

A gasp from Anand, '*Empress!*'

Laseen raised a hand to silence all objections. 'It is decided. We must leave immediately.'

Though clearly unhappy, Anand gathered himself and bowed stiffly. Havva bowed as well. *So shall I too go. As will Possum and the majority of the Claw. In the field again, as it was so long ago.*

'I shall raise a magnificent monument to your future victories on this very site,' Mallick said, bowing.

'Wait until I have won them,' Laseen said, her unreadable gaze steady on the man.

* * *

In an urban garden servants brushed ash from laden tree-branches while workers dismantled one of its collapsed brick walls. A man in loose trousers and a long plain maroon shirt stood at a planting bed, examining a potted flower. His long black hair hung loose. A woman with a heart-shaped face and short black hair entered the garden and walked swiftly upon him. Without turning, he said, 'A rare specimen from Avalli, Kiska. Undamaged, thankfully.'

The woman covered her nose. 'It stinks.'

'Its scent imitates the smell of weakness: rot and death. Attracting flies and other insect scavengers. Which it then eats.'

'Disgusting.'

'Revelatory. There is a lesson here for anyone who cares to reflect upon it.'

'Avoid stinking plants.'

Tayschrenn sighed, set down the pot. 'You are too much the child of the city, Kiska.' He faced her, set his darkly tanned hands on his waist. 'Could not stay away, could you? I suppose I should have known better.'

Kiska studied the workmen, the usual local labourers hired to maintain Tayschrenn's home, all cleared by Hattar. 'I just kept an eye on things.'

'Good. I see that some wisdom has penetrated your thick stubbornness. But one does not merely "keep an eye" on men such as Cowl.'

'He left by Warren.'

'Which?'

'Hood's.'

Tayschrenn grunted. 'How appropriate. So, what did you witness – other than futility and waste?'

Flicking back her short bangs, Kiska tilted her head to one side, frowning. 'I saw a number of Claws fleeing Avowed open ways into the Imperial Warren.'

'Yes?'

'They never returned.'

'Indeed.'

'I saw an Avowed named Amatt break a barricade of burning wagons and piled timbers simply by walking into it and pushing a section aside. I counted seven crossbow bolts in him. He then walked down to the ships, pulling the bolts out as they struck him.' She shook her head, amazed. 'I tell you, I do not want to face those Guardsmen again.'

'I agree. It would be a great waste.'

'Waste?'

Tayschrenn merely rubbed his face, gestured for Kiska to continue.

'Mostly I shadowed a female Claw – or someone who resembled a Claw. She was hunting Avowed. I saw her stalk and kill two, bare-handed. I say she looked like a Claw in that their – our – training resembled her skills in the way a child's sketch resembles a masterpiece.'

'Indeed.'

'And there was another woman out there as well. One who moved with ease in and out of Warrens. Like nothing I've ever heard of before.'

He stilled, his gaze in the distance. 'Is that so? Interesting . . .'

Kiska swung a kick at the planting bed. 'Is that all you have to say? *Interesting*? What's going on, damn it all to Trake!'

Dark eyes focused on Kiska; the long shaved jaw writhed, tightening. 'A trial is approaching us. I ask a difficult thing of you – restraint. I foresee a chance of . . . *chaos* . . . arising out of the coming confrontation. I may have to act quickly and there is someone among us who will try to take advantage. Do you understand?'

Kiska bowed. 'I will inform Hattar.'

'My thanks.' As she turned to go he called after her, 'Tell me, Kiska, why did you not remain in the Claw? You could be a Hand-commander by now, perhaps more.'

She shrugged. 'I came to understand that I'd always wanted to serve something greater than myself. It became obvious to me rather quickly that those in the Claw serve only themselves. Why?'

But the tall mage was now bent over regarding his plants. 'Just wondering.'

Kiska bowed and left. *Someone*, he says. Well, she had a pretty good idea who that might be. She and Hattar would have to put their heads together to figure out a way to counter that fat conniving priest. As for the Claw who hunted Avowed, Kiska felt a thrill shiver through her. Could it have truly have been *her*? Tayschrenn hadn't seemed surprised – after all, he'd seen her in action so many years ago. Yet by now everyone seemed to have forgotten, or been deliberately led to forget, that long ago when the fighting had been the thickest, and Dancer guarded Kellanved, it had been Surly, Mistress of the Claw, who had stalked and slain their enemies.

CHAPTER III

See the little blackbird,
Dappled and grey.
See the fallen soldiers,
Dappled and grey.
It hunts a tasty morsel,
Dappled and grey.
It looks in eyes unseeing,
Dappled and grey.

Children's rhyme,
Streets of Heng

AND SO THE SOLDIER OF LIGHT HAS DELIVERED HIMSELF. BUT JUST
what does he herald? A hand gentle on the *Kite*'s tiller, Ereko
looked down at the calm face of the sleeping lad. His gaze
travelled to the sword at his side wrapped in its sheath and belt. Even
hidden away its power appalled him. A blade too great to be wielded
by any being cognizant of its potential. And so an innocent youth
carries it – or perhaps it only allows itself to be carried by such a one.
Ereko knew only that *he* dared not touch it. Thinking back to that
delicate meeting on the beach he breathed again a prayer of thanks
to Goddess Mother that violence had not visited them. That blade is
a match for Traveller's – if only in its singleness of purpose. And
these clansmen from Assail, they carry secrets that should never have
left that land. Rising, his eyes met the bright steady gaze of Traveller
across the length of the vessel. And what of you, my friend? Why do
I fear for you even more with every passing league? I suspect the full
dregs of what you must endure yet await you. So why such a fell
gathering of power and pregnant histories? Are we all here to escort
you, my friend, or do you escort us? Who is to know save the

317

Enchantress and Queen of Dreams, T'riss, in the arc of whose vision we all act?

The lad shifted, stretched and awoke blinking in the early light. 'Sleep yet,' Ereko told him.

Kyle rubbed his eyes. 'It's all I seem to do these days, sleep.' He rubbed his arm where Ereko's High Denul had mended torn ligament and ruptured flesh. 'What of you? You man that tiller day and night. Won't you rest?'

Ereko lightly laughed the suggestion aside. 'No, lad. I am so old now that sleeping and waking have melded together into one and I know not which I inhabit.'

Watching the lad struggle through that, Ereko shifted course slightly to avoid a looming ice-spire.

'Truly? So old? As old as the mountains?'

Ereko raised his brows. 'Goodness, no. Not *that* old. Only half so old, I should think.'

The lad pulled his blanket closer, eyed him sidelong as if gauging the degree of his sincerity. Unsure, he raised his chin to the ice-dotted waves. 'What is that light to the south?'

Ereko did not turn his gaze. *Even yet the power of that ritual bruises!* 'That pale bluish light?'

'Yes.'

'A great field of ice, Kyle. Quite perilous. To travel there is to risk wandering accidentally into another Realm. A place of eternal cold. The home of another race.'

'And these ice mountains?' Kyle indicated the largest one nearest them: a towering peak of deep sapphire blue, wind and water sculpted into sweeping arcs and blade-like curves.

'Yes. Children of the ice field. They break off and wander the seas. Some say they each carry some small part of the power that binds the ice here in the world. And so does it diminish over the ages.'

'Well, it's a good thing we have all this ice.'

'Why?'

'We're getting low on water.'

'Burn Forefend, lad! We mustn't touch this ice.'

'No? Why ever not?'

'Why ever—' Ereko ducked his head. Lowering his voice, he continued, 'Haven't you been listening? Have your people forgotten everything, lad? Don't you know that such ice is the feat of the Jaghut?'

The lad looked away. 'We know of them.'

'Yes. Your people are their enemy though they are not yours. In any case, such ice fields on land and at sea are the highest accomplishment of their arts. Omtose Phellack crystallized here upon the world. Your people spread in great migrations over land and sea. Such fields of ice were raised as barriers against your expansion. We skirt now the remnants of one such.'

'And how do you know this?' the lad asked with the bluntness of youth.

'Because I saw it happen.'

A snort confirmed the lad's disbelief. Ereko fully expected the reaction. He shifted into a more comfortable position, crossed his arms on the tiller. 'I will tell you a story.' Kyle said nothing but Ereko noted the Assail native, Stalker, shift to turn an ear to the stern. 'Know you not that Elder Night, Kurald Galain, possesses its children, the Tiste Andii? Well, what of the world and its many races and beings? Who are its children? Are they what some name the "Founding Races"? Or can some other kind lay claim to being the true children of the earth? Myself, I believe the term "founding" refers to those races that established civilizations or societies complete with writing and tools, either flint knives or the complex mechanisms of the K'Chain Che'Malle. In any case, the question is, were any of those the children of the earth? Well, of course, all are to one degree or another. Any beings of bone, muscle and blood partake of Mother Earth. Only those of the Eldest, those of most ancient lineage, entities born of pure energy such as some believe the Elder Gods, or the Eleint, what you call "dragons", may stand apart in that. Aside from such beings, what of the Thelomen, the Toblakai, the Teblor or Trell? What of their many kinds? Well, these are the varied descendants of one common ancestor. The first children of the earth. Those of my race, the Thel Akai. Those Who Speak.'

'Quite the story,' Kyle said, again with the unthinking innocence of youth.

Ereko gave an easy shrug. 'Oh, yes. I may be lying, or more likely self-deluded by memories twisted over the ages. But I lived through those times. I was there when an isolated flowering of civilization of your people arose on Jacuruku. And I suppose it was my people's nurturing that helped things along – not that I say we gave you civilization as some Jaghut claim they have – no, we merely advised and supported. In any case, in time a warlord arose. One who showed a genius and a lust for conquering all his surrounding states. We were not a warlike people, not in the least, but we lent our support against him. We raised our voices in opposition, gave

319

succour to his enemies. For that we earned his eternal enmity. He swore to wipe us from the face of the earth. And he almost succeeded. Of my people only I remain.'

'I'm sorry,' Kyle breathed. He was staring out over the waves, squinting against the glitter of dawn's light from the ice. Ereko thought him half-awake.

'Thank you. Since then, for the most part, your race has been kind to me.'

'Who was this warlord?'

'Who was he? Ah, yes. He became King, of course. Eventually even his own people became so sickened by his cruelty that they attempted to rid themselves of him. And thereby they brought great misery to this world. But that is a story too long to be told now. Let us say he anointed himself with the name High King. Originally, his name was Kallor.'

Stalker sat up, draped his long forearms across his folded legs. 'I've heard the name Kallor.'

Ereko shrugged. 'No doubt there are others named such.'

'He was mentioned among the Guard. An ally of Brood against the Malazans in Genabackis. They called him the "Warlord".'

Again an easy shrug. 'This world has seen too many warlords.'

* * *

Crouched on his haunches, Toc the Elder took up a handful of the dark rich prairie soil and rubbed it in his hands. He held it to his nose and inhaled the rich scent of humus. No matter what might come, success or failure of this toss of the bones, he was thankful that he would see it here in his adopted homeland. He would offer up a blessing for that gift to Wind, Earth and the ancient spirits of the land. At some point in his younger days – he wasn't sure when it had happened – but at some time he'd fallen in love with the plains landscape. Some he knew found it empty and desolate – the Great Central Desert, many called it in Tali and Unta, even Heng, here right upon its doorstep. Yet to him it was far from empty. To him it was in fact full of a grim yet enthralling grandeur. This, to his mind, was the key to why so many professed their dislike. The simple truth was that it was too big for those small people.

He stood, stretched his back and nodded his assent to the waiting atamans and message riders. Choss waited at the flaps of the command tent and they embraced. 'Almost all together again,' Choss said, grinning behind his thick gold and russet beard.

'Almost.'

Toc greeted the atamans and they all reclined on the blankets within. Trays of sweetmeats and flatbreads made the rounds. 'Firstly,' Toc said, dipping his hands in a water bowl, 'may I thank the gathered atamans for the trust and honour they have been generous enough to place upon me. And secondly, may I apologize that the walls of Heng yet stand.'

The atamans spoke all at once, dismissing any need for an apology. Ataman Ortal, of the Black Ferret Assembly, raised his hands to speak. 'Warlord, it was understood from the beginning that we would not take the city immediately. You asked us to wait for allies to arrive. And now they are here – now we need wait no longer. Now we will attack together.'

Toc exchanged a glance with Choss, shifted his seat and selected a handful of grapes. 'I wish it were so simple, Ortal. Our allies from Tali have brought many men, yes, but not enough to take Heng.'

Gazes moved to Choss. 'Not enough?' said Ortal. 'Then why come at all? Explain.'

'We ask for further patience,' Choss said with a grimace. 'We have more men coming.'

'More? From where?' asked the Plains Lion Assembly ataman, Redden Brokeleg. 'Wait, you say. This is your answer for everything. Where can these warriors be coming from? There are no more in all your lands. You may have as many men and women as there are blades of grass, yet they would be useless when there is no will to fight.'

The other atamans all shouted their disapproval of such harsh words. Toc raised his hands to speak. '... If I may ... Redden, your words are strong but I hear them. Are they yours or do you speak for other voices that I have heard are raised against our alliance?'

All eyes turned to Redden. He shrugged his indifference, dug at the bare earth with a stick. 'I merely speak openly what others only dare tell their Hands.'

'And what are these things?' Toc asked.

'There are those who heard promises of great booty but have found none. Promises of honour in fighting but who sully themselves riding down women and children. Who see Seti blood spilled to further the ambitions of outlanders ... as it was in the past.'

'The Wildman of the foothills,' sneered Imotan, the White Jackal shaman sitting cross-legged to one side.

Redden nodded his agreement. 'Yes. The Wildman. He speaks against all alliances.' He raised his gaze to Toc. 'Especially those with Malazans.'

'He should have been slain long ago,' Imotan growled.

'You are welcome to try,' Redden said with an easy shrug. 'He is coming.'

The shaman's face darkened. 'What? Here?'

'Yes.' The stick scoured a line in the dirt. 'He calls for all warriors to rally to him. Some say he means to challenge for leadership . . .'

'Of what Assembly is he?' Toc asked.

An insouciant shrug. 'Who is to know? He renounces all such bonds – he names them chains upon the mind and body.'

For a time no one spoke. Toc shook his head. 'I wish it were so easy, but you cannot turn your back upon the world – it will not go away. You must adjust to change. Or be consumed by it . . . In any case,' he bowed to Redden, 'my thanks, friend, for bringing this news to us. We all have much to think about. I ask for further patience and I promise you this, many more men are close. Very close. Enough to take Heng. They will be arriving soon.' He bowed to the gathering and all answered in kind.

After the hugs and assurances of loyalty, Toc was left with Choss and Imotan, the White Jackal shaman. Servants lit lamps against the gathering darkness. Toc listened to the susurrus of the field crickets.

'What more do we know about this Wildman?' Choss asked Imotan.

The shaman waved a clawed hand dismissively. His sun-darkened face puckered in distaste. 'Very little. He is called this because he emerged from the woods and they say he's as hairy as a wild bhederin.'

Choss poured himself a glass of wine. 'Just what we need – some fiery prophet denouncing all contact with outlanders. You Seti are ill-served by him, I think, Imotan. What does he expect? You're inviting the world to bite your arse when you stick your head in the sand.'

'Colourful but accurate,' said Toc. He eyed Imotan and his mouth drew down in thought. 'Perhaps some demonstration of fighting spirit is called for. We should contact our people in Heng. A co-ordinated, targeted attack . . .'

'Would be a waste of resources,' Choss countered, waving the glass dismissively.

'An investment in improved relations.'

'Damned expensive.'

'Required, I think.'

Choss's thick, expressive brows rose and fell. He scratched his beard in thought. 'Well. I'll pull something together.'

'Good.' Toc stood. 'We are finished, then?'

Grunting, Imotan pushed himself up with an effort. 'I am too old for these long talking sessions, I think.' Choss offered an arm but the old man waved him off.

'What of you?' Choss asked him. 'I'd think you'd agree with this Wildman.'

The old shaman assented, bobbing his head in approval. 'Oh, yes, I agree with most of what he says . . . But for one thing – he does not have the sympathy of our people's spirits. They whisper to me that Heng must be besieged. That out of this will come the salvation of our people. So, in this you and I are allies. And I will fight him with all the resources at my command.'

'I see. Thank you.'

'Do not thank me, Choss. It is chance only. We might just as easily have been enemies.' And smiling he left the tent to be surrounded by his white-cloaked bodyguard.

Choss clasped hands with Toc. 'Well, on that reassuring note . . .'

'Let me know what you've cooked up.'

'Aye.'

Toc watched Choss go, waving his lieutenants to him, then raised his chin to a man in studded leather armour, a blackened iron helmet and a long mailed skirt. The ivory grips of twin sabres curved bright at his sides. The man approached, bowing, 'Sir?'

'Captain Moss, you've heard talk of this Seti Wildman?'

'Yes, sir. I have.'

'Who is he? Where is he? Track him down and report back.'

Captain Moss saluted. 'Sir.' He jogged down the gentle hillside. As he went, he called to his troop, 'Mount up!'

Toc remained for a time in the tent opening testing the night air. It carried a hint of the stink of Li Heng, now a glow on the southern horizon. Toc smiled at his own conceit; here he was, son of a nameless speck of a hamlet in Bloor, naming the Seti prairie his home and damning cities as stinking shitpits. He wrinkled his nose . . . still, it did smell of shit. He supposed he'd been away from all human settlements for too long. He thought he could also detect a distant pine stand – the sap would be thickening. Autumn was coming. They didn't have much time.

* * *

It was worse than Cowl's most pessimistic forebodings: the instant they entered the Warren he scrambled to raise the most potent protections he could muster. Yet even now, sheltered from direct exposure, he could feel the rabid energies gnawing at his wards. Should they corrode their way through, he and Skinner would not last a heartbeat. Here, at the most far-flung reaches of Thyr, within sight of the effects of Kurald Liosan, Elder Light, inaccessible and far more inhospitable than all the other elders.

He crouched with Skinner within the shadows of a narrow, deep ravine of cracked, baked earth. Overhead, curtains and streamers of energy lashed and snapped across a blinding white sky. Cowl imagined he could almost hear them singing.

'You prefer this to Chaos?' Skinner growled.

'I preferred to *chance* this over Chaos, yes.'

'You are too cautious. Why not Shadow, or Tellann?'

'Too crowded. And eyes are everywhere. Here there are no eyes.' He gestured the way ahead. The two shuffled along, wincing against the raging storm of energies above.

'What do you mean, no eyes?'

'Can't you feel it? This place is wild, feral. It is without a guiding presence.'

'What of Father Light?'

Cowl raised an arm across his face. 'Well, if you must cite the first mover, the prime originator, then, yes, I suppose he is here, yes.' He pinched shut his dazzled eyes, grimacing. 'If only in spirit.'

'I mistrust it. I have heard the air is poisoned. That those who come here die of it later.'

'It's not the air that's poisonous,' Cowl said, and he took a right-hand turn where the ravine met another, wider channel. 'This way.'

'You said something about crowds?' Skinner said.

Cowl turned. Skinner was pointing to the channel's dry dirt floor: a Path. Twins' laughter! How had he missed that? Damn. He waved Skinner on.

They followed the channel for some time. How long Cowl could not be sure, of course; no sun rose or fell, nor was there any discernible change in the natural variations in the streamers and coronas of unleashed energy lashing across the sky. They had reached a position, roughly, where his instincts told him he might attempt to reach out to the churning power to manipulate an opening, when four figures suddenly stepped out in front of them.

Surprised, Cowl stopped short; obviously, he could not count on his heightened senses and perceptions here in this inimical place. The figures wore a kind of white enamelled armour, now caked in dust, and pale yellow cloaks. Their features reminded him of Tiste Andii, though the hair of each hung white and long. One barked something in their own tongue. Cowl signed his lack of comprehension.

A wave from one and the spokesman tried again, 'You understand us now, worm?'

Cowl gave a half-bow. 'Greetings, honored Liosan.'

'Relinquish your arms and armour, trespassers. You are now our slaves.'

Cowl turned to Skinner – the full iron helm, blackened yet glittering as if dusted in sand, disguised the man's face but Cowl could imagine the raised brows. In answer, Skinner waved Cowl aside and advanced upon the four.

Perhaps it was incomprehension, or an inability to accept what was occurring, but Skinner was able to close on the first two before they acted to draw their weapons. As the nearest went for his grip the Avowed commander grasped that arm and swung the Liosan aside to crash into the defile wall, bringing down a rain of baked clay soil as jagged as kiln-dried potsherds. The second he backhanded aside into the other wall. Both slumped unconscious. The remaining two, swords readied, raised their white triangular shields. Skinner continued to close, still empty-handed. The first swung, the curved creamy blade striking an upraised armoured forearm and shattering into brittle shards. The Liosan gaped in unbelieving amazement. A punch from Skinner drove his shield into his chest and knocked him backwards from his feet; he lay stunned. The remaining Liosan sliced Skinner's chest but the blade merely skittered from the Avowed's glinting deep-crimson armour. An arm lashed out to clout the Liosan across the side of his helmeted head, spinning him from his feet. Without pausing, Skinner stepped over the fallen Liosan. Cowl followed, not even bothering to look down.

After a time one of the Liosan sat up groggily. He yanked off his helmet and threw it to the dirt. 'Brother Enias, I am coming dangerously close to losing my faith.'

A second sat up, coughing, and gingerly pressing his chest. 'Hold on to your faith, Brother Jorrude. These are tests, are they not, of its strength?'

'Well, I cannot speak for you, Brother Enias, but I am tested sorely.'

Groans sounded from the other two and Jorrude helped them to their feet. 'And who were they?' he demanded of Enias.

'I know not. Humans yet, though I smell vows, pacts and patronage about them. Enough that they insult us by trespassing with impunity.'

'We must follow! Bring justice to them!' said a third.

Jorrude. retreived his helmet, brushed dust from it. 'Perhaps it would be best that we continue our quest . . . what think you, Brother Enias?'

'Yes, Brother Jorrude. Satisfying though justice may be, we ought not to neglect our purpose. Father Light has turned his face from us brothers! Some failure or lack within ourselves or our ancestors has severed our connection. We must find a way to bring the warmth of his gaze upon us once more.' Brother Enias adjusted his armour, wincing. '*That* is our purpose!'

'Yes, Brother Enias,' the other three recited.

Cowl waited until enough distance lay between him and the Liosan – guards, or fellow travellers like themselves, or whoever they may have been – before deciding to try to exit Thyrllan. He did not look forward to it; so abandoned were the energies here that enforcing the control of manipulation would try his skill to its limit.

He was flexing his gloved hands when Skinner stopped. 'There, Cowl. What is that?'

He looked ahead, then up. Just visible above the narrow gap of a side ravine rose an ochre-brick tower. Cowl stared. *Great Mother Dark – who might possibly* . . . He hurriedly stepped aside into cover. 'We should go. Now.'

Absently, Skinner raised an iron-gauntleted hand to shake a finger at Cowl. 'I think not. I am curious.'

'Do not fool yourself. There are entities here far more powerful than those Liosan.'

'Then let us go meet these great powers.'

'Are you insane? I will take us out, now.'

The finger pointed. 'No. You will accompany me in case you are needed.'

The Avowed High Mage stood silent for a time, stroked the scars that traced a pearly thatching along his neck. *Even more imperious than when he left us is our Skinner. Still, he was powerful even then, and now this Ardata seems to have invested even greater potentialities within him. Why would she have done so and then apparently meekly allow him to go? There is a greater mystery here. And perhaps it would be interesting* . . . He waved an invitation to proceed.

After investigating for a time they could not discover any way up to the tower. It seemed that whoever built or occupied the structure had no use for the sheltered ways all other travellers were forced to walk in order to pass through this deadly reach of the warren. That alone made the sweat cold that soaked Cowl's silk shirt, layered thin hauberk, pocketed vest and many weapon belts. They also had to pause while he renewed each of the layered protections he had woven around them. After this, Skinner selected the shallowest ravine wall and punched out depressions as hand-holds. Cowl waited, face averted, while the dry clay clumps rained down.

Eyes shaded, he waited until his seemingly irresistible commander had almost reached the top then took a breath and launched himself at the rotten wall. A soft moccasin touch within one gap, a deft pull upon a protruding rock, and in an instant he had ascended the wall as if flying up.

Reaching the top and pulling himself erect, Skinner grunted to see Cowl standing before him. He gestured to himself. 'I don't suppose you could have . . .'

'No.'

A blasted landscape of harsh shadows and brilliant whites assaulted their vision. The energies pulsing outward felt like a hand thrusting Cowl backwards. The commingled roar of its rush was a thunder almost beyond his capacity to hear. Face averted, he ran for the cover of the tower. Even Skinner joined him, hunched against the raw, yammering aurora. The bricks of the tower scorched Cowl's fingertips. 'You're not going in, are you?' he shouted.

'Of course. And you are coming with me.'

In the end, he followed, if only to avoid the indignity of being dragged by his belts. They found an opening leading to an empty ground floor and stairs up. All was built of the same clay bricks – all of which had equally bulged and sagged in the unrelenting kiln heat. Skinner led the way up. The brick stairway circled the tower three times before ending at an empty circular chamber, roofed and featuring one slit window that faced directly upon Kurald Liosan. They kept to one side, wary of the blade of brilliant light cutting across the chamber's middle. Cowl noted that the motes of dust that drifted into the blade puffed into wisps of smoke. Skinner crossed his arms. 'Your evaluation?'

'Some sort of a research, or observation or communication tower, I should think.'

A grunt from Skinner. 'Very well. Let us then communicate.'

'You're not going to . . .'

'Yes. I am.'

'We don't know what will happen!'

The mailed finger pointed once more. 'Exactly, Cowl. And this is where you always fall short. You don't know what you can do – until you do it.' And he stepped up before the slit window. Instantly his surcoat burst into flames. Grunting anew, this time in pain, he averted the vision slit of his full helm. So great was the force driving in that Skinner shifted a mailed foot back, leaning into the stream. 'Do you see anything?' he bellowed.

Cowl attempted to send his awareness out ahead but it was like trying to push a boat up a foaming set of rapids. Still, he could sense *something . . . something very potent . . . approaching . . .* 'Something's coming!'

A shape, a presence, occluded the stream of power. It seemed to hover before the slit window. Through eyes shaded and narrowed Cowl had the impression first of a coiling, shifting serpent, then a winged entity, then a globe of roiling flame. Whatever it was it seemed entirely protean, without any set shape.

'*Who are you?*' came a thought so powerful as to ring the chamber like a bell.

'Skinner. Avowed of the Crimson Guard. Who—'

'*These titles are meaningless. You are not he – that is plain.*'

'Who—' Skinner began, then a blast struck the tower, which rocked. Raw, yammering power seared through the slit window throwing Cowl backwards to the floor. Dust as dry as death swirled in the desiccated air. The blade of light returned. Carefully Cowl straightened, coughing, peering into the shifting curtains of brick dust. A groan brought him to the rear of the chamber. Here, Skinner straightened from the wall. Behind him crushed and broken brick tumbled to the floor. He patted his chest, sending the black ash that was his surcoat floating out into the chamber. The helm shifted to Cowl. 'You are going to say something. I can see it in your face.'

Cowl raised a hand to his neck. He struggled to keep his mouth straight. 'If I were to say something, Skinner, I suppose it would be that what goes around comes around.'

The Avowed commander ground out a long, slow growl.

*　*　*

The entire trip to the Golden Hills Lieutenant Rillish spent surrounded by a moiling horde of Wickan cavalry. Mounts had been

328

provided for all; recovering, he could ride now with major discomfort, but he could ride. A large cart, a kind of wheeled yurt, had been assembled for the youth and it now constituted the centre of the churning mass of yelling, chanting horsemen. Early on Rillish had leant to Sergeant Chord, asking, 'What is that they're repeating?'

'Well, sir, they seem to think the youth carries the spirit of Coltaine, reborn.'

The name impressed Rillish no end. Coltaine. Leader of the last Wickan challenge to Malazan rule. Through negotiation he had then become one of the Empire's most feared commanders, and had died battling a rebellion in Seven Cities – though some claimed he had actually led it himself. That news had come four days ago. Plenty of time to ruminate on the truth, or suspicious convenience, of the timing of such a manifestation. After mulling it over – Nil and Nether seemed to accept it explicitly – he decided that it wasn't a *truth* for him to judge. He wasn't a Wickan. Not that he would endorse just any culture's practices – slavery of women, for example. Sure, it was a tradition among many peoples not to allow women access to power. Fine, so long as the 'tradition' was recognized for what it was: just another form of slavery.

So he would go along with the story. Never mind, whispered that scoffing sceptic's voice within him, how convenient it might prove for *him*.

Five days of wending up and down steep defiles and crossing rocky rushing streams brought them to a high broad plateau dotted with encampments of yurts and surging herds of horses. A great exulting war call went up from the column followed by a ululation of singing from the many camps. Mounted youths charged back and forth, spears raised. Some climbed to stand on the bare backs of their mounts; others leapt side to side, running alongside their horses, hands wrapped in manes.

'You'll have your hands full with this lot,' Rillish said to Nether who happened to be at his side. Her answer was a long, amused look, then she kneed her mount ahead.

A bivouac was set aside for Rillish and his command. He set to its ordering along with Sergeant Chord. 'Now what do you think, sir?' Chord asked while they inspected the soldiers' work, some raising tents, others assembling imitations of the yurts in blankets and cloaks over a framework of branches. Fires were going and water was heating in clay pots over the flames.

'Don't know for certain, of course. Some kind of an army will be organized, I imagine. They obviously intend to swoop down and clear the invaders out.' Rillish caught the eye of the soldier who had helped him escape from the fort and nodded his greeting. Smiling broadly, she saluted.

As they walked along, Rillish asked his sergeant, 'What is her name, anyway, Chord?'

'Ah, that would be Corporal Talia, sir. Designated instructor in swordsmanship. The lads, they don't care a fart for technique. They think a thick arm and a thick head will see them through. But the lasses, sir, they know it's their edge.'

'True enough, Chord. Thank you.'

'Perhaps we could arrange some training, sir. While we rest and regroup. You've been on your back for some time now.'

'Thank you, Chord. But you know regulations. Only commissioned ranks can spar together.' Rillish rubbed the side of his nose. 'Too many officers found run through, if I remember correctly.'

'As you say, sir. But it seems to me that command is far away now, and there's some as might question whether we're really even in the army now, sir, if you follow my thinking.'

Rillish stopped outside the yurt the Wickans had given for his use – though obviously desperately short of shelter themselves. 'Thank you, Chord. But the day I follow your thinking is the day I tear off all my clothes and jump into the ice of the Cut.'

'I blame the drink, sir.'

'You wouldn't have any of it left, would you?'

'Used it to poison the enemy, sir.'

'And a sad waste it was too.'

'The bottle got a promotion out of it though, sir.'

'True enough – wait, don't tell me – it's now known as Korbottle Dom.'

Looking away, Chord grinned. 'Heard that one before have you, sir?'

'Many times. And about this yurt . . .'

'Yes, sir?'

'Give it back to the Wickans tomorrow.'

'Yes, sir.'

Later that night Chord stopped beside Corporal Talia's bedroll. He tapped her awake with a foot. She opened an eye. He produced a bottle from under his cloak. 'Why don't you go offer to share this with the lieutenant?'

'Why isn't *he* here instead of sorry-arsed you?'

'All traditional, he is. Thinks rank's a problem.'

She sat up on one elbow. '*Oho*, so that's the way of it. Questions of coercion.' She took the bottle from Chord. 'Well, we'll just have to hammer that out.'

Chord offered a mock salute. 'Don't take too long. That yurt's disappearing tomorrow.' He walked away thinking that it was good to see the lieutenant up on his feet again, but that it was the duty of any sergeant to see to the fullest recovery of his commanding officer . . . at least those worth saving.

Over the next few days Rillish saw little of any of the Wickan youths he'd got to know during the march. They had all been adopted into families of their clans while Mane, Nil and Nether were absorbed in the furious debates that swirled night and day around the central ring of yurts as participants came and went, sometimes sleeping then returning to pick up old arguments where they'd left off. He was glad to have no part in it. What part awaited him now troubled him enough. Resignation seemed increasingly the compelling path. Especially now with his new-found intimacy with Corporal Talia. To his mind it was too complicated for the command structure. What if an opening for promotion came up and he gave the sergeancy to her? Grumblings of favouritism? What if he did not? Unfairly penalizing her? There was no way either of them could win. Unless he was no longer her superior officer.

That settled it then; problem was, there was no one to resign before.

Sitting cross-legged on his bedding, Untan duelling swords across his lap, Rillish wrapped his sharpening stone in a rag and sheathed the blades. Unless he could report to someone who – technically – outranked him. He stood, gestured a soldier to him. 'Find Nil or Nether and tell them I wish to speak with them.' The soldier saluted, jogged off.

A formal letter might be necessary. Rillish picked up his kitbag of bits and pieces that he'd pulled together since losing everything at the fort. Perhaps he had a scrap of vellum or two.

The soldier returned. 'Sir, Nil and Nether wish to speak to you at the central ring.'

'Thank you.'

Rillish straightened his torn and faded surcoat, belted on his swords, pushed back his hair that had grown too wild and long of late and carried more grey in it than he wished. He crossed to the main ring. As he went, the constitution of the population of Wickans here in the plateau impressed him once again – so many youths and elders and almost no one of middle age. All those had gone away to fight in foreign wars and precious few had returned. As he neared the ring he noticed the quiet; things had apparently finally been settled. Only Wickan elders faced him – no youths had the stomach, or patience, for these sorts of interminable disputes. Or perhaps *they* had things to do with their time. Many of the elders wore torn and dirty leathers, and many betrayed the gaunt and ashen pallor of hunger, that grim companion of all refugees. They parted to let him pass. Some glared open hostility. Fists even rested near the bone handles of long-knives.

So fares the reputation of the Malazans now in the company of Wickans. And deservedly so, too. He found the twins next to that special youth's yurt. Here he got his first good look at the child who sat cross-legged on a blanket, a small sheep's wool cap high on his domed head. It was true that the youth's black eyes held an unusual amount of self-awareness for one of his age.

'Rillish Jal Keth,' began Nil, 'it has been decided. My sister and I are now guardians and councillors to this youth who since his birth has been unquestionably recognized as Coltaine reborn. In this capacity we wish to enlist you as captain and military adviser to the Head of All Clans. Do you accept?'

Rillish stared. Had he correctly understood? He came to offer his resignation and this is what he hears? Shocked outrage had taken the crowd – everyone was awaiting his reply. Many now glared open hatred. Rillish struggled to find his voice. 'Adviser? I? Surely there must be a Wickan officer among you—'

'There are a number. But we have chosen you.'

As the moments passed, a wall of objections now firmed up in his mind. 'With all due respect, a Wickan would be more suitable, would know the land better—'

'That is all true, assuming we intend to fight a war of defence,' said Nether. 'We do not. Foreigners have invaded our lands and brought war to us and so we intend to return the favour. We will not ride down into the steppes to drive them off. No, that we leave to Temul who commands on the steppes. We, instead, will lead the counter-offensive. We shall ride south into Untan lands bringing war and invasion to them. What say you to that, Malazan?'

Rillish felt as if he couldn't breathe. Good Gods, the two mean it. Could it be done? How many could they muster? A few thousand at least, many old veterans to steady and instruct the young bloods. The finest skirmishers and horse raiders anyone knew of. And last he'd heard there weren't enough soldiers left in Unta to hold a drinking party. Still, there remained questions of loyalty. 'To what end, Nether? Nil? To what end?'

Angry calls sounded from all around. 'He spits in our faces!' someone shouted in Talian. Nil raised his arms for silence. The twins exchanged glances, their eyes glittering like sharp stones. 'To force a renegotiation of our treaties with the Empire.'

'I see. Then I can only answer in one way – I offer my resignation. Do you, Nil or Nether, as senior officers, accept?'

A roar as the crowd of enraged elders surged inward, raised blades flashed orange in the afternoon light. A clot of dirt struck Rillish's chest. Both twins threw their arms up for silence, shouting down the crowd.

'Yes,' sounded a piping voice that cut through the din like a whistle. The elders were silenced instantly, almost as if abashed. The twins stared down, astonished.

'Accepted,' said the toddler, grinning up at Rillish.

It occurred to Rillish then that in the view of many, the twins were *not* the senior officers present. 'Very good,' he stammered, shaken despite his scepticism. 'Then I, Rillish Jal Keth, accept your commission.'

The child clapped his hands, clearly delighted. The twins quickly, and loudly, swore their confidence. After a long tense silence, the surrounding elders shuffled forward one by one, taking turns to bow and acknowledge his selection.

At the end of the ceremony Rillish was left with the twins, an old woman and the toddler, who had fallen asleep. The old woman picked him up and nestled him in her arms. As she did so his eyes popped open and he said something to her. She gestured Rillish to her with an impatient twist of her wrist.

'Yes?'

She was looking down at the child who now rested, eyes closed. 'He said, "Turn their swords. Turn them."'

'Turn their swords?'

'Yes.'

Turn their swords? Had the old woman heard correctly? Perhaps he'd just babbled some gibberish. But she had ducked into the yurt, taking the child with her, and pulled the flap shut. He turned to Nil. The young man had pressed both hands to his face as if to cool it.

'That went better than I'd hoped,' the youth said through his fingers.

'Really?'

'Yes. No one was hurt.' He tucked his hands under his arms, grinning.

'You set high standards.'

'I know my people. We're a fractious lot.'

'Well, now it's my turn.'

'Oh?'

'Yes. Now I have to explain to my people why and how we've just switched armies.'

* * *

When his worthless nephew stuck his head between the cloth hangings of his palanquin shouting, 'Ships, Uncle! Hundreds of ships!' Nevall Od' Orr, Chief Factor of Cawn, nearly had a heart attack. Not from the prospect of Cawn being sacked by some fleet out of nowhere – invaders can be milked just as easily as anyone – but rather from the fact that his nephew had managed to get within arm's reach of him.

'Groten!' he bellowed, massaging his chest with one hand and smoothing his beard with the other.

The captain of his bodyguard thrust his shaven blue-black bullet head through the cloth hangings, 'Yes?'

'That's "Yes, Chief Factor".'

A nod of agreement. 'Yes?'

Nevall stared at Groten; Groten stared back. Sighing, Nevall covered his face. 'Groten,' he began, speaking through his hands, 'how did my idiot nephew get through your oh-so-vigilant cordon of guards?'

'He's your nephew.'

Nevall threw his arms down to slap his thin crossed legs. 'I know he's my Lady-damned nephew! I myself hired the mage who through no mistake of mine actually reported honestly on his paternity. Now, because of the egregious oversight of allowing one of my relations near me I penalize you one month's wages.'

Groten's thick brows pressed together. A large meaty hand rubbed his sweaty pate. 'A month's?'

'Yes. That is, unless you'd prefer to go back to whipping slaves on one of my merchantmen?'

The hulking Dal-Honese frowned his assent. As he did so the palanquin jerked from side to side and Nevall braced himself with a hand at the low roof. 'What was that? What's going on out there?'

'Ah, the crowd, sir. All headed to the waterfront.'

'Well? Why aren't we?'

The captain of the bodyguard opened his mouth to answer,

thought better of it and clamped his mouth shut. The head withdrew. Soon after that orders sounded and the palanquin rocked as Nevall's bearers started up again. He found the paper fan he'd dropped when the terrifying apparition of his nephew's head had assaulted him and he set to cooling himself. Gods above and below, did any of the smelly populace of Cawn have the least idea of what he had to endure as their Chief Factor?

Comforted by the crack of his bodyguard's whips and the thump of their truncheons clearing the way, Nevall turned his thoughts to this fleet of mystery ships. Could it be the Empress's forces? His sources spoke of her intent to sail after the disastrous assault of those mercenary raiders. And where else would she sail but for Cawn? Port of choice for any inland expedition. Yet how could she have arrived so soon? It would take more than two weeks for a fleet of that size to make its way from Unta – and that barring any of the usual delays. No, logic compelled that this must be some other force. Therefore, eliminating the possible but improbable invasion from Korel, Genabaris, storied Perish, enigmatic Nemill, legendary Assail or that empire his most distant trading partners whisper about – Lethery, or some such absurd name – that left the rumours his field agents had been picking up of a massing of ships in Western Falar. But an invasion fleet from Falar? To what end?

The stink of the waterfront, old sun-rotted fish and human excrement, penetrated the palanquin and Nevall scrambled to find his pomander; he dug it out of one of the small drawers and pressed it to his nose. Dead Poliel! How could anyone live like this? How could he be expected even to think? The palanquin slowed. Voices all around babbled. 'Groten!'

The captain of the bodyguard stuck his head between the hangings. 'Yes?'

'What is it? What's to be seen?'

'Lots of ships. All kinds. Even Moranth Blue merchantmen.'

'Moranth Blue vessels? How could you possibly know a Moranth Blue vessel from any other?'

The captain of the bodyguard shrugged his wide shoulders, shaking the palanquin. 'Because the sails are blue?'

Nevall stroked his beard. 'Oh, yes. Flags? Any flags? Did you think to look for those?'

An uncertain frown. 'Well, they're still pretty distant. But there's an old woman here who claims to be a witch. Says she can see though the eyes of birds. Says she'll look for a half-silver.'

'A half-silver! Tell the hag I'd look through the anus of a mole for half a silver. No, wait, let me guess what she'd see looking through the eyes of a bird – fish! Fish and water! What else would a blasted bird look at!'

Groten flinched away, hurt. 'It was just a suggestion. Anyway—' he looked out, spoke with someone, glanced in again. 'Tali. They're flying the blue of Tali.'

Nevall hissed a breath while pulling at his beard. Tali. The old hegemonic power itself. So much for these rumours of a return to independent states. Looked like they'd merely be changing one hat for another. So be it. The Cawnese were famous for their pragmatism. They would join – until fortunes changed.

'Very well. Groten, take me to whoever's in charge down there when they arrive.'

'Yes, ah, Chief Factor.'

Even as the sullen dockworkers kicked at the mooring ropes thrown from the *Keth's Loss*, a palanquin carried by six extraordinarily tall men and escorted by ten cudgel- and whip-wielding bodyguards bulled its way down to the dockside. At the railing, Ullen clenched his teeth, knowing who that would be: the current Chief Grasper and Extorter of Cawn, whoever that was this year. While he watched, members of the bodyguard stood on the gangway planking where the dockworkers were lazily sifting, and name-calling led to pushing which led to punching and soon a gorgeous, indiscriminate row erupted between labourers, dockhands, general onlookers and the bodyguards. Caught in the brawl the yellow-clothed palanquin pitched about like a ship in a storm while its occupant screeched, 'Cawn welcomes . . . its liberators! Long . . . live the Talian forces! We open our doors . . . to your noble . . . warriors!'

Ullen could only hang his head. Gods, Cawn, how he hated the city.

That night Urko rode west with a force on all the horses that had survived the crossing in serviceable health. He claimed to be scouting the trader road to Heng, but Ullen knew he was fleeing any dealings with the Cawnese authorities. He also knew why – Urko would have throttled the lot of them. The warehouses Ullen leased were falling-down ruins awash with a fetid sludge of rotted fish. The wagons he rented fell apart even as they were loaded. The horses were either diseased or broken or both, not one animal among them fit even for light scouting. Meanwhile, the fees, tithes and bills piled up in the wallets of his secretaries, exaggerated, inflated and outright false. He had bills for material and labour for repair of ships he didn't even recognize.

Meanwhile, V'thell had formed his Moranth Gold into columns and marched off without speaking to anyone and Bala had somehow claimed a fine carriage – probably threatening to curse a family – and attached herself to that brigade. By the time Ullen was organizing the rearguard and supply trains Urko's entire campaign chest was emptied. Toward the end of his stay Ullen was handing out scrip and referring bills to Tali's ruling Troika. Nevall Od' Orr and Seega Vull, the richest factors in Cawn, sent him on his way with a sneer and the fluttering of handfuls of his scrip to the wind.

It surprised him that he kept his humour through the entire ordeal. Standing with the rearguard, hands at the reins of the scrawny and bruised ex-carthorse he'd purchased for the price of a Grisan war-mount, he bowed an ironic farewell to Cawn – may it rot in the effluvium of its own sour rapaciousness. For what seemed not to have occurred to these factors in their myopic focus on the immediate gain was that once the League had taken Heng, the road to Unta led back this way.

*　*　*

Shaky had been motionless at an arrow-loop of the westernmost tower of Heng's north wall for some time now. Hurl was glad; she didn't want him bothering her while she worked her calculations.

'Would you look at that . . .' he said, amazement in his voice.

'What?' Hurl did not look up from her scratches on the slate board resting on her crossed legs.

'They're attacking.'

'I don't hear anything.'

'Take a look. They're prepping.'

Sighing her annoyance, Hurl pushed her piece of chalk into a pouch and cautiously uncrossed her numb legs. 'It's almost bloody dark, for Fanderay's sake!'

'Guess they think they need all the help they can get.'

She looked out, studied the Talian entrenchments, and was displeased to have to admit that Shaky was right. 'Well, so do we,' she said absently as she watched the fires lighting down the lines, moveable shield platforms being raised and buckets of water being tossed on hides hung over every piece of wooden siege equipment. The increasing activity of the besiegers extended as far as she could see east around the curve of the outer wall. 'Looks like a general assault,' she said, amazed.

'It's ridiculous. They don't have the men to take the walls.'

'And *they* know we don't have the men to defend them.'

That silenced Shaky. He glanced up and down the top of the curtain wall. 'You think maybe they've got a chance?'

'There's always a chance.'

'Yeah. Well, maybe someone ought to do something.' He was looking straight at her. Hurl stared back until she realized that that someone was her. She stepped into the tower archway, leaned out. 'Ready fires! Prepare for assault!'

'Aye, Captain!'

Hurl fought the urge to look behind her whenever anyone called 'Captain' her way. She heard her orders repeated down the curve of the defences. She adjusted the rank torc at her arm – the damned thing just didn't seem to fit right. 'Get up top and ready the Beast,' she told Shaky.

The old saboteur winked, bellowing, 'Oh, aye, Captain!'

'Just get up there.'

Laughing at her discomfort, Shaky climbed a ladder affixed to the stone wall and pushed open the roof trap. 'Stoke the fire!' he yelled, pulling himself up.

The squat, broad figure of Sergeant Banath entered the stair tower, saluted crisply. 'Sergeant,' Hurl greeted him.

'Orders?'

Hurl eyed the Malazan regular, a red-haired Falaran veteran of the Genabackan campaigns, tanned, always looking as if he needed a shave, even at the morning muster. She'd yet to detect any definite sign either way of his attitude to this new command structure. A careful career soldier, she was coming to think. She said nothing at first. Orders should be blasted obvious, she thought. 'How do the urban levies look?' The levies were the majority of their forces: citizens hired, cajoled and plain coerced into the apparently distasteful duty of actually defending their city. She'd been given four hundred to hold this section of the wall. Banath led the three garrison squads that formed the backbone of her command.

The sergeant frowned the usual professional's distaste for amateurs. 'Nervous and clumsy. Not pissing their pants, yet.'

'Keep an eye on them.'

'Aye.'

'And hold fire until I give the word. Dismissed.'

Another crisp salute, a regimental turn, and exit. Maybe, the thought occurred to her, the exaggerated parade-ground manner was one long extended finger for her to spin on. Well, that was just too

338

bad. His buddy isn't the Fist. She peered out of the loop to gauge the activity. Metal screeched and ratcheted overhead, vibrating the stones of the tower. The Beast was being wound. Hurl could hear Shaky gleefully cursing the lads he had helping him and she couldn't keep down a smile; Gods, Shaky was never so happy as when he had a machine to pour destruction down on someone. And the Beast was his own special design. A winch had been installed at the rear of the stair-tower to bring up the enormous clay pots, big enough for a kid to bathe in, that were its ammunition. Only you wouldn't want to bathe in these. Sealed they were, and filled with oil. World's biggest munition.

Hurl watched while flagmen signalled out at the lines. Sappers took hold of the broad-wheeled shield platforms, and bowmen were forming up behind their cover. A lot of bowmen. Narrowing her eyes, Hurl tried to penetrate the gathering dusk. They looked like Seti tribals. Dismounted horse bowmen? What in the name of Dessembrae were they up to? Horns sounded in the night, and Talian siege engines, medium-sized catapults and onagers, fired. Burning bundles of oil-soaked rags arched overhead streaking smoke and flames in their wake. Stones cracked from the walls. Hurl ignored it all: the Talians had yet to field a single engine capable of damaging Heng's walls. It was just nuisance fire meant to keep everyone's heads down. A flight of arrows darkened the sky, climbed, then fell full of deadly grace. Though she had cover, Hurl winced at the havoc such salvos would cause along the walkway. While she watched, a staccato of answering fire darted from the lines. Hurl ran to the archway, yelling, 'Who fired? Hold, I said!'

She returned to the loop. The besiegers could waste all the arrows they wanted; they had something Heng would never get: resupply. She squinted again far out to the small hill behind the Talian investments. It was an inviting hill with a view of the river, and a good chance of a steady breeze to keep the midges away. She and Sunny and Shaky knew all this because weeks ago they'd spent a few nights clearing away rocks to make it even more attractive. And sure enough, their work had paid off because the first thing whoever it was commanding this flank had done was obligingly raise his, or her, command tent right on the spot. Hurl couldn't keep from shifting from foot to foot. C'mon, man, fire! Now. It was all calibrated and set! What was Shaky waiting for?

The mantlets were close now, the bow fire more targeted on the parapets. Hurl leaned out the archway, 'Fire! Fire at will!' She watched the exchange of salvos with a critical eye – wrong, it was still going all wrong. No matter how many times you had them practise . . . She returned to the portal. 'Aim up, for Hood's sake! Up, dammit!'

Banath stalked the walkway, bellowing, 'Into the sky! Rain it down on them, damn you dogs!'

Something strange caught her eye on the darkening field of burnt stubble and flattened burned hovels. Something low but moving. She stretched to stick her head out through a crenel. Arrows pattered from the stones around her, the iron heads sounding high-pitched *tings*. A catapulted rock exploded against the wall of the stair-tower above sending shards raining down. Everyone hunched, cursing. A nearby Heng levy raised a tower shield over Hurl. Leaning forward once more she could see that the object was some kind of low rectangular platform covered in sod and grass stubble. It was edging up toward the base of the wall and there were more of them all up and down the lines. 'Cats!' she yelled. 'Sergeant, we have cats! Bring up the stones – I want them broken!'

'Aye, Captain.'

'Come with me,' she said to the soldier who had raised the shield.

At the loop she leaned forward to try to get a look straight down. Not that mining the wall would do the poor bastards any good – the foundations went down a good three man-heights – she should know as she and Sunny had spent most of their time lately digging around down there.

The tower shuddered then as if it had taken a terrible blow from a stone as big as a horse thrown by a monstrous trebuchet such as those Hurl had seen rotting and broken after the siege of the island fortress of Nathilog. Dust and stones sifted down and she coughed, waving a hand. The Urban Levy had instinctively crouched. Hurl darted to the loop. At first she saw nothing, the brightly lit white command tent remained. Shadows moved against the canvas, messengers came and went. Then she flinched away as a blossom of orange and yellow flame suddenly lit the night. The eruption reached her as a shuddering boom echoing along the curtain wall. Hurl jumped up and down, yelled to the roof, 'You nailed it, Shaky! Beautiful. Just beautiful!' War whoops reached her from above. She could imagine the old saboteur doing his war dance. 'Reload,' she yelled, and went to the portal. The soldier joined her, a portly older fellow, probably a shop-owner. 'What's your name, soldier?'

'Ah, Jekurathenaw, Captain.'

'Jeck-your-what? Never mind. Cover me, Jeck.'

'Yes, sir.'

Hurl stepped out on to the walkway; Jeck held the tower shield between her and the parapets. Soldiers knelt among the litter loading and aiming. Arrows pelted around them. She stepped over the wounded and fallen alike. The sergeant, Banath, ran to meet her. 'How's it going?' she yelled.

'They should just pack it up and go home, sir.'

'I agree.'

Hurl studied the too-empty curve of the walkway. 'Stones, sergeant? Where are the stones?'

Banath spat. 'Ran out. Trouble at the winch. Some kind of mess up.'

'Hood's bony arse! All right. You stay on the levies – I'll check it out.'

'Aye, sir.'

Hurl edged further along. Jeck followed, shield extended. She jumped a section of walkway burning with oil where levies beat soaked cloth at the flames. The main winch was idle, and a team of three men and one woman sat next to it, staring down. 'What in the name of Gedderone is the problem here?'

One fellow rubbed a greasy rag over his neck. 'Don't know. Maybe flames spooked the oxen. Or a broken block.'

Hurl leant far out past the inner edge of the wall, grasped the thick hemp rope. 'What's going on down there!' she bellowed as loud as she could.

Catapulted fire-bombs arching over the walls lit for Hurl a milling chaos of soldiers and citizens below. Growing fires dotted the crowded buildings of the Outer Round. For as far as she could see torches danced up and down the roads around their curve where men and women surged in seeming headless panic. Ranks were forming up around the base of her section of wall from the West River Gate to half-way to the North Gate. More Urban Levy? Reinforcements? Who had sent them? Storo?

Down at the base of the winch a fellow holding a torch was yelling something back up to her. '*What?*' The fellow waved his torch, gesturing to the platform. Snarling her disgust, Hurl pushed herself upright. 'Oh, to Hood with this.' She pointed to the crew, 'Get this thing working or I'll toss you over the side!' She waved Jeck to her. 'Let's go.' She went to find Banath.

She found him with two Malazan regulars next to the wall of the stair-tower assembling a cache of casks, flasks and skins of oil. Hurl took in the supplies, the rags, the torches, and nodded her approval. 'Good. How soon?'

'Working double-time, sir,' said Banath without pause in tying together the fat goatskin bladders.

'How much do we have?' Hurl asked. She crouched and lent a hand.

Banath spat again, scowling. 'This is it.'

'Not nearly enough.'

'No.'

'Did you send word for reinforcements?'

Banath looked up, blinking. 'Reinforcements? No, sir.'

'There's more Urban Levy below, waiting.'

'Maybe someone's on to the Talians.'

Hurl thought of Silk and returned to work soaking rags. 'Maybe.'

The regulars lifted a cask and set off. Banath shouldered the bombs of oil-skins. 'Good hunting,' Hurl called. The ginger-haired veteran straightened his helmet and cracked an evil smile. 'Aye, sir.'

Hurl returned to the parapets. She wiped her hands, looking out. Jeck raised his shield over her. Below, more cats were inching their way to the walls. So many . . . And the archers seemed mainly Seti tribals . . .

Cheers brought Hurl's attention around; the men were waving to Urban Levy ranks now climbing the open stairs lining the walls. Hurl gaped – *who in the Abyss ordered that?* She retreated to the stair-tower for a better look. Inside, stamping sandals echoed up the circular stairwell.

A strange silence then descended all along the wall. Hurl was momentarily frozen when suddenly the cries of the wounded dominated the night. Voices pleaded for water, for relief. From the darkness a woman cursed the besiegers in a string of obscenities worthy of any Jakatakan pirate. Hurl stood still, straining to listen, and a shiver ran down her arms. The bow-fire had ceased; the catapults had stopped. Up and down the wall the men were straightening, looking to one another in wonder. Had the attack been called? Had they beat them off?

Hurl stood motionless but her thoughts gyred the same circle. *They've stopped firing – new cohorts she didn't request – they've stopped firing – Gods Below!* She bolted to the archway and there across the inner curve of the curtain wall she caught a glimpse of the unmistakable tall slim form of Captain Harmin Els D'Shil, Smiley himself, leading a column of urban levies charging up the stairs. She pointed, bellowing, 'Don't let them—'

An arm at her neck yanked her back. Pain lanced her side. She was thrown to the stone floor where she curled around a wound that felt as if it passed entirely through her. Blinking back a veil of pain she saw Jeck over her, his face expressionless. He sheathed his dagger and drew his shortsword. He raised it in both hands above her, paused. 'Amaron,' he said, 'sends his regrets.'

Hurl could only stare up dumbly. *Oh Storo, I'm so sorry. Outgeneralled from the start.*

Then the man was gone. Hurl blinked her confusion, peered around. Jeck lay now all crumpled up, bloody vomit at his mouth. Arms straightened her, leaned her up against the wall. She looked up at the dirty torn robes of a chubby ugly fellow with a slack mouth and one drooping eye. '. . . situation?' he said, slurring the word.

Hurl stared at the man blankly. Who in Soliel's Mercy was this? Yet had she any choice? She took a deep breath, fought her dizziness and nausea. 'Urban Levy turned. Working with the attack.' The man closed his eyes, cocked his head as if listening to someone or something Hurl could not hear. Then he nodded and opened his eyes.

'Retreat. Defend River Gate.'

'Says who?'

'Your commander.'

'Storo? Help me up.'

Showing astonishing strength, the man lifted her, held her erect with an arm under hers. Pain blackened Hurl's vision but she fought it back. 'Who are you?'

'City mage . . . old friend of Silk's.'

She gestured to the archway. The mage dragged her over. What confronted her was like a vision out of Hood's Paths: waving torches lit figures seething, locked in hand-to-hand fighting, some panicked, even leaping, or pushed, from the walkway. Grapnels now lined the parapets and some Urban Levy chopped at them while others defended them. Two Malazan regulars were crouched behind shields facing the tower entrance, ready to stop any further enemy. Upon seeing her their eyes widened within the visors of their helmets.

'Soldiers,' she tried to bark, but could only gasp. They straightened, saluting. 'Spread the word – retreat to the River Gate.'

'Aye, sir.'

The mage turned round, taking her with him, and Hurl now saw that the circular stairway had been reduced to broken rubble. She craned her neck to face the man directly. 'Who *are* you?'

'. . . Ahl . . .'

'Well, Ahl, my thanks, I—' But the mage kept walking, taking Hurl out through the westerly tower arch. 'What are you doing?' she snarled, her side biting at her with teeth of acid.

'Retreating.'

'No, I have to see to—'

343

But Ahl kept going. They passed Urban Levy who stared and gabbled questions. Hurl just shook her head. 'Defend. Defend the wall here.' They came to a grapnel that had yet to be cut. As they passed Ahl reached out one hand, and, grunting his effort, yanked it free of where the iron tines had dug into the stone, held it out beyond the lip of the parapet and released it. Screams accompanied its fall. Hurl stared at the man. *Who in Serc's regard was this?* A scent now wafted up from the fellow as well: the sharp bite of spice.

At Hurl's stare, Ahl smiled lopsidedly, the one side of his mouth edging up, and he winked his good eye. 'We could've held off any besiegers. But not those damned undead Imass of the emperor's.'

Queen preserve her! One of the old city mages who defended Heng so long ago. And, a friend of Silk? So, he, too . . . But of course he as much as confessed such to her. Yet it was one thing to hear of it abstractly. Another to see it in action. 'Set me down here.' Ahl shot her a questioning look. 'We have to hold this section for the retreat.' He grunted his understanding. She waved an Urban Levy to her as Ahl gently sat her against the parapet. 'Any regulars here?' A frightened nod. 'Good. Go get one.' She asked Ahl, 'Can you do anything for me?'

He shook his head. 'Not my . . . speciality.'

'Well, bind it, would you?'

The mage began undoing the lacings and buckles of her armour. A Malazan regular, a woman, arrived to kneel next her. Hurl waved her close. 'Forces should be retreating to us,' she said, her voice falling. 'We must hold this section.'

'Aye, Captain.' She squinted aside, smiling, 'I think I see them.' Another regular arrived.

'Who're you?' Hurl slurred.

'Fallow,' he said, and brushed aside Ahl's hands. 'Squad healer.'

Hurl laughed, almost vomiting in pain from the convulsion. Fallow held something, a vial, under her nose. She jerked up a hand to slap it away. 'Don't dope me!'

'Then stop bloody moving!' Fallow pulled up Hurl's undershirt, began wrapping her middle. He jerked his head to Ahl, asked low, 'Who's the civilian?'

'Mage,' she whispered. 'Maybe Soletaken.'

'Hood's dead breath . . .'

'What's going on? Have to know.'

The man's hands were warm on her stomach and side. Hurl felt the pain retreating. He was looking away. 'They're close now. A slow retreat in ranks. Banath is organizing crossbowmen . . .'

A terrible thought struck Hurl. 'Close?'

'Yes.'

'Past the stair-tower?'

'Yes.'

'Good Burn, no!' She struggled to rise. Fallow's hands pressed her down.

'Don't you dare ruin my work! What is it?'

'Shaky! In the stair-tower. We have to—'

'It's lost. The Talians have it.'

All the strength fled from Hurl. 'Oh shit, Shaky . . .'

They lifted her, set her on a rough litter made from two shields over spears. Ahl retreated at her side. She caught his eye. 'Where's Silk? Where's Storo, Jalor, Rell? We've lost the wall!'

'You think . . . you're alone? The Inner Round Gate . . . as well. It was . . . priority. Rell broke them there . . . fighting now . . . to take the Outer. Troop rafts on the Idryn. The River Gate . . . must hold.'

Great Fanderay, it was worse than she imagined. She let her head fall back on the litter. So, now they knew what it was like to face the Old Malazans. Terrifying. They charge over you like a flashflood. What a gambit. And it may yet succeed.

They reached the short tower that secured the most westerly reach of the wall together with the north arch of the bridge supporting the River Gate. Hurl planned to hold the Talians here. She ordered barricades assembled. Banath's slow methodical retreat fell back to them. He gathered what levies he could as he went. The salute he offered Hurl was as crisp as his earlier ones despite a round shield hacked to kindling, a bloody slash across his mouth exposing both upper and lower teeth, and two missing fingers. Hurl decided that maybe it hadn't been an act after all. 'Well done, Sergeant.'

Banath nodded, saluted, and turned to the soldiers, pointing and shoving men. Hurl realized that with a wound like that the man could no longer make himself understood. She gestured Fallow to see to him. Arrows sang into the tower over the barricade. A tossed incendiary burst flaming oil over the piled table, barrels and chairs. Everyone flinched, then quickly straightened to return fire through the flames. More Malazan regulars, crossbows rattling on their backs, climbed the ladder to the trap in the tower roof to pour fire down on the walkway. After a time it became quiet out on the curve of the curtain wall beyond the knot of mixed Talian troopers and Heng levies besieging the barricade. But now sharp yells reached them: shouts full of sudden panic and open fear.

'What is it? What's going on out there?' Hurl demanded, hoarse.

The female Malazan soldier came to her side. 'Don't know. It's dark. All the torches have been thrown aside. There's no light.'

'I smell oil,' a soldier called from the barricade. 'Lots.'

'What is that?' another said.

'What's going on?' Hurl snarled. 'Look!'

The female regular stood tall, peering. 'Something's pouring down the walls from the walkway. Water?'

Hood's Laughter! Shaky! 'Get down!' Hurl shouted. 'Everyone! Take cover!'

Ahl turned to her, his good eye narrowed. 'Why?'

Brilliance suddenly silhouetted the man. A yellow-white chiaroscuro of blinding light and shadow seared Hurl's vision. A roar such as that of a landslide slammed into the barricade, pushing it backwards. Soldiers rolled away slapping at themselves, clothes aflame. Screams quavered an undertone of hopeless pain beneath the furnace roar. A howling thing of flame crashed through the fallen barrels and furniture and thrashed about until soldiers stabbed it repeatedly. Ahl, a hand raised to shield his eye, turned to look down to Hurl once more. 'You saboteurs . . . you fight dirty,' and he frowned his distaste.

Likewise I'm sure, friend.

In the morning orders arrived to withdraw to the southern Inner Round Gate. Talk was they were abandoning the entire Outer Round. Too many rods of wall and not enough men. Hurl grated at the news; all those men dead, Shaky's sacrifice, and for what? All to hand the wall over to the Talians?

A dishevelled, hollow-eyed Storo met her as she was being carried to the gate. He took hold of her shoulder. 'I heard you took one in the side.'

'A gift from Amaron.'

He winced, looking away. 'Yeah. Well, I guess we've all got one coming. Listen, don't take it bad. It was chance. You just happened to have that section last night. That's all. Could've been anyone. Don't take it personal.'

She laughed hoarsely. 'I'll try not to.' She eyed the man, gauging his strength. He was exhausted and had taken a slash across the arm – he'd been in the fighting – but he didn't have the look of a man sliding down into despair. 'We lost Shaky.'

'Yeah. I heard.'

'We were betrayed. The Urban Levy . . .'

He raised a hand. 'I know. We'll get to the bottom of it.'

'And don't *you* take it personal. There was nothing you could do about it. Betrayal's always the way sieges end.'

The man smiled his rueful agreement and his eyes brightened for a moment. He rubbed the back of his neck then pulled down his mail hood to scratch his head. 'Yeah. I understand. Who could beat Choss and Toc, eh? But listen.' He waved her bearers on, walked alongside the litter. 'They did us a favour. We were stretched too thin out there on the Outer anyway. And they tipped their hand too early with that move. To gain what, the Outer Round?' He waved the success aside. 'They should've held out for the Inner. Now we know.'

'We should've suspected . . .'

'We did.'

Hurl raised her head to eye Storo directly. 'What do you mean? Do you mean that city mage, Ahl? What's his story? Do you trust him?'

Storo would not meet her eye. 'You'll have to ask Silk.'

'I will . . . What happened, anyway?'

A shrug. 'Cohorts isolated your section at the Outer Round while a second group secured the North Gate. Shaky took care of the gang who took the wall but the other groups opened the gate. They overran the north ring of the Outer Round but we stopped them at the Inner Gate. Rell earned his pay there; he held the gate. Everyone's full of what he did there.'

'On that subject, my sergeant, Banath, he deserves a commendation.'

A nod. 'Good. I'm glad.' He offered a big smile. 'These noncoms, they're only as good as their officers,' and he squeezed her shoulder.

It's OK, Storo. I ain't broke yet.

* * *

Seti warriors whooped and sang their war-chants through the next day, riding circles around Toc's command tent where he reclined together with Choss and the Assembly leaders. Occasionally a warrior would ride past the opened flaps and Toc would glimpse a piece of booty held high, a sword, silver plate, silk cloth, a severed human head. His gaze shifted to Choss who lay back, an arm over one knee, his mouth sour behind his dirty-blond beard, eyes downcast. *Sorry, Choss. Things did not go as hoped. We were stopped on two counts by acts eerily reminiscent of Old Empire tactics.* Toc shifted his numb elbow, straightening it and wincing. It was as if they faced themselves – and he supposed in fact they were. Malazan-trained military engineers, masters of siegecraft. Poor Captain Leen, blasted from the face of the earth by what was probably the largest mangonel ever constructed on the continent. Then that same engineer dumps his ammunition to immolate the curtain wall. It cost almost an entire battle group. But they took the Outer Round. Yes, the Outer. When we'd planned to have the Inner. Plan was . . . Toc let his gaze slide up to the bright canvas roof of the tent. Well, plan was to be nearing Unta by now.

'Why so grim, Malazans?' Imotan called across the tent.

Toc forced a smile. 'We'd hoped for more.'

'Yes, yes. That is plain. But you should rejoice for what you have accomplished! Never before have the walls of Heng been breached! We have entered! Soon the rest will fall like a tree wounded and tottering.'

Toc raised a tumbler of tea to that, which Imotan answered. *The walls weren't breached, you fool. Can't you see this was but the first blooding in what would surely prove to be a fight to the death for the both of them? And they'd shot their best bolt first. All to bind you lot to the siege. Now this Fist, Storo, will be wary. It won't work a second time. But then you can rejoice, can't you, Imotan, and your lackey, Hipal? Heng wounded all without your warriors hardly spilling a drop? It's our war, Malazan versus Malazan while you watch us bloody each other – no wonder you're grinning!*

Raising the tumbler a second time, Toc held Imotan's gaze. *That's the deal, shaman. We'll remove this thorn from your side, which you have failed to reach for so long. In return, you will accompany us east with every living soul able to mount a horse to burn, harass, worry and harry, harry, harry any force she might field against us.*

Imotan answered with his tumbler. His smile behind his grey beard was savage, and his glittering black eyes held the knowing promise of bloodshed – for Malazans.

*   *   *

Riding with her commander, the Marquis Jhardin, and her Sentry of a hundred horse, Ghelel had her first good look at Heng since the attack. They travelled the trader road north-east to the old stone bridge over the Idryn. To the west, the orange morning light coloured the distant walls ochre. Smoke rose from fires still burning throughout the city. She couldn't see the north wall where a horrific firestorm had incinerated so many of her men but she'd heard stories of that amoral, almost petulant, act. How destructively childish! They'd lost the battle and so they should have shown the proper grace and simply bowed out. What were they going to do, burn down the entire city out of plain spite? It was – she searched for the right word – *uncivilized*.

'So, a rendezvous?' she said to the Marquis, who rode beside her.

He gave an assent, drawing on his pipe. 'Yes, Prevost. Reinforcements.'

'From the east, sir?'

'Yes. Landings at Cawn. Recruits from Falar and abroad. Commanded by no less than Urko Crust himself.'

'Urko? I thought he was dead.'

The Marquis showed stained teeth in a broad smile. 'He's been reported drowned more times than a cat.'

Ghelel thought about all the names now assembled against Laseen in this 'Talian League'. So many old lieutenants and companions. How must it feel to be so betrayed? So alone? But then, she'd brought it all upon herself, hadn't she? Yet that was the question – hadn't she? Ghelel also thought of herself as alone. How much more might the two of them have in common? Anything at all? Perhaps only this condition of isolation. It seemed to her that while she was the leader-in-waiting of the Talian League, in truth she controlled nothing. And, she wondered, how much alike might the two of them truly be in this regard as well?

A plume of dust ahead announced another party on the road. An outrider stormed up, pulled her mount to a halt, saluted the Marquis and Ghelel. 'A religious procession,' she reported to Ghelel.

'Oh?'

'Common here,' the Marquis said. 'This road passes over the bridge to meet the east–west trader road. A major monastery sits at the crossroads—'

'The Great Sanctuary of Burn!' Ghelel said in wonder.

'Yes.' If the Marquis was offended by the interruption he did not show it. 'You've heard of it, then.'

'Of course. But wasn't it ruined long ago?'

'Yes. Struck by an earthquake.' A wry smile. 'Make of that what you will. Yet the devout still gather. They squat among its fallen walls. Persistent in their faith they are. This road was lain over the old pilgrim trail. The first bridge was built ages ago to accommodate the traffic.'

As the Marquis spoke they came abreast of the procession: old men and women on foot, some carrying long banners proclaiming their status under the protection of Burn. All bowed as the Sentry rode past, even the ones already on their hands and knees genuflecting in the dust every foot of their pilgrimage, all to the great increase of their merit. As she passed, Ghelel had an impression of brown and grey unkempt dusty hair, tattered rags, emaciated limbs showing bruising and sores. From their darker complexion they looked to have originated from the Kan Confederacy, though it may just have been the grime.

They descended the southern flank of a broad shallow valley, the old flood plain of the Idryn. Upriver, intermittent copses of trees thickened to a solid line screening the river. Ahead in the distance the old stone bridge lay like the grey blade of a sword, long and low over the water. A great number of dark birds circled over the river and harried the shores. A gust of warm air greeted Ghelel, a current drawn up the valley. It carried the aroma of wood smoke from Heng, plus the stink of things not normally burned. As they neared the muddy shores a much worse, nauseating reek assaulted Ghelel and she flinched, covering her nose. 'Gods, what *is* that?'

The Marquis turned to her, pipe firmly clenched between teeth, his broad face unreadable. He exchanged a glance with Sergeant Shepherd riding behind, and took the pipe from his mouth. 'Heng uses the Idryn as a sewer, of course. So there's always that downriver from any city. But now, with the siege, it's much worse . . .' Riding closer, Ghelel saw that the garbage and broken wreckage of war littered the shore. Among the shattered wood and flotsam lay tangled bodies: a stiff arm upraised like a macabre greeting; a pale bloated torso, obscene. And roving from corpse to corpse went contented dogs, stomachs distended. They flushed clouds of angry crows and kites with their bounding. 'Because, you see, in the city, there's no room to bury the dead – it's just easiest to . . .'

'It's criminal!' Ghelel exploded. 'What of the proper observances?'

'Who knows? Perhaps some basic gestures were made . . .'

Ghelel was in no mood to share the Marquis's forbearance. For her this was the final outrage from these Loyalist forces, the convincing proof that whoever these men or women were, they truly deserved to be wiped from the face of the earth. They had no common decency such as any reasonable man or woman. They seemed no better than animals.

The horses' hooves clattered on the worn granite stones of the bridge. The Marquis raised his chin to indicate the far shore. 'See there – the caves?'

Past the north shore, the ascent from the valley was much steeper; the road switched back and forth up cliffs of some soft layered sedimentary rock. Dark mouths of caves crowded the cliffs, forming a sort of abject settlement.

'Hermits and ascetics squat in them. Purifying themselves for better communion with Burn, I suppose, or Soliel, or Oponn, or whoever.'

Figures that seemed no more than sticks wrapped in rags squatted in some of the dark openings. Beards and ragged clothes wafted with the wind. Children played in the dust with frisky grinning dogs. Beside the road an old man wearing only a loincloth despite the chill air leaned on a dead branch torn from a tree: As they passed he shouted, 'Why struggle against our universal fate, brothers and sisters? Every step you take brings you closer to the oblivion that awaits us all. Repent this life that is a delusion for the blind!'

Ghelel twisted in her saddle. 'That is blasphemy!'

'Ignore him—' the Marquis began.

'May the Gods forgive you,' she shouted.

'The Gods forgive nothing,' came the man's dark answer.

She stared back at the tall lean figure until a twist in the road took him from sight. 'As I said,' the Marquis began again, 'hermits and mad ascetics infest these hills. Here you'll find all kinds of profanation and heterodoxies. Like the babbling of a thousand voices. You might as well yell for the wind to stop.'

'Still, I wonder what he meant . . .'

'Perhaps he meant that what we name as Gods have no concern for us.'

Ghelel and the Marquis turned to face Molk, who rode behind. He shifted in his saddle, shrugging. 'Perhaps.'

Both turned away. Ghelel did not know what the Marquis made of the pronouncements, but they crawled on her like some sort of contagion. She felt an irresistible urge to wash. Just words, she told herself. Nothing more than words.

After climbing the slope they reached the north plains. Dark clouds bruised the far north-east where the Ergesh mountain range caught the prairie winds. North, the road would bring them past an isolated sedimentary butte, or remains of an ancient plateau. Here, climbing its steep slopes and jumbled atop, rested the crumpled fallen remains of the Great Sanctuary of Burn. Entire wings of its boxy, squat architecture had slid down the cliff on massive landslides and faults while other quarters appeared untouched. From this distance, its canted maze of walls appeared to Ghelel as if a God had tossed down a handful of cards. Traces of grey smoke rose amid the ruins. 'It must have been enormous.'

'Yes. Largest on the continent. It housed thousands of monks. Now the cries of prairie lions sound instead of the drone of prayer.'

Ghelel glanced to the heavyset man; his pale eyes, hidden in a thick nest of wrinkles, studied the far-off remains. 'You sound like a poet, Marquis.'

His thick brows rose. 'I had hoped to be, but circumstances have made of me a soldier – Prevost.'

'Yet the sanctuary does not seem entirely abandoned.'

'Yes. As I said. The devout still gather. They slouch amid the wreckage, forlorn.' He glanced to her. 'Perhaps they dream of the glory that once was . . .'

Ghelel shied her gaze away to the ruins. 'I see no scaffolding, no efforts at rebuilding.'

'Perhaps their dreams are too seductive.'

'Or they are too poor.'

Grinning, the Marquis nodded thoughtfully. After a time he cleared his throat. 'I am reminded of some lines from Thenys Bule. Are you familiar with him?'

'I have heard of him. "Sayings of the Fool"?'

'Yes. It goes something like – "While travelling I met a man dressed in rags, his feet and shoulders bare. Take this coin, I offered him, yet he refused my hand. You see me poor, hungry, and cold, he said – yet I am rich in dreams."'

Ghelel eyed the man narrowly. 'I am not sure what to take from that, Marquis . . .'

'Yes, well. The man was a fool after all.'

Past noon they reached the crossroads. Here the road south to Kan and Dal Hon met the major east–west trade route. The freshly burned remains of wayside inns, hostels and horse corrals lined the way. Ghelel knew this to be the work of the Seti and she bridled at the destruction wrought in what some might come to construe as her name. Trampled and now neglected garden plots stretched back on all sides. All was not abandoned, however; a tent encampment stood on a north hillside overlooking the crossroads. What looked to Ghelel like several hundred men and horses rested. A contingent was on its way, walking its mounts leisurely down the gentle slope.

'Urko's men?'

'Yes.'

'They are to join us in the south?'

The Marquis fished his pipe from a pouch at his side. 'That is the question, Prevost. They were to deploy against the South Rounds. But things have changed. Now we must discuss strategy – and much will rest on our decisions. As it always does, I suppose, in matters of war.'

The contingent did little to strengthen Ghelel's confidence. Among their numbers she saw the robes over mail of Seven Cities, the embossed boiled leather of Genabackis and the bronze scaled armour of Falar. No order or effort at regimentation seemed to have been made save for pennants and flags of Falaran green. The soldiers seemed to treat the rendezvous as some sort of outing; they joked and talked amongst themselves while kicking their mounts on to the road in complete disorder. Ghelel glanced sidelong to the Marquis – the man's heavyset face revealed nothing of any anger or disgust at what, after all, could be interpreted as an insult. The foremost one, a ginger-bearded fat fellow in a leather hauberk set with bronze scales, inclined his head in greeting. 'Captain Tonley, at your service, sir,' he said in strongly accented Talian.

'Marquis Jhardin, Commander of the Marchland Sentries. Prevost Alil, and Sergeant Shepherd.'

'Greetings.'

'Is Commander Urko with you?'

'Yes, he is. But he's unavailable just now.'

'Unavailable?'

'Yes. He's . . .' The man searched for words.

'Reconnoitring,' one of his troops suggested.

Captain Tonley brightened, his mouth quirking up. 'Yes, that's it! Reconnoiting. Come, join us,' and he reined his mount around.

'Thank you, Captain,' the Marquis said. 'I hope we will see him later.'

'Oh, yes.' The captain waved such concerns aside. 'He will be back tonight. For now, join us. Rest your mounts. Tell us about this attack we are hearing of.'

The Marquis nodded to Sergeant Shepherd who raised his arm in a 'forward'.

With the gathering of dusk the bivouac came to resemble less and less a military encampment and more a gathering of brigands. From under the awning raised on poles that served as the command tent,

Ghelel watched drunken fights break out around campfires, betting and wrestling over what meagre loot had been gathered so far, and a virtual army of camp followers picked up at Ipras and Idryb who circulated among the men and women. Captain Tonley entertained them with stories of the crossing while the Marquis sat calmly on a camp stool and smoked his pipe. Molk, Ghelel noted, had disappeared the moment they entered camp. Gloriously drunk by now, no doubt.

Almost no one noticed when an old man bearing two leather buckets of stones stooped under the awning. He dropped the buckets then pulled off his oversized wool cloak revealing a wrestler's broad shoulders and knotted, savagely scarred arms that reminded Ghelel of oak roots. Captain Tonley sprang from his stool to offer the man a tankard. The fellow drank while eyeing them over its rim. The Marquis stood and bowed. Ghelel followed suit. Finishing the tankard he thrust it at the captain who staggered back.

'Another. It's dusty work in the hills.'

The man extended a hand to the Marquis who took it. 'Marquis Jhardin, Commander of the Marchland Sentries.' He indicated Ghelel. 'Our new Prevost, Alil.'

The man grunted, turned to her. She extended her hand, which disappeared into his massive paw. Ghelel had an impression of a brutal blunt Napan-blue face with small guarded eyes under a ledge of bone, brush-cut hair white with dust, but what overwhelmed everything was the pain in her hand. It felt as if it had been cracked between stones. 'So this is our new Prevost,' he said, eyeing her, and she knew that, somehow, this man also knew. 'Commander Urko Crust.'

'Commander,' she managed, her teeth clenched against the pain.

Sighing his ease, Urko sat on a stool. Captain Tonley set another tankard next to him. 'Captain Tonley. Just because I'm away for the day doesn't mean that the entire camp has to go to the Abyss.'

The captain flinched. 'No, sir.' Saluting, he ducked from the awning.

Urko dragged the buckets close, nodded for the Marquis to sit. Ghelel sat next to him. 'What word from Choss?' In the distance, the sharp commands of Captain Tonley filled the dusk.

The Marquis set to repacking his pipe. 'She's on her way. Is right behind you, in fact.'

Startled, Ghelel stared at Jhardin. *She?* The Empress? Coming here? Gods! Then, this could be it. The battle to decide everything.

But Urko merely nodded at the news, as if he'd half-expected it. He selected a stone from a bucket and studied it, turning it this way and that. He spat on it, rubbed it with a thumb. 'So, deploying to the south is out of the question. Can't have the river between our divisions.'

'No. Choss requests that you take the north-east flank.'

He grunted, set the stone on a table. 'And the south?'

'We'll keep an eye on the south. They haven't the men in Heng for a sortie in any strength.'

Urko selected the next stone, frowned at it, threw it into the darkening night. 'So. I will hold the north-east, Choss the centre, Heng will block the south flank, and the Seti will harass and skirmish.' He let out a long growling breath. 'Probably the best we can arrange for her.'

Gathering herself, Ghelel cleared her throat. 'With all due respect, she marches to relieve Heng, doesn't she? Shouldn't we stop her before she reaches it?'

Urko's grizzled brows clenched together. He lowered his gaze to retrieve another stone. The Marquis took a mug from the table and filled it from an earthenware carafe of red wine. 'Ostensibly, she marches to relieve Heng, yes. But she should know enough not to trap herself in it. No, the best way for her to relieve the siege would be to take the field.'

'Do we have any intelligence on the size of her force?' Ghelel asked. Urko cocked a thick brow at the question, peered up from his inspection of the stone.

'Amaron has his sources,' Jhardin answered. 'I have been informed that, at best, she can field no more than fifty thousand – and that is assuming she conscripts all down the coast at Carasin, Vor, Marl and Halas.'

'Then we well outnumber her.'

'Yes. But numbers count for less than you would think. The emperor was almost always outnumbered. Wasn't that so, Urko?'

The old general grunted his assent while buffing the stone in a cloth. 'She has other assets . . . the Claw. The mage cadre. And there is always the possibility that Tayschrenn may choose to dirty his hands.'

Ghelel sat back on her stool. Great Togg forefend! She hadn't considered that. But the High Mage had yet to act in any of this. Why should he now? Clearly everyone was assuming he would not. To think otherwise was to invite paralysis.

'So,' Urko said, taking a long draught from the tankard. 'We'll wait here for the rest of the force to catch up. Then we will deploy to the north-east.' He handed a stone to Ghelel. 'Take a look at that.'

One side of the oblong stone was coarse rock but the other revealed a smooth curved surface that glistened multicoloured, reminding her of pearl. After a moment the likeness of a shell resolved itself, spiralled, curving ever inward with extraordinary delicacy. 'Beautiful . . .' she breathed.

One edge of the general's mouth crooked up. 'You like it?'

'Yes! It's wonderful.'

'Good!' He sat back and watched her turn the stone in her hands. 'I'm glad you like it.'

* * *

These last few moons strange dreams had dogged Kyle. He slept restlessly, often waking with a start, in a cold sweat, as if having seen or heard something terrifying. And always, the images, the ghost-memories, receded just as he reached for them. This last week on board the *Kite* had passed more calmly, however. Perhaps it was the monotonous rocking, or the slapping rush of the waves, or the melodies Ereko hummed to himself during his long nights at the tiller, but he'd slept either more easily, or far more deeply.

One night Kyle dreamt, or thought he did; he was not sure. All that he knew was that suddenly he became aware of himself walking through mist, or what seemed like mist, or clouds. And he was not alone.

He walked just one pace behind, and slightly to the right of, a slim pale figure who wore layered thick robes that dragged on the ground behind – a ground, Kyle now saw, of dry baked dirt. He walked slowly and deliberately with long strides, his wide hands clasped behind his back, his head bowed, perhaps deep in thought. Long white hair hung to the middle of his back. The man's similarities to the Magus, the Wind Spirit upon the Spur, made Kyle's eyes well with suppressed emotion, but there were differences as well; this man was not as powerfully built and he seemed taller. Yet even as he watched the man's figure rippled, shifting and wavering before returning once more to the slim snow-pale man. In that moment Kyle swore he glimpsed *another* shape, a bestial form unfolding.

He should not be there and it terrified him. Had they somehow trespassed or wandered too far in their journey? The man's sandalled feet raised clouds of dust but no sound reached Kyle of their fall. The dull pewter vault of the sky made his eyes ache to look at it; it seemed to blur when he studied it too carefully. Shadows flew across the two of them, cast themselves on the ground around them, all without any seeming source.

Eventually, after Kyle knew not how long, a destination detached itself from the horizon ahead, a low dark hill or structure of some sort. It resolved into a heap of gigantic darkly smoky crystals, as large as a building. Upon reaching it, the man planted his feet firmly, and from what Kyle could see, set his chin in a fist as he made a survey of the formation, carefully, from right to left. Coming to a decision, he took hold of one crystal with both hands. He strained, grunting and hissing his breath, and with a massive grinding crack the huge shard gave way. It stood twice the height of the man who himself stood far taller than Kyle. The man pushed it aside and reached for another.

'Hold!'

Kyle and the man spun.

A slim figure came walking upon them, dark-skinned in a night-black cloak over sombre clothes, tall with long white hair. Noting the hair, Kyle wondered at a common ancestry between these two.

'Anomandaris,' the man greeted the newcomer, straightening, and loosening his arms at his sides.

Anomandaris bowed. 'Liossercal.' Closer now, Kyle saw that the man was no Dal Hon or of any other darkly-hued tribe, but non-human: his black skin seemed to absorb the dull light that fell upon it, yet his eyes were bright gold lamps that shone now with a kind of reckless amusement.

'What business have you here?'

'I may ask the same.'

Liossercal crossed his arms, rumbling, 'Research.'

The brow over one gold eye arched. The newcomer kicked at the broken crystal. 'It would seem that the subject may not survive the investigation.'

The arms fell again, large hands splayed. 'What of it?'

A shrug. 'It is young yet, Liossercal. A child. Would you dismember a child?'

Liossercal, whose back was still to Kyle, seemed surprised. 'A child? This is new, yes, the weakest of these strange invasions into our Realms and thus so very appropriate to my purposes. But a child? Hardly.'

The one named Anomandaris took a step closer. 'This is my point. It is new and thus unformed. Who is to say what is or is not its character or purpose? You? The universe you inhabit is one of certainties, I have learned. So you can say for certain you know of the future then?'

'A poor argument. You play to my own point. What I can say of a certainty is that we will never know unless we investigate.' And Liossercal turned to the formation.

'I will not allow it.'

Liossercal stilled. He slowly returned to face the newcomer. 'An ocean of blood birthed the hard-won accord between our Realms, Anomandaris. You would risk that? For this? It is not even of our existence! It is alien – very possibly a threat. I would resolve this mystery.'

Anomandaris's eyes seemed to glow even brighter in the gloom. 'It is my interpretation that this house is of Emurlahn and Emurlahn exists as proof of the accord between our Realms. Threaten one and you threaten all.'

Liossercal drew himself up straight, head cocked to one side. After a time he nodded thoughtfully. 'Very well. I will reflect upon this new light you bring to the situation. A reprieve, then, for a time, for this Shadow House.'

Anomandaris inclined his head in agreement. A smile lifted his thin lips and he gestured an invitation to the empty plains. 'Tell me of Resuthenal, then? How fares she?'

Liossercal clasped his hands behind his back, accepted Anomandaris's invitation. They walked off side by side. 'She is in fine health, though the mention of your name still enrages her. Especially when I point out that she lost as a result of her own stupidity.'

Anomandaris laughed. 'Yes, that would enrage anyone.'

Kyle wished to follow the two; he certainly knew that he ought not remain. The things the two spoke of were complete mysteries to him, but he feared being left behind, becoming lost in this strange dream. If only he could have seen the man from the front – he would know then for certain that he dreamed of the patron of his tribe, the Wind King himself. Now dead, killed by Cowl. He struggled to will himself to follow the two receding figures.

'You have come far enough, I should think.'

Kyle turned. He faced a woman, an extraordinarily beautiful woman with deep black eyes and long straight black hair wearing a flowing dress that shimmered white and silver. He attempted to throw himself face-down in the dirt before this Goddess but found that he could not. He closed his eyes, face averted. Who was this? Sister Dawn? Queen of the Night? Great Mother Goddess?

The woman laughed and the sound brought shivers to his spine. 'Come with me, Kyle. It is time that you returned. You are in powerful company, lad, and it is drawing you along with its wanderings. Your dreams are not your own. And I have to say, they are quite perilous.' She led him off.

After a time he dared ask, 'Who were they?'

She waved a hand dismissively. 'Memories. Nothing more than old clinging memories.'

Kyle glanced back to the heap, the 'house'. He was startled to see yet another figure now standing beside it – this one tall and slim as well, but by his silhouette quite ragged and carrying a longsword at his back. Kyle raised a hand to point but the woman, Goddess, who-ever she was at his side, urged him on. 'Some things,' she said, 'are best left unnoticed. Now,' and she faced him, 'it is time for you to move along.'

He opened his mouth to speak but found that he could not. He was frozen, immobile. His vision darkened. He heard water, nearing.

'Lad? Kyle?'

Kyle opened his eyes. Stalker crouched over him, his hazel eyes narrowed. Seeing Kyle awake the scout grunted and moved aside. 'You were fast asleep. Something's come up.'

'What?'

In answer the scout gave a disgusted wave to the sea beyond. Kyle pushed himself up. The sky and sea held a formless grey pre-dawn light. Mist enclosed them on all sides. The sail hung limp. They were becalmed. He glanced back to Ereko who sat motionless, a hand still on the tiller, squinting off into the fog. Kyle shifted to the stern, whispered, 'What is it?'

A shrug from the giant who did not take his eyes from the mist. 'Something. A presence. But,' and he gave a lopsided smile, 'I am not afraid.'

'We've moved.' This from Traveller at the bow.

'Yes. Question is . . . are we closer, or farther . . .' Ereko raised a hand, took a long deep sniff of the air. 'Land,' he announced, smiling.

Stalker went to the gunwale, sniffed the air. He looked to the giant. 'Desert?'

Ereko agreed.

'I hate deserts,' said Coots.

'Lizard gives him god-awful indigestion,' Badlands explained.

'Man the oars,' said Traveller.

The brothers readied the oars. Kyle sat at one, flexing his arm – Ereko had healed it their third night out. 'I think everything gives you indigestion, Coots.'

Sitting, the brother strained furiously on the oar and let out an enormous fart. He looked surprised. 'By the Dark Lady, you're right. Even rowing gives me indigestion.'

Stalker cuffed him on the shoulder. 'Pay attention. I hear breakers.'

The mist dissipated and the wind rose revealing a long flat coast of dunes guarded by a reef. Ereko stood tall and scanned the shore. He nodded to himself, satisfied. 'North around the coast a space yet,' and he sat heaving the tiller around to face them away from the waves breaking over the reef. 'Ready sail.'

* * *

Captain Moss's search for the Seti Wildman of the Hills brought him and his troop of thirty horse north to the rugged High Steppes that formed one heartland of Seti territory. On their way they encountered bands of Seti young bloods, soldiers of the Jackal, Plains Lion, Ferret, Wolf and Dog warrior societies, male and female. Some demanded payments in weapons or coin before allowing the troop of Malazan horse to proceed; others challenged Moss to single combat, but when he told them he was on his way to find the Wildman they laughed and said they would leave Moss for him.

The troop entered the Lands of the Jackal, so named for Ryllandaras, the legendary man-beast, brother to Treach who was now ascended as Trake, god of war. The bands they passed no longer continued on southward, but trailed them instead, coalescing into an informal escort of considerable numbers. Moss also noted that many no longer carried fetishes or colours proclaiming their allegiance to one or another clan Assembly.

On the third day smoke ahead announced a large encampment. Moss's slow pace brought him to the very lip of a grassed escarpment that fell steeply to a wide valley dotted by hide tents and corrals. Moss waved away the fat biting horseflies that circled his head, eased forward in his saddle. 'Near a thousand, I should think,' he said to his sergeant who nodded. The sergeant, a great wad of rustleaf bunching one cheek, raised his chin to the east where an erosional cut offered a way down. 'Have to do,' Moss sighed, and waved his men on.

They crossed a thin stream, an undersized remnant of what once must have been a massive flow. On the opposite shore a crowd was gathered. A raised hand from one Seti elder stopped Moss, who inclined his head in greeting then cocked a knee around the pommel of his saddle, watching. By way of his height advantage, he could see that the crowd surrounded an oval of open ground. At one edge stood a tall muscular Seti youth, his bare chest and legs smeared in paints proclaiming his many victories. His knife-brothers and sisters laughed with him, wiping more paint across his face. One pressed a functional-looking fighting blade into his hand. Moss cast across the oval for the youth's opponent but saw no likely figure. Eventually, straightening from a crouch, an unlikely candidate did appear. An old man, wild-haired with a gnarled grey beard. The Wildman? If so, he was from that much older Seti generation, back when it was unusual to meet any who stood taller than the backs of their mounts.

Moss leant aside to a Seti warrior, asked in Talian, 'What's going on?'

The woman answered, reluctantly, 'A challenge.'

'Who would challenge such an old man?'

She looked up, smiled sharp white teeth. 'The old man challenged *him*.'

'Why?' But the woman didn't answer because the old man had drawn a knife from the back of his deerskin trousers and strode ahead. Waving the blade, he beckoned the tall youth forward. Moss could see him more clearly now; other than his trousers he wore only a thick leather vest revealing a barrel chest matted by silver-grey hair and equally hairy bent arms that seemed to hang unnaturally long. His lips were pulled back from canine-like yellowed teeth in an eager, almost scornful grin. The young blood laughed as he came forward but Moss knew he was in for more than he expected – the old man was fully as wide as he was tall.

Moss had always thought these ritual challenges raucous, chaotic mob scenes but an eerie silence now took the crowd, as of a collective holding of breath. The two combatants crouched, arms reaching out to one another. Moss straightened in his saddle, more than a little anxious since the target of his mission might just be eviscerated before his eyes.

Blades slashed, hands grasped, a grunt, crunch of a solid blow, then the youth spun away, hand at his face where bright blood smeared his chin. Many in the crowd let out breaths in a knowing exhalation. The old man straightened, made a throwing gesture as if to say, 'we're finished,' and turned to go.

But the youth angrily slapped aside the hands of his friends and advanced to the centre of the oval. Warnings brought the old man about. Turning, he called something; the youth's answer was a growl and a ready stance. With a shrug, the old man complied, advancing. This time he held his arms out wide, his hands empty. The surrounding crowd tensed, shocked, edged back a step to offer up more room. The two circled warily, the youth shouting – perhaps demanding that his opponent arm himself. The old man just smiled his feral toothy fighting grin. After two circuits the youth gave up, yelled something to the crowd – probably asking they witness that he'd given the old fool every chance to defend himself – and pressed the attack.

This time the exchange lasted longer. The youth slashed, hunting an opening while the old man gave ground, dodging. Moss could only shake his head; it was so damned obvious to him. A swing from the youth and the old man seemed to casually step inside and twist, throwing his opponent yet keeping a grip on the arm. That arm forced backwards farther and farther. A shriek from the youth. A sickening bend and wet snap of that elbow. And the old man straightened leaving the youth hugging his arm, rocking it like a crippled infant.

The Seti woman at Moss's side murmured something and Moss gave her a questioning look. 'He should consider himself lucky,' she explained. 'The Boar showed great patience with him.'

'The Boar?'

'Some call him the Boar. Many elders swear he reminds him of the Boar of their youth.'

'Who was he?' Moss noted that from across the oval the Boar was now watching him steadily.

'He was our last great champion from a generation ago. No one could defeat him.'

'What happened to him?'

The female Seti warrior gave Moss a strange penetrating look. 'Your Dassem Ultor came to us.'

The Wildman, or Boar, was now coming straight to Moss's horse. The crowd parted before him, some reverently reaching out to touch him as he passed. 'You, Captain,' he called in the Talian dialect. Moss moved to dismount. 'Stay up there!' Shrugging, Moss complied.

He stopped beside Moss's mount. Small brown eyes well hidden within ledges of bone studied Moss, roved about his figure. He sniffed, wrinkling his flattened nose. 'I'm smelling a stink I haven't smelled in a long time, Captain. And I don't like it. You can stay the night. But don't you step outside your camp.'

Moss bowed his head. 'Warlord Toc sends his regards and extends his invitation.'

'He can keep both.'

'You may bring an escort, perhaps fifty of your most loyal—'

'I'm not interested in reminiscing. I'm looking to the future. One without any of you foreigners.'

'Wouldn't a future without Heng help in that regard?'

'Heng?' the old man snorted. 'Heng?' He smiled his unnerving, hungry, bestial smile. 'You've been on the trail for some time now, haven't you, Captain? Well, word's come. Heng's a sideshow now. *She's* left Unta. Coming by sea.'

Moss stared. *So, she's coming. Now his choice would matter even more.* He bowed as best he could while mounted. 'My thanks. This is welcome news. I hadn't heard.'

The old man, Wildman, Boar, now scowled ferociously. 'Yeah. It's welcome all right. I have a few things to pick over with her, I'll tell you, if I could be bothered.'

He waved Moss off. 'Now go. We're finished.' He marched off without waiting for a reply.

After a minute Moss dismounted. Seti warriors pointed him to an empty field; he waved his command over. While his men led their mounts to the bivouac, Moss watched where the Wildman now crouched shoulder to shoulder within a circle of elders, sharing a pipe and a platter of food. Who was he? Such men do not simply appear out of nowhere; he must have a history. A Malazan veteran, that much was obvious; he knew Moss's rank. Fought abroad and learned much of the world. A Seti officer returned from overseas. How many of them could there be? Toc and the atamans would have the resources to find out. Once he returned the mystery would be solved. Then he would also know whether this man might prove a factor in his mission – or not. He pulled his mount's reins to urge it on after his men.

CHAPTER IV

Battle is for an army to win or lose; war is for civilization to win or lose.

Wisdom of Irymkhaza
(The Seven Holy Books)

NEVALL OD' ORR, CHIEF FACTOR OF CAWN, WAS BREAKING fast with tea and a green melon on his terrace overlooking the Street of Virtuous Discretion when his worthless nephew shouted up from below, 'Another fleet, Uncle! A fleet!' Nevall gagged, scalding the inside of his mouth – and spat the offending liquid over the terrace. '*What? Already?*' He stood at the railing and sure enough a cloud of sails was closing on the harbour mouth. His perfidious nephew had taken off down the street to the waterfront carried in his new sky-blue palanquin. Gods, even the village idiot travelled in style these days.

So. Already she had arrived. Must have killed all her oar-slaves or squeezed the life from a mage of Ruse. All as his sources had told: and why not, he paid them a fortune. Yet another expeditionary force to be milked. Hood's infertile member: after they've squeezed all the gold from this one even the dogs will go about on silk cushions. He tossed down his half-melon to the mud and shit-smeared cobbles below for the beggars to fight over and called for his robes of office to be readied. His last thought on the terrace was that he would have to get a much bigger palanquin.

The wharf was heaving with onlookers but his bodyguards beat a passage. 'Make way for your elected representative!' Groten bellowed as he kicked the citizens of Cawn aside.

'What is it? What do you see?' Nevall called through the hangings. Groten stuck his glistening bullet-head through the cloths. He wiped a hand across his slick brow. 'Small for an Imperial fleet, sir.'

'That's Chief Factor. And what do you expect? It must be the lead element.'

'If you say so, sir.' He batted aside the filmy hangings.

'Groten! You're getting the cloth all sweaty!'

'Sorry.' Ducking his head he glanced out. 'Pretty damned shabby too, sir.'

'Well, she was probably forced to commandeer the scows and bay-boats left behind in Unta harbour. I heard that attack from mercenary raiders had cost her dear.'

'So you say, sir.'

Nevall waved him away. 'Just take me to whoever docks.'

'Yes, sir.'

As the labourers tied the ropes to bollards and the gangway was readied, Nevall had his carriers set him down. He waved a hand to demand help in straightening from his palanquin. A representative stepped down the gangway – a commander or captain. Nevall rearranged his thick velvet robes of office and peered nearsightedly up at the fellow. To the Chief Factor's surprise, the man wore a long set of mail that dragged along the gangway, a tall full helm and scaled, articulated iron gauntlets. And the equipage was not new either. It was blackened and scoured, as if having been thrown into a smith's furnace.

'Cawn welcomes – welcomes . . .' Nevall searched the masts, the lines, for flagging or any heraldry at all, '. . . your forces. Consider yourself among friends.'

The fellow stopped before him. The tall helm turned as he took in the waterfront. 'We require drayage and mounts. Wagons, carts. All the food you can supply for an army in the field.'

'Of course! Our pleasure. But a secessionist force has preceded you. They left us nothing. What little we have is vitally needed to feed us and our children.' Nevall gave a self-deprecating laugh. 'In our defence, I must warn you, it will take much for us to part with the least of it.'

Metal ground and scratched as the helm edged down to regard him directly. 'It will take *what*?'

Flames lit the column of the Crimson Guard as it climbed the road west out of town. Afoot, Shimmer paused to look back to burning Cawn as the buildings collapsed into charred ruins. Wagons piled high with hoarded and hidden foodstuffs rumbled past her drawn by straining, sweaty racing thoroughbreds, their eyes rolling white at their unaccustomed treatment. A column of impressed Cawn levies also marched by, pikes and spears awry, the youths' own eyes also wide from their unaccustomed treatment. She rubbed her side where Shell had cut deep to cure the infection from that crossbow bolt – one of the worst woundings she'd ever yet received.

She had spoken against any impressments at the field meeting. But she had to admit that their numbers were needed to flesh out the base of the Guard forces. An officer cadre of nearly one hundred Avowed commanded a force of nine thousand Guard veterans, swelled now by close to fifteen thousand recruits from Bael, Stratem and Cawn. A force small in numbers, she knew, in comparison to Imperial armies, but the Avowed were worth much more than mere numbers, and twelve were mages.

She watched the flames licking the south horizon and the coiling haze of smoke and wondered just how many towns and settlements they had left behind in similar straits. So many! Did all now count their name a curse? As surely did the Cawnese. Yet hadn't they come as liberators? She drew off a soot-stained gauntlet to pinch her eyes for a time as if attempting to blot out the sight. A cough brought her attention around; the Malazan renegade, Greymane, at her side. Helmet under an arm, his thinned ice-blue eyes seemed to regard her with real concern. 'Yes?'

He raised his grey-stubbled chin to the west. 'The column's well past, Lieutenant.'

Frowning, Shimmer followed his glance; sure enough, while she stood lost in thought the column had marched completely past. She was noticing such moments more often now that she and the other Avowed moved among – how should she put it – normal men and women. Occasionally, she or and another Avowed would stand sharing a conversation, or their reminiscences, only to find an entire afternoon had fled. It was as if they had entered into a different time – or more accurately a differing *perception* of it – from the rest of humanity.

She inclined her head and invited Greymane onward. 'Shall we join them?'

A half-smile pulled at the man's fleshy mouth and he bowed.

'Many of the Avowed wonder at your being with us here, Greymane,' she said as they walked. 'Once more we will face Imperials – perhaps those of your old command.'

A thoughtful nod of agreement. 'We will face Imperials, but none of my command. They remain trapped in Korel. The truth is I am even more pleased to be among the Guard with what we hear of this civil war, or insurgency, call it what you will, and this Talian League. It would seem to me that any domestic, ah, reorganization, would hopefully work against the continuance of, ah ... overseas entanglements.'

Shimmer regarded the wide-shouldered ex-commander. The wind pulled at his long, straight grey hair; sun and wind had tanned his round, blunt features a dark berry hue. Obviously, the man had benefited from his share of the life-extending Denul rituals the riches of Empire allowed. It occurred to her that here was one of the few people alive who could be considered close to an Avowed himself. Yet so far what had he demonstrated while among them? Very little. The majority of her brothers and sisters were – to be honest – dismissive of the man. They regarded him a failure, a flawed officer who had broken under the strain of a difficult command. She however sensed within him something more. A veiled strength great enough to have defied not only his own superiors but the Korelan Stormguard as well. '*Overseas entanglements*.' Obviously, here also was an officer who felt keenly the responsibilities of leading soldiers.

'I have been considering my staff and I'm offering you a captaincy and command of a flank in the field.'

The man's grey-shot brows climbed. 'A captaincy?'

'Yes. Do you accept?'

'I am honoured by your trust. But perhaps there will be objections—'

'There damn well will be objections, but no challenges. Do you accept?'

'Yes.'

'Good. Now, what can we do to make these recruits reliable?'

A grin of square white teeth. 'A few small victories would go a long way.'

* * *

The chambers of Li Heng's ruling High Court of Magistrates were known officially as the Hall of Prudence and Conscientious Guidance; to others it was the Palace of Puckering and Spluttering. Predictably, it mirrored the city as a round room where a raised gallery looked down on a central floor. A continuous table of pink marble circuited the upper gallery where the magistrates held court over all petitioners below.

Hurl, her torso tightly bandaged beneath her leathers, now

occupied that floor, alongside Storo, Silk, Liss, Rell and Captain Gujran. Gritting her teeth, it was all she could do to stop herself from walking out on this absurd proceeding immediately. But Storo had *requested* her cooperation and so she was present, despite the strong need for a drink. It was also only the first time she'd seen Silk since the attack – the mage had been busy or making himself absent of late. She still had a lot of pointed questions for him regarding that city mage, Ahl.

The magistrates fiddled and shuffled their papers, or rather, their servants did, sitting behind them and acting as their amanuenses. Many eyes, Hurl noted, watched not Storo, as one might expect, but rather the wiry Genabackan youth Rell, who stood with his head lowered, long greasy hair obscuring his face. Rumours abounded of what this man had accomplished at the North Gate of the Inner Round. Hurl was not surprised; she'd seen him in action enough not to be surprised by any of his unbelievable acts of swordsmanship.

Magistrate Ehrlann tapped the butt of his switch on the table, cleared his throat. 'Honoured fellow magistrates, assembled citizens, appellants. We are gathered here to discuss a serious course of action arising from the recent catastrophes inflicted upon this city by its current military leadership.' Behind Ehrlann his servant, Jamaer, scribbled awkwardly on a vellum sheet balanced on his knees. The magistrate pointed the switch at Storo. 'Sergeant Storo Matash, temporarily promoted Fist, do you have anything to say in your defence at this time?'

Storo unclasped his hands from behind his back, his broad face impassive. 'Nothing.'

'Nothing?'

'Nothing.'

High above them, the magistrates exchanged uneasy glances. Ehrlann shook his switch as if dusting the table of the case. 'Very well, commander. You leave us no choice but to pursue the painful course of action this court has decided upon.' He pointed the switch. 'You, Fist, are stripped of all rank, dismissed and placed under arrest for gross negligence.' The switch flicked to Captain Gujran. 'You, Captain, by the power invested in this court, are promoted to rank of Fist – on a provisional basis only, of course – and charged with military command of this city. Your first action as commander will be to open negotiations with the besieging force to explore terms of surrender. There you are, Fist Gujran. You have your commission. Please act upon it.'

Hurl turned to peer about the room, at the set faces of the magistrates glowering in a full circle down upon them. It occurred to her that the place didn't have one window. Just seven old men and five old women blinking inward at one another from across a circular room. A single window looking out on the city, it seemed to her, would have helped this court a great deal. As it was, Captain Gujran standing beside her just scratched a flame-scorched brow and said, 'No.'

The switch froze. 'No?'

'No.'

The switch trembled. 'Think, Captain. You are risking your future, your career. You are being offered a rank far above that which your breeding could otherwise ever allow.'

Gujran's hands went to his belt. 'You're doin' yourself no favours with that, magistrate.'

'Enough of this charade,' Magistrate Plengyllen burst out from where he sat a quarter of the way around the room. 'Arrest the lot of them.' He waved his switch at a guard. 'Summon the soldiers of the court. Arrest these criminals.'

The guard glanced to the centre of the room. Storo gave the smallest of assents. The guard left. Three of the twelve magistrates also sprang to their feet and hurriedly left the room. Hurl grasped Storo's arm to point but Storo waved her concern aside. Shortly the magistrates reappeared, backing into the chamber, forced in by soldiery filling all exits.

Magistrate Ehrlann glanced about, took in the soldiery, their Imperial colours, and swore. He threw his switch to the tabletop. He slipped his fingers over the forward edge of the table, his mouth twisting his disgust. 'So,' he hissed. 'It comes to this. Usurpation of legitimate republican rule. Once more you Malazans are revealed for the pirates and thugs you are. *Your* rule is the sword and the fist. Ours authority arises from the consent of the ruled. We shall see of which history approves.'

Storo inclined his head to the guards, who motioned the magistrates from their seats. 'It seems to me, Magistrate Ehrlann, that you are only legitimately blind to the truth that oppression comes in many forms. Consider, if you are capable, the rather narrow constituency you and your circle claim to speak for in this city for the last hundred years.'

The magistrate gaped at Storo – as did Hurl. Never before had she heard the man speak in such a manner. It occurred to her that many hours of expensive private tutoring stood behind such opinions.

Contact with rulership seemed to be bringing out the man's hidden talents.

As a guard reached for him, Ehrlann spun to his servant. 'Do something, Jamaer! They're arresting me!' Jamaer's feather pen scratched as he dutifully copied down the magistrate's words. Snarling, Ehrlann slapped the papers from the man's lap. 'No, no! Do *something*, you fool. You've worked for me for over thirty years! Doesn't that count for something?'

Slowly, solemnly, Jamaer handed the magistrate his umbrella.

Hurl suppressed a laugh while Liss chortled. The stunned incomprehension on Ehrlann's face was worth it.

Once the magistrates had been taken away Storo ordered the guard to withdraw. He waited for the room to clear, his hands reclasped at his back, and studied the flagged black marble floor. Silk paced, and Hurl noted that despite the opportunity, even in a besieged city, the mage had yet to replace or mend his tattered finery, or even repair his worn boots. He also noted that while the mage paced from one side of the room to the other, his glance unfailingly returned to Storo. While Storo, it seemed to her, with his downcast eyes, was avoiding the man's attention.

Then Liss straightened, hissing, and faced the single lower floor entry portal. Silk stopped pacing. Three men entered – or, rather, three versions of what seemed to Hurl to be the same man, though each was dressed differently – Ahl, the very mage who had saved her. Hurl rubbed her eyes. Liss visibly shrank from the three's advance. Reacting to the tensions of the room, Rell shifted to stand next to Storo, his hands on the grips of his twinned swords now returned to his shoulder baldrics.

Liss's heated gaze darted to Silk. 'How dare you invite this man – this creature – back into the city.'

'We need allies, Liss.'

A fat arm shot out, pointing. 'That Path is an abomination!'

As one, the three grinned – though their smiles were not identical; the one Hurl was sure had introduced himself as Ahl, the left side of his face drooped as if dead, while another's right side hung slack, also as if dead. The third seemed to suffer no such affliction at all. Studying them more closely now, Hurl noted many more differences: one had his hair cut short while it hung long and unkempt on another. Each also bore differing wounds: a facial slash on one, a mangled, mishealed hand on another.

'Nice to see . . .' said the one in a soldier's light leathers.

'. . . You too . . .' said Ahl, wearing his dirty frayed robes.

'. . . Liss,' finished the third, in a reversed sheepskin tunic sashed at his waist.

'Explanations, Silk,' Hurl demanded in the silence following the three Ahls' eerie, mangled form of communication. Six glittering black eyes shifted to Hurl and she felt the power of that regard, like a red-hot iron plate held just before her face.

'Later,' Silk said, and the weight of the three's eyes slid from Hurl leaving her able to inhale.

Liss obviously had more to say but Storo straightened, letting out a long breath, and turned to study everyone present. Smiling at a sudden funny thought, he scratched a thumb across his chin. 'Ehrlann was closer to the truth than he realized. We are gathered here to consider a very serious course of action.'

Silk was shaking his head, his thin blond hair tossing. 'No,' he barely mouthed, hushed. 'Don't do it.'

Liss took a step to Storo, her eyes now narrowing to slits, the three forgotten. 'Do – *what*?'

'We're far outnumbered, Liss. Have to shorten the odds. And a way does exist to do just that. Here, in the city.'

The Seti shamaness, who claimed to be the reborn Vessel of Baya-Gul, patroness of all Seti Seeresses, stood frozen for an instant, then, it appeared to Hurl, her matted greasy ropes of hair actually seemed to stand on end and her eyes, raw red with exhaustion, widened in horror. 'So,' she said, now nodding her comprehension, 'this is how it will be fulfilled – his last words: "Those who hate me most shall set me free".

'Who—' began Hurl.

'What of the containment wards?' Liss demanded.

'Between all of us, we have a chance,' Silk said, hugging himself.

Liss snorted her disdain. 'Us? Wards set by Tayschrenn, the emperor himself and Gods know how many mage cadres?'

'We think . . .'

'. . . we can . . .'

'. . . manage.'

A fat arm shot out to point in the three's direction. 'You stay out of this.' Liss faced Storo. 'Please, consider all the lives that will be lost. The bloodshed.'

'That's the idea, Liss. I'm sorry, but he'll tear them to pieces out there and that's what we want.'

The old woman shook her head. 'And after all this is over, Storo? All the lives to be lost in the centuries to come? What of them?'

Storo lowered his gaze. 'We'll deal with that then – assuming any of us remain alive.'

Hurl had had enough. 'What are you two talking about?' she shouted. 'What's going on, Captain?'

The three regarded one another in silence for a time. Then Silk turned to her. 'The man-jackal's still alive, Hurl,' he said, still hugging himself. 'He was imprisoned beneath the city. Probably yet another of the hidden assets Kellanved seemed to love salting away for emergencies.'

'I heard he was cast over the cliffs of the escarpment.'

'He was,' said Silk.

'What? Am I just slow or am I missing something here?'

'Many have claimed to have destroyed him but he just keeps showing up again. Some say he is unkillable. That so long as the plains remain, so shall he. But . . .' and the mage's gaze slid to the three brothers, 'there are other theories.'

The three gave Silk their mix-matched unnerving grins. The avid glitter of their eyes made Hurl's skin shiver. They struck her as unhinged.

'In any case, Silk knows how to get to him,' Storo said.

Hurl looked from face to face. *Gods no. Ryllandaras. The eater-of-men. Heng's Curse. A God, some said.* She shook her head, appalled by the vision of centuries of slaughter. 'No, Captain. Don't do it. They'll curse your name for a hundred years.'

'There!' Liss pointed again. 'That from the most level head among you.'

Storo kicked at the polished black flagging. 'Rell?'

The Genabackan did not answer immediately. He kept his head low. 'Do not ask me strategy,' he finally said.

Waving that aside, Storo took hold of one of the man's sheathed weapons and shook it. 'Think tactically.'

A shrug. 'In that case there is nothing to discuss. We are engaged in a duel. We have an opportunity to wound the enemy. We must take it.'

'That's good enough for me.' Storo motioned Silk to the exit.

'Wait!' Liss raised a commanding hand. 'There is more going on here than just this. I must speak now as Seeress. Have you forgotten that Ryllandaras is said to be brother to Trake? Of the First Heroes? Trake ascends as god of war and now war comes to Heng and his brother is released? Is this coincidence? Just *who* do we serve here – have you considered any of this?'

Broad, feral smiles had been spreading on the crippled lips of the three Ahls for some time now. The madness that seemed to sparkle in their eyes kept dislodging Hurl's thoughts. Looking away, she offered, 'It would serve Trake, I imagine.'

'Or weaken him? Might he challenge his brother? Are we releasing a rival claimant to the Godhead? And what sort of god? You forget, Ryllandaras is the enemy of humanity.'

'He's . . .'

'. . . no . . .'

'. . . god.'

'You fool!' Liss stamped a sandalled foot, cracking a marble flag in an explosion that echoed like the eruption of a Moranth munition and rocked Hurl where she stood. In the stunned silence following, all recovered from their flinch and stared at the fat woman in her tattered layered skirts and stained muslin wrap. 'The Seti have worshipped him for ten thousand years!'

Storo rubbed a hand over his balding pate, glanced to the others. 'Well. They'll be spared the brunt of his savagery. He'll fall on the Talian forces. Just what we want.'

'You remain determined?'

'Yes.'

Liss tightened her wrap, shaking her head. 'Do not expect my help.'

'Very well. I'm sorry.' Storo motioned to the exit. Coming aside Hurl, he said, 'They can curse my name, Hurl, so long as they die doing it.'

* * *

The ancestral castle of the D'Avig family of Unta was burning at night. Flames gouted from windows and painted the keep in writhing shadows. The town of the same name it overlooked echoed with screams and the harsh clap of hooves as Wickan raiders looted and burned. *But no slaughter*, Rillish told himself. *Please, Lady, little of that.* Nil and Nether had been stern in their warnings – take all you want but no killing. Not that some would not die this night. Rillish had witnessed enough sackings to know it inevitable, as hot blood demanded it. Still, the twins' warning ought to carry weight – they'd threatened the most ignoble punishment imaginable to any Wickan – death by drowning.

With his Malazan command Rillish had been assigned the barricading of a crossroads on the main road south out of D'Avig. They found it to be the centre of a small hamlet. A wayside inn, a corral and a carpenter's workshop lined the crossroads. Rillish promptly had the men toss everything big and moveable across the road. Watching the glow of the sacked castle, he took the waterskin from his side and drank, easing back on the high cantle of his saddle. His leg throbbed; the wild ride through the hills and down in the rich Untan farmlands had re-torn the freshly healed muscle. He sought out and caught his sergeant's eye. 'No one gets past, Chord.'

'No chance, sir. There's Wickans crawling all over the hillsides. Like the old days it is, so I understand.'

Yes. The old border warfare all along the Wickan frontier. How appropriate; the central authority collapses and it's a quick return to the tried and true old ways of doing things. No one's learned a thing. Cocking his head, he listened: distant panicked cries only, no clash of sustained resistance. From where he sat it looked as if D'Avig had well and truly been overrun. Surprise had been complete. His job was to keep it so. 'Sergeant.'

'Aye, sir.'

'Gather the freshest horses and send a squad all the way south to the fortress at Jurda. I want eyes on that stronghold.'

'Aye, sir.' Chord spat out a wad of rustleaf, bellowed, 'Talia! Get your squad provisioned and ready to move!'

Rillish shot a glance to the rear. Talia – newly promoted squad sergeant and his lover – signed her acknowledgement to Chord and flashed a bright mocking smile to Rillish. The lieutenant spun to stiffly face the front. *Were those grins he'd caught on the faces of his soldiers? Damn Togg, woman, show some discretion.* He ached to glance back once more but dared not now. The most dangerous assignment he'd be asking of his command and she pulls it. What if he was to countermand Chord's selection? He'd just undermine the man's authority – never mind what he'd be doing to his own. No, he would just have to trust his senior sergeant's judgment in the matter. *And wish her Oponn's favour.*

'Cavalry, sir!' came a shout. 'And it ain't Wickan!'

'Form up!' Chord barked.

The double ranks of regulars levelled the spears they'd collected to assemble the traditional hedgehog. Rillish glanced to the second-storey windows of the inn and the lofts of the stable and woodworking shop opposite, and eased his swords in their scabbards. Soon the crash of horses at full gallop reached them and the horsemen – perhaps twenty – reined up before the barricade of upturned carts. Untan white and red surcoats declared their allegiance. Among their milling numbers one pointed, ordering, 'Remove the barrier, fools! Are you blind! We're no Wickans!'

'Then who are you?' Rillish called.

'Who? *Who!*' the man yelled, outraged, his face darkened above his full grey and black beard. 'Dol D'Avig, you fool!'

Rillish felt his insides twist sickeningly. Curse Fener, it was the man. He recognized him now, brother to the count. They had met once or twice at functions in the capital. Rillish tightened his stomach muscles and clenched his jaw against a vertigo as it came home that now was the time he would cut his own past from himself as surely as if he had lost a limb. Either with this man or another, sooner or later – it was just a shock for it to have come so soon. 'Then I ask you, Dol, for the sake of your men, to throw down your weapons and surrender.'

The brother to the count yanked the reins of his mount, shearing the beast's head aside. '*What!* Surrender?' His thick brows clenched as he studied more closely the forces arrayed before him. 'You wear Imperial colours – where in Hood's Arse did you come from?'

Not there, I assure you. 'Never mind. I ask you again – throw down your weapons.'

Teeth shone white in a savage, knowing smile. And something surfaced in Rillish's mind, a memory of chatter during those dreary social gatherings at the capital: 'Dol D'Avig – a better mage than his brother is count.' *Queen take it!* He drew breath to shout but at the same instant Dol waved curtly and Rillish's throat constricted shut. All around him spears and swords clattered to the cobbles as his men gasped, choking, tearing at their throats.

The same overwhelming need for breath flamed in Rillish's chest and it was all he could do to draw a sword and hold it high. The shutters of the inn's second-storey windows banged open and in the loft doors opposite crossbowmen rose to their knees. Bolts raked the Untan cavalry. *Get him! Gods, please!* His sight was darkening, the sword fell from his grip.

Then, *thank Soliel!*, breath, sweet clean air. Rillish sucked great lungfuls deep into his chest. 'Where is he?' he gasped as soon as he could manage, righting himself in his saddle.

'Gone, sir. Rode off.'

'Well – get him!'

'Where?' asked Chord.

Cursing, Rillish sawed his mount around and kneed it into motion. 'South, of course!'

'Sir! Wait!'

But Rillish could not wait. Only he was mounted. Only he stood any chance of catching the man. Storming through the modest hamlet he left it behind almost immediately and entered the un-relieved darkness of an overcast night. Empty flat fields lined the way in monochrome pewter, interrupted occasionally by black lines of low stone walls and the darkness of small copses. His leg screamed its pain at him, making him squirm in his saddle. A cool mist, the beginnings of rain, chilled his face and neck. Where he imagined he should have caught up with the fellow his mount balked at the road ahead, almost throwing him over its neck. He grunted the agony of using his legs to rescue his seating. When he'd recovered a mounted rider blocked the way. Rillish reached for one sword but found an empty sheath only. *Damn!* He drew the left.

'Wrong rider,' called the figure in a young woman's familiar voice. Rillish peered into the gloom. 'Nether?'

'Come. We must hurry.'

Rillish kneed his mount forward, clenching his teeth. 'How did you . . .' But of course – the Warrens. He sheathed the sword.

'He's good, this one. Eluded us all night but betrayed himself at your roadblock.'

'He is headed south?'

Nether tossed her wild black hair, hacked unevenly to a medium length and damp with sweat. 'You could ride all the way to Fist and not meet him. He's taken to the Warrens but I have his scent – come!' Her mount lunged away at a gallop.

Cursing, Rillish struggled to urge his sweating horse onward. 'C'mon, boy. That's a handsome mare she's riding. C'mon.'

Either she reined in to wait for him or he had coaxed renewed vigour from his mount but he gained upon her and they raced single file. She glanced back, grinning the pleasure of a daughter of the steppes who had ridden before walking. 'Hold on, Malazan!'

Not knowing what to expect Rillish flinched and thereby missed the transition. When he opened his eyes the fields were gone as was the road and the low rain clouds. Instead, his mount's hooves sank noiselessly into deep moss and rotting humus while all around squat trees loomed from a shadowed silver night. Nether pulled up savagely.

'The arrogant fool! He has no idea the risks he runs here!'

'Where is *here*?' Rillish's mount shuddered beneath him, muscles flinching in exhaustion, and perhaps in fear.

'Shadow. Meneas and Mockra skeined together I sensed in his

weavings. Now we have proof. But illusion will not save him from this,' and she waved to the forest.

Rillish slipped a hand to the grip of his remaining weapon. 'What is it?'

She regarded him closely. The flat light of shadow cast her face into sharp planes of light and dark. Gods, she looked to Rillish like the ground-down mother of nine who had seen most of those into the dirt. Yet she was young enough to be his daughter. Child, life has been so unfair to you. She asked, 'What do you know of the houses of the Azath?'

He shrugged. 'Some. Stories, legends.'

'They capture any foolish enough to enter their grounds. Sometimes with vines or trees.' She gestured to the forest. 'As those trees are to the Azath, so is this forest to Shadow. None who enter escape . . .' Cocking her head she raised a hand to forestall any comment. 'And this raises a disturbing question – what could be so difficult, or important, to imprison that an entire forest is required?'

Rillish stared at the girl, or rather young woman. Damn these mages and their unfathomable academic minds. He waved the question aside. 'He's getting away.'

'Is he?' And she smiled again. 'I do not ask that you accompany me, but will you?'

'Yes.'

'Then stay close – as your saboteurs say, things are about to get hairy.' She kneed her mount forward. Rillish followed, gasping as he too kneed his mount. What trail Nether followed he had no idea – some sort of magical wake of warren manipulation perhaps. In any case, she did not hesitate, leaping fallen rotting logs, dodging trunks and ducking low branches. Rillish struggled to keep up. Glancing ahead, it seemed to him that the thick leafless branches were becoming more numerous, were perhaps even swinging into their path. Now, a yellow glow spread out ahead of Nether, almost like ripples, which pushed back against the branches while she and he slipped through. Then, in the distance, Rillish heard a sound that raised the hairs of his neck and forearms: the angry baying of a hound. Nether's head snapped around, and though her face was no more than a pale oval, Rillish thought he saw fear in the witch's eyes.

Roots now writhed through the moss and heaps of steaming fallen leaves. Nether's mount stumbled, legs stamping, snorting its alarm. Pulling up, she pointed. 'There! His horse was taken. He is afoot.' She urged her mount onward but it baulked, dancing aside. 'What?'

A yell of outrage reached them from ahead, then the ground

erupted, sending their mounts rearing. Rillish shielded his face from a driven spray of dirt and smoke. Blinking, arm raised over his eyes, he made out Nether standing tall in her saddle, peering ahead. 'What was that!' he yelled through the roaring in his ears.

'I thought I saw . . .'

Bellowing as loud as a bull's snapped their heads around. Something huge thrashed in the forest back along their trail. Wood cracked sounding like explosions. He and Nether shared a grin of terrified amusement – the forest, it seemed, wasn't too particular. 'We have to go!'

Nether was nodding, but her gaze was captured by what lay ahead. 'He has escaped again. But I believe I know . . .' She snapped a gesture and the surroundings wavered, lightening to a grey dusk. At that instant her mount shrieked a death-cry.

The transition felt like the worst hangover Rillish had ever experienced. He held his blazing forehead, blinked away tears. As his eyes refocused, he found he was still mounted, but Nether lay on the ground at his horse's hooves, her mount splayed dead in a pool of its own viscera. Half the animal had not made the shift. 'Nether!'

An arm wrapped around her side, she pointed, snarling, 'Get him!'

Rillish kicked his mount into motion. He had a blurred impression of a dirt plain scattered with boulders, a flat dull sky, then his mount carried him over the lip of a ridge to slide dancing and side-stepping down a long scree slope to a narrow, dry valley floor. Coughing, he waved at the dust cloud while dirt and rocks skittered down around him. Nearby, someone else was coughing.

As the dust thinned Rillish saw Dol lying among the rocks, both hands clenching the empty rags of one trouser leg. He was looking up at him, anger and a touch of bitter amusement twisting his face. 'Damned trees took my leg,' he said, his teeth flashing behind his beard. Rillish allowed himself to relax, massaged his thigh.

'You know,' Dol said conversationally, 'in the songs, the hero jumps from Warren to Warren always landing on his feet. He never appears on a Hood-be-damned hillside and falls on his arse.'

Rillish nodded his tired agreement. 'I don't think the minstrels have been there.'

A fierce grin of suppressed agony, then the man squinted up at him. 'The Keth family, right? Rillish?'

'Yes.'

'Gone over to the barbarians, hey?'

'Let's say I disagree with the Empress's policies.'

Dol stared, then laughed ending with a snarl of pain. 'The Empress? Oh yes, *her*.'

Rillish eyed the man uncertainly and opened his mouth to ask the obvious question when the man glanced aside and gaped his surprise. Someone else was walking up, picking his way between the rocks of the valley: slim, wild grey hair, the tattered rags of what once must have been expensive finery hanging from him. 'What in Hood's paths is *that*?' Dol said, speaking Rillish's own thoughts.

The bizarre figure closed on Dol to peer down with an antic grin that seemed about to break into laughter. Dol gaped up doubtfully at him. Rillish clasped his sword grip. 'Who—'

A foot lashed out, taking Dol in the throat. The mage's blood-splashed hands leapt from the ruins of his thigh to his neck. His eyes bulged his disbelief.

'*Damn you!*' Rillish drew, but his numb leg couldn't restore his balance and he slid sideways off his horse. He lay on his back like an upturned turtle, his leg twisted in the stirrup.

The man came around the horse. He rubbed a hand over the animal's quivering sweaty flanks and studied it with open approval. 'Falling off your horse like that . . . was that some sort of fiendishly cunning manoeuvre meant to confuse me?' Rillish had no idea what to say or do; his leg was useless and he lay helpless before this insane murderous beggar.

'No, I just fell off my horse.'

A barked laugh. 'I like you,' a sudden frown, 'a pity.'

Closer now, the man's wild filthy hair was perhaps very light beneath the dirt and the hue of his flesh underneath the caked grime was quite dark. Rillish wondered if the fellow were part Napan. But the eyes were wrong; the eyes were . . . almost inhuman. 'Who are you?'

The quick rictus of a smile, gone just as suddenly as it appeared. 'A lie. A lost letter. A message whispered to the wind. A dart tossed into a cyclone.'

A madman. Rillish wet his lips. 'What do you want?'

'Nothing you—' the man stopped himself, glanced up the valley slope. His brows rose. 'Not who I was expecting,' he said. He may not even have been aware he was speaking aloud. 'No, not yet, I think.' He backed away, pointed to Rillish. 'The Lady is with you today. Do not imagine she will be tomorrow.'

'Who . . . ?' But the harlequin figure disappeared among the boulders.

Moments later Nether came hobbling around the horse, still

clenching her side. She nodded to Rillish then returned her stare to where the apparition had gone. 'You saw him?' he demanded, as if doubting his own sanity.

'Yes. You spoke with him?'

'Yes – you know who he is?'

A long slow affirmation. 'Oh yes. And I will tell you in all honesty, Jal Keth. I seriously debated whether or not to come down here.'

'Well, who *is* he?'

A shake of the head. 'No. It is safer for you not to know – for now. Someone who was supposed to be out of the game.'

Rillish allowed himself to lie limp on the ground. 'Gods, woman! Well, at least help me up.'

'Who, me?' Together, each aiding the other, with much trial and error, they mounted with Nether behind holding Rillish steady. She nickered to start his mount walking; it picked a path between the boulders.

'Just where in all the Realms are we anyway?' Rillish asked.

'The Imperial Warren.'

'Oh. I thought no one was supposed to come here any more.'

'That's right.'

'Did we perhaps just meet the reason behind that prohibition?'

She whispered in his ear, 'How could we when we've never been here?'

While Nether gently weaved their transition from the Warren Rillish tried to fight his sudden keen awareness of the warmth of the young warlock's embrace. It did not help later that night, close to dawn, as Nether and he and their exhausted mount were walking the road north through a cold drizzle, when soldiers straightened from hedgerows alongside the road and Rillish pulled up suddenly to see Talia watching him from over the stock of a levelled crossbow. She did lower the weapon, but the look she gave him there on the horse in Nether's arms was a caution for when they next met.

* * *

To Kyle the coast of this land seemed to consist of nothing more than league after league of empty sand beaches leading up to dense jungle. Ereko skilfully wove the *Kite* through gaps in reefs as they skirted north-west. White and black seabirds hovered and dived in their wake. Peering over the gunwale was like staring down from a great height – undersea mountains of coral passed majestically beneath them. The sun glared with a ferocity Kyle had never known. It seemed to bake the top of his head. The brothers had used leather strips to tie rags over their heads and Stalker had even removed his armour and now sat in his leathers, a sash around his head and face like a scarf. Only Traveller and Ereko seemed unmoved by the oppressive heat. Kyle itched with sweat and rashes seemed to be creeping over his entire body.

'Won't we land now?' he asked Ereko yet again, rubbing a finger over his cracked lips. 'We're low on water.' Blood smeared his fingers.

'This is a dangerous land, Kyle,' the Thel Akai giant answered, as patiently as the first time Kyle had asked. 'We have to be careful.'

Careful! Kyle almost pointed to the bow where Traveller reclined in the shade of a sailcloth. With an obvious master swordsman like *him* on board? And you, a giant nearly twice the height of a man? And these three veterans from Assail who quit the Crimson Guard because they found it boring? Gods and Spirits, what kind of a land was this?

Still, they did not pull in – even when the last of the water was shaken from the last keg. The afternoon golden light faded to the red sunsets that came with disorienting suddenness. He almost asked again why Ereko made no effort at landing and would they simply career along like this until they all died of exposure when he realized that no one else was asking. Everyone else, even fiercely independent Stalker, seemed content to defer to the giant's experience. Clenching his teeth, Kyle sat back against the warm, damp and now mouldy planking of the *Kite*.

As the evening deepened Kyle dozed in the deadening heat and humidity. A grunt from one of the Lost brothers woke him. Everyone was staring ahead. Kyle sat up straighter. Distant torches lit the edge of a long low spit of sand. Behind the torches stood a large tent, the thin cloth of its sides billowing lightly in the weak night wind. Ereko turned the bow to shore.

Traveller stood, rearranged the simple padded mail hauberk he wore beneath his dark leathers, and belted his long, slim black-hilted sword at his side. Kyle found he could not take his eyes from that weapon. As the bow scraped up into sand Traveller leapt down into the wash to steady the vessel. Stalker and the brothers joined him. They pulled the *Kite* as far up the strand as they could. Kyle belted on his own tulwar and jumped into the wet sand. Ereko stepped down unarmed. When his feet touched ground the giant stood still for a time, head lowered. Kyle thought he heard him whispering something that may have been a prayer. Straightening, his usually smiling lips were set, his brow lined. He had the air of a man facing a trial. Traveller led the way to the tent.

As they neared, a man stepped from the open flap. He was a large fellow, tall and well-padded in fat. The torchlight glimmered on his bright silk robes and his round head was shaved. His flesh held the hue of oiled ironwood. He bowed. 'Welcome to you all,' he said in accented Talian. 'Welcome to the lands you call Jacuruku.'

Within, carpets covered the sand. Lamps on tall iron tripods lit the large interior. Pillows lay scattered, as were silver platters containing covered bowls, cups and carafes. Traveller eased himself down to sit cross-legged. Their host sat opposite. Stalker, Coots and Badlands sat together uneasily, glancing about. The tent was tall enough to accommodate Ereko who sat near the entrance. Kyle sat with him.

'Greetings all,' their host continued. 'Please . . . eat, drink. My name is Jhest Golanjar. How it is I know your language you are wondering. That is simplicity. It is the language spoken by an invading army that conquered a neighbouring kingdom decades ago. They rule as a caste of warrior-aristocrats who enforce their will with sword and magery. All in the name of that kingdom's ancient Goddess – the Queen Ardata. Know you them?'

Their host seemed to be addressing everyone, but his dark glittering eyes remained fixed upon Traveller. Coots, his mouth stuffed full of bread and meat sauce, slurred, 'No.'

Untroubled, Jhest continued. 'In our language we call them the *Isturé Forlan Edegash*. In your language,' he lifted a meaty hand to Kyle, 'the Crimson Guard.'

Kyle stared, speechless, then he remembered the sigil still pinned to his chest and he felt his face redden in embarrassment. *Fool, to have kept it!*

'Are we enemies, then?' Traveller asked, his voice low, yet Kyle now felt attuned to the man's moods and he heard the coiled warning behind the question.

Jhest's smile was broad and easy, yet oddly flat. He raised both hands. 'Not at all. We admire the *Isturé* for what they have accomplished.'

'Which is?' Ereko asked.

Jhest answered without so much as a glance to the Thel Akai; it was as if the giant did not exist. 'They have advanced far in the path that is our . . . how shall I put it? . . . our passion – my brothers and sisters' speciality of interest and research.'

'That being?' Stalker prompted.

Again, the broad yet oddly empty smile. The man's black eyes unmoving on Traveller. 'Why, the Paths of Ascension, of course.'

No one spoke for a time. Badlands and Coots ate noisily; Stalker picked up a flatbread and tore off a bite. Kyle poured himself a drink that proved to be some sort of sweetened water. Traveller pressed a hand to his brow, sighing. 'Thank you for your hospitality, Jhest, but we are tired and should sleep. Perhaps tomorrow we could trouble you for water and supplies?'

'Of course.' The man stood, brushed at the folds of his robes. 'Until tomorrow, then. Goodnight.' Bowing, he left the tent.

Chewing a mouthful, Stalker caught Badland's eye and cocked his head to the flap. Badlands crossed to the opening. 'Gone.'

'Anyone around?' Stalker asked.

'Hard to say. It's damned dark. Probably someone.'

Grunting his assent, Stalker gestured Coots out. 'You two, first watch.'

Glowering, Coots picked up the tray and carried it out the door. 'Figures. First decent meal in months . . .'

Stalker now turned his attention to Ereko. 'What do you think?'

During all of this, Traveller merely ate, eyes downcast. It was as if the man had given up on everything and was willing to accept whatever might come to him; it was either the worst sort of pathetic fatalism, or a kind of enlightened understanding that expectations, plans, ambitions, were no more than deluding vapours that, in the end, could not change anything. It was maddening to Kyle that he couldn't decide which.

Ereko lifted a pot of a thick yellow cream that Kyle thought might be yogurt. He sniffed it, set it down. 'I have been away for a very long time, of course. But I have heard rumours. It seems they may be true. This portion of the continent is ruled by a magiocracy, an oligarchy of powerful mages who bend all their resources and research to unravelling the mysteries of Ascendancy. It is said they are masters of the Paths of Denul, and even conduct rather horrifying surgeries and experiments upon the bodies of their people to that end. No doubt they see Ascendancy as their way to power and immortality, and so on.'

'Yet he ignored you,' Kyle said.

Ereko laughed, smiling. 'Ascendancy holds no interest for me, Kyle. To them, I am probably just some sort of wretched failure. Nothing more than that.'

383

'You are the Eldest of all living things here of the world, Ereko,' Traveller suddenly announced. 'Father to us all.'

'*Father?*' Kyle echoed, his wonder and amazement obvious.

Ereko waved the words aside. 'Our friend is speaking poetically, Kyle. When one considers such ancient times one's only recourse is the language of poetry. Thus legends, myths, creation accounts, history. All are no more than stories shaped to justify the present appearance of things.'

Rolling his eyes, Stalker tossed back a drink. 'I was hoping for rather more practical information.'

Ereko laughed, smiling self-consciously. 'Sorry, yes. To the point then. They are torn. They want to move against us – but they are of course anxious as to our capabilities. The question for us is which faction will prevail. The voices for caution or the voices for action.'

'They will act.' This from Traveller as he sat, head lowered, studying one of the land's unfamiliar yellow fruits. 'When it becomes clear that we will perhaps get away, a small faction will take matters into their own hands and will move. Once they do so the rest will have no choice but to commit themselves.'

Kyle stared, unable to breathe. 'You have *seen* it?'

The eyes rose, met his. The intensity of that gaze drove Kyle's gaze aside, but not before he glimpsed a well of terrifying emotion kept locked under an almost inhuman control. 'I have seen it all before, Kyle.'

Ereko gestured to the cushions. 'Sleep for now, lad. You can have the last watch.'

Having eaten and now sitting comfortably on soft cloth Kyle already felt his eyelids drooping. He lay back and curled up without argument – Ereko would wake him if anything happened. Sleep took him almost instantly.

A tap of his foot woke Kyle. Stalker stood looking down at him; the scout gestured him out and left. Kyle grabbed up his armour, helmet and weapon belt and followed. Outside, a false dawn of diffuse light made the sea look strangely flat, the beach lifeless and the jungle a dark mystery. Stalker unbuckled his tall conical helmet. 'Been quiet.'

Over his linen shirt and padded aketon, Kyle pulled on his hauberk of iron rings laced to leather, adjusted the leather wrappings at his legs. 'No one at all?'

'Only if you count the soldiers surrounding us.'

'*What?* When?'

An indifferent shrug. 'Who knows? Right away maybe. Coots has been watching them all night. Says it ain't right the way none of them have moved. Not even to take a piss, apparently. Coots thinks that's downright unnatural for any soldiers.' Stalker gestured around. 'You can maybe make them out on the dunes and the forest edge.' His watch done, the scout ducked inside. Kyle adjusted the weight of his tulwar on his left hip, pulled on his helmet. For the thousandth time he wished he had a shield, a bow or even a fistful of javelins. Squinting, he could just distinguish the tall dark shapes standing still as tree trunks in the mist and pre-dawn gloom. Big bastards, with good discipline, sounds like. He didn't relish having to tangle with them.

Nothing stirred during Kyle's watch. The day brightened and the sun rose like a ball of fire over the jungle. Kyle thought it a wondrous sight, quite unlike anything he'd seen on the prairie. It was as if the entire east jungle was aflame. Traveller eventually emerged behind him. The tall swordsman was tying back his long, kinked black hair. He gestured Kyle in with a nod. 'Break your fast.'

Over the remains of the platters Badlands and Coots worked the edges of their weapons with the small sharpening stones they carried with their gear; Badlands his two long-knives and Coots his single-edged longsword with an extended two-handed grip. Out of their rolls also came helmets – iron and bronze, with faceguards that curved down to nasal shields. 'Haven't seen those recently,' Kyle observed.

'Haven't faced a stand-up fight recently,' Coots said. 'We prefer to avoid them.'

Badlands pulled his helmet on. 'Yeah. They can get you killed.'

Kyle almost burst out laughing: the helmet looked two sizes too small on the hairy burly fellow, like a bull wearing a pot. After mastering himself Kyle reflected that he mustn't look much better in his hand-me-down mismatched armour. He drew his tulwar, examined its edge – as bright and keen as the day Smoky inscribed it. Nothing seemed able to mar it. He turned to Ereko who sat cross-legged with no weapon in sight.

'Where's your spear?'

The Thel Akai looked up and in his golden eyes something flashed that stabbed Kyle to his heart before it was hidden away and the familiar wintry smile returned to his lips. 'Not here, Kyle. Not in my homeland.'

The brothers continued fussing with their equipment. Stalker checked the positioning of more weapons than Kyle had even guessed he might be carrying. He wondered what they were waiting for then, then Traveller re-entered the tent, and he understood.

The man examined each of them in turn, his face dark with churning emotions Kyle couldn't name, a kind of impatient anger, even disgust. The lines that bracketed his mouth slashed down like cuts. He nodded his approval and the Lost brothers jumped to the tent flap, flanking it with hands on their weapons. Stalker ducked out first. Traveller exited, then Kyle and Ereko. The brothers brought up the rear.

Jhest awaited them down the beach near the *Kite*. He stood next to a collection of bundled fruits, foodstuffs and wooden casks that Kyle presumed held water. Also present were the tall soldiers, positioned in a wide semicircle. They wore no uniforms or colours, only a strange sort of armour made from a mosaic of small stones, each a slightly differing shade of green, varying from dark sea-blue-green to a pale yellow-olive. Helms completely enclosed their faces and gauntlets their hands – all of the same shimmering mosaic surface. The weapons at their waists were hidden in wooden sheaths clasped in worked bronze, but from the shape they appeared curved and perhaps flaring out toward the point.

Jhest bowed. 'I trust you slept well and are refreshed. Please do not be alarmed by the presence of our soldiers. They are here to help load your vessel. You must find them somewhat familiar, yes? They are inspired by the many insights gained by those Malazan allies, the Moranth.'

'Yes,' Traveller answered curtly. 'Thank you for the food and water. We *will* be leaving now.'

'If you must. But I must ask that you reconsider your goal.'

Traveller, who had bent to a cask, straightened to face Jhest. 'Yes?' Ereko picked up two casks, one under each arm, and began loading the *Kite*. Kyle and the Lost brothers all spread out around Traveller.

'You really do not expect to succeed, do you? It is impossible. You would only be throwing away your existence in a futile gesture. Your presumption is beyond arrogance. It is a sad waste.'

Traveller was silent for some time. Kyle, his back to them and eyes fixed on the soldiers, could only hear their exchange. He adjusted his footing – the sand was strangely loose and yielding now, unlike earlier when they had landed the *Kite*. Traveller finally answered, his voice so low Kyle barely caught it, 'Do not come between me and my vengeance, Jhest. My response will be felt not just by you, but by all those who speak with you as well – and who are no doubt listening at this very moment. Think on that!' he suddenly yelled, startling Kyle.

'That is the question, is it not?' Jhest answered, his voice still eerily flat, unperturbed. 'Are we interposing ourselves when said goal is then abandoned? An interesting philosophical point, yes? Room enough, perhaps, for the risk.'

'Finished,' Ereko called. Kyle and Stalker, on one side, began edging backwards.

'You risk far more than you comprehend,' Traveller said, sounding almost regretful.

'It would not be a risk otherwise.'

Beneath Kyle's sandals the beach shook, churning. A hissing flow of sands sank his feet to the calves. He jumped, staggering, to keep his footing. A shocked yell from Ereko snapped his head around. Traveller was gone. Kyle gaped at Ereko who stared at the empty sand.

'*No*,' the giant mouthed, appalled.

'*You fools!*' the giant roared at Jhest. 'You have no idea who – *what* – you are interfering with!'

'What may, or may not, happen far away in another land is of no interest to us,' said the mage and he gestured. As one, weapons slid from the soldiers' wooden and leather sheaths. Ereko sank to his knees, pressed his hands to the sands.

'Get him on board,' Stalker snarled, drawing his curved blade. Kyle grasped an arm, but he might as well have been pulling at a tree trunk. The giant dug at the yielding sand, yanking free of Kyle's grip.

'You really did not think we would be so foolish as to cross swords with *him*, did you?' Jhest said – his voice still as flat as when they exchanged pleasantries last night.

'Oh, just kill the bastard, will you?' Stalker said over his shoulder. Kyle ignored him, a hand at Ereko's arm.

'We must go – please!'

The soldiers advanced, swinging, and the Lost cousins parried once, twice, holding their ground, ripostes gouging scatterings of the small stones to the sands.

Jhest's bland smile drew down and his smooth brow furrowed. 'What is this?' he murmured.

Ereko raised his head and Kyle was shocked by the rage roiling in his molten eyes. 'You and your cabal have erred, Jhest. You should not have chosen D'riss. Any Warren but that. For you seem to have forgotten who, in truth, *I* am.'

'You are Thel Akai, yes. An ancient race of this land – a useless remnant of a sad past.'

'And who were we before we named ourselves, before any other sentient kind arose? Our forebears were the children of the earth!'

'Kyle!' A yell from Stalker. One of the soldiers had caught Badlands in a bearhug. The man stitched the armoured giant in thrusts of his long-knives but to no visible effect. Kyle darted forward, drawing. He swung at a shoulder and the tulwar slid through the stones with a grating screech. The arm hung half-dismembered, accompanied by a gout of black blood as thick as tar. Badlands fell to the sand and lay stunned. Kyle stared. He was so amazed that a ponderous attack from another of the armoured giants almost decapitated him. He ducked, swung two-handed at the leading leg and severed it at the knee. The soldier collapsed to lie flailing in the sands like an upturned beetle.

'*What?* How is this?' Jhest gaped his disbelief.

Kyle leapt to one of three soldiers Stalker had kept at bay, severing an arm at the elbow and crippling a leg on the backswing.

'*No!*' Jhest bellowed. 'You are not of the *Isturé*!'

Unhesitating, Kyle continued hacking the lumbering giants – none of whom uttered a sound or even flinched from their attack though it was obvious they were doomed. Once down, the brothers finished them off.

After the last, Kyle spun on Jhest. He was exhausted, his arms numb and tingling from the jarring impacts of swings that he'd had to give every ounce of his strength. The Jacuruku mage eyed him in turn. 'You should not have been able to do that,' he said flatly. 'It is therefore the blade. Allow me to examine it.'

'Allow *me* to kill *him*,' Stalker said to Kyle, panting his own weariness.

'Not yet.' He crouched beside Ereko who still knelt on his hands and knees, his arms sunk to his elbows. 'What should we do?' he asked, pleading.

Ereko did not answer. His eyes were screwed shut, his teeth clenched, lips drawn back in a rictus of effort. 'Almost,' he hissed on a breath. '*Almost . . .*'

Jhest clapped his hands, barking an order. Stalker raised his sword. 'Wait!' Kyle yelled.

'Why is this shit still alive?' Stalker demanded.

'Damn right,' Badlands added.

'Because we may need him.'

'For *what*?'

'To retrieve Traveller.'

Hesitating, Stalker slammed home his blade. 'Damn the Dark Hunter!'

Jhest, however, appeared utterly unconcerned. His gaze was directed far off to the jungle-line beyond. A one-sided smile crooked up his thick lips. Kyle, a cold presentiment shivering his flesh, slowly turned following the mage's gaze.

'Trouble,' Coots said laconically, spitting.

Movement shivered the treeline all up and down the beachfront for as far as Kyle could see in either direction. Armoured soldiers identical to those dismembered around them stepped forth. Tens, hundreds. '*Ereko!*'

But still enmeshed in his efforts the giant did not answer.

'You have no choice but to abandon him,' Jhest observed blandly.

Snarling, Stalker drew and thrust in one movement. The mage did not flinch. Instead, he looked down calmly at the sword impaling his abdomen and cocked one brow. 'You will find me a great deal more difficult to kill than my servants.'

Stalker stepped back. His blade sucked free, glistening with a clear, thick ichor. '*Kyle . . .*'

'Wait!'

Ereko, grunting his effort, was withdrawing his arms from the sands. His hands came free, clasped in a shared wristlock with another's arm – Traveller's. Up and down the shore, the beach shuddered, rippling beneath everyone. Even the mage, Jhest, was rocked. 'No!' he bellowed. 'Impossible!'

Beneath Ereko was revealed a gap, a wound into darkness. Sands disappeared, sucked in a growing vortex that appeared to lead to . . . dark nothingness. Kyle leaned forward to lend a hand.

'No!' Ereko gasped. 'It will take you.'

Traveller's other hand appeared, pushed down against the surface. Gasping, Ereko straightened his legs, drawing the man free. The gaping void disappeared with an explosion like the burst of a Moranth munition. The report of its closure echoed from the tree-line. Traveller lay supine while Ereko straightened, drawing in great bellowing breaths.

'They're still comin',' Coots drawled into the silence.

The swordsman pushed himself to his feet. Jhest watched, his face eager, almost avid, lustful. 'You live,' he breathed, awed.

Traveller rolled his shoulders, wincing. 'My life is now my own, magus. It can no longer be taken by anyone.'

The statement seemed to transport the mage. His eyes lit up and open glee twisted his mouth into a frog-like leer. 'Then it is true! It can be done!'

Traveller seemed merely to gesture and the mage's head flew from his shoulders to roll to the sands. 'Not by you.' He sheathed his sword.

'Time to run away,' Coots suggested.

Blinking, Kyle stared at the headless torso of the mage that remained standing, immobile. He had the unnerving impression that should he touch it a hand would leap up to grab him. Glancing away he saw the army of armoured soldiers almost within reach. '*Run!*' They leaned their shoulders to the *Kite*, pushed it out into the surf. The Lost brothers pulled themselves in. Ereko, Kyle saw, glanced back and cursed, slogging away. Traveller had remained on the shore.

Cursing as well, Kyle threw himself back into the surf. When he arrived Ereko was pleading with the swordsman. 'It is of no use!'

'Go,' Traveller said. 'I will deal with all of these and their masters as well.'

'There is no need!' Ereko was fairly weeping.

'They came between myself and my vengeance.'

'Traveller!' Kyle called sharply.

The dark-skinned swordsman pulled his gaze from the relentless advance of the soldiers. He glanced to Kyle, puzzled, 'Yes?'

'Your vengeance is elsewhere, isn't it?'

A hand rose from his sword grip to massage his brow. He clenched his eyes shut, pinching them.

'Well?'

The front ranks of soldiers met and trampled the body of Jhest. They drew their weapons in a clash of iron that echoed all up and down the treeline. Traveller allowed Ereko to drag him backwards into the surf. 'Yes. Elsewhere . . .' he murmured, sounding confused.

The waves buoyed them, darkening Traveller's leathers. Ereko continued pulling the man backwards. Kyle forced himself out against the waves. Glancing back, his chest clenched at the sight of the statue-like soldiers marching on, not even hesitating, to push into the surf. 'Don't stop!'

The cousins reached for them over the side of the *Kite*. Ereko slapped their hands aside. 'Trim the sail!'

Springing up, Kyle grasped hold of a rope. Ereko had an arm around Traveller who still held his head, his eyes closed. The sail snapped, filling. The *Kite* pulled on Kyle. Behind them the soldiers marched on, disappearing beneath the waves rank after rank. Hanging from the side, Kyle could not help but raise his legs as tightly as he could from the water.

*   *   *

390

Impatient strikes on the tunnel wall next to his alcove brought Ho from his meal of stewed vegetables and unleavened bread. He swept aside the rag hanging across the opening, a retort on his lips, to meet no one. Peering down he found the bent double shape of Su, an aged Wickan witch whom gossip in the tunnels had as once member of the highest circles of tribal councils. 'What is it, Su?'

She closed her dark knotted hands on a walking stick no longer than his foreleg. Her fingers were twisted by the swelling of the joints that afflicts the aged – those who cannot afford the Denul treatments or have access to them – and she cocked her head to examine him with one eye black and beady like the proverbial crow's. 'Just thought you might want to know. They caught those two newcomers. The Malazan spies. Caught them poking around down at the excavation. I do believe Yath intends to kill them.'

Ho started, shocked. 'Kill them? How in Togg's teats is he to manage that? Talk them to death?'

A cackle. 'Ha! That's a good one. I don't know how. But he does intend to introduce them to our guest down below.'

Introduce them? Sweet Soliel, no. Who knows what might become of that? 'I'll get my things. Many thanks, Su.'

'Oh, I'm coming with you.'

At the tunnel he paused, pulled on his jerkin and sandals. 'I'm rather in a hurry.'

The Wickan witch was tapping her way along the uneven tunnel. She waved a hand contemptuously. 'Faugh! There's no rush. You know how these things go. Everyone has a stick to throw on to the fire. They'll be talking through the night watch.'

They came to the broad main gallery and Ho was surprised to find it nearly deserted. 'Where is everyone?'

Su jabbed her stick to the beaten earth floor. 'Didn't I just tell you, fool? They're down below!'

Slowly walking along, down a side gallery, Ho tucked his hands into the sash he used to hold up his old worn pantaloons, so loose after he'd lost so much weight. 'And no one came to tell me . . .'

'*I* came! Thank you very much!'

'Other than you, Su.'

She leaned heavily on her stick, a bit out of breath. 'Poor Ho. You really didn't think that you could simply stand aside, did you? Yath has been whispering against you for years! Undermining you constantly! Haven't you noticed?'

A shrug. 'No . . .'

'Bah! You blind idiot! Not much of an infighter, are you . . .' She sighed. 'Ah well, we all have our strengths and weaknesses. I suppose I'll just have to work with the material the Gods have mockingly cursed me with.'

Ho stopped short. 'Your innuendo and vague pronouncements might impress the others, Su, but I have no time for them.' The witch caught up with him, peered aside.

'Oho! Some spirit! There's one segment of spine left in there after all!'

Ho refrained from commenting that she, of all people, should not talk about spines. He collected a full lamp from a nearby alcove and lit it from another, then crossed to a steeply sloped side tunnel complete with guide-rope. He led while Su huffed and puffed her way down behind. Small stones they kicked loose bounced and rattled down the slope until so distant their noise was lost in the dark. Hot, humid air wafted up the tunnel in a steady stream, licking at the lamp flame. 'All right,' Ho finally announced, 'what did you mean by that comment?'

A cackle from the dark above. 'Ha! Takes you longer than anyone to admit you're human just like the rest of us, doesn't it? Makes perfect sense! Ha!'

Ho slowed his descent. *Was the hag merely casting darts into the dark? Yet every one falls just that degree of uncomfortably close . . .* 'I've no idea what you're talking about.'

The stick echoed from the dirt behind. 'Oh, come, come! The ore inhibits any new castings but the old remain! I . . . *smell* . . . you, Ho.'

Queen, no. He froze. 'Unkind, Su. Precious little water down here, after all.'

The crone's long face loomed into the guttering lamplight. The flame danced in her black eyes; she leered conspiratorially. 'I smell the old ritual on you, magus. The forbidden one. How did you manage it? Everyone thinks it lost.'

And so it must remain. He pulled away, descending. 'I've no idea what you're talking about.'

'Very well! Be that way. It seems trust is in as short a supply down here as initiative. I don't begrudge you your caution. But you could end the farce below should you wish. Just bring forth a fraction of what sleeps within, magus. I believe it is possible despite the ore.'

Possible! Aye, it may well be possible – bringing madness with it! And I have a strong aversion to madness, witch. Very strong.

*

392

After a long gentle curve and another long descent the narrow tunnel met a natural cavern, its floor levelled by dirt that Ho knew had been excavated from elsewhere further within. Its walls rose serried like the teeth of a comb, climbing in teardrop shape to an apex lost in the dark. A knot of men and women, a selection of the Pit's inmates, filled the floor. Lamps on tall poles lit the gathering in a dim gold light. Without slowing down Su pushed her way through the crowd, elbows jabbing and stick poking. 'Out of the way, fools!' she hissed.

Ho, following, squeezed past, nodding to inmates he knew who glared, holding shins and sides. 'Sorry.'

Broaching the front he found the two newcomers, Treat and Grief, surrounded by a gang of the more hale men armed with spears. Both looked healthy and, if anything, bored by the proceedings. Grief especially radiated contempt, standing with arms crossed and mouth crooked as if ready to laugh. Yath and Sessin stood nearby. Catching sight of Ho, Yath pointed his staff. 'Here he is! Of course he has come. Their Malazan confederate. We'll deal with you next, Ho.'

'Confederate?'

'You have been seen on many occasions secretly meeting with these two spies. Do you deny it?'

Ho scratched his scalp, shrugging. 'Well, we've talked, yes. I've talked with everyone here at one time or another.'

'Brilliant,' Su muttered under her breath. 'What are you doing here, Yath?' she barked. 'Is this a court? What are the charges? Under whose authority are you empowered?'

Yath stamped his staff on the soft ground. 'Quiet, witch!'

'Or you will deal with me later also? When will it end? How many will you kill?'

Behind his full beard Yath smiled and Ho realized that Su had overplayed her hand. He opened his arms, gesturing broadly. 'No one here is going to die. What do you think I am? We are all civilized people down here – a description I extend even to you, Su. I am merely planning a small demonstration. A little show for our new friends meant to impress upon them the importance of our work.' Yath glanced about the crowd entreatingly. 'It is, after all, what they have come for. Is it not?'

From the nods and shouts of agreement, Ho understood that, as Su said, he had been withdrawn from the community for far too long now. How could their small brotherhood of scholars and mages have come to this? Singling out 'spies' for punishment; arming themselves; sowing fear? Those who would speak against Yath were obviously too disgusted to even bother coming down. *Like himself.*

'We don't know what might happen, Yath. It's too dangerous.'

'Silence! You have discredited yourself, Ho. Plotting with your fellow Malazans.'

'Malazan? I'm from Li Heng, Yath.'

'Exactly. From the very centre of the Malazan Empire.' Yath waved the spearmen to move the prisoners forward. Sessin stepped up between Yath and the two, his hands twitching at his sides. Ho could only stare; the ignorance the man's statement revealed was stunning. How can one possibly reason one's way across such a gap?

'Yath,' Ho called, following with the crowd, 'you know about as much about Malaz and Quon Tali as I know about Seven Cities! Many on the continent consider the Malazans occupiers just as you do!' But the tall Seven Cities priest was no longer listening.

Amid the spearmen, Grief peered back to Ho. 'What's gonna happen?'

'Quiet,' warned a number of the guards. Grief ignored them.

'They're just going to ... show you something. It's nothing physically threatening.'

The man's mouth pulled down as he glanced away, considering. 'I'm kinda curious myself.'

Su, Ho noted, was watching the two with keen interest, her sharp eyes probing. After a moment she let out a cawing laugh. She edged her head up to Ho and smiled as before, touched the side of her hooked nose, winked.

'What is it?' he murmured.

'Something else I smell. Took me a while to place it. Was a long time ago at the Council of All Clans.'

'What?'

'You'll see. You and Yath, I think. Ha!'

Ho snorted. 'More of your games.'

'Ha!'

The path led away to a crack in the stone wall of the cavern. Beaten earth steps led down through the narrow gap to another cavern, this one excavated from the layered, seared sedimentary stone that carried the Otataral ore. The spearmen pushed Treat and Grief to the fore where yath and Sessin waited. Beyond them, a walkway of earth climbed the far wall that appeared made of some smooth and glassy rock.

Grief glanced around. 'This is it?'

Yath had at his mouth a grin of hungry triumph. He urged, 'Look more closely. Raise the lights!'

Poles were taken down, lamps affixed, and re-straightened. The light blossomed, revealing a wall of dark green stone that held hidden depths where reflections glimmered. Ho watched as, stage by stage, slow realization took hold of Grief. 'No – it can't be . . .' the fellow murmured. His gaze went to the bulge excavated at the base, the slope up to a gaping cave opening, the jutting cliff above this cut off by the roof of the cavern. 'Of all the forgotten Gods,' he said. He looked to Yath, open unguarded wonder upon his dark Napan face. 'A jade giant . . . I'd read of them, of course. But this . . .' He shook his head, staggered beyond words.

Ho shared the man's astonishment; no matter how often he came down to look it stupefied, and humbled, every time. The oval cave, taller than two men, now transformed itself in his mind's eye to a mouth, yawning – or screaming. The bulge below, the chin. One then scaled this lower half of the face to the upper, then face to head, head to neck, and . . . and that was as far as Ho's imagination could carry the exercise. It became absurd. Unimaginable. How could such a thing possibly be constructed? Would it not collapse under its own colossal weight?

But of course, they come from elsewhere. Yet would not such a Realm, no matter how alien, possess its own properties, its own set of physical laws which could not be contravened? It was too much for Ho – as it had proved for this entire battalion of professional mages, scholars and theurgical researchers who had made the mystery their primary fixation for the last three decades.

All these revelations were lost on Treat who nudged Grief. 'What is it?'

Grief just shrugged. 'A fucking big statue.'

'Come, come,' urged Yath, starting up the walkway. 'Come for a better look.' He waved Grief to follow. The man's eyes were narrow in open distrust, but he clearly could not turn down such an opportunity. *One of us after all*, Ho decided.

Grief followed the Seven Cities priest up the walkway of beaten dirt. It ended at the edge of the dark cave, the open gaping mouth. Yath gestured within and backed away. Keeping a wary eye on the priest, Grief leant forward, cast a quick glance in and flinched back, stunned. 'A throat!' he called down. 'They carved a throat!'

Ho, his eyes closed, nodded, almost despairing. Yes, a throat. And none of our sounding stones have yet to reach bottom. There is not enough rope in all the island to descend the innards of this statue. And so the mystery only confounds us further: as there is a throat, what of a stomach? Intestines? Ought one continue deeper into this route of inquiry? Perhaps not. What would a giant statue of jade eat? More reasonably, it would have no need for sustenance. Why then a throat?

'And what do you hear?' Yath urged, a hand clutched at his own throat, his eyes feverishly bright.

Grief cocked his head, crouched, silent for a time. Everyone below stilled as well. 'I hear a breeze . . . sighing, or whispering . . . like the wind through a forest in the fall.'

'He's a strong one,' Su whispered to Ho. Edging her head sideways, she glanced up. 'What did you hear?'

'Screams of the insane. You?'

She dropped her head. 'Inconsolable weeping.'

Yath now spread both his hands over the carved jade face, his long fingers splayed. He pressed the side of his own face to it, his mouth moving silently.

'What in Oponn's name is the fool doing now?' Ho murmured in wonder.

Sensing something, Grief peered up. 'What?' He shifted to the lip of the walkway, glanced down to them uncertainly. 'I am amazed, I'll grant you that. And if we had—'

'Wait,' Yath interrupted, moving away from the opening.

Something drew Grief around. Ho felt it as well, in the stirring of his own thin hair, the pressing of the cloth of his shirt against his chest. A hiss of alarm escaped Su's lips.

Roaring burst from the mouth in a rushing torrent. Grief ducked but an explosion of air erupted from the mouth like the giant's own exhalation of breath. It plucked the man from the landing and threw him flying across the cavern. Everyone clapped hands to their heads as their ears popped. Several fell, screaming excruciating pain. A storm of dust roiled about the cavern blocking all vision, while above them Yath laughed and howled like a madman possessed.

As the dust settled Ho found the knot of inmates who had gathered around the fallen Malazan. He pushed his way through; Treat was there, kneeling at the side of his friend, who lay motionless.

'Bring the next one!' Yath ordered from the walkway, but no one listened. Everyone was shouting at him at once: when did he discover this capability? Why hadn't he shared his knowledge? How had he come to it? Was it conscious, or merely reflexive? What of the qualities of the air?

Ho stood silent, looking down at the dead man. The fellow had been difficult, brusque, highhanded even, but he had liked him. And none of them had even suspected what Yath had intended. That is, none except Su.

Treat raised a hand and slapped it hard across his dead friend's face. Inmates took hold of the man to pull him away, but Grief coughed, wincing, and covered his face with both hands. He groaned. 'Hood take me, that hurt.'

Ho gaped – this was impossible! The man flew right over their heads! How . . . without magic . . . how? Treat pulled Grief upright and he stood swaying, brushed the dust from his leathers. He cupped his neck in both hands, twisted his head side to side. 'Well, now that that's out of the way maybe we can get out of here.'

'*What!*' came a bellow of consternation from above.

The inmates flinched away leaving a broad empty circle around the three Malazans. Su burst out laughing her contempt. 'Difficult to kill, these two.' She cocked her head, addressed Grief. 'Come recruiting?'

Grief examined her up and down. 'Wickan? Definitely.'

Yath arrived, his eyes wild. 'What is this? Still alive?' He gestured to the spearmen. 'What are you waiting for? They are obviously a threat! Kill them now.'

Treat snatched a spear from the nearest, levelled it against Yath. Sessin was suddenly there to slap his hands on the haft just short of the knapped stone point. The two men yanked back and forth, spear between them, sandalled feet shifting in the dry dirt. 'Stop this now!' Ho shouted. Yath waved everyone back. The tug of war continued, Sessin grinning, his back hunched, Treat's mouth tight, eyes gauging. They strained, motionless, as if engaged in a pantomime of effort, until with an explosive report the spear burst in half between them. Each staggered backwards.

Yath raised a hand, shouted something in the Seven Cities dialect. He addressed Grief: 'Who *are* you?'

'An ally.' Grief raised his voice to address everyone. 'We've come to bring you all back to Quon to fight the Empire. What say you? Revenge against those who imprisoned you?'

Yath stared, eyes bulging, then he laughed his madman's laugh. 'You idiot! What use can any of these old men and women be? What of the Otataral?'

Grief shrugged. 'The Pit has long since been mined out. It's just a prison now. The little ore that remains that you have been digging out contains the barest trace element. And that raw, unrefined. It can be cleaned off.'

'It's in the food!' someone called out.

397

Again the shrug. 'A change of diet. It will pass.'

Yath smoothed his beard, thinking. 'If its presence is as mild as you say – then why can none of us draw upon the Warrens? Why is all theurgy closed to us?'

'Proximity. It's our location here on the island. Once we get away it will come back.'

'But we've been breathing it in!' a voice objected.

'There are many alchemical treatments, expectorants.'

'That's true,' someone said. 'D'bayang powder inhaled with sufficient force can—'

'Will you shut up!' Yath snarled. He clasped his staff in both hands across his middle. 'Believe me, Mezla, I want revenge upon your Empire more than you can possibly imagine. But we are down here in this – prison – as you name it and I do not see how you propose to get us out!'

Grief was rubbing and rolling a shoulder, grimacing. 'Fair enough.' He glanced around. 'What time of day is it above?'

'Before dawn,' someone answered, nods all around.

'OK. Let's go up to the mine-head and we'll have you lot out by dawn.'

Yath sneered. 'Lies! Once there you'll call for the guards to rescue you.'

'So stick us with your spears.'

Yath subsided, glowering, his mouth working. Su laughed her scorn. The two headed to the tunnel; everyone moved from their path.

Ho brought up the rear, waiting for Su. Once the rest of the inmates were sufficiently ahead he asked, 'So, who are they then?'

The witch cast him a creamy self-satisfied look. 'Have you not guessed by now?'

'No. So, they're not Malazan.'

Her stick lashed him across his shin and he danced away, wincing. 'Please! Of course they are Malazan. But then there are Malazans and then there are Malazans.'

'I don't understand.'

'Obviously.'

They walked along in silence for a time. 'So they're with this secessionist movement we've been hearing of.'

Su waved him away like an annoying insect and headed off. At the long ascending tunnel he waited while she caught her breath. 'I am old,' she said suddenly. 'Strange how those of us who have benefited

398

from manipulating the Warrens, or by ritual, to linger on – continue to do so here in the mines?' Ho did not answer; what was there to say? That it was a mystery? 'For a time I feared I would spend eternity here. Or until the wind eroded the island down around me and I could simply walk away. Do you have no such fears?'

Ho shook his head. 'I've never thought about it.'

She studied him keenly once more, frowning. 'You have no imagination, Ho. In fact, you lack many things that would make a man whole.'

'Is that an insult?'

'A temper, for example. I don't recall ever seeing you angry. Where did your temper walk off to, magus? Your ambition? Your drive?'

'That subject's closed, Su,' he growled and headed off.

He waited for her where the sloping tunnel met the side gallery. From here they walked along side by side, though quiet. They met no one. Coming to the main gallery they found this deserted as well. Ho wondered if Grief and Treat had already whisked everyone off – perhaps they'd dug a tunnel climbing all the way to the surface, with toothpicks.

The murmur of many voices, however, reached them from the round mine-head. A milling mass of what appeared to be the entire Pit's population, all talking, mixing, exchanging opinions and rumours. Ho caught the eye of the nearest. 'What's going on?'

'Two of the newcomers climbed the wall.'

Ho's brows rose. 'Really.' *Just as they'd said.* 'But everyone's tried that.'

A helpless wave. 'Apparently one had two short sticks that he jabbed into the wall, climbing like that, one then the other. The second followed along his path, punching and kicking the holes deeper.' Ho thought of the short batons he'd seen Grief whittling. *So not weapons after all.*

'Since then?' Su asked.

'Nothing. Silence. Yath says they've run off.'

'He would say that.' There was something pathological about that man's hatred. If they did get out he'd have to keep an eye on him. Who knew what he might try; he'd already attempted murder.

Grating and ratcheting above announced the hanging platform moving. All talking stopped. A number of inmates fled the mine-head, perhaps afraid it was the guards on their way to bash heads. Ho thought it possible, but unlikely. Why come down here to dirty their hands when they could just withhold food?

As the platform descended it became obvious that it held only one occupant, Grief. After it touched down, rather clumsily, he unclipped a safety rope and waved an invitation. 'Five at a time, please.'

No one spoke, or moved. Faces turned to examine one another in wonderment as if searching for some clue as to what next to do. Grief frowned his disappointment. 'Well, aren't you all an eager lot. Don't trample anyone.'

Taking a steadying breath, Ho stepped forward. 'What happened up there, Grief?'

'C'mon up. Take a look around.'

'I'll come,' said a female inmate, stepping up. Ho recognized her as another of the latest newcomers who had arrived with Grief and Treat. Three other inmates joined them. On the platform, Ho asked the woman, 'You know each other?'

She looked Grief up and down. 'No.'

Grief pulled a cord strung among the fat hemp rope suspending the platform and shortly afterwards the mechanism jerked upwards, climbing. Ho saw that two mismatched swords now hung at the man's belt.

The grey, yellow and gold sedimentary layers of the excavated rock edged past as they rose. The rope creaked alarmingly. Ho glanced down, thinking, how many decades kicking through that dust? Six? Seven? Had he simply lost count? Somehow the future now alarmed him. What would he do? Where would he go? He'd gone too long now without even having to consider such questions. He eyed Grief; not a mark on the man and how many guards? Twenty-five, or thereabouts. How had the two accomplished this? All without any Warren magics either. The achievement irked Ho in a way – he felt as if he'd been rendered obsolete. What need for mages if they can manage this?

The platform bumped to a stop, swinging. With a screeching of wood on wood, the cantilevered solid tree-trunk supporting them began turning aside, carrying the platform over to rest on the dirt beside the opening. Grief unhitched the safety rope. Ho blinked in the unaccustomed dawn light, shaded his eyes. The Pit's infra-structure had not changed much since he'd last seen it. A long clapboard house looking like a guard barracks stood where, when Ho had been processed, had only been a tent. A lean-to blacksmith's shop, a corral for donkeys, a dusty heap of open piled barrels and a squat officer's house completed the penal station. Broken barrels and rusted pieces of metal littered the landscape. Beyond, dunes tufted by brittle grasses led off in all directions. Curtains of wind-blown dust obscured the distances. Treat was busy watering the four donkeys hooked to the spokes of the broad, circular lifting mechanism. 'Where is everyone?'

Grief raised his chin to the barracks. 'Inside.'

Ho wet his lips, forced himself to ask, 'Alive?'

'See for yourself.'

Ho decided that, yes, he would. But he could not bring himself to step from the platform. The others had walked off immediately. He looked down, edged a sandalled foot forward, brought it down on the surface, shifted some weight on to it, bounced slightly up and down as if testing its soundness. Only after this could he bring his other foot from the wood slats.

Grief watched all this without comment, his lips pursed. 'I'm sorry,' he finally said as they walked along to the barracks.

'For what?'

'I hadn't thought about just how hard this might be for some of you.'

'For most of us, I think you'll find.' Then Ho stopped. Something had been bothering him about the installation. He glanced around again, thinking. 'Where are the wagons? Where's the track to the coast to deliver the ore?' He pointed to the haphazardly piled barrels. 'Those are empty. *Where are all the full ones?*'

Grief was looking away, squinting into the distance, the wrinkles around his eyes almost hiding them. 'I'm sorry.'

'Sorry? *You're sorry?* What do you mean, Hood take you!'

'He means they've been dumping them,' said the woman. Ho spun; she'd followed along.

'Dumping them? They dump them!' Ho raised his dirty, broken-nailed hands to Grief. 'Seventy years of scraping and gouging – halved rations when we missed our quotas – and they ... they just . . .' Ho lurched off for the barracks.

Grief hurried to catch up. 'Not at first, I understand. Only the last few, ah, decades. It was all played out, not worth refining. I'm sorry, Ho.'

The door wouldn't open. When Ho turned his shoulder to it as if he would batter it down, Grief stepped in front, pulled out two wedges. Ho pushed it open. He found the guards on the floor, lying down and sitting. Seeing Ho, those who could, stood. Seeing Grief they flinched. Almost all carried bloody head wounds, bruising blossoming deep black and purple. Ho thought again of the short batons Grief had whittled. *So, yes, weapons after all.* 'Who is the senior officer?'

A short, broad fellow with a blond beard stood forward. He straightened his linen shirt. 'I am Captain Galith. Who in the Abyss are you?'

'Am I to understand that you have been dumping the ore that we have been sending up?'

A smile of understanding crept up the man's mouth. 'Yes, it was policy when I arrived five years ago. We tested each delivery and dumped anything below refinable traces.'

Ho ran a hand through his short hair and found drops of sweat running down his temples. 'And tell me when . . . how often were these standards met?'

The smile turned down into mocking defiance. 'Never.'

Ho grasped a handful of the man's shirt. 'Come with me.' He walked the man out towards the gaping ledge.

Grief followed along. 'What are you going to do, Ho? Toss him in? I can't allow that.'

'You can't—' Ho stopped, faced the short, muscular Napan. 'Who do you think you are? You hang around for a few months and you know everything? This goes way back.'

'These men surrendered to me. Not you. They're under my protection.'

Facing the Malazan officer, Ho took a deep steadying breath then forced his fist open; Captain Galith pulled his bunched shirt free. 'You didn't have the guts anyway,' he grated.

Ho swung a backhanded slap that caught the man across the side of his head, sending him off his feet to lie motionless. Grief leapt backwards clasping the grip of one sword. 'How did you do that!' he demanded, eyes slitted.

'How did you have Treat defeat some twenty guards?'

Grief straightened, inclining his head in acknowledgement of the point. He smiled in a wicked humour. 'We surprised them.'

'If you two have finished your pissing contest then perhaps we can discuss how we're getting off this island?'

Grief and Ho turned to the dumpy, grey-haired female inmate. 'Listen,' Ho said impatiently, 'what in the Lady's Favour is your name anyway?'

She crossed her thick arms across her wide chest. 'Devaleth Omptol.'

'Where are you from?'

'It wouldn't mean anything to you.'

Ho rolled his eyes. 'Gods, woman, there are over forty scholars, historians and archivists here.'

'Mare. Ship's mage, out of Black City.'

'You're from Fist, then.'

The woman's brows rose, surprised. 'Yes. That name's not in common usage.'

Grief took the feet of the unconscious captain, began dragging him back to the barracks. 'Ship's mage, hey? That'll be damned useful.'

'If either of you think I'm going to summon my Warren with all this Otataral around you're the insane ones.' She shouted after Grief, 'How are we getting off this blasted island anyway?'

'Treat's going to get the rest of our, ah, team, tonight. We have a ship.'

Devaleth snorted something that sounded like 'Fine!' and walked away.

'Where are *you* going?' Ho called after her.

She pointed to the dunes. 'There's an ocean out there. I'm going to wash my clothes, scrub my skin with sand, scrub my hair, and then I'm going to do it all over again!'

Ho plucked at his threadbare, dirty jerkin, lifted a foot in its worn leather sandal. All impregnated with the ore. He looked to the barracks, his eyes widening, and he ran after Grief. 'Wait a moment!'

*　*　*

Ghelel wanted to curry her own mount. It was an eager mare she'd grown quite fond of, but Molk had warned against it saying that the regulars took care of such things and that she, as a Prevost, ought not to lower herself. She personally saw nothing odd in an officer caring for his or her own horse; Molk, however, was insistent. And so she found herself facing another empty evening of waiting – waiting for intelligence from Li Heng on any development in the siege, which appeared to have settled into a sullen stalemate despite the early victories. Or waiting for intelligence from the east on the progress of the Empress's armada. Or of a new development: the coastal raids of a significant pirate navy that had coalesced to take advantage of the chaos, pillaging Unta and now Cawn. Just two days ago word reached them that these raiders had become so emboldened they were actually marching inland. The betting around the tents was on how far they dared go. Raids on Telo or Ipras were the odds-on favourites.

She therefore faced the same choice that wasn't really a choice this last week since General Urko's army had marched through: lie staring at the roof of her tent, sitting at the main campfire or visiting the command tent. Spending another useless evening at the campfire meant watching the Falaran cavalrymen led by their fat captain, Tonley, share barbs and boasts with the Seti while swilling enormous quantities of whatever alcohol his men had most recently 'liberated'. Most often beer, though the occasional cask of distilled spirits appeared, and even skins of mead. Visiting the command tent meant, well, getting even closer to Commander Ullen. Something she found frighteningly easy to do.

What would the Marquis think? Or Choss? Would they approve? Ghelel pulled her gloves tighter against the chill night air, glanced to the east where the land fell away into the Idryn's flat, rich floodplain. Somewhere there just days away marched a ragged horde of pirate raiders. Idly, she wondered why Ullen didn't simply uproot his rearguard battalion together with the Falaran lancers, the Seti scouts and the Marshland cavalry and wipe the brigands from the face of the continent. Well, damn them anyway; they maintained she was the heir of the Talian Hegemony, the Tali of Quon Tali. Therefore she outranked the Marquis and Choss wasn't here. She headed to the command tent.

Reaching a main alley in the encampment, she saw ahead the torches and the posted guards, Malazan regulars of the Falaran brigades, and she slowed. If the League *should* win the coming confrontation and she were installed as the Tali of Quon Tali . . . how would her behaviour here now come to reflect upon her in the eyes of these regulars everywhere? The thought of their mockery burned upon her face.

The eyes of those guards had her now, glittering in the dark beneath their helmets, and she forced herself to keep moving. Well, damn them too; right now she was nothing more than a lowly cavalry captain, a Prevost. Lowly, and lonely.

As she approached, the guards inclined their heads in acknowledgement and one pushed aside the flap. Ghelel gave as courteous a response as she dared and ducked within. It was warm inside. The golden light of lanterns lit a cluttered table, a scattering of chairs and a low table littered with fruit, meats and carafes of wine. Commander Ullen straightened from pouring wine at the table and bowed. The Marquis Jhardin straightened and bowed as well, though more slowly and perfunctorily – a mere observance of aristocratic courtesy. For her part, Ghelel saluted two superior officers.

Ullen waved the salute aside. 'Please, Alil. How many times must I ask?'

'Every time, sir.' Ghelel drew off her gloves and cloak, draped them over a chair.

'We were just talking of this pirate army,' the Marquis said, easing himself back down. 'They say that at Unta they must have tried to rob the Imperial Arsenal. Blew up half the city and themselves for their trouble.'

'There's enough of them left,' Ullen growled into his cup, and sat, stretching out his legs. Ghelel liked the way he did that; and liked the way he watched her from the corner of his pale-blue eyes, almost shyly. She sat at the table, picked up a carafe. 'I quite understand why we aren't swatting them. I mean, since they number so many . . .'

A smile from Ullen. One that held no mockery at all, only a bright amusement shared by his eyes. 'How gigantic have they become now?'

'I overheard one trooper swear them to be at least thirty thousand.'

The Marquis whistled. 'Prodigious multiplying indeed. Forget them, Alil. They're just a mob of looters. We don't care about the vultures. We've come for a lioness.'

But Ullen frowned, the lines of care around his mouth deepening. Ghelel caught his eye, arched a questioning brow. 'We aren't ignoring them, Alil. I have Seti scouts watching from a distance. There have been some rather disturbing, admittedly contrary, rumours about them. But they are – how shall I put it? *Difficult* to credit. And our mage with Urko, Bala, has sent the message that she is troubled. She suspects powerful mages shielding themselves from her questings.'

'There must be one or two forceful personalities keeping the horde together,' the Marquis opined. 'We'll spot them and eliminate them and the mob will evaporate. They should not have come inland – they are obviously overconfident.'

'Was Kellanved overconfident?' Ullen mused aloud, eyeing his glass, 'when he marched inland with his pirate raiders from Malaz? And Heng was one of his first conquests.'

Neither the Marquis nor Ghelel spoke for a time. The Marquis inclined his head to concede the point. 'I suppose you could say he was the exception that proves the rule.'

Ghelel studied her wine glass. 'Speaking of the Throne . . . why don't we go to meet her? Excuse me for asking, but as new to the command – could we not stop her in the narrow plains west of Cawn?'

Another smile from Ullen. 'True.' He stretched, ran both hands through his short blond hair. 'But then she would simply withdraw to Cawn and wait for us. That we cannot have. As an advocate would say, the burden of proof lies with us. We have to *beat* her; she merely has to stand back and wait for our support to erode.'

For all Ghelel knew Ullen was patronizing her just as Choss and Amaron had, only his manners were smoother. But there was nothing in it that *felt* that way to her; they were merely talking through the options together and he was giving the benefit of his greater experience. She wondered again just how much the man knew of her, how much Urko or the Marquis had told him. It could mean a great deal to know that. 'Why should our support be eroding – not hers?'

'Because if we can't take Heng, how can we take anything?'

Ghelel pursed her lips at the truth of that sobering evaluation. Indeed. Why should any of the League's supporters stay with them if they should fail here? They would face wholesale desertions. A return to independent kingdoms with the old war of all against all not far behind. Continent-wide strife, the inevitable dissolution into chaos with starvation, brutality and petty warlordism. Something Ghelel would do anything to avoid.

The Marquis drained his glass and stood. 'If the Empress commits to the field then Heng can hang itself.' He saluted Ullen: 'Commander.' Bowed to Ghelel: 'Prevost. I will leave you two to sort out the rest of the problems facing our army and will expect appropriate orders tomorrow. Good night.'

Laughing, Ullen waved the Marquis out. When the heavy canvas flap closed Ghelel faced Ullen alone. For a time neither spoke. Ghelel poured herself another glass of wine. 'Did the Marquis tell you I am new to his command?'

Ullen nodded. 'Yes . . . Your family goes back quite far in Tali?'

Ghelel felt her face reddening and damned the reaction. To cover it, she shrugged. 'Rich in ancestry, poor in cash. Yourself?'

An edge of his mouth crooked up. 'Like you. Rich in experience, poor in cash. I have served in the military all my life.'

'Then you have been overseas? Genabackis? Seven Cities?'

He shook his head. 'No.' A mischievous smile. 'Unless Falar counts?'

She answered his smile. 'Oh, I suppose we could allow that – just for this one night.'

Ullen raised his glass. 'My thanks. Now I possess a more soldierly exotic flair.'

But Ghelel was troubled. The man looked to be in his late forties, yet had never served overseas. Where had he been all these years?

Had he seen only garrison duty for the last twenty years? Yet Urko seemed to have every confidence in him; could he be nothing more than a competent manager, more clerk than soldier?

A knock at the front post. 'Yes?' Ullen called.

A guard edged aside the thick canvas. 'Seti scout here, sir, with word from the raiders.'

Sighing, Ullen pushed himself to his feet, crossed to the work table. 'Send him in, sergeant.'

A slight wisp of a figure slipped through the opening and Ghelel stared. A child! What had they come to, sending children into the field? The girl-child's deerskin trousers were torn and muddied, her moccasins worn through. A sleeveless leather jerkin was all else she wore despite the bitter cold night. Her long hair hung in a tangle of sweat, knots and lengths of leather and beads, and a sheathed long-knife hung from a rope tied round one shoulder. Despite her bedraggled and hard-travelled appearance the girl-child surveyed the contents of the tent with the scorn of a princess.

'Ullar yesh 'ap?' she addressed Ullen in obvious disapproval.

'Aya,' he replied easily in Seti. 'Tahian heshar?'

'Nyeh.'

Ullen looked to Ghelel. 'Excuse us, please.' To the girl-child, 'Bergar, sho.'

The child launched into a long report in Seti. When she gestured Ghelel was wrenched to see that her fingertips were blue with cold, as were her lips. Gods! This child was half-frozen with exposure from riding through the night. The Seti youth tossed a fold of torn cloth on to Ullen's table and turned to go. Ghelel intervened, 'Wait! Please!'

A hand went to the grip of the long-knife and the girl glared an accusation at Ullen. 'What is it?' he asked of Ghelel.

'Ask her to stay. To warm herself – anything.'

He spoke to her and the tone of the girl's reply told Ghelel all she needed to know. She offered her own cloak. 'She can take this.'

Ullen translated; the girl responded, shooting Ghelel a glare of ferocious pride that would be humorous if it were not so obviously heartfelt. Ullen translated, 'She thanks you but says she would only be burdened by such a possession.'

Ghelel squeezed the thick rich cloth in both hands. 'Then will she not stay?'

'No. I'm sure she means to return immediately to her scouting party.'

'She'll die of exposure! Can't you order her to stay until tomorrow?'

Ullen passed a hand through his hair, sighing. 'Alil . . . her party probably consists of her own brothers, sisters and cousins.'

Ghelel leant her weight into the chair, let the cloak fall over its back. 'I . . . see. Tell her . . . tell her, I'm sorry.'

In answer the girl reached out a hand to cover Ghelel's who hissed, shocked, so cold was the girl's grip. She left then, and Ghelel could not raise her head to watch her go.

After some moments Ullen cleared his throat and came around the table. He squeezed Ghelel's arm. 'Your concern does you credit, Alil. But it is misplaced. She was born to this. Grew up with it, and is used to it.'

Ghelel flinched away, shocked by the man's words. 'So they are less than us, are they? Coarser? They feel less than we do?'

Ullen's face froze. He dropped his arm. 'That is not what I meant at all.' He returned to the table, picked up the scrap of cloth the messenger had left. 'Ehra – that's her name by the way. Named for a tiny blue flower you can find everywhere here – she reports that her party captured a runaway from the raiders. And since they're under my orders to find out what they can about these pirates, they questioned him. The fellow claimed the sigil they wear is important.' Ullen waved the fold of cloth. 'He sketched it here.'

Sitting heavily, Ghelel poured herself another glass of wine. 'Commander . . . I'm sorry. I forgot myself. No doubt you meant that she was used to such privation; that she's grown up riding in such weather all year round. You are no doubt right. I'm sorry. It's just that we Talians border on the Seti. There is a long history of antagonism and I have grown up hearing much that is . . . how shall I put it – bigoted – against them. You have my apology, commander.' Hearing nothing from him, she glanced up, 'Commander?'

Ullen had backed away from the table. His gaze was fixed upon the opened cloth. He appeared to have had a vision of Hood himself; his face was sickly pale from shock. His hands had fisted white. Ghelel threw aside her glass and came to his side. 'What is it?'

'*Gods no . . . it's true*,' he breathed.

She picked up the scrap. Sketched in charcoal and ochre dust was a long rust smear bearing a weaving undulating line. 'What is it?'

Ullen swallowed, wiped a hand across his glistening brow. 'Something I prayed I'd never see again. Sergeant!'

The guard stepped in. 'Sir?'

'Summon the Marquis and Captain Tonley, quickly.'

'Aye, sir.'

Ullen went to the low table and poured himself a glass of wine.

'What is it?' Ghelel asked again.

Downing the drink, Ullen said, 'It means nothing to you? A red field, a long sinuous beast – a dragon perhaps?'

'No.'

He spoke into the depths of his empty glass. 'How quickly so much is forgotten.'

The Marquis threw open the tent flap; he wore only an open felt shirt, trousers and boots. 'What news?'

Ullen nodded to Ghelel, who held out the torn strip. The Marquis took it. 'Surely you are versed in liveries, Marquis. What do you make of that insignia?'

'A red field, a long beast or perhaps a weapon – it could be any number of things.'

'And if the thing were a dragon?'

'What would that mean?' Ghelel asked.

'Then—' Snorting, he tossed the cloth to the table. 'Imposture, surely. An empty boast.'

'I think not. This confirms rumours out of Unta.'

'What rumours?' Ghelel asked more loudly.

'You cannot be certain though,' said the Marquis.

'No, but certain enough to treat them more warily. I ask that you return to your command south of the Idryn.'

'Agreed.'

Captain Tonley pushed aside the canvas flap. Wincing, he shielded his eyes from the bright lantern light. 'What is it – ah, sirs?'

'Yes!' Ghelel added. 'What is it, damn it to Hood!'

'The sigil of the Crimson Guard,' Ullen said.

Ghelel stared, her brows rising. The Crimson Guard? That hoary old-woman's bogeyman? Mere mercenaries? Was this what so unnerved Ullen? Only her tact stopped her from laughing out loud.

Captain Tonley scratched his auburn beard. His face betrayed an utter lack of recognition. 'The Crimson Guard, you say? That so, sir? Amazing.' He took a great deep breath, noticed the carafes of wine and scooped one up. 'Orders, sir?'

Ullen either didn't notice or was inured to the man's manners – or lack thereof. 'Send your best rider to Urko at Command.' He scratched a message on a scrap of vellum, handed it to Tonley. 'The invading army confirmed as Crimson Guard.'

'Anyone could use that symbol,' Ghelel objected.

'No one would dare,' the Marquis answered. 'Come, Prevost. We leave immediately.' He bowed to Ullen. Ghelel did not move. She watched Ullen who bowed his farewell to her while, she thought, keeping his face carefully empty of emotion. The Marquis took her arm. 'Prevost.'

Outside, the Marquis said low, 'Change quickly, we ride within the hour,' and he was off to his tent. Feeling somehow drunk, stunned by these quick developments, Ghelel walked slowly away. Inside her tent, she found Molk lying across the entrance, an arm over his face. 'Get up. We're going.'

He moved his arm to blink up at her. 'Going? So soon?'

'Yes. And hurry – you have to pack.' She began changing to dress in her armour.

He sat up quickly. 'What's the news? Is it her?'

Pulling off her shirt, Ghelel paused. Her? Oh, yes, *her*. 'No. Not her.'

'Who then?'

A laugh from Ghelel. 'Yes, who indeed.' She shook out a silk undershirt, pulled it on. 'Apparently our glorious commander believes these raiders are the Crimson Guard returned. Can you believe that?' She straightened the front lacings, looked up. 'Molk?'

She turned full circle, peering around the tent. The fool had disappeared. Well, damn the man. Now who was going to pack?

It was not until the column started off south for the Pilgrim road that Ghelel had an opportunity to speak in relative privacy with the Marquis. Side by side just behind the column's van riding with lit torches, she leaned to him. 'So you believe him then? That this is the Guard, returned?'

Helmet under an arm and reins in one hand, the Marquis turned to examine her. His eyes were dark pits in the night and his black curly hair blew unbounded about his face. 'I believe Ullen,' he called back.

'Why should Ullen be so certain? And why so fearful? They are only mercenaries. Famous, yes. But just a band of hireswords.'

The Marquis's mouth straightened in a cold humourless smile. 'Have you not heard the stories then?'

Ghelel thought of the bedtime tales her nanny had told of the Guard and how they opposed the emperor. Romantic heroics of great champions and fanciful unbelievable deeds. 'I've heard them. Troubadours' tales and romances. But that was all long ago. Why should Ullen fear them now?'

It was now the Marquis's turn to look confused. 'Do you not know who he is, was?'

Ghelel stared, taken aback, then cut off a snarled reply. She pulled her mount closer to the Marquis. 'How in the Queen's own Mysteries am I to know anything if no one tells me anything!'

The Marquis raised a hand in surrender. 'Apologies. I thought you knew. The man served on Dassem's staff! Was Choss's adjutant for a time. That's why I believe him.'

Astonished, Ghelel relaxed and fell behind the Marquis. Ranks of her cavalry thundered past while her mount slowed. *Served with Dassem! Served all his life yet had never left the continent – the man had fought during the wars of consolidation!* Damn the fellow! She was half tempted to turn her horse around and confront him. Why didn't he just out and say so? *Yet why should he have to?* Why shouldn't she have faith in him regardless? Urko chose him for a reason, didn't he? Didn't she accept *his* competence unquestioned?

She slowed her mount to a canter, gazed back to the encampment, a distant glow in the clear starry night. Her and her mount's breath steamed in the frigid air and Ghelel thought of a bony Seti girl riding east dressed far more poorly than she. Ahead, four of her cavalry had held back from the column, awaiting her. Idly, she wondered where Molk had got himself off to and whether she'd ever see the man again. The stars blazed down with a hard cold light from horizon to horizon and suddenly new ones appeared in the east. Ghelel squinted, surprised. No, not stars, yellow flickering lights, torches. A handful appearing and disappearing in the dark above the horizon where . . .

Gods turn from her! Ghelel raked her spurs, leaning high and forward. Ride! 'Haugh!' She dashed between her startled guard, racing for the column. When she reached the van, the Marquis took one glance at her face and raised an arm in the halt.

His mount rearing, he called, 'What is it?'

Also struggling to control her own mount, she pointed, 'Look! Lights! It must be them. They're taking the ruins of the monastery.'

The Marquis studied the east. His mouth twisted his disgust. 'Trake take us, we'll never lever them out of there! It's a rat warren.' Then he stared at Ghelel as if seeing her for the first time, his eyes widened, and he yanked on his helmet, securing the strap one-handed. 'Outriders! Form up! We ride for the bridge!'

A guard of the cavalry formed around Ghelel and the Marquis. Scouts stormed ahead. The Marquis signalled the advance. The column gathered speed to a gallop into absolute darkness.

*

They met no one, though fires burned fitfully beside the road where bands of travellers lay sleeping. Down toward the Idryn dogs rushed out of the dark, snarling at the mounts. Fires burned before the black openings of caves. Ghelel's face was numb with cold, her hands frozen claws around her reins.

Before they reached the bridge their scouts emerged from the dark, barring their way. 'Armed men at the bridge.'

'Hood bugger them!' the Marquis exploded. Then he inclined his head to Ghelel. 'Pardon me, Prevost.' To the scouts, 'Can you identify them?'

'No, sir. No colours.'

'It's them,' Ghelel said, feeling oddly like laughing. Strange how she was the one to deny even the Guard's existence yet now she felt completely certain of their presence ahead. She thought of those stories from her youth; of the romantic yet tragic figure of Duke, then Prince, K'azz. 'We should go to meet them. Parley.'

'Parley?' the Marquis answered, annoyed. 'Whatever for?'

'Passage south, of course.'

'Passage? Why in Fanderay's name should they grant us passage?'

'Why ever should they not, Marquis?'

He studied her for a time, his head cocked to one side. Then he raised a hand in consent. 'Very well, Prevost. Let us go down and speak with these mercenaries. I admit to no small curiosity myself.'

They took a guard of four men. With torches held high they advanced slowly on the bridge. Four figures, that they could see, awaited them, blocking the way across. Torches on poles stood to either side where the flagged way met the broad granite blocks of the bridge. The figures themselves stood far back from the light.

'Far enough!' a man called in Talian as the Marquis and Ghelel entered the flickering light.

'Who are you? And how dare you block this way?' the Marquis called. 'This is a pilgrim road, open to all.'

'It's still open to pilgrims,' the man responded. 'Well armed for devotions, you are.'

'Come forward,' Ghelel invited. 'Let's discuss passage.'

A tall man and a very short and broad woman came forward into the light. Both wore helmets wrapped in dark cloth that wove around under their chins and surcoats of a thick dark cloth over blackened mail shirts that hung to their knees. Gauntlets covered their hands. The man bore a shield at his back, a longsword at his side, while the hilts of two curved blades jutted forward from the woman's wide sash.

'Identify yourselves,' the Marquis demanded again. 'Are you part of a legitimate army or mere brigands?'

'Questionable distinction,' the woman said, a dark brow arching.

'It's just a matter of scale, really,' the man said to her.

'Or success,' Ghelel added.

Both looked up, surprised. 'Hello,' the man said. 'I am Cole, this is Lean.'

'Prevost Alil, the Marquis Jhardin of the Marchland Sentries.' While they had been talking, Ghelel's sight had been adjusting to the light and she could now see that the cloth wrapped around the helmets and the jupons as well was of a very dark, almost black, crimson.

'Prevost, Marquis, greetings,' the man said. 'That you have chosen not to charge down here with your cavalry to overrun us means that you already know who we are. I congratulate you on your intelligence services. We've tried to keep as low a profile as possible.'

'Obliterating half of Unta?' the Marquis snapped. 'Burning Cawn to the ground?'

The man smiled, baring sharp teeth. 'As I said – a low profile.'

Ghelel leaned forward, crossing her arms on the tall pommel of her saddle. 'Cole, we formally request passage south for our detachment.'

Waving an invitation, Cole bowed. 'Granted, Prevost. All, ah, combatants wishing to withdraw south are invited to do so. But none may come north. Spread the word if you would, please.'

The Marquis glared his disgust. 'Expecting a flow of desertions, are you?'

'In the near future, to be brief . . . yes.'

With a curt nod the Marquis sent a man back with word to advance. 'I suppose we should *thank* you for our passage.'

Cole and Lean stood aside. 'Just doing our job.'

∗   ∗   ∗

Hurl found Storo on the parapet of the Inner Round wall, chin on hands, staring north. Talian soldiers in the cover of a tower in the lower Outer Round wall were taking pot-shots at him and the nearby soldiers manning the wall. 'Collect those bolts,' Storo called to the men as Hurl came to his side and ducked behind a merlon.

'What are you doing up here?' Hurl demanded.

'Being useful.'

'You'll be pincushioned!'

'Occupational hazard of straw targets.'

'You're in a mood.'

Storo lay his chin on his hands once more. 'How're you feeling now?'

Hurl couldn't help rubbing her side. 'Better. Thanks.'

'Thank Liss. Where is she now anyway?'

'Watching the east. Won't turn from it for an instant.'

Storo frowned, tilting his head. A crossbow bolt ricocheted from the merlon next to him, spraying stone dust. 'We know she's coming. Just a matter of time.'

'No, not that. She says something else is out there, a blank spot where there shouldn't be.'

'A blank spot, hunh? We have bigger worries.' He swept his arm to encompass the broad arc of the army camp that spilled out beyond the Outer Round. 'It's now official – they have enough men.'

'Why don't they attack?'

'They will. In the next few days. Escalade all around the north curtain wall, I imagine.'

'Sir?' A soldier further along the wall pointed. Hurl glanced through a crenel, saw double ranks of crossbowmen standing atop a nearby tower, all aiming in their direction. She yanked Storo down as a fusillade of bolts staccatoed into the parapet around Storo. Mocking shouts sounded from across the way requesting more target practice. Storo set his forearms on his knees, brushed the dust from his stubbled pate. 'So, how's our leveller coming along?'

Hurl could only shake her head. Was the man mad, or determined not to survive the siege? She decided then that however it went she'd have everyone keep a close eye on him. 'That's the news. Silk says they're ready.'

He faced her, his eyes red-rimmed and sunken, but still hard. 'Ready? Well, it's about bloody time. They can go ahead with it.'

'Says you should be there, you want it done.'

The eyes rolled to the sky. 'Tell him I'm busy.'

'Getting yourself killed, I know.' She tilted her head to the nearest soldier, lowered her voice, 'Not exactly what you'd call confidence inspiring.'

The Fist stood once again in full view of the besiegers. 'The men like a commander with endearing eccentricities.'

Hurl grabbed his arm to pull him along while crossbow bolts ricocheted from the parapets with sharp metallic *tings*.

Silk met them at the central city temple. Rell was with him, as were Sunny and Jalor. Hurl realized that they hadn't all been together like

414

this since the beginning of the siege. She felt a pang of loss for Shaky – unreliable son of a bitch that he'd been.

The city mage looked worse than he had after the attack. His worn silk finery hung from him in lank sweaty folds. His greasy hair gripped his skull like a cap, and his hand, when he gestured for them to follow, shook with a palsy. 'Follow me,' he croaked.

Storo fell into step with Silk, Hurl with Rell. She'd spent little time with the Genabackan lately. The man was ever on the move around the city leading a company of some twenty elite. Wherever he went morale soared – the Hengans thought him some kind of champion. As far as Hurl was concerned, they didn't know the half of it. 'How are you doing?' she asked.

'Well.' His voice was different now, distorted by his burnt lips. He wore a helmet complete with a faceguard of gilded bronze and a long camail that hung to his shoulders. She still wondered if all that was for protection or to cover up the scarring. A cuirass of iron banding, mail sleeves and greaves completed his serious accoutrement. She doubted the man had ever worn that much iron in all his life. But the same twinned, single-edged, slightly curved swords hung at his sides.

She nodded to Sunny who now commanded a party of emergency response sappers pulled together out of city masons, glassblowers and builders. They'd already blocked a number of attempts upon the Inner Round north gates and had countersunk two tunnels dug by Talian sappers. Jalor, for his part, had somehow fallen even further into a sort of worship of Rell and had elected himself chief body-guard, accompanying him everywhere.

And what of her? Somehow she had fallen into a role as well. For some reason everyone seemed to consider her second in command after Storo.

Silk led them through the city temple, which Hurl noted had been cleared of all the new shrines to the various Quon Talian gods and spirits that the conquering Malazans had forced upon the Hengans: Burn, Osserc, Hood, Oponn, Soliel, Fener, Togg, Fanderay, even the brand new gold incense bowl dedicated to Trake. Hurl came to Silk's side. 'House cleaning?'

A tired glance aside and weak smile. 'Re-consecrated, Hurl.'

'To who?'

'Not who, what. The city itself.'

'The city worships itself? Sounds incestuous.'

'Just old-fashioned.'

'That's what my uncle said.'

'What happened to him?'

Hurl cocked her head to study the ceiling as they walked along. 'Come to think of it, nothing happened to him. He lived a long life in a rule of terror over a huge family of idiots. Choked to death on a bird bone.'

Silk gave a long thoughtful nod to that. 'There you go.'

'Yup. There you go.'

He opened the door of the Inner Sanctum that they'd first entered through during the night of the insurrection. 'This way.'

'Wait a minute,' Sunny growled, stopping. 'This leads to the shit.'

'Indeed it does – more than you would know.'

'Well, I'm not going back down there to get all covered in crap again.'

'Came off, did it?' Hurl said.

Sunny bared his jagged teeth. Sighing his impatience, Storo waved a forward.

True to Sunny's forebodings they ended up ducking back out by the gigantic stone jackal head. It slowly ground shut behind them, closing with a boom that shook the floor and leaving them in darkness but for the shielded candle Silk carried. It was gloomy, but it looked to Hurl as if someone had cleaned most of the excrement from the chamber leaving only a dry flaking layer of scum on the limestone floor and a quarter of the way up the walls. 'Now what?' Sunny asked in what Hurl thought forced bravado.

Silk motioned to a row of lanterns. 'Light those.' Hurl and Jalor complied; Silk turned his attention to the jackal head. Standing directly before it he inscribed in the air a complicated twisting pattern with his arms then spoke in a language Hurl did not recognize. The grinding of stone announced the jackal's maw grating open once more.

'Why didn't you just do that the first time?' Sunny asked resentfully.

'Because we're going somewhere different now.'

Indeed, behind the open jaws, where the throat would open up was now a dark stone pit set with iron rungs. Of the tunnel they'd followed out, no sign remained. Silk led the way in and down. Hurl imagined that were Shaky still with them he'd be asking something like 'How'd he do that?'

They climbed down a long chute that, thankfully, bore the dry dusty air of never once having had shit poured down it. The chute ended at a claustrophobic rectangular chamber of roughly shaped limestone blocks. Intricate drawings of geometric designs covered the blocks of the roof, all four walls and the floor. A layperson to theurgy, even Hurl could recognize multilayered linked wards, or inscribed incantations, or investments of overlapping Warrens. A section of one wall had been deconstructed, and the huge blocks, far larger than Hurl imagined any man could move – except perhaps Ahl – had been tossed aside. Beyond ran a low descending passage that looked to have been carved from the very igneous rock underlying the city. Again, Silk led the way, followed by Rell. Coming along close to the rear, just ahead of Jalor, Hurl's lantern lit the wrenched and torn remains of a series of barriers set across the passage: first a slab of copper as thick as three of her fingers, blasted as if by some physical blow; then a slab of what she recognized as hardened silver, melted; lastly a slab of iron, shattered and bent outward. Surely not Ahl?

The passage debouched into a large chamber that echoed their footfalls and groans as they straightened their backs and stretched. Three ghostly figures emerged from the gloom to meet them: Ahl and his brothers Thal and Lar. Grime and sweat smeared their clothes almost black. Lopsided grins leered at them wetly making Hurl damned uncomfortable.

'Is this it?' Storo asked, his voice booming in the immense quiet of the chamber.

Silk nodded.

'Kellanved didn't build all this, did he?' Hurl asked, awed by the sheer scale of the construction.

'No. It was built long ago. All in the hopes of eventual occupation. He merely fulfilled its purpose.'

'*Merely*,' Sunny echoed, sneering.

'What next?' Hurl asked.

Silk waved to the darkness. 'This way.' An object ahead dimly separated itself from the surrounding shadow. It resolved into a circular ledge, then finally into the raised border of what appeared to be a common well. A chain of black iron descended from the darkness above, and on down into the well. It was constructed of enormous square links each as thick as Hurl's forearm. But of all these wonders what caught Hurl's eye were the two bright objects thrust through the opening of the link level with the top of the mortared stones of the well: two longswords, their blades spanning the diameter of the opening. It seemed to Hurl that to pull the swords would free the chain to continue its descent.

'The last barrier,' Silk said into the silence of them all gathered around studying the amazing arrangement. 'Or last link. Pull these and he is released.'

'Where?' Storo asked. 'Released where? Into this room?'

'Gods no!' Silk laughed – more than a touch feverishly, Hurl thought. 'Far below. He will be released to make his escape to the plains, north.'

'Who can do it?' Storo asked.

Silk waved a hand. 'Oh, anyone strong enough, I imagine. But I wonder if you, Rell, might . . .'

The engraved visor turned to Storo who waved for him to do so if he wished. Rell stepped forward, studied the arrangement. Hurl looked to Silk – it seemed to her that there was more going on here than the mage was letting on. And Silk was now more animated than he'd been so far the entire evening; watching the Genabackan swordsman the mage's eyes glowed, his hands were fists at his sides. The three brothers, Hurl also noted, appeared uniformly sour, almost uncomfortable. She took a strange sort of reassurance from this.

Rell took firm hold of the grips, set one booted foot against the side of the well, and yanked. The first time nothing happened. Sunny snorted. Rell adjusted his grip, hunched his back. He yanked again. The screeching of iron on stone pierced Hurl's ears; she flinched, covering them. Finger's breadth by finger's breadth, the blades scraped towards Rell. Ominous rattling ran up and down the length of the chain above. Finally, with an explosive shattering of the stone, the tips fell. Rell was yanked forward, disappearing, and only the quick hands of Storo and Jalor at his thighs saved him. He straightened with the swords still in his hands, blades intact. The enormous length of chain, each link as large as a child's head, jangled and knocked, descending. Hurl felt the movement of something distant shuddering the ground beneath her feet. Dust sifted down around them. She brushed it from her hair and shoulders.

'It is done,' Silk exhaled into the dark. 'He will have to dig a long distance but that won't stop him.'

No one spoke. The chamber was quiet but for the distant rumbling. Storo rubbed a hand down his stubbled jowls. 'Let's go, then. We've been away for damn long enough.'

'Aye,' Sunny ground out, and he spat into the well.

Walking away, Rell admired the blades still in his hands. 'You should use them,' Silk said. 'I think you'll find them . . .' his voice trailed off into silence.

Hurl turned to the mage. 'What is it?'

Silk raised a pale hand for silence. Hurl listened, straining.

Something ... sounds from behind them, from the well. Words? The hair at her neck and forearms stirred as Hurl recognized the sounds for hoarse, growled Talian, distorted, but understandable, echoing up the pit of the well:

> 'Those who free me,
> be my enemies.
> Those who enslave me,
> kneel to me.
> When the end of all things comes,
> as surely it does,
> on which scale stand you?
> In the final balance
> And the accounting?'

A long low chuckle, more a panting than a laugh, followed. Hurl sought out Silk's gaze but the mage's eyes were resolutely downcast. The three brothers, however, grinned insanely at everyone.

'Let's get out of here,' Storo rumbled.

CHAPTER V

Only the dead should be certain of anything.

A scholar's ancient warning
Jacuruku

'SHIPS, UNCLE! A CONVOY OF SHIPS!' NEVALL OD' ORR'S nephew
called from outside the tent. Nevall Od' Orr, once Chief
Factor of Cawn, gagged on the mouthful of chewed charcoal
he used for ink as he sat attempting to bring his books up to date. In
a fit of coughing he clutched the edges of his high table.

'Ships, uncle!' his nephew shouted again.

The factor took a drink from a cup, rinsed and spat on to the bare
dirt floor. 'What of it?' He drew his blankets tighter about himself.

'They fly the Imperial sceptre!'

'Wonderful. Yet another fleet to sack us. Will they take our hoard
of turnips, I wonder?'

'You have turnips?'

Nevall slammed shut his scorched book. Sighing, he rubbed his
blackened hands across the back of his neck. 'I suppose I should go
down and grovel picturesquely. Perhaps she'll toss me a copper
moon. I wonder if I am attired appropriately to receive an Empress?'

Nevall listened, arms open. Silence. He hung his head, 'Lout.'

He stepped down gingerly on to the damp dirt ground, crossed to
the front flaps and peeked out. Downhill, over the blackened ribs of
burnt Cawn, a rag-tag flotilla of ships of all sizes and ages was filling the harbour. *Now* she comes. Still, better than if she had come
before the mercenaries. They had at least a small chance to recoup
their losses. He sniffed the air and wondered if any of the day's catch
was left. He should send his other nephew for a fish.

'Nevall Od' Orr.'

He stiffened then, slowly turned. A man occupied the rear of the tent, nondescript in a loose dark shirt and trousers. Nevall inclined his chin in greeting, shuffled back to his table. He tore a pinch from a dark loaf and popped it into his mouth. 'Ranath. It's been a while. The Claw, now, is it? I've lost track of all the changes.'

A shrug. 'It's all the same shell game.' Ranath straightened the front fold of his shirt. 'Listen, Nevall. She's here. She means to wipe this League and the Guard from the face of the continent, but . . .' and he opened his hands, '. . . she needs the funds to do it. Lots of funds.'

A burst of cackled laughter. Nevall opened his arms wide to gesture all around. 'She's welcome to all of it – even the blanket from my back.'

Ranath's lazy gaze did not waver. 'Come, come, Nevall. The spies you have placed everywhere report to us as well. The Guard took everything not nailed down. Horses, oxen, cattle, goats, wagons, carts, preserves, flour, rice, pots, timber, rope, nails. Everything. Everything, that is, except . . .' he raised a hand and turned it over to reveal a gold coin. 'Except cash.' He tossed the coin from hand to hand, his eyes on Nevall. 'They didn't find the vaults of the trading houses, did they?' He snapped the coin from the air, opened the hand to show its empty palm. 'You know, I wonder if they even knew to ask for them? Now there's an irony – charitable mercenaries.'

The pointed tip of Nevall's tongue edged out to wet his lips. 'Now, Ranath. Let's not be hasty here. We back the Empress, of course. The Empire was ever superb for business. But,' he shrugged his bony shoulders beneath the thin blanket, 'our hands are tied – it's all spoken for. You know that.'

Ranath sighed. He raised his gaze to the tent ceiling while he searched for words. 'Nevall . . . how shall I put this – oh yes.' He smiled, raising his hands. 'The gloves are off. And lo and behold, the claws are unsheathed.'

'Whose?'

The smile hardened. 'Careful, my friend. The Throne's, let us say. You say you support the Empress. Excellent. Let us collect the entire contents of every trading house's vault to hold as pledge to said backing. You will notify the Ruling Convene of the province that all their writs have been called in immediately. We will expect the complete commitment of all troops from across Cawn province as the honouring of said debt. Understood?'

Nevall sat heavily on his stool, lay a hand on his blackened ledger book, nodded.

'As you merchants say, Nevall – a pleasure doing business with you.'

The factor hung his head. Tent cloth shifted. He looked up and the Claw was gone. Yanking open his book, Nevall took a bite from a stick of charcoal next to it and chewed furiously. He jammed a feather nib into the corner of his mouth. 'Damn Laseen and Mallick both.'

* * *

'The place is a dump!' Nait exclaimed from the crowded rail of the fishing scow that had carried its contingent of seven hundred – limping and wallowing – all the way from Unta to Cawn harbour. Least, in thin torn buckskins only, his fists white on the rail, mumbled abjectly, 'I just want off. Please Hood, kill me and take me from here.'

Nait eyed the stricken giant halfbreed Barghast. He leaned close to whisper, 'Want some fish?'

'Baiting!' Hands yelled from nearby.

Rolling his eyes, Nait leaned over the side, made a great gagging show of spitting out the wad of chewed rustleaf bulging his cheek. Least paled, swallowing.

Hands dragged Nait from the rail. 'Staff meeting,' she smiled gleefully. Nait slumped, groaning.

At mid-deck they met with their old sergeant, now captain, Tinsmith. Many of Tinsmith's old command from the Untan Harbour Guard were gathered around, Hands, Honey Boy, together with many faces from other guard companies within Unta such as Lim Tal, one-time chief bodyguard, and rumoured lover, to Duke Amstar D'Avig. Also sitting with the captain was the old tanned and scarred veteran for whom many had already come to nurture a precious hatred for having drilled them mercilessly day after day since casting off from the capital. A man Tinsmith simply referred to as Master Sergeant Temp, but whom the men called 'Old Clozup' after his constant badgering of 'Close ranks! Close up!'

Tinsmith looked to each of them, cleared his throat. 'We'll have to wait our turn to off-load. Cawn's as bare as Hood's bones, so we'll shoulder what rations we have left and march right on out. Orders are to make six leagues a day—'

'Six leagues!' Nait squawked. 'After sitting on our backsides for so long?'

'Put *Captain* after your whining,' Hands snarled.

'And another thing,' Nait continued, 'everyone's a sergeant around here. Hands, Least, Lim, Honey Boy—'

'That's Honey, now.'

'Yeah, fine, *Sergeant Honey*. Why ain't I a sergeant too?'

''Cause you lead our saboteurs, Corporal,' growled Master Sergeant Temp. 'And no saboteur rises to the dizzy heights of a sergeancy.'

'I heard o' one or two.'

'Then show me what you got . . .'

Nait looked away from the veteran's icy pale eyes, waggled his head mouthing, '*show me what you got.*'

'We are part of one battalion of the Fourth's heavies,' Tinsmith continued, stroking his long silver moustache with a thumb and forefinger. 'The iron core of this army. Now, we got us hardly any cavalry to speak of, some spotty noblemen, a few mounted scouts. What we do got is thousands of skirmishers, light infantry – enough crossbowmen to depopulate a country. That's the hand we've been dealt. So, what to do? They need a centre, an anchor. That's us. The ferocity of their fire will wither any force stupid enough to show their heads like they did the Guard, and will do to any cavalry. But when we do hit strong resistance, they'll melt through us to the rear and reform. We don't melt. We hold. Understood? So, all the old veterans,' Tinsmith inclined his head to the Master Sergeant, 'they sent a contingent to High Fist Anand – and the Sword, Korbolo Dom, too of course—'

Nait blew a farting noise.

'To hash things out,' Tinsmith continued blithely, 'an' what they came up with is four main battle groups, mutually supporting, each anchored by a battalion of heavies. The Sword has the lead one, o' course. Braven Tooth will command us on the left. The right flanking battalion is under Fist D'Ebbin, and High Fist Anand co-ordinates from the rear. Now, the lot of you might think that the Master Sergeant here was just to train you up, but I'm sure you'll all be right pleased to know that he'll be the anchoring right corner shieldman on the front line.'

Nait eyed the old veteran; sure, he looked tough, but him march six leagues in a day? The geezer'll drop and he'll be sure to step on him on the way past.

'You sergeants,' Tinsmith added, 'you have your men follow his lead. Stand with him, follow his orders and I guarantee you our ranks will hold. That's all for now. Dismissed.'

'One last thing, Captain,' the old-timer threw in, his scarred cheek

pulling up in a one-sided smile, 'while we're out here on this beautiful day waiting for our turn to off-load . . .' Nait caught Honey's
gaze, rolled his eyes. '. . . I thought I might have the men and women
practise some close order drills.'

Tinsmith smoothed his moustache to hide his smile. 'All yours,
Master Sergeant.'

From the rear ranks of the Imperial retinue of court functionaries, it
appeared to Possum that the Empress was in a hurry. Marines
formed in parade ranks guarded the wharf where a glittering crowd
of nobles and functionaries, Possum included, awaited the Imperial
presence. All the usual ceremonies and speeches of reception had
been waived. Behind the ranks of marines the citizens of Cawn stood
waiting, silent and – Possum had to admit – looking rather down-
trodden and desultory. But then, the town had just been sacked. She
appeared at the top of the gangway without fanfare or announcement – just one more passenger disembarking, yet Possum was
surprised by the collective inhalation from the Cawnese that her
appearance evoked. *How could they have known?* She wore no finery,
no crown or tiara; no sceptre weighted her arms; nor was she carried
by palanquin or raised throne. No, she merely stepped up un-
announced, wearing only her plain silk tunic and pantaloons. Her hair
was short, mousey-brown and touched by grey; her face, well, plain,
and rather sour in its tight thin mouth, lined at the eyes and brow.

Yet everyone knew it was *her*. Perhaps it was the glance she cast
over the waterfront and all assembled. Severe. Utterly assured. And
frankly rather disappointed with what it saw. The nobles knelt
followed by the citizens. The marines saluted.

She did receive the local factors of the Cawn trading houses: they
were allowed to crawl forward on their knees like a gaggle of beggars
on the street. She acknowledged their abject loyalty with a brief in-
clination of her head, then was assisted by a groom in mounting her
horse. Everyone else then mounted, and the whole cavalcade set off,
the screen of cavalry, the honour-guard, the Empress and her bodyguard accompanied by High Fist Anand and staff, the court retinue
following along, Possum among them. The other High Fist, Korbolo
Dom, also Sword of the Empire, was where he insisted upon being,
leading the van, where everyone seemed content to leave him. For his
part Possum was dressed in rich silks, Untan duelling sword at his
side. He played the part of a minor noble whose job was to sneer
haughtily at anyone gauche enough to ask him what position it was
he actually filled.

As he rode along, he spotted operatives standing alongside the road. From signs from them he learned that Cawn had been secured, that spies left behind by Urko had been identified, and that the deal that Ranath, the region's old chief of intelligence, had proposed to Possum had been accepted. The deal was a sweet one and would double Laseen's forces – eventually – but its appearance out of seemingly nowhere troubled him. What had Ranath been up to lately? Where had the intelligence behind the deal come from? And yet, was it not the man's job? Why question him for being competent and resourceful? Was he, Possum, now the sort of leader who dreaded talent among his subordinates? Had he not in fact deliberately cultivated the opposite managerial style? Did he not signal in so many ways to his subordinates that ways and means were of no interest to him so long as the job got done? That they could count on him appearing only when things got botched up? He forced himself to ease back further into his role, flexed his neck and glanced – scornfully – around at the efforts the Cawnese were making in demolishing and rebuilding their city. His gaze fell on the rider next to him and he was startled to see there, dressed in the cream flowing robes and headscarf of a Seven Cities noblewoman, Coil, the most insolent of the five commanders who constituted his second echelon.

'What are you doing here?' he demanded.

An arched brow, a regal wave to the surroundings. 'Is this not delicious? Is it not bracing to be out in the field once again?'

Glancing about, Possum smiled thinly. 'Indeed it is. I am reminded of the old days, my more *active* times.'

The woman's painted lips could just be made out curling behind the sheer scarf. 'It seems to me that you should have been getting out much more often all this time.'

It seems to me that both of us were damned lucky not to have been on Malaz just recently. But he inclined his head in assent to the point. *Whatever it is she's getting at – yet more useless taunting, no doubt.* 'But we are not here on a pleasure outing.'

'No. Sadly not. We have the Guard before us and the insurrectionists and their traitor ringleaders. A tall order for anyone, yes?'

What was the fool getting at? She knew as well as he that Laseen in no way intended to actually fight the Guard if she could avoid it. So, the ringleaders. He glanced away, touched a silk handkerchief to his nose. Yes, a tall order. And what order? Or orders? 'Our primary concern is the safety of the Empress, of course.'

For a mounted rider, Coil performed an admirable curtsied bow, and reined to fall back. Possum turned away. *So – has she just announced herself as the source of all these initiatives and unexplained actions on the part of so many of the Claw? All running through here? Sadly for her I cannot risk not acting. There cannot be a parallel command structure. I should strike now, but I cannot forget what lies ahead. After all that, woman, should you still be alive . . . I'll kill you myself.*

* * *

Captain Tazal, career soldier, of no famous family, newly installed, marched up to the Throne room of Unta, helmet under one arm, hand on the grip of his sword, and sweat slick on his brow. Guards opened the doors and entering he bowed just within the threshold. Raising his head he saw the throne empty, draped in a white satin cloth – *of course, fool!* He glanced about. Aside, rinsing his hands in a washbowl, he saw the current authority in the absence of the Empress, Mallick Rel, spokesperson of the Assembly.

Mallick turned from the bowl, dried his hands in a white cloth. 'You have news, Captain, of this barbarian stain offending our lands?'

Our lands? But Tazal carefully held all emotion from his bearded face. 'Fortress Jurda has capitulated. Insufficient garrison to withstand an assault.'

The Assemblyman held out the cloth and a servant took it. He clasped his hands across his wide stomach. He glanced down as if studying them. 'I see. And whose decision was this to make?'

The captain sought to disguise a frown. What was this? Retribution? 'The commander, the current Lord Jurda.'

'Competent?'

'In my view? Yes.'

'Unfortunate . . .'

How so unfortunate? Unfortunate that the fortress has capitulated? Or unfortunate for the commander that he capitulated without permission? Or unfortunate for you that thousands of Wickan were now storming down upon you howling for your blood? Or, to give the Assemblyman some credit, unfortunate that a competent military commander viewed the situation so hopeless he capitulated? The captain wiped a sleeve across his brow, striving to keep his face flat. The man did appear admirably calm given the hole he'd dug for himself. Made of strong stuff, this fat conniver.

Still lowered, the Assemblyman's gaze slanted aside to the

unoccupied throne. His pale round face appeared even more bloated. 'The Sword of the Empire has left for the west, Captain. What advice would you offer us?'

Us? From all accounts the captain had heard of this self-proclaimed Sword it was damned lucky the man was in the west and not with them. Then the captain realized the enormity of what had just been requested. *Good Soliel! Here he was, a mere garrison commander just raised to captain, never dreaming of seeing the inside of the throneroom, being asked for advice from the most powerful man in the Empire? Well, at least his wife will be pleased. Yet what on Burn's Earth should he, or could he, say to the man? Perhaps, as his father used to say, if you're going to get drunk, might as well throw in the whole deck.* He coughed into a fist to clear his throat. 'One war at a time, sir. Their timing is exquisite. We can't beat them. We must negotiate. Buy them off. Deal with them later.'

Sallow eyes still on the throne, the Assemblyman's thick lips pursed. His fingers, entwined across his stomach, stirred restlessly, reminding the captain of some sort of pale undersea creature. 'The urge to lash out is almost overwhelming,' the man muttered almost as if he'd forgotten the captain's presence. 'Exterminating these vermin from the face of the world my most dear wish . . .' Tazal wondered if he ought to hear any of this yet he dared not say anything, or even breathe. Mallick announced more loudly: 'Tactical frankness is like a smooth clean cut in battle, captain – much appreciated. I cannot dispute the straight thrust of your thinking. Ruthless cold pragmatism. Refreshing.' He nodded to himself as if what he'd heard confirmed his own thoughts. 'Yes. We will send an envoy to open negotiations.'

Tazal clashed a fist to his newly fitted cuirass. 'The envoy, Assemblyman?'

The fingers stopped weaving. 'Why, yourself, of course. Promoted under my authority to the rank of Fist.'

After the captain exited the Throne room and the doors closed Mallick also left, but by a small side door, leaving behind the court functionaries, clerks and servants for a small private audience chamber. After a moment Oryan entered the room by another door. Mallick fixed the dark-skinned, tattooed man with a long hard stare. 'Why, servant of mine, are you still here?'

The old man remained unperturbed, his long dark face impassive. 'The Wickans are not important enough.'

Tight-lipped, Mallick grated, 'I gave you strict orders.'

'Your problem in the past has been your nurturing of grudges and your predilection for vendetta.' The slim old man, limbs no more than bone and writhing, faded blue tattoos, made a casting away gesture. 'You must learn to abandon such urges if you wish to actually succeed.'

Mallick's eyes bulged his outrage, hissed splutterings escaped his lips bringing spittle with them. He brought his pudgy fisted hands to his face. 'You would dare!'

Again, unperturbed, the Seven Cities shaman's eyes remained bland. 'Which do you wish? Petty satisfaction or achievement of your ambitions? *Choose!*'

Mallick sucked in a great shuddering breath, forced his hands down. 'Past failures would indicate flaws in my choices, yes. Though I dearly wish them utterly destroyed they are currently no dire threat, true. No fearsome Wickan curses winging my way. Yes, Oryan. At this time attention to them would be counter to productive, yes? Very well. Annoying distractions, they are, from the main stage. Like a loud man at the theatre. An irritation to be endured by us – the more cultured.' Mallick crossed an arm over his chest then propped his other upon it and pressed the tips of his fingers to his forehead. 'And so further insult is to be endured from these unwashed illiterates, as my advisers suggest.'

An insouciant shrug. 'As I say. They are of no importance.'

'Very good. So, the west, then. And speaking of the west – any word from our beautiful murderess?'

'None since she left with the fleet. I believe she secured a position as an officer's whore.'

'Careful, Oryan. Your biases are showing. No doubt she has the man enslaved.'

'As I said – a whore.'

'Yes, well. You may have a point there.'

A discreet knock at one door. Mallick gestured Oryan out, crossed to it. 'Yes?'

'Matter of a property dispute, Assemblyman,' a voice quavered through the door. Mallick pulled it open. 'A *what?*'

A court clerk bowed extremely low. 'As the authority present in the capital, sir. A property dispute has arisen out of the rebuilding efforts . . .'

Mallick stared at the man, his bulging eyes blinked. 'And this is a matter you bring to me *now?*'

'The parties involved are most insistent, and of the highest rank and most prestigious families . . .'

'Then perhaps a city magistrate would no doubt be appropriate.'

The clerk bowed again. 'Sadly, said magistrate's family has been proven to be distantly related to one of the claimants . . .'

Mallick clasped his hands at his stomach, his eyes narrowed to angry slits. 'Very well, court clerk. Here is my judgment upon the case that said self-important appellants are so keen to bring before me to the exclusion of all else I may have to attend to. Said plot of land or property is to be divided exactly in half and fifty per cent given to each party – even if said property constitutes a slave. Am I understood?'

The clerk bowed deeply again – perhaps to hide the tight grin that he fought to disguise. 'Excellent, sir. I shall write up the papers immediately.'

'That should winnow the line of petitioners, do you not think?'

'Most drastically, sir.'

*   *   *

For the next few days while they skirted the Jacuruku north coast, Traveller lay at the bow gripped in a fever of sweats and shuddering chills. Ereko guided the *Kite* while Kyle and the Lost brothers slept in turns. The third night Traveller suddenly cried out, weeping inconsolably, his body wrenched with the violence of his convulsions. Kyle went to the Thel Akai's side. 'What did they do to him, those mages?'

Ereko was surprised. Under their broad bone ridge, his argent eyes flicked to Kyle, smiled their reassurance, then returned to scanning the shore. 'They? Nothing. He carries his illness with him. It has been whispering to him all these months. I have seen it growing upon him day by day. Those fools with their interference have weakened him and now he feels its pull keenly.'

'You cannot cure it?'

A shake of his shaggy head. 'You have not guessed, Kyle? It is the sword he carries. That is not a blade meant for any human, no matter who. It brings with it the memories of terrible things. Bloodshed, yes. But much worse – acts of cruelty and of soul-corroding anguish. It was forged ages ago by the one known as the Son of Darkness, Anomandaris. Know you of him?'

'Yes. We have legends of him. Stories of the Moon itself floating overhead and dragons soaring.' Those fireside tales no longer sounded so incredible to Kyle.

'It has held many names over the ages. Anger. Rage. Vengeance. Of them all, he chose for himself *vengeance*. A choice we should perhaps be grateful for. Now that choice eats at him like acid. I pray it will not taint his spirit.'

Kyle watched the man, curled up under a cloak, hands clenched in his sweat-slick hair, his face hidden behind his forearms. 'Then we should take it from him.'

The giant grasped Kyle's upper arm in his massive grip. '*No*. You mustn't. He would strike without thought. Would you add yet another burden to his conscience?'

'Then what can we do?'

Without turning his head, Ereko slid his bright gaze to Kyle in a strange sort of sideways regard. He bared his tusk-like teeth in a one-sided grin. 'You can pray, Kyle.'

Kyle flinched away. *Pray? Is there so little hope?* He moved off to lie down next to the Lost brothers wrapped in cloaks and blankets. *Pray? To who?* He thought of the bewildering array of Gods, spirits and heroes he'd heard mentioned since leaving Bael lands. None appealed to him. That left his old guardian and tribal ancestral spirits going back all the way to their legendary progenitor, Father Wind. Perhaps that very entity taken from him by the very company he joined? Yet, as time has passed, it all seemed so unreal to him.

The gentle night waves rocked the *Kite*, and the susurration of the nearby surf whispered rhythmically. Kyle eventually did slip into an uneasy sleep. He repeated his people's ancient invocation:

Great All Father,
Whose breath cleanses, brings life,
Guide me. Show me my path.

Kyle awoke, spluttering and coughing on a mouthful of smoke. He lay in a tent made of roughly sewn hides. But not a tent like the one he'd recently slept in; this one was cramped and dark, its ceiling low. A hunched figure, a man or a woman, occupied half the sagging quarters. A brazier next to the occupant sent out gouts of smoke that made Kyle's eyes water and his breath catch in his throat. Outside, a strong wind blew, gusting at the sides of the frail construction. The figure waved a hand wrapped in tatters of cloth. Its shape was unnervingly strange and distorted. 'Apologies for the poor domestic arrangements. Recent setbacks have reduced my circumstances.'

'Where am I? Where is everyone?'

'You are not so far away from your ship and your friends, Kyle.'

'Who are you?'

'Who am I?' The shape rocked back and forth, cackling. 'A friend, of course. One who has, how shall I put it – intervened – to help.'

'Help?'

'Yes. Help you. Whereas those you erroneously pray to ignore your pleas, I, however, am always responsive.'

Kyle attempted to wave the choking fumes from his face. 'How did I get here?'

A great gust of wind kicked the frail tent and the figure hissed indistinct mouthings under its breath. 'Never mind that, Kyle. Time is pressing. Your friend is ill. It lies within my power to ease his sufferings. What say you? For a small price I will sooth his misery, calm his nightmares. Do you not wish to see him revive?'

'Yes, of course – but what price?'

'Oh, nothing awful, I assure you. Nothing like your blood or your spirit or anything absurd like that. No. However, I am interested in that sword you carry. It has unusual characteristics. You could say I have an interest in uncommon weapons.' The arms opened in a shrug. 'There you have it. Nothing unreasonable. Surely you do not value this blade above your friend's health and recovery?'

Kyle blinked to clear his blurring vision, coughed into a fist. 'No, of course not. But why—'

A wind slammed the tent with a thundering boom, completely flattening one side. The figure pressed both hands against the bulging hides, snarling, 'No! I am master here! Be gone!'

A woman's voice came cutting through the howling wind then. It rose and fell as if calling from a great distance. Kyle cocked his head, straining to listen. 'You are not the master *here*, Chained One,' the voice seemed to scold. 'Come, Kyle. Come away.'

Unable to stand, Kyle crawled on his hands and knees towards the entry. 'You!' the figure roared. 'How *dare* you! There will be retribution! I will remember this!' Kyle reached the flap, scrabbled under it. 'Wait! I can tell you what you carry – don't you want to know? Aren't you curious? How you've been betrayed? *Used?*'

'Speak not of *using* others, great deceiver,' the voice answered.

On his elbows, Kyle pulled himself out from under the hide into the night to find himself before the bare feet of a woman. She stood above him, her pale slim body wrapped in loose gossamer scarves the colour of darkest night that whipped sinuous in the wind. The long veil over her face flicked like a banner and her black hair lashed about her face. She turned and walked away.

'And you! Speak not of *deception*,' was the last thing Kyle heard spat from within the tent.

Stumbling, crawling, he followed the woman. Broken wood and

tatters of cloth littered the beach; it looked as though a shipwreck had crashed ashore. None of it seemed to obstruct the woman yet Kyle had to pick his way carefully. At one point the wind brought a long-drawn-out mournful howling like that of a hound. The woman's head snapped aside, to the north, and she raised a pale languid hand as if waving something away, then continued on. Kyle joined her far down the strand, the surf licking his sandals. 'Where am I?' he gasped.

Back to him, scanning the sea's starry horizon, she said, 'It is a dream, Kyle. Only a dream. Nothing more.' She turned her oval, achingly beautiful, veiled face to him. 'And you are haunted.'

'By you?'

A teasing smile; a cool hand at his brow. 'Among others,' and she gestured down the beach. Kyle squinted – there, through the curtains of blowing sand, a figure, shouting, a hand at his mouth. An old man, one-handed . . .

'Stoop! Yes, I see you! *What? What is it?*'

'He was banished to Hood's most distant Paths,' the woman explained. 'Yet not utterly, for the Vow holds him still in bindings that cannot be broken. And so he is caught between Realms. Cast away yet linked to you.'

'To me?'

'Yes. He chose you to speak to – as is the custom among the fallen Avowed. Their "Brethren" I believe they are named.'

Brethren. So, that is who they are.

She extended a naked arm, pointed a long finger out to the expanse of water. 'And there you are.'

Kyle squinted out to the dark sea. Far out, past the phosphor glow of breakers at a reef, was the pale patch of a sail passing east to west. 'What? Is that me?'

His vision blurred and he fell to his knees. 'Sleep now, soldier,' the Goddess whispered, and he pitched forward into the surf. Water splashed his face.

'Kyle? Kyle!' He opened his eyes: Ereko's anxious face loomed above him, his long stringy hair hanging down. The giant shook water from his hand. 'How are you now, lad?'

Kyle wiped his wet cold face, blinking. 'Fine, fine. What is it? What happened?'

'What happened?' Pain clenched Ereko's brow and looked away. 'What happened was my fault. I am sorry. It was . . . more perilous

. . . than I imagined. But it turned out well in the end. My Lady won't thank me for it, though.'

'Who was that *thing*?'

'That was the poison corrupting the Warrens, Kyle, and more. The Outsider. Some call him the Chained God, others the Crippled God, for he, or it, is broken, shattered. His presence here has infected this land.'

'He seemed . . . *sick*.'

'We are no doubt a sickness to him – for he is from *elsewhere*. He was brought here unwillingly, and now suffers eternally. Myself, I pity his plight.' Ereko took Kyle's arm in his huge hand, his eyes searching. 'I'm sorry, Kyle. I did not expect such a strong reaction from all involved. But it forced her to act and now all is well. It is Traveller. He's awake, and he's asking for you.' Ereko handed him a skin of water. Kyle gulped it down then crab-walked hunched to the bow. Traveller sat with the Lost brothers, propped up against the bow, a blanket at his shoulders. His long dark hair was plastered across his brow, hung lank about the blanket. He appeared exhausted but his eyes were sharp and clear. Kyle squatted in front of him.

'How are you?' the man asked.

'How am *I*? Fine. What about you?'

Traveller looked past him to the stern where Ereko watched. 'I am fine now as well,' he said, his eyes on the Thel Akai. 'They were just dreams. Bad dreams. I see that now.' He offered Kyle a hand; Kyle took it and he squeezed. 'My thanks.'

'Thanks? For what?'

'For your patience. Your faith.'

Confused, Kyle shrugged. He moved to leave but Traveller held his hand. 'We are close now. Very close. Whatever happens do not interfere. This is between Ereko and me. Yes?'

Kyle shrugged again. 'Certainly.'

'Thank you.' He released Kyle's hand.

Still confused, Kyle headed back to his blanket. Stalker had moved to lie there, an arm over his face. 'Maybe we can all get back to sleep now,' the man grumbled. Kyle looked to Ereko who winked.

The next morning saw a coast of ruins. Sun-bleached pillars of cyclopean stones stood canted amid dunes. Jetties of stone lay submerged just visible beneath the clear cerulean surface, overgrown by coral and seaweed. Inland, the remains of an immense dome of blindingly white stone hung half collapsed at an angle. Next to

Ereko, Kyle peeled one of the local fruits. He looked to the giant who nodded. 'The Dolmans of Tien. We are close. Close to many things.'

After the ruins of the ancient city they came to where a smooth plain of hard wind-scoured sands met the coast. Here all remains of occupation ended and menhirs, or stone pillars, stood, isolated and distinct. Coming around the headland of a bay Kyle saw that the menhirs continued on in even more numbers, like a forest of stone, for as far as he could see inland. 'The Dolmans,' Ereko said. He swung the tiller for the shore.

'And K'azz?'

'From what you have told me I imagine he must be imprisoned within one of these.'

Kyle stared. Imprisoned within one of these? 'But there's thousands of them!'

'Yes.'

'How will we even know where to begin?'

Ereko tapped Kyle as lightly as he could on the back, rocking him. 'Do not despair, lad, we'll know.'

A collection of ramshackle huts occupied the beach whose ragged inhabitants stood staring, too beaten down or famished even to run. Jumping ashore, Traveller adjusted his hauberk beneath his salt-stained leathers, drew the mottled magenta blade a hand's breadth from its black wooden sheath and slammed it home. Before the man turned away Kyle glimpsed a clenched ache on his features that made him wince. Having secured the *Kite*, Ereko tried speaking with a few of the cringing fisher-folk but quickly abandoned the effort.

'They know nothing,' he told them. 'The interior, the Dolmans, are just sources of terror for them. They have turned their backs upon them.'

'What do we do then?' Kyle asked, unable to keep an edge of irritation from his voice.

His back to them, Traveller said, 'We will follow Ereko.'

Stalker, at Kyle's side, nodded silent assent. He signed to the brothers, who checked their blades then jogged off to the right and left. 'I'll bring up the rear.'

Kyle was surprised. 'Shouldn't you—'

'Walk with me, Kyle,' Traveller invited.

Smiling his reassurance to Kyle, Ereko set off ahead. Traveller handed Kyle a strip of smoked fish taken from the bundles supplied by Jhest. He took a bite and handed it back as they walked.

The pillars were built of stones carved to sit one atop the other, diminishing smoothly on six facets to a blunt tip just taller than Ereko himself. They stood some five paces apart in immensely long rows running east–west and north–south. Looking carefully Kyle could discern a curve to the east–west rows, as if they described a series of nested arcs, or vast circles. 'What is this?' he asked of Traveller.

Ereko answered, 'A cemetery, mainly. However, it served many other functions for those who built it. Ritual centre, timepiece, observatory, calendar, temple and prison.'

'Did your people build it?'

'Goddess, no, Kyle. We were not builders. No, this was raised ages ago by a people long gone. Humans, like yourself, of a close lineage.'

'You have been here before?'

The Thel Akai glanced back, a smile of amusement at his lips. 'No.'

'Then where are you leading us?'

A shrug of the massive shoulders. 'To the centre. I find that the centre is often a good place to start.'

'Do not worry,' Traveller said, also smiling at Kyle's discomfort. 'Ereko knows what he is doing. Can you say the same?'

'What do you mean?'

'I mean that I gather you intend to try to rescue or release this Prince K'azz D'Avore, commander of the Crimson Guard. Do you think that wise?'

'Wise?'

The man's dark-blue eyes watched him sideways, gauging. His beard of silver and black bristles gave him a grave, priestly look. 'Yes.'

'The Guard's become a band of murderers. Skinner has——'

'*Skinner!*' Traveller interrupted, then mastered himself with an effort.

'Yes . . . He killed one of their own right before my eyes. Only K'azz can restore the Guard to what it should be.'

Traveller's gaze was averted, but in it, and in his tight down-turned mouth, Kyle read sadness coupled with a strange amusement, as if at some grim joke known only to himself. 'Indeed. To what it should be. And what might that be, I wonder?'

'I – I don't know, but it would have to be an improvement. Only the Duke can bring Skinner to heel.'

'Can he? I wonder . . .'

Ahead, Ereko stopped, raising a hand. Coming abreast of him Kyle saw that they had reached the innermost ring of pillars. Before them lay a flat circular plaza the size of a city centre floored entirely by pale, off-white, wind-scoured gravel. The gathering shadows of the afternoon revealed that the pavement was not smooth, but that the stones were intricately set in lines. Some lines bisected the expanse, some curved, some were straight, each was marked out only in shadow by the arrangement of the stones. Indeed, from where Kyle stood, it appeared as if a forest of lines, some gently curving arcs or tight curls, others straight as sword blades, crawled about the gravelled floor of the plaza like, well, an infinity of paths. But all were marked only in shadow. The stones were all identical, all the same shade of creamy off-white. One could not tell which stone was part of which line. And even as they all stood staring in fascination, Coots and Badlands coming to stand with them, the sun moved a fraction and all the lines writhed with it like shadows jumping to new tracery.

'Incredible,' Ereko breathed. 'Would that I had known its makers. A construct worthy of the great artificer Icarium.'

'Do we cross?' Stalker asked.

'Our goal is across the way.'

'We go around,' Traveller said.

Kyle felt unaccountable relief at that pronouncement. But he also felt a deeper unease, for here was a man who surely must have no need to fear anything, yet even he was wary of this place. They slowly traced their way around half the circumference. All the while, Kyle watched the plaza: no bird landed, no leaf blew, no twig or dry weed tumbled across the expanse. All was still. It was as if the space were somehow sealed off from the normal littered, overgrown expanse of sand surrounding it.

Eventually, Ereko stopped at a pillar that, as far as Kyle could see, was no different from any other. He knelt to study its base for a time. 'This is where we must dig, I believe.'

'Dig?' Kyle asked in disbelief.

'Oh, yes.'

'But, is he . . . dead . . . ?'

The giant frowned. 'From what you have told me of these Avowed, I presume not.'

'Then . . .' Words failed Kyle. *Father Wind! To be buried alive for so long, unable to die. His mind must be gone . . .*

The brothers set to without question. They fell to their knees, began dragging armfuls of sand aside. Seeing Kyle watch, Coots commented aside, 'The sooner we're outta here the better . . .' Kyle got to his knees to help. An arm's length down they met harder

436

ground, firm tough dirt, a deeper hue of yellow, damp and cold. Out came boot-knives and short blunt eating blades. The fighting blades stayed sheathed. It came to look to Kyle as if the Thel Akai must have been right in selecting this one particular pillar out of the countless thousands, for the ground was broken, the lower matrix mixed with the sands from above. Someone had dug here before them.

They reached a flat stone barrier, roughly hewn. Feeling about the edges Badlands revealed a paving stone or lid, roughly square, about an arm's length in each direction. He pushed his fingers under one edge and, straining, lifted. The stone grated, rose and fell leaning. Badlands edged aside to reveal a small dark cavity, like a large urn. Within, arms wrapped tightly around knees tucked to its chest, was a desiccated corpse.

Badlands gestured. 'This the guy?'

'How should I know? I've never seen him!'

'He don't look so good,' Coots said, brushing sand from his beard.

'Oh, you think so? Ereko?' But the Thel Akai had turned away and was scanning the grounds. 'Ereko?'

The giant glanced down, his amber eyes churning with heavy sadness. 'I'm sorry, Kyle. I'd hoped you'd be successful. It would make . . . well, I'm sorry.'

Puzzled, Kyle peered about the surrounding dunes, his eyes narrowing. 'What's going on?'

Traveller had stepped down and crouched over the corpse. He lifted its skull to examine its ravaged face, wrenched its right hand free to examine it, then straightened.

'Well?' Kyle asked.

Traveller too was looking aside. 'It might be him,' he said, distractedly. 'Hard to say.'

'What's going on, Lady take it!'

Stalker's head snapped up and he leapt aside, facing east, a hand at his sword. The brothers crouched behind the cover of the piled sand. Traveller straight-armed Kyle to fall backwards into the pit. '*Hey!*'

Peering up over the lip, Kyle saw that a wind had arisen, a twisting dust-devil that kicked up clouds of sand. Within, darkness gathered, a ragged gap that Kyle recognized as the opening of a Warren. Greyness moiled behind the fissure. Then, with a clap, it was gone and the sands settled. An armoured man now occupied the space between two pillars. He was tall, gaunt, looking exceptionally old. His face was dark and lined, ravaged by age, and his long grey hair hung lank. His mail shirt hung to his ankles, a plain bastard sword was at his side. He approached, scanning everyone briefly. The open scorn of his gaze set Kyle's teeth on edge. The eyes fixed upon Ereko and a hungry smile twisted the old man's mouth. He called something in a language unknown to Kyle.

'Talian is a common tongue here,' Ereko answered.

The man paused, inclined his head fractionally. 'Very well . . . I had lost hope, Ereko. Yet here you are. Seems we've played the longest waiting game in history, you and I.'

'I play no games, Kallor.'

'Coy to the end, then. Come,' he gestured Ereko forward impatiently, 'let me complete my last remaining vow.'

'Let me take him,' Stalker said, straightening.

Ereko shot out a hand. 'No! No one must interfere. This is between him and me.'

'You aren't armed, Ereko,' Kyle called.

The giant turned a wistful smile to Kyle. 'It is all right. Don't worry, Kyle. This is what I have chosen.' He took a long ragged breath. 'I'll not meet you with a weapon in my hand, Kallor. That would dishonour the memory of why I am here.'

The man shrugged. 'As you will. It would make no difference, in any case.'

'Traveller, do something!' Kyle begged.

The swordsman did not answer. Kyle was shaken to see tears staining the man's face. He gripped and regripped the hilts of his sword. 'I'm sorry, Kyle,' he ground out, almost gasping. 'This was our agreement.'

'Well, I made no such Hood-damned agreement . . .' Kyle climbed from the pit, went for his tulwar. Traveller grabbed his arm, twisted it behind him. Pain flamed in his shoulder. 'Damn you!' he gasped.

'I sometimes think that is so,' the man answered in a voice almost broken in emotion.

Ereko stepped forward, arms open. 'Come then yourself, High King. I know no fear.'

Despite facing an unarmed opponent, the one named Kallor retreated. Perhaps he wondered if this were some sort of elaborate trap. Or was incapable of understanding what was unfolding. After a few steps back he scowled anew, drew his sword. 'Do not think that I will be moved by such a display.'

'Be assured that in your case I am under no such misapprehension.'

Badlands and Coots jumped atop the piled sands, weapons out. 'Hold!' Traveller barked.

'He's gonna get killed!' Badlands called.

'It is his decision.'

'No,' Kallor snarled, shifting forward. 'It is mine!'

For all his apparent age, this 'High King' moved with stunning speed. The bastard sword's long blade thrust high then was quickly withdrawn to slash down Ereko's front. The giant clenched his arms around himself and fell to his knees. Kallor thrust a second time. The blade pierced the back of Ereko's shirt then withdrew. Silent, Ereko toppled to his side.

Kyle covered his face, horrified. Yet he knew he should bear witness and so he forced himself to look up again, his eyes searing.

Kallor drew his blade across the fallen giant's clothes to clean it. He looked down for a time, musingly. 'Too easy by far. Though oddly satisfying all the same. But—' he leant forward. 'What's this – breathing still?' He shifted to stand closer to Ereko's shoulders. 'I think I will take the head.'

'No, you will not,' Traveller announced.

The High King straightened, blade rising. 'A little late for your friend, don't you think? Pangs of delayed guilt? Then again,' and the man struck a ready stance, 'please do. I came for a fight. Perhaps *you* can provide me one.'

Traveller edged forward carefully. 'I speak now because the terms of my agreement with my friend have been observed.'

'And now you wish revenge. Yes, yes. It's all so drearily predictable.'

Traveller flinched as if stabbed. He raised a hand, pointing. 'Speak not to me of vengeance, Kallor.' Kyle was shaken, hearing in Traveller's words echoes of the night before. 'The one who lies before you made me swear off any vengeance in his name and I respect his wishes. And so I say to you – go now! You have struck mortal blows. Ereko will die of them soon enough.'

Kallor drew himself up tall. His mouth curled his contempt and disbelief. 'You dare dismiss *me*! Had you the least idea of who and what I am you would run now and not stop until beneath the waves!'

Traveller eased his blade in its scabbard. 'There are those who would say the same of me . . .'

A smile broke through the man's glower and he stepped free of Ereko, sweeping his blade wide in an invitation. 'Then by all means, come. I will take both your heads.'

'Flee now, High King, or I will act.'

439

The man made a show of peering first to the right and then the left. 'I appear not to have fled.'

Traveller drew his blade. 'That is good enough for me.'

The two closed, feet shuffling slowly and carefully, blades extended. Kyle was worried, for the High King had just demonstrated amazing speed and his bastard sword was a much heavier blade than Traveller's. Not to mention that the man was more heavily armoured.

The blades touched, scraping. Both held two-handed grips. They clashed once, iron snarling. They clashed again, parrying, then Traveller was somehow before Kallor, his fists at the man's chest, blade thrust completely through to the hilt. Kyle gaped and Kallor stared as well, just as astonished. One of his mailed hands went to Traveller's grip while the other swung his weapon. Traveller snapped up a hand to clasp the man's forearm. They held like that for a time, circling and straining, Kallor's blade held high while Traveller's slim dark blade thrust straight from Kallor's back. Kyle was chilled to see no blood upon that blade.

Fury changed to consternation to disbelief on the High King's lined face as his eyes widened and his lips peeled back from grey teeth. 'Who . . . are . . . you?' he ground out. Edging his head closer, Traveller spoke, his words lost beneath Kallor's gasped breaths. The High King blanched, flinching away. '*No!* Chained One, aid me!'

A wind gathered around the two. The High King glanced behind himself where darkness blossomed. He gave Traveller a mocking smile. 'As you can see, apostate, though you have the better of me this time, I am just as difficult to overcome as you. And my Patron is very strong here. In this place, especially . . .' He threw himself backwards, sliding off Traveller's blade into the darkness of a gap that cracked open that instant. Traveller appeared ready to throw himself in, but Stalker, leaping forward, pushed him aside.

The gateway disappeared with a sharp explosion of air. Traveller stood motionless for a time, staring at where the portal had been. Beside him, it was Stalker who was gasping for breath, his face sweaty. 'I thought you weren't going to strike him,' he said. Traveller sheathed his sword. 'That was long overdue for another friend.'

Kyle ran to Ereko, threw himself down at his side. The Thel Akai was conscious, panting shallowly. Traveller knelt with Kyle. 'He is gone,' he told Ereko.

The giant gave a curt jerk of his head. 'I go too,' he said, laboured, 'to join my people. I have been a long time from them. I have missed them. Thank you, my friend.' Glancing to Kyle, he offered a weak smile. 'Do not mourn me. And do not give in to sorrow. I will always be with you, yes? This is necessary, here and now. Necessary . . .'

Traveller stood. 'Farewell.'

Kyle remained on his knees, thinking, someone ought to do something. *Why wasn't someone doing something?* The Thel Akai's skin took on a grey pallor, roughening. Before Kyle's eyes the flesh transformed to gritty grey stone. The stone cracked, crumbled and flaked. Kyle could not help but pull away, unnerved. 'What's happening?'

'He's returning to the Earth. To his mother,' Traveller said softly, reverently. 'As it should be . . .' and he scanned the horizons, hand on his sword grip.

Even as Traveller spoke Ereko's flesh crumbled to a dust that the wind pulled away. In moments nothing remained. Traveller whispered something that sounded to Kyle like a prayer.

Behind them, the brothers spoke with Stalker who then approached. 'We'd best go,' he said, his voice low.

Traveller nodded, 'Yes.' He moved to take Kyle's arm but Kyle flinched away.

'How can you just leave him here!'

'He's gone, Kyle. The wind has taken him and he will be of the earth once more. It is what he wished.'

The burning in Kyle's chest flared at those words. 'And how could you have let this happen! You could have stopped it!'

The swordsman's dark-blue eyes widened in shock, then he lowered them and turned away. 'We should go,' he said, his voice thick.

Stalker took Kyle's arm. 'Don't be angry with the man,' he mumured. But Kyle pulled his arm free.

'He might as well have killed Ereko himself!'

'Kyle – that's not . . .' but the scout could say no more. He shook his head and walked away, signalling something to his brothers.

Kyle fell to his knees next to where the giant had lain. He reached out to pass his hands over the sands. Gone. He felt as if his heart had been torn from his chest. He'd sworn never to feel this way again, yet somehow this affected him so much more than that day atop the Spur. Someone so kind and wise – how could this have happened? It was not right. Drops of tears wet the sands. His hands found a leather thong and a stone, the necklace he'd seen on Ereko. The stone had a hole through which the thong ran and was smooth and translucent, like amber. He clenched it in his fist and stood.

Feeling oddly as if he were sleepwalking, he headed back, retracing their steps. Distantly, he was aware of Coots and Badlands keeping an eye on him. Reaching the shore and the *Kite* pulled up on the strand only pained Kyle further. The Lost brothers worked together with Traveller to ready it. Kyle sat and watched them, the ocean and the steady surf. An old man came walking up the beach from the direction of the village. 'Greetings,' he called in Talian.

Kyle looked to Traveller who merely returned to his work. Shrugging, Kyle faced the man. 'Yes? You speak Talian?'

'Yes. I'm of Gris. Was shipwrecked here years ago.' His long, straight, greying hair whipped in the off-shore wind. His beard and moustache were a startling white against his lean, sun-darkened features. He wore the ragged, bleached remains of a shirt, leather vest and trousers. His feet were bare and cracked.

'And?'

The man's eyes narrowed to slits and he glanced away. 'Was hoping you'd offer a berth – passage anywhere but here.'

'I don't think so. We're not really—'

'I know these waters well. I could guide you through them. Been fishing here for years. Where are you headed?'

Kyle was at a loss. Yes, where were they headed? He looked to Traveller; the man's back was turned as he was stowing the bundles and refilled water casks. 'Quon Tali,' the man finally said.

'Quon! Then please, Lady's Mercy! You must take me.'

Kyle glanced sharply to the man – *Lady's Mercy?* But no, why read anything into that. No doubt it was a common enough Talian oath. 'It's not really for me to say . . .' he looked again, a little sullenly, to Traveller.

The man was coiling rope. His back to them, he hung his head then raised it as if entreating the sky. 'It's your decision, Kyle.'

'Then I suppose so. What's your name?'

'Jan.'

Kyle made the introductions. The Lost brothers greeted the man but Traveller did not turn around. 'We should catch the night tide,' was all he said.

Jan gestured to the village. 'I'll just get some supplies.'

'Be quick about it,' Traveller called after him.

They had the *Kite* out in the shallows when Jan returned burdened by skins of water, bundles of fruits and pale root tubers. Pushing his way out into the surf he tossed the goods over the side then climbed in. Stalker yielded the tiller. Kyle and the brothers handled the sail. Traveller sat at the bow, arms crossed over his knees. Jan turned them north.

After a time, as the stars came out, Kyle sat against the side and set his chin on the gunwale. He stared back at the dark line on the horizon that was the coast of Jacaruku. His suggestion to come to the Dolmans had been a disaster for them. K'azz dead or gone. Ereko slain. And, Kyle now worried, he may have insulted Traveller beyond forgiveness with his words back at the Dolmans. He saw that now. But he'd been so *angry*. He'd given no thought to the fact that the man had known Ereko far longer than he. And now Traveller was taking them to Quon – the very destination of the Guard. Perhaps he meant to hand Kyle over to them. It suddenly occurred to him that Traveller might actually blame him for his friend's death; if he hadn't suggested this destination of Jacuruku out of all possible headings then Ereko would still be alive. He glanced to the bow. The man was awake, brooding, it seemed to Kyle. His eyes were glittering in the dark, fixed on the seemingly oblivious Jan at the tiller, whose gaze held just as steady to the north-east horizon.

* * *

For Toc the assault began with a burgeoning roar that shook the hooves and flesh of his mount before it struck his gut. To the south, what seemed the entire horizon lit up behind the Outer Round curtain wall as incendiaries flew tall arcs in both directions over the Inner Round walls: inward from Talian catapults and outward from Hengan onagers. Remnants of the Talian legion that had participated in the original assault watched from the pickets alongside the gathered camp followers and support staff of armourers, cooks, drovers, washerwomen, prostitutes and trooper's wives and their children.

Beyond the encampment bands of Seti roved the fitfully lit hill-sides, chanting warsongs, waving lances, bellowing their encouragement and cursing the Hengans. Toc longed to be in the thick of things with Choss, though well could he imagine the horror of it: frontal escalades were always high in body counts. Pure naked ferocity versus ferocity.

As the assault dragged on into the night, the constant low roar not abating, up out of the night came the White Jackal shaman, Imotan, and his bodyguard to Toc and his staff. The shaman urged his mount to Toc's side. A simple leather band secured the old man's grey hair and his leathers were mud-spattered. Instead of a lance he carried a short baton tufted in white fur held tight across his chest. The old man's eyes blazed bright, either in excitement or alarm, Toc wasn't sure. 'What is it?'

'You must get all your people inside,' Imotan called.

'Why? A sortie?'

'No. Something is coming. For you, something terrible. Yet for us, a prophecy fulfilled.'

Toc stared his confusion. Was the man mad? 'What do you mean?'

'Ryllandaras is coming. I feel him. I can almost smell his breath.'

'*Ryllandaras?*' The man must be mad. It was impossible. He'd been imprisoned long ago. 'No. You must be mistaken.'

Imotan flinched away, glowering. 'Do not insult me, Malazan.' He sawed his mount around. 'Very well. I have done my part. Ignore me and die.' The White Jackal shaman stormed off into the night surrounded by his bodyguard.

Toc watched him go then straightened up tall in his saddle, peering to the left and right, squinting at the lines. Surely the old man would not have come to him unless he was certain. But still, Ryllandaras, after all this time? And why now?

'Rider!' he called.

One of his staff urged his mount alongside. 'Sir?'

'Go to Urko's command. Tell them the Seti warn of a dangerous presence out in the night.'

'Sir.' The messenger kicked his mount and rode off.

'Captain Moss?'

'Sir?'

'Take a troop and do a circuit of the perimeter. Warn the pickets to be sharp.'

'Aye, sir.' The captain saluted and reined his mount away.

There. But had he done all he could? Should he warn Choss? No, the man had more than enough to handle, electing to direct the assault from the front. He would wait to see if anything came of this – on the face of it – utterly outrageous claim.

It was a full hour later, close to midnight, when a woman in a dress torn and stained dark came walking out of camp. She headed straight to Toc, as silent as a ghost, her eyes empty, hands held out before her dark and wet. His men shouted, pointing. Toc stared. He could not speak; would not believe. He slid from his mount and took her hands sticky with blood. '*Where!*' he shouted. '*Tell me where!*' She stared up at him, uncomprehending, her brow clenched in confusion.

'They are dead,' she told him. 'Everyone is dead.'

'*Where, damn you!*'

'By the creek.'

'Blow to arms,' he yelled. 'Form square. Escort all civilians behind the walls!'

Far to the back of camp, screams sounded – not human – the shrill shrieks of terrified dying horses. Toc straightened. *Gods preserve all of us.* He remembered. He remembered Ryllandaras. He'd been there. Not even Dassem could kill him. They had nothing. Nothing to counter the Curse of Quon, eater of men. The man-jackal, brother of Trake, god of war.

* * *

Escorted by a bodyguard of Malazan regulars, Storo climbed the Inner Round wall where Hurl waited. His surcoat was rent, blood smeared his gauntlets and his face glistened with sweat and soot. 'This had better be good,' he warned, his voice hoarse from shouting commands. 'We're barely hanging on out there. We'd be overrun if it weren't for those three brothers. They're a right horror, they are.'

Hurl said nothing, her eyes avoiding his. Storo drew breath to speak but something in the timbre of the noise here stopped him; it was different from the tumult elsewhere: rather than rage, screams sounded alongside shouts of panic. And no escalade persisted here. He drew off his helmet, pulled back his mail hood revealing smeared blood where a blow had struck. 'What is it?'

Hurl raised her chin to the parapet where, opposite, the north gate of the Outer Round wall stood. 'It's begun.'

Storo climbed the parapet. A milling mass of humanity. Torches waved, Talian soldiers shouted and fought to maintain lines facing the half-closed North Plains Gate. Civilians crammed the portal, fought to pass the soldiers, screaming, pale hands grasping at armour. Nearby in the press, one of the few mounted figures gestured, shouting orders, his short grey hair and moustache bright in the gloom. He held a black recurve bow in one hand, emphasizing his orders with it.

'*Gods*,' Storo blurted as if gut-punched. 'Toc. Toc himself.' He glanced to Hurl. 'Have you any bowmen here?'

'No.'

'Huh! The man's luck still holds.' He stepped down, faced Hurl squarely. 'Wait 'til they're clear then do it.'

'Must we?'

'Yes, dammit! Otherwise we're lost.'

'They'll be slaughtered. Soldiers and civilians alike.'

Storo pulled up his mail hood. 'Then they should've stayed home. As for the civilians, they were warned. I have to go. May the Lady favour you.'

'And you.'

Storo tramped back down the stairs. Hurl remained with her sergeant and squads of regulars guarding this section of the curtain wall. While she watched, passage was made for the clamouring civilians. The Talians formed lines of crossbowmen facing the gate as others struggled to close it. The last man staggering through was memorable, his dark surcoat and mail coat hanging in tatters, the remains of a shattered helmet swinging from his neck, twin sabres in his hands. Had he actually survived a mêlée with the man-eater? She'd probably never know. The second wing of the gate was levered shut and iron crossbars frantically lowered into place. Hurl turned to Sergeant Banath. 'I want you down there.'

He saluted, jogged down the stairs. Along the Outer Wall Talian soldiers climbed to the parapets, scanned down beyond. Hands pointed, alarm was raised, crossbows fired. Hurl waited until the civilians were far clear of the gate then went to the inner lip of the stone walk. She peered down to torches lighting a crew, Sergeant Banath with them, in a trench dug tight against the wall. She looked to her right and left up and down the wall. 'Brace yourselves!' she shouted to the men. She raised a hand, thinking, with this hand I doom more men and women than I can imagine. What has happened to me that I could do such a thing? Was it Shaky's death? The attack of Fat Kepten's men? What did she care if Heng fell? Not at all, to tell the truth. No, the mean selfish fact of it was that she wanted to live and if the city fell she'd no doubt be executed.

She dropped her hand and threw herself down, covering her head. Below her, she could imagine a sledge being swung to bash a pipe that ran out underground across the entire breadth of the Outer Round to a stash of carefully ordered and bound Moranth munitions snug against the left gate jamb. There its pointed end would crack a sharper nestled within four cussors. The resultant explosion—

A shockwave kicked the breath from her. The thunderous blast of the munitions was lost on her deafened ears. A bloated roaring filled her head. Tiny rocks peppered her back. Blinking, shaking her head, she climbed to her feet. Smoke obscured the gates. Down in the Outer Round, strewn in wreckage, men and women were picking themselves up. Wounded staggered from the smoke carrying appalling wounds and Hurl's stomach churned. She'd known that not everyone had been far enough away, but most had – or so she told herself. Nearby buildings burned in ruins. And through the smoke *something* ran. She couldn't be sure; it had been too fast. Just a glimpse of paleness, but huge, smooth and terrifyingly fluid. Then it was gone.

She slumped down against the parapet. It was done. Now she too shared Quon's Curse. The blood it would spill from this night forward would now also steep her. She covered her face and great shuddering sobs shook her.

The report of the explosion startled Toc's mount and it sidestepped into a stall, became tangled in ropes and boxes, tripped and fell. He hit the cobbled road hard, losing his breath. The press around him closed in, hands raised him. Shouts and screams continued, only doubled now by the blast. Everyone was asking what had happened; Toc ignored them. He pushed to where his mount thrashed screaming among the shattered slats of the stall, leg broken. He drew his sword – poor animal – one of his favourites, but he couldn't leave it like this.

The instant the report of the eruption reached him he knew what had happened. They'd blown the outer gate. The fierce calculated cruelty of the plan left him awed. Enfilade. Here they were drawn in and trapped between high walls. Death hunting them. By morning the Outer Round would be one long slaughterhouse as Ryllandaras slaked a near century of blood thirst. He had to get to Choss. He raised his sword high in both hands and swung.

Picking up his bow he straightened, shouted, 'Get indoors, hide. Defend yourselves.'

Soldiers looked to him and the pleading in their eyes clawed at his conscience. He wanted to offer reassuring words but he had none. The most despairing of the men and women did not even bother searching out his gaze for commands. He gathered himself, set one tip of his horn recurve bow to the cobbles and, leaning all his weight upon it, strung it in one quick motion. 'Form square here for a fighting retreat. Spears, lances, poleaxes, anything you can find on the outside. Crossbowmen and archers within.'

A civilian woman shrieked at him, '*What of us!*'

'And get these people off the street!'

A nearby soldier, a lieutenant by his arm-torc, snapped a salute. 'You heard the commander! Set to. Form up!'

'Slow retreat, lieutenant,' Toc repeated. 'I have to find the commander.'

'Aye, sir. Oponn with you, sir.'

Toc answered the man's salute and jogged up the street.

Burning buildings near the Inner Round wall lit the night. Toc met soldiers assembling hasty barricades on the main thoroughfare. He almost ordered them to abandon the effort but decided not to add to the confusion and chaos of the night. Yet it was a forlorn hope: the beast would easily sidestep any such position. Soldiers directed him to the rooftop of a sturdy brick warehouse. Here he found Choss, surrounded by staff.

'Thank Beru!' the big man exploded upon spotting him. 'What in the Chained One's name is going on out there? I'm getting all kinds of outrageous reports.'

'It's Ryllandaras returned, beyond a doubt. And we're pressed in here with him.'

Choss's horrified stare was the worst vision yet for Toc that night. A wind, pulled up by all the fires, blew the commander's great mane of hair across his face. He spat to the roof. 'So they've been saying. Well, you'd know, Toc.' He looked to the sections of curtain wall visible from this position, drew in a deep breath, held it, then released it in a long slow exhalation of regret. 'We captured a tower, Toc,' he said, wistful. 'We were so close. Now I have to turn around and come up with a way to salvage this.'

Screams of utter terror pulled their gazes aside to the maze of streets and lanes. Toc's back crawled at the hopelessness of those cries. Ryllandaras was murdering their soldiers – and he would not stop. Toc studied Choss. The man's regard had returned to the distant battlements where figures could be seen firing down, dropping torches. Toc was silent, thinking of how closely this man had worked with that great general, Dujek, and how it was he who saw the army through the shock of Y'Ghatan where Dassem fell. 'If I remember rightly,' Choss said, his gaze narrowed, 'his feud is with Heng. It's Heng he hates. You could say we're just in the way.' The hazel eyes shifted to Toc, calculating. 'Is that not so?'

'I think you could say that.'

'All right then. If this Storo wants to play for all the stakes then we'll match his roll.' He turned to a messenger, 'Bring up all the munitions! Tell the sappers, every single last secret cache upon pain of death! Double-time.'

'Aye, sir.'

Toc watched as Choss returned to studying the walls. What did he intend? Toc had spent most of his time with the cavalry and so didn't know the man as well as he would like. But munitions? Would it work? Every trap and trick known had been tried on the man-beast and none had succeeded. The creature's wariness and cunning were legendary. Still, munitions ought to be new to the cursed fiend.

*

Hurl found Storo at a stair-tower close by the Inner Round Gate. 'They're retreating to the Gate of the Dawn,' she told him. 'Abandoning the assault.'

He wiped a bundled handful of his surcoat across his face. 'Looks like. Can't fight *him* and us at the same time.'

'What do you think they'll do?'

'Withdraw. Redeploy to face Laseen. Get off the plains as fast as Oponn will allow.'

Yells and firing at the Inner Round Gate drew Hurl's attention. She peered out to see that the assault continued there. Bowmen behind mantlets and among the ruins of the burnt buildings close by exchanged fire with their crossbowmen. Ladders lay broken like straw on the road amid bodies, some burning. 'What's going on there?'

'Keeping up appearances. They're running sappers up against the gates, to no use.'

'Why? Are they digging?'

'Yes. But the foundations go down far too deep. You know that.'

Hurl's chest tightened with an inchoate dread. 'I don't like it, Storo. Clear them off.'

'Fast as we can.' He turned to a messenger. 'Tell them to bring up more stones.'

'Aye.'

Storo pulled his helmet off, sighed his exhaustion and obvious unshielded relief. 'I thought they really—'

A blast rocked their footing, throwing them both down. Hurl smashed her head to the stone floor. 'Hood preserve us!' Storo gasped. Together they leapt to the east arch. Hurl held her head and fought back a darkness gathering at the edges of her vision. Smoke and dust obscured the gate but from the strength of the eruption Hurl knew it was shattered. Storo's eyes met hers. Her legs buckled and he reached out quickly to support her. He cupped her head then brought his hand away wet with blood. Hurl tried to say what she now knew but there was no need; she saw it in Storo's stricken gaze.

Ryllandaras was now their curse.

Hurl awoke to screams and a guttural snarled bellowing that raised the hair at her neck and shook the stones beneath her back. She lay in a room crowded with many other wounded. Groans and cursing along with the tang of blood and spilt bile assaulted her on all sides. She pushed herself up, dizzy, her head throbbing as if a spike were being hammered into it. Her munitions bag still hung from her side.

She made her way to the door, stepping carefully over wounded, some of whom helped steady her. At the door a guard watched the street, crossbow raised. Hengan urban cohorts ran past the opening, weapons abandoned.

It was still night. The fitful light from fires lit the street. Hurl peeked out to see that she occupied a guardhouse hard up by the blown gate. A shuffling, yelling wall of men armed with spears and poleaxes fought something. A thing that when it reared back rose fully three times their height. It was covered in pale creamy-white fur with darker streaks down its back in grey and dirty yellow. A great maw, black-lipped, twisted from enormous canines. Carmine eyes as dark as heart-blood glared hotly and blood stained its entire front. It punched out with unnaturally long cabled arms ending in black talons to claw men and toss them aside like handfuls of straw.

A sound like a whimper brought Hurl's gaze around; the guard met her gaze. Terror and uncomprehending despair filled the man's wide staring eyes. 'It is *he*,' he gasped. 'The man-eater.' After a last look of utter hopelessness, the guard threw down his crossbow and ran.

Hurl reached down to gently take up the weapon. Yes, it was he. The creature some named a God, brother to an ascending God. Some even claimed him to be a last remnant of those ancient primordial terrors who hunted humanity's ancestors so long ago out beyond the firelight. Hurl did not know; she knew only that he had sworn to level Heng, and that should he get within he would do so. And the Talians would lay claim to what was left with the sunrise.

She pushed her way out on to the rubble-strewn street, pulled the bolt from the weapon. She slid round the crowd to begin climbing the heaped fallen stones to one side of the blasted opening. At times dizziness took her and she paused on all fours, breathing heavily. She reached a vantage on the piled stones and spread her booted feet for stability. She could now see that one soldier led the defence: he wore a long coat of armour and a visored helm, and wielded twinned longswords. Rell. The monster racked at him but he slipped every swing and the blades flicked inward, slashing so fast only the reflected torchlight marked their movement. The beast's roar of rage and pain shook the stones beneath Hurl's feet. From the bag at her side she took a bolt armed with a sharper, slotted it and punched the air. Warning shouts sounded below. Grunting her effort, she raised the weapon, steadied it. She marked the littered ground just behind the beast, fired. The kick knocked her backwards from her feet. An instant later an explosion spat stones against her entire

450

front. She lay among the broken smoking rocks until roused by renewed roaring that was a constant thunder snarl of rage. Using her elbows and knees she pulled herself up to a sitting position. Men still faced the fiend but it had pulled down or swept aside most. Blood now flecked the pelt on its back. It dodged right and left, blurringly quick, but always the same fighter forestalled it, twin swords raised. Hurl was hardly conscious but even she could sense that something miraculous was occurring – no man ought to be doing what Rell was managing. Through the blown gate she saw Talian troops standing still, watching, mouths open. They held bows and crossbows loose at their sides as if it were inconceivable to interfere in the duel. Ryllandaras's wild swings, ducked or slipped by Rell, knocked the very stone blocks of the wall flying – stones heavier than any man could lift. Spittle flew as the beast threw back its head in such a bellowing eruption of blind incandescent rage that more stones were torn from the fractured walls and Hurl cried, attempting to cover her ears.

Through eyes slitted and blurred, she saw that Rell alone now faced the man-beast. He struck a guard position, one slim blade low, the other high above his head, point down. Ryllandaras' jaws worked, taloned bloodied hands gestured. Was it speaking to him? The thunder in Hurl's ears deadened them to all sounds. A sudden leap inward made her flinch, so quick was it, yet Rell met it in a flurry of counter-attacks that slashed arms, torso and legs. Now Hurl was amazed by the man-beast: how could any living thing absorb such punishment? Was it truly something of a god itself – akin to Trake? Was Rell doomed to tire, to slow and fail?

Rousing herself, she fought to cock the crossbow, gave it up as futile. She threw it down, drew another bolt from her satchel, pulled the sharper from its mount. With it held high in one fist she struggled to climb down the rubble slope closer to the beast. Now Rell was shouting something, pointing a blade. Hurl looked up to meet the lambent flame-red eyes of the beast watching her. The eyes tracked the munition in her hand. A leg moved as it stepped toward her – *Gods, what a stride!* An arm stretched out, talons closing – *what reach!*

Hurl threw at its feet, falling flat.

Some unknown time later she came to as hands pulled her, stones scraped along gouging her back. She tried to cry out, couldn't. Soldiers bent over her; it was still night. The clash of fighting still nearby. Someone took her shoulderbag, another cupped her head on

451

his lap. She looked up into the worried face of Fallow, the squad healer. 'I'm getting to be a regular,' she chuckled.

'You and your commander. Now quiet.'

'Storo? What . . . ?'

'Quiet. Relax.' He closed her eyes with his palm and that was the last she knew.

Toc and Choss remained behind at the Gate of the Dawn with a contingent of seventy spearmen backed up by fifty archers and crossbowmen. They waited until the last of their elements had withdrawn, then their men pulled the gates shut behind them. Smoke, dust and exhaustion made Toc's eyes gritty and he pressed his fingers into them. As it was after every battle his mouth was as dry as dust and held an iron tinge of – and he could admit it – terror. He spat into the charred remains of a building next to the road burned by the defenders to deny them the wood for siege engines. When he turned from the gate dawn's light struck his gaze and he raised a hand to blot it out. Horsemen were galloping up from the east. Choss and he went to meet them.

'Felicitations from Commander Urko!' the leader announced, a fat ginger-haired Falaran in bronze scale armour. 'I am to report that as per your intelligence Urko has begun excavation of ramparts and is raising a palisade to fortify his position.'

Choss nodded. 'Thank you, ah . . .'

'Captain Tonley.'

'My thanks, Captain Tonley. Tell him our divisions will redeploy to join him by tonight.'

'Very good, Commander.'

While they spoke, spare horses had been brought up led by the bloodied Captain Moss. Toc took one, nodding his thanks. Choss mounted as well. Captain Tonley leaned forward on his saddle. 'Ah, tell me, sirs . . . what's this I hear of a great giant beastie?'

Toc, Choss and Moss exchanged exhausted glances. 'It's the truth,' Choss said flatly.

Captain Tonley shook his head, amazed. 'You Quon Talians seem fearful of everything. First a band of hireswords and now a beastie. How you ever got the better of us I'll never know.'

Choss stared at the man. A grin pulled at his lips and he chuckled, then laughed outright. 'It's a mystery, Captain. You may report back.'

A sloppy salute. 'Very good, Commander. Let's go, boys. No drink to be had here.' The troop stormed off. Toc turned to Choss.

'So, now Laseen . . . And what of the Crimson Guard?'

'We'll make them an offer. They want the Empire broken, don't they?'

'And Heng?'

'Heng and Ryllandaras can bugger each other. What of your Seti?'

Toc scanned the empty hillsides. 'I don't know. I'll have to speak with them. Imotan's spent all his life praying for his patron God and now that he's come he's probably terrified.'

Choss grunted his scepticism. 'Well, go. We still need them.'

'Aye.'

They rode back to camp, silent for a time. 'That soldier,' Toc finally said, 'who faced Ryllandaras. Have you ever seen the like?'

'Dassem drove him off as well,' Choss said. 'But he was favoured by Hood.'

'I've seen it,' Moss said.

Toc and Choss glanced to the captain. He shifted uncomfortably in his saddle, touched the raw livid tear across his face. 'Well, not seen exactly. Had it described to me by someone who had seen it in Genabackis. That style of fighting. That fellow, he's Seguleh.'

'Seguleh?' Choss repeated in wonder. 'I've heard the name. What's he doing here?'

'Storo's company was stationed in Genabackis,' Moss said.

Toc studied his captain sidelong. 'You know a lot about this Storo . . .'

Moss rubbed his gouged nose, wincing. 'Ah, yes, sir. Gathering intelligence. Know your enemy, and such.'

'In which case, captain,' Toc said. 'Would you like to go on a mission to the Crimson Guard? We have a proposal for them.'

The man smiled. The talon slash across his face cracked and fresh blood welled up. 'Yes, sir. It would be a privilege.'

Though exhausted, his joints aflame with pain, Toc mounted a fresh horse that morning and set out alone to track down the Seti. He found their camp deserted, but here he also found unusual tracks. Something had visited the camp before him. Like wolf tracks, they were, except far larger, more the size of the largest bear track. And of an enormous breadth of gait. He knew this man-beast Ryllandaras could cover ground faster even than a horse. Though it was common lore that the creature hunted only at night, Toc suddenly felt very exposed out all alone on the plains. A part of him wondered if that was just a detail of atmosphere the jongleurs had tossed into the songs they recited of him. He could just hear Kellanved snarl: *never mind what you imagine to be the case, what do you know?* Not one to let reputations or legends stand in his way, was he. After all, he trapped the fiend, didn't he? And how did he manage that? A piece of information perhaps relegated to some archive somewhere is suddenly now not so trivial any longer. Knowing how wild Kellanved had been back then, he'd probably used himself as bait.

Towards noon, as he crossed a shallow valley, horsemen appeared in small bands all around him and moved in. He stopped to await them, crossed his arms on the high cantle of his saddle. They circled him from a distance until one broke through and closed. He was a burly fellow, wearing only deerskin trousers, a thick leather vest and wide leather vambraces. His curly hair was shot with grey, as was his matted chest hair. He looked Toc up and down in open evaluation. 'You are Toc the Elder,' he said in Talian.

'And you are the Wildman of the Plains.'

A nod. 'You ride to speak with Imotan. I think you shouldn't go.'

'May I ask why?'

'He has his white-haired God now. What need does he have for you?'

'There's a lot of history between us. We've exchanged many vows.'

'Between you and the Seti, yes. Not him.'

Toc flexed his back to ease its nagging pain. He studied the man before him: sword- and knife-scarred, speaks Talian fluently. An Imperial veteran, perhaps a noncommissioned officer. 'What of you?' he asked. 'You might not accept Imotan's authority but we could use you and your warriors to throw off the Empire just the same.'

The man bared his sharp yellow teeth. 'Do not insult me. Empire, League. It's all the same.'

'Not at all . . . You and others would be nearly independent.'

'Empty promises at best. Lies at worst. We've heard all that before.'

'You should consider my offer carefully, veteran. We are set to defeat Laseen. She is so short of proper troops she's desperate. I've heard she's even dragooned all the old veterans on Malaz to bolster her numbers.'

The old Seti veteran grew still. His tight disapproving frown vanished. 'What was that?'

Toc shrugged, puzzled. 'I just said that she'd sent out the call to gather up everyone she can, even from Malaz.'

The Wildman tightened his reins. 'I'm going now. I will tell you one more time, Toc – do not pursue this allegiance.' He clucked his mount into motion and signed his warriors to follow. They thundered away.

Toc sat still for a time, watching them while they rode from sight. Something. Something had just happened there, but exactly what it could have been, he had no idea. Shaking his head, he urged his horse on.

He rode through most of the rest of the day before catching any sign beyond empty horse tracks. Dust rose to the north-east. He kicked his mount to pick up his pace a touch. He was just becoming worried about being caught out in the dark when he topped a gentle grassed rise to see below a horde of mounted warriors circling in a slow churning gyre, calling war chants in crowded rings around tents of the shamans. The clouds of yellow dust they raised plumed into the now darkening sky. He approached and waited but the young bloods ignored him. Most of the youths carried white hair fetishes on their lances, around their arms or in their hair. Eventually, perhaps at a command from within, grudging space was allowed for Toc's mount to push through.

In past the flank-to-flank pressing rings of hundreds of horsemen the atamans were sitting before the central tent, that of Imotan, the White Jackal shaman. Toc bowed and Imotan gestured him forward, patting the ground next to him. He sat and greeted the atamans while Imotan eyed him with a steady, weighing gaze. Toc met it, waiting. 'I am sorry for your dead, Toc,' the shaman finally said.

'My thanks. It is him, then? The very one named Ryllandaras?'

Imotan used a short eating knife to cut meat from a haunch. 'Yes, it is he. We've hoped and prayed for generations and now he is returned to us.'

'Hoped? You hoped? If it is him, who do you think he'll turn to once we're gone?'

'That is our concern, Malazan. We lived with him long before you ever came.'

'We rid you of a predator.'

'You interfered.'

'We freed you!'

The old man stabbed the knife into the ground between them. '*Freed us!* Can you free a man from himself? A people from themselves?' Taking a long hard breath to master himself he turned to the platter of food and gathered a handful of grapes. He laughed and shook his head at some thought that struck him. 'Liss's curse! We *are* a lost people, wandering lost. Lost from ourselves. But now our way has returned to us.'

'I see no true path.'

'You are not Seti.' The shaman was silent for a time. He appeared troubled while he pulled and studied the blade of his knife. 'Toc the Elder,' he began carefully, 'we honour you for what we have accomplished together in the past, but you should not have come.'

'The old agreements still stand, Imotan.'

'Do they?' The shaman glanced aside to Hipal, the ferret shaman, who grinned, evilly, Toc thought, then he scanned a circuit of the men and women sitting in a circle before him. Many glanced away when his gaze reached them. Toc was struck by how much had changed in one night. Before, at the councils, Toc spoke with the atamans, the warrior society warchiefs and tribal Assembly chiefs, while Imotan and Hipal sat relegated to the rear. Now, though, Imotan occupied the seat of honour while the atamans sat at his feet, looking like no more than supplicants.

Having reviewed his council, Imotan sighed, thrust his knife into his sash. 'What is it you ask, Toc?'

'This coming battle will be the final arbiter of all. After it, you may consider all agreements fulfilled, all obligations met. It is the last and final request I shall make of you.'

The White Jackal shaman had nodded through Toc's statement. He held his thickly-veined hands up open. 'So be it. We will be there. Now, for obvious reasons I suggest you spend the night here in our encampment. You will be safe with us. Tomorrow you may join your command.'

Toc bowed. 'I thank you, Imotan of the White Jackal.'

* * *

Nait threw another handful of dried dung on to the fire and sat back in disgust. 'I'm tellin' you guys, if he says "clozup" one more time I'm gonna knife the old fart.'

Least let out his own loud fart while Honey pointed into the night. 'You're welcome to it – he's over that ways.'

'That's offensive,' Hands commented to Least who looked abashed. Lim Tal, the Kanese ex-bodyguard, undid a clasp in her hair allowing its full black shimmering length to fall down past her shoulder to her shirt front. Nait, who looked about to say something, appeared to have forgotten what that was and stared along with everyone except Heuk, the company mage, who lay snoring wrapped around a brown earthenware jug. Hands watched as well, sighing. 'I wish mine would do that.'

456

Brushing her hair, Lim smiled, flexed her bare bicep. 'I wish I had your arms.'

'Listen,' Nait called across the fire, 'you two wanna compare any more body parts I got me a nice big ol' blanket over here . . .'

'Should we bring him naked to the line tomorrow?' Lim asked of Hands. 'Push him out front?'

Hands snorted – either at the image or at the idea of Nait at the front of anything. 'They might die laughing . . .'

'Tomorrow?' Nait asked, leaning forward. 'You think maybe it's tomorrow? You heard that?'

Lim shrugged. 'Tomorrow or the next.'

'I hear there's a demon out there who will eat us all,' Least said.

Beside him, Honey stared. 'Where'd you hear that?'

Least pointed to the fetishes of wood and bone tied in his hair.

'No – really?'

A sombre nod.

'G'wan! No! I heard it from a guy in line.'

Least's eyes widened. 'They speak to other people?'

A youth in an oversized studded leather hauberk came out of the night and squatted at the fire, warming his hands. He carried large canvas bags at each side hung from leather straps crossed over his neck. A crossbow hung ungainly on his back and a wooden-handled dirk was thrust through his belt. 'You got any food?' he asked them.

'Who in the Abyss are you?' Nait demanded. The youth looked confused. 'Listen, kid. This fire's for sergeants only, right? Bugger off.'

The boy straightened, sneering, pointed to Nait. 'You're no sergeant.'

All except Nait laughed. Honey handed over a cut of hardbread. 'You tell him, kid.' The youth snatched the bread and ran into the night.

'Too full of themselves, they are,' Nait grumbled, and he took a stick from the fire to examine the blackened, shrivelled thing at its end. He pinched it in his fingers, frowning.

'I'd say it's done,' Least offered.

'I'd say we're all done,' Nait said without looking up. At the long silence following that he raised his eyes. 'C'mon – you all got ears, eyes. I heard what they were sayin' in Cawn.' He pointed to the darkness. 'They got ten thousand Moranth Gold! They got twenty thousand Falaran infantry – plus the Talians! Plus the Seti!' He threw down the stick. 'An' what have we got? A horde of civilians is all, maybe ten thousand real soldiers?'

'That horde beat the Guard,' Hands said, her voice low and controlled. 'I heard seven Avowed died. Those Gold come marching against us and they'll find themselves so full of quarrels they won't be able to fall over.'

'The Seti will sweep those amateurs from the field.'

'They're so hungry out there they'll be happy to see all those Seti horses.'

'They'll—'

'Enough!' Honey bawled. 'Hooded One take you both! Quit bickering like you're already married. We already got us two High Fists.'

Snorting, Hands dismissed Nait with a wave; Nait chuckled at Honey's comment. 'Two,' he mocked. He picked up the stick and dusted off the burnt wrinkled thing at its end.

'Where'd you get that anyway?' Least asked.

'Found it dead.'

'You ever been outside a town?'

Nait took a test nibble at the thing, looked to Least, puzzled. 'No, why?'

Heuk suddenly jerked upright, making everyone flinch. His rheumy bloodshot eyes rolled, scanning the dark. 'Something's happening,' he croaked.

Nait threw a handful of dung at the man. 'Not again! All the time, old man. Things happen all the time.'

'He's here. I can taste his lust and hunger. All our blood couldn't slake it.'

Everyone stared. Leaning over, Nait cuffed the man. 'Will you cut it out! You're giving everyone the willies.'

Heuk raised the earthenware jug, gulped down a mouthful of its dark contents. He spilled much over his beard and dirty robes. Honey waved a hand in front of his nose. 'Faugh, old man. What's in there?'

'Blood and bravery.'

Shouts suddenly sounded from the dark. Everyone stilled. The shouts took on a panicked note, followed shortly after by the beginnings of a scream suddenly cut short. Hands jumped to her feet. 'What in the Abyss was that?' She scanned the surrounding fields, dotted in campfires. 'North, I think.' She picked up her sword and belt. 'C'mon!'

Everyone, even Heuk, climbed to their feet. 'Anyone have a torch or a lamp or anything?' Lim asked. Shrugs all around. 'Great. Just great.' She picked up her longsword and helmet and jogged after Hands who had not waited.

Least picked up a piece of burning bhederin dung. 'I got this . . .' he called after Lim.

It was chaos out on the dark shadowed slopes of tall, wind-lashed grasses. Men and women shouted, ran together, split up. Crossbow bolts flew, snapping overhead, making Nait duck. Another scream shattered the night in the distance. Nait ran into Honey, who was shaking a crossbowman by the shirt. 'No shooting, Hood take it!' He threw the man aide. 'Almost skewered me . . .'

'What is it? An attack?'

'Don't know. Hope not, 'cause we're beat already.'

Torches brightened the night to the north. A bellowing voice sounded across the hillside, '*Assemble! Asssemmbblle!* Form up! Close! *Close up!*'

Nait's shoulders slumped. 'Oh, Gods Below. I don't believe it.'

Honey slapped his back. 'C'mon – he's got the right idea.' He jogged off. After peering about at the dark, Nait followed.

The formation was a broad swelling rectangle swallowing all it met; swordsmen held torches at its edges, crossbowmen behind. The master sergeant was there, and commander Braven Tooth, whom Nait had heard called a walking enraged hairball, a description with which he was inclined to agree. Also keeping order were Hands, Lim and the other sergeants.

After marching for a time, being chivvied into ranks with cuffs and kicks, orders sounded from the front to halt and to hold ranks. Nait pushed his way to the front. Here the stink of spilled bowels, vomit and blood almost choked off his breath – all that plus another reek like that of some kind of sick animal. It reminded him of the village butcher's, only this time instead of goat and pig guts and portions, it was human torsos, limbs and smears of viscera. Master Sergeant Temp and Braven Tooth were huddled over one corpse, torches held high. Both either slept in mail coats or had had the time or where-withal to pull them on.

'Looks like Soletaken, don't it?' Braven Tooth said, his guttural voice kept low.

'He could be. Not all are known.' The master sergeant raised his head, calling, 'Any cadre mages?'

Shortly later Heuk either pushed his way or was pushed to the front. The old man took one look at the splayed corpses and strewn entrails and fell to his knees and hands vomiting up great gouts of dark fluids.

'I feel so much safer now,' Honey commented to no one in particular.

'That thing's a demon!' Nait blurted out.

Both the master sergeant and Braven Tooth winced, glaring. 'Will you stop your gob, soldier,' Braven Tooth grated.

'He's no demon,' Master Sergeant Temp announced loudly to the crowd.

'How in the Abyss would you know?' Nait demanded.

The master sergeant crossed to Nait, peered up at him – he was a very squat, but very wide, man. ''Cause demons don't smell like that.' He walked off to study the trail of slaughter. Braven Tooth clenched a hand on Nait's shoulder, grinned behind his bushy black beard. 'You can trust the master sergeant on that one, soldier. Knows his demons, Temp does.' Squeezing the shoulder painfully, he pulled Nait close to growl, 'You keep your yap shut or I'll give you your real name, soldier.'

'What d'you mean, my real name?'

His mouth tight in distaste, the commander looked him up and down. 'Like Jumpy, soldier. You are definitely Jumpy.' He pushed Nait aside, raised his head to the column. 'All right! That's far enough! I want all the veterans, guards and Malazan regulars front and centre, now!'

Nait followed Hands to the master sergeant, who had returned from the trail. She asked, 'What's going on?'

'We're splitting up. Most of you guards and regulars are gonna escort the skirmishers back to camp—'

'What?' Nait blurted. 'That's stupid, splitting up.'

Master Sergeant Temp just watched Nait for a time, saying nothing. He turned to Hands. 'The recruits are too green to see what's ahead. It might break them. We need to get them back.'

'Aye.'

While Braven Tooth was ordering the column, a troop of Imperial cavalry came riding out of the dark, torches sputtering. It was led by none other than Korbolo Dom, High Fist and Sword of the Empire, in full regalia of layered iron-banded armour and iron-scaled sleeves and hose. A black jupon displayed the silver Imperial sceptre while his mount supported long black and silver trappings that brushed the trampled grass. Master Sergeant Temp and Commander Braven Tooth saluted.

The High Fist pulled off his helmet. 'You are wasting time here, Commander. You should give pursuit!'

Braven Tooth frowned thoughtfully as if considering the

proposition. 'We were thinking that if we did that he might just swing around and take a bite outta our arses.'

The Sword's bluish Napan features darkened even further. 'You have been long from the front, Commander. You have perhaps lost the proper fighting spirit. Very well, stay hidden among your men. *I* go to hunt him down!'

'I wouldn't go out there if I were you,' Master Sergeant Temp said. 'He'll just string you along then turn on you.'

The Sword sawed his mount over to look down at the man. 'And who are you?'

'Master Sergeant Temp,' and he saluted.

'Then that, Master Sergeant,' Korbolo explained loftily, 'is why *I* am the Sword and you are not.' And he kicked his mount to lunge away into the night, followed by his troop. Commander Braven Tooth and the master sergeant exchanged glances of arched brows.

'Think we'll ever see him again?' Braven Tooth asked.

'With his luck and ours? Yes.'

After more cajoling and cuffing the commander led the main column of skirmishers, escorted by regulars, back to camp. Master Sergeant Temp led the smaller column of ex-guards and Malazan regulars, including the cadre mage Heuk, onward, tracking the way the beast had come. As they walked through the night Nait complained, 'Jumpy? I ain't jumpy. Who in the Abyss does he think he is? It ain't even a name. Might as well call someone Stone, or Stick.' He cuffed the fellow marching ahead of him who, from his size, must be a heavy. 'Hey, what's your name?'

The fellow turned, blinking slowly. 'Fish.'

'*Fish?* Your name is *Fish?* What in the Abyss kind of name is that?'

A shrug. 'I dunno. The commander gave it to me.'

'Hey, Jumpy,' someone shouted, 'Shut the Abyss up.'

They backtracked the beast until they lost the trail along the rocky bed of a dry creek that wended across the plain. Straightening, Master Sergeant Temp waved Heuk forward. The old man came puffing up, looking as if he was about to pass out. His curly brown mop of hair hung stringy and sweaty. He hugged his earthenware jug as if it held his deliverance – which, Nait presumed, wasn't too far from the truth. 'Well?' the master sergeant demanded. 'Try your Warren – track him down!'

The old man raised the jug and took a long pull then wiped his mouth with a greasy sleeve. He squinted blearily at the trail, shook his head in a long drawn out negative. 'No, Temp— that is, Master Sergeant. I'm not a Warren-mage. Blood and the Elders is my path. And you don't want me opening it. Not yet.'

The master sergeant looked like he was about to savage the man with a few good curses, but then he stopped. He scratched his stubbled cheeks while studying the old mage and actually appeared unnerved. He tilted his head, accepting the explanation. 'Yeah. Let's hope it don't come to that.' He raised a hand to sign a return. It was dawn before they sighted camp and when they returned they found everyone packing for another day's march.

* * *

Ho came and kicked Grief – that is, Blues – awake where he dozed in the shade under canvas hung at the bow of the *Forlorn*. 'Yath's drowning another of us.'

The man cracked open one eye. 'Why're you telling me? I'm not his keeper. You lot can rule yourselves – like you were so proud of.'

'We're on board your ship! If you can call this rotting wreck a ship. You have authority.'

Blues groaned, fumbled to his feet. Ho still could not get used to calling the man by his real name. Real? More like his earlier alias. Who knew what his real name was? To him, he'd always be Grief. Ho chuckled aloud – he liked that. Blues gave him a puzzled glance. 'The stern.'

'Right. The stern.' He motioned to two of his companions. 'Get Fingers.' Grumbling, the two headed below.

The Seven Cities cargo ship *Forlorn* boasted two decks, the main and a raised second stern deck. The gap between was tall enough for most save the tallest of the men. At the very stern, where the keel rose up tall and curving, Yath and Sessin were overseeing a party of his most enthusiastic supporters teamed on a rope. Seeing so many of the inmates all crowded together almost made Ho laugh aloud again; what a ragged, seedy and just plain scrofulous spectacle they all presented! Most had hacked their hair to brush-cut length to rid themselves of the clinging dust; most wore no more than blankets or rags taken from the ship's stores. All the pale-skinned ones were sunburnt red with cracked, bleeding skin. Ho ran a hand over his own shaved head and winced as he was sun-burnt just as badly. And to make it worse, they were already nearly out of water.

'That's enough,' Blues called.

The men looked to Blues then glanced at Yath. After a moment the

Seven Cities priest allowed an indifferent shrug. The men hauled on the rope. It was amazing, Ho reflected, how the revelations that followed the arrival of the *Forlorn* with the rest of Blues' squad, or blade, had instilled a spirit of cooperation among the fractious band of inmate mages. The truth that Blues and Treat and his squad were not just' secessionists working against the Empress, but in fact were Crimson Guardsmen, and not only that, all six were of the Avowed: well – it certainly ended the talk of throwing them overboard.

The rope team pulled an old man up over the railing to splay naked and unconscious on to the deck. He had tightly curled greying hair and brown skin, and scars of swirling designs covered him. Ho recognized him as Jain, a Dal Hon warlock. 'Yath! You idiot!' Blues snarled. He knelt over Jain, listened at his chest, then tilted his head back and blew into his mouth. The man coughed, spluttered, inhaled a great gasping breath.

'Wasted effort,' sneered a voice from behind Ho and he turned to see the skinny, almost skeletal shape of Fingers, the mage, with Treat and Dim. While of the Avowed, the mage had the appearance of a gangly apprentice.

'He must be cleansed of the taint,' Yath said. 'All of us must be.'

'Have you gone under?' Blues snapped.

'I have.'

Blues waved curtly to the grinning Sessin. 'Has he?'

'Yes.'

'Then you're finished. Everyone's gone.'

Yath stepped closer. He appeared even more hungry and wiry now that he'd shaved his beard. He leant forward on his staff – a new staff he'd found on board – to tower over Blues. 'Not everyone . . .'

'Now wait a minute. Why should we—'

'You were in the Pit.' Yath raised a brow to Fingers. 'Your friends nearby were exposed to the dust. Your continuing contamination spreads dust anew. All of you must wash. Cut your hair. Scour your skin with stones. Just as we have. And wash again. Your people and the women inmates as well – all, Su, Inese and that Korelan sea-witch.'

Blues eyed the man as if he was insane. 'Why in the Abyss would we do that right now, right away? I mean, I plan on getting cleaned up – eventually. What's your rush?'

The Seven Cities priest's dark wrinkled face broke into a self-satisfied grin. He caught Ho's gaze and Ho realized that the man knew – that somehow he'd sensed what was going on – or had been informed by one of those he'd browbeaten into following him. 'Tell him, Ho,' Yath invited.

Blues turned to him. Ho rubbed his scalp and winced again. He pulled his hand away. 'Something's going on at Heng. A lot of us can sense it – bits and pieces – glimpses, now that we're far from the islands. Something important. And Laseen is there.'

'This insurrection you're talking about?'

'. . . Yes . . . and more.'

'More?'

'Your mercenary company is involved,' Yath said.

Blues' gaze narrowed on Ho. 'Is that true?'

Ho was unable to meet the man's eyes. He lowered his head. 'Yes. They've come back. They are in the field near Heng.'

Blues was silent for some time. Jain continued coughing. Waves washed the sides of the *Forlorn*. Cordage creaked and rubbed overhead. 'Why didn't you say anything?'

Ho raised his eyes, tried to plead for understanding. 'I said nothing because I do not agree with Yath's proposal. What he is talking of is too dangerous. Far too risky for all of us. We will most likely all be killed.'

Blues' mouth twisted in his clenched anger. He took his hands from the twin blades he now carried at his sides – his own swords had been left behind when he came to the Pit. Without moving his gaze he said, 'Talk, old man.'

The Seven Cities priest made no effort to conceal his triumph. He bared his sharp yellow teeth. 'A ritual, mercenary. We have among us more than thirty mages of considerable power. We will enact a ritual of movement through warren by ship. It is more common than you might imagine. Ask our Korelan friend – with her aid we are assured of success.'

'Provided we can cleanse ourselves of the Otataral.'

'Yes. Provided.'

Blues' gaze slid past Ho to question Fingers. 'Interesting . . .' the mage said.

'Now I'm *definitely* nervous,' Blues muttered. But he waved a hand. 'All right, Yath. We'll get cleaned up. In the meantime, set your people to scrubbing the deck.'

The Seven Cities mage actually bowed. 'Excellent – Captain.'

Blues ignored the man, pointed to Treat. 'Take down the sails, wash 'em.'

Treat just rolled his eyes.

*

That night Ho sat with Su in the empty cargo hold. 'If you don't go, they'll come down and carry you up.'

'I'd curse their manhoods – if they still had them.'

'It's just water. A quick dunk and they'll leave you alone.'

'I'm too old for too many things, including dunking.' The hull groaned around them. Rat claws scratched on wood. Ho felt the dark pressing in upon him, damp and gravid. 'And what of you,' Su said, tilting her head back to eye him. 'They are all so much less than you – why fear them at all?'

'We're not talking about that, Su. We could lower you in a net.'

'A net? Am I a fish? Does your friend Blues know the real reason why you did not tell him of Heng? Why you are so frightened to return?'

'Quiet, witch.'

'Let us make a pact, magus—'

'No pacts, witch. Just washing.'

'A washing for me and a reunion for you.'

'You're going under regardless, witch. It's just a question of coercion.'

'Yes, it is always a question of coercion in the end, is it not?'

Ho sighed his impatience. 'Su, I told you already I'm not impressed by these vague empty pronouncements you toss off hoping people will think they're wise.'

She smiled. 'Is that what I do?'

'*Su . . .*'

The old woman lifted a crooked finger. 'Wisdom lives only in hindsight.'

Ho pushed his head back to hit the hull planking.

'Is that anger I'm seeing, Ho? A temper, perhaps?'

'Right, that's it.' He stood, gestured Su up. 'Let's go. On deck. Right now. There's something going on you should see. C'mon.'

She stared up at him, fiddled with her walking stick. 'What? Right this minute?'

'Yes. Come on!'

'Well! Give an old woman a moment, would you?' She struggled to rise, slapped away his offered hand. 'As if anything could be so pressing! You would think Hood's Paths themselves had opened up above vomiting up all the dead!' She grasped the steep gangway in one gnarled hand. 'Just a trick, I'm sure,' she grumbled, climbing.

On deck, torches and a bright moon in a clear night sky lit a crowd of inmates gathered around the Avowed at the larboard side of the

Forlorn. Fingers sat gripping the sides of a slat seat perched atop the gunwale. By turns he peered down with pure dread and at Blues with pure venom. Treat and another of the Avowed, Reed, were tying ropes to the seat and to Fingers – who was already tightly strapped in.

'It ain't gonna work!' Fingers was shouting. 'You're taking advantage of me right now is what you're doing! I'll drown.'

'We'll keep a close watch,' Dim assured him. 'Don't you worry now.'

Fingers glared bloody fury at the man.

'OK,' Blues said. 'All secure?'

Treat slapped Fingers' back. 'All secure.'

'Bastards!'

'Over we go,' Blues ordered.

Treat and Reed lowered the stretcher by the ropes, backed up by Blues and Dim. Fingers had stopped cursing them all and, sinking out of sight, his pale white face stretched even tauter over his sharp cheekbones. The crowd of inmates pressed forward to line the side.

'Room, dammit,' Blues complained, raising his elbows. 'Room!'

Ho observed aside to Su, 'We're a little short on entertainment out here.'

'Somehow this is not reassuring, Ho.'

'Don't worry.' He waved to a solid woman, her greying hair hacked short, who had come to his side. 'Su, this is Devaleth. She's been over already but she and you and Inese – and Opal also – can wash at the stern. We'll put up a spare canvas or blankets. It's that or they'll throw you over in a net.'

The old witch's thin mouth curled in condescension. 'If I must.'

Whoops and laughter sounded from the gathered inmates. Treat and Dim were hauling on the ropes. A sodden, shivering Fingers appeared at the gunwale. His torn linen shirt hung from his lank form. He stuttered something – curses probably – as they lowered his stretcher to the deck. Dim held out a blanket that he snatched and wrapped around himself. Ho watched, wondering, how could anyone be so skinny?

'This does nothing for the traces we've ingested, or are ground into our calluses, or under our nails, or such,' Su observed.

'We've used the pumice stones on our flesh and knives under our nails,' Devaleth said. 'Myself, I would cut off my left hand to regain my gifts.'

'Yes, well, let us hope it does not come to that,' Su observed, turning away to limp to the stern.

466

From the broken wall of what was once one of a series of outlying gatehouses, hostelries and pilgrim inns for the sprawling complex that was the Great Sanctuary of Burn, Shimmer watched the envoy of the Talian League mount and ride off. The doubts and small suspicions that had gnawed at her since their return had lately coalesced into one dark, smothering feeling of wrongness that seemed to choke her. She turned back to the other two occupants of the room, Skinner and Cowl. 'Was that wise?' she asked, though she knew nothing would come of her objection – yet again the sensation struck her of being a player in a charade, of merely going through the motions in some tired play. Had she been here before? Done this countless times? Whence came this mood?

Skinner, his helm under one arm, revealing his scarred face and matted reddish-blond hair, waved her concerns aside. 'This League is no different from the Malazans. I no more credit their offers of territory than I would any from Laseen.'

'They may unite against us.'

The swordsman's gaze slid aside to Cowl. The High Mage, who had been looking off across the plain to the south, frowned a negative. 'Unlikely for the near future – but a growing threat admittedly. Yet more forces are approaching.'

'Laseen's?' Shimmer asked.

A sly smile pulled at the curled tattoos beneath his mouth. 'Who is to say? The choice is their commander's, I should think.'

'It would precipitate matters, would it not,' Skinner rumbled, 'if Choss believed them Laseen's?'

'Indeed.'

Skinner waved Cowl away. 'I leave it to you.'

A curt bow from Cowl. The High Mage backed into shadow and disappeared. Shimmer turned to Skinner, surprised. 'I thought Warren travel was extraordinarily dangerous these days.'

Heading to the shattered door jamb, the commander paused, considering. 'So is Cowl.'

Alone, Shimmer suddenly felt the heat of the day seep into her – as if the commander's presence drained something vital from her. Catching his eyes still made her wince. What had become of the man who had led the First Company into the diaspora? He had been ambitious and fierce, yes, but not – inhuman. Now, something else looked out of those eyes. Something that felt more terrifying and menacing than anything that might be awaiting in the field.

'Captain?'

Blinking, Shimmer turned. Greymane stood there along with Smoky and a regular, Ogilvy. 'Yes?'

'Turned them down, didn't he,' Smoky said.

'Yes.'

A sour nod. 'Thought so. Makes sense.'

Shimmer straightened, ill at ease once more. 'Explain yourself, mage.'

'Me 'n' Grey been talking. Got us a theory.'

'Yes?' Shimmer said calmly, though her breath seemed to die in her throat.

'First, though, this Guardsman here has something to say.' Smoky urged Ogilvy forward with a curt jerk. Saluting, bobbing his bald bullet-head, the regular saluted.

''Pologies, ma'am, sir. Kept my drink-hole shut I did, sorry. Seemed most discretionary. Circumstances as they was, 'n' all.'

Shimmer blinked again, her brow crimping. 'Sorry, Guardsman . . . ?'

'Was first at the scene of Stoop's killin' there in Stratem. Saw tracks – tracks that was later smoothed away. By spell.'

'And those tracks told you what?'

'Accordin' to those tracks the lad never entered that clearing.'

'I . . . see.' Shimmer swallowed a tightening sickness. 'Is there anyone else who saw these tracks? Who could corroborate your testimony?'

The Guardsman glanced to Greymane, then down. 'No, sir.'

'No. Well then, Guardsman, I suggest you continue to keep this to yourself until such time as further information comes forward.'

Ogilvy saluted. 'Yes, ma'am, sir.'

'You are dismissed.'

'Yes, ma – sir.'

Ogilvy left. Shimmer turned on Smoky. 'You presume too much, mage.'

Smoky's long face hardened. 'I got more to presume. The men won't say, but there's a lot of grumbling. Skinner's gathering Avowed to himself, treating everyone else like servants, not brothers or sisters. There's sides drawing up. Everyone's looking to you to do something. You or—' he stopped himself, then barrelled on, 'Greymane.'

Shimmer finally faced the massive ex-High Fist. 'I would take great care if I were you, Malazan. You are not of the Avowed.'

'A condition that perhaps allows me the proper perspective.'

'Proper – explain yourself, soldier.'

'It is plain that Skinner intends to defeat both Laseen and this Talian League. And once both are crushed, what then?'

Brows wrinkled, Shimmer shrugged. 'Why, then, the terms of the Vow will have been fulfilled – the shattering of the Empire.'

Greymane and Smoky exchanged troubled glances. 'And yet not. Any new force could then step into the vacuum, such as an alliance of Dal Hon and Kan forces, or any other such, yes?'

'Possibly . . .'

'Unless this position were already occupied by another organization, another force ready to act. Is that not so?'

'I do not see what you are getting at, Malazan.'

Smoky gave an impatient snarl. 'The Vow has you in too tight a grip, Shimmer. Open your eyes! Skinner intends to occupy the throne himself!'

Shimmer could only stare. Then she laughed outright at the absurdity of the assertion. 'Smoky, you know as well as I that the terms of the Vow would never allow such a thing.'

'You're not a mage, Shimmer. Even I can see a few possible ways around it and Cowl is leagues ahead of me. One way to construe it is that the Malazan Empire remains an impossibility so long as the Avowed occupy the throne. There? How's that? Life and power eternal. Worth a throw, wouldn't you say?'

Shimmer felt almost dizzy. She steadied herself at a wall. 'But that would be—'

'A monstrous perversion? Yes.'

'No.' She shook her head. 'No, Smoky. You are inventing threats, conspiracies. Seeing enemies everywhere. Perhaps that is the Vow affecting *you*. You've never made a secret of your distaste for Cowl. Have you considered that?'

The mage was silent for some time. His stare was hard, gauging, and Shimmer was shaken to see disappointment colour the man's eyes. 'Greymane is not Avowed, Shimmer,' he said, and pushed his way past. Greymane remained, but Shimmer would not face him. She turned her back. After a time he bowed and left.

We are so close. Queen's Prophecies, the completion of the Vow is within reach! We can break them! Why then these doubts, these worries? None afflicted at the beginning. Everything was so clear then. The sides so cleanly drawn, our cause so pressing. Now, though, I can hardly muster the effort to go through with it. For

whom did they fight? Not the Untans, nor the Cawnese. Then who?
Skinner on the throne, and through him, what else?

Riding out alone into the night from the remains of the Sanctuary of Burn, Lieutenant-Commander Ullen felt extremely ill at ease until the detachment of Talian cavalry escorting him rode up to rendezvous. Leading them was Commander Amaron, accompanied by Toc's new aide, Captain Moss.

'They rejected the offer?' Amaron called.

'Yes.'

A sour shake of the head. 'The fools. They're going to get themselves wiped out.'

'You're so sure?'

Amaron smiled knowingly, signed for a return to the fortified encampment – Fort Urko, some called it. 'You are not?'

Ullen merely raised a brow; he motioned to the ruins. 'I've just come away from speaking with Skinner, Amaron. I never did meet him before, and I have to say he looks every bit as nasty as his reputation.'

'Oh, I don't doubt that.' The commander shifted his considerable broad weight on his tall horse. 'I'm not saying we'll pull down the Avowed. What I'm saying is that if they are so foolish as to take to the field their regular force will be broken and the surviving Avowed will have to withdraw alone. Then what can they do? A handful of men and women cannot hold territory. They will have to flee once again. No, the whole thing, their recruiting and return, will all have been for nothing. A sad waste, really.'

Behind the commander's mount, Ullen and Moss shared a glance, saying nothing. Moss flicked his eyes to indicate the fifty troopers walking their mounts along behind and Ullen nodded. Amaron was not speaking to them; he was speaking to the men, fulfilling one of the obligations of command, bolstering morale.

The Napan turned to Moss. 'So, Captain, served in Genabackis, did you?'

'Yes, Commander.'

'With Dujek?'

'No, sir. Not directly. I remained up north. Rotated out.'

'Up north? Why, so you've faced the Guard before, then! Didn't they have a contract with a warlord there, that fellow named Brood?'

'Yes, sir. I've faced them.'

'And they were beaten there, weren't they?'

470

Moss shot Ullen a glance of veiled amusement. 'Oh yes, sir,' he responded loudly. 'They were beaten.'

Half of the cavalry officer's expression told Ullen that he could play Amaron's game too – and had said what the men would be helped to hear. The other half of the expression told Ullen just how far from the truth were the man's words.

* * *

The Wickan camp occupied a stretch of the east shore of the River Jurd, just north of Unta. Circular yurts dotted hillsides in a sudden new township of some four thousand. The surrounding Untan villages and hamlets supplied fodder for horses, firewood and staples. Nil and Nether promised eventual payment in trade goods. Rillish and his Malazan command occupied a large farmhouse and compound in the middle of vineyards where bunches of white grapes hung heavy on the stems. Since his night foray with Nether, his sergeant, Talia, had been even more insistent on their intimacy – to his great relief and pleasure, he had to admit.

So it was they lay in bed together one morning when a discreet knock sounded on the door of his room. He pulled on his trousers, while Talia dressed as well, quickly strapping on her swordbelt. 'What is it?' he called.

'Beggin' your pardon, sir. Riders from the south.'

'Yes?'

'They carry the Imperial banner.'

'I see. Thank you, sergeant. I'll be down shortly.'

He turned to Talia and she laughed at the embarrassment that must have been obvious. He splashed his hot face in a basin. Outside in the courtyard, horses readied by Chord waited. Rillish mounted, invited Chord to attend him, gave command of the compound over to him, and rode off with a troop of ten.

Wickan horsemen had already met and stopped the small column, which consisted of some twenty Untan cavalry. Room was made for Rillish to edge to the front. He inclined his head to the man leading the column, who, by the markings on his helmet, held the rank of Imperial Fist, though Rillish did not recognize him. The man's dark eyes glanced to him but in no other way did he acknowledge Rillish's presence. Eventually, Nil and Nether arrived from their more distant camp. They pushed through to the front, nodded to the Fist who saluted, bowing. 'Allow me to introduce myself. I am Fist Tazil Jhern. I am come as envoy from the capital, empowered to discuss terms.'

Nether inclined her head in acknowledgement. 'I am Nether, this is my brother Nil. And this is Lieutenant Rillish Jal Keth. Greetings.' The man continued to studiously ignore Rillish.

'What terms, may I ask?' Nil inquired. 'Terms of your surrender?'

'Terms of cessation of hostilities. You have grievances, conditions you wish to discuss, surely?'

The twins exchanged narrowed glances. 'We have *demands* and conditions, Fist,' Nil corrected.

'You say you are empowered, Fist,' Rillish asked. 'Empowered by whom?'

The envoy said nothing, continued to stare straight ahead. Nether's brow furrowed. 'The lieutenant asked you a question, Fist.'

'I am sure you understand that I feel in no way obligated to speak with a traitor,' the man told her.

Nil flinched, stung, and tightened his reins. 'Then I am sure you understand that we—'

So, the day has come when I am repudiated. Rillish raised a hand. 'It is all right. Please, take no offence. I will go.'

'*Stay where you are!*' Nether ordered, startling Rillish. 'You will remain and listen to all this envoy has to say. Then, my brother and I will expect you to advise us afterwards.'

Struggling to keep his astonishment from his face, Rillish bowed stiffly. 'As you order.'

Nil invited the Fist onward. 'This way, envoy.'

Later that day, the Fist begged off early to retire to the quarters prepared for his party. Once the man left the large tent a fury of debate leapt to life among the gathered clan representatives, elders and surviving warlocks. The twins sat quietly, letting the storm blow itself out. Rillish was alarmed by some opinions he overheard: sacking the province, ravaging the countryside, even claiming the Throne. When that suggestion, taking the Throne, was called across the tent to Nil, he merely observed, 'What would we do with it? It's too heavy to sit on a horse.'

A new round of debate began, this time peppered by escalating retorts, condemnations and insults. It seemed to Rillish that the discussion was veering further and further into the territory of past transgressions, slights and ages-old grudges. He glanced to Nil and saw him watching – the lad winked, tilted his head to invite him outside. Rillish uncrossed his numb legs, bowed to the assembly and ducked out of the tent.

Without, twilight was gathering. The hillside sloped down like a dark green swath of silk to the Jurd, which glimmered, tree-lined, wide and black. The air was thick with the scent of ripeness, pressing into rot. Night moths and flies clouded around, attracted by the light. It occurred to Rillish that he was home yet this was no longer his home. Where could he call home now? The Wickan plains? They could hardly be expected to be welcoming at this point. Nil ducked out, joining him. The lad hugged himself over his plain deerskin jerkin. His unkempt black hair was a tangle, yet Rillish said nothing – one does not tell the premier Wickan warlock that he needs a haircut.

'A rich land,' the youth said, viewing the green hillsides. 'You people have done well by it.'

Rillish eyed the Wickan adolescent, blinking. 'Pardon . . . ?'

A blush and duck of the head. 'Sorry. All this once belonged to my ancestors.'

'No, Nil,' Rillish managed, his stomach clenching, 'It is I who am sorry.'

The youth blew out a breath. 'So different from Seven Cities.'

'So, what will you do?' Rillish asked, gesturing to the tent.

'We will let them talk, then give our opinions, then let them talk some more, then give our opinions again and let them talk. Once they begin saying our opinions back to us as if they are their own, then we will agree with their wisdom and we will have their unshakable support.'

Rillish eyed the lad, who was looking down the slope, unmindful of his regard. 'Nil?'

'Yes?'

'You are far too young to be so cynical.'

A bright smile. 'My sister and I are far from young, Lieutenant.'

Yes, you have come so far too swiftly and for that I am sorry. 'What are those opinions then? What should you do?'

'Ah . . . you've hit upon the problem. We aren't sure yet.' Horses nickered in a nearby corral, stirring restlessly and the lad's eyes moved to the noise. 'What do you think of our envoy?'

'It's possible we're intended to judge the offer by its bearer – candid, honest and practical.'

A boat appeared floating down the Jurd, sail limp, long sweep raising a bright wake. The eyes of both tracked it. 'Yes,' Nil said. 'An honest offer honestly given, to be just as honestly disregarded at earliest convenience.'

In that statement Rillish listened for echoes of sullen resentment, sneering disdain or suppressed rage, but heard none. Only a sad sort of resignation that the world should be so ordered. 'You are caught,' he said. 'You've done everything you can but you still have no true leverage.'

A long slow assent. 'We are in a strange situation, Lieutenant. We ought to have all the advantages, camped as we are on the capital's doorstep, yet we find ourselves a sideshow. Unta has been sacked already. We can hardly threaten that. What will be our fate is in fact being determined far to the west – and we are not even there.'

'You must still work to achieve the most advantageous terms you can.'

'Yes,' the lad sighed. 'We must. Yet I wonder – have we done *all* that we can?' Nil turned to face Rillish, and his gaze slid to the tent then back, cautious. 'Thank you, Lieutenant.'

'For what?'

'For listening. Unlike many of my countrymen I think it useful to talk through things. I find that it helps unravel knots.'

Rillish motioned to the tent once more. 'Your countrymen do not seem averse to talk.'

'Most use it only to tighten existing knots.'

'Ah. I see.'

The warlock took hold of the tent flap. 'You need not endure any more of this tonight. Nether and I will manage things. I understand you have much more pleasant company awaiting you,' and he grinned.

An adolescent effort at adult banter? 'Yes, thank you.'

The grin faltered. 'Now, if only I could find someone for my sister . . .'

Rillish bowed quickly, 'Goodnight.'

On the dark road back to the farmhouse Rillish found two mounted figures waiting. Sergeants Chord and Talia. Sergeant Chord saluted, turned his mount, and rode off ahead. Rillish brought his mount alongside Talia's. 'Sergeant . . .'

'Lieutenant . . .' She leaned aside and they kissed. There was something about her tonight; her smile was so bright in the dark, her eyes so full of a hidden humour.

'You are looking . . . mysterious . . . this night.'

She turned her mount while watching him sidelong. 'I have a secret.'

He stilled, his eyes narrowing. 'Oh?'

'Yes. I am, as they say in your fancy aristocratic society – with child.'

'*What?*' He stared, utterly shocked. 'But that's impossible!'

An arched brow. 'Has no one told you how all this works, then?'

'No! I mean, what I meant was . . . how could you know so soon?'

'The horsewives told me. They're beside themselves. You should've heard them clucking over me.'

'Well, you'll have to leave the ranks, of course.'

She faced him squarely. 'I certainly will not. I'm a sergeant now. Got a pay increase.'

'I could bust you down.'

'For what?' she snapped. 'Misconduct with an officer?'

Rillish opened his mouth then quickly shut it, thinking that perhaps another assault would be inadvisable at this time. Reconnoitring and observation were clearly called for. Perhaps some judicious probing. Talia rode in a loud pointed silence, her back stiff, face averted. He cleared his throat. 'Not the reaction you were expecting, I imagine.'

'Damned straight.'

'I'm sorry. It's just . . . quite a surprise. My first reaction is that you don't take any risks . . .'

'You think I want to?' She sighed, eased her mount closer, took his arm. 'Old Orhan and I can swap duties.'

Orhan, Rillish reflected. The company quartermaster and horsemaster. Demanding work, potentially dangerous, but not a battlefield position. A gimp leg and getting slow, yet a canny veteran who'd been in the service all his life. Was a sergeant on the listings.

'. . . then I'll find a wetnurse among the Wickans. After that the little tyke can go to stay with my brother in Halas. He's a woodwright there. Or what about your people?'

Rillish thought about his people. He thought of the high-season house in Unta and the off-season house in Haljhen. The family lands along the Gris River where vineyards, fields and orchards stretched for more than a day's ride in any direction. He thought of the barrels of wine ageing beneath the great manor house, the countless families who lived on and worked those lands.

All lost to him. Lost to Rillish Jal Keth, the family traitor.

And now he had an heir. An heir to the two swords he carried, the bag of coin under his shirt and a name he or she could never claim. He took Talia's hand. 'So where is this Halas?'

* * *

One of their remaining Seti scouts came roaring up and pulled short at the last moment, his mount stamping, sweaty and lathered. Ghelel recognized Toven, the young smartarse who had teased her and Molk earlier. Now, she was grateful for the lad's love of excitement.

'They're headed for Heng,' he reported.

The 'they' in this case was a huge Kan Confederacy army that had come marching out of the south, consisting of some four thousand lancers and twenty-five thousand infantry. The 'they' being the reason the Marquis and his command were now hunkered down in a copse of trees south-west of Heng.

The Marquis nodded his acknowledgement.

'Thank you, scout. Get yourself a fresh horse.'

'Aye, commander.' A leering grin to Ghelel and the lad kicked his mount onward.

'Going to get himself killed,' Prevost Razala said with a kind of reluctant affection.

'I hope not,' the Marquis murmured, 'we're running out of scouts.'

'So this Kan force – they're our allies?' Ghelel asked.

The Marquis drew his pipe from his shoulder-pouch, clamped it unlit between his teeth. 'Not necessarily, they may be with Laseen. But, if I were to lay any wagers on the matter, I'd say they're on the side of the Itko Kan Confederacy.'

'Meaning what?'

'Meaning that they may be here to try to take Li Heng.'

'What? But that's ridiculous! With our army here, and Laseen's!'

A thoughtful frown. 'Not at all. Itko Kan has always resented the establishment of the Free Cities. Heng is the only reason the entity exists. Now's their chance to rid themselves of it. Not to mention possibly keeping hold of Heng. No, I imagine they plan to negotiate with whoever wins up north, using Heng as their card. Sound strategy.'

'That's—' Ghelel stopped herself from saying anything that would reveal any more of her lack of . . . well, cold-bloodedness.

'Makes me wish the beast would cross the Idryn,' Razala grated.

Jhardin shot the woman a look. 'Believe me, Prevost, you do not wish that.'

'What of us, then, Marquis?' Ghelel asked.

'We withdraw west. To the Falls.'

'West? West to Broke Earth Falls?' Ghelel repeated, disbelieving. 'But that would take us completely from battle! We are needed up north! Choss is facing off against Laseen. Every man and woman is needed!'

'Five hundred would make precious little difference, Prevost Alil. In any case, our way north is blocked. We are cut off from the Pilgrim Bridge, from Li Heng. The only place we *may* be able to cross is the Falls.'

'I differ with you on that point, Commander. A charge of a hundred heavies could make all the difference in any battle. Razala? What of you?'

The commander of heavy cavalry held her gaze long and hard on Ghelel, who caught a storm of suppressed emotions writhing just beneath her sweaty, plain, scarred face: resentment, anger, shame and finally regret. Then the woman lowered her eyes as if studying the backs of her gauntlets crossed before her on the pommel of her saddle. 'I wish it more than I can say, Prevost. *But* . . . I'm sworn to follow the Marquis.'

'So we go west,' Jhardin said. 'The Seti will keep us informed.' And he kicked his mount into motion.

* * *

'Kanese forces,' Sergeant Banath snorted next to Hurl. 'Ploughboys, fishergals and runaway 'prentices. Not a backbone in the lot. Don't know why they bother. Might as well pack up and go home.' He spat over the edge of the tower next to the South Outer Round gate. ''Cept their mages. Plenty tricky, them Kan mages. Like the Dal Hon – only not so bad.'

'Thanks for the tip, Sergeant,' Hurl said, head in hands. It still hurt. Liss said she was all healed up, but it still hurt. And this Kan parley did not help at all. Gods help its commander; she was in a mood to bite stone. 'All right. Let's go.'

Hurl rode out accompanied by Silk, Sergeant Banath and a detachment of twenty Hengan cavalry – a good fraction of all that remained to them. Liss was watching the north, Sunny was handling repairs and reconstruction, while Storo lay in bed, barely alive, recovering from the savaging the beast had inflicted upon him. And Jalor; Jalor had fallen doing his job – standing next to Rell. As for Rell, he made it plain these sort of negotiations were not for him. And so it came to Hurl, now Acting-Fist, and commander of the city's defence.

Kan outriders stopped them just a short ride along the road south. Here they waited for the Kan representatives. They had a long wait. Hurl took the opportunity to get as much room as possible between her and the horses. She walked to an abandoned farmhouse and grounds – the trampled garden plot picked clean, the rooms emptied of all furniture, tools. All hints of the family that had occupied the homestead gone. Standing in the thatch-roofed, single-room house, watching the dust swirl in the light from the open door, all she felt was a sense of sadness and loss. Who had lived here? She wondered if their own scavenging parties had been responsible, or the Talian force reportedly in the south, or these very Kanese outriders keeping an eye on them. Eventually, a large carriage drawn by four oxen came rumbling up the south road. Lancers escorted it, and a van of five horsemen preceded it. Hurl went out to meet them.

One dismounted and approached, a man wearing functional armour of banded strips and a long jupon bearing the seven entwined blossoms of the Itko Kan Confederacy – an insignia last seen some hundred years ago. He pulled off his helmet and cloth cap revealing a middle-aged man, darkly featured with a moustache and closely trimmed beard. He bowed to Hurl. 'Commander Pirim 'J Shall at your service.' He motioned to the riders. 'Invigilator Durmis.' The short robed man bowed. The rest of the riders were obviously guards. 'Within the carriage is Custodian Kapalet. Sadly, the demands of the expedition have proved wearying for the custodian and she is indisposed.'

'Acting-Fist Hurl.' She motioned to her own escort. 'And this is Silk.' The commander bowed. Exhaling noisily, he sat on the edge of the broken water trough.

'Congratulations in forestalling the Talians. It must have been very difficult.'

'Accepted.'

'Yet . . .' and he was looking off to the west, 'it has no doubt left you sorely diminished. You must ask yourself, how much more can your men take? How much more must they have left within them?'

'Enough to turn away your dog and pony act.'

He flashed a tolerant smile and motioned to the surrounding countryside. 'We of the Confederacy did not come empty-handed, Acting-Fist. We know these lands well – they used to be ours. We know of the shortage of wood and so we brought our own. Enough for many siege towers.'

'There's nothing I like more than a good fire.'

Again, a smile of forbearance. 'Consider, commander, can you face us in the south and keep adequate watch on your north? I very much doubt it. Consider well, and offer terms – if only for the sake of your men.'

Hurl pulled on her gloves. The formalities had been observed; she had no interest in jousting with the man. 'Our terms are that you withdraw to a day's march to the south. Otherwise we consider you a target. Am I understood?' She finally succeeded in wiping away that smile. The man stood, gave a curt bow and gestured to the horses. Hurl led.

Readying her horse, Hurl saw that the fat bald Invigilator and Silk were locked in something of a staring match. As she mounted, the Invigilator addressed Silk: 'Many of my brothers and sisters in the south say that now that the Malazan peace has been broken the man-eater has returned, summoned by the bloodshed. What say you?'

'I would say the current hostilities have much to do with it, yes.'

'Those responsible for his return deserve to die in his jaws,' the Invigilator called as Silk turned his horse. 'Just as the ancient curse prophesies. Wouldn't you agree?'

Silk did not turn. His back stiff, he snapped his reins and rode off.

'How many has he taken so far?' the man yelled.

Hurl followed, but she could not help glancing back: the Invigilator pointed a damning finger at her. She urged her mount on to catch up to Silk.

'What in the name of D'rek was all that about?'

Looking ahead, the mage pushed aside his wind-tossed hair. 'Nothing, Hurl.'

'*Nothing?* You mean there's a *real* curse? Jalor's dead. Storo is nearly. Shaky's gone—'

'Shaky died before we did anything, Hurl.'

'Don't split hairs. I see a trend. How long have you known about this *curse?*'

Silk gestured helplessly. 'Hurl, it's nothing to take seriously. Nothing specific. It's probably just something made up by minstrels and such who love the subject. That's all.'

'Probably . . . *probably*? How do you know?'

'Because neither Kellanved nor Tayschrenn deal in curses, yes? It wasn't to their taste.'

'So I'm supposed to trust to that?'

'Yes.' He faced her, gave his best reassuring smile that she'd seen him lie through hundreds of times. 'Listen. He was just trying to shake you up. Undermine your confidence. That's all.'

'Yeah, well, he succeeded.'

They met up with the rest of their detachment and by mutual consent neither said anything more on the subject. Reaching the city, Hurl travelled with her newly assigned six bodyguards to the North

479

Outer Round to check on the repairs. There the seething activity astonished her. Hundreds of workers clearing up, repairing walls, salvaging material. It seemed that the residents of Li Heng had finally come around to their own defence. The cynic in Hurl wondered whether Ryllandaras's appearance had anything to do with their sudden new enthusiasm. But there *was* another explanation. She could not deny that after Rell's performance forestalling the beast the city had embraced him. It was now common to hear them shouting 'Protector!' after him and even throwing flowers. It had got to the point that he didn't go out on to the streets any more. The city, it seemed, had convinced itself that, in its hour of most dire need, it had found its new Protector. And for her part, Hurl was not entirely certain that they hadn't.

At the North Plains Gate she spotted Sunny surrounded by a crowd of shouting tradesmen, and he raised a hand to acknowledge her while heaping insults on them. She climbed stairs to the wall ramparts. The gate, beyond repair, was being permanently sealed. A wall of stone blocks was being raised up behind temporary wood and rubble outer barriers. At the battlements she found Liss. The Seti shamaness, or mage, or whatever she might be, was staring north over the prairie, empty now but for broken, abandoned equipment, humped burials and wind-lashed tatters.

'How's Storo?' Hurl asked.

A cocked brow. 'As good as can be expected. Mending a clean sword cut, a blade puncture, or knitting a broken bone is easy compared to trying to align flesh torn and mangled by talons. He's lost his arm, an eye, and we may yet lose him to his internal wounds. But why ask me? You should go to see him yourself.'

Hurl shook her head. He would not want her to see him as he was, helpless and broken. Liss pursed her lips but said nothing. She returned to moodily watching the plain.

'Will he be back?' Hurl asked. Both understood that by *he*, Hurl now meant someone else.

Liss nodded weakly. 'Yes. Eventually. Right now there's easy pickings out there.' The shamaness's demeanour seemed to be falling by the hour. Her hair hung in greasy strings, her skin looked unhealthily pale and, unbelievably, she smelled worse than when Hurl first met her – something which had she been asked at the time she would not have thought possible.

'And the Seti? Are they safe?'

A tired smile. 'Thank you, Hurl, my gal. Yes. For the time being. They are safe. Yet can a people be said to be safe from themselves?

This White Jackal worship must not be allowed to gain its stranglehold once more. It is a regression for us – a childlike dependency.'

'I'm sorry.' Indeed, she felt very sorry. More and more it was coming to seem that they should not have done what they did. That she had made a terrifying mistake that would haunt her for the rest of her life. Perhaps there really *was* a curse.

The shamaness slapped Hurl on the back. 'Don't worry yourself, lass. What's done is done. Now, it's up to me to do something.'

'You?' She eyed her suspiciously. 'What do you mean?'

Liss turned her hands back and forth before her eyes, examined her layered ragged skirts. 'Just something I've put off for maybe too long, that's all. Maybe the time's come.'

For what? Hurl wanted to ask but something stopped her, a vague unformed dread that whispered *you do not want to know*. It occurred to her that perhaps she was a coward after all.

* * *

The journey north had been smooth, though the *Kite* did not perform nearly so lithely as before without Ereko's steady hand at the tiller. Jan, Stalker and Kyle traded off keeping the sail as taut as possible. The brothers kept to the middle of the open boat, preparing the food and generally getting on each other's nerves. Traveller was a dark brooding presence at the prow that everyone avoided. It was as if Ereko, though not human himself, had been the only thing keeping a human presence within the swordsman. Kyle knew that the Lost brothers believed he blamed Traveller for Ereko's death. And for a time he had. But now he wondered how much choice the man had – the entire confrontation had had the air of an inevitable convergence, the long-delayed closure of a circle. Unavoidable. And Ereko had warned of the melancholy spell of the weapon at the man's side. It was clear now to him that what had happened had been just as hard on Traveller, if not harder. Hadn't he been friends with the Thel Akai for so much longer? It seemed to him unhealthy that the man be allowed to brood for so long and he realized that if anyone was going to do anything, it could only be him. On the fifth day he worked up the resolve to approach and sit near the prow.

'So, Quon,' he said after a time.

Through his long black hair hanging down, the man's dark ocean eyes shifted from his hands hanging limply at his legs to

Kyle. Something stirred, flickering within them, a kind of distant recognition, and a hand came up to squeeze them. He raised his head. 'Yes. Quon.'

'May I ask why?'

A tired shrug. 'You have a case to make with the Guard. That is where the Guard is headed.'

'And you?'

'I will make my way from there.'

'Will you help?'

A smile of amusement. 'No, Kyle. My presence would only . . . complicate matters.'

'Cowl will just kill me out of hand.'

'No. You'll be safe enough with the brothers. And there is the blade you carry. You have no idea what you really have here and that I think is the way things were intended.'

His sword? 'What do you mean?'

An easy shrug. 'It is a powerful weapon. Others might have used it to gather riches, power. But nothing like that has even occurred to you, has it?'

Kyle thought about that – the fact was he didn't have the first idea how to go about such things.

'Then, what about you?'

'Me?'

'Yes.'

The man took a deep breath, scanned the waters. 'I'm hunting someone, Kyle. Someone determined to avoid me. But eventually I will corner him. Then there will be an accounting long delayed.'

'Vengeance?'

A sharp glance, softened. 'Yes. But not just for me, for a great deal. A very great deal.'

An errant wave sent spray across Badlands who howled his shock. Coots laughed uproariously, his mouth full. A smile touched Traveller's features, though it appeared to Kyle to be the wintry, distant smile of an adult watching the amusing antics of children. Or . . . what was that word he'd overheard the Guardsmen using when discussing the leader of the race they called the Andii? And the Magus? An *Ascendant*.

'Well, perhaps we can help?'

Traveller looked to him, his smile holding. 'Thank you, Kyle. But no. This is something I have sworn to do. I must pursue it in my own way.'

'Well, if that is as it must be.' He rose to go.

'Kyle?' Traveller called after him.

'Yes?'

'Thank you. And . . . I'm very sorry. I know you were very fond of him.'

'Yes. I'm sure you were too.' Kyle turned away and his eyes met those of Jan, watching from the stern, who looked away, back out over the water, as was his habit.

The next morning Kyle awoke to find Stalker at the tiller, standing, peering ahead, and at the bow Traveller standing as well. 'What is it?' he asked Coots. The man was tending the small cooking fire in a metal bowl, cutting up the roots they boiled for a starchy stew. He gave an unconcerned shrug.

'Some kind of storm ahead.'

At the stern he caught the eye of Stalker, who gestured forward. A dark bruising of clouds darkened the sky. 'Can we go around?'

The scout merely arched one dusty blond brow. 'This is my third course correction since dawn. Each time – there it is.' To one side Jan lay curled up in blankets. Kyle considered questioning him but decided against it; if Stalker or Traveller wanted to, they could do it.

'What does Traveller say?'

'He said to stop trying to go around. Just head on north-east.'

Kyle went to the bow. Traveller's gaze was fixed ahead. He was wearing his armour coat beneath his leathers and his sword belted at his side. A sizzling anger rode his taut shoulders and stare. 'What is it?'

'Someone's interfering. Someone who should know better than to get in my way.'

'Who?'

The man looked about to answer but stopped himself, shaking his head. 'Never mind. Just keep your eyes sharp.'

'What should we do?'

'Do? Eat, check your weapons.'

Coots prepared a meal of boiled mush with fish and mouldy old bread. The Lost brothers busied themselves testing the edges of the multitude of blades each carried at belts, vests and boots. Jan had no weapon at all that Kyle could see so he fished around to come up with an old long-knife that he never used and offered it to the man. Jan looked up, surprised and pleased. Then his gaze slid aside and Kyle followed it to find Traveller watching, his face held rigid, unreadable. Jan pushed the weapon through his belt.

The edge of the unnatural cloudbank drew close. The sea curving around its front held its normal swell and trough of tall smooth waves touched by the thinnest of spume at their crests. Beneath the clouds, under the gathering dark of thick shadow, the sea appeared calm, the wind diminished. Traveller turned from the prow. 'Get down. Secure yourselves. Tie the rudder.' Stalker roped the rudder's long arm. The brothers twined their arms in taut ropes. Kyle found a secured rope and pushed an arm through. Jan sat against the ship's side, his legs out. Eerily silent, the tall looming wall of darkness rose above them like a cliff, severing the light. The *Kite* was engulfed.

Loss of headway was immediate. Kyle was thrown forward. Equipment and stores shifted, tumbling. The *Kite* groaned, planks creaking, the sail flapping loose. Waves surged around them, flooding the freeboard. In the disorienting diffuse light everything seemed flat and distant, colourless. Traveller was shouting something from the prow but his words sounded strange, distorted. Kyle was punched forward once more. Stores crashed over the brothers who roared their anger. The grinding of the keel and planking announced the *Kite* scraping up on a shore where no shore should be. A savage blow stunned Kyle.

After a time his vision cleared – he'd been disoriented for a moment. Blinking, he stood, steadying himself. A dark plain of mud stretched into the distance to an even darker treeline. Behind them, a sullen sheet of water as flat as black glass but for the wake of their passage. Overhead, dull sky the colour of slate. 'Cheerful place,' Jan observed, rubbing his shoulder.

Coots erupted from a pile of stores, cursing, a hand pressed to one eye. Badlands laughed uproariously. Stalker rubbed his hip. Traveller was examining the planking at the prow. 'Damaged?' Stalker called to him.

'Can't say. We're stranded in any case.'

'Travellers! Greetings!' someone called in Talian from the distance. Kyle peeked over the side. A man was standing in the muck. A great thatch of black hair framed a long pale face. His robes hung down in the mud and he was either very short or sunk in the slime.

Traveller vaulted the gunnel to land before the fellow only to promptly sink past the shins of his boots. Regardless, he managed to grasp hold of the front of the fellow's robes and twist a grip. The man flailed at Traveller's arm, the long loose cloth of his sleeves – long enough to hang in the mud – slapping wetly.

'Take us to the scheming rat,' Traveller snarled. 'He's finally earned a few choice words from me.'

'Yes!' the man squawked. 'That is, no. No screeching bats here. They're in the woods.'

Startled, Traveller released the fellow, who straightened his robes, smearing mud all over his front. 'I am come to deliver you to my master, Shadowthrone. You are blessed by his condescension.'

'Who are you?' Traveller asked.

'Whorou?' the man said, squinting. 'Damned awkward name. Common enough though, isn't it?' He stuck out a muddy hand. 'Hethe.'

Traveller did not raise his. After a time the fellow lowered his, wiped it on his smeared robes. 'Yes, well. We must be off! Come!' The fellow waddled away, his robes dragging behind, curls of green-brown mud falling from its trailing edges. After a few paces he turned, beckoning. 'Come, come!'

'Aw, for the Lady Thief's sake,' Coots grumbled. He collected a few stores and skins of water, and lowered himself from the side. His sandalled feet sank entirely beneath the quivering gelid surface. He shivered, gasping. 'Damn, that's cold!'

The rest followed, dropping one by one into the muck then labouring on after Traveller and their guide. Soon Kyle was almost short of breath as each foot became encased in a leaden weight of clinging mud. Stalker and Badlands had drawn knives and were shaving the layers from their feet and flicking it away. The stink was ripe with the fetid reek of decomposing sea creatures. Kyle had to turn his face away when he reached down to shave off the mud.

'Damned undignified, hey?' Badlands said to his brother, and Traveller turned sharply at that, his gaze narrowing, only to snort as if at some joke known only to himself, and set off again slowly shaking his head. The brothers exchanged mystified looks.

Ahead, the mudflats yielded to a climbing strand of black gravel. To the left stretched a dark forest of tangled grey underbrush and squat trees. Their guide was leading them to the right where the shore climbed to eroded hillocks thatched in thick tangled grasses. Kyle wondered if he was falling behind. Either that, or their guide was sinking further and further into the mud, or getting shorter. Most of his robes now trailed him in a long train and his sleeves dragged as well. Stalker and Kyle exchanged uncertain looks.

Beneath his hanging robes, the man, or whatever he was, now clearly stood no more than waist-high to Kyle. Taking a few quick steps Traveller lunged ahead to grab the sodden trailing cloth and yank it. It came away revealing a short, hairy, winged, monkey-like creature that spun, hunching and snarling.

Everyone froze, staring.

Surprised, the creature drew itself up and, with an uncanny mimicry of wounded dignity, snatched the robes back from Traveller and marched off. Traveller turned to face everyone, completely astonished. He bent his head back as if entreating some unknown blessing from the sky – patience, perhaps – then rubbed his neck and exhaled loudly. 'Apologies. It's my fault. An old argument between myself and the one awaiting us. He was always of the opinion that . . . I took myself too seriously.'

Ahead, the creature had reached the gravel and now struggled to dress itself. The effort degenerated into a battle of life and death between beast and garment. The creature flailed amid the wet folds, hissing and kicking, squalling its rage. Its bullet-head emerged, fangs clenched on a mouthful of the cloth. It mimicked throttling folds in its hairy hands then disappeared again amid the sagging wet mess. Traveller simply walked on past. Everyone followed, stamping the mud from their sandals and boots. Last, Kyle saw the creature pop its head up. Its yellow eyes deep beneath prominent brow ridges blinked their confusion. It scampered ahead dragging its tattered adversary after it.

Cresting the eroded hillock, Kyle saw a plain dotted with abrupt hills, or what resembled hills. Their sides appeared too steep to be natural. Traveller was walking on, heading in the direction of a dark lump in the distance, though just how far away it might be Kyle had no way of judging. Everything seemed strangely distorted here, wherever here was. He jogged up to Stalker. 'So, where are we?'

The scout was adjusting his studded leather hauberk and kicking mud from his knee-high leather moccasins. He scowled his disgust. 'Shadow Hold, I'd say.'

'Shadow Hold? What's that?'

'That's what we call it where we're from. You could call it the Warren of Shadow, or Meanas, or whatever you like. Take your pick – it don't care a whit.'

Kyle slowed. So, Shadow. The Wanderer, Trickster, Deceiver. A power to avoid, or treat with most carefully, according to the shamans and warlocks of his people. Now they were in its grip. And the swordsman with them claimed to know its master personally – and to have an argument with him. True, so far it did not strike Kyle as particularly menacing. If anything, it struck as, well, disorganized and slightly deranged.

The beast had gained the advantage once again and, throwing the ragged robes over its shoulders, stuck its chest out and marched in a direction slightly askew of their line of advance. Eventually, finding itself off alone, it would squawk and run to gain the front once more, raise its chin and set off resolutely in the wrong direction. All these antics took place under the very nose of Traveller who displayed no outward hint of noticing, though Kyle thought his back increasingly rigid and sword-straight as the journey continued.

The hills proved to be domes constructed of cyclopean stones, ancient, overgrown, some displaying cracks or collapsed sides where the blocks scattered the plain as if having been thrown outwards by some tremendous force.

At one point a sudden cloud of darkness boiled over them as if the unseen sun were obscured even further. Kyle was unnerved to see shadows flickering over the dry dusty ground, even over his arms and legs. It was as if someone were waving tatters of cloth between him and the sun. Just as suddenly the 'storm' of shadows swept on. Seeing that no one appeared harmed, he and Jan exchanged uncertain shrugs and continued.

Their goal resolved itself into one of these domes, larger than the rest and with straighter sides. Reaching the open dark portal, the creature scampered in without a backward glance leaving a trail of mud across the threshold. The party halted by mutual unspoken consent. Traveller turned to them, his eyes lingering on that portal. 'I'll go in. No one else need come. Though I can't forbid anyone from choosing to do so. It's up to you.'

'I'd rather remain out here. If you don't mind,' Jan said with something like distaste in his voice. And he sat on a nearby block.

'Us, too,' Stalker said. Coots and Badlands gave their curt agreement.

Traveller looked to Kyle.

'Is it dangerous?' Kyle asked.

'Dangerous? Well, if you mean will we be attacked . . . no, I don't believe so.'

'All right. I'll come. I mean, we're kind of in already, if I understand things aright.'

Traveller's brows rose, impressed. 'True enough. I believe so.' He started to the portal. Kyle followed.

The entrance tunnel was dark, cool and humid. Torchlight flickered ahead. They entered the main chamber, a round domed vault containing shattered stone sarcophagi, the occupants of which lay scattered about the chamber, desiccated limbs askew, clothes dusty dry tatters, teeth gaping in yellow grins. Traveller scanned the chamber and his fists clenched.

'*Enough!*' The eruption of his voice shook the stones and brought down wisps of dust. 'Was that your wizened monkey face we followed all this way?'

'*Wizened!*'

A shadow against the far wall started forward, rising. 'I'll have you know I am quite well preserved.'

'No more games – *Ammanas*.'

'Games? No more games? What, then, to do? All is a game.'

'Ammanas . . .' Traveller ground out.

'Oh, very well.' Translucent shadow arms gestured. The chamber blurred, shadows churning, to resolve into a long hall, stone-walled, a roof of sturdy timber crossbeams sunk in gloom, and at the far wall a broad stone fireplace. 'More to your liking?'

A shrug. 'Yet another façade, but it will do. And Cotillion?'

'Here.' A soft voice spoke from behind Kyle, who spun to see a man in a doorway, unremarkable but for a rope coiled around one shoulder. Traveller bowed shallowly to the man who continued to watch, motionless.

'And who is this?' Ammanas asked. Kyle was alarmed to see the figure approach, a walking stick now in one insubstantial hand. Its features resolved into that of an elder, darkly hued, mouth a nest of wrinkles. 'Kyle,' he said, his voice faint. Could this be the Deceiver himself? He struck Kyle as dangerous, yes, but also oddly frail, even vulnerable.

'A companion,' Traveller said.

'And why are you here?'

Kyle had no idea how to answer that. Why was he here? Curiosity? Hardly adequate. No – he came simply because Traveller did. Kyle motioned to the swordsman, 'To accompany Traveller.'

'Ah yes.' The figure, no more than a gauzy patchwork of shadows, turned to the man. 'Such a valuable quality. So . . . useful it proved.'

Traveller merely snorted his dismissal. 'Do not speak possessively of that which you never possessed.'

'That is open to debate.'

'I did not come here to debate.'

'Then why did you come?'

'You brought me here!'

'I merely invited you – you did not have to come.'

'Did not—' Traveller bit the words off, pressing a fist to his lips. He exhaled a great harsh breath, flexing his neck. 'You have not changed a damned bit. There's still nothing for us to discuss.' He turned away. 'Come, Kyle. My apologies. This was a mistake from the beginning.' He faced the other man, Cotillion, who stood aside, a mocking smile at his thin lips.

'Come, now,' Ammanas called out. 'Let us stop this bickering. You know what I offer.'

Traveller stopped, turned, keeping both Ammanas and Cotillion in view. 'No, I do not. You haven't made your offer yet.'

The shadow figure's shoulders slumped their exasperation. 'Really, please! I rather thought my hairy messenger made it all quite plain in his eloquent pantomime . . . you can never succeed in your goal, my friend. I'm sorry, but there it is.' The figure shook, giggling. 'Quite inspired, his display. Emblematic, you might say.'

Kyle had decided that he really ought not be where he was. Traveller, however, blocked the exit. Since he was stuck, then, he decided he ought to be useful and guard the man's flank. He rested his hand on the grip of his tulwar and found the sword surprisingly warm – hot, almost. He yanked his hand away, alarmed.

'And your offer?' Traveller ground out.

'*My offer?*' Ammanas fairly squawked. 'Gods! Need I spell it out?'

'From you? Yes. Exactly so.'

The god – yes, the god of deceivers, Kyle reminded himself – hissed a string of curses beneath a breath, drew himself up as tall as he could manage – a height yet far below even that of Kyle, who was considered squat – and swished his walking stick back and forth through the air, mimicking swordplay. 'You strike at shadows. You chase ghosts. Yet always your quarry eludes you . . . Well, I know something of shadows and eluding. I can help you along, old friend. A nudge here; a hint there. What say you?'

'And the price?'

The walking stick set down with a tap. Translucent hands rested upon its silver hound's head grip. 'A mere service. That is all. One small service.'

Traveller was silent for a time, his gaze steady upon the wavering transparent figure. Kyle's sword had become intolerably hot. He pulled it away by stretching his belt. Yet instead of alarm what he felt was embarrassment – how dare he interrupt such talk so far above his ken with a complaint about his weapon?

'I will agree, Ammanas, provided you agree to a condition.'

The shadow figure hunched, almost wincing. 'A condition! What's this of conditions? I ask no conditions of you! One does not raise a finger to the one you seek and insist upon conditions!'

'Hear me out. Don't fly to the winds.' A harsh laugh sounded from Cotillion at that. The figure turned a dark glare upon the man. 'What is it?'

'Two requests.'

'Two! *Two!*'

'Hear him out,' Cotillion said wearily.

'I'm handling these negotiations.'

'Is that what you call this?'

489

The figure wavered closer to Cotillion. 'Don't—' Though appearing to float, Ammanas seemed to suddenly trip, stumbling. 'What?' He poked with his walking stick and came up with limp folds of muddy torn robes. '*What is this mess?* Look at it! Mud all over the floor! Who is going to clean this up? Where is he! I'll skin the rat.' He shot a finger into the air. 'Wait!' The finger lowered to point to Kyle. 'What are you doing?'

Kyle could not help but back away. 'Nothing. Nothing! It's just my sword. Something's—'

'*Cotillion! I sense an emergence!*'

A hiss accompanied Cotillion's coiled rope seeming to come to life of it own accord. It leapt to twist around the sheathed weapon at Kyle's side. A flick and Kyle's belt snapped, the tulwar flying loose. A coil then snapped around his neck, tightening. Traveller motioned and the rope parted, snipped cleanly in two. Cotillion and Traveller faced one another, Cotillion spinning his foreshortened length of rope, Traveller with his sword held in a two-handed grip above his head, point down. Kyle yanked the now limp coil of rope from his neck and gasped in a breath.

'*Halt!*' Ammanas bellowed. Surprisingly, both men obeyed the Deceiver, edging back into guard positions. He raised a finger it to where the tulwar had fallen. 'An uninvited guest.'

The sheathed weapon had fallen in a tangle of Kyle's leather belt. Smoke now climbed from the equipment, then flames as the wood and leather burst into fire. Incredibly, molten iron poured out over the stones, bubbling and hissing. It steamed like boiling water. The clouds became biting, forcing Kyle to cover his eyes and nose. Even Traveller, at Kyle's side, was batting an arm through the mixed steam and smoke.

As the smoke dispersed Kyle caught sight of a tall shape hunched where the sword had fallen. The figure slowly straightened, climbing taller and taller, stretched out his long arms. A bunched mane of white hair fell down his back. He was barefoot in loose trousers and a long loose shirt.

When the newcomer turned, Kyle was astounded to see the Archmagus of the Spur. *It was he! The Wind King!* Closer now, Kyle was certain that he must also be the figure from his dreams.

Ammanas, Cotillion and Traveller all edged together to face the intruder and Kyle almost laughed to see them shrinking from the entity. His second thought was: *all that is Holy! Who was this being?* Ammanas eventually slid forward, planted his walking stick. 'Osserc! You are trespassing upon my demesnes!'

So! It was he! Skyfather of his people. Alive after all! Known to these – an Ascendant?

The blunt, almost brutal features of the being did not even register recognition that anyone had spoken. His gold eyes scanned the room, avid. A smile of satisfaction tightened his heavy lips. 'After so long . . .' he rumbled in accented Talian.

'You must go! You are not permitted here!'

Kyle's stomach clenched in dread upon seeing Cotillion and Traveller, flanking Ammanas, exchange narrowed glances. The doorway was now unoccupied but Kyle did not move. He longed to approach yet dared not interrupt. From the distance, muted by the walls of the ruin, or building, or whatever sort of construct it was, came the long and low baying of hounds. Ammanas straightened to rest his hands on the handle of his walking stick. A creamy satisfied smile crept up his lips.

Osserc merely turned his back upon everyone, stretched his hands out, running them over the walls. 'Yes, yes. I *see* . . .' he breathed, his tone almost reverent.

Ammanas's insubstantial features twisted his frustration. He stamped his walking stick. 'Do not be so foolish as to provoke me!'

'And do not be so foolish as to repeat the mistake you made with my compatriot Anomander not so long ago,' Osserc growled. 'How many guardians did you lose bickering with him, little shadow crow? Two? Three?'

Flinching away, Ammanas turned to Cotillion. The two appeared to share unspoken communication. The rope in Cotillion's hand twitched as if it were part of the thoughts. Traveller slid forward, sword raised, the light gleaming from the oily magenta blade. His back to the room, Osserc murmured, 'I know that weapon better than you and we have no business, upstart.' Traveller carefully edged back, his eyes slitted.

A rumbling snarl shook the stones beneath Kyle's feet. He turned his head aside to see there in the entrance a crouching hound, a monstrous one that appeared as if it could be fully as tall as Kyle himself, mangy brown and scarred. Its snout, longer than Kyle's forearm, rested on its outstretched forepaws. Ammanas crossed to it, set a hand on its head, murmured reassuringly.

Into this tableau came the little monkey-like messenger. He was pushing a mop ahead of himself as he came from further within. All eyes, but for those of Osserc, moved to track the creature as it became increasingly obvious that his path would take him straight into the giant. The mop bumped up against Osserc's bare foot. The giant did not move, though he clasped his hands behind his back in what Kyle thought might have been irritation. The creature repeatedly banged the wet mop-head against Osserc's foot. Its face screwed up in vexation. The giant edged his head down. The monkey-like thing jumped up and down, waved its arms, stamped a foot. Letting out a deep rumbling sigh, Osserc stepped aside to allow the fellow to pass. The creature slathered the mop over the flagging, muttering to itself.

Ammanas straightened, his gauzy face relieved. 'The House is unconcerned. We need not bother ourselves with this rude intrusion. We may ignore it as one might an irksome fly.'

Osserc snapped a glare to Ammanas that just as quickly eased into indifference and he turned away. His gaze found Kyle and the eyes swirled molten, his lips pulled back in what one might generously call a smile, revealing prominent tusks at his lower jaws. 'Well done, son of the steppes. I am in your debt.'

'Father of Winds,' Kyle began, stammering, 'I had no idea . . .'

'You were not to. And I am not father to winds or to your people. Your ancestors merely adopted the ancestral totems of sun, sky and winds – all of which shine, turn and blow without my intervention. So are traditions invented. It is up to you to keep them – or not. Here,' and he gestured and a weapon appeared in his hand. 'I owe you a weapon. Take mine with my thanks and we are even. Goodbye.' The giant abruptly turned and walked away, disappearing into the gloom further within. Kyle stared after him as one might a phantom.

'Good riddance!' Ammanas called loudly. 'Now, the rest of you, out as well! Out! Is this a grubby tavern? Am I social host?'

The hound had left and so Kyle backed into the doorway. It opened on to a hall that led past an alcove containing a huge and ornate set of bronze armour, then on to another door that opened as Kyle approached. Kyle almost stumbled here as he glanced back to see the same old beehive-like tomb behind him.

Outside, Jan and the Lost brothers sat up, weapons out. 'Thank the Dark Hunter,' Stalker called. 'A hound as large as a horse came running in after you.'

'Yes. It didn't attack.'

'And Traveller?'

Kyle looked back, surprised. 'He should be with me . . .'

After a moment the swordsman did emerge. He glanced anxiously among them, then relaxed. 'Good. I was worried that perhaps the hound . . .'

'It ignored us,' Stalker said. 'So? What happened?' and he looked between them.

'An agreement was reached and you are free to go,' Traveller said.

'*You?*' Kyle and Stalker echoed.

'Yes. I am not going with you.'

'I didn't agree to that,' Kyle said, his voice rising.

'Don't worry. There's no danger – either for you or for me.'

'*No danger?* That man, or god, or whatever he is, is a *lunatic*.'

'I've had that impression for some time, Kyle.'

'So, just like that? You'll stay?' The scout could not have been more sceptical.

'Yes.'

'Do we go back to the boat?' Jan asked.

'No.'

'No? Why not?'

'You no longer need it.' The swordsman scanned the horizon, inclined his head to indicate a direction. 'You should go that way.'

'What do you—' Stalker began but something flew out of the open portal to land in the dust with a wet slap. A torn muddy robe.

Everyone traded glances. 'I suppose,' Coots said, 'that means we ought to be on our way.'

'Yes. You should.'

'Traveller,' Kyle begged. 'Don't . . .'

'It's best this way. I'm endangering you. Attracting unnecessary attention.' He walked to stand before Jan. The two locked gazes for a time, neither looking away. Finally, taking a deep breath, the swordsman studied Jan directly for the longest time, his gaze moving up and down; the old man did not move at all, his mouth clenched tight as if he dared not speak. After a moment Traveller sighed, nodded at some unspoken evaluation and turned to Kyle. He set his hands on Kyle's shoulders. 'Farewell, Kyle. Bring your case to the Guard. I hope they will prove worthy of you.' He released Kyle's shoulders.

'Please come with us!'

The swordsman gently reached out to touch the amber stone hanging at Kyle's neck. 'You were right to pick that up. But I know he will always be with you regardless. I know he will always be with me. Farewell.' And he turned away, blinking.

Kyle felt the hot tears at his cheeks. 'Traveller . . .'

The man's shoulders tightened. 'It is how it must be, Kyle. I . . . I am sorry.' He faced the brothers. 'Stalker, Coots, Badlands. An honour.'

They tilted their heads in goodbye.

Traveller ducked into the tomb, disappearing into the darkness.

'Farewell Whorou!' a voice called from aside. 'Fare thee well!' Kyle spun. Their guide, the dirty-robed fellow, had returned. As they all watched, he blew his nose on the arm of his torn garment. Kyle glanced back to the entrance; it was of course gone. 'Come, come,' the man beckoned, the loose wet sleeves hanging empty. 'Come.'

Reluctantly, Kyle last, they started away from the beehive-shaped tomb, striking a direction that to all appearances seemed no different from any other across the flat dusty plain dotted by its ancient sepulchres. Overhead, in the slate sky, things flew, looking like nothing more than folded shadows.

CHAPTER VI

It was an act driven by a profoundly inward – and backward – looking movement. Who are we outsiders to judge? It was, after all, also
driven by the honest (if we may claim misdirected) desire to improve
the condition and prospects of the Wickan people . . . In this regard it
must be seen as completely earnest and not in the least duplicitous.
Especially when bracketed with the act it then allowed.

The First Civil Wars, Vol. II
Histories in Honour of Tallobant

SURROUNDED BY COMMAND STAFF AND BODYGUARD, ULLEN STOOD
next to Urko and the Moranth Gold commander atop a modest
rise to one side of the marching columns of Talian and Falaran
infantry. Toc, together with a troop of some forty, came riding up
and reined in. 'A good day for battle,' Urko called and Toc gave his
assent. 'Not too hot.' Ullen peered at the sky; yes, overcast, though it
might rain. He didn't look forward to that. They had left the fort
before first light and been marching through dawn. The night had been
relatively calm – the beast, Ryllandaras, if indeed it was he, had probed
twice but been driven off by the massed ranks of Gold, backed up by
a liberal dose of their munitions. Already flights of gulls, crows and
kites crowded the skies over the line of march. How many generations
of warfare, Ullen wondered, had it taken them to learn what the
massing of so many men and women in armour might presage?

'Commander V'thell,' Toc greeted the Moranth in his armour hued
a deep, rich gold like the very last gleam of sunset. The Moranth
inclined his fully enclosed helmed head.

'Still unmounted, I see,' Toc said to Urko with something like a
nostalgic smile.

Urko shrugged beneath his heavy armour of banded iron. 'It

reassures the soldiers. They don't like their commander being mounted when they ain't. Makes 'em suspect you're gonna ride off as soon as things get hot.'

Toc's staff, all mounted, shared amused glances. Captain Moss caught Ullen's eye and winked. 'And the carriage?' Toc asked, gesturing down the gentle slope to where a huge carriage painted brilliant red and green waited while grooms fought its fractious team of six horses.

Urko rolled his eyes. 'Bala. She'll be with me at the centre rear. I'll have the reserves. The Falaran cavalry and elements of the Talian and Falaran infantry. Choss is already with the south flank. You'll have the north – and where are those blasted Seti anyway?'

Toc scanned the north horizon. 'Bands are appearing. They'll be here soon.'

'Bloody better be.'

'What of this force in the south? The Kanese?' Toc asked.

'Still arrayed around the south side of Pilgrim's Bridge. None too eager to take on the Guard – can't say I blame them. Amaron has some hints that they are to come out for Surl—' Urko stopped, correcting himself, 'for the Empress. But he's not sure. They might decide it's worth it, though, at any time.'

'We'll keep an eye on them.'

'Aye.'

'And the Marchland Sentries?'

Urko paused, glanced away, his mouth drawing down even more. 'Withdrawn to the west. Out of harm's way 'n' all. Too bad. Could've used them. But perhaps for the better, all things considered.'

'Perhaps.'

V'thell bowed to the general. 'Permission to join my people.'

'Granted. And V'thell . . .' The Moranth Gold turned back. Urko raised a fist. 'You're the hammer. Break them.'

V'thell bowed again. 'We shall.'

'I should track down an ataman,' Toc said. Urko nodded his assent. The cavalry commander rode off with his troop.

'And myself?' Ullen asked.

'I want you here. If things go to pot I'll have to wade in and I want you to take over.'

Ullen was alarmed but struggled to disguise his unease. *Wade in? You're not young any more, Commander.* 'Aye, sir.'

The general waved to the carriage. 'Now go down and see what Bala has to say.'

Ullen less successfully hid a smile. 'Yes, sir.'

Toc and his troop combed the rolling hills north-west of the assembly point. From high ground the dust of Laseen's forces was clear to the east. Midday, his instincts told him. They'd finish manoeuvring by midday. Where were Brokeleg and Ortal? It was unthinkable they should let him down. After all the years he'd spent among the Seti; after he'd fought with Kellanved for their interests. He'd even raised his own children among them: Ingen, Leese and little Toc the Younger.

A messenger pointed to the north where a broad cloud, more like an approaching dust storm, was darkening the sky. Soon, a van of horsemen could be seen galloping down a far broad slope. Tall pennants of white fur flew prominently, along with white fur capes. *Imoten, not the atamans. Has the man usurped them completely?*

He waited while the column closed. A standard-bearer led, a tall crosspiece raised above him hung with white pelts and set with what looked like freshly skinned animal skulls. The sight of that grisly standard made Toc profoundly uneasy. Imotan followed directly, together with his bodyguard, which had swelled to some seventy men and women, all sworn to their White Jackal god. Imotan drew his mount up next to Toc's and smiled, inclining his head in what seemed an almost ironic greeting. 'Well met, Toc the Elder.'

'Imotan. Where are the atamans? We should discuss the coming engagement.'

'You will discuss the matter with me. I have direct authority over all warriors.'

I see. What has been the political infighting there in your encampment these last few days, shaman? Clearly, I have been away for too long. 'Very well. Let us find a vantage point.'

Imotan nodded to the standard-bearer who dipped the pennant forward. Blood, Toc noted to his distaste, dripped liberally from the skulls and pelts of the macabre standard, having soaked the shoulders and hair of the bearer. The massed bodyguard burst into howls of enthusiasm. Moments later, in the distance the calls were echoed and a great thunder of hooves kicked to life, shaking the ground. All along the north horizon of hilltops and crests of mounds horsemen advanced. Toc stared, his heart lurching; it was a massing such as he could not have imagined. Where had Imotan gathered such numbers? Seemed the coming of their old foe and totemic animal Ryllandaras might have given Imotan limitless reach.

The bodyguard surged ahead and Toc and his troop kicked their mounts to join their numbers.

Forward Seti scouts – the small bands Toc had seen riding the grounds – directed Imotan's column to a rise that offered a prospect of the assembling forces. Toc rested his new horse, a slim grey youngling, next to the shaman's large bay. A heavily overcast sky frowned down on a wide, very shallow basin. To the south-east, the top of the tall promontory that supported the Great Sanctuary of Burn could just be made out as a smear of yellow and umber. After jockeying and scouting through the night, elements of both forces had settled on this front in a mutual, unspoken accord. Small flags could even be made out marking the marshalling points for various units. Forward elements from both armies were already forming up.

Opposite, the skirmishers of whom Toc had been hearing so much were pouring into the basin from the south like a flood. *So many. Where did Laseen get them all? She must have emptied the gutters of Unta and every town in between. And they seemed eager enough, too.* Within their formless tide could be made out the ruled straight columns of marching infantry. *Malazan heavies. The very forces he'd counted on in the past to anchor his own light cavalry and skirmishers now arrayed against him. It was an intimidating sight. And what was this? A banner at the fore, the sceptre underscored by a sword! The Sword of the Empire! So it was true. That Fist – what was his name? – from the Seven Cities campaigns had claimed the title. Wait until Urko sees that! He'll wrap the man's own sword around his neck.*

Seti bands, Imotan's outriders, had stormed down into the basin and were already beginning to exchange arrow and crossbow fire with the skirmishers. Choss's own light infantry and skirmishers, pitifully few in number, were scrambling to catch up. Three separate columns of Moranth Gold then entered from the west, escorted by troops of Talian cavalry. They made for the centre where the standard of the Sword of the Empire had been planted.

'That horde of skirmishers must be contained and swept aside,' Toc told Imotan, who nodded, stroking his grey-shot beard. 'Our intelligence tells us Laseen hasn't the cavalry to oppose you.'

'So you say. Yet if that is true then why is she here?'

Toc's brows rose at the question. 'Well, I suppose I would have to say that she has no choice. She has to oppose us – to do otherwise would be to admit defeat. And that is hardly in her nature.'

'Is she counting on some hidden asset to deliver her? What of the Kanese?'

Toc shook his head. 'I don't believe they'll cross. A lot to lose and too little to gain.'

'They could gain much by arriving in time to deliver her . . .'

'Imotan,' Toc said, gesturing to the battle grounds, 'once it looks as if she will lose they will throw in with us. If she wins, her rule will be absolute. No one will rise to oppose her for a generation.'

The White Jackal shaman flinched at that, glowering. 'There is more to this continent than just Tali and Unta.' He turned to his guards. 'Send word to the warbands.' The guard bowed and rode off. 'What of this mercenary army? Why are they not with us? Didn't Urko offer enough?'

Toc almost laughed, mastering himself in time. 'The Crimson Guard wants the Empire crushed. That's their goal. I suppose they're thinking – why bloody themselves when we'll mangle each other for them, hey?'

'Then why not get rid of them?'

'It's Choss's estimate that despite the Avowed they are not a viable threat. He believes they don't have sufficient forces.'

'*Estimates?*' Imotan echoed. 'You would gamble when so much is at stake?'

Toc edged up his shoulders in a small shrug. 'Every engagement is a gamble. You make your best choices and hope you made no major mistakes.'

The shaman grunted a reluctant acceptance of the point. 'And Laseen? Where is she?'

Toc scanned the east. 'Hasn't arrived yet. She's probably in the rear.'

A coarse laugh from Imotan. 'So why don't I send my warriors to the rear and rid us of her?'

'Because she's probably guarded by all the Claw and mage cadre on the continent, that's why.'

'Ah, yes,' the shaman sneered. 'Your vaunted mages. Where are they now? Where is the Tayschrenn, the Hairloc or the Nightchill now? Why are we even here assembling soldiers when in the old days your mages would turn this valley into an inferno?'

Toc eased his seat in his saddle, eyed the man edgeways. *What odd directions the man's thoughts were flying in. Pre-battle jitters, perhaps.* 'We formed rank back then too, Imotan. Even with Tayschrenn. Because mages can't hold territory. In the end, it always comes down to leather on the ground – the plain spearman or army regular. They win the wars.'

'Myself, I would say otherwise.' Imotan hooked a leg around the pommel of his saddle. 'I would say that you Malazans foolishly squandered your talent. Burned them up and drove them mad as your reach exceeded your grasp.' He regarded Toc squarely. 'And now you have none left worth the name.'

Toc answered the man's steady gaze from under knitted brows. He wasn't certain how to respond to that claim – or provocation. Could it even be denied? What was the man getting at?

Imotan gestured to the field. 'Ah. Something is happening.'

Toc glanced down. What was happening was complete murderous chaos. Laseen's skirmishers were not waiting for their own heavies to complete their formations. They charged forward in waves, kneeling and firing, then retiring while the next rank took their place. A steady hail of bolts punished the Gold, who displayed astonishing discipline in retaining ranks. The Talian and Falaran flanking phalanxes were forming clean enough. Toc turned to a staffer. 'Send word to Urko to sign the advance!' To Imotan, 'I'm surprised Laseen unleashed her skirmishers so early; but then she may not have had any say in the matter. They seem to think they can win this battle all on their own. Your warbands should retake the open ground – if you would, Imotan.'

The shaman nodded his assent, signed to a guard who rode off.

Below, signal flags waved frantically between the League elements. As one the Gold drew their heavy curved blades and advanced. Urko seemed to have sent the command already – or V'thell had simply lost patience. The flanking phalanxes moved forward as well, covering them. The skirmishers palpably shrank back. Far across the basin tall Imperial banners signalled Surly – Laseen, Toc corrected himself – entering amid a column of Untan cavalry, many bearing noble banners, and flanked by marching Malazan heavy infantry.

A Talian message rider stormed up to Toc, reined savagely. 'General Urko inquires as to the disposition of the Seti,' the man panted, his face flushed.

I don't doubt that he does – though not in those words. 'Sweeping back the irregulars momentarily.'

The rider saluted. 'Aye, sir.' He reined around and gouged the iron spikes of his stirrups into his mount's flanks, galloping off in a flurry of thrown dirt.

Imotan caught Toc's gaze, directed it to the ridge line. 'The Seti are here – just as promised, Toc the Elder.'

Riders climbed the ridges and crests to the north, a curving, undulating skirmish-line of thousands of light cavalry lancers. Below, on the broad open plain a great moan went up among the Untan irregulars. The flights of crossbow bolts – so thick at times it was hard to see through their waves – faltered, thinning to nothing. The exposed men and women swarmed, bunching up like ants around three squares of infantry in their midst, seeking sanctuary within. Toc could well imagine the brutal exigency of those infantry pushing back their own allies – to allow entrance to any would mean compromising the integrity of their own formation. *Still, so many! If they should recover, take a stand of any kind . . .*

'And now, Toc,' Imotan said, a hand raised, his voice climbing. 'Because we Seti remain a free people – free to choose! We choose to go!' And he signalled to the standard-bearer, who circled the tall crosspiece hung with its freshly skinned white pelts and animal skulls. Droplets of blood pattered down on Toc's bare head and he flinched, ducking. *Go? Does he mean attack?*

All along the crests of the shallow hills, the mounted figures turned and rode off, descending out of sight. Toc gaped, turning left and right. *What? What was this?* Imotan's white-caped bodyguards pushed their mounts between him and the shaman as the man turned his horse around.

What? 'Wait! Wait, damn you! You can't do this!' He reached for his sword. All of the nearest bodyguard, some twenty, went for their weapons and Toc's staff set their hands to their grips. Toc lifted his hand away carefully. 'Imotan!' he bellowed to the shaman cantering his mount. 'This is wrong! You can still salvage your honour! Imotan! Listen to me!' *Listen . . .*

'We should get word to Urko,' a staffer said, his voice faint.

'I'm sure he can see clearly enough,' Moss suggested.

Still staring after the retreating back of the shaman, his shoulders as rigid as glass, Toc said, 'Everyone go to Urko. He'll need all the cavalry he can get.' None moved; all sat regarding their commander. He turned to scan their faces one by one and all glanced away from the complete desolation written there in the man's eyes. 'Go! All of you! . . . And tell him . . . tell him, I'm sorry that in the end, I failed him.' Toc kicked his mount to ride after the White Jackal shaman.

After glancing amongst themselves for a time, uncertain, the assembled staffers and messengers turned their mounts down on to the plain. All but one, who lingered behind.

For a few leagues the Seti ignored Toc, the lone rider attempting to push his way past the surrounding screen of the escort. The dull roar of battle had fallen away long ago. The guards swung their lances,

501

urging him off, laughing, as if he were no more than an unwanted dog.

Eventually, either in disgust or from a feeling of safety that the battle had been left far enough behind, the group slowed and halted. After they searched him and took his every weapon, including his famous black bow, Toc was allowed to pass through the crowding guards. Still mounted, he was led before Imotan, who waited, glowering his impatience.

'Do you wish to die, Malazan?' he snarled.

'What you have done is wrong, Imotan,' Toc said, calmly. 'You have stained the Seti with the name of betrayers. But you—'

'*Wrong!*' the shaman shrieked. '*You* betrayed *your* promise, Malazan! You promised us Heng! *You* turned away from that promise and so now we turn away from *you*.'

Toc knew it was useless but he held out his open hands. 'Imotan, after this battle we can turn all our resources to Heng—'

'*Too late, Malazan!*' Spittle flew from the man's lips. His hands knotted themselves within the strips of his reins. 'Another false promise! More of your empty words. All too late. Now we have our ancient patron returned to us! With him we will level Heng ourselves. Why should we die for *you*, eh?' The rheumy, lined eyes slitted as the man eased into a satisfied smile. 'And now such alliances as this are no longer necessary, Malazan. Have you any last words?'

Toc forced himself to relax. *Useless, how useless it all was.* 'Ryllandaras can't destroy Heng, Imotan. Never could, never will.'

'We shall see,' and he signed to his guards.

Two lances pierced Toc's sides, physically raising him from his saddle, then withdrew. He gasped at the overwhelming pain of it. His world narrowed to a tunnel of light and roaring agony. He was only dimly aware of the troop heading off leaving him hunched in his saddle.

After a time his mount moved a restless step and he unbalanced, sliding off to fall without even noting the impact. He lay staring at the sky through a handful of dry golden blades of grass until a dark shape obscured his view, sat him up.

A sharp stinging blow upon his face. He blinked, squinted at someone crouched before him, wet his lips. 'Ah, Captain Moss. Thank you . . . but I don't think there's much hope . . .'

The captain was studying him. The scar across his face was a livid, healing red. Sighing, Moss sat, plucked a blade of grass and chewed it. Slow dawning realization brought a rueful grin to Toc's lips. 'But . . . you're not going to try.'

'No, sir.'

Toc laughed, convulsing, and coughed. Wetness warmed his lips. He touched it, examined his bloody fingers. 'So. She sent you, did she? I thought the Claw was compromised.'

'I'm freelance. I sometimes tie up loose ends for her.' Moss looked away, scanned the horizons. After a moment, he said, 'I've come to admire you – I really have. I want you to know that. I'm sorry.' He shifted his sitting position, checked the grounds behind him. 'She wants you to know that she's sorry too. So long as you kept away she was willing to look the other way. But this . . .' he shook his head, took out the blade of grass, studied it and flicked it aside.

'I suggest you try Urko next,' Toc breathed wetly. 'Get real close first . . .'

'Tell me about these Marchland Sentries. What or who are they guarding?'

His head sinking, Toc tried to edge it side to side – perhaps he succeeded – he wasn't sure. He dragged his fingers through the dirt, raised the handful of black earth mixed with blood to his face. 'I'm glad to die here,' he said, slurring. 'Glad. The sunlight. The wind. Beautiful . . .'

The man rose, dusting his leathers. After a moment hoofbeats shook the ground. Then, nothing. The wind knocked the heavy grasses. Insects whirred. The sun warmed the side of Toc's face. Then came movement again. He had no idea how much time had passed; each breath seemed an eternity of pained inhaling followed by wet exhaling. Someone else now stood before him – a Seti in moccasins and leathers. The man examined his wounds, raised his face, but Toc saw only a dark blur. The man said something to him, a question, but Toc only noted how the sunlight now held such a golden glow. The man left accompanied by many horses. The silence of the prairie that was in truth no silence returned. Toc felt himself join it.

* * *

At first Nait couldn't believe it when the Seti withdrew. He thought it was some kind of diversion or awful cruel trick. He'd been sure they were goners. Now, though, he joined in the great roaring cheers that followed their disappearance. The tall banner marking where the Sword's command was locked in combat with the Moranth Gold waved its encouragement. The steady crushing advance of the Gold into the Malazan phalanx faltered. In front of Nait the irregulars punched their arms into the air, hugged the infantry who moments before had been beating them away with the flats of their blades.

Then almost as if with one mind the skirmishers melted away and Nait saw the Falaran infantry phalanx closing double-time. Obviously, they now saw their only chance in breaking the Imperial units. Iron mail skirting chased in bronze flashed as the Falarans stepped in unison. They held broad, engraved leather-covered shields locked and steady. shortswords thrust straight out between the shields. Squared Falaran helmets framed eyes, some narrowed in calculation, searching their targets, others wide in eager bloodlust. 'Hold!' the master sergeant was bellowing to Nait's right. '*Hold!*'

Nait would have run if he could have. This wasn't what he'd signed up for! To be cut down in some stupid pointless battle! But he was pressed within the second rank and couldn't even raise his elbows. He could only watch as the opposing ranks closed, the marching feet shaking the ground, the stink of piss and fear assaulting him from the men and women around him, and perhaps from himself as well. His mouth was cracked dry in terror, his hand numb on the grip of the light duelling longsword he'd picked up during the Guard's assault of Unta.

The front lines crashed, jamming together as shields slid clashing into shield. Nait was squeezed breathless in the press. He couldn't even raise his sword, so ruthlessly were the two bodies of soldiers jostling for momentum. Dust kicked up by the shuffling pushing feet blinded him and caught in his throat as he sucked in great gasping breaths. Soldiers screamed around him, in rage, in pain, in panic, the noise melding with the clash of sword and crack of shields, until it all became a meaningless unintelligible roar that simply sounded like a beast thirsty for his blood. *Not me*, was all his mind could repeat like a personal prayer, *not me, not me. Not me!*

The man before him fell to a blow to the neck and the press forced him forward though he had no wish to step into that gap. In a ferocious will to preserve his skin he smashed his shield into the Falaran opposing, flicked the longsword to his eyes then down around his shield to catch the inside of his thigh and cut, withdrawing. The man fell to one knee and Nait punched his face with the boss of his shield. Immediately the Falaran behind lunged forward to smash Nait's own shield into his face. Stunned, he barely fended off the man's attacks. That taught him, though, and he settled into a stubborn, reserved defence, using his longer reach to thrust his opponents back.

What was happening just two soldiers away came to be completely irrelevant to him. His world shrank to just the enemy facing him and his shieldman and -woman flanking. For fleeting moments when the line of locked shields moved smoothly as one he had the feeling of being part of something far greater than himself. Something far stronger, almost omnipotent. It was the most intoxicating sensation of his life. Something he'd never even suspected could exist in the world. And almost immediately he felt addicted to the power of it.

How much time passed he'd no idea. All he knew was exhaustion such as he'd never imagined. Everything was wrung from him in the panicked heart-hammering effort to live. Yet he drew the strength from somewhere within to raise his shield one more time, to thrust and block. For to do otherwise would mean his death. Eventually, in a haze of pink, he sensed the pressure against him lessening. Falaran soldiery were breaking off, turning and running. Crossbow bolts took them in a withering gale like dark wings passing overhead. Nait flinched, rocked, as a number of bolts punched his shield. He opened his mouth to complain but no sound came.

Before him the men and women of the Untan Volunteer Citizen Militia now scrambled over an open field of fallen. 'Right! Right face!' came a roaring order. The phalanx turned, armour clashing. '*March!*'

Through the screen of the shifting, darting irregulars, Nait could see only the tall shields and helms of Moranth Gold closing in their slow deliberate pace. Then, Imperial infantry appeared, jogging from the front. A troop of Imperial cavalry came roaring back and in their midst bobbed the tall banner marking the Sword.

The leading Imperial phalanx had broken.

And now, Braven Tooth's command, with him jammed inside, was moving across to seal the gap. Nait felt his own flesh cringing from the coming confrontation. '*Halt!*' The phalanx froze, feet stamping as one. '*Left face!*' They turned. '*Relief!*' The ranks shifted, edging past one another. Nait found himself three ranks back from the front. An extraordinary weight left his shoulders and suddenly he could breathe. But the feeling was short-lived for he knew that if things went badly it would be his turn again too soon.

'Corporal! Corporal Nait!'

The woman next to Nait nudged him. 'Someone wants you, Jumpy.'

Movement behind through the ranks and a hand cuffed Nait's shoulder. He turned, fist rising. Captain Tinsmith caught the hand. 'Still with us, I see,' Tinsmith said, impressed.

Nait tried to speak, had to struggle to wet his mouth. 'Ah, yes, sir.'

The captain's brows rose. 'Sir, now, is it? Well, collect your saboteurs. There's fallen Moranth out there and those fool irregulars are collecting munitions. Confiscate it all. Saboteurs only! Quickly!'

'Yes, sir!'

Nait edged down the ranks picking men and women from the lines as he went. Reaching a flank, he pushed outside the phalanx, slung the heavy broad shield on to his back. Suddenly he felt completely exposed, naked. He cuffed the lads nearest him. 'Let's go! Collect munitions – search the Hood-baiting skirmishers for it!' The men and women saluted him and he jerked, startled. *Oh yeah – and don't that feel good too!*

The open plain of battle was a seething mass of running skirmishers jockeying for position. Troops of Talian and Falaran cavalry would suddenly appear without warning, scything through, running down irregulars, swords flashing, only to circle away before concerted fire could be brought to bear. Yet the League cavalry were too few. For the instant the horsemen passed, the skirmishers straightened and once more fire returned to punish the shield walls of the Gold and Malazan League formations.

Nait ran, directing his squad of ten to the trail of the Gold advance. In the middle distance a great shout went up from the north League phalanx. Swords thumped shields like a roll of thunder. Nait stopped, straightening; through the charging surging mass of skirmishers he glimpsed Imperial infantry fleeing the north – Fist D'Ebbin's phalanx had broken. Now, only Braven Tooth's command faced the remaining League elements. Part of him longed to return to the newfound security of that formation – part of him was damned glad he wasn't. He curtly gestured his squad on.

A troop of Falaran cavalry came charging past running down skirmishers. Sabres flashed, red and silver. A fat bearded fellow on a huge dappled warhorse led it. He sported crossbow bolts stuck to his scaled armour like decorations. Nait's squad hunched low until they thundered past, then headed on. They reached the trail of fallen Gold Moranth and Nait crouched down next to one body thatched in crossbow bolts. Everything not attached to the corpse was gone. The irregulars had thoroughly looted the trail. Someone had even tried prising the Gold's chitinous armour from his arms, but the plates appeared sutured on. One of his squad, May, called, waving, and Nait ran to the woman. She was kneeling holding a leather satchel containing a wooden box divided into compartments. It was empty. Nait tossed it away – *Hood-damned fools! They're gonna blow themselves up!* 'Let's go before we get chopped to pieces.'

'Aye.'

Nait led them back around, heading for the flank of Braven Tooth's command. One of his squad, Brill – was that his name? – called to him, pointing in a panic to the west. There, past a screen of intervening irregulars, Nait saw a moving line of blue and green soldiery, shields raised, marching forward. It extended far to the north and south. *Shit!* League reserves advancing in a skirmish-line! They're going to try to sweep back the Imperial lights.

'What're we gonna do?' Brill asked, wiping his running nose.

'How in the Abyss—' Nait caught himself, cursed under his breath. 'Let's find someone in charge out here in this mess. C'mon!'

They hunched low, jogging, and passed a natural depression in the rolling plain where a knot of irregulars had gathered, all clustered around something, crossbows loose at their sides. Nait ran over.

'Do you crack 'em?' someone was asking within the crowd.

'Naw. I think you scratch 'em.'

'You try'

'No – *you* try.'

Nait's bowels tightened in sudden gelid terror. He surged forward. 'Who's in charge here!'

Sullen, sneering faces turned on him. 'Who wants to know?'

'I do!'

'Who're you?'

'Corporal Jumpy, that's who!' Brill bellowed, pointing a warning finger.

Silence, then gales of raucous laughter all around. 'Corporal Jumpy! That's a good one!'

Nait hung his head. *Gods, Brill* . . . 'Yeah, yeah. Listen, you're gonna blow yourselves up – worse than that, you're gonna blow *me* up. I know how to use those so hand them over . . .'

'Piss off!'

The crowd melted. Men and women legging it in all directions. 'Wait, dammit!' None halted. In seconds all that remained were four skirmishers; the youngest of the lot. They wore plain leather caps and soft leather hauberks set with rings and studs. The faces of three were ravaged by pimples and pox scars. They peered up at him suspiciously.

'You a real sapper?'

'Yeah, kid.'

'You'll show us how to use 'em?'

'Yeah.'

They exchanged narrowed glances. 'Well, OK – but we get to throw 'em!'

In a heroic effort, Nait squelched the urge to grab them by their ankles and shake them until they dropped the munitions. 'Sure, kid. You'll get to throw them.' He motioned everyone to the lip of the depression. There, they knelt for a peek. The lads cocked their crossbows. The smallest lay on his back, pushing both feet on the goat's foot lever, straining, until it caught. Nait was amazed, and appalled. *He did that just as fast as any soldier could. Crazy brave kids. Just what he needed.*

The Imperial skirmishers were now facing a fluid, shifting battle on two fronts. To the west, the League skirmish-line was making steady progress against the irregulars, who were giving ground. The line was long and loose but three deep, staggered. Shieldmen advanced, covering their own bowmen or crossbowmen. Their superior discipline was showing over the Imperials who simply retreated, making no effort to pull together an organized line. The remaining League cavalry swept back and forth across the grounds before the skirmish-line, swords scything, scattering any knots of resistance.

To the east waited the swollen merged wedge of League elements and Moranth Gold. And it was obvious to Nait that the skirmishers were now bunching up dangerously close. Braven Tooth's command must have absorbed enormous punishment holding all that back, but it still held. Behind, the reserve phalanx under High Fist Anand was closing to reinforce. With it came the Sword's banner. *Oh, great! Now he's gonna wreck another one.* Nait motioned aside.

They ducked and wove through the massed irregulars. Crossbow bolts sang overhead like angry insects, so close that Nait almost stopped to chase down one or two offenders but they scattered when he turned and he gave it up as useless. He led his squad to a position as close to the Gold shieldwall as he dared. All around skirmishers knelt, loading and firing. The whine and singing of bolts through the air was unrelenting. They'd passed a number of skirmisher bodies displaying bolts in their backs – the occupational hazard of friendly fire. Occasionally, the irregulars would dare to advance and a wave of javelins arcing out of the Moranth formation drove them back. The shouting and clash of weaponry from the ferocious engagement of heavies just beyond was deafening. Hunkered down, Nait waved his squad close. 'Okay,' he shouted. 'I want you lot to spot one of them Gold carrying something – it might be on his back or at his side. It'll be about so big – a pack or a box . . .'

* * *

From his position on the modest hillside overlooking the battle, Ullen felt sick. That horde of skirmishers was savaging their forces. Soon they might have no cohesive units left. If the Gold and Talian heavies could push through, force the Empress to retreat, then they would have a chance to bargain for terms. Otherwise, they faced a slow gnawing down to nothing. He wish Urko continued luck with his skirmish-line. Gods! A line! Forming line with Imperial cavalry still in reserve! But it was all they had. He turned to one of the messengers who waited along with his staff next to Bala's cumbersome carriage, now unhitched of all its horses, much to her annoyance. 'Any news of Toc?'

'None. Apparently he went after the Seti – hasn't been seen since.'

Poor man. They probably killed him out of shame. He examined the field. It was hard to tell – the dust kicked up by all those shuffling feet obscured any details – but it looked as though the skirmishers were bunching up favourably. He was about to tell Bala to send a message to V'thell when across the field Imperial pennants and battle-flags dipping and circling caught his attention. The Imperial cavalry – many boasting their own noble family banners – was on the move. Two wings came cantering out from the rear where a tall grey horizontal banner bore the Imperial sceptre. They arced around the battlefield to the north and south. But few. Very few. Less than a thousand all told, he calculated. His gaze flicked to Urko's thin skirmish-line. The risk they'd invited had been delivered. It suddenly seemed to him that perhaps they'd waited too long. 'Bala! Bala!'

'Do not bark! I am here!' came her scornful voice from within the carriage.

'Tell V'thell, now's the time! Open up!'

'Yes, yes!'

A flash from the battlefield made him flinch. It was followed by an eruption of dirt and bodies that arced up high above the Gold formation, flying outwards in all directions, armoured bodies pinwheeling, then spinning down. The thunderous echo of the explosion reached him like a distant roll.

Hood preserve us! A lucky crossbow bolt? Who could know? He almost laughed. His order might well be irrelevant now that the first munitions had been unpacked. V'thell would probably just go ahead now. And he watched sideways, half wincing, for the firestorm to come. His gaze caught the top of the distant outcropping to the south, golden now in the late afternoon sun. And the Guard. What would they do? Should Laseen win would they throw their weight against her now that she was weakened? Yet what could they hope to accomplish?

Someone else would merely claim the Throne. And what if Urko and Choss down in the chaos below should prevail? Would the Guard simply leave, the terms of their Vow sufficiently fulfilled?

'What do you sense of the Guard?' he asked of Bala.

'Ahh! You are perhaps no fool after all, little Ullen. They have not deployed – yet. But they watch. And wait. And bide their time.'

Some ally this mage of theirs was proving to be!

A moment later a rider charged up from behind Ullen's position, sawed his reins. 'Seti approaching from the rear, sir,' he gasped. 'A long column.' Ullen's staff and guards repositioned themselves, swords drawn. Shortly afterwards five Seti horsemen galloped up. Ullen raised a hand and kneed his mount to the fore. The lead Seti was a bull of a man in layered ringed armour bearing a score of lances, javelins and two long-handled axes crossed over his back, long-knives sheathed at his hips. Under his blunt bronze helmet his scarred, sun- and wind-darkened features were those of a startlingly old man.

An intuition whispered to Ullen and he inclined his head, 'You are this Wildman of the Plains?'

'I am. And I am come to offer a measure of restitution, Malazan, for my countrymen's betrayal.'

'That is?'

'We will ride against the Imperial cavalry – just the cavalry and only them! What say you?'

This unlooked-for offer, the answer to his despair, made Ullen's gaze blur. His throat clenched so tightly he was unable to talk. *Thank the capricious laughing Gods!*

'Well? Speak, damn you!'

Ullen fought to breathe. 'Yes, yes, of course. Your arrival is timely.'

'Damned right – we've been watching.' The man straightened in his saddle, raised a hand signalling and rode onward. A roar of cheers arose from behind Ullen's position; then came a rumble of hundreds of galloping horses. They came charging past, yipping and chanting, lances raised. Most carried no animal fetishes at all, though some bore wolf, lion and ferret pelts and tufts tied to their lances or worn over their backs.

Thank you, whoever you are. And thank whatever old grudge it is that drives you to lend a hand.

* * *

The detonation that followed his boys all tossing their sharpers at the Moranth Gold carrying a munition box exceeded Nait's expectations by a hundredfold. It kicked him and his squad backwards though they were lying down. Dirt, gravel, shattered equipment and other wet pieces of things he didn't want to think about came pelting down in a thick passing rain. After the echoes of the concussion ceased, he sat up, knocked a hand to his ear to try to regain some hearing. All around the battle had paused, and a shiver seemed to pass through every soldier present as each now realized the very terrible turn this engagement had just taken. His squad, recovering, jumped up and down in what to Nait was silent, childlike glee. Around the circle of fallen Gold Moranth, helms, he noted, were turning their way. He frantically motioned for a retreat and started hustling his squad back. A flight of javelins hurried them on.

They pushed their way back while the crowded irregulars babbled at them asking how they did that, and whether they could have one too. Brill, his big chin thrust out, told them all that Corporal Jumpy had just blown up half the Moranth Gold and that there was more of it to come. Nait just slapped his shoulder. 'Would you shut up!' He turned to the youths. 'How many more you got?'

Their grins disappeared. Their eyes darted. 'I dunno – how many you got?' one asked another.

'How many *you* got?' he retorted.

Gods, they're saboteurs already. 'All right! All right. Let's just put everything we got down here on my shield. OK?'

Eyeing one another sullenly, the youths knelt. Nait unslung his shield. Reluctantly, they dug hands into pockets and pouches and one by one, piece by piece, the extent of their haul was revealed. Nait was thrilled and horrified at the same time. *Lad turn away! Eight sharpers, two melters and a collection of smokers! And . . . Lady's Grace!* He ran a hand over the dark gold ovoid. *A cussor. They're carrying cussors into battle! So that's what happened.*

A band of skirmishers came jogging up, bent over, crossbows held high. Nait's lads threw themselves on top of their treasure. 'Hey!' one called, 'Was that you? We got some too. Show us how you did that!'

Nait waved them in. 'That was a one-off. We ain't gonna see anything like that again.'

'You Jumpy?'

Nait raised his fists as if about to grasp a handful of the fellow's shirt. Then he let them fall, his shoulders slumping. 'Yeah. That's me.'

'OK! We want some of this.'

'All right—' Beyond the lad, from the Gold shieldwall, Nait glimpsed a wave of dark objects flying high out over the crowded ranks of skirmishers. His heart clenched. '*Down!*' He threw himself on top of the lads and the assembled munitions.

A staccato of punching eruptions burst all up and down the field. Skirmishers shrieked as the jagged slivers packed into Moranth sharpers lanced through their crowded ranks. '*Retreat!*' Nait hollered with all his strength. '*Retreat!*'

He and the lads picked up the shield and ran. But they could not get far. They quickly bunched up against irregulars firing at the advancing League skirmish-line. Behind them the punishment of Gold munitions continued. Staggered explosions split the air. Smoke wafted over the field in white and black clouds. It seemed from where Nait stood that the skirmishers were being slaughtered between the two lines, and that unless someone did something he'd join them soon enough.

He motioned to the lads to pick up their munitions, then hefted his shield and faced his squad. 'We're gonna break the skirmish-line here, or die!' He pointed to the youths. 'You lot. You're gonna throw when I shout! Then keep throwing at any damned Talians who come running to reinforce. Understood?' Sweaty pale faces nodded, terror-strained. 'Good! OK.' He drew his longsword. 'Follow me!'

Nait ran for the skirmish-line. As soon as he judged the distance right he yelled, 'Throw!' Then, 'Down!' and he knelt behind his shield. Moments later sharper bursts buffeted him. Slivers sliced into his shield with high-pitched trills. He straightened in the dense smoke, bellowed, 'Charge!' and ran forward. He hoped to Trake that enough stupid and crazy brave men and women were within earshot to follow.

Pushing through the smoke, he suddenly faced a Talian infantry-man holding a shattered arm. Nait shield-bashed that arm, raising a shriek of pain, then ran his sword through the man as he lay writhing. Another Talian heavy nearby still held a shredded shield and Nait tried to knock him backwards and though he was obviously stunned by the explosions the broad fellow didn't yield a hair's breadth. He chopped at Nait and the two exchanged blows. Three more Talian heavies straightened from where they'd lain to take cover and Nait knew he was in deep trouble. Over his shoulders and past his elbows crossbow bolts snapped through the air, pluck-ing at his surcoat. One nicked his arm, another his leg. The heavies grunted, raising their shields. Brill and others crashed into them at a full run, overbearing them backwards, long-knives flashing. Nait passed that writhing mob to clash shields with yet another Talian heavy running to close the gap. A thrusting shortsword gouged Nait's side, caught in his hauberk and punched the breath from him. He bowed double, stepping back, and a blade crashed from his helmet. Another fusillade of crossbow bolts whipped around him singing in his ears; something smacked into the back of his mailed hand knocking the sword flying from his grip. The Talian shield-bashed him, sending him staggering backwards. Then a horde of skirmishers trampled both of them. The Talian went down beneath a storm of thrusting blades and the flood continued on. Nait halted, gasped in great lungfuls of the choking, smoky air. They were through. He leaned on his shield, his legs suddenly weak. He sat heavily in the crushed, smouldering grass. *This wasn't what he'd signed up for. No, not at all.*

Horrified, Ullen watched while the tide of Imperial lights slowly engulfed section after section of the League skirmish-line. Even the Seti column, engaging the heavier Imperial cavalry, could do little to stem the bleeding. At the front, the Gold and Talian phalanx had advanced with the shock of the munition barrages, but a good wedge of the Imperial formation, including the banner of the Sword, yet remained. And that was it; all either side could do. All reserves had been committed on both sides. Soon the irregulars would be free to concentrate their fire once more. As he watched, another barrage of munitions punished the Imperial phalanx facing the Gold, plus the surrounding irregulars. The Imperials refused to break; Ullen had to admire their inspired obstinacy.

After a number of passes the Seti drove the Imperial cavalry from the field. Many bright and shining Untan family pennants had fallen to the man leading the charges. This man, the Wildman, peeled off from the column with a small escort and rode back to Ullen's position. He reined in his mount, hooves stamping. Blood and lather soaked the animal's forequarters. The rider's lances were all gone, as were his javelins. One war-axe was missing, shattered perhaps. His armour was rent across the hips, shiny where blows had fallen, scraping the iron. His helmet was gone and blood sheathed his neck. Blood and gore darkened his gauntlets. The fellow appeared to be ignoring wounds that would have left anyone else prostrate.

'My thanks,' Ullen called to him. 'Though I do not think it is enough.'

The man wiped a handful of bunched cloth across his face, gestured back to the field. 'It isn't. Let's just call that the settling of old debts.' He regarded Ullen levelly, his eyes hardening. 'What will you do? Will you yield the day? Men and women are dying down there for no good reason.'

Ullen was already nodding. Yes, that was all that was left, though he could not bring himself to actually speak it. He gestured to a messenger, swallowed the tautness of his throat. 'Raise the surrender.' This messenger glanced about the assembled staff, none of whom spoke. His face paled to a sickly grey but he nodded, kneed his mount forward.

The Wildman inclined his head to Ullen in grudging admiration of what it must have taken to reach that decision, and he turned his mount to descend again to the battlefield.

'Bala!' Ullen called, his voice savage.

'Yes, yes,' she answered, just as testy. 'I am still here. Do you think I have fled already?'

'No, of course not! Send word to Urko, Choss and V'thell. Surrender.'

'Shall I inform the Imperial High Mage?'

Ullen's clenched stomach lurched. 'The what?'

'She's been watching. Had I intervened in the battle she would have struck. And though I do not consider her worthy of the title, her attack would no doubt have eliminated you and your men.'

'Thank you so *very* much, Bala,' Ullen ground out. He waited for a retort but none came. 'Bala?' Silence. Ullen dismounted, walked to the carriage on legs weak and numb from sitting all day. He wrenched open a door and peered in. Empty. Completely empty. Not even a dropped cloth or a fleck of dirt.

* * *

Possum spent the entire battle keeping an eye on the grand pavilion raised to house Laseen. Certainly, a number of Claw operatives had no doubt been posted by his lower echelon commanders. But Possum no longer knew whom to trust. Frankly, he'd always been of that policy, and it had served him well all through his career, saving his life more often than he could count. Now, however, he had more than his usual nagging suspicions and doubts. He had material indications of a parallel command structure organized by a subordinate, Coil, pursuing her own ends. This he could not tolerate – mainly because those ends no doubt did not include him.

And so he did what he did best, watched and waited. Laseen had imposed a moratorium against any head-hunting for the time being and so he did not have to be on the job. He could wait. He did not think Coil so clumsy as to ignore that edict. He stood, sorcerously hidden, in the shade of a small tent that offered a view of the rear of the Imperial residence, and waited. He kept watch both over the mundane grounds and through his Warren of Mockra.

The noise and turmoil of the battle to the west rose and fell and frankly Possum did not give a damn. It was not his job. Staffers, higher-ranking soldiers and nobles came and went. Noncombatants as well – servants, cooks, craftsmen, chamberpot emptiers – everyone necessary to the maintenance of such an august dwelling. It was these who interested Possum the most. The faceless servants who came and went without notice. How often had he himself taken advantage of the selective blindness of his social betters?

The day waned; the late afternoon sun broke through to clear sky far to the west and found his position against the tent canvas. Possum squinted. Sweat dripped down his arms. Nothing. All day and nothing. He was offended . . . No, more than that: he was disgusted! What was his profession coming to? Surely he was not alone in his – how should he put it . . . his professional curiosity? He decided to replay through the day's comings and goings, searching for a pattern. Some betraying slip or detail. And after sorting through so many individual moves, glances and gestures of those who passed, he believed he found it. A woman. Civilian. An officer's woman – wife or mistress. Seven times the woman's errands and apparently random wanderings had taken her in a near circum-navigation of the tent's walls. And her walk and carriage! No camp-follower her. Each time she made a show of coming to watch the battle but she spent more time studying the tent and its guards than looking west. A pity, really; more training and experience and she'd be almost undetectable.

Possum edged up and down slightly on his toes to keep his legs limber, ran his fingers along the pommels of the knives slipped up his sleeves. *Come back, little lady. Who are you? But more importantly – who do you work for?*

He waited and he waited. The noise of battle waned. A flurry of message riders came and went. Had someone won the blasted dreary battle? They had, he supposed. A crowd gathered of the camp-followers, wounded and servants, kept distant by the Imperial guards. Yes, from everyone's excited smiles he imagined they must have won. And then there she was. He stepped out after her, wrapped in veils of Mockra, deflecting attention.

No raised Warren flickered about her that he could sense. She gawked westward for a time, shot glances to the Imperial tent, then headed away back to the encampment. A slim wisp of a thing; a pleasure to watch. Long black hair. From time to time Possum wasn't the only one following her. Her path took her back to the officers' tents. He saw no gestures that betrayed her awareness of his presence. She entered the tent of a rather lower-ranked officer, a lieutenant perhaps, lifting the canvas flap then letting it fall behind her. Possum paused next to the neighbouring tent. Really, now. That's a give-away. There's no way talent like that would settle for a lieutenant. Her walk alone rated a captain. He sensed as passively as possible past and through the tent. No active Warren magics that he could detect. She was there, sitting. *Very well.* He dropped his favoured blades into his hands. *Time to earn his pay.*

He pushed aside the tent flap, his Warren dancing on the tips of his fingers, both blades raised, faced where she had been sitting and a hand clasped itself at his neck like the bite of a hound and pushed him to the dirt floor. Face jammed into the dirt he slashed, kicking. He raised his Warren once again but the hand clenched even impossibly tighter, grating the vertebrae of his neck. *Such strength! Inhuman!* A woman's voice breathed in his ear: 'Don't.'

He recognized that voice. He'd heard it before the day of the attack of the Guard. This was the second time this girl-woman had got the better of him. He let his Warren slip away. 'Good.' She yanked the blades from his hands as if he were a child, dug one against the side of his neck. 'Now,' she whispered, so close her breath felt damp. 'What should I do with you? By that I don't mean let you go . . . oh, no. What I mean is – how shall I kill you? I will let you choose. Do you want me to push this blade up under your chin or into your eye? Shall I ease it through your ribs into your heart?' She crouched even lower so that her lips touched his ear. 'Tell me what you want,' she breathed huskily.

Despite the stark certain knowledge that he was about to die a lustful rush for this girl-woman murderess possessed him. He wanted her more than he could express. He opened his mouth to tell her what he wanted when the tent flap opened and a woman shouted deliriously, 'They've surrendered!' Then she screamed.

The murderess snarled something in a language unknown to Possum. He twisted, throwing her off. He jumped up, fresh weapons drawn but she was gone. He pushed the screaming woman aside to search outside. Of course there was no sign. He calmed the woman with a wave of Mockra.

'Thank you. You know, their surrender saved my life.' He bowed to leave then paused, turning back; he looked her up and down – not bad. A little bit more his type and he might've . . . well, duty and all . . . He headed to the Empress's tent.

Far along the western horizon the setting sun had passed beyond low clouds and Nait sat letting the slanting light warm his old bones. Old! Ha! Just this morning he'd thought of himself as young. But now he felt old – especially in the company of these sprouts. Old and wrung out. It was too much effort even to open his eyes. He thought of all the stupid things he'd done and he vowed never to ever do anything like that again. And it wasn't like he was some kind of glory-seeker or any dumb shit like that; no, he'd done all of it merely to preserve his precious skin.

Someone tapped his outstretched booted foot. Squinting, shading his eyes against the orange-gold glow, he peered up to see an Imperial officer. 'Yeah? Ah – yes, sir?' He saluted.

'Are you Corporal Jumpy?'

'Ah, no and yes, sir.'

'Your captain wants you. Something about a commendation.'

'That so, sir? Thank you, sir.'

The officer moved on. Nait made an effort to stir himself, failed. He fell back against his shield right where he'd sat when the skirmish-line broke. He felt as if all the brothers of all the girls he'd stolen kisses and gropes and more from had caught up with him and beaten him all over with wooden truncheons. Incredibly, his worse wounds had been inflicted by the skirmishers themselves. After the adrenalin rush of battle drained away he'd been surprised to find that a crossbow bolt had passed entirely through the inside of one thigh. Another had gouged his neck with a slice that would not stop bleeding, while another had lain open the back of his hand, and another had almost cut his ears off by knocking his helmet all this way and that. And he knew he was damned lucky.

More shapes moved about the darkening battlefield; stunned wounded walked aimlessly; camp-followers searched for loved ones and secretly looted on the sly; healer brigades collected wounded. Nait could not be bothered to get up. Around him his squad sprawled, equally quiet, sharing waterskins and pieces of dried flatbread. He took a mouthful of water, washed it around his mouth and spat out the grit and blood. He searched around for loose teeth – he'd taken such a clout in the jaw.

Someone else approached. Glancing over Nait recognized him and stood up wincing, favouring his leg. Tinsmith. The captain looked him up and down. 'You look like Hood's own shit.'

'Thank you, sir.'

'But you're alive.'

'Yes, sir.' His eyes tightened on the captain. 'Sorry, sir?'

Facing the west, the captain smoothed his moustache. 'You and Least. And Heuk.'

Him and Least. And Heuk. That was all? So Hands and Honey Boy bought it. Big sensuous Hands dead and cold. Hood be damned – what a waste! He thought of all the awful things he'd said and done to her and his face grew hot, his breath shortening. She'd taken all those things to Hood with her; no chance for him now to take them back, or apologize, or tell her she was probably damned right. 'I'm sorry, sir.'

'Yes. Me too. But . . .' and he cuffed Nait's arm, 'congratulations. You are now officially a sergeant.' He held out a grey cloth armband. 'From what I hear you earned it.'

Nait took it loosely in his fingers. Him a sergeant! Now what would they think back home! It was what he'd wanted all this time but now that he had it he realized he was just a damned fraud. It would be an insult to Hands and Honey Boy for him to wear this. He suddenly remembered the captain still standing there with him. 'Ah, yes. Thank you, sir.'

'You're welcome, Sergeant.' Tinsmith inclined his head aside, 'These your boys?'

'Yeah. Squad of ten, sir.'

'Very good. Your first detail is to help with the fortifications around the encampment. They've been going up all day. High Fist Anand wants a ditch and a palisade, or a wall of spikes. Whatever you 'n' the other sappers can manage.'

Eyes still on the cloth, he said, 'Yes, sir.' Puzzled, he looked up. 'Why, sir?'

'Why?' Tinsmith's pale watery eyes watched him with something like compassion, or gentleness. 'A sea of blood's been spilt here, Nait. Night's coming. *He'll* be coming. We have to get ready for him.'

Him. *Him!* Oh, Burn save them! Him! He faced the squad. 'Up, you louts! We have shovel detail! C'mon! At the camp. They got hot food up there, I hear! Now, c'mon.'

He turned back to Captain Tinsmith, called after him, 'Sir! What happened to that old duffer, what's his name, the master sergeant?'

The captain was still for a time. 'You haven't heard?'

'No, sir.'

'He faced down the Gold the whole time, Nait. Stopped them cold. He's the reason we didn't break, him 'n' Braven Tooth. They finally got him though. Blew him up with their munitions there at the end.'

'Too bad.'

'Aye. Too bad. See you at camp.'

Damn. Another one. He waved his men on. Seemed the old fart knew his business after all.

It was a grim crossing to the east. The stink of spilled entrails and loosened bowels drove Nait to cover his face. In places it was difficult to find a clear spot to walk. From the sprawled bodies it was plain the lightly armoured skirmishers had taken a savaging while at the same time inflicting mass murder on the Talian and Falaran regulars. Wounded called, or just moaned, gesturing helplessly to them as they passed. His boys and girls promised to send help to each – what more could they do? Gulls, crows and vultures hovered overhead and hopped among the bodies, glistening with fluids and quarrelling. Nait threw rocks at them.

'Sergeant,' a man called in accented Talian. Nait turned. It was that Falaran cavalry commander. He lay pinned on his side under his dead horse. Crossbow bolts stood from the two like feathers. Nait squatted next to him, pulled off the fellow's helmet. 'My thanks,' he said, smiling behind his big orange-red beard.

'What can I do for you?'

'Nothing. I cannot complain. I've a good horse with me.'

'Maybe some water?'

The man grimaced his revulsion. '*Water?* Gods, man, whatever for? No – but there is a flask of good Falaran brandy in my waistbag there . . .' he gestured with his chin. Nait fished through the bag and as he did so he saw that one of the man's arms was pinned beneath him while the other was stitched to his side by three crossbow bolts. He found a beaten and dented silver flask, uncorked its neck. He tipped a taste into the man's mouth. Pure bliss lit the commander's face as he swallowed. 'My thanks.'

Nait waved his squad on. 'We have to go.'

'Yes, I know. But I've a favour to ask of you, soldier.'

Oh Gods no. Not that. 'No . . . I'm sorry.'

'Ah, well, I understand. It's just the birds, you see. Evil beasties flapping closer all the time. And I . . . well . . .' he glanced down to his useless arms.

Soliel's mercy! How could he leave the man to . . . *that*? But he was no killer. What could he— 'Brill!'

'Sir?'

Nait shoved the flask to the man. 'Stay here with this wounded officer – wave down a healer.'

Brill saluted, his long gangly limbs jerking, thrust out his chin. 'Aye, sir.'

'OK. Let's go.'

As they turned away, Nait heard the cavalry commander asking Brill, 'So, have you ever been to Falar then?'

By the time they reached the Eastern border of the battlefield their trousers and cloth leggings were painted red to the knees from pushing through the soaked grasses. Flies tormented them, and the setting orange-red sun cast its light almost parallel with the plain, limning the field of slaughter in rich honey tones. Nait glimpsed dun-hued shapes loping across the hills in the distance and he shivered. Jackals or wolves. They were already here – and *he* was coming. He waved to his boys – that is, his men and women, all gone quiet now over the harrowing course of their trek – to pick up their pace.

* * *

The rain that had been threatening all day fell with the cooling night. After labouring in the downpour beside his men finishing the defences of the Imperial compound, deepening the pooling outer trench, helping to shore up the logs of the palisade, Ullen, along with a handful of other officers, was separated out. They were marched to the main gate. Entering, he strained to look back to the set, grim faces of the Talian soldiers watching him go within while they remained without. Many saluted their farewell. He was escorted to a brig of sharpened stakes. Here he found Urko, V'thell and other surviving League officers, including Choss, who lay in the lap of a Captain Roggen, near unconscious from loss of blood. Urko was hunched nearby, wearing only a torn padded linen jerkin, apparently unhurt despite everyone attesting that he'd been trampled by horsemen three times. V'thell sat nearby as well, his battered and cracked armour reflecting deep red-gold from the torches. Ullen knew that Urko could walk right out if he wished, but he – and Laseen no doubt – also knew that he wouldn't because of reprisals against his men.

He knelt on his haunches before his commander. The chill rain slapped against his back. 'General – the men are being kept outside the compound.'

Urko slowly raised his head. 'What?'

'All the Talian regulars. They're being kept out.'

'*What?*' Urko lurched up, peered into the slanting mist of rain. He crossed to the wall of stakes, grasped hold and shouted to a guard, 'Get me your commander! Right now!'

'No need for that,' a voice answered from the thin rain. A dark shape approached flanked by guards. Squinting, Ullen made out the bulky armoured figure of Korbolo Dom. 'Urko and Cartharon Crust,' the man called, stopping at the wall of stakes. 'Amaron, Grinner, Nok, Surly . . . Do you have any idea what it was like to grow up on Nap in the wake of such names?'

'Fener can shit on that! My men are outside the compound with that *monster* on the loose – on whose orders?'

'Mine.'

'*You!*' A stake shattered in Urko's fist.

'Kill me and your men will surely die!'

Urko subsided, his shoulders twitching beneath his padded gambeson.

'Anonymity,' Korbolo continued. 'You doomed us all to anonymity. Can you think of the name of any Napan of the last generations?'

'There's my grand-nephew Tolip.'

'Well, a new name has finally eclipsed yours. All the mouths on the island and in the Empire will finally be speaking that new name – Korbolo Dom – Sword of the Empire. And it is only right and proper that a fellow Napan has finally defeated you.'

'I'd say it was just Oponn's decision. The fortunes of war. Listen, let the men in . . . I'll guarantee their cooperation.'

'The loser would invoke fortune, wouldn't he?'

'And the winner wouldn't, would he?' Urko hunched his shoulders, biting down anything more. He finally asked, 'What do you want from me?'

Korbolo straightened, adjusted his layered cloaks against the rain. 'I have what I have always wanted. Look at you, squatting in the mud like an animal. You are defeated, squalid. I need not even attend your execution in Unta – you are already dead to me.'

Urko bared his teeth. 'You don't want to know what I'm lookin' at.'

Korbolo turned away, walked off into the night escorted by his guards.

'Listen, Hood take you!' Urko called. 'Never mind about me. Do what you want with me – but let my men in!' He wrenched another stake from the wall, broke it in his fists, almost launched himself out after the man, but mastered himself to finally sink down into the mud.

Ullen sat as well. To one side Choss coughed wetly, murmuring. Roggen held a cloth out over his slack face. Reaching out, Ullen tried to warm the man's ice-cold hand in his. The chill damp was sapping even Choss's strength. He doubted his old mentor would see the dawn.

Lights approached, torches flickering and hissing held by guards, and in their midst a short slim figure, the rain beading and running from her dark hair, the wet silk cloth of her tunic outlining her muscular arms, slim chest. Ullen had not seen her in decades but she looked exactly as when he had last set eyes upon her. Surly – Laseen. So small and unprepossessing! Yet all those around were unable to ignore her presence; even the captive Talian officers found themselves drawn to stand in respect. She acknowledged their gesture with a slight nod. Urko, however, refused to look up. She simply waited, clasped her hands at her back. After a time Urko finally glanced up, then away, and kept his face averted.

'I expected better of you than this, Surly,' he grated.

'I've come with a request, Urko,' she said.

He pushed himself awkwardly to his feet. 'A request? You come with a request of me? Well, it just so happens I have one for *you*.'

'Yes. Strange, that. I would speak with you and V'thell.' At the mention of his name the Gold commander bowed. His right arm and side were a weeping, gouged and mangled mess.

'I would want their cooperation. Urko. V'thell.'

'You'll have it,' Urko swore. V'thell bowed again.

'I will still have to keep you and the officers as guarantors . . .'

'We understand,' V'thell said.

'Very well.' She signed to a guard.

'What of Korbolo?' Urko asked.

'He is not your concern.'

That statement, delivered with such assurance and command, struck Ullen as a true note of Imperial rule and it must have echoed similarly with Urko as well for he straightened, giving a small nod of his head, with a look of something like surprised wonder on his craggy, rain-spattered face.

* * *

Nait, followed by the two heavies of his squad, Tranter and Martin, and one of his regular infantry saboteurs, Kal, walked the lines of the defences. 'You seen a soldier named Brill?' he asked every picket he met. 'A stupid-looking gawking awkward fella? Anyone? Out on the field?' But no one had and the fellow hadn't reported back. How stupid could he be? Had he just fallen asleep somewhere without reporting? If so, he was gonna tear his head off!

A soldier caught up with them and tapped his arm. 'You lookin' for a man out on the field?'

'Yeah. Brill.'

'Brill. Brill? Maybe. I was with a healer detachment. He waved us over but wouldn't leave the field. Said he was ordered to stay with his man. Don't know why though – the fellow was dead.'

Nait stared, then shuddered with cold. He wiped the rain from his face, saw the soldier regarding him curiously. 'Right! Ah, thanks, solider.' The man saluted. Nait stared again until he realized that he ought to respond; he answered the salute and the soldier jogged away into the rain. He looked to Tranter, Martin and Kal. Their eyes slid aside to the darkness out beyond the crossed stakes. *Poliel's Pustules! Hood's Kiss! Fucking dumbass anus-for-brains!* Nait threw his helmet into the mud.

'I haven't heard anything about no inspection,' the guard at the gate said, frowning in his confusion. Nait shrugged under his cloak. 'It's not like it's official or anything – we're just worried about the wall of the palisade collapsing – that's all.'

The guards exchanged alarmed looks. 'Collapsin'?'

'Yeah. In the rain.' He pointed to the wall of sunken poles. 'Look – they're tiltin' out already.'

'OK, OK. You wanna go out there, that's your worry.' The guards lifted the barrier aside. Nait waved forward the five with him but out of the rain came four more, the young new recruits shuffling up beneath outsized capes that dragged in the mud. Nait glared, motioning them away, but they saluted.

'Reportin' for the *inspection*,' the eldest, Kibb, said, winking.

His back to the guards, Nait raised a fist to them. The youth tapped something bulky with him under his cape. Nait's brows climbed his forehead; the youth gave a smirking, knowing assent.

'You goin' or what?' the guard asked.

'On our way, Cap'n.' Nait waved the squad through impatiently.

Out of earshot, in the dark with the rain pelting down, he turned on the youths. 'What'd you think you're doing! This ain't no pleasure hike!'

'We know!' Kibb said, annoyed. 'We came armed for bear.' And they pulled up their capes.

'The Gods' golden shit!' The exclamation was torn from Nait as if he'd been poleaxed. Under their capes each carried one of the Moranth munition boxes. The rest of Nait's squad flinched back a step.

'Will you put those away!' Nait yanked down their capes, glared out at the darkness as if expecting to be arrested. 'How did you get them?'

Kibb tapped a finger to the side of his nose. 'We marked the tent they was hiding all the confiscated munitions. An' in the rain an' the dark an' all it was easy.' He shrugged.

'Well, you're not comin' with us. It's too dangerous. You're going to stay here and wait until we come back and then you're going to return those like nothing's ever happened! OK?'

'Bullshit!'

'*Bullshit?* Don't shit me, soldier!'

'Well, you're talkin' it.'

Nait set his fists on his hips. *Why, the little runts! It's just like he was back home dealin' with his swarm of younger brothers.* 'OK, fine. You wanna come then you have to follow my orders and . . . Abyss, I don't even know all your names – what in Fanderay are your names anyway?'

'Kibb.' *Yes, Kibb. What a dumb name. What's it supposed to mean?*

'Poot,' said one. *Poot? Aw, you poor skinny pox-faced kid! What were your parents thinking? Maybe I'll start calling you 'Pimple'– that'd be an improvement.*

'Jawl.' *Jawl? What kind of a name is that for a girl?*

Blushing furiously, the smallest just shook his head. 'No name at all?' He squirmed.

'Stubbin.'

Stubbin? Stubbin! You poor kid. Your parents really did a number on you. Gods, he couldn't have come up with a worse selection than their parents had managed spontaneously. 'Okay. Let's go.'

As far as Nait was concerned, he was the only person he knew entirely free of any self-delusions. He knew he wasn't brave or a particularly good fighter. He knew sure as Beru that he wasn't exactly an inspiring figure. He also knew that he wasn't leading his squad out on to a gruesome battlefield at night haunted by the worst curse ever to afflict Quon because he was some kind of glory-drunk fool. No, he was just gonna collect his man then get the Abyss off the field all real quiet and as fast as his little pitter-pattering feet could carry him.

The rain let up though it was still as dark as the inside of a cave and for that he was thankful. He misstepped a few times, slipped on things all slithery and occasionally stuck his hand into something wet and soft that sucked when he yanked it free but he didn't look, didn't want to know what that thing was. His squad was real quiet and for that he was thankful as well. No talkers. Some men or women get all talky when they're scared or nervous; that was something he couldn't abide.

The stink wasn't quite so bad yet – not so bad as you'd lose your meal. The flies, though, they were vile. Assaulting his nose, eyes and ears as if they preferred live meat over the endless banquet prepared for them. He had a fair idea where they'd found the Falaran commander and he led his squad as quickly as he could to that spot, without detour or bothering to keep to low-lying ground. Growling and snarling warned them off the skulking carrion-eaters and he figured they wouldn't attack – not when their stomachs were full and there was plenty left for everyone.

. They found the man's big horse and him still beneath it – unmarred by the sharp beaks of any birds. But no sign of Brill. The image flashed into Nait's mind of the man asleep in the compound and he almost fainted in a gasping white fury. Then Martin hissed, pointed to his feet. There the man lay, blissfully asleep amidst all the gory horror. What could allow such a thing? A clean conscience? An utter lack of any imagination? It was one of the Queen's own mysteries to Nait. They kicked him awake and he sat up, yawning and rubbing his face.

He peered at them, completely unsurprised. 'Yeah?'

Nait waved everyone down. '*What are you doing?*' he hissed.

'Waitin' for you.'

'Waitin'—' Nait stopped himself from reaching out to throttle the ape. But he had to do something – he pulled off his helmet and hit him with it. 'You damned fool! Don't you ever do anything like that again!'

'But you ordered me to—'

'I don't care what I said – you use your blasted empty head! Now, c'mon. Let's go.' He started up but Stubbin waved everyone down. 'What?'

Stubbin made a motion for quiet.

'What is it?' Nait whispered.

The boy waved furiously for silence.

Oh, right. He listened. He didn't hear a damned thing. That is, except for the wings of night feeders, the growls and snapping of fighting jackals and plains wolves, the moaning of one or two wounded still alive somewhere out there in the dark. 'I don't hear—!' A hand grasped him and another covered his mouth, stifling his yell of surprise. He was yanked around to face the sweaty, dark, scarred features of Master Sergeant Temp. He relaxed and was released. 'It's you!'

'Yeah. Damned unfortunate.'

'They said you were blown up.'

'That's the story. 'Preciate you keeping to it.'

'Uh, OK. Why?'

'Let's say I first left Imperial service under sharp circumstances.'

Nait's squad gathered around. 'What's up? Kibb asked.

The man was a gruesome sight, hacked and slashed, the front of his layered iron hauberk and scale gauntlets dark with the remains of blood and gore. His shield was gone, but from his short time in the phalanx Nait knew it was common to go through two or three or four shields in any one engagement. 'What're you doing out here?'

'Same as you, I expect.' He flicked the cloth tied around Nait's arm. 'What's this?'

Nait thought maybe he blushed and was thankful for the dark. 'Made sergeant.'

'Handin' them out to anyone these days.'

'Listen – we're headin' back. You coming or not?'

'No, you're coming with me.'

'Coming with you? What in Fanderay's ass for?'

'There's Seti poking around out there and I want to know who and why.'

'*What?* Who cares? Ryllandaras is out here. We gotta get back!'

The master sergeant dragged Nait up. 'Ryllandaras ain't gonna bother with little ol' us so don't bother with your cover story.' He motioned to the squad. 'Fall in, double-column.'

'Cover story? What d'you mean cover story?'

'I know why you came out here with your saboteur squad.' He shook Nait by the arm. 'Got yourself some munitions, don't cha? Gonna bag yourself the big one, ain't ya?'

'*What?* No!'

'The old fart's got a point,' Kibb said aside.

The veteran waved a gauntleted hand. 'It's all right. You'll get your chance for everlastin' fame and glory. I just want a quick parley with these Seti here, then we'll hustle back to camp and I'll help you ambush Whitey.'

'For the last time, I don't—'

'Shhh.'

The master sergeant led them west past the killing fields out on to horse-trampled prairie. Farther west Nait could just make out a party of Seti horsemen, dismounted and gathered together. They seemed to be just waiting, watching the east, towards the Imperial encampment.

The master sergeant whispered into Nait's ear: 'Call for the Boar.'

'*What?*' Nait hissed. 'No, you call!'

The veteran nudged him none too lightly. 'G'wan.'

Eyes on the master sergeant, who winked his encouragement, Nait cleared his throat. The Seti all dropped from sight as if felled. 'Ah – is the Boar there?' he called in a strained whisper.

After a time the answer came in Talian: 'Who is asking?'

'Tell him,' whispered the master sergeant, 'his sword-brother.'

Nait cleared his throat once more. 'Ah – his sword-brother.'

A man stood, short and very stocky, long arms akimbo. 'Sword-brother? Stand up then, damn you!'

The master sergeant stood. 'I know that voice!'

'And I know that silhouette.'

The two men started forward towards one another through the grass, slowly though, warily, until close they threw themselves into each other's arms, pounding each other on the back.

'Am I seein' things,' Kibb asked. 'Or are those two guys hugging?'

The Seti chief, or warleader, Nait wasn't sure what he was, gave instructions to his band. They mounted and rode off to the north-east without him. 'Gonna ambush Whitey on his way back if they can,' the master sergeant explained. The man then came east with them. Turns out he was some kind of Malazan veteran who'd served with the master sergeant. The two led the way back, talking in low gravelly tones.

'I thought the Seti was all for the jackal,' Jawl whispered to Nait.

'Seems this Boar fella's against him.' He studied the faces of his squad as they pushed their way through the cold wet grass. Here he was asking them to pick through the killing fields for the second time. If they hadn't yet had all their delusions about warfare squeezed from them by now, they would have before this night was done. Tranter and Martin humped their broad shields on their backs, their eyes scanning the dark, never resting in any one place. His infantry saboteurs, Kal, Trapper, Brill and the woman, May, walked more or less together while the Untan kids kept together. He was proud of them, the way they'd handled the horror of seein' all this. But then, they'd been here when it was delivered. Gone was the fear

527

– you can only sustain a terror-pitch for so long – but gone also were the grimaces of pale nausea and flinches of disgust. It looked to Nait as if walking through the field of the fallen was pushing them down into the worst mood for any soldier, flat sadness. He crossed to them.

'Hey – when we get back maybe I'll see about getting you lot kitted out proper. How 'bout that?'

Looking up, Poot brightened. 'Really? Like with real armour 'n' such?'

'Yeah, could be.'

Kibb and Jawl started taking about what kind of weapons and armour they'd want. Poot just smiled dreamily at the thought of it. But little Stubbin wouldn't be drawn in – nothing could pull his eyes from scanning the fields.

Ahead, the master sergeant and the Seti had stopped to let them catch up. Temp signed for everyone to stay low. 'What is it?' Nait asked. Both veterans signed angrily for silence. Kneeling, everyone listened. At first Nait couldn't hear anything unusual over the same noises of snarling of the sated jackals and the moans of wounded suffering out there among the many, and now tormented by thirst. Then came a distant roaring, as of countless throats shouting – a riot far away, or battle. And a louder echoing bellow and snarl. Everyone's eyes brightened in the dark. The master sergeant and the Seti leapt to their feet. 'C'mon! Forward!'

*　　*　　*

It was the worst engagement of Ullen's life though he himself was in no danger. Men and women, his soldiers, pulled themselves by their clawed hands up the mud-filled trench they'd just worked to dig. They threw themselves three, four, five deep against the crossed spikes and makeshift palisade of timbers and logs, begging for weapons, for mercy, for everyone inside to die miserable deaths. Soldiers at the barricade pushed them back with spears, poleaxes and lances. And he and Urko could do nothing. Guarded, they'd been marched close to wagons where Imperial soldiers tossed swords and shields out over the barricade to the clamouring horde beyond. Swords and shields only, no armour or bows or crossbows. Nearby stood Laseen, surrounded by her guards, making it clear what authority lay behind this relief – if delayed.

Out in the darkness beyond the reach of the compound torches, the man-eater, Ryllandaras, roared and slaughtered. His explosive bellowing shook the boards of the wagons, vibrated the mud upon

528

which they stood. Ullen caught fleeting glimpses of a huge grey shape, astonishingly fast. But the Talians and the Gold fought. Weapons were passed along or thrown further across the press to the front where new hands carried them against the beast, or picked them up from dead ones.

Fists at his head, Urko spun to Laseen, pleading, 'For the love of Burn, allow a sortie!'

'What would stop your men from attacking them, pillaging their arms and armour and fleeing? Or attacking?'

'My word! My bond!'

The Empress's gaze snapped to Urko. 'You pledge to me?'

'Yes!'

Stepping closer, she said, her voice so low Ullen barely heard, 'You did before.'

'I—' the man's stricken gaze was pulled inexorably to the tumult outside, the shrieks and the cries of the wounded. 'Please – for the men! Yes, I pledge!'

'Your life? Obedience?'

'Yes! I swear.'

Laseen's face betrayed no emotion, though the lines bracketing her thin mouth were severe. This was the only hint of her passion Ullen could see. 'Very well, Urko. I accept.' She turned to the captain of the guard detachment with her. 'Send Fist D'Ebbin with a hundred heavy infantry.'

The clash of a salute. 'Aye.'

'I was to lead!' Urko called.

'I did not agree to that,' Laseen snapped. 'Did I?'

Urko's jaws worked as he ground through all that he might say. Finally, he admitted, reluctantly, 'No.'

'Now go speak to them, Urko.'

A slow salute. 'Aye.'

Laseen nodded to the guards who allowed him to pass.

A cavalry detachment rode up led by Korbolo Dom. He took in the wagons, the weapon distribution, and shook his head. 'It will do no good.'

'Nevertheless,' Laseen said.

'A useless gesture. I go now to collect its head!' And he pulled on his helmet, kicked his mount forward, his troop following.

'Oponn go with you,' the Empress called after him.

Ullen turned to V'thell, who had not turned away from the barricade the entire time. 'Still they fight,' the Moranth commander said, musing. 'Despite everything. They know it is their only hope.'

'They could run.'

'No. Your hapless civilians might but your soldiers know their strength resides in the unit. The group. Your soldiers are like us Moranth in this regard. It is one of the reasons we allied.'

Ullen was struck by the amazing things one learned at unlooked-for times. 'I didn't know.'

V'thell's helmed head cocked aside. 'Very few do, I imagine.'

At the barricade Urko was bellowing: 'I have begged the Empress for a sortie and she has agreed! Relief is coming! Imperial infantry! They come to defend you and to fight at your side! Honour that! Do you hear me! Honour that!'

A column of heavy infantry came marching to the nearest gate, double-time; the Empress had been assembling them already. Ullen could only shake his head. What chance did they have against such planning? Yet – had it not been a close thing? What if the Seti hadn't turned against them? What if— He cut off that line of thinking. The 'what if's were infinite and meaningless. All that mattered was what occurred. Align yourself with that, man, and perhaps you will stand a chance of remaining sane.

A great thunderous cheer went up outside the barricades. Ullen could imagine the armed and armoured heavy infantry working to interpose themselves, attempting to push back the beast. Certainly many of them would fall, but with far less ease, and at far greater cost. The timbre of the battle changed. The raw, naked screams of men and women being torn by talon and teeth lessened. The clash of armour and shield rose. Snarls of frustration rent the air. The thump of hooves now joined the turmoil, together with the high-pitched shriek of wounded horse. And so the battle continued. At one point a shield came winging through the air like a kite. Before it fell into the massed crowd Ullen thought he saw that an arm still gripped it. Eventually, however, numbers told – or so Ullen assured himself, listening to the tide of the attack. Perhaps the beast had simply sated his bloodlust for the moment – or perhaps easier targets could be found elsewhere. In any case, Ryllandaras withdrew. A massive, swelling, raucous cheer gripped those gathered outside and within. Ullen yelled; Urko shook his fists at the dark. Men and women rattled the barricade. It was gone. The horror had been pushed back.

Urko returned, directed a salute behind Ullen, who turned, startled; Laseen had remained through it all. 'I still wish I'd led that sortie,' he growled.

'I still need you.'

His brows knotted, his eyes slitted almost closed. 'The Guard.'
Laseen nodded her assent.

The damp flesh of Ullen's arms prickled with a chill. *Gods, the Guard! She anticipates an attack. But why? For who? They have no sponsors. The Talian League has been crushed. Defeating this army, even killing Laseen, would not destroy the Empire. The times cannot be reversed to how they were before the consolidation. What possible purpose could it all serve? But then, by that measure, what purpose did today's battle serve?* He pressed a hand to his slick forehead, took a long slow breath. *Stop it! I am so tired. My thoughts turn darker and darker.*

Ullen jerked as the unmistakable reports of bursting Moranth munitions echoed from somewhere out on the plain. His first reaction was to turn to V'thell who was nodding his helmed head. 'Excellent,' V'thell said. 'Knowing he would come allowed the opportunity for ambush.' He bowed his admiration to Laseen.

Urko now also turned to the Empress. The old commander's surprise was obvious. 'Hood's Gate, Surl – *Laseen*. Seems we've done nothing but underestimate you.'

'So have a great many others . . .' she answered absently. Her dark eyes glittered as she studied the night. 'I wish I could take credit but I cannot.' She motioned to a member of her staff. 'Find out who that is.' The woman saluted and ran to a horse. 'And now,' she said, 'I suggest we try to get some sleep before dawn. Urko, V'thell, you may speak with your soldiers but only through the barricade. Until tomorrow.'

V'thell bowed. Urko gave a curt jerk of his head. Both crossed to the spikes of the barricade. Wiping his hands down his face, Ullen joined them.

*   *   *

Knocking on the front pole of her tent woke Ghelel. She rose, found the sheathed dirk she kept next to her cot then pulled on a thick warm cloak, tucking the blade under it. 'Yes?'

'Apologies, Prevost,' came the Marquis's voice, 'but news has arrived.'

'Come in.'

The thick canvas hissed, brushing. She heard the man moving about within the outer half of her quarters. The light of a lamp rose. She pushed aside the inner hanging. 'Yes, Marquis?'

The man was pouring himself a glass of wine. He wore a plain long shirt and trousers; his considerable bulk plainly consisted of equal muscle and fat. He turned to her. 'We've lost.'

'Lost?'

'The battle.' He frowned down into his glass. 'The Talian League has been shattered. Toc presumed dead. Urko, Choss, the Gold commander captured.'

Her knees went numb; she searched for a chair then stiffened herself, refusing to display such weakness. 'So quickly . . .'

'I'm sorry.'

'Yes . . .'

'Will you have a drink?'

'Yes. Thank you.'

He poured another, crossed to hand it to her. 'Had been there you would now be captured – probably dead.'

Ghelel took the glass, smiled sadly. 'Had we been there, Marquis, we might have won.'

'Yes, well.'

'Now what?'

'We must move. No doubt the Kanese will come to hunt us down to curry favour with the Empress.'

'Where will we go?'

'Back to my province, north Tali. We'll be safe there. There will be *some* reprisals, of course. A winnowing of the aristocracy. Reparations. Funds will be extorted to weaken Tali. But that will be the worst, I expect.'

'And myself, Marquis? What will I do?'

The man's face flushed and he glanced aside. 'That should be obvious . . . Ghelel. You will be the Marchioness. My wife.'

Ghelel felt the need for that chair. *What? How dare he! I would die first!* She tossed the glass aside. 'So, what now? Throw me down on the cot? Rape me?' She slipped a hand within her cloak to close on the dirk.

'Nothing so melodramatic, I assure you. No, in time you will come around. You will see the union of our families as the political necessity it is. The Tayliin line must be preserved, after all. I'm sure you understand that.' He returned to the table, set his glass down. 'We failed this generation – but perhaps our sons or daughters or theirs . . .' He glanced back, his blunt features softening. 'I know it . . . *I* . . . am not what you've dreamt of. But think carefully. It is for the best.' He gestured to the entrance. 'And do not try anything foolish. You are of course under guard for your own safety. Good night.'

She longed for that wine glass to throw at him as he left. Once the cloth flap fell she dropped into the nearest chair. Where could she go? What could she do? She was his damned prisoner! Stirring herself, she went to the table for that wine. Perhaps she could collect the food and slip out the back. Movement behind her spun her around, her hand going to the dirk. It was Molk. The man was pulling himself up from under the edge of the tent where she'd thrown the glass.

'Still hard on your tableware, I see,' he commented, studying the broken glass.

'*Where have you been?*' she hissed.

The man rolled his bulging eyes, his mouth widening. 'Around. Listening. Watching.'

'Some bodyguard you are! I'm a prisoner!'

'Keep your voice down,' he warned. 'You've been safe so far, haven't you?'

'*So far!*'

'Exactly. But now I'm worried you're about to try something stupid.'

'*Me?*'

'Yes. Such as running off in a huff without thinking things through.'

Lowering her voice even further, she whispered, carefully, 'There's nothing to think through.'

'Yes, there is.' The man went to the table, selected a cut of smoked meat, poured a glass of wine. 'Why should you be the one to leave?' he asked, innocently.

'I'm sorry . . . ?'

He turned to her, shrugging. 'I could make it look like the Claw . . .'

Ghelel stared, her hand fell from the dirk. *Make it look like the . . . Dessembrae, no! What a terrifying offer!* She felt sick, wiped her palms on her cloak. 'What an awful thing to suggest.'

He gave a thoughtful frown. 'Yes, I suppose it would be best to wait until you are actually married. *Then* kill him.'

'That's not what I meant!' she shouted, then slapped a hand to her mouth. Molk listened, cocking his head. After a moment he waved off any worries. 'No? Really? Well, of course the problem is that the man's already married.'

'*What?*'

'Oh, yes.'

'Then what . . .'

A shrug of regret. 'Well, her blood is not nearly as rich as yours . . .'

'He wouldn't . . .'

Molk sipped his wine. 'An ambitious man, our Marquis.'

Through clenched teeth Ghelel hissed, 'You're enjoying this far too much, Molk.'

He stepped closer, lowered his voice even further. 'This is what I do, Ghelel. What I'm good at. My business . . . Now you face an important choice. A major fork in the path of one's life, so to speak. Do you want to stay in the business or do you want out? Which will it be?'

Ghelel almost said immediately that she wanted out but a small voice whispered: *just what are his orders from Amaron regarding me? To guard me and, if failing that . . . to kill me? Is that what he means by 'out'?* She walked away, saying, 'I have to think,' then turned back with the dirk bared and ready. 'What if I said I did want out, Molk. What would you do?'

His broad mouth stretched in a large smile. He gave a rueful shake of his head. 'I would say too bad – you have the right crafty turns of mind. But no, nothing like that. Suffice it to say that if I wanted to kill you – you'd be dead already.'

Ghelel did not lower the blade. 'So you say now. But how can I believe you?'

The smile melted away. He raised a hand, cupping the fingers, and a darkness blossomed within. A dancing flame of night. 'Believe me.'

Oh. She straightened, sheathed the dirk. 'I see. Now what?'

'Get dressed for travel. We'll leave tonight.'

Assenting, she pulled aside the inner hangings.

When they were ready, Ghelel having gathered all the food and water they could pack, Molk went to the rear wall of the tent and stood listening for a time. He waved her over then pulled up its staked lip. She gave him a glare and he shrugged. 'Simplest is always best,' he mouthed, and urged her on.

She didn't know if he used his arts to disguise their passage, but they made it out of the camp without being seen or any alarm sounding. They climbed a hill north of the sheltered, hidden forest depression the Sentries had chosen as their retreat and she could now hear the roar of the distant falls, Broke Earth Falls, where they tumbled down Burn's Cliff on their way to Nap Sea. 'Now what?' she asked him.

'We'll cross at the falls. Lots of rafts 'n' such there. After that I'll escort you back.' He looked to her. 'I presume you do mean to return to Quon?'

'Yes. And you'll . . . let me go?'

A waved agreement. 'Oh yes. It's plain to me you don't have the, ah, stomach for this life. Way too many scruples. No, best get out before you're killed, or become something you despise . . .' He looked away, clearing his throat. 'And I wish you luck.'

The night was perilously old by the time they reached the lagoons east of the falls. The flat diffuse light of a false dawn lit the swampy shore with its ghostly tangle of logs, uprooted trees and broken timbers all clogged downriver of the falls. A cool mist kissed Ghelel's face. The roar of the falls was a deep bass rumbling that seemed to vibrate her entire body.

They crouched for a time in the cover of the nearest treeline. Molk studied the apparently deserted lakeside. Standing, he waved her forward. They reached the littered shore. 'Now, we just have to find one of the rafts or a small boat. There's lots about. Locals—'

The man was knocked backwards off his feet and lay face up, the finned end of a crossbow bolt standing from his chest. 'Oh shit!' he gasped.

Ghelel cried her shock and surprise and spun, drawing her sword and heavy fighting gauche. There, a slim man in charcoal-hued clothes tossed away a strange thin crossbow. He flexed his arms and long-bladed throwing daggers appeared in his hands. Coming towards her, he waved them in a knife-fighter's dance. She shifted to face him sidelong, struck her guard.

He straightened then, cursing, and quickly disappeared in a flurry of shifting shadows. *Oh come on!* Ghelel cried to herself, outraged. *As if this wasn't bad enough!* She spun, slashing the air around her and saw that Molk was gone as well. *The Warrens! They're duelling! Get him, Molk!* Not knowing what else to do she slashed again. Then she thought – the water! She ran.

Where she'd stood something burst like a branch exploding in a fire but she did not turn, did not slow. She slogged into the swampy muck until the water reached her thighs, then she tuned to face the shore. *Come for me now, bastard!*

She scanned the clutter of fallen branches, the stands of wind-brushed marsh grasses, her heart almost choking her. She strained, listening for any betraying sound; logs bumping out in the current spun her round; an animal splashing into the lake upstream almost made her scream. *Come on! End this one way or another!*

Within the root mat of a fallen tree grey shadows suddenly writhed. A shape of darkness squirmed from the shadows. It writhed, limbs twisting, black flakes exfoliating from it, and a high keening of excruciating pain reached her. Gods! Not Molk, she prayed. It disintegrated into nothing while she watched. Ice stabbed as a blade slashed the meat of her forearm followed by a splash. She gasped, throwing herself forward. Two bodies grappled in the water behind her. Blood bloomed. Wincing, hunched, she watched, sword raised one-handed. The water foamed, steaming and churning as if boiling, then stilled, hissing with bubbles that spread, dissipating. A body touched the surface and by the barbed crossbow bolt standing from its back she recognized it as Molk. She pushed forward to grab him. The water burned her legs and hand. Snarling her pain she dragged him back, flipped him over and pulled him to shore with one hand, the other at her side, useless.

She fell next to him, studied his boiled beet-red face. 'Molk!'

He coughed, spat up a great gout of water. His face twisted its agony. 'Damn! That . . .' he gasped a breath '. . . went poorly.' He cracked open an eye. 'Ghelel?'

'Yes.'

'Apologies. Should've guessed. Hubris, hey? Thought I was so smart.'

'Relax, don't talk.'

'No, have to. Won't last. You'll have to hide deep now. Those two were mages. It will be noticed. They'll send someone even better to take up the trail. Run now. Cross over, head west. Best of luck staying . . . free of all this ugliness. I hope you succeed.'

'I might as well run back to the Sentries now. They'll just track me down.'

Molk smiled smugly, then coughed, spitting up blood. 'No,' he whispered. 'I let the Kanese know where they are.'

'No! You didn't! You scheming, tricky . . .'

'Knew you'd come around. Now go. I'd like to think that a little good might've come of all of this . . .'

She rested a hand at his brow. 'Yes. I'll go. I'll get away, thanks to you.' She kissed his cracked blood-wet lips. 'Thank you. You're not . . . you're not what I thought at all.' She grabbed the dropped pack and ran to find a boat.

Behind her, alone, Molk lay flat on his back. His breaths came slower, more shallow and laboured. Finally, he offered a weak rueful laugh to the brightening sky. 'Neither of us were.'

After abandoning the leaky boat in the weeds she jogged west, keeping to the wettest, soggiest patches of land she could find. At dawn she reached the great escarpment of Burn's Cliff. South of her now ran the main beaten road that switch-backed up one of the shallowest portions; she decided against it. Instead, she selected a slim meandering path traced out by locals. A mule-trail. This she followed to the top then found a copse of trees to hide in. She sat for a time on her knees, thinking through her options. As the day brightened and the insects gathered, she pulled off her helmet and, one-armed, began stripping off her armour. She used her dirk to dig a pit and into it went the armour, her surcoat, leggings, gauntlets, helmet, even her boots. Ghelel Rhik Tayliin and Prevost Alil, she decided, had to die.

But her sword. Her old familiar blade. Without it she'd be defenceless. How could she give up her weapon knowing what was after her? No, it had to go. It all had to go. *What good would a sword do if a Claw should find me in any case?* She lengthened the hole and pushed the blade down. Even the pack she emptied and jammed in. She filled the depression, stamped down the dirt. Wearing only a linen shirt, the dirk underneath, her hair unbounded and mussed, her arm bandaged and the food and remaining skin of water in a shoulderbag, she set out.

The sun on her back warmed her and seemed to help push her on her way. *Here I am in the most dire straits so far of my life, alone, undefended, yet I feel incredibly free and light. Even reborn. I could go anywhere, do anything. So, what am I to do? And I will have to be careful. These people will never give up.* Still, the future, once no better than a prison, now seemed completely unbounded. For the first time since that bloody day at the Sellath estate she felt in control of her own destiny. Come what may, at least she would be the one deciding.

At the shore of the Idryn she came to a squalid hamlet so small it no doubt boasted no name. She passed the few wattle-and-daub buildings to walk straight down to the shore where a shallow, single-masted cargo-boat was being readied for a trip upriver. The youths loading stopped their work to watch her and she smiled. 'Who's the owner? I'd like to ask about heading upriver. I came following the army but my man's dead, so I'm going home. I have a few coins.'

'M'father,' said one, his eyes growing huge.

'Could you get him?'

The lad dropped his basket to run down the shore. 'Da! Da!'

Ghelel winced at that but followed. She did have coin – more than this fellow had probably seen in all his life. Enough, she hoped, for his silence. Enough, she hoped, to cover whatever cost the Gods deemed necessary to buy one's life back.

BOOK III

Fates and Chances

Light strikes
Dark smothers.
Shadow goes round.

Ancient saying,
original meaning lost

CHAPTER I

All bow to the Eternal Round,
Save the Avowed.

All sink down into dimming Night,
Save the Avowed.

All to the wither of time must go,
Save the Avowed.

None gainst Hood's touch make defence,
Save the Avowed.

Yet to lure of the eternal return they did yield.

Lay of K'azz
Fisher Tel Kath

SKINNER HAD SELECTED SHIMMER AND ONE OF HIS AVOWED MAGES,
Mara, to ride out to with him to discuss terms with the Empress.
Just after dawn on a slight rise south of her encampment he
pitched the tall cross-piece standard with its long crimson banner
and they waited. They had dismounted and Shimmer walked a
distance off, her thoughts very far from the coming meeting.
The Brethren of course were triumphant. Soon would come the
fulfilment of the Vow. All they had dedicated their lives and deaths
to. Not one whisper of reserve or disquiet could she detect among
them. Smoky's and Greymane's case, so compelling at the time,
now seemed utterly implausible, even shameful. *Smoky, the
Brethren whispered, jealous of Cowl now that he stands next to
the commander, not him. Greymane – Outsider! – they sneered.
Ignorant. What does he know of us?* And yet, she wondered, what

of Stoop? *Deserter! He must have snuck away, abandoned the Vow!*

'Shimmer,' Skinner called. 'You have been quiet of late, reserved. I have noticed. Now is not the time to be troubled – we are close to achieving our ambition.'

She adjusted the fit of her silver-chased helmet, its hanging camail. 'I wish we had more men to achieve it with.'

'We Avowed will rule any engagement.'

'Any engagements, yes. But our reception in Unta—'

A dismissive wave from Skinner. 'We do not need their approval.'

Shimmer turned to study the man more closely. *Approval? For just what . . .?*

'Someone comes,' Mara called, pushing back her thick wind-tossed curls. 'Four. No mage.'

'Has she any worth the name at all?' Skinner asked, more to himself.

'Very few. But Heng is close. And there are extraordinary presences there.'

'Thank you, Mara.'

The Dal Hon woman bowed, adjusted her robes. 'They come.'

Four riders closed. All four male, Shimmer noted. So, no Laseen. Not that she'd expected her to come, but still. It rankled. Surely she and her councillors must understand that they were not to be brushed aside. The lead rider was a Napan, as was common enough among the highest ranks of the Imperium – predictable cronyism, Shimmer knew – and rode under the banner of the Sword of the Empire. So, here the man was, the inheritor of Dassem's position come to treat with one of the very few opponents, if not the only one, who had survived a clash with his predecessor. She wondered whether this was a man capable of appreciating such finely layered irony. Probably not.

With him rode one surprise – a Moranth Gold – perhaps the very commander who had opposed Laseen yesterday. Ah yes, the notoriously businesslike, or perhaps *adroit*, attitude the Moranth take to alliances now showing through. The two others, one tall, poplar-slim older commander and one younger, appeared commonplace.

They reined in; the Sword drew off his helmet, inclined his head. He appeared flushed, sweaty. 'Korbolo Dom, Sword of the Empire. Gold Commander V'thell, High Fist Anand, Commander Ullen.'

'Skinner. I command the Crimson Guard. This is Mara and Shimmer.' The four inclined their heads in greeting. 'So, the Empress does not deign to speak with us. Did she give a reason?'

'The Empress does not treat with hirelings.'

Skinner's arms uncrossed with a scraping of armour. The gauntlets clenched at his sides. 'I wonder if you have any idea with whom you are dealing.'

'To the contrary – I know a great deal of you,' Korbolo answered, undeterred. 'It is you who knows nothing of me.' And the man glared his challenge, his hands twisting in his reins, his breath short.

Studying the man, the Crimson Guard commander slowly nodded his helmed head, re-crossed his arms. 'I believe I now know all I need know.' He raised his voice, addressing all four. 'Our terms are these: The Empress Laseen is to formally abdicate all authority and to stand down as sovereign over any and all lands or holdings, or we will prosecute her forces in the field into unconditional surrender.'

The Sword of the Empire openly sneered his disdain. 'And these are our terms, *mercenary*. You are an unsanctioned body of armed men and women, no more than brigands in our lands. You will throw down your arms to be escorted to the nearest port for transport or be crucified to a person. The choice is yours.'

Shimmer almost laughed aloud. Gods, could a greater gulf be found this side of the Abyss? This is the man the Empress sends to treat? Did she deliberately wish to goad them beyond endurance?

Skinner had gone still, as had the others of the Imperial delegation. The Moranth remained a mystery to her of course, but the older man, the High Fist, showed flinching reservation in the face of such a blunt statement, yet he did not dispute the terms. The younger commander, Ullen, made no effort to disguise his dislike of the Sword but his face held no reservations, only a measure of . . . regret. Reconciled to battle and his probable death this one was, perhaps all are, if for foolish or supportable reasons. A shame. They cannot win.

Nodding ponderously, as if in reluctant acquiescence, the Crimson Guard commander, raised a gauntleted hand in dismissal. 'Very well. The Gods, it seems, are determined that blood shall be shed on this day. We must not disappoint them.' And he bowed.

The Sword yanked his mount around. V'thell, the Gold commander, bowed as well, saying, 'A privilege to meet with you upon the field.' The older High Fist merely inclined his head, his mouth sour and tight. The young commander Ullen's reaction was the only one which gave Shimmer pause; he studied them for a time, an expression in his eyes that one might hold when seeing for the last time something rare or precious. She watched him go, wondering just what he had intended by such a regard. Was he saying goodbye to his own life? Or was there more here than she was aware of? These unknowns troubled her.

Skinner mounted. 'We will deploy across the south. We must keep the Kanese force bottled up.'

'Agreed,' Shimmer said.

He turned to her, gathering his reins. 'And I am in no rush. I hope to extend this into the night.'

'I understand.' *Yes. The night. The men exposed, pinned down in the open field. The dread of Ryllandaras's return may alone win the battle for them.* 'Cowl, the Veils and the mages?'

'Will all be unleashed. I mean to inflict the lesson here, Shimmer, that none should oppose us.'

* * *

'What d'you think they're saying, Sarge?' Kibb asked, his gaze shaded to the south.

They're steppin' on each other's bloated ideas of their own self-importance and now we're all gonna die because of it! That's what they're talkin' about!

'Nothin' important, Kibb. Just a formality.' *A formality before we all get buried by the Guard.* Still, Nait had a hard time putting aside what he witnessed last night. Those two old veterans actually blocking Ryllandaras! How'd they do that? How could anyone? It was like the old stories of the clash of champions from before Dassem's fall. Like he'd heard some of the Talians saying they saw at Heng. Then the beast moving so fast – they only brushed it with their munitions – and it was gone like a ferret down a hole. How could anything that big move that quick? *Because he's a damned Ascendant, that's why, Nait my boy.* And those two stopped him cold for a time, think about that! It occurred to him that the survival potential of his own skin – and that of his squad – might go way up the closer he managed to get to those two. Something to keep in mind out there on the field. In the meantime, though, he had to select a corporal. He'd rather not – no need to give someone the actual authority to sniff at all your commands and dispute all your plans . . . but he had to select someone to take over when Hood finally managed to pin him down long enough to squash him. Not that he'd care after that anyway! He'd be holding tight with both hands to Hood's Gate then.

Other than Kibb on watch his squad was all splayed out, snoring. Let 'em sleep a little longer – they'd earned it. None of the new recruits, that was plain. Not Martin or Tranter. Calling them saboteurs was like calling a shovel a jeweller's pick. No, have to be one of the regulars. May, he supposed. She was smart. Too smart, truth be told. He didn't like the way she watched him. Saw right through him, she did. So how was he gonna shut her up? Make her part of the hierarchy, that's how! Shame she was no Hands with her hair all hacked short, the old scars on her nose and chin, all bones and angles she was. Yes, he didn't think he'd be like to meet another like Hands; she'd been the one for him. What a Hood-damned fool he'd been! This May, though: a hard life, he supposed, before she'd joined. Beat on all her life growin' up by her da probably. He'd seen it before.

He stood, groaning and stretching, and kicked May's sandalled foot. The slight woman sprang up into a fighter's crouch, a belt-knife in her hand. *More than just beat on by her da, most likely.* He waved for her to follow him. She picked up her padded gambeson and weapons to follow.

'Finally worked up the guts to run off?' she said as they crossed the encampment.

'Kept us all alive so far,' he answered from the side of his mouth.

'Well, I haven't decided whether we'd all be better off with or without you, frankly.'

'Well, you're corporal, so you are officially now part of the problem.'

'Thank you *so* much.'

They came to a crowd of officers and noncoms – a general briefing for Braven Tooth's command, now 7th Battalion. Nait pushed his way into the circle. He searched for familiar faces – saw Least and Lim Tal, and Heuk with two very nervous-looking old gaffers he presumed to be the sum total of the company's mage cadre. *Poor bastards – soon to be smeared by the Guard Avowed.*

Braven Tooth, his hair a black and curly tangle standing in all directions, was talking: 'So, a new kind a battle so a new strategy. Truth is, it's an old strategy – one we used to use when confronting mage-heavy enemies. Been a while since we faced such so it must seem new to everyone here.' He cracked his hairy knuckles, scanned their faces. 'Main order of battle is this: no concentrations of forces! Any big mass is an invitation to the mages. Stay broke up in small units, companies and squads ideally. Circle yourselves, watch all directions. Keep any eye on the flow of the field – move towards any strong resistance to blunt it – but don't bunch up! Wait your turn!'

'What's to stop them from overwhelming, encircling?' one officer asked.

'Because we'll be moving within the screen of our own skirmishers tryin' to do the exact same thing to them, only we'll succeed! That's why, right? OK. Now, the Guard veterans will be doing the same –

moving in small units, their "Blades". The new recruits they'll probably have form line and flanking phalanx. OK?'

'What about the Kanese in the south? They helpin'?' asked another officer Nait didn't know. In fact Nait knew none of them, only his own, Tinsmith, who was keepin' quiet and not asking any damn-fool questions that Braven Tooth would be getting to answering anyway, in good time.

'Right, the Kanese,' said Braven Tooth with a look that said the same thing Nait was thinking. 'If we can be said to have an objective – that's it. We want that bridge! There's twenty thousand Kanese infantry on the other side just wettin' themselves to prove how loyal they are to the Empress. We want to let them through and the Guard wants to stop us. Simple as that. All right? OK.' The commander adjusted the soft leather shirt that served as an armour under-layer, crossed his arms tucking his hands up under his armpits. 'Dismissed! Except for you saboteur sergeants. Want a word with you.'

Nait waited for the crowd to thin. Lieutenants and captains passing gave him a nod of approval – some a shake of their heads – in acknowledgement of last night's action. Apparently, word going around was that he'd snuck out with his men to try to ambush Ryllandaras. Come on! How could anyone be so stupid?

Not that he was gonna disabuse them.

Least passed, cuffed his shoulder in a gesture of consolation; Nait was surprised and touched – he didn't think his past behaviour warranted anything like that. It must have been damned ugly in that phalanx.

Braven Tooth cast a gimlet eye over the slouching, grimed, disreputable assortment left behind. Nait knew none of them. One greasy fellow was slumped under a dirt-smeared wool cloak; a fat Dal Hon wore a rusted iron pot helmet and a shirt of rent mail that was nothing more than a ragged patchwork of wire, leather ties and cloth knots. The last was a swarthy, skinny woman who had the look of a constipated stork.

'Introductions, I suppose,' Braven Tooth rumbled. He waved to the fellow in the cloak, 'Gant,' the Dal Hon, 'Bowl,' the woman, 'Urfa. This here's Sergeant Jumpy.'

'So you're the guy,' Urfa said, studying him like he was something she'd found growing inside a damp felt boot.

'The guy who what?'

'Stupid enough to go after Ryllandaras.'

'I ain't that stupid.'

She nodded, squinting cross-eyed. 'Good. I hoped you weren't.'

'Naw,' Gant opined, leaning back. 'You was just out hunting

dropped munitions, weren't cha? An' Ryllandaras jumped ya . . .'
and he winked.

'Yeah. Something like that.'

Bowl's bulging eyes narrowed to slits. 'How many did you
find . . . ?'

'All right,' Braven Tooth cut in. 'You'll all get your fair share. But I
have to warn you – the Gold keep most of it. They know it best. Now,
as to you sorry-assed excuses. We're short on mages – that's no secret
– so you're going hunting. That's your assignment and the assignment
of the saboteur squads in all the other companies. You keep your
heads down and wait for an Avowed to show him- or herself then you
let them have it. You got it?'

Nods all around. A chorus of slovenly 'Ayes'.

Braven Tooth scowled his disappointment from under his matted
tangled brows. 'All right. Dismissed – all except you, Jumpy. A word.'

The other saboteur sergeants sauntered off, Gant offering a mocking laugh to Nait. Braven Tooth waved him close. 'Met someone out
there, did you?' he said, his voice low. So close was the man Nait
flinched back – he stank of rancid animal fat, old sweat and stale
beer. *Gods! Has he never washed?*

'Yeah. Met the master sergeant, Temp.'

'No, you didn't, right?'

'That's what no one out there told me.'

'Good . . . Now, what was he doin'?'

'He met up with some old Seti veteran he knew from before.'

Braven Tooth's bhederin-like brows climbed his blunt forehead to
his greasy tangled mane. 'This Seti,' he rumbled, his voice oddly
faint, 'what did he call him?'

'Called him his "sword-brother".'

The commander stepped backwards as if reeling. 'Hood's bony
prang!' he breathed, awed. '*Two!* Two of Dassem's old bodyguard
here with us now! The Avowed have no idea what they're facin'.'

'What's that?' Nait asked.

The man's faced clouded over. 'Nothin'. You saw nothin'– heard
nothin'. Clear?'

Nait shrugged his indifference. 'Fine. Anything else?'

'Yeah. You've got munitions. They're all supposed to be handed in
for distribution. Return 'em.'

'I'll return half.'

'*Half!*'

'Deal?'

Nait swore he could hear his commander's teeth splintering and grinding. 'Deal,' Braven Tooth spat. 'Now get outta my sight before I throw you in the brig.'

Nait saluted and sauntered away. Out on the compound grounds May edged up and said aside: 'I'm comin' around to thinking maybe you're not so bad for the unit after all.'

'All this lovin's making me just dippy,' Nait grumbled. 'Now let's take a look to the south.'

They climbed the south palisade wall. Far out of sight beyond the gently rolling hills the Guard were deploying. Within the compound horns blared to sound formation. Laseen's combined forces, the remaining Talian, Moranth and Falaran soldiery all now serving beneath the Imperial sceptre, were gathering to march south.

'All open ground,' Nait said, thinking aloud. He stroked a thumb across his lips. 'Lousy for us.'

'At least they got no cavalry to speak of,' said May.

'Who does? Horses are as rare as gold these days.'

'So won't be much manoeuvring, then, maybe.'

'No. Toe-to-toe. It'll be ugly. Nothin's gonna be held back today. Say – remember that siege equipment in the train? Take a few of the lads and get a hold of one of those stone arbalests. Biggest you can find. Break it down if you have to. I want to be able to reach anywhere on that field.'

May's thin lips crept upwards at the images that came to mind. She tilted her head in agreement. 'Aye, Sarge.'

* * *

Silk had settled Storo in a better-class inn. That dawn Hurl paced the hall outside the door. She was leaving, nominally commanding a Hengan detachment of volunteers to join the Empress's forces to the east. It seemed probable to her that she'd never return so now was her only chance to say goodbye. Still, she could not bring herself to enter. It had been days and all this time she hadn't yet come to see the man. Now maybe it was just too late . . .

'C'mon in, Hurl,' he called through the door. She froze, cursed the noisy floorboards. She opened the door. He lay on the bed. An open window let in the early morning light and air. She stood in the entrance. He waved her in. 'C'mon, I don't smell so bad now.'

She didn't want to and didn't mean to but she flushed, embarrassed. She came and sat at the end of his bed. The man's face was torn, a great ragged zig-zag that had taken an eye, cheek and edge of his mouth – he now spoke with a slur. That side's arm was gone as well, amputated. An abdominal wound was covered by the sheets. 'I hear you're headin' out. Wish you wouldn't. The Seti will probably attack – it's their last chance.'

'Rell's staying, and Silk and Liss. And the city's full behind us now. You have full cohorts and Captain Gurjan. More than enough men and women for the walls.'

'Still don't like it.'

'I'll be fine. Got a good sergeant in Banath.'

'You won't be safe. You're safe here in the city. And you're takin' those three. I don't trust them.'

'Can't say I like them myself but they fought for the city and Silk agrees Laseen's short on mages – these three could make a real difference.'

He took a laboured breath – was this tiring him? He was weaker than she thought. 'Still don't trust 'em. Why go? Why're they all so eager to go?'

'I don't know. But they are. So we're going. Now take care – heal up.' She stood.

He struggled to straighten himself higher. She came and gently eased him back. 'What . . . ?'

'Come back. Y'hear? Come back. I don't want . . . this fight to take you.'

'All right. I'll keep my head down. Now, we'll see you later.'

His hand on the sheet rose to her, opened, fell away. 'Yeah. Be careful out there. Real careful.'

'I will.' She backed away, closed the door. Pressing her back to it, she considered the very real possibility that they were both of them damned cowards.

Outside, her escort of twenty waited; she was, after all, second in command of the city. They rode to the Gate of the Dawn where six hundred cavalry were assembling in a double column. The call had gone out some time ago and, with Rell's very vocal support, six hundred viable mounts had been selected from the city's remaining horses. Many were on their last legs, hardly better than swaybacked nags. But they would do for a day's ride on a good road. At the gate, a sliver of dawn's light still slanting through, Hurl pulled up short. There waited the three brothers, but also Rell and Liss, both mounted. Near them stood Silk, his arms crossed over his still unmended tattered shirt, and Sunny, his glower even more sour than usual.

'What's this?' Hurl asked of Rell.

'We're coming,' said Liss.

549

'I asked them not to,' Silk cut in.

'You shouldn't. The city—'

'He won't come here this night,' Rell said from behind his visor, his voice still harsh and distorted from his scarring. 'We know where he's going to be.'

Hurl nodded. True, from all she'd heard there was no way the monster could resist all the blood about to be spilled. Obviously Rell and Liss wanted to be there when he came. So be it. At this point, with so few, she wouldn't turn anyone away. She raised her shoulders to Silk who hugged himself tighter, frowning his helpless disapproval.

Sunny came to her side. 'I ought to be the one goin',' he growled.

'One of us has to stay and I seem to be the field commander.'

'You weren't such a week ago.'

'No, but somehow suddenly I am. Keep any eye on the north wall.'

His sneer told her not to tell him his job. She signed to Sergeant Banath who raised himself in his stirrups, waving. The banner-men dipped their colours forward and the column slowly made its way out of the east-facing Gate of the Dawn. Hurl raised a hand in farewell. The mage bowed, arms tight about himself, a strained smile of encouragement at his lips. Sunny raised a fist.

*　　*　　*

Lieutenant-commander Ullen's brigades had already marched, but he rode with his aides to the battlefield where a detail was piling corpses for burning. The bonfire nearest the compound contained wounded who had succumbed since the engagement. And among these was the body of Commander Choss, once High Fist under Laseen.

Ullen reined in, crossed his mail-backed hands before him on the pommel of his saddle. Such a damned waste. So much knowledge, cunning and experience gone now just when it was needed so vitally. The Empire was marching to face its oldest – possibly its most dangerous – foe and it had lost one of its most gifted commanders of men in what now seemed to him useless internal squabbling. *Nothing like an external foe to put things into perspective, hey, Choss?* He'd probably appreciate the irony.

An aide's mount nickered in what Ullen hoped was inadvertent impatience. To these youths just beginning their officer training this man was nothing more than a name, a last remnant of legendary times as distant to them as the T'lan Imass. What did they know of campaigns more than twenty years old – before some were even born? But Ullen had been there. He'd been younger than they on his first posting, just a messenger attached to Choss's staff during the final conquests.

To one side two soldiers stood up from where they'd been sitting in the grass and pulled on their helmets. Come to offer their own respects no doubt – old-looking veterans – men whose memories go back even further with Choss, perhaps back to the earliest campaigns. The urge to speak with them washed over Ullen, to share memories of the man they'd come to see off, but they didn't seemed eager for company and so he had to respect that. Still, watching them go, there was something familiar about seeing the two of them together. Perhaps they'd crossed paths more than once over the years.

One of his staff cleared his throat and Ullen tightened his lips, exhaling. The smoke from all the burning was thick and he had to fight his own urge to cough. *Goodbye, old friend and mentor. You deserved better. But then, so may we all.* He clicked his tongue to urge his mount onward and pulled the reins aside.

They rode alongside the main line of march south, passing first the laden wagons of the train and the camp-followers on foot, a ragged mob of the combined Talian and Malazan noncombatants. Wives with children in tow waved, as did girlfriends and prostitutes, even husbands of some female officers who held down a trade, smithing or leatherworking, or cooking. Then came the rear guard and the Empress's personal train surrounded by its own guard of Malazan heavies and troops of noble cavalry. Securely ensconced within rolled the Imperial carriage, pulled by a team of eight oxen. Idly, Ullen wondered whether Laseen was even in the damned thing and whether it was all just for show. What little he knew of her made him suspect such to be the case. After this they came to the columns of the reserve elements; here was to be Ullen's assignment, coordinating with High Fist Anand. But he was curious to see the grounds ahead and so continued on. Crossing the east–west trader road they next came upon elements of the main body, spreading out, forming up. Ahead, the ground sloped gently downward. Here awaited the Guard, straddling the south pilgrim road. Beyond, the slope continued on to meet the cliffs of the Idryn River valley.

The mercenaries had deployed themselves in a broad arc, widely spread, with large phalanxes holding their extreme flanks. Clearly they were inviting a thrust down the middle. The Avowed appeared supremely confident in their capability to blunt and pin down any advance. Ullen was inclined not to doubt them. He cast a glance to the sun – close to noon and the day was humid, fast heating up. Not a good day for any long-drawn-out struggle. To the east rose the enormous eroded butte upon which the ruins of the Great Sanctuary of Burn could just be made out. Idly, he wondered whether the Guard intended it as a retreat and rallying point – but they did not seem the type to set contingencies for defeat.

The Imperial skirmishers, the Untan Militia, call them what you like – the murderous midges, his own heavies named them – had already spread out over the hillsides of tall sun-browned grass. Ground-nesting birds took flight, disturbed by their movement. Stooping down, many of the crossbowmen disappeared entirely from sight and Ullen had to smile: *yes, good cover, but it won't last. The Guard's mages will burn it away.* He'd seen it before. Unlike most here he'd witnessed full-scale mage clashes where Warren battled Warren and swaths of ground and men were churned under. He'd been there when the Falaran island capitals fell and his stomach clenched in dread of what was to come. Still, he consoled himself with the knowledge that such a full-on field engagement was not to the Guard's style; they never were a stand-alone force. More an attachment to any main army, a special service good for narrow, specific objectives or duties. He hoped this less than ideal position would help even the odds.

Lead elements of Malazan, Talian and Falaran infantry spread themselves out. They had already broken down into units of just one or two or three companies. They pushed their way through the irregulars like ships through a heaving sea. Many of the units had organized themselves with hollow centres – a good strategy when facing battle-mages. Urko was down there somewhere on the west flank with his Talians, V'thell on the east with the Gold. He studied the distant Crimson Guard formations: they too followed such dispersal, mixed with lines. Yet the Guard must know that Laseen was weak in mages. *The Claws remain! Don't forget them! Simply because she elected to spare the League officers such culling doesn't mean that her forbearance would extend to the Guard. No, on the contrary, the Avowed will no doubt find themselves swamped.* And thinking of that Ullen suddenly knew why not one Claw had assaulted him or any other League officer. *She needed them for this! All this time! She'd been planning even for this!*

He almost fell from his horse, so great was the anger that clamped his chest. *Had they no chance all along then? All useless? For nothing?* Stopping, he pulled off his helmet, wiped the sweat starting from his brow. His staff pulled up as well, to cast him curious glances. *But no – she could not have known for certain.* Just plain prudence. A husbanding of resources. He and Urko and others of the League had been spared. Laseen had intended all the time to win over their men and assassinating beloved leaders such as an Urko or a Dujek was no way to manage that. No such considerations, however, applied to the Guard. All the Claw shall be unleashed upon them.

While he watched, the standard of the Sword reached the centre field, this time dismounted. This new Sword, Korbolo Dom, had elected to fight on foot backed by a legion of heavies. Ullen knew little of the man except what he'd heard before and seen just recently. The man's ferocity and fighting ability were certainly not to be doubted; but he appeared to lack that certain aura or élan that had so bonded the men to Dassem. With the old Sword, the soldiers had known that should they come to a tight spot Dassem would be there to defend them no matter what. Ullen knew this. He'd seen Dassem trailed by his Sword bodyguard repeatedly cut a swath across battlefields to come to the aid of hard-pressed formations and positions. One could not confidently expect the same from this Sword.

'Sir?' one of his staff ventured, rousing him from his reverie.

'Yes?'

'Should we not be returning?'

Ullen squeezed his eyes. Already he was tired. 'Yes. No doubt High Fist Anand is wondering where we've got to . . .' He gently urged his mount around.

* * *

Harbour-Assessor Jenoso Al'Sule of Cawn, newly appointed, gauged with something akin to horror the wallowing, limping progress of this current entrant to their busy docks. *God of a Thousand Moods, please do not sink in a berth! His superiors would note the loss of income! Still, if it did sink, it would technically be occupying the berth and its owners would then be legally obliged . . .* Jenoso smoothed his crisp new uniform, Imperial black trimmed with burgundy, and waited while harbour launches towed the vessel in. Once lines were firmly secured to bollards he started forward, fully expecting a gangway to come out to meet him, yet none came. He stopped abruptly at the edge of the dock, scanned the railing. Gods! What a wreck! Had it been in a storm?

'Hello? Vessel . . .' Jenoso scanned for the name – *Beru, no! Who would name a vessel that?* 'Ah, *Ragstopper*?'

A pale-faced, sickly-looking sailing hand appeared at the rail. 'No one comes aboard!' he fairly howled, pointing.

'Very well – that is your business. Mine is registration and inspection. Now, let me aboard.'

'No! Go away!'

'Do not be ridiculous. Your cargo must be inspected, fees levied. Come, come. I haven't all day.'

The man yanked at his long, unkempt, mangy hair. 'Plague!' he shouted. 'Yes, that's right! We've plague! Look out! Ooo!'

Jenoso blinked his confusion. 'Well, in that case you are in contravention of standard procedure. You must anchor in the bay, raise a black flag . . .'

An old man with a shock of grey-white bristly hair and a seamed, wind-darkened face pushed the sailor aside. 'Did I hear the words "standard procedure"? What's happened to all the ports these days? Why, times were in Cawn a few silver moons would – *Holy Dessembrae forfend!*' the man cried, staring at the town. 'You must've tried to tax the wrong people!'

Jenoso struggled to ignore the accuracy of that off-the-cuff observation. 'Never mind – more so, greater funds are now needed for reconstruction – ergo, the matter at hand.'

The old captain, his thin, sun-faded shirt barely hanging on his bony frame, gestured a clawed hand to him. 'Why the Imperial colours? I thought Cawn was open to the highest bidder. Or has the bidding closed?'

Again Jenoso struggled to keep his features, and tone, even. 'I'll have you know that not just yesterday a massed army of close to thirty thousand Cawnese provincial forces marched through here on their way west to the support of the Empire.'

The captain rubbed a hand over his face, grimacing. 'That so. Yesterday or not yesterday? Which?'

'Ah . . . pardon?'

'You said "not yesterday" – so, which was it?'

It seemed to the harbour-assessor that somehow control of the situation was slipping away from him yet he couldn't exactly put his finger on just how and when it happened. 'Ah, yesterday, or so . . .'

'Well, why didn't you just say so, man! Gods!'

Jenoso's grip tightened so hard on his wax tablet he felt his hot fingertips pressing into it. 'Sir! The matter at hand . . . !'

'What's the matter with the hand dealt to us here is that we're throwin' in our hand. Looks like the Empire's got all the ports in the fist of her hand so we're pushin' off!'

The harbour-assessor's knotted brows hurt. 'I'm sorry . . . ?'

'So am I. Cast off!'

'What – me?'

'Why? Are you enlisting?' He gestured aside, 'Cast off!'

'Aw, no, Captain! Please!' someone pleaded. 'Soliel's mercy, sir! We want water, food . . .'

'What you want is a chance to desert! Now move!'

'Sir . . .' Jenoso called, 'Sir!'

'Yes? You still here?'

'Sadly so.'

A fey laugh from the captain. 'That's the spirit, lad.'

Sailors, barefoot, dressed in ragged trousers and shirts climbed over the sides to slide down the mooring ropes. Jenoso pointed. 'Wait. You can't do that – wait. Mooring and unmooring at a whim! You owe fees – docking, launch crews must be paid . . .'

'Tell you what,' the captain announced, 'here's a down-payment,' and he tossed something, a small ball of some kind.

In his panic, Jenoso dropped his tablet to catch the dark ball. He juggled it in his hands, staring. 'What is this?' he fairly squeaked.

'It's what you think it is.'

Jenoso froze, the ball, or ovoid, held at arm's length. His mouth gaped but no sound emerged.

'Raise sails!' the captain ordered, 'we've a seaward breeze. It's less than the gas passed from a countessa during a reception, but it'll do.'

Canvas and ropes rasped, feet pounded the deck. Jenoso remained frozen. His arms ached.

'Farewell to all these bureaucracy-choked lands!' The captain bellowed. 'A curse upon all you assessors and collectors and all you state-run bandits! May you choke in Hood's craw! Goodbye to all fees, tithes, taxes, bills and levies! Damn you all to the darker side of the Abyss!'

The sails caught the weak breeze. Sailors struggled to push off with poles. The captain continued his rant. Unavoidably, this strange activity attracted the attention of the harbour guard and a detachment marched down to investigate. Its sergeant found the harbour-assessor white-faced, arms quivering, a death-grip on an object in his hands. The sergeant gently pulled it from him to study it. 'Stamp of the Imperial Arsenal,' he said musingly.

'Is it . . .' the harbour-assessor stammered, weak-voiced, 'is it . . .'

'It's just a smoker,' the sergeant said, tossing it hand to hand. He raised his chin to the ship easing into the bay. 'Who was that?'

'The *Ragstopper*,' Jenoso gasped as he flexed and massaged his hands together. Peering down he saw that his tablet had slipped neatly through a gap in the dock slats to drop into the harbour.

He pressed his hot hands to his face and fought an urge to cry.

'The *Ragstopper*, you say? Well, we'll be waiting for him. No matter where he puts in – we'll be waiting for him.'

* * *

The seas were climbing and heavy clouds prefaced a squall, but Yathengar stamped his staff to the deck of the *Forlorn* regardless, calling assembly of the ritual participants. Ho sat at the stern with Su and Devaleth; the Wickan witch perfectly miserable in the rough weather and the Korelan sea-mage perfectly at ease.

The participants, some twenty-three, not including Yath, shuffled together and again Ho was struck by the sad spectacle. *We look like a collection of village idiots, all of us. Hair hacked and badly shaved, dressed in rags scrounged on the ship – all old clothing and sandals and such thrown overboard. Some men even shaved their body hair. Those pale are sun-burned. The skin of all is raw, cracked and bleeding from repeated scrubbing. You'd think plague had broken out on board. Yet it's working – that and having left the islands far behind. I can feel my powers returning. They are there; I just have to dare to reach for them.*

The participants arranged themselves in rows before Yath, Seven Cities priest and mage. Ho, of course, had researched ritual magics to a degree far greater than most scholarly mages and Su, he knew, must also be familiar with its demands. Wickan warlocks and witches employed it regularly. Devaleth, he imagined, must also be conversant – Ruse was infamous for the complexity of its rituals.

And none of them had elected to participate. Was this the mere product of personal dislike of Yath, or was there more here – a deeper suspicion, or healthy dread, of the consequences for any participant should things go wrong? Maybe both.

It began well enough. Ho detected only the most negligible interference from the presence of any lingering traces of Otataral. Around the sitting, concentrating mages, the mundane sailing of the vessel continued. The Avowed crew shortened the sails and secured everything against the coming storm. Blues was at the stern-tiller with Treat while Fingers sat beside them propped up against the side. The skies darkened, the thick low clouds churning. Ho wanted to call it all off, but he understood that time was pressing. Events were converging on Quon. A cusp of a kind was approaching during which they must act or thereafter lose any chance of influencing its outcome.

He studied his own rasped-raw palms and the soles of his feet, his bloodied nails cut short by a knife – and all self-inflicted! Was there a metaphor here of some kind for the pursuits of him and his companions? If so, it was not a pleasant one.

Mouthings pulled his attention to Grief – Blues – at the stern tiller along with Treat and Dim. The man's eyes were on Yath, his lips moving as he followed along in the invocation, nodding to himself at Yath's choices in his groundwork for the merging to come. Ho straightened, amazed – the man's a mage! *Yes, one of us indeed!*

'You're a mage as well,' he said to Blues.

The man shared a glance with Fingers, a sardonic smile raised one edge of his lips. 'Don't spread it around. Fingers and I like to surprise people with it.'

'What Warren, may I ask?'

A shrug. 'D'riss.'

So, the Paths of the earth. A Warren very appropriate to their researches in the Pit. Was this how the man was able to so shrug off what happened to him there? Yet had he? He also, Ho noted, was not participating in the ritual. But Blues and his fellow Avowed now fought the heavy tiller arm, swinging it hard over. Devaleth stood, studied the waves surging towards them like slate towers.

'Shorten the sails further,' she called to Blues. 'Now.'

Blues did not waste time thinking or reacting, he merely nodded to Treat who ran to relay the order. 'We're much too damned light,' the woman grumbled under her breath. 'Should've taken on more ballast at the Pit . . .'

'More Otataral?' Ho asked of her, mockingly.

As an answer the sea-mage gestured ahead. 'This will kill us just as surely.'

Icy spray slashed Ho's face. He wiped it away. 'Then let's hope Yath succeeds.'

The Mare mage was now the only person standing unaided on the deck. Everyone else was sitting or clung to ropes or the sides. She stood with her feet widely spread, her hands clasped at her back. She looked down to Ho. 'You and I both know it'll take all day to bring everyone into harmony for the casting. A wave could swamp us any time before then.'

'Then you best help us,' Su said, her dark face wrinkling up in a smile.

Devaleth raised her eyes to the clouded sky, muttered curses to her self in Korelan. Ho thought he heard echoes of the old Malazan accents in the language. 'Oh, very well,' she hissed in Talian. She took the tiller arm, pushed at Blues. 'Let go, you damned oaf.' He shot an uncertain glance to Ho who gave his assent. Taking a deep breath, he and Dim relinquished the arm to Devaleth's control. Immediately the *Forlorn* steadied, its progress smoothing. She pushed the arm with just the finger and thumb of one hand and the prow fairly leapt to meet an oncoming wave. 'Too light,' the woman muttered, distastefully.

'Is there no interference?' Su called, eager.

'Yes, there's bloody interference!' the sea-mage snarled. 'The Otataral is a rasp gouging my mind! But I can push that aside – no, there's something else . . .' Her eyes narrowed to slits as she sought within, searching. '. . . Something I cannot identify. But it's there. It's pulling, like a tide or current, urging me aside . . .' She shook her head. 'Too ephemeral. Can't spare the time or effort – you chase it down!' And she turned her back, putting an end to any further distraction.

Su offered Ho a knowing conspiratorial smile, and again he wondered: what did the old woman mean by such gestures? Was it no more than an invitation to read whatever suited his own fears or plans? Would she later claim to have known all along how everything was going to unfold? The affectation annoyed him no end. No one can know another's mind or their own deepest motivations, hopes or feelings. People were all of them strangers – sources of continual surprise – at times disappointing but at other times affirming. And so it must be for everyone, he imagined.

At the mid-deck Yath had sat as well, staff across his lap, struggling to weave the commingled contributions of the participants into one seamless flow of channelled power to be held, coalesced and distilled, then released in one awesome revelation of willed intent: the transference of the ship through Warren from one physical location to another.

* * *

'What're they waiting for?' Brill asked, an arm over his shovel, gazing off at the Guard lines to the south.

Nait didn't stop hacking furiously at the dry earth. 'How in the Abyss should I know? Now stop your shirking and get to work!' Grinning, Brill set once more to deepening their trench. *Just hold up a while longer*, Nait pleaded, *an' we'll have us a nice defensive perimeter. Just a mite longer* . . . He swung a leg up and crouched in the grass, peering left and right. Not much movement. Pot-shots from the skirmishers, nothing serious. *What's everyone waiting for?* It's damned unnerving is what it was. *No one eager to get killed, I guess.* May had chosen a good hill – not high enough to attract unwanted attention, but not too shallow neither. Not close to the centre, but not too far to the side. Once he'd snuck his squad down Nait had set everyone to digging a long semicircle of trench – their hidey-hole when the mages and Veils came hunting. May and the regulars were setting up the stone arbalest. This engagement, instead of stones, it will be throwing something far more deadly at any Avowed or mage who's fool enough to reveal his or her position.

Speaking of mages, Heuk was with them. A number of saboteur squads had been assigned cadre mages, though what use the old soak was going to be was beyond Nait. He pulled at his iron and leather brigantine – liberated from the quarter-master wagons by his light-fingered recruits. They too now sported better armour, as well: padded and layered leathers set with rings and studs, iron helmets, greaves and boiled leather vambraces. Too much armour, in truth. But they were young; if they lived long enough they'd come to find the proper balance between protection and weight.

Mixed League and Malazan cavalry patrolled the outlying edges of the field – too few to do anything more. Most of the field commanders had dismounted to stand with their battalions. At centre front the Sword standard threatened advance but never quite committed; waiting word from Laseen. Nait wondered how long that would last. What was the woman waiting for? Why not unleash the skirmishers, sound the advance? Mid-afternoon now and still no one had exchanged blows in anger.

A brown grasshopper landed on Nait's mailed sleeve and he blew to send it flying. *Get along, little fellow – things are about to get far too hot for the likes of you.* Untan militia fire, he noted, was thickening to the west flank. Some Guard Blade or line had pushed forward or done something and the irregulars responded. Now, seeing their brothers and sisters firing, more and more of the crossbowmen and women were popping up to fire. The flights of bolts became a constant pattering, then a darkening rain, thickened to a punishing storm. *This was how it would start: some inconsequential move would invite retaliation, would spur a countermove, would become an escalation in resources and before either side knew it they were committed.* Being utterly without personal delusions Nait knew he was a neophyte, but such a scenario of chaos, of blind forces groping at one another in the dark and reacting without thought, made sense when compared to what he'd seen so far. And it would be dark soon enough – *shit! As if things couldn't get any worse! The dark! There's no way they'd be off this field before night.*

Nait cast about for the cadre mage. 'Heuk! Get up here!' The old man appeared, greasy-haired, squinting. 'What good you gonna do us anyway?'

Heuk shaded his eyes from the afternoon sun. 'You pray you don't need me—'

'Yeah, yeah. That's all we ever hear from you. Well, you know what I say? I say *bullshit*! We're gonna need everyone!'

The mage scanned the field from under his palm, bobbed his sour agreement. 'I think you're right.'

'So?'

'So . . .' he ducked back down into the thin trench, 'wait for night.'

Nait restrained himself from tossing a shovelful of dirt on to the man. He kept one eye on the gathering firefight. From the unit absorbing the storm of bolts on the flank came twin arcs of flame that shot skyward then came crashing down, bursting into billowing orange-red infernos. In their wake arose swaths of flames as the sun-browned grasses took up the fires like the rarest of tinder. Skirmishers ran like ants from a kicked nest.

Nait squeezed himself down into the shoulder-width trench. *Lady save them, it's started. And things were not looking good.* 'Water!' he bellowed. 'Douse yourselves!' He fought with shaking hands to unstop a bulging skin.

The popping of distant sharpers sounded: his cohorts punishing whichever mage that was – *as if he or she was still there!* Yet the pattern was now set. Mages would reveal themselves to smash any point of strength and the saboteurs would seek to stalk and hammer them. The hammering part Nait loved . . . but he wasn't too keen on that stalking part. *Gonna get hammered ourselves draggin' our asses across this field. No – won't do.* 'Heuk!'

Jawl showed up, crouched above Nait, her long hauberk touching the ground down past her knees. 'Do we have to keep diggin'? We've been diggin' all the damned day. I mean, the fighting's startin'.'

'Will you get down! Fire's comin'!'

'Naw – it was snuffed out.'

Nait straightened. 'What do you mean, "snuffed out"?' He squinted out over the field. Plenty of smoke hanging in the still air but very little fire. Heuk had dragged himself over, hugging his tall brown earthenware jug. 'What happened to the fire?' Nait asked.

'Put out by one of ours.'

'We got one c'n do that?'

A shrug. 'Sure. Serc Warren. Maybe Bala.'

'Bala? Who's that?'

A rotten-toothed grin: 'Oh *you'll* know her when you see *her*.'

Jawl was still squatting next to the trench. Nait gave her a glare. 'What in the name of Rotting Poliel are you doin' there? Get to work! Keep diggin' – it's what saboteurs do.' The youth pulled a long face, sulked away. Nait studied Heuk. 'Listen, I don't want to be run all over Hood's playground out there . . .'

'Sound policy.'

'But we need a way to spot the targets 'n' such. Can't you do anything to help us out?'

The mage lowered his greasy seamed face to the open top of his jug as if studying its depths. He looked up, winking. 'I think I can maybe do that.'

Nait's brows rose. *Damn – we're gonna actually see some action out of this broken-down old fart?* 'So? Do it.'

'Wait for night.' And he ducked down.

Smartarse. Nait studied the lines. The Sword standard kept edging forward yet not *quite* committing. The Guard lines remained immobile. *Why'd they put their backs to a cliff? True, they gotta hold the road to the bridge, but still . . . Neither side wants to get bloodied. We know there's Avowed waiting for us; and they're outnumbered more than four to one.*

* * *

Shimmer could not believe the punishment these Untan irregulars were inflicting on her lines. They were like biting flies – or hornets – and her forces the blundering bhederin attempting to swat them. Something had to be done; how much longer must her men and women hold the line – no more than obliging targets?

Brethren! She called within her thoughts to her fallen brother and sister Avowed. *Speak with Skinner. We must advance! Sweep the field of this threat! We cannot delay any longer.*

Your concerns shall be conveyed, came the distant response.

Concerns? Her tactical judgment no more than a concern? Was she not second in command?

Skinner warns you to put aside your panic. These pests shall be dealt with in good time.

Panic! *Panic!* She took hold of the grip of her long whipsword. Who did he think he was? She almost set out from her flank commander position to confront the man, but refrained knowing she could not abandon her post. *Damn him! Well, she would act, even if he wouldn't! Brethren! Orders for Smoky, Twisty and Shell: you are given leave to punish those skirmishers – and keep moving!*

Orders shall be conveyed.

Damn right they will be conveyed. Skinner may have no regard for the third investiture common soldiers of the lines – but she was going to do everything she could to protect the men and women of her command!

Orders acknowledged.

Good. Now those pests will be made leery of approaching her flank!

Moments later a great sheet of flame arose across the intervening field and began sweeping north. Distant figures writhed, caught in the sudden eruption. The great mass of skirmishers recoiled, fleeing. The wedge of fire broadened, swelling, a runaway grass fire threatening to engulf the entire field. Then, just as suddenly, the flames were snuffed, as they had been before. *Who in the Queen's Mysteries was that mage?* The irregulars crept forward once more, began targeting her lines where her soldiers hunched behind shields. *Damn, they're brave bastards!* Sudden wails of surprise and alarm – the barrage stuttering, thinning. Twisty and Shell at work. Less showy than Smoky but just as effective. She could imagine Twisty ruining their weapons, Shell softening the ground beneath their feet. Enough to send them running.

Something flashed across her vision then. Men and women of her bodyguard fell, one clutching at a bolt in her neck, another in his chest. Cold iron punched into Shimmer's back and she spun, pinned the attacker's arm and struck, crushing the man's throat. *Claws! Two full Hands!* Another crouching figure aimed and she ducked; a bolt sang overhead. She leapt, rolling to take the woman down, clasped her head and twisted, breaking the neck. She stood, drawing long-knives from her belt and something struck her, a wave of pressure that when it passed left her surroundings darkened, quiet. Suddenly it was dusk, the sky colourless. The field remained but now stretched empty. *Shadow!* She spun, found what she searched for: the mage some distance off. Ignoring the pain of the thrust in her back, she made for him.

Shadows closed, coalesced before her. She pushed through. Something clutched her throat, cutting off her breath. She felt at her neck but found nothing. *Shadows throttling her! How to . . .* She fought to breathe but nothing came. Her lungs charred. Her chest tightened in a rising frenzied panic. But still through the blurring haze she saw him, the Claw mage, and she made for him. Amazingly the man did not move; he watched her advance with disbelief in eyes that widened and widened as she closed. The shadows tightened like a hangman's noose. She felt her pulse throbbing, clenched off.

'No . . . *impossible* . . .' the man breathed, astounded.

A more thorough briefing may have been required regarding the Avowed, Shimmer reflected as she swung, slitting his throat in one slash, then she fell, her vision blackening.

Brethren! I join you . . .

* * *

Olo sat smoking his pipe, lying back in his skiff, his arms crossed, legs out, hat pulled down over his eyes against the sinking late afternoon sun. 'Boatman,' someone called, 'for hire?' His boat rocked slightly, and he roused, reluctantly.

'What?' A fat man in rich dark-blue robes stood on the dock peering down at him, a strange unnerving grin on his thick lips. Olo stared back, suspicious. What in the God of a Thousand Faces was a rich fellow like this doing hailing him? He looked like some kind of eunuch or functionary from the Empress's court. Was he lost? 'Ah, what can I do for you?'

'Use of your craft, good boatman, to take me across the harbour.'

'Across? You mean to the spice and silk docks p'chance?'

'No. I mean straight across. West.'

Olo sat up straighter, glanced over, shading his gaze. 'But there's nothing there . . .'

'My concern, do you not think?' and the fellow produced a gold coin. Olo goggled at the coin then held out a hand. The man tossed it. It felt hefty enough, not that he'd held many gold Imperial Suns in his life. 'Be my guest.'

Whoever he was, the man was at least familiar with the water as he smoothly eased himself down on to the light craft of hand-adzed planks. Olo readied the oars, pushed away from the dock. 'Been quiet since the attack and the Empress leaving, hey?'

'Yes.'

'A course, she took all of Unta with her, didn't she!' and he laughed.

Silence. Olo cast a quick glance to his passenger, found him moodily peering aside, a slight frown of puzzlement wrinkling his pale face. Olo squinted as well: the fellow appeared to be watching a shoal of clustered leaves bobbing in the waves. Old prayer offerings. Not a man for small talk, obviously. Olo rowed on, taking a moment to pull down his loose woollen hat. A bottle of Kanese red maybe, and that Talian girl – the one who was so full of herself. Or maybe rice-piss for as many days as he could stomach it. And thinking of that – Olo shot a quick look to his self-absorbed passenger, pulled out a gourd and took a quick nip.

'What *are* you up to, Mael?'

Olo gasped, choking. 'Me sir? Nothing, sir! Just a touch thirsty 's all.'

But the eunuch wasn't even looking his way; he was turned aside, looking out over the water. Olo squinted as well but saw only the smooth green swells of the harbour, the forest of berthed ships. The boat slowed.

Without so much as turning his head the man said, 'Row on or jump out. Your decision.' And he held his hands over the side.

Olo gaped at the fellow. *What? Who was he to—*

The water began to foam under the man's hands. It churned as if boiling, hissing and paling to a light olive green.

Olo almost fell over backwards as he heaved on the oars. *Gods forgive me! Chem Bless me! Thousand-fold God favour me! What have I done to deserve this – other than all those things I've done but never told anyone?*

'Those folded leaves. The flowers and garlands on the water. What are they?'

Pulling harder than he had in thirty years, Olo gasped a breath. 'Offerings. Prayers.'

'Offerings to *whom*?'

'The God of the waters, sir. God of all the seas. God of a Thousand Moods, a Thousand Faces, a Thousand Names.'

'No! Mael! You shall writhe in agony for this!'

Olo gaped at the man. *Mael who?* Then, remembering, he renewed his pulling. The skiff bucked, bobbing in suddenly rough waters.

'Speak! I command you!'

Olo somehow knew that his passenger was not addressing him. The tiny skiff sped up, but not from any efforts on Olo's part. The water was swelling, climbing upwards, bulging beneath them like a blanket billowed by air, and his skiff was sliding down its slope. He abandoned his oars in futility, scooped up the gourd and emptied it over his face, gulping. And horribly, appallingly, he heard something speak: '*Mallick. What is there for us to talk of?*'

564

'What have you been scheming!' the passenger demanded.

'*I? Nothing. Your prohibitions forbid this. I have merely been here – awaiting your summons. Am I to be blamed that others have sensed me, sent their offerings? Their prayers? Is it my fault that somehow have been recalled the ancient titles and invocations?*'

'What are you babbling about!' his passenger fairly howled, hands now fists at his temples.

The voice took on a harsh edge. '*I am free of you now, Mallick. Your bindings upon me have frayed, unravelled by the plucking of countless thousands. We are done, you and I. Finished. We shall speak no more. I could crush you now – and I should for all the crimes you have committed. But I will withhold my anger. I have indulged it too much of late. My last gift to you is this passage. That, your life, and my mercy – may it gall you.*'

The skiff suddenly spun like a top, whirling on foaming waters. Olo had the sickening sensation of falling, then water heaved over the sides, the boat rocking, settling. He scrambled to use his cupped hands to toss out the water. His passenger sat slumped in the stern, soaked in spray. Olo then grasped the oars, rowed for his life. The west shore was close now, though it looked too wild and steep. Had they drifted out into the bay? As his boat neared the rocky shore he looked around and gaped, stunned. Where in the Queen's Teasings was he? This was not Unta! There was a town to the north, but it was much too small. Though it too did look as if it had seen an attack. He steadied the craft at a rock, setting a sandalled foot out to hook it. Waves threatened to break the skiff on the shore but he pushed back, fighting the surge. Movement announced his passenger stirring.

'We're lost, sir,' he called over the waves.

A long pause, then, 'Yes. I am. But perhaps not completely.'

The man was obviously one of those crazed mages he heard all about in songs and somehow his insanity had touched him – Gods, may it pass! 'What I mean, sir, is I don't know where we are.'

The man edged his way forward, set a cold damp hand on Olo's shoulder. 'We are in Cawn,' he said, and he pushed off Olo to reach the rock.

Olo gaped up at him. 'Really, sir? I mean, I've never been.'

The fat fellow pushed back his wet hair, clasped his hands across his broad stomach, his fingers weaving, and he regarded the town to the north through lowered eyelids. 'Well, you have now.' Something must have caught his eye then for he stooped, reaching down, and came up with a folded leaf votive offering. It held an old wilted geranium blossom. So, even here in Cawn too, Olo reflected. The fellow regarded it for a time, quite pensive, his fat lips turned down. 'Patience, this lesson. Patience, and – acceptance of the unalterable. Will I finally learn, I wonder?'

'Pardon, sir?'

But it was as if Olo had not spoken at all. The fellow tossed the offering back into the waves and turned away. Further up the shore, where a short cliff rose from a steep strand of gravel, driftwood and black, angular rocks, a group of men and women now waited where just before none had been. Olo recognized the dark-cloaked figures from stories and was now glad to have simply been left alive. He lifted his gourd for a drink but found it empty and threw it aside in disgust. Then he remembered the coin and fished around inside his shirt. He found it and shouted his glee then glanced hurriedly to the shore but the figures were gone, and his eerie passenger with them. May they fall into the Abyss!

He pushed off from the slippery algae-lined rock and back-oared. Now for Cawn. He hoped they were civilized enough here to boast a brothel or two. And what a tale he had to tell! It might even be good enough for one on the house.

* * *

Ullen picked up a fallen soldier's helmet only to find it heavy with gore. He dropped the wet thing. Four of Cowl's Avowed assassins. The reserves in turmoil. Some sort of flesh-bursting Warren magics only stopped by an end of bodies to feed it. He caught the eye of the healer treating High Fist Anand, bloodied and prone on a cloak, cocked a question.

The healer rose to put her face to his ear. 'He may live.'

Ullen turned to the pale, shaken staff officers, Imperial and Talian. 'Reorder the brigades.' Relieved jerked nods all around. 'The rest of you, follow me. From now on we'll keep moving.'

Salutes. 'Aye, Commander.'

He headed south to the best vantage of the field he could find. Ahead, smoke draped the entire slope where fires rose raging only to suddenly whip out as if by invisible tornadoes. The heaving mass of irregulars still fired their withering flights of bolts into the hunched lines of Crimson Guard soldiery. So far the thrumming and singing of the crossbows was the main noise of battle. Behind the lines, the Blades waited, veterans and Avowed all. On the west, Urko's command of Talian heavies had broken through and now faced a number of coalesced Blades. *Good luck, old friend.* The tall standard of the Sword was still pressing in the centre, now facing the thickest of the lines. Ullen had to admire the man's bravery and martial spirit, even if it was accompanied by a rather appalling lack of imagination. He waved forward a messenger. 'Ride to V'thell. Give him my compliments and have him break that east phalanx at all costs, then head west to the road to cut the main Guard elements from the bridge.'

'Aye, sir.'

A staff lieutenant cleared his throat. Ullen turned, a brow raised.

It was an Imperial officer. 'With all respect. That is not Korbolo and Anand's battle plan.'

'No, it is not. But I served under Choss who has faced the Guard before and his lesson is not to treat them as an army but as individuals. Separate the Blades, isolate them, bring superior numbers to bear and bury them.'

The Imperial staff command officers stirred uneasily. 'Again, with all due respect, Lieutenant-commander. *We* defeated *you*.'

Ullen merely blinked, puzzled. 'We were not the Guard.'

Another staff officer, a young Dal Hon woman, spoke. 'Should we not check with the Empress? What if she is not safe?'

Ullen returned his gaze to the field. 'That is not my concern. My job is to win this engagement if at all possible.' And he headed off again – he'd been standing in one place long enough. The assembled staff and messengers of command could choose to follow or not.

He climbed up on to the south road, a high point, its bed raised by Imperial engineers. The deep amber slanting light of late afternoon now gathered over the broad slope. Cries snapped his attention to the centre field where a swirling in the light revealed a Warren opening. Darkness blossomed and out came something night-black and angular, winged. *A demon. And not one of ours.* The staff officers shouted their alarm. Ullen turned on them, 'Have the skirmishers concentrate their fire on that thing!'

The Dal Hon woman saluted, 'Aye', ran for the nearest mount.

Good. A lesson from Choss: even if you know it's not enough – do *something*! And where was their damned mage cadre? Done in by the Veils already?

While the entire field of gathered men and women watched, the thing swooped over Urko's heavies and stooped, slashing left and right. It then rose, carrying a victim that it dismembered in full view of all, limbs spinning, fluids splashing. Ullen swore that his complete command flinched at the spectacle. *Damn it to Hood! They had to show everyone they possessed the firepower to counter that thing! That display alone was enough to break morale.*

Wings beating heavily, the demon swung next to the east where V'thell's Gold were mauling the Guard phalanx. Sharpers burst beneath it among the ranks indiscriminately, revealing missed throws of munitions. *Where was their blasted mage cadre!* As the creature passed over a hillock something struck it and a flash of actinic light made Ullen wince and glance away. A grating shriek such as cracking stone echoed over the slope. When he looked back the thing was flailing, white flames engulfing it, pieces dropping away in fluid globules. It began to sink, limbs spasming as its outline changed, thinning, drooping. It struck the ground, bowled over irregulars and crashed into a shieldwall of Malazan regulars who hacked at its twitching flesh. A great cheer went up among the Imperial forces. Everyone on both sides had paused in horror and fascination to watch the spectacle. *Gods, a melter. What an awful way to go.* He marked that hillock, bare but ringed by a dark line, a trench. Something odd about the crest struck him. The grasses bowed, fluttering as if in a constant hard wind – *fanning! Bala.*

'Name a strong reserve unit,' he called out.

'We have a detachment of Gold,' someone answered from the mix of Ullen's own personal guard and the command staff surrounding him.

'Send it to defend that hillock on the east flank. Someone's established a redoubt there on the field.'

'A redoubt, sir? Isn't our goal to advance?'

'Push back the Avowed? Hardly. But we can break them up. Penetrate their lines. As to the redoubt,' Ullen lifted his chin to the west, 'night is coming.'

His thoughts obviously returning to the horrors of last night, the officer paled and bowed. 'Aye, sir.'

A disgraced ex-High Mage and a saboteur squad dug in. A strong position. Should V'thell succeed they might be able to lever the Guard from the road. 'What news from the bridge? What of the Kan forces?'

A pause as staffers discussed things among themselves. 'Latest intelligence is that they've yet to commit,' the Imperial lieutenant said.

Ullen stopped pacing the set cobbles of the road. '*What?*'

Confusion, exchanged panicked glances. 'Sorry, sir—'

'You are all agreed on this?'

Nods all around. *Damn the tightfisted calculating bastards!*
'Send messages across the river. By arrow, if you must. The Empress
demands they initiate an attack on that bridge! Further – any
continued delay will be considered rebellion and we will march on
Kan next!'

'*Sir!*' someone objected, shocked. 'Ah, that is, do we have the
authority . . .'

Ullen pointed to the south. 'We could lose any and all Hood-
damned authority we may have thought we had. Now go!'

'Aye.' A man ran for the mounts.

Movement on the road caught his eye. A pink mist had appeared,
swelling, rolling towards them like a cloud. It engulfed screaming
soldiers who disappeared before his eyes, their flesh, armour, even
bone, flensed into a suspended mist that was heading straight for
them. Soldiers jumped aside. *Too long in the same spot, fool!*
'Magery!' Ullen leapt from the road.

*   *   *

Shimmer did not lose consciousness but after a moment's reflection
this did not surprise her. She was after all joining the Brethren. The
dead Avowed chained to their living brothers and sisters. Enslaved by
the Vow, by those awful impetuous terms – *eternal opposition.*
Cheating Hood, yes, but unable to rest, ever agitating for the Vow.
Remember, they had always come to whisper in her sleep, torment-
ing her.

You swore! Remember your Vow . . . Remember . . .

A hand turned her over. She blinked up at a pewter sky occluded
by a skeletal, withered face. *Hood himself?* 'You are dying,' said the
vision of death. 'Despite your great vitality, it is draining away.'

'Are you . . . Imass?' she whispered, hoarse.

The dried flesh of the face could not express emotion but Shimmer
had the impression of surprise. 'No. I am Edgewalker.' Shimmer had
nothing to say to that as the name meant nothing. 'I am sending you
back. Your engagement is spilling over into Shadow and that I cannot allow. I want all of you gone. You, that murderous trespasser –
even the binder of your Vow – though he is being shielded.'

Shimmer stared up at the bizzare entity. 'Binder of my Vow? You
mean K'azz?'

'Whatever his name. He must go. I will send you now.'

K'azz! Shimmer cast out her thoughts as she did when summoning
the Brethren. *Are you there? K'azz?*

Distant shocked surprise. *Shimmer? Is that you? In truth? K'azz! Where are you?*

Shimmer – I am close. I'm coming! Listen. It was Skinner and Cowl! They betrayed me!

'You go now,' Edgewalker intoned in a voice like dry dust falling. A dessicated hand, all sinew and bone, rested upon her chest.

Shimmer tried to move – the effort blackened her vision. 'Wait!'

Pain made her gasp. Hot smoky air choked her and she coughed, wincing with the memory of the stab wound. 'Here she is!' Someone threw herself down next to her: Shell. 'Back with us!'

'What's happened?'

'Shh now.' She nodded to someone out of Shimmer's vision; she turned her head – Twisty – their best healer. He gave her an encouraging nod. Shell eased her up, handed her a gourd of water. The cacophony of battle assaulted her: closer now, much closer. The Imperials have been advancing. And it was dark, sunset. Twisty opened her armour, slid a hand in around her side. 'The east flank's collapsed,' Shell explained. 'Those Imperial allies, the Moranth, they're pushing to the centre, trying to cut us off from the bridge. And we are hard pressed in the west. But reports are that Cowl and the Veils have a free hand. They say that the High Fist has fallen, the Sword has fallen, Urko has fallen—'

'Who says!' Shimmer cut in, wincing and gasping for breath.

Shell wiped smeared dirt from her face and short blond hair, her brows wrinkled. 'Why, the Veils, of course . . .'

Shimmer stood, rolled her shoulder on the side Twisty had healed. 'Yet the Claws found me.'

Further puzzlement, the lines at the woman's mouth deepening. 'And others, yes . . .'

'Who else?'

'Sart, Betel, Ketch. Those I know of.'

None friends of Skinner. 'Summon Greymane and Smoky to me – now. And remain with me.' Shell bowed. Who else could she count on? The majority of her command, she imagined – and hoped. How she wished Cal-Brinn's company had come through! They'd understood each other. Bars and Jup Alat would make a great difference. And Blues' Blade – what in the Mysteries of D'rek has happened to them? They seemed to have disappeared from the face of the world.

She took hold of Twisty's arm and gently pushed him away.

'Not yet, Commander,' he said, anxious.

'It will have to do.'

He shook his head, moved to speak, but stopped himself and nodded. 'Very well.' He helped her up. She studied the field. The current assault looked like a very strong effort to take command of the ground. The Guard could not fight the Empress and themselves at the same time. Should that happen she must consider how to withdraw – but to where? Skinner's arrogant disposition had crippled them. The bridge was too narrow and the Kanese were waiting for them in any case. A fighting withdrawal, then, to a defensible position. And the only real possibility within reach lay to the east . . .

Still, ought she not make one last effort? She faced a still puzzled Shell. 'Stay here. Ask Greymane and Smoky to await me here as well. Will you do that?'

'Of course. You're not . . .'

'Await my return. Tell Smoky – he was right all along.'

The mage caught at the mail of Shimmer's arm. 'Don't go.'

'What?'

'You're going to him, aren't you. Don't.'

Shimmer studied the nest of winkles at the woman's entreating eyes, her mouth bracketed by furrows, wanting, perhaps, to say so much more. 'I have no idea what you're talking about.'

The hand tightened. '*Shimmer!* You're not the only one Smoky spoke to.'

'He spoke out of place, then.' She gently removed the hand.

'Twins take it, woman! What are you hiding from?'

'We are wasting time here, mage. See to your duty – as I must mine.'

Shell urged her off with curt wave. 'Go then, fool! He'll not listen to you.'

Shimmer turned and walked away. *The Vow. Remember your Vow.* She picked up a shield from some fallen soldier, held it between her and the skirmishers as she crossed the field of assembled Blades. Avowed called but she did not answer. Thrown sharpers burst, scattering shards and dirt, but she did not flinch. Bolts hissed, hammering the shield and plucking at her, but she did not pause.

And we were so close . . . so close to finally, utterly, being rid of the Vow that has damned us all.

She found him at the standard, arms crossed, helm lowered as always. Crossbow bolts slashed the air. One struck him full on, glancing away, unable to penetrate the strange night-black glittering mailed armour. His company Avowed were gathered around him – though what Claws would marshal an attempt upon him she could not imagine. Dancer, of course; Topper, perhaps, if he was still competent – their intelligence told them he'd let himself go completely. Who, then, was left? No one. For an instant she wondered if the man was fully justified in his almost magisterial self-assurance. Who was there to face him? Save – and the thought came with a gut-tightening shock – herself.

'Shimmer,' he called. 'You have left your post.'

'A full Hand has taken out my guard. The Gold have broken through. We need reinforcements.'

He inclined his helmed head. 'A timely request. I am collecting blades to meet the threat. I will go with fifteen of my Avowed to break them.'

A wave of tossed munitions suddenly blasted earth and sod skyward over everyone – all ducked save the Avowed. 'And after that?' Shimmer shouted, her ears ringing.

'Then we march north on the Empress's position.'

'She'll hardly remain to meet you,' Shimmer said with far more scorn than she intended to reveal.

The man's arms uncoiled, an iron gauntleted hand going to the black stone – polished jet? – that served as his blade's pommel while the other reached to her, clenching. 'Then Cowl will hunt her down and slay her like vermin!'

Shimmer flinched away. *I see.* 'And then what?'

'Then? Why, then our ambitions will have been fulfilled.'

'The *Vow* will be fulfilled, you mean.' Two bolts struck her shield, momentarily pushing her weight over on to one foot. She hefted the massive rectangle to straighten it.

A pause. The man gestured forward his guard of Avowed mages: Mara, the Dal Hon, her wild matted hair like a lion's mane; Gwynn, in his severe black tunic, sash and trousers; and Petal, grey-haired, crippled Petal leaning on his staff. 'Do your thoughts not cast beyond the Vow, Shimmer? Have you not considered – what then?'

'We return to Avore.'

'Avore has been wiped from the map! There is no more such entity. Kellanved was quite thorough.' Skinner waved the possibility aside. 'So, the question remains . . . what then?' The helm edged aside to look beyond her and he backed up a step. Shimmer turned. Avowed approached through the dusk and smoke: Halfdan, Bower, Lucky, Shell, Smoky, as well as the broad hulking Greymane who had yet to draw his sword.

No, not now! Now while we dance with the Imperials. Shimmer bowed to Skinner. 'My command from the east flank. You say you march on these foreign allies from across the sea. Very well. We will master the west. What say you?'

Skinner's mail-backed fingers flexed upon the grip of his sword. The helm swung to the west. 'Very well, Shimmer. Take control of that flank and I will do so in the east. Between the two of us we should hold the field by midnight. Done?'

'Done.'

The two bowed slightly – the Avowed, all equal in theory, held to no salute. Waving to his gathered Avowed, Skinner marched away. Shimmer watched after him, slowly let out a long oh-so-taut breath that sent agony through her side. She regarded Smoky – the man was scorched and sweaty, robes torn, his nose bleeding – so far of all the Avowed mages he had been pressing the assault, and receiving the brunt of the mage cadre counter-attacks. 'I told you to remain on post.'

He jabbed a finger after Skinner. 'Who knows what he might have done . . .'

'*Now* is not the time.'

'Then when?'

Dare she tell them? But what if it were no more than delirious wish-fulfillment? K'azz indeed? So close? Gods, let it be true! Yet . . . No . . . it would be too cruel. 'After the night is won. Agreed?'

A sour scowl. 'Agreed.'

Shimmer twisted aside as a crossbow bolt shot across her front, plucking at her crimson surcoat. She gestured close Smoky, Bower and Shell. 'Gather all those you can. Bring them to me on the western flank. There will be a choosing of sides come the dawn!'

They bowed, hurried off. She turned to the Malazan renegade, studied him, hands on hips. He too had picked up a large Malazan infantryman's shield. 'And what of you? Will you kill Malazan soldiers?'

The man glanced away, his bright sky-blue eyes clearly troubled. 'I will fight to defend myself,' he rumbled.

No. Not good enough. Not good enough by far. 'Then stand in the way and defend yourself, Hood take you!' She snapped a wave, calling loudly to all, 'Come! We march to take the west! Smash every unit! Break all organized resistance!'

A great roaring shout answered her, swelling through the ranks. 'For the Duke!'

Aye – for the Duke. May he return and not prove a mere spectre of all my hopes and fears.

CHAPTER II

And in that year, at that conflagration, there was revealed once again
upon the world that presence that had been withdrawn for so long. All
else must be disregarded as mere commentary. That new old lurking
presence asserted itself and the Night acquired the taste of blood and
iron.

Street Prophet, Kan

THE BREATH OF RILLISH'S MOUNT FOGGED IN THE COOL NIGHT AIR.
He stroked her muzzle, waiting in the courtyard alongside his
readied troop. *Prepare for travel and battle*, Nil's message had
said and so he'd had Sergeant Chord fall everyone out. Though
where within riding distance could any battle be found? Negotiations
were still proceeding with the envoy along predictable lines – the
same phrasings as in earlier treaties signed decade after decade and
similarly broken one after the other. Were the twins so fed up they
planned an attack on Unta?

'Riders,' Chord said aside though Rillish could hear them just as
well.

Shortly afterwards the twins followed by a guard of some twenty
veterans thundered into the courtyard. They reined in close to
Rillish. The brother and sister wore thick dark-blue tunics sashed
with trousers and leather boots. Nether's long hair was pulled back
and tied in leather strips. Horn-handled long-knives thrust forward
from under their arms. Nil looked down at him and the severe set of
his mouth tightened further. 'Just you, Captain.'

He glanced between them – something had changed. They looked
. . . intent upon something neither were happy about. Talia appeared
at his side, took his hand while disguising the gesture between their
bodies. 'Just me?'

Nether motioned to the road. 'Come. We must hurry.'

'Very well.' He mounted, caught Sergeant Chord's eye. 'Take care of things for me here, Sergeant.' Chord tilted his head in assent, spat on to the ground.

Talia had a hand on his boot. 'What's going on?' she asked, her voice low.

'I don't know. Listen to Chord.' He adjusted the weight of his new hauberk of banded iron, the hang of his swords. 'Take care of yourself. I'll . . . I'll see you later.'

'Come back to me,' she said, her voice so tight as to be almost breathless.

'Yes.'

The twins urged their mounts onward and the troop exploded forward, hooves hammering the beaten earth of the court. Rillish noted that almost all the guard accompanying Nil and Nether were old veterans of the Seven Cities campaigns – a hard-bitten if ancient lot. They drove hard, taking the road south, and as they went they passed contingent after contingent waiting strung out along the darkened road. *Sweet Fanderay! Must be a thousand!* All waiting in the night. He urged his mount forward and room was made for him next to Nil at the van.

'What's going on?' he shouted.

He was relieved when Nil offered him a familiar smile. 'You remember our conversations some days ago? We are setting out to seal our agreement with the throne. And in such a way that cannot be denied! We, above all, have reason to detest Laseen but here we are riding to her deliverance.' He shook his head. 'Such is politics.'

'Is this what the envoy—'

A negative wave. Nil pushed his wind-tossed hair from his face. 'No. This is nothing to do with him. We and the witches have been sensing the west. All are agreed a confrontation is gathering such as Quon has not seen in a century. We go to tip the balance and our price of Laseen will be sovereignty!'

Sovereignty? Oh, Nil, Nether, I hope so for your sake. A high goal for your people. Worthy of . . . Rillish craned his neck, scanning the riders within sight . . . all the oldest of the lot, many bearing what would otherwise count as incapacitating wounds: crippled arms, missing hands, eyes. So. They ride to give their all in this one last throw to win the highest goal for their children and grandchildren. Self-rule.

And he rode with them. He leant to Nil once more. 'I am honoured, Nil. But why me? Why am I here?'

A fey, easy laugh. 'Should we win through, Captain, someone must negotiate. You know your own court's ways. You must study every word, every statute. Make sure the terms are binding!'

'I shall, Nil.'

'Good! I know you will,' and he laughed in a completely unrestrained boyish manner. 'That's why I'm so relieved – I won't have to do any of that!'

The column reached a bridge and rumbled across, the hooves sounding like a thunderstorm over the cut and set limestone blocks of its sturdy arches. Torches appeared at nearby guardhouses, inns and farmhouses, but the column passed on, heading west into what was once the sovereign state of Bloor.

Rillish knew, of course, that the Wickans had no intention of riding all the way to Heng. That left travel through Warren – another reason perhaps that he alone had been chosen to accompany them, having just recently endured such a mad journey. And he frankly dreaded any revisit.

Yet he had to admit to some curiosity: how would it be done? All some thousand of them? Such a passage would be unheard of. From what he had pieced together mage-invoked travel through Warren was similar to that of a mouse daring a daylight raid upon a cat's milk-pan. Done most timorously.

Again, however, the grim and deadly intent upon the faces around him determined his answer: none intended a return in any case. Therefore, no price, no matter how high, would prevent their going. Gods! And he was part of this charge!

He urged his mount close to Nil once more. 'What Warren?' he called.

The young warlock pulled his gaze from ahead, appeared puzzled for a time, then grinned. 'Much debate and snarling surrounding that, Captain. Which would afford quickest passage? One was finally agreed upon – the one least likely to invoke the wrath of any guardian – the Abyss itself!' And he laughed, kicking his mount on ahead.

Stunned, Rillish let his horse ease back into line. *Yes, least likely to arouse the wrath of anyone: because there was nothing there!* Would they fall for ever, as some said? Ride off the edge of the world? Or sink into the great ocean that some believed encircled all lands? Which would it be? Well, soon he would find out. Though he didn't imagine he'd have the chance to pass the knowledge on.

Ahead, the starry sky swirled, blurring and smearing in a sickening way. The road broke up in wavering lines like those of heat-mirages, though the night was cool. Rillish chanted prayers to Fanderay, Soliel, the Queen of Dreams, Dessembrae, and Trake: may they find a firm something under the hooves of their mounts and air to breathe. The column's van, led by Nil and Nether together with a troop of other warlocks and witches, disappeared into the void revealed beyond, opening the way. The column pressed onward, unflinching, and Rilllish felt a scream gathering itself in his chest. It clawed its way up to his throat as his place in the ranks neared the void, then burst forth along with other shouts and calls from those alongside him as many drew swords, mounts leaping, '*Hood look away!*'

* * *

From cover lying flat within tall grass at the crest of a hill, the setting sun behind, Hurl, flanked by Sergeant Banath, scanned the battle-field. It looked to her as if the Imperials were doing far better than she'd imagined. The Malazan forces controlled the ground in the east and the west, but the Guard still held the centre. Banath motioned to where the Pilgrim Way descended into the Idryn river valley. 'Will they move on the bridge, you think?'

'I don't think so.'

'What if the Guard breaks through – what's to stop them from heading north?' and Banath raised his chin to where the tall glowing pavilion advertised the presence of the Imperial person herself.

'They might. But I don't think she'll hang around for them.'

'So, what's the objective here?'

Hurl motioned him back down the hillock. 'Annihilation.' They jogged back down to the copse of woods where her troop waited with Rell, Liss and the three brothers. Hurl came to Liss's side. 'You'll keep us hidden?'

The shamaness nodded. 'As well as I can, but I'll confess, the magic unleashed on the far side of those hills is like a return to the old campaigns where the mage cadre ruled the field. And I fear we'll see much worse through the night.'

'We're just here for Ryllandaras.'

'Oh? What of relieving the Empress?'

'Keeping him occupied would be more than enough of a contribution, don't you think?'

Liss's gaze skittered aside and she pursed her lips. 'Too true.'

Hurl came to Rell who had dismounted, out of necessity, for Hurl had never before seen a more awkward rider – other than herself. 'Regret coming?'

The man edged his helmet and gilded visor side to side. 'No, I do not. Though I do regret not having the chance to match swords with the Avowed. I have heard much of them.'

Hurl studied the man for a time, his repaired armour, the twin milky spheres serving as the pommels of the swords at his sides – said by Silk to have been the very weapons carried by Li Heng's ancient Protectress. 'Why did you ever leave your homeland, Rell? All these years it's been obvious to me that you miss it greatly.'

The man clasped his hands at his back, his visor sinking as he peered down. 'I had no choice. I was exiled – no, that is not true. I left of my own choice, for to stay would have been untenable.'

'I don't understand.'

'No.' In Rell's tone Hurl imagined a regretful smile. The man turned half-aside as if he could not bear to speak aloud to her – or to anyone. 'I was young. Very full of myself. I had been promoted to the highest martial body of my people. One of the youngest ever to have been so honoured. I fought many duels – but not as you and your people seem to understand them, to the unnecessary death or sloppy exhaustion. At the level I fought, blood was rarely spilt. All could be decided by the judging body in a mere one or two passes. Speed, technique, execution. Perfection of form and precision of application. Indeed, some matches were lost merely because of what one contestant *failed* to do. An opening overlooked. A technique not pursued to its uttermost realization. For us, in short, fighting had become a form of religious dedication and expression.'

Hurl's mouth had gone dry. *Ye gods! This would explain a lot.* She swallowed to speak, said, her voice rough, 'Well, then, why leave?'

'As I said. I was full of myself. I did the unthinkable – I disputed a ruling. The judges, all my superior in rank of course, re-emphasized their judgment. I, then, dared to question their interpretation. For this presumption I was expelled from the martial order of my society. Forbidden to carry arms. All that was left to me was a life as a crafts-man, farmer or servant. I would remain free, but would never fight again. Well, you can imagine . . . How could I in my hot youth bear to watch my peers – men and women far less skilled than I – walk by exalted in rank while I bowed before them? No. I chose exile instead. Now, however, I would return if I could. I think I would farm. Raising something from seed to fruitful crop would, I think, prove very satisfying.'

Yes, Rell, you have come a long way. But perhaps your only fail-ing was being too headstrong in a society too rigid to accommodate it. 'You could think of Heng that way.'

A tilt of the helm. 'My thanks, Hurl.'

A grating shriek echoed through the twilight from hill to hill and Hurl's back shivered, the hair on her arms rising. She ran to Liss. 'What was that?'

'Another summoned creature met an ugly end over there. Things are heating up. We can expect Ryllandaras soon, though I suspect that even he would think twice before stepping out on to that conflagration. Mage duels, I think, to the misery of all, will settle that engagement.'

Hurl looked to the east where the crests of hills flashed in silhouette lurid red and yellow and where the echoes of sharper bursts staccatoed like falling rocks amid the roar of battle. Above the field swirled an eerie reflected glow such as that of the green and blue banners that sometimes flickered in the northern sky. *Earthquake, firestorm and typhoon all rolled into one. Gods aid the common soldiers in that maelstrom! All they can hope to do is keep their heads down and avoid notice while the Avowed mages flex their muscles to clear the field.*

*   *   *

'What in the name of stinking Poliel was that!' May called out from down the trench.

'I don't know and I don't wanna know!' Nait shouted. 'Just keep firing!' A gaggle of skirmishers ran past, heads down, and Nait called to them, 'Over here! C'mon, take cover!'

They dived into the trench. 'Gettin' hot out there,' one said, an idiotic grin on his smoke-smeared face.

'Just fire!' Nait told him. As far as he could see all order had been lost. The lines were intermingled. No clear front remained. But hanging smoke, real and damned Mockra illusion blocked his vision of portions of the field – he knew when the smoke was Mockra because he couldn't smell it. Crimson Guard Blades stalked the field breaking all resistance where they found it. Since May's lucky toss with that melter took out that demon they'd been getting a lot of unwanted attention. So far the focused fire of Nait's squad had driven off three attempts upon them, blunted and deflected the Guardsmen to seek out softer targets. That, and the Moranth Gold who showed up out of nowhere to help defend their position. And speaking of fire, it appeared to be thinning to his left – Nait rose up out of the trench to squint down the line. Heuk was there, talking with Jawl and the boys at their lobber. What in the name of Hood's all-too-close breath was the damned fool up to? The mage then headed to him. 'Will you get down!' Nait yelled.

'Drink this,' the old drunkard said, shoving his jug at him.

'Go to the Abyss.'

'Drink!' and crouching he pressed it into Nait's hands.

'All right!' Nait took an experimental sniff and pushed it away. 'Gods, no!'

Heuk was unsympathetic. 'You want help? This is it.'

Reluctantly, Nait raised the jug to his mouth, forced himself to take a mouthful of the cloying fluid, swallowed, gagging. He swiped his leather-palmed gloves across his mouth. 'Gods! What is that?'

'Horse blood, mostly.'

'Horse blood? What're you trying to do? Poison us?'

The mage slapped him on the back, chuckling. Since the battle began the fellow seemed to come into his own; where everyone else ran ducking and wincing he strode straight and unconcerned. He motioned Nait up out of the trench. 'Come with me. There's someone who wants to talk with you.'

'Talk with me? What'd you mean?'

'C'mon.' And the man took hold of Nait's arm and lifted him from the trench.

Nait stared, rubbing his wrenched shoulder. 'Take it easy . . .' Heuk pushed him up the hill.

The wind that had been blowing constantly down the hillside now intensified. Something came throbbing overhead, a pressure, and he ducked, but Heuk gestured, muttering, and the pounding retreated. Nearby, the ground shuddered, dirt and ash flying into the air along with a few fleeing irregulars.

'What in the Abyss . . .' Nait gaped.

'Never you mind – just keep the boys firing,' Heuk said. 'Here we are,' and he pushed Nait forward. Suddenly, the air stilled and he saw that someone sat in the grass at the crest of the hillock. A very broad and heavy Dal Hon woman, a fan in one hand waving furiously at her sweaty, glistening, dark face. Sweat also drenched her silk clothes, darkening them and draping them over her wide bosom. Despite being absolutely terrified for his life, Nait was instantly captivated. *Dear Gods, what a figure of a woman!*

'This is Bala,' Heuk said. 'She's the reason you're still alive.'

'Yeah? Well, *I'm* the reason *she's* still alive!'

The mage's sweat-beaded, thick arms shook as she laughed a throaty chuckle that made Nait faint with desire. 'Well said, soldier.

Your fighting spirit remains, I see. Good – you'll have need of it. To be brief, I am exhausted. I have defied, deflected and blunted the Avowed mages' efforts to turn this slope into one long killing ground all this long evening. But now I am done. Finished. I thought I was up to anything – that I was a match even for Tayschrenn, but now I find I must withdraw where before he alone faced down these and more. Heuk here will be taking over for me.'

At Nait's obvious alarm she threw up a hand up for silence. 'If half of what he has shown me is true then you are in good hands. In fact, if any of what I suspect is true I am frankly glad to be withdrawing. So, soldier. Goodbye and good luck. I see from your stupefied gaze that you are of course entranced by our meeting. I would be pleased to remain to torture you with my unattainability but that will have to wait until we meet again.' She snapped her fan closed with a loud snick like that of a sword sheathing and she disappeared. Nait stared blinking at the empty flattened seat of grass. *Just my luck. Meet the woman of my dreams the day I'm gonna die.* He knelt to press a hand down on the earth where she'd sat. It was warm to his touch. *Lady, let me meet that one again!*

Heuk cleared his throat. 'So you could see her.'

Nait turned on him. 'Yeah, I could see her!'

'Good. Look around. What more do you see?'

Wanting to tell the old man to stuff it, Nait reluctantly glanced away to scan the field. Lights moved through the dark of gathering twilight – bright glowing figures among those milling, running and fighting. 'I see people all lit up.'

'Good. You have a touch of the talent now. The blood has given you this, as it has everyone down in the trenches. You can see anyone with raised active Warren magics. Now get down there and use that arbalest to blow them to Hood.'

Nait did not have to be told the advantages of this. He grasped hold of his shoulderbag and jogged down the slope. 'Kibb! Load the lobber!'

* * *

Laseen had been very strict in her last orders: do not enter the Imperial Pavilion. No matter what. And though Possum was dearly tempted to edge aside the thick layered cloths of its walls to peek within, he restrained himself. *No sense offering myself as a target to whatever awaited hidden inside.* Planted torches lit its outside perimeter, Malazan regulars stood guard at intervals. No messengers or attendants came or went. Possum watched, as before, hidden half in veils of Mockra and slanting shadows of Meanas. Night gathered, thickening. He would wait. Eventually someone worth his attentions would make a mistake; then he would pounce. In the meantime he entertained himself imagining tableaus of what was occurring within. Had Havva Gulen woven multiple layers of wards and Warren-sprung traps for any attackers? Gods knew she didn't seem useful for anything else; he hadn't seen her dirty, lank hair or stained robes since they'd arrived. Perhaps the Veils had already taken her out. How would they ever know? In any case, he could wait. The Hand-commanders all had their orders – the sum total of which amounted to little more than hunt down any isolated Avowed and take them out. What more could they do? Laseen had ordered no Claw bodyguards remain with her. Very well. Who was he to disagree? Technically, he wasn't really *with* her, was he? He was watching from a safe distance. And should anything untoward happen . . . well, someone would be needed to step in to take charge . . .

Movement of the thick overlapping cloths brought Possum to the balls of his feet. A shriek tore from within, inhuman, gurgling, bubbling down into the mewling of incandescent agony. Possum ran for the pavilion. Guards backed away, swords out, as something dragged itself out from under the staked edgings of the cloths. A demon, its limbs and taloned hands twisted, almost melted. Smoking patches ate at its shaggy pelt. It trailed smears of ichor and dustings of red earth behind as it writhed free of the pavilion. Possum knelt, touching the strange rust-red dust. He rubbed it between his gloved thumb and forefinger. Smooth, like chalk.

Sighing, the tortured thing expired. Its flesh melted into a bubbling, hissing mess before everyone's eyes. Possum backed away. Queen preserve them! What could do such a thing to a summoned creature – an inhabitant of Gods knew what Warren or Realm? Then the thought struck him: summoned! A creature of magic! As if stung Possum wrenched off his glove, turned it inside out and flicked it away like a viper. *Gods! He'd almost . . . too horrible even to consider!* He backed away further – at least none of the guards appeared to have perceived him – his Warren magics remained active. He found another vantage point, his back covered by the spear wall of an impromptu horse corral.

Pure Laseen. Vicious and efficient. A floor dusted in Otataral and she in the centre. The dust negates the magics of any entering, levelling the field. As to the fight that followed, well, she had been mistress of the Claw after all. And the pavilion's thick cloth walls disguised the fates of all who entered from those who waited without. How many have fallen within? Five? Ten? And by dawn how many? How many would Cowl send before entering himself? And when he did . . . the vaunted Avowed High Mage would find himself crippled – as would that mystery female mage who'd got the drop on him before. Yet Cowl duelled Dancer in his time. *It was a pairing I'd almost step within to watch.*

Almost.

It appeared that for the meantime Laseen had things well in hand. Perhaps there was time for a tour of the field fishing for targets of opportunity. Yes, perhaps so. And he ought to gather a feel for the engagement – in case the situation was such that discreet withdrawal was called for. Warren raised, half within natural shadow and half within Meanas, Possum jogged unchallenged on to the field.

What he found appalled him. Never had he witnessed such indiscriminate slaughter. Hanging curtains of Mockra drifted about, perhaps bringing to those it covered a crushing demoralization, or certitude of defeat. Thyr-induced walls of flames stalked the already burnt embers of the ravaged grassland. Skirmishers huddled in defensive knots firing on all who approached. Malazan regulars were digging in, forming shieldwalls against attack from roving bands of Crimson Guardsmen. Smoke wreathed all amid the dark. As far as he could make out things had descended into little more than chaos, murder and mayhem in which anything that moved was a target.

An enormous eruption of munitions battered his ears and buffeted him. He ran for the nearest vantage. The explosions rippled on in an incessant crashing that seemed to grow and grow in waves, climbing into a continuous roar. He reached the top of a modest hill to see down the slope toward the cliff to the Idryn valley. There, the Moranth Gold phalanx had been met by a Crimson Guard force ludicrously small by comparison. But it was not the mundane attack that captivated and horrified: the phalanx was under assault by ritual battle magics. A tornado of Serc squatted over the unit plucking up Moranth into its gyring maw. There they twisted, doll-like, limbs flailing, some being swept down to bowl over entire ranks. There they collided and, sometimes, erupted, disappearing in clouds of burst flesh and fragmented armour. *Hood refuse this!* This was not war. This was slaughter. And the thought clenched his chest, almost stopping his heart: they have no mages!

They have no mages. Stop this! Someone must put an end to this!

'It's begun,' a coarse, gravelly voice announced beside him. Possum leapt, spinning: an old bearded man in dirty robes hugging a chipped brown earthenware jug.

'*Who are you?*'

'Heuk. Cadre Mage. Sixth squad, Second Company, Fourth Division, Fourth Army.'

'What's begun?'

'Our duel.'

Possum eyed the man up and down as if he were mad. '*Your* duel? There are at least twelve Avowed mages out there.'

'Less than that. The boys got maybe three. In any case,' and his eyes looked directly into Possum's, 'that's not your concern, is it?'

Possum could not help but back up a step: that smell, blood? The man's eyes – midnight black upon black? And at his mouth – blood? 'Who *are* you?' he breathed.

The fellow gestured to the south. 'Look. They've broken.'

Indeed. The Gold phalanx was disintegrating under the pressure of the widening ravenous cyclone. Knots of soldiers fled in all directions.

The man's smile twisted, revealing black, crooked teeth. 'We're next.' His glance returned to Possum. 'Who am I? Your recruiters named me a mage, but I am no mage. And now,' he hiked up his jug, 'you'd best fly away, little death crow. Keep to your games in the shallows of shadow. As for myself – I plumb the infinite depths of Night Eternal!'

Possum continued backing away. 'No – that Warren is beyond us.'

'Fool! As I said, I am no mage. I am a mere worshipper of Night. And as the old saying goes, my blood is up. Now flee, because I am about to call upon my God for he has returned and the time is long overdue for a demonstration of his gathering presence upon this world.'

While Possum watched, revolted, the man upended the jug over his head. Thick fluid – clotted blood, he imagined – ran down over the man's hair, face and shoulders. Possum turned away, his gorge rising. Madness! Utter insanity. And the night had barely begun! At the base of the shallow rise he stopped short as cocked crossbows in the hands of tens of soldiers kneeling and lying in the grass jerked to train themselves upon him. He froze.

'Lower your Warren,' someone shouted. 'Or die.'

Possum complied. *They see him. How could they see him?*

'Ach!' someone snorted. 'It's only a fucking Claw.' The crossbows all swung away.

Feeling rather piqued, Possum sought out the owner of that voice. He found the man – a sergeant – in a trench arguing with a Moranth Gold who towered above. 'I don't give a rat's ass,' the sergeant was saying. 'Your orders are to stay, so you stay!'

'Our brothers need us,' the Moranth rumbled. 'They are sorely pressed.'

'They've broken,' Possum said. Both looked over, annoyed, it seemed to him, by his interruption. The sergeant made a tossing away gesture. 'There you go.'

'You could have them rally to this position,' Possum suggested.

The Moranth swung his helm down to peer to the sergeant who glared at Possum then waved the Moranth away. 'Fine!' And he muttered under his breath, 'Might as well paint fucking bull's-eyes on our heads.'

'Too late for that, Sergeant . . . ?'

'Nai—' The man took a deep breath. 'Jumpy. Sergeant Jumpy.'

Ah! Of course, the man crazy enough to go out into the night to try to stalk Ryllandaras. Who else would it be? 'You already have the Guard's attention. I can guarantee you that. You have a lunatic mage, or priest, above your heads with delusions of omnipotence. And with the Moranth broken, yours and the centre are the last remaining Imperial strong-points in the field.'

The man was scanning the dark field before the trench where mixed Moranth and Malazan regulars held lines defending coalesced skirmishers against probing Guard infantry. 'Then I guess you best run away,' he said, offhanded.

Possum's mouth clamped shut; his hands twitched to fill themselves. 'Do not presume to be beyond the reach of the Empress,' he ground out.

'Don't you presume yourself safe.' And he pointed down the trench. Possum glanced aside: four saboteurs held crossbows trained upon him, each set with a sharper. 'We're in the trench and you ain't,' the sergeant observed laconically.

Possum straightened, carefully adjusted his dark-blue tunic. 'Continue defending this position, Sergeant,' and he stepped over the trench, raising his Warren to pass through the lines of assembling Imperials. The sergeant called after him, 'No kidding! Like I was going to go for a blasted swim or something.'

Impertinent shit. Possum calmed himself with the certainty that – even with the deluded priest's claims – they would all be dead by the dawn. He just hoped they would savage the Guard brutally enough for the Claws to then at their leisure pick off the remaining exhausted and drained Avowed.

* * *

Her Blades found the west flank in a shambles. Shimmer sent her lieutenants ahead to organize what scattered forces remained. All that stopped a solid Imperial advance was the lack of support from the rest of the field – the Guard centre still held and the appalling display of battle magics on the east was a pause for every ordinary soldier.

Shimmer advanced with Greymane, Shell and Smoky, gathering to her a growing following of Avowed, most of which she sent ahead to help firm resistance. The closer they got to the front, or scattered sections of the front, the thicker became the punishing flights of crossbow bolts. Every Avowed, and many regular Guardsmen and women, had picked up a Malazan heavy infantryman's solid rectangular shield, which they hunched behind like moveable walls. Shimmer had to occasionally sweep away the bolts hammered into hers in order to keep it usable.

An Avowed, Daneth, waved her over to a pile of fallen Guardsmen. 'Look at this.' On her knees, she raised a corpse to rest its head on her lap. Despite the man's mangled features Shimmer recognized him as an Avowed, Longlegs. The body displayed a number of wounds, as one would expect, but what was surprising was that fatal head wound: it was singular. Someone, or something, had struck him a blow on the face shattering his nose and jaw, driving the fragmented bones back into his brain, killing him instantly. 'A club or mace?' Shimmer opined.

'The heel of an open hand,' Daneth said, her flat tone matching her set grim face.

'*What?* Who could possibly . . .'

'Urko!' Smoky gasped as if the name itself were a curse. 'He's here.'

Urko – the man who needs no weapons. No wonder the west was in such disarray; no unit could hold against him. She glanced around, caught the gaze of nearby Avowed. 'Halfdan, Bower, Lucky! Find him and kill him.'

They three inclined their heads in concurrence, jogged off.

'They won't find him,' Smoky said aside.

'No? Why not?'

'He's probably standing in line like any other heavy infantryman. He's already hiding from the Veils. He could be any of them.'

'Lucky is no fool. He'll wait and watch.'

A shrug. 'I hope so.' He motioned to Shell. 'In any case, Shell and I have done a few head-counts and we think we have some thirty of our brothers and sisters.'

'And Skinner?'

'Slightly more.'

'I see. So, we remain split in our sympathies.' Again, doubt stabbed at her, squeezing her breath and churning her stomach almost to the point of retching. *What if she'd been dreaming? Hearing voices? It was Shadow after all.* She turned on Greymane, snapping angrily, 'What of you? Are you a match for a man who breaks armour with his bare hands?'

Nearby eruptions from a wave of tossed munitions shot dust and dirt over everyone. Greymane hefted his scavenged shield, shook dirt from his shoulders. 'I've never met him,' he shouted. 'But from what I've heard – no.'

'No?' She was incredulous. 'Just like that – you admit you could not defeat him. Is this a refusal to fight?' All remaining nearby Avowed turned to watch warily.

'I did not say that, Shimmer,' Greymane said calmly, his hands kept loose at his sides. 'I merely said there would be no match between us.'

'So, all you have heard of him leads you to fear him that much.'

'No, Shimmer. All that I have heard leads me to admire him that much. But I will say this. I vow that I would give my life in defence of you.'

Shimmer remained motionless for a number of heartbeats, her dark gaze slitted on Greymane's own pale unguarded eyes. She let her shield fall then hiked it up again as a crossbow bolt sang past, biting at the crimson silk tail that hung from her helmet's wrapping. She let go a snarled exhalation through clenched teeth. 'Damn you, Greymane. Must you always walk the knife's edge?'

'I must be true to myself.'

And look at what it has brought you, renegade! But she left the retort unsaid. The man seemed all too desolately aware of it. She gripped her sheathed Napan whipsword. 'Then I'll have to take you up on your offer and head to the front ranks until we find our friend . . .'

He rubbed his broad, flattened nose, wincing. 'I was worried you'd propose that.'

'Father Light preserve us!' Smoky breathed, suddenly fixed upon the east. Shell too stared, speechless. Her hands rose as if to fend off what she was seeing. Shimmer squinted but could only make out a darker patch against the general night. 'What is it?'

Eyes still on the far edge of the field, Smoky murmured, almost inaudibly, 'The impossible.'

'Explain yourself, mage,' Shimmer snapped.

Blinking, the man turned back to her, ran his soot-blackened hands up through his tangle of wild hair. 'Someone has unveiled Kurald Galain here on the battlefield. And whoever that mage is, he or she ain't one of ours.'

'Kurald Galain?'

'The Tiste Andii Warren of Elder Darkness,' Shell explained. 'Home of their Goddess, Mother Dark.'

Shimmer eyed the coalescing, gently turning smear of darkness low over the field. 'But there are no Tiste Andii here . . .'

'Exactly. The impossible.'

Buffets of wind announced the arrival of mages through Warren: Opal, Lor-sinn and Toby. The gathered Avowed mages all cast taut glances to Smoky who agreed with a tart downturn of his mouth to whatever had been communicated. He faced Shimmer. 'The escalation in magery has begun. Skinner's invoked ritual magics, the Imperials have responded. We, all five of us, together with the recruited mages, Twisty, Palla and whoever else – we'll probably all be needed here.'

'*All* of you?'

Smoky dragged a hand across his face. 'Whoever raised that, Shimmer, is beyond me.'

Shimmer forced herself to remain rigid. Show nothing! They are all looking to you! *Could no battle go as planned? We expected sword and shield to settle this engagement. Now Smoky claims things have spiralled to a clash such as the sorcerous conflagrations of old. Well, so be it. Short of the appearance of Tayschrenn she was confident of the Guard's mage cadre. At least that thing, whatever it was, was now Skinner's concern as it stood directly between him and the Imperial pavilion. K'azz, if you really are close – we need you.* 'Very well.' She nodded to the sergeant with her, Trench, who raised a hand signing 'advance'.

'For'ard!'

Greymane followed Shimmer, obviously meaning to guard her back, while the assembled mages flanked her. The Avowed of her command spread out through the phalanx of second and third investiture men and women, rallying all the disparate knots into one swelling, widening wedge of shielded soldiers.

* * *

'Great Goddess protect us,' Liss murmured, her head turning abruptly to the east. The three brothers, Hurl noted, had all turned as well.

'What is it?' she asked.

'Amazing . . . Like nothing I have ever seen, nor expected to see.'

'What, dammit!'

'Elder Darkness, Night Eternal, unveiled there on the battlefield.' She pulled her gaze from the silhouetted hills to look down to Hurl who stood next to her mount. 'Things, Hurl, are rapidly sliding out of control out on that field. Forces are being summoned that would give even Ryllandaras pause. He is, after all, just one creature.' She pointed. 'But out there, magery such as that which consumed armies is being primed for wielding.'

'So?'

'So – we must find him before we ourselves are consumed.'

'Let us . . .' said one brother.

'Leave him . . .'

'To die,' finished the last.

Liss turned on them. 'He's too cunning. He will flee. I intend to make sure of it!'

'I, as well,' Rell added.

The three shrugged, their indifference raising the hairs of Hurl's neck. They moved not one after the other, or raggedly, but identically, at exactly the same moment in exactly the same way despite the sagging paralysis of shoulders, lips and arms. It was as if they were one. And there had always been something eerie about them. Something unsettling. Everyone felt it. For Hurl it was a prickling that struck right at the very centre of her being but which she couldn't exactly pin down. Intuitive. Something was very wrong about them.

Yet what could she do? They'd done nothing suspicious. Nothing to call them on. Quite the opposite, in fact. They'd been vital to the city's defence. And so she was stuck with them. Like horses, she reflected, sourly. They made themselves useful so you couldn't just kill them all. But she knew their true side – she was on to them. 'So?' She sighed. 'What do you suggest?'

'We should move. He's close. In the north. The brothers and I should be able to find him.'

Find him? Great Lady, they're actually going hunting for him! Well, it was what they came for. Personally, she'd hoped to wait till he got himself tarred by the Imperials then they could just step in and finish him off. But there was still hope.

She went to her mount, gathered the reins. The red mare turned its head, watching her. *Try anything and I'll kill you – you know it too.* The mare shook her auburn mane. Hurl patted the bulging saddlebags strapped tight and padded in sheepskins. *Yeah, she meant to make sure of it too.*

* * *

A squad healer, name unknown to Ullen, gave his left arm a squeeze to let him know he was done, then moved on the next wounded man. Standing, Ullen spared a glance from then field to see that the man had fashioned a sling to tie the dead meat that was his right arm to his chest. One of Cowl's Veils, a tall slim woman with long white hair, had appeared out of nowhere, slaying guards and staffers, making for him until a saboteur sergeant briefing him, Urfa, had thrown something that burst a spray of razor fragments, some of which had lacerated his arm, slicing tendons and nerves. It left the Veil staggered, slashed in zig-zags of blood, then, and only then did a full Hand appear to jump her. The resulting mêlée had tumbled away into the night in a frenzy of leaping bodies, thrown blades and tossed Warren magics.

Ullen saw in that same all-encompassing glance that his command staff of relatively green lieutenants and messengers had been profoundly shaken. *First time's always the worst.* He cleared his throat, drawing their attention from the night. 'Now we know what a visit from Dancer must have been like, hey?' and he offered a self-mocking, almost sad smile. The gathered men and women eyed one another; some wiped at their shining sweaty faces. Then: appreciative chuckles and even blown breaths.

A chorus of 'Yes, sir.'

'Reports, people! What's going on?'

The Imperial lieutenant brushed at a trail of blood from a slashed cheek. 'Reports are we're losing ground in the west. Urko is pulling his people to the centre.'

'I have unconfirmed accounts that the Sword is wounded, possibly fallen,' added the Dal Hon lieutenant, Gellan.

'Moranth and other elements remaining in the east are rallying to the redoubt,' said another. 'I have also had intelligence from the

Claw that Skinner is leading a phalanx north, making for that very strongpoint.'

Gods, what a clash that will be. It could determine the victor. 'And that darkness gathered there . . . ?'

'We have confirmation that it's one of our own cadre mages, apparently,' came the grudging admission.

Don't count the mongrels out, you son of an aristocratic house. Even though they don't have vaunted titles like High Mage many actually know their trade. 'Very good. Have all broken elements assemble on the redoubt. Order the skirmishers to concentrate fire on that phalanx – grind them down!'

'Aye.'

'What of the Empress?' a staffer asked. 'If the Veils have—'

'Never mind the Empress,' Ullen replied, angered. 'She is fighting her battles as we must fight ours.' *And if you think we've been cursed by Veils – you don't want to be anywhere near her.*

'The Empress sends her compliments,' said a new voice and Ullen turned, surprised – and pleased – to see the scarred figure of Captain Moss. He extended his left hand and they shook, awkwardly. 'I have been seconded to your staff.'

'You are most welcome.'

'She bade me inform you that you have her fullest confidence. She commends your actions as field-commander.'

Ullen's brows rose. *Just what the Imperials on his staff needed to hear. Thank you, Moss.* He cleared his throat into his left fist again. 'Very good, Captain.' He turned to his people. 'What of the Kanese?'

'They have attacked but Avowed still hold the bridge,' said one.

'How many?'

'Reports are,' and the fellow swallowed, his voice failing, '. . . five.'

'*Five?* Five Avowed against twenty thousand?'

'Ah, yes, sir.'

Hood – are you pleased? What a ferocious confrontation! He didn't envy the Kanese the effort it would take to lever the Avowed from that narrow pass. *And how many did they face – thirty? Forty? No, don't go there! Avoid the scenarios of despair. At least these are in the open. These can be cut down from afar.* 'The Kanese will break through soon enough,' he said. 'We just have to hold on.'

At least a few of his staff mustered the effort to murmur, 'Yes, sir.'

His haunting the field, scanning in turn through Meanas then Mockra, paid off when Possum sensed his quarry to the north-west. Moving quickly through Shadow he arrived on the darkened slope to see Coil bent over still forms lying twisted in the grass – a full Claw Hand. *Damn the woman! They need all their strength and here she is eliminating rivals! That is more than enough justification* ... Drawing his blades he launched himself forward through Shadow. Just as he arrived her own senses moved her to twist, but not quite quickly enough to avoid the thrusting iron as it entered through her ribs in the back and front, puncturing lung and pricking her heart. He wriggled the knives, lacerating the organs to make sure of it.

Coil stared back at him, stunned, horrified, eyes full of the knowledge of her own coming death. 'You fool . . .' she breathed. He thought nothing of such death-babblings. Strange things are said as life flees. Curses, claims to innocence, innermost longings. 'These . . . Mallick's . . . I was all that stood between them . . . and *her*.'

Possum withdrew the blades, straightening. *What?*

Life dimmed in the woman's dark eyes and she fell. She smiled, her teeth red with blood. 'Chance,' she gasped, chuckling ruefully. '*Chance* . . .' Her shape writhed, blurring, changing. Possum recognized artistry of high Mockra – and that far greater than his – until the body resolved itself clearly once more for him to see lying at his feet the fat messy form of High Mage Havva Gulen.

Soliel forgive him! What had he done? Why hadn't she told him? Told anyone? Because – fool! – she was running her own game just as he. Now what? First, go! Let the fog of war obscure all. He raised his Warren and stepped into Shadow—

To be hammered down by a blunt blow to his side.

He lay gasping amid dirt and clumps of sharp cactus-like grasses that gouged at his exposed skin. A tall thin shape loomed over him. Blinking, he made out a dead ravaged face of desiccated skin, peeled-back lips, yellowed teeth and empty sockets above tattered torn armour and hanging rags. *An Imass? Here?*

The Imass reached down, grasped a handful of his shirt and pulled him upright. 'Your trespassings annoy me,' the thing hissed. 'Shadow is not to be used so lightly.' The being shook him like a child. 'Now go, and do not return.' And it thrust him away.

Possum staggered, righted himself. He straightened his clothes. 'And who are you?'

The Imass – was it, though? – clasped a fist of bone and sinew to the sword sheathed at its back. 'Go! Keep your disputes out of Shadow!'

'Yes! Yes.' And Possum waved, removing himself from the Warren. The night slope reasserted itself around him. The cacophony of battle returned. Who – *what* – in the Enchantress's Name had that been? Renegade Imass? Ascendant of some kind? Revenant? *Never mind. Irrelevant. Focus!* He attempted to centre himself, calm his breath. *Gods, what had he done! Slain the High Mage. A woman who claimed to be helping! Drop it, man. Think of your own back. According to Havva, Mallick held the Claw while he was the puppet! What options did he have? Laseen! She was all that was left to him. He had to reach her.*

Possum summoned his Mockra Warren. Shortly afterwards just another soldier of uncertain allegiance scrabbled hunched across the slopes. He was in the west and found the field now commanded by the Guard. The Avowed had entered the fray, sweeping all before them. Skirmishers and Imperial heavies still ran in clumps here and there like field mice, but the only solid formations were Guard squares, and these far separated as a precaution against mage assault. In the east, the cadre mage's deep unmitigated darkness still hung like a flat cloud over his hillock, apparantly doing nothing – a slowly turning vortex of night – while Malazan forces coalesced around the mage-protected strongpoint. To the south-east the tall silver dragon banner of the Guard was advancing before a broadening phalanx.

Just then from the north a brilliant yellow-orange light illuminated the darkness – the Imperial pavilion bursting aflame. It pushed back the night for a half-league all around. The flames climbed like those of an immense bonfire, a celebration of light and vitality, if short-lived. Possum stared, his arms falling to his sides. Oh, Cowl! Master-stroke! So much for such careful preparations and precautions! I bow before your unbending ruthlessness.

What now for poor Possum? Imperial forces routed, the pavilion aflame, and he himself assassin of the Imperial High Mage. What could possibly be left? Was not all lost? A giddy, almost fey mood took him and he laughed aloud. He felt like dancing amid the dead. *His anxious oh-so-important worries of rivals amid the order? Utterly irrelevant! A life-time of scheming, positioning, manipulating? A life wasted! His own ambitions, hopes, dreams? Completely thwarted!*

He walked down on to the field between the fallen, laughing

593

aloud. *Come Cowl! Come Lacy, Tarkhan or Isha! Let us put an end to the comic tragedy!*

* * *

Nait knelt in the trampled grass just up from the trench together with a mixed collection of sergeants and officers from three different brigades. Captains Tinsmith and Jay K'epp, or Captain Kepp as everyone called him, and a battered Moranth Gold who gave the name Blossom, were the highest ranking officers present; Commander Braven Tooth was reportedly still active but elected to remain in the field to help rally splintered elements; the Sword was reportedly wounded somewhere amid the carnage of the centre strongpoint where Urko, it was rumoured, was organizing resistance.

Captain Tinsmith lay having his slashed leg re-bandaged while Kepp sat silently by – he could only sit silently as the fist of an Avowed had shattered his jaws.

Of the lesser officers and sergeants present, Nait shared nods with Least, Lim and others, and watched while these conferred in whispers and grunts. Everyone was whispering because they squatted on the border of the Darkness. All was quiet here; even the battle's roar just a few paces away was a feeble distant murmur. And it was cold; Nait's damp sweat-soaked shirt and padding chilled him. He knew of course what was coming before they said a thing. So he shared an all-suffering roll of the eyes with Least when Tinsmith called out, 'Sergeant Jumpy, a word.'

He jogged up and knelt on his haunches. 'Aye.'

'We want you to go up and talk to him.'

'I ain't goin' up there to talk to him. You go.'

A savage glare from the old sergeant, now captain. 'In case you hadn't noticed – I can't walk.'

'Then Kepp, here.'

Through clenched teeth: 'He . . . can't . . . talk.'

'Then Blossom, here.'

'He doesn't speak Talian!'

Fucking troop of carnival clowns, we are. Fucking hopeless. 'Fine!'

Tinsmith stroked one side of his long silver moustache, smiled evilly. 'He's your squad mage.'

'Yeah, yeah.' He straightened, grunting and wincing – *so tired, and things ain't even come to a head yet* – and started up the slope. The grass crackled brittle with hoarfrost under his old falling-apart sandals. The dark was extraordinary, unrelieved, yet he could still see and he thought of Heuk's swill – the iron tang of which still caked his tongue. It was as if he were wrapped in layers of the thickest, darkest, finest cloth imaginable. Sable, maybe, he decided, though he'd never seen or touched it. The chill bit at him; lacings of frost appeared on the iron backings of his gauntlets.

'Heuk!' The dark seemed to swallow his voice. A silence answered; but it was not a true silence. Something filled it. He strained to listen: the faintest rumbling and rattle of chain? Deep reverberations such as wheels groaning somewhere in the dark? 'Heuk?'

'Here.'

Nait started; the fellow was practically kneeling right before him. 'Ah, you all right?'

'Yes. Why?'

'Why're you kneeling there?'

'I was giving thanks, of course.'

'Ah.'

The mage pushed himself to his feet, weaving slightly. He was a sight. Blood dried black, or what appeared black in this strange place, covered his face and shoulders, and had run in streaks down his robes. Oddly, he seemed taller and straighter than before. 'What is it?' he asked, as if there was nothing strange in any of this.

'Ah, well. The boys down below want you to know we have Avowed headed our way. An' I guess, they're worried. C'n you handle them?'

'I will give it everything I possess,' the man said, sounding more lucid than Nait could ever recall. But it was unnerving as well: he was so calm, his gaze so steady and self-possessed. And that eerie all-black pupil, iris and orb.

'Ah! Great! Everyone'll be happy to hear that. We'll keep them off your back then.'

'I know you will, Nait. Good luck to you. I will do what I can to protect all of you. If I am overcome, there will be no mistaking it.'

'Right.' Nait almost saluted. Strange how an aura of unassuming command seemed to have suddenly enveloped the old bird. After a sort of half-bow, Nait started down the slope. He had no idea of where the trench was, of course, as the dark was so unremitting – yet he could see to walk in it. He decided it must've been that sip from the jug.

It all thrust itself at him in one pace as it had before: the yells, clash of weaponry, rattle of shields. Hands pulled him down and he crouched, blinking. Far down the modest slope, curving arcs of layered defences of heavy infantry behind shields protected a screen of skirmishers who took turns stepping up to fire then withdrawing. Behind these, an inner defence of Moranth Gold and more Malazan heavies, and behind these the trench where a dense thicket of cross-bowmen and women, skirmishers and saboteurs, rained a punishing hail of bolts down on the ranks of Guardsmen pressing the defences.

Yet so few. So few left on both sides. Where was everyone? Could the fallen number so many? Thousands remained in the centre, though, of course, and in the west. Thankfully, the Guard elements here had been reduced to so few that all they could do was harass and pin down – yet why do more? Why bloody themselves further cracking this hard nut when all they had to do was wait for their Avowed to arrive and break us open for them?

Yells went up around the curve of the defensive line as two figures were spotted charging the trench. Nait jumped up, running, 'Hold fire! Hold fire!' The two shouldered aside closing regulars, straight-armed Moranth Gold from their path, and tumbled into the trench. Nait arrived as they straightened, sharing mad grins. 'You damn fools!' he snarled. 'You could've gotten yourselves killed.'

The shorter of the two, Master Sergeant Temp, wearing an ox's load of layered mail and banded iron armour, flinched back his grey-stubbled chin behind the cheek-guards of his helmet. 'Why, it's our old friend Sergeant Jumpy himself. Sounds like he's gone all responsible on us, Ferrule. Command does that, I hear.'

The two climbed up out of the trench. 'I told you, it ain't Ferrule no more,' the other, the burly Seti, complained. 'It's . . .' and his thick brows clenched in concentration, '. . . Bear.' His face lit up, all pleased. 'Yeah, Bear.'

'*Bear?* That's just plain stupid. Don't you have any imagination? How about . . . Dainty?'

The Seti struck Temp a blow on his chest that would've broken Nait's ribs. 'No! That don't take any imagination – that's just saying the opposite. Like Rock.'

'Oh, yeah, Rock. I forgot about that guy. Lady, could he run!'

'Hey! *Hey!*'

The two glared at Nait. 'What?'

'What in the Abyss are you two doing here?'

Temp shrugged, winking. 'We heard this was the place to be.'

Oh great! They were gonna get hammered.

Almost as if reading Nait's thoughts, silence gathered over the lines. The Guardsmen had pulled back all around the length of the curving front. Figures pushed forward to the front of the makeshift Guard shieldwall: both glowing like miniature suns to Nait's blood-enhanced vision. *Here we go!* Damned Avowed mages come to answer the challenge. Through the blazing auras surrounding them he could just make them out: a man leaning on a staff, twisted-looking like he'd been wounded bad, or had survived childhood rickets. The other was a Dal Hon woman in thick dark robes gathered at one shoulder, her hair bunched and wild.

The men and women around Nait shouted, pointing off to the side. He squinted into the night lit by fitful fires over the field cluttered with broken equipment and piled bodies. A long column of soldiers was marching by and at their fore a tall banner, dark with the bright silver dragon rampant. Skinner circling around to head north. Why? Was he that confident of his mages?

Temp struck Ferrule's, or Bear's, shoulder, motioning to the distant banner. 'There's our boy.'

'What? Circlin' around?' The Seti was affronted. 'Fener take it! After all the trouble we went to.'

'C'mon,' the master sergeant called, and jumped the trench. 'He's gettin' away.'

'*Wait!*' Nait called but they were gone, jogging hunched down the hillside like two boulders launched against the Guardsmen line. They crashed into it and kept going, men falling backwards before them, weapons flying, to disappear into the night. '*Shit!*'

It had got perceptibly colder, as if the darkness were gathering itself for what was to come. The two mages in Nait's sight raised their arms. Crossbow bolts flew at them like a hailstorm but none came near. From the Dal Hon woman's position pressure mounted against Nait like a wind that was no wind. Waves of it advanced up the hill before the woman, each stronger than the last. First they pressed the broken grass stalks flat. The next waves gouged the stalks and dense root matrix from the ground. The next then began pushing a ridge of loosened dirt up the hill like a chisel. Just in time the trench was abandoned by scrambling men and women as it collapsed, pushed back and filled by the shifting earth. Some soldiers fell, hands clutching at their ears, helmets torn off. Nait fell to his knees. Hunched, he glimpsed much worse appearing before the other Avowed mage. In a slow advance up the slope soldiers fell as if scythed, shrieking, gagging. They writhed in wordless agony, limbs twisting up like drying roots. The sight brought Nait's gorge to his throat. He fell to his hands and knees and vomited.

And just two on this side! Two of how many all around the refuge?

Four? Five? Had all the soldiers assembled here just to pile the hill in dead? Something tickled his hand – a black snake. He flinched away, his hand passing through the snake. *What?*

It was no snake; its length ran all the way up the hill and it was weaving down through the grass. Others followed, slithering down around him, making for the Dal Hon mage. Nait pushed himself to his feet, wiped his mouth. 'Saboteurs!' he bellowed louder than he had ever before. '*Ready munitions!*'

Weak calls answered him up and down the line. He readied one of his few remaining sharpers. The Dal Hon mage slammed her hands together before her, fist to palm, and a bell-like reverberation sounded, tearing Nait's hearing from him. The ground moved beneath his feet like the sea. Malazan and Gold heavies buckled as waves seemed to pass through them shattering armour, bursting chests. Lines of soldiery heaved backwards as if rammed. Nait threw himself down into the loose soil of the collapsed trench. It felt as if a sledgehammer struck every inch of his body: his feet, his shins, his knees, thighs, hips, stomach, chest and head. Something punched him down into the yielding earth. Not only did he have his breath hammered from him, he lost the ability to inhale. Dazed, punch-drunk, he flailed in a blind panic, dug himself up to stand, tottering. *Fucking bitch! Where was she! He'll ram this beauty up her – there she was! The glowing bitch!*

Something warm was soaking his neck and shirt front. He pressed a gauntleted hand to his neck and it slipped up his slick chin and over his mouth and nose to come away clotted with blood and dirt. He eyed the bloodied leather in horror, then fixed his eyes on the mage.

'Throw!' he roared, his eyes tearing, blood flowing from his nose and mouth, dripping from his chin. 'Throw, throw, throw!' He heaved the sharper, the effort unbalancing him and he fell to lie groaning at the pain.

The peppering burst of munitions brought a smile to his face. Got the bitch! *Must've!* It seemed to him that a shriek followed the eruptions, but not one of pain, a cry of soul-rending surprise and utter terror.

After a time soldiers lifted him up; he recognized Jawl, Kibb and Brill. 'What happened?' he croaked and spat out a mouthful of blood and catarrh.

'Drove 'em off,' said Jawl.

'Blew 'em up?'

'Naw. Was the dark. Looked like it actually tried to eat them. They

598

jumped like Hood himself had snuck up and goosed them with his bony finger. They ran.'

Maybe not his bony finger, Jawl. 'Get me up.'

Brill and Kibb raised him to his feet. 'What happened to you, Sarge?' Kibb said. 'You look like someone beat you all over with boards.'

'Tell May to load the lobber – toss all we got at the Guard column, break 'em.'

'Lobber got broke, Sarge,' Brill said sadly.

Oh, for the sake of Fener! 'Then get them firing – fire! Now!' He pushed both away.

'OK, sheesh!' said Kibb. He asked Brill as they went: 'Is he always like this after a fight?'

Nait staggered up the hill. The dark and cold was the same. The smeared blood, sweat and grime began to solidify on his armour. 'Heuk!' Silence. He pulled a small skin of water from his belt, found it had burst, threw it aside. 'Heuk!' After just two paces more he suddenly burst in upon two figures near the flat crest, one lying curled as if dead or asleep, the other standing over him. It was the standing figure that captured Nait's attention. He'd never seen a Tiste Andii, but had heard them described often enough. This one resembled such: tall, black as night, almond eyes, long straight shimmering black hair. The calm, almost contemplative expression that Nait had seen upon Heuk rested now in this man's features. He wore a coat of the finest mail that descended all the way to his ankles, shimmering like night itself. And it seemed to Nait that the figure was not entirely there; he could see through it. Something hung at its side. Nait almost looked there but pulled his gaze away in time: a void hung there yammering terror at him. It seemed to suck in the night. The figure inclined his head to him.

'Keep them here, soldier,' he said. 'Keep them close. Worse is to come. Much worse.'

Worse! What could possibly— But the figure walked off, hands clasped at his back, disappearing into the dark. *Shit!* He knelt at the curled man and found it was Heuk, apparently asleep, but deeply so, unresponsive and shivering badly. He grabbed him by his collar and dragged him down the slope. *Worse? Worse than this? Damned unlikely unless Hood himself hiked up his rags and elected to shit on them.*

* * *

599

Hurl was surprised by the lack of outriders and pickets north of the Imperial encampment. They rode slowly, ready for any challenge, a call to halt. But none came. The night was cool. Their horses' breath steamed the air. Hurl caught her sergeant's eye and raised a brow in a question. The man shifted in his saddle, glowering, evidently even more uncomfortable with the situation than she. He directed her attention to a torch lying nearly extinguished. They rode over. Before reaching it their mounts shied away from dark shapes lying splayed in the tall grass. Banath dismounted, studied them. He remounted looking far more pale. Hurl cocked another question and he gave a sickly nod.

So, found him. But the rear elements? Soliel, no – that would be camp followers, noncombatants, families, craftsmen and women, and even . . . no, please not that. She urged her mount on with a kick. The troop picked up its pace.

They found the camp a shambles. Wrecked wagons, torn tents, scattered equipment, and everywhere mangled dismembered bodies. Survivors wandered, blank-faced, turned to watch them pass without even challenging their presence. Banath slowed his mount. 'Shouldn't we . . .'

'No, not yet. The trail goes on, yes, Liss?' Riding behind Hurl, the mage gave a tight bob of her head, her lank hair swinging. 'It goes on. And . . . I'm afraid I know where he's headed.'

Banath could only eye her, puzzled, but he acquiesced.

To the south the green and yellow glow of battle-magics was plain. A muted roar reached them, punctuated by the eruption of munitions. Hurl felt someone close and turned to see that Rell had moved his mount up to her left. She felt infinitely better with him at her side. A field of tents and blankets spread on the ground lay ahead and Hurl made for it. Closer, fires could be seen burning among them and many tents hung twisted and canted, some torn in strips. Banath, at Hurl's rear, groaned as realization clenched him. 'No. Oh, no.'

'I'm sorry,' Hurl murmured. But she was far more than sorry. What lay ahead, no matter how horrific, was all her fault, her curse. *I killed these men and women.*

Finally, as they almost reached the field hospital, a soldier stood before them and raised a hand. A company cutter by his shoulder-bags. 'Who are you?' he demanded, dazed.

'Detachment from Heng,' Hurl answered. 'We ride under the sceptre.'

'Heng? *Heng!*' He gaped up at them. Hurl saw that gore stained his uniform, his hands; none seemed to be his. A chuckle escaped the man. It grew into a deep gut-heaving laugh that he made no effort to suppress. 'Well,' he said, tears now mixed with his laughter, 'you are just too Burn-damned late, aren't you?'

'I'm sorry . . .'

'Sorry! You're *sorry!*' The officer took hold of Hurl's leg, smearing blood on her trousers and boot. 'All our wounded. Hundreds of men and women. Wounded. Helpless. Unarmed . . .'

Something like jagged iron thrust at Hurl's chest. She took a shuddering breath. 'I could not possibly tell you how—'

'*He butchered us like sheep!* Like sheep!' He tugged at her leg as if to pull her from her mount. 'Aren't we human? Men and women? How can this happen now? In this day and age? *Will he slay us all?*'

'Calm yourself . . .'

'*Calm myself?* You! You of all people, from Heng. You should know!' He pushed her leg aside and backed away, disgusted. 'This is your curse! You brought this upon us!'

Hurl flinched as if fatally stabbed; she stared, feeling the blood drain from her face, her heart writhing. *Yea Gods, so it was now true. Was this foreordained, or did I walk voluntarily, of my own choosing, into this nightmare?*

'Well?' he stared up at her, demanding an answer, some kind of explanation for the horror that bruised his eyes. Hurl opened her mouth, but no sound came. She tried again, wetted her cracked lips.

'We're going to put an end to this.'

'Good. Do so. Or do not come back. Because after this night . . . this atrocity . . . you are no longer welcome here.'

Part of her wanted to object, to argue the injustice of that charge. But another part accepted the judgment. So be it. History's condemnation made clear. They were damned. Unless – unless they managed to end things this night. She gave a rigid curt nod to the man and pulled her reins aside, kicking her mount.

After they exited the camp, riding north across the plain lit silvery in the clear night, Hurl waved Liss to her. 'Can you track him now?' she demanded, her voice unrecognizable to herself.

'Yes, now that we've found his trail.' The Seti shamaness was uncharacteristically subdued. 'Hurl,' she began, 'it's not your—'

'Yes, it is.'

The shamaness appeared about to object or dispute further, but reconsidered. She pursed her lips, looking away, then frowned. 'Where are the brothers?'

'What?'

'The three – I don't see them.'

Hurl raised a hand for a halt. The troop slowed, stopped. 'Sergeant!'

Banath rode up. 'Sir?'

'Find the brothers.'

The man jerked a nod, sawed his reins around, rode off. After a brief time he returned. 'Not with the column, sir. Left us.'

Hurl turned to look back, the leather of her saddle creaking. Flashes lit the distant battlefield like lightning, and a dark cloud hung low over it like a thunderstorm – smoke? 'They never wanted Ryllandaras,' she said, thinking aloud. 'They came for something else.'

'Should we go back?' Banath asked.

'No – let them go. Personally, I hope never to see them again.'

'Agreed,' Liss added, sounding relieved.

Hurl eyed her – the shamaness had hated them from the start. Named them an abomination. She'd never asked what she'd meant by that exactly. But after having spent some time with them she knew in her gut that she'd felt it all along. 'You still have the trail, Liss?'

'Yes. He's had his fill for one night. Heading north.'

'Good. We'll follow for as long as it takes.'

'Agreed,' Rell said. 'He's a menace to all.'

Hurl urged her mount on. *But we didn't stop to think about that, did we – or at least we were willing to turn a blind eye to it. Well, now we're paying the price. Heng's curse, reborn. We're pariahs. No one will come within a hundred leagues of us until we can rid ourselves of him.*

* * *

Shadow was damned monotonous. Such was the conclusion Kyle was drawing. They walked and walked and then walked some more. It occurred to him that he ought to be tired, or hungry, but so far nothing like that came upon him. What he felt instead was a kind of draining lassitude, a strange feeling of eternal waiting – not despair – no, not hopelessness, but rather a sensation of time suspended, of eternity. Just how long had the five of them been walking? Who was to know? Their bizarre guide would presumably let them know once they'd reached Quon. No sun rose, no day, or night, came. Eternal dusk. He felt like a ghost walking he knew not where.

All of them, Jan, the Lost brothers, seemed to have fallen beneath the same spell, as conversation stopped and all walked apart, alone with their thoughts. For a time they drew abreast of a large lake.

Figures fished it from boats, casting nets; they appeared huge, in-human. Their guide swerved them away from the coast. The ground became rougher. Steep-sided canyons rose to their right, cutting through flat-topped hills of layered rock. The Shadow priest Hethe led them around the canyons and out on to a level desert-like land-scape of broken rock and thick, sword-like clumped grasses.

Jan, it seemed, had finally had enough and he jogged ahead to take hold of their guide's frayed robes to pull him to a halt. 'Where are we?' he demanded.

Hethe's hood fell back revealing his wild, kinky black hair like a thin halo around his bumpy skull. His tangled brows rose. 'Wearwy?' he said. 'No, my name is Hethe.'

'No,' Jan snarled. 'Where . . . are . . . we . . . going?'

The man looked insulted. He pulled his robes from Jan's grip. 'That's rather personal!' and he stormed off.

'Where are you taking us!' Jan yelled after him.

'Wartegenus?' he called back. 'I know of no such place.'

Jan pressed a hand to his brow, hung his head. Coming abreast of him, Stalker urged him on with a hand. They continued on. This desert, or what resembled a desert, extended for leagues. Ruins dotted it: no more than scattered fragments of wind-gnawed worked stone.

After a time all but their guide halted as the calls of more than one hound echoed across the bleak landscape. They exchanged uneasy glances. Some unknowable time later Jan suddenly let out a surprised gasp. His hands went to his neck. The rest of them, but for the guide, halted. The man stared ahead into the distance, amazement in his eyes. Kyle looked to Stalker and the scout shrugged, at a loss. A moment later Jan staggered, caught himself from falling and glared around at the empty landscape. 'We're close,' he said, and he set off at a faster pace leaving the four of them to eye one another in com-plete confusion. Finally, Stalker shrugged again and set off. The brothers followed.

Kyle refused to move. The thought came to him: what difference would it make? Why should they walk on and on forever like this? He sat down on the gritty, pebbled desert plain. Why return to Quon, to where the Guard was, when they'd just kill him? Unless Jan was who he thought – but could he trust his life to a chance like that?

Footsteps crunched on the wind-scoured dirt around him. He looked up to see the four of them peering down at him – their guide was nowhere to be seen. Stalker bent down on his haunches in front of him. 'You comin'?'

'Maybe.'

The scout glanced up to the others, puzzled. 'Maybe?'

'If this guy comes clean,' and he tossed a stone to Jan's feet.

Stalker gave a long thoughtful nod, looked up at Jan. 'Well, how about it?'

The old man pushed back his hair, long and thin enough to be blown by the feeble wind that seemed to haunt the warren. He gave a quick nod of consent, motioned Kyle up. 'Very well, Kyle. From what I understand, you deserve better.' Kyle stood, brushed off the dust. Jan fished out the object he carried around his neck, broke the thong, and put what was a ring on his finger. 'As you suspect, Kyle. I am K'azz D'Avore. Jan, by the way, is part of my full name.'

'I knew it all along!' Badlands exclaimed, elbowing Coots. 'Didn't I say so?'

'You didn't say.'

'But you're—' began Kyle.

'Old?'

Kyle shrugged, sheepish. 'Yeah.'

'I wasn't when I made the Vow, Kyle. Since then, though, I have aged. But I don't think ageing is the right word for it. I find that I am toughening up, losing flesh, so to speak. I eat little, hardly sleep. It is as if I were transforming somehow.'

'Into what?' Stalker asked, his gaze narrowed.

'I don't know for certain. I suspect that something in the Vow is transforming me, perhaps all of us Avowed, preserving us. Sustaining us so long as it should hold. Until we complete it.'

The brothers shared shocked glances, Stalker scowling. 'That's impossible.'

A shrug from K'azz invited Stalker to come up with his own explanation. The news meant nothing to Kyle. All it did was confirm that something strange was going on – as though he needed to be told that!

'Where's the little rat?' Coots asked.

Everyone glanced around. K'azz pointed, 'There.'

Kyle squinted: a tiny dark dot out on the unrelentingly uniform wind-scoured waste.

'For the love of the Infinite,' Badlands breathed, 'doesn't he even know we've stopped?'

K'azz set out at a jog, waving them on, 'C'mon. We mustn't lose him.'

They all set out at a jogging run. At first they seemed to make no progress; the tiny dot seemed to get no larger. Kyle already knew distances and proportions were strange here in Shadow. They trotted for a time, then set out at a run again; they were gaining ground. Kyle's lungs burned, his feet and thighs ached. None of the others evidenced any signs of exertion. He bit down on the pain and kept going. Quite suddenly, they caught up. The man had stopped and was waiting for them, an irked expression on his wrinkled, hairy face.

'Yes?' he demanded.

They halted. Kyle bent over to pant, hands on his knees. Stalker faced the fellow, 'Well? Is this it?'

Hethe cupped a hand to his ear. 'What? What was that? You think I can't hear? Well I can! Perfectly!' He turned around and set off again in his awkward bowed-legged walk.

'I swear I'm gonna kill 'im,' Coots ground out.

K'azz waved them forward. 'Let's go.'

They continued on. Coots muttered darkly about strangulation and torture, then, louder, 'I swear he's leadin' us in circles!'

'We have no choice,' K'azz answered tiredly.

Kyle shifted to walk alongside K'azz. The man caught him studying him sidelong. 'Yes?'

Wetting his lips, Kyle ventured, 'So – you're really him?'

An amused smile. 'Yes, Kyle.'

He'd done it! Actually found him! But they were a long way from Quon. 'I knew Stoop.'

The smile broadened. 'Yes, Stoop. I learned a lot from him when I was a lad.'

'Are you really a Prince?'

K'azz tilted his head aside, thinking. 'Some call me that. I was a Duke. During the wars I defended a principality for a time. But that fell too . . .'

Kyle glanced away. Oaf! Reminding him of all that.

Coots shouted, pointing ahead: 'Look there! There's some poor bastard he led out here to die before.'

It was a skeleton in verdigrised armour sprawled in the desert sands. The wind had piled little dunes of dust and sand up over its limbs. Reaching it Hethe stopped, jerking as if startled. They caught up with him.

'What is it?' K'azz asked.

In a sighing of sands and creaking of leather-cured sinew and tendons, the skeleton stood. All five of them leapt back, drawing weapons; their scout remained where he stood. The animated corpse took hold of the front of Hethe's robes and raised him from the ground, shook him like a dog. Coots edged forward for a blow. The thing raised a hand. 'Hold!'

Out of the bottom of the ragged robes fell the little winged and tailed monkey they'd followed before. It hung its head before the skeleton, kicked at the dirt like a guilty child. 'This has gone far enough,' the being said. 'I do not want Shadow becoming embroiled in this. Now go.' Brightening, the monkey-thing puffed up its chest and marched off. After it had gone a few paces it shot back a glance, wrinkled up its wizened features, stuck out its tongue, then scampered off at a run.

All six of them watched it go. It seemed to Kyle to shrink down into the distance with impossible speed. He faced the corpse – for upon closer inspection it resembled more a desiccated body, dried cured flesh and all. Like the Imass he'd heard so much of. Thinking of that, he glanced to K'azz who likewise was examining the creature, wonder – and suspicion – on his face. 'Who are you?' K'azz asked.

'My name is Edgewalker,' came the breathless dry response, like wind over heated sand. 'Though it means nothing to you. What is important is that you do not belong here. I am sending you back.'

'About damned time,' Coots said aside to Kyle.

'To Quon?' K'azz asked, but the being merely waved. 'Quon Tali!' K'azz shouted, demanding. The grey gloom of the Warren gathered around them, choking off all vision. It was not dark or night, merely so dim Kyle could barely see. Ahead, a pale glow asserted itself; he and the rest headed for it. Kyle found himself in a cave hacked from loose sandy rock. He headed for its opening where starlight shone cold but bright. He had to step over several figures wrapped in thin blankets asleep around a dead fire-pit. He came out into a clear cold night. Cliffs surrounded them, marred by dark openings, a multitude of caves. A road passed before them climbing the incline. In the distance roaring and flashes bruised the night like lightning to both the north and south. K'azz climbed down ahead and now faced the south, staring. They joined him.

The road switchbacked down cliffs to a long, narrow stone bridge over a wide river. The far bank was swarming with figures lit by countless torches. The mass of them were all crowded around the far end of the bridge and filled its length to about the halfway point where the press stopped, held back by what appeared to be just a few men. Avowed? He looked to K'azz; the man was studying the bridge, his eyes narrowed to slits. 'Cole,' he whispered, 'Amatt, Lean, Black and Turgal.'

'Brethren!' K'azz roared. 'Attend!'

Silence and stillness. Dogs ran away, loping through the rocks, tails down. Kyle studied the bridge. Such a mass of soldiers facing such a thin barrier . . . why not just cut them down with arrows and bolts? But then, the bridge appeared to have stone sides, and the press was so close – any flights of missiles would account for far more of the attackers.

Stalker nudged him, lifted his chin to across the way. Something obscured the many dark cave openings opposite – gauzy grey shapes came emerging from the shadows. They filed down, approaching, silent. Kyle jumped as more stepped out from behind him. Shades in the hundreds. All the Avowed dead. They surrounded the party. All empty dead sockets stared fixed upon K'azz and Kyle could feel the heat, the awful will of that regard. It seemed as if the rest of the party need not even have existed to these shades. Just a year ago such a visitation would have sent Kyle screaming into the night; but by now he felt inured to any horror. He even recognized two of the fallen.

K'azz studied them in turn, nodding to many. 'This attack is against my wishes. Who leads this invasion?'

Hissed from hundreds of indistinct throats: '*Skinner.*'

A nod from K'azz, who'd known all along. 'Obey no more orders from him. He is expelled from our company. He is *disavowed.*' The Brethren inclined their heads in acquiescence.

'Not so easy, I suspect,' Stalker whispered aside to Kyle.

'Now, give my regards to those defending the bridge and ask if they can hold much longer. And send word to all – I am returned.'

The Brethren bowed and as one they bent to a knee. Then, to Kyle's eye they seemed to slowly disperse, disappearing as a haze in the sun. All but one: the shade of a short thin man with one hand – Stoop – who approached, smiling. 'Well done, lad. Well done. Knew you'd pull it off.'

To this outrageous claim Kyle could only shake his head.

A shade materialized next to K'azz. 'Cole sends his welcome and asks how many days you require.'

A tight grin from K'azz. 'Tell Cole I'll send relief as soon as I can.'

The shade remained. K'azz, who had started for the road, stopped short. 'Yes?'

'The truth is they are badly wounded and may not last much longer.'

The Crimson Guard commander spun, faced the bridge – glanced back to the north where battle-magics glowed like auroras brought to earth and combat shook the ground.

Kyle glanced between the two as well. Gods, what a choice! He faced Stoop. 'What do you think?'

The shade examined the bridge and the thousands behind. He scratched his chin. 'Don't know what's goin' on up north but we can't let them through.'

'I agree,' K'azz said, making Kyle jump – he didn't think him close enough to overhear. 'Thank you, Kyle.' To Stoop: 'Tell Cole I'm coming.'

'Queen forgive me,' Kyle breathed. Beside him, Badlands sent an entreating look to the sky as if asking – *why me, Hood? Why me?*

* * *

Ullen was in the north-west when word came of the attack and complete slaughter of the field hospital. He stared for a time wordlessly to the north, numb of all feeling. *What had he not done that he should've? A larger rearguard? More messengers? A tighter distribution of the command? I've failed my soldiers. The men and women who look to me to protect them.* Standing before him, the pallid-faced messenger cleared his throat. 'Sir?'

Ullen blinked, confused. 'Yes?'

'Your . . . orders, sir?'

He raised his weak, newly healed right arm to wipe his brow, found it slick with sweat. 'Relocate the field hospital closer to the reserves.'

'The only reserves are those with us, sir.'

Ullen looked up. 'Only my legion?'

'Yes.'

'Then . . . move it . . . closer to the field.'

'Yes, sir.' The messenger saluted, departed.

Ullen studied the south. He would not, could not, face his staff. He clasped his sweaty hands at his back to quell the urge to wipe them on his uniform. The darker smear of night, empty of all stars, still hung over the redoubt in the east – bless that mage whoever he was – he'd saved that flank. Now, if he could only salvage some order out of the west. He could not understand the Guard's reluctance out there on that flank. They could have routed them if they'd pressed their advantage. A phalanx marched now up the middle, standard in prominence, making an obvious effort to lay claim to overall control of the field. And what did they have left to throw against them? Nothing. If they could not be stopped then the Guard would have effectively won. His lines would have been cut in half.

A young girl came running up to his position, one of the Untan irregulars. His guards grabbed hold of her leather hauberk to yank her back. She fought the man, punching him. 'Commander Ullen!' she shouted. He waved her through. The oversized crossbow on her back rolled side to side as she came. 'The Guard, sir – they're fallin' apart!'

He studied her, disbelieving. 'What do you mean?'

'Units are breakin' up. Crimson Guardsmen runnin' this way and that. Some even fightin' each other. I heard Avowed even attacking Avowed.'

'But that's incredible. Why . . . ?' he glanced around, searching for confirmation. 'Who else says so?'

'I saw it with my own eyes, sir.'

'Fist D'Ebbin approaching, sir,' a lieutenant called out. Ullen dismissed the girl then jogged ahead to meet the Fist. He found the short, round commander surrounded by his bodyguard. All had seen fighting. The Fist's armour was hacked, a cheek and his lips swollen from a blow. The man pulled off his helmet and gauntlets to wipe his face.

'My compliments, Fist,' said Ullen, and he meant it.

D'Ebbin gave a small wave as if to say it was of no great importance. 'Been some kind of falling out among the Guard. Two camps appear to be organizing. One is firming up around the standard with the phalanx. The other is pulling together out of the Blades facing us. That phalanx, though, looks like it's determined to take control of the field.'

'We have to meet it.'

A curt nod of his bullet-head. 'Understood.'

'How many can you spare?'

'We have to keep the main group contained.'

'Reinforcements will come once the Kanese have broken through. They should some time soon.'

His hairless bony brows rose. 'In truth? Then when they come we'll swing east.'

'Done.'

'You'll wait?'

Ullen shook his head. 'We can't leave the challenge unanswered. It would look like capitulation. The men will break.'

'I understand. The column numbers about two thousand. But you know, my people estimate there are some forty Avowed among them?'

Forty Avowed? How could any force meet such a potent body? Still, there were twenty thousand Kanese on their way – enough to keep them pinned down, surrounded. Grind them down one by one. But how long will it take them to break through? He had to hold until the Kan forces arrived. 'I have four thousand Malazan regulars with me, Fist. The commander's, Anand's, reserve. I will meet them.'

The Fist drew his gauntlets on. 'I ask that you wait. The day is within your grasp. You have done a masterful job. I commend you. Do not throw it away.'

Ullen saluted. 'I go now to save it, Fist.'

'D'Ebbin nodded his assent, saluted. His face settled into grim resignation. 'For sceptre and throne, Lieutenant-commander.'

'Sceptre and throne.' Fist D'Ebbin jogged away. Ullen turned back to his staff. 'Relay my orders. We march to meet the Crimson Guard standard. We must keep them engaged until the Kanese arrive. Now is our turn to bloody our swords.'

'We are with you sir,' said the Imperial lieutenant, and Ullen was surprised and pleased to hear the support in his voice.

'Very good. Order the march.' His officers saluted and ran to their commands.

* * *

'Is this the truth?' asked an astonished Shimmer.

The Brethren shade before her, once Lieutenant Shirdar, bowed. 'We offer no excuse. We were ... blinded ... commander. The Vow—'

'Damn the Vow!' Shimmer grated. 'Cowl used your damned fixation to manipulate you!'

The shade wavered, fading, then reasserting its presence as if attempting to go but being held against its wishes. '*It is yours too,*' it murmured.

Shimmer raised a gauntleted hand as if she would strike it. 'Gather the Brethren. There are second and third investiture soldiers abandoned in the field, alone, beleaguered. Find them, protect them, guide them here!'

'And K'azz?'

'We will be—' She cast about, pointed to a hill in the west. 'There. Our rallying point.'

Shirdar bowed his head. 'As you order.'

'Yes! As *I* order. Now go!'

The shade disappeared. 'Avowed!' Shimmer yelled, raising her arms and turning full circle. 'There are soldiers abandoned in the

610

field! Our brothers and sisters! Go! Find them! Bring them to me! The Brethren will guide you!'

A great shout answered her call, arms raised. The Avowed spread out for the field. Smoky, Shell and Bower paused to eye Shimmer – she waved them on. Even Greymane bowed, obviously meaning to go. She cocked a brow. 'Where are you going? The Brethren will not talk to you.'

The man's thick lips turned up in a one-sided smile. His eyes now laughed with some hidden joke. 'Skinner, you say, has been cast out. Very good. I go now to do what should've been done some time ago.'

Her breath caught. 'I forbid it!'

The smile broadened with the hidden joke. 'As you have constantly reminded me, Shimmer, I am no Avowed.' And he bowed, leaving.

You fool! There are too many! He is not alone.

'Commander,' a Guardsman sergeant, Trench, asked.

'Yes?'

'The rallying point?'

She pulled her gaze reluctantly from the back of the renegade as he jogged into the fire-dotted night. 'Yes. This way. We withdraw to that hill.'

A Brethren shade appeared before her. 'The Claw comes.'

Shimmer pushed Trench from her. 'Go! Assemble. Go on.' And she backed away. The man hesitated, hand going to his sword. 'I order you to go!' Grimacing his unwillingness, the sergeant turned and ran.

Shimmer continued backing away. She unsheathed her whipsword and it flexed before her, almost invisible in profile so thin was it. Darker shapes arose in the field around her. She turned, counting. Ten. Two Hands. She flicked the blade, weaving it, and she turned, spinning. Slowly at first, then quickening, the blade nearly invisible. *And so the dance*, Shimmer heard again the dry voice of her old instructress lashing her. *The sword-dance of spinning cuts. Beautiful – but oh so deadly.*

The Claws closed, knives out, crouched. Thrown weapons glanced from the twisting blade. Training of a lifetime refined over a further century flicked out the tempered blade to lick arms, legs and heads as she spun. Claws flinched away, gasping at razor cuts that sawed through flesh to scrape bone, sever wrists, lacerate faces and slit throats.

A second wave challenged, ducking, probing. The blade licked whipping through them all, extending suddenly to its full length. Shimmer spun, twisting and leaping. The blade's razor edge flicked, kissing all remaining, and she landed, arms extended, panting.

She stilled, weapon extended before her, quivering, blood running from its length. All ten were down, some weeping, holding faces, bloodied stumps. Three more stood a few paces off, their eyes huge. Shimmer saw them and at the same instant each raised a crossbow. *Damn – no momentum.*

Then another jumped among them, kicking, rolling, and they rocked backwards to fall, immobile, felled by blows of feet and hands. This new figure strode up to her – female, slim and wiry, wrapped head to foot in dark cloth strips. Those strips wet with blood at her feet and torn away from her bloodied hands by the ferocity of her blows. Shimmer inclined her head in greeting. 'I could have handled them.'

'Perhaps.' Only dark, calculating eyes were visible in her face and these shifted away. She raised her chin to the retreating Guardsmen. 'You are withdrawing.'

'Yes.'

'Then go with my permission and never return to these lands.'

Shimmer's brows rose. 'And you are?'

The female Claw ignored the question.

Another Claw came running out of the dark, this one a man with a pinched rat's face, dark mussed hair and an unsettling crazy grin. Shimmer recognized him from briefings on the Claw – Possum, Clawmaster. He crouched behind the woman as if guarding her back. The Master of the Claws following around a woman like a pet dog? Then this must be . . . Shimmer froze in shock. *Gods! It's her! Of course, Mistress of the Claw, once rival of Dancer himself!*

Trench with a full Blade was running their way. Shimmer raised a hand to forestall them.

Unconcerned, the woman motioned aside, to the east. 'And those?'

Shimmer knew who she meant. 'Disavowed. Disgraced. Stricken from our ranks.'

'I see. May I ask the reason for this falling out?'

She doesn't know! 'Skinner exceeded his authority.' *All too true.*

'How depressingly familiar . . .' Musing, still gazing away, the woman – Laseen in truth? – spoke. 'Very well. We are done here. Go! Return and you will be hunted down and slain. Accepted?'

Shimmer offered a shallow bow. 'Accepted.'

The woman turned away, paused before the Clawmaster, who bowed profoundly on one knee. 'Come, Possum. We have much to discuss – now.' And she walked off into the dark, and, after a courtly mocking bow – that grin, *unbalanced* – Possum followed.

Trench jogged up. 'Who was that?'

'A . . . Claw officer. We have struck a truce.'

'A truce? What of Skinner?'

'I don't believe he's interested in any truces.'

Trench adjusted his hauberk. 'No, I suppose not.'

'Come, Sergeant, we've a defensive perimeter to build. No sense trusting to the Empire's good graces, yes?'

'Aye, Commander.'

The sergeant headed off but Shimmer lingered. She gazed back to where the two disappeared into the night. *So, met at last. Is your word good, Empress? Shall you simply allow us to withdraw? Or will other voices, other councils, sway? I wonder . . .*

* * *

The smearing, shifting land, spiralling sky and blurring, meteor-like stars forced Rillish to close his eyes else vomit or faint. He lowered his head into the smoky mane of his mount. He clenched his eyes, wondered just what it was they rode upon then wished he hadn't. Gay laughter from ahead forced him to look – Nil and Nether sharing grins of victory, laughing their confidence, hair flying. *As if they'd feared they all could've died immediately!* He glanced back and wished he hadn't. The land they rode upon was disappearing behind them as they passed, collapsing, falling away, revealing emptiness – Abyss – behind. *Ye gods! Ride!*

Overhead the great empty bowl of the night sky turned so fast the stars blurred like spun torches. A sun rose, fat and carmine – a bloated travesty of what he knew as the sun. Was it ill? Some peoples, he knew, worshipped the sun as a god. Its crimson light revealed that ahead lay . . . nothing. A dirt surface appeared before their column as if called into existence by the will of all the witches and warlocks bound to the twins. The surface supported them only to fall away once more into the miasma of the Abyss.

Ride, lads and lasses! Ride!

The glow of the horses' eyes shocked him – all whites! Unconscious! But of course, what animal could endure such chaos? And so they ran, pulled along by the will of the warlocks. And he and all those who followed as well! He saw that at some point he'd unsheathed a sword, and, laughing, he awkwardly resheathed it. What use such a pathetic instrument?

Something moved upon the face of the unformed, churning sky – distant yet immense – wings outstretched, long tail lashing. A body

613

of rib and spine only – *a skeleton dragon?* And why not? In such a place where everything yet nothing is possible. And farther yet, if such things as distance applied here, a great dark fortress. Static, brooding. Appearing to float upon nothing. What were these things? Hallucinations?

He glanced back and the hair on his neck and arms rose, charged. *It was gaining!* The land was falling away closer and closer upon their rear. Nothingness was overtaking them!

Ride, fools! Death's reaching!

The twins pointed ahead where a dark smear stained the churning miasma ahead. Our gate? *But so far!* Rillish glanced back again and screamed. The rear ranks were slipping off the edge, hooves scrabbling, horses tumbling, men and women spinning backwards from sight. He kicked his mount savagely, almost weeping.

Ride to the Abyss!

* * *

Ullen ordered his legion into two arms, each of which would meet the Guard phalanx leading face at angles, hopefully to then wrap around and envelop. That was the best he could hope for. The Crimson Guard standard was held just a few ranks back from that face. The Avowed, he knew, would overcome any individual soldier who might oppose them, but eventually, if numbers should tell, they would find themselves beleaguered from all sides to be cut down by these stolid, grim Malazan and Talian heavy infantry veterans. Or so he told himself.

The two forces came marching towards one another out of the dark. The ruins of the Imperial pavilion smouldered just to the north. Ullen knew the Empress was nowhere nearby; yet for the Guard to march unopposed this far would be tantamount to victory, a tacit acknowledgement that the Imperial forces could no longer muster the wherewithal, or will, or spirit, to face them. The closest thing to defeat that becomes defeat in its realization.

When only a few paces separated the two lines Ullen raised his sword for the final charge. The Imperials sounded a low animal roar that swelled to a ferocious demanding invocation of rage, hate and battle-lust. They raised shields, leaning forward, the pressing shields of the ranks behind at their backs forcing them on. The two formations smashed together with a bone-breaking clash of shields smashing, blades probing, legs thrusting at the dirt. Line pushed against line; ranks slid across one another, mixing, milling. Men died but could not fall, so crushing was the press. The screaming cacophony melded into one undifferentiated rumble that punished Ullen's ears into a ringing, oddly muted, din. He knew he was yelling but he could not hear his own voice.

Sword held awkwardly in his left hand, for his right remained too weak, he thrust savagely between shields. The ground beneath the grunting, scrabbling mass became glutinous with shed blood. Sandalled feet slipped, bodies fell. Men and women cursed fallen friends and enemies alike when they entangled their feet, tripping them. As the lines shifted back and forth these fallen became trampled down into the mulch of mud and gore.

Anything that moved before him, Ullen stabbed. Blades hacked at his shield, cutting, some sticking. He flicked his sword over the top, slicing arms. A hand yanked at the shield, almost pulling it down; he bashed, pushing, sliced a leg. Men and women fell around him. Footing became treacherous. The Malazan regular on his right was hacked down by a stupendous blow that shattered his shield then helm, the sword continuing on down to split the skull, face, lodging in the collarbone and upper ribs. Without thinking of the terrifying power of that blow, he swung, severing the arm holding that blade at the elbow. An eruption of rage rocked him back. Ignoring the severed limb, that Guardsman turned on him. *Lady's Pull, he'd found one.*

The Guardsman threw his shield down, gripped Ullen's and yanked it, snapping the leather grip and breaking Ullen's elbow. A figure pushed forward at Ullen's side, Captain Moss, his twin blades slashing, but the man ignored the blows. His berserk all-white eyes remained fixed on Ullen. The Guardsman's fist lashed out and Ullen's head snapped backwards so far he saw the night sky. The rear of his helmet struck his own back between his shoulder-blades, flew from his head.

Things seemed to slow down. He watched while the man pulled his fist back once more. Scintillating lights gathered in his vision. All noise became a blurred murmur. All sensation seemed to flow away leaving an odd feeling of ease.

From behind Ullen's shoulder and sides spears thrust, impaling the man in a series of impacts. Snarling, he fought to push forward against the hafts, reached with his one remaining clawed hand for Ullen. Other hands pulled Ullen back into the ranks. He fought to remain. The Dal Hon lieutenant, Gellan appeared before him, held his face, fought to look into his eyes: 'Commander!' she shouted, or he thought she shouted, she sounded so far away.

He blinked, frowning. *Commander?*

'We're breaking! We can't hold them!'

Breaking?

'Where do we rally?'

What? Rally? He searched the grounds with his swimming vision. Knots of men and women were recoiling – too many Avowed, too closely concentrated. *Ye gods, forty of them! Who could stop such a formation? They had nothing left. All that remained was to hunker down, hope to resist for the best terms.* He tried to shake his head – the spinning! It would not stop. 'The redoubt! Rally to the redoubt. We'll make our stand there.'

'Aye,' she shouted, still holding his head. 'I will spread the word.' Aside, she ordered: 'Take him south.' Arms grasped him, urged him on. He pushed at them – *leave me alone, damn you!* He recognized one of the men, Captain Moss, and he relaxed. He'd lost a gauntlet, wiped at his cold head. The hand came away blood-smeared. He stared at it, surprised. When had that happened? *That punch, fool! It shattered your helmet!*

He and his escort staggered, fumbling, southward, across the burnt black field littered in bodies. Ullen knew he'd taken a serious head-wound when he saw walking past them out of the gloom a figure from his youth – the unmistakable broad, armoured silhouette of Greymane. His guard pulled their weapons, arranged themselves around him. He raised his hand, 'It's all right! I know him. Greymane!' he called. The man swerved their way. 'Greymane!'

Closing, he halted, breathing hard. His eyes appeared preternaturally bright within the confines of his full-helm. They narrowed on Ullen. 'You know me?'

'Ullen Khadeve. I was with Choss long ago.'

'Ah.' The man glanced down. 'I heard. I'm sorry.'

'So am I – *what are you doing here?*'

The helm turned aside, he gestured north. 'I'm here for Skinner.'

That statement from any other man or woman would've made Ullen laugh. He shook his head, dizzying himself. 'There's too many Avowed. They'll cut you down.'

The hands in their iron gauntlets tightened into fists that almost shook. A curse sounded from within the helm. 'Yes – you're right . . . for now.' A chuckle of self-mockery. 'So much for simple-minded delusions of satisfaction demanded on the field of battle, hey?'

'Come with me. We're headed to that hillock, our last strongpoint. He'll be headed there next.' Ullen pressed a hand to his searing brow. *Had the man shattered his skull?* 'But I warn you – I may ask for terms. If the men agree, I'll not have you break them.'

A nod. 'I understand.'

'This way.'

But the armoured giant did not move; he was staring off to the north.

'What is it?'

'Something . . . something's coming. I'm sensitive to the Warrens. I can feel a damn huge disturbance . . . Coming very fast! Get down!'

The man stepped up before them, drew his blade – a slim longsword that looked comical in his huge hand. Ullen's guards ranged themselves behind him, Captain Moss included.

Ullen knew that through the darkness he could not see half of what was occurring but what little he did see terrified him. The air up the slope to the north began to ripple as if heated. Flashes like those of stars flickering permeated it. Before it, Skinner's phalanx paused, the tall standard hanging limp in the still night air. The ground suddenly shook as if hammered. *An earthquake?* The flickering coalesced into a dark-blue aurora that made him squint, shading his eyes and turning his head. Out of this light burst a hurtling wedge, striking the slope with a booming thunder that echoed from all the hills. Ullen had one glimpse of a massive column of riders, swords raised, mouths open in soundless yells, before that wedge slammed into Skinner's phalanx.

The solid ranks of Guardsmen melted before the onslaught like a stand of sticks before an avalanche. They disappeared beneath the crush of massed hooves. The standard snapped, mowed down. While Ullen watched, stunned, astounded, more came, rank after rank passing, trampling the same ground where before a solid formation had once stood. Its front rank curved away to the west and the column rode on, horses lathered, riders yelling their war cries. Wickans, Ullen saw as they swung by. Come through Warren!

After they passed, the deafening roar of their hooves diminishing, only dust swirled over the furrowed and churned ground of the slope. One rider closed upon them, reining up: an old man, his one good eye wide, the other a white, milky orb. A death-grin seemed frozen on his face. 'That should put an end to your pogrom against us, eh, Malazan!' he yelled with a crazed laugh.

'You obliterated them,' Ullen answered, his voice faint with shock.

The Wickan pointed a bloodied scimitar, his horse rearing to be off. 'Witness! Give witness, Malazan!' And he rode off, shouting a great ululating war cry.

Ullen watched the man disappear from sight. 'Yes . . . I shall.'

Yet incredibly, unbelievably, shapes now stirred among the trampled and punished ground. Here and there Guardsmen stood, weaving, shaking themselves, straightening. The sight chilled Ullen's flesh and he stared, utterly appalled. *Great Gods! Will nothing stop these Avowed? They are relentless. Like the Imass.*

Greymane turned to him, wry humour in his eyes. 'As you said, Ullen. They're too many. But the odds have levelled somewhat, I think. Now is my chance.' Before Ullen could object the man ran down to the churned slope. If Ullen had had a helmet he'd have thrown it to the ground in frustration. 'Dammit!' He turned to his guard. 'We have to follow him. We can't let him go alone.'

His guards, a mixed body of seven Malazan and Talian infantry, eyed one another, clearly unsure. 'Our orders . . .' one began.

'Your orders are to follow me,' Ullen said. Clenching his jaws, this one bowed his curt concurrence. Ullen turned to Moss, who nodded then lifted his chin to the field. 'And we're not alone . . .'

Ranks of Imperial infantry were advancing from all around, small units pulling together from every direction. 'Come!' Supported by Moss, Ullen limped after Greymane.

The field was a charnel-house of trampled broken bodies. Stunned survivors staggered, blood-bespattered, ignoring them as they passed. All fighting, as far as Ullen could tell, seemed to have been snuffed by this cataclysmic charge. Sadly, a number of his own infantry seemed to have been caught in the charge as well. Ahead through the night, however, two swords clashed, ringing in the silence following the prolonged detonation of that charge. Ullen searched the dusty night for the combat. The grunts, blows and ringing of iron drew them on. They came to the wreckage of a train of Imperial supply wagons. Ullen glimpsed the duel as a blow from one threw the other backwards into a burning wagon, knocking it sideways, its wheels gouging the dirt. Greymane. The man was battered, helm gone, face a mass of blood. Bands of iron armour had been hacked away leaving hanging leather strapping. Skinner loomed forward into the light. A ponderous two-handed downward swing from him was dodged by the renegade to crash into the wagon's siding and bed, breaking it in two in a terrific explosion that sent up clouds of obscuring smoke and ash. Greymane answered but his blade skittered from the Avowed's unearthly glittering armour. They clashed again, grunting their effort in blows that would fell trees. A swiping riposte was met by Greymane's slimmer blade which burst like a sharper, shattering beneath the strain. But instead of flinching

618

away the ex-Fist closed, grappling, and the two struggled from view. Ullen dodged through overturned wagons, butchered horses and burning spilt matériel in a frantic effort to catch sight of them again. Moss and the guards ran with him.

This was lunacy! Here he was with a broken right arm and a probable fractured skull searching for a nightmare out of the old wars of continental subjugation – and the worst of those! A champion that, should Greymane fail, could not be matched by anyone alive today; what could he possibly do? Ullen honestly did not know.

He glimpsed them, wrestling, crashing into wagons, rolling amid the wreckage, trading blows that echoed through the night. Greymane arose bent behind Skinner, a grip up under his chin, straining, his face writhing with effort. Yet, incredibly, the Avowed commander straightened beneath him, raising the man clear off the ground to heave him, armour and all, off into the night. A crash and clattering of iron from stones revealed a gully or slope nearby.

Skinner adjusted his long mail shirt, rolled one shoulder, grunting. He bent to pick up his helm and drew it on again to walk off towards the field. Ullen was torn – dare he challenge him? But what of Greymane? The man was wounded. His guards had already scampered down to find the renegade. That settled the matter for Ullen and he followed.

It was a shallow, rocky gully. They found Greymane lying amid stones at its bottom. The man was conscious, but barely so. Together all of them strained to drag him up the side. They laid him on the ground. His eyes – one carmine with blood from broken vessels – found Ullen's face and he snorted, shaking his head. 'Cheating bastard. His blade's poison. Bastard poisoned me! Got me all riled up, he has. Lucky bastard. I almost used the sword on him – but not here . . . too close to the sanctuary it is. Who knows what might've happened?'

Ullen ignored the man's ramblings. *His sword? What was the man on about?* 'Relax – we'll bring a healer.' Ullen motioned one of his guards away. The man saluted and ran.

Ullen caught Captain Moss's eye, tilted his head after Skinner. The officer held his gaze for a long time, his own eyes dark and flat, his mouth held expressionless. A hand rose to rub at the scabbed gashes crossing his face and he nodded his assent. Ullen straightened from Greymane. He pointed to another of his remaining guards. 'Stay with this man. The rest of you – follow me.' He jogged after the Avowed commander, left hand hot and sweaty on the grip of his sword. *Left! His bloody left hand!*

Conversation guided him through the detritus of burning equipment and scattered corpses. He caught sight of two men confronting Skinner. They were speaking with him, their words lost amid crackling flames and the shrill shrieks of a wounded horse. The two burly soldiers looked familiar yet he couldn't quite place them. Across the way figures emerged from the gloom, five Crimson Guardsmen, all Avowed, no doubt. They drew blades and began edging out to surround the two.

Ullen started forward but stopped as another man stepped directly in his path – *where on earth had he come from?* Moss lunged forward, sabres raised, but the fellow held up empty hands. He was an ironwood-hued Dal Hon, scarred, in a fine mail shirt. His long kinked hair was pulled back tied in a leather strip and he regarded Ullen as if he knew him. And the man did look . . . *but no, that cannot be . . . he was dead!*

The ghost rested a hand on Ullen's shoulder. 'You've done more than enough, Ullen,' he said in that voice that sent chills down Ullen's spine. 'The field is yours. My congratulations. Choss, I'm sure, would have been proud. Now leave this to us.' Then the man's closed features softened with affection and he motioned to the gathering duel: 'Those two, I swear they did this deliberately. Knew I couldn't let them face him alone.' And he jogged off. The encircling Avowed flinched from his approach and he slipped within, to the side of the two facing Skinner.

No – it cannot be. How could it be him? Was it no more than a ghost from his past?

The three formed a triangle while the Avowed completed their encirclement. The newcomer faced Skinner who pointed a gauntleted hand, saying something lost in the roar of the burning wreckage. The newcomer didn't deign to answer. He drew his sword, a dark slim length. At a signal from Skinner all lunged in upon the three at once.

Ullen was stunned by what he witnessed, blades flashing in the firelight too fast for him to comprehend. Of the three defenders, one hunkered behind a square heavy infantryman's shield, calmly sliding blows that would batter walls only to jab, forcing back any of the Avowed who edged too close; the other, a burly Seti, fought with two sturdy long-knives each bearing bronze knuckle guards, parrying and delivering awful blows, lashing out to rock one Avowed with a swipe to the head. Ullen winced, thinking of his own wound.

But it was the duel between the Dal Hon and Skinner that took his breath. The man's smooth, economical grace was beautiful:

tremendous swings from Skinner brushed aside with the seeming lightest of touches to be followed by lightning ripostes. *It must be him! But how? In answer to a prayer?*

Yet those ripostes all slid, rebounding, from the Avowed's stained dark armour. And Skinner laughed. In that laugh Ullen heard certainty of victory.

At his side, Captain Moss breathed, awed, 'Who *is* that? I've never seen anything . . . He knew you – who is he? But that armour . . . Skinner will wound him. And then . . . just a matter of time.'

But Ullen shook his head. 'No. He knows. He must know.'

The Avowed pressed, struggling to overbear the two guarding the Dal Hon's back. They took horrendous wounds attacking, but the two would not be forced or drawn out from guarding each other's flanks. One Avowed grasped the shield only to have his hand nearly severed: it flapped uselessly at the end of his arm as he continued fighting. The Seti was more aggressive, slashing at faces, torsos, inflicting wounds the Avowed silently absorbed until their legs ran glistening with blood and the ground darkened at their shuffling feet.

Try all you like, Avowed! No one ever penetrated the Sword, his bodyguard. He only fell to treachery. The Dal Hon continued punishing Skinner, landing blow after blow; yet each glanced away, turned by the man's seemingly impenetrable armour. While for his part, the Avowed could not pierce the man's virtuoso defence. All for naught, Ullen thought, for neither could bring the other down.

Didn't he comprehend? Why continue hacking at that mail coat? It was obviously Warren-invested, perhaps even aspected. Useless, utterly useless. Perhaps his dark thoughts tinged his vision but it seemed to Ullen that the two guarding the Dal Hon's back were tiring. It was to be expected – who could forestall Avowed forever? Soon, they would fall, then it would all be over. Skinner would finally prove victorious. He would return to the field to rally his Avowed, and they would sweep away any remaining organized resistance. The Guard would win.

The squat heavy infantryman's shield had been reduced to no more than a slivered handle of shattered slats. He now only parried with his shortsword. The Seti had abandoned counter-attacks and now merely defended. Only one of the Avowed had fallen: a woman who staggered off, hands pressing in her stomach where wet curves bulged out. She toppled face first a few short paces away where she lay, her appalling Avowed vitality sustaining her as limbs shifted weakly, kicking and writhing.

Still the Dal Hon riposted and counter-attacked. Just one of his cuts would have flensed any other attacker to the spine, yet Skinner remained unharmed. Ullen almost screamed: *You fool! Give it up! Disengage!* Suddenly it was too much for him. For *this* man he would act; it was not even something to question. Ullen lurched forward, raising his sword left-handed. Moss's arm encircled his neck to yank him back.

'Don't be a fool!'

Then, in the midst of yet another exchange of heavy cumbersome blows from Skinner and the Dal Hon's lightning flickering counterassault, the Dal Hon lunged forward farther than he ever had before, the tip of his blade in one pass flicking upwards just under Skinner's helm. The Avowed commander snapped his head back. He clutched a gauntleted hand to his neck where blood coursed down his front. He backed away, hand gripping his throat, sword still raised, still steady. The four remaining Avowed shifted to cover his retreat. The Dal Hon alone followed, pressing the attack.

Backing away, parrying, Skinner shouted some garbled wet command or entreaty and the air behind him boiled. It seemed to froth, lightened from night-dark to ugly streaked grey. The Avowed all backed into the jagged mar to disappear, two supporting Skinner. The Dal Hon halted, motionless, his breath still calm and level. He sheathed his dark-bladed sword.

Ullen ran up to the two soldiers who leaned together supporting each other. When he glanced back to the Dal Hon swordsman, he too was gone. A curse from his side revealed Captain Moss making the same discovery. The broad squat infantryman threw down the shattered slats and loose bronze strapping that remained of his shield. He pulled off his helmet and took a skin of water from his belt to squeeze a jet over his head and drink, gasping. He tossed it to the Seti.

'Where is – the other . . . the Dal Hon?' Ullen said.

'Weren't no other,' the old bald infantryman ground out, his voice so hoarse as to be almost inaudible. 'Never was, hey?'

'But . . .'

Panting, gasping in great lungfuls and swallowing with effort, the veteran waved Ullen's objections aside. 'No, just the two of us. Ain't that right, ah, Slim?'

'Slim?' the Seti growled. He wiped his glistening face with the back of a hand, leaving a smear of blood. 'Naw. It's . . . Sweetgrass.'

'Wha—' The infantryman faced the Seti directly to stand weaving, exhausted. 'Sweetgrass? All these years . . . none of us even knew?'

A truculent glower on the man's battered and cut face, chin thrust out. 'What of it?'

'Nothin'. Just surprising 's all.' The two bent down attempting to pick up fallen gear, couldn't bend far enough and gave up, then turned away to head back to the field. They limped, stretching their backs, pausing now and then to bend over gasping for breath, coughing. Ullen, Moss and his guards following along exchanged mute glances of wonder.

'What about you?' the Seti, Sweetgrass, asked of the old veteran.

'You don't want to know.'

'What?'

'No.'

'C'mon.'

The old veteran stopped to lean over. He dry heaved, gagging, then hawked up a mouthful of catarrh that he spat. 'No.'

'Boulbum?'

'No.'

'Ishfat?'

'No!'

Ullen looked to Captain Moss, who walked with the back of his hand pressed to his grinning mouth.

They returned to find mixed Malazans, Talians and Falaran elements being ordered into phalanxes by a battered and bloodied Braven Tooth and Urko. The four old veterans greeted one another with great back-slapping hugs. Then, to Ullen's shock and horror, Braven Tooth and Urko saluted him, sharing wicked grins. He answered the salute then waved aside their gesture. 'No – you command, Urko.'

'No. We ain't done yet. These ones all run off but we got a pocket of Guardsmen yet. Dug in on a hill. Fist D'Ebbin and his remaining forces and the Wickans are keeping them tight. Time we contributed. I'll be with one of the units. You can coordinate. Congratulations, Commander.'

The four veterans went to join units leaving Ullen to face his last remaining guard. He rubbed a hand at his wrenched, aching neck, feeling overcome. 'Well . . . find a mount and send word to Fist D'Ebbin that we're coming.'

The guard saluted, jogged off. Horns sounded a general advance. After some ragged reordering the columns began marching south. It was now well past midnight. The fires had died down and the field of battle was a dark tangled nightmare of fallen twisted bodies, broken equipment and wounded, dying horses.

With Moss at his side, Ullen picked his way south carefully. After a time, the captain leaned close and glanced about, troubled. The savage gashes that crossed his face appeared livid, raw. 'Where's your staff?'

'Scattered.'

'You need more of an escort.' He gestured aside. 'We should join that column.'

Ullen shrugged. 'If you think it best.'

But the man halted. His hands snapped to the bright ivory grips of his sabres. 'Something . . .'

Dust swirled up around them; Ullen shaded his gaze, wincing. 'Captain?' The clash of blows exchanged, iron grating iron. Ullen fumbled to draw his sword left-handed. Then an impact into his back like the clout of a sledgehammer. Cold iron slid deep inside him. Gasping, he turned to see a woman, her long white hair wild in the wind, eyes slitted, lips snarling. A flash of silvery-grey then that head tilted, falling, blood jetting, body jerking. Ullen fell as well.

Starry night sky then Captain Moss leaning over him, saying something, but all Ullen could hear was his pulse roaring in his ears. He couldn't breathe! He strained, but nothing would enter his burning, aching lungs. Damn! This wasn't *right*.

What of—

Couldn't he—

The roaring pulse slowed. Night closed, obscuring Moss's face, his mouth moving. One beat sounded like a heavy, slow hammer echoing.

Wait—

CHAPTER III

Vision dims, memory fades,
All forestalled is discounted,
And so returns upon the ignorant
In violent refrain.

Lessons from the field of the Crossroads
Waden Burdeth, Unta

KYLE, K'AZZ AND THE LOST BROTHERS FOUND THAT A
flotilla of makeshift rafts had been pulled up along the north
shore of the Idryn. Lying sprawled on the approach to the
Pilgrim Bridge and piled in its mouth lay a trail of slaughtered
Kanese soldiery. Facing the dead was one Crimson Guardsman. He
was leaning against the stone wall of the bridge, legs wide, sword
planted before him, his body and limbs feathered in arrows.

'Baker,' K'azz said, his voice thick.

The man stirred, his head rising. A sad smile crept up beneath long,
tangled ginger hair. 'M'Lord.' He struggled weakly to straighten.

The Guard commander eased him back. 'Stay here,' he ordered
gently. 'We need you to guard the north.'

A wry smile pulled Baker's mouth to one side. 'Oh, aye, sir.'

The brothers were collecting shields from among the fallen. Kyle
joined them. Each held as many as they could carry under both arms.
Kyle offered one to K'azz who took it with a bob of his head. They
jogged up the bridge.

Ahead, a deep sonorous roar, like the continuous detonation of
thunder, raised the hair on Kyle's neck and arms. It was a low,
reverberating, animal growl of anticipation uttered from thousands
of throats, so loud it almost drowned out the clangour of weapons

clashing and shields striking. They met the struggle near the bridge's mid-point. Four Avowed, back legs braced, faced the pressing solid wedge of Kanese infantry. Shield thrust against shield, spears and other pole-weapons jabbed, while a fifth Avowed remained a step back, watching, resting. Armour hung hacked and torn from all, helmets battered, arms black with drying gore. The rear Avowed, a short, broad woman, saluted them. The side of her head glistened, one raw wound; her sliced scalp hung down as a flap. Underfoot lay a litter of broken shields, fallen swords, spears, lances, arrows and shattered pieces of armour. Blood darkened the set stones of the bridge crimson.

'You are most welcome, my Lord!' the woman shouted to be heard through the din. 'But we didn't call for reinforcements.' The woman frowned then, eyeing K'azz up and down. 'Being away didn't agree with you, I think. But you should leave. We will hold until we fall!'

'So will I! Good to see you too, Lean.' K'azz readied his shield, raised his long-knife. Other than this, the man was unarmed. Lean shook her head. 'No – you're reserve.' She nodded to Kyle and the cousins. 'Don't I know you?'

'Stalker, Coots, Badlands, Kyle,' K'azz shouted. 'They're up to it.'

'Wecome, brothers!' She pointed to the Avowed hacking at the exposed front line of massed soldiery, rank upon rank of which held spears and javelins which they raised high or thrust at the defenders in a forest of jabbing, waving stalks. 'Amatt, Cole, Black and Turgal.'

There was room for only eight or so Kan soldiers to stand shoulder to shoulder, though the layered ranks behind could reach with spears and halberds. Lean bashed her own spear to her shield and the four Avowed yielded a step, adjusted their footing and hunkered down. The Kan soldiery surged forward to be met by quick ruthless thrusts from the Avowed. Their wounded and fallen comrades choked and encumbered all those who struggled forward to fill the ranks. Eyeing the fighting, Stalker threw down his load of shields. He kept one and picked up a fallen spear. Instinctively, the brothers followed suit, as did Kyle.

Lean paced back and forth behind the defending Avowed, keeping close watch, and perhaps making sure K'azz did not push forward to join the line. She tapped Black on the back of his leg, waved Badlands forward.

'Relief!'

Black curled away, spinning, and the startled Badlands was caught surprised. But he leapt forward, knocking aside the hafts of jabbing spears to thrust himself in, bulling in with all his weight. Lean watched narrowly, gauging.

Stalker came and touched Kyle's arm. He pointed to his waist: 'Use that.'

Kyle glanced to the sword strapped into the outsized scabbard. His gift from Osserc; he hadn't even drawn it yet. 'No reach,' he yelled back.

'It must be something!' Stalker answered.

Kyle shrugged.

One by one Lean relieved the Avowed until only Cole – whom Kyle recognized from Kurzan – remained, and it was Kyle's turn. K'azz objected but apparently Lean was in charge of this particular contingent and so her judgement ruled. The relieved Avowed, Black, Amatt and Turgal, stood panting, faces glistening. They bore horrific wounds; Amatt coughed up blood; Black's iron cuirass leaked blood at every overlapping band; Turgal, who bore a huge Malazan infantryman's rectangular shield, had it strapped to his mangled, broken left arm.

His turn coming, Kyle readied his spear, tucking it tightly under his arm. He was suddenly deathly thirsty but knew that while he needed water it was best to be thirsty in case of a stomach wound. He tried not to think of what was about to come, and Lean, perhaps sensing his gathering dread, did not wait. 'Relief!' she bellowed, and Cole ducked away. Kyle lunged forward. Almost immediately his spear entangled amid the forest of jabbing, swinging pole weapons. Strikes on his shield rocked him, numbing his arm and shoulder. He could not bring his weapon to bear. It was hung up, useless.

The Hooded One's laughter! He was going to die, spitted like a boar.

Javelins thrust around him, Lean and others driving back the ranks for him to straighten out his spear. He recovered, bending forward into the press. From the edges of his vision he saw that the Lost brothers were up to the challenge. Coots and Badlands fought like grinning, savage dogs, at home in their element, while Stalker was calm, pacing himself, yielding nothing. They were holding their ground and again Kyle wondered: who were these men seemingly equal to the Avowed in their strength, ferocity and endurance?

As for himself . . . Kyle and the Kanese soldiery opposite both sensed almost immediately that he was the weak link in this line. A thrown javelin cannoned from his helmet, briefly stunning him. A solid blow to his shield snapped it backwards to smack into his forehead, sending blazing agony across his vision. Blinking, everything a blur, he missed a strike to his own haft that levered his spear from his grip. The two Kanese facing him and the ranks behind roared, surging forward. Hands steadied him from behind, javelins thrusting. In a panic Kyle pulled his sword free, snapping the straps that kept the slim curved blade in the scabbard. He brought it up, fending off thrusting, clanging spears and halberds, and was dumbfounded as the dark golden blade cut through each haft as easily as if passing through a candle.

The Kanese flinched away, eyes huge under the lips of their helmets. The severed hafts clattered to the stones, loud in the sudden silence. 'Beru Bless us!' Lean cursed behind him, awed.

Osserc's own weapon! Could it be, truly?

Kyle edged forward, recovering his lost footing. He crouched down behind his shield. *Now I am ready.* Beside him Coots and Badlands exchanged savage, elated grins.

Kyle remained in line while the others traded off. After his blade sliced shields in half and shattered swords no one would face him. The respite allowed the Avowed to recover, though for Black and Amatt the fight was over. Loss of blood left them unable to stand. The rest traded off in quick succession and in this system, presided over ruthlessly by Lean, they held.

K'azz was in communication with Shimmer through the Brethren. She reported that Skinner and his remaining Avowed had quit the field, abandoning their remaining loyal Guardsmen regulars. Shimmer and the majority of the surviving Guard had established a strongpoint. She claimed to have reached a temporary truce with the Imperials. In any case, the Wickans that had smashed Skinner's command now merely encircled Shimmer, content with containment. Later K'azz reported that Shimmer expected formal negotiations to begin any time and that they had to hold off the Kanese in order that she could press for as favourable terms as possible. K'azz concurred.

Just after this report from Shimmer, Kanese horsemen came fording laboriously up the middle of the bridge. They forced their way through the press of soldiers like ships over a heavy sea, beating their way through the men with switches and kicks. At a bellowed command from the leading figure the infantry stepped back, spears levelled. Into the resultant ringing silence the fellow yelled, 'Who commands here?'

'I do!' Lean answered, stepping forward. She pushed her scalp up and pressed it in place.

He drew off his helmet. He was a dark fellow with a neatly trimmed moustache and beard. He bowed as well as he could while mounted. 'Commander Pirim 'J Shall at your service.' He motioned to the rider behind: 'Invigilator Durmis.' The robed man bowed far more awkwardly, his pained gaze fixed far beyond them to the north cliffs.

'We commend you, Guardsmen, on a heroic defence – though it has cost us dear. But we come bringing news. Are you by any chance in communication with the main body to the north?'

An unsure glance back from Lean. 'We are.'

'Then, the Invigilator Durmis is most insistent—'

'What do they sense?' the robed man cut in.

'Sense?'

'Yes, damn you! Inquire through your Brethren.'

Lean glanced back again, bloodied brows wrinkled. K'azz nodded. 'A moment,' she reported.

K'azz straightened, calling, 'They report disturbances among the Warrens.'

'And growing,' the Invigilator added. 'Something is coming blasting its way through the Warrens like a collapsing tower and it's headed right for here!'

Commander waved a hand deprecatingly. 'He may be exaggerating . . . the Invigilator's job is to be wary of such irresponsible abuses among the men and women you name *Talents* – such as may threaten our Confederacy. A main reason, by the way, why we did not resort to such extreme measures to eliminate you from our path. For to do so would be to invite retaliation and escalation from your formidable Avowed mage cadre, yes? Thus costing us significantly more personnel than otherwise, yes?' A smug smile. 'In any case, the office's more *enthusiastic* members have been known from time to time—'

Invigilator Durmis kneed his mount to bump into the commander's. 'This is real,' he ground out.

'Like the warning earlier this night? Of impending thaumaturgic transgression? The mere arrival of a few horsemen?'

'Who knows who they could have been? They may have been allies of the Guard! In any case, those horsemen won the battle for the Empress.'

'A point curiously moot to us here on this bridge!'

Lean cleared her throat. 'Gentlemen! We are still in parley?'

Commander Pirim returned his attention to the front. He pulled on his long, cream-hued jupon to straighten it, adjusted his helmet under his arm. 'Invigilator Durmis insisted upon this exchange of intelligence. To my mind formalities have been observed. We are done.' He bowed.

Lean answered the bow, her hand still pressed to her head.

The commander struggled to turn his mount and, from the gathering rage and dismay on his face, found that he could not. He cut his switch viciously at the men pressed in around him. 'Make way, damn you! Way!'

Lean turned an arched brow on Kyle and those of the line. Coots gave a mocking hoot. Invigilator Durmis, however, remained motionless on his mount. He sat slumped, hands folded before him. 'It is here,' he said, sounding defeated.

Kyle risked a quick glance behind. Above the cliffs the night sky of the north-west seemed to swirl, stars rippling. A pink and orange glow gathered, streaming into banners and crown-like circles that widened, fading. 'What is it?' he breathed.

Then a flash like an immense distant fire blossoming only to be snuffed out. Shortly afterwards a muted roll of thunder reached them. Lean looked to K'azz. 'Something has struck the battlefield,' he reported. 'Cut a swath through units on the west flank. Left a trail of wreckage.'

Commander Pirim's brows rose in almost comical surprise and alarm. He looked to Lean. 'I suggest a truce – for the time being.'

Lean bobbed her head, wincing. 'Agreed.'

*   *   *

Whether the sea would swallow Ho and his mage escapee companions had become immaterial. As Yath's control over the disparate chords of his ritual participants gradually asserted itself he took steps to protect the vessel. A cocoon of power edged round its sides. Through the barrier's pulsing multicoloured walls the sea appeared to have been left behind – the *Forlorn* seemed to float on nothing.

Sighing her profound relief, Devaleth sat with a heavy thump next to Ho. She massaged her hands. Sweat coursed down her ashen face. Unnerving groans now sounded from the vessel as timbers creaked, popping and flexing. The masts shivered, their tops shorn off where they met the aurora of power above. The deck juddered beneath them and she and Ho shared uneasy glances.

'Where are we?' Treat asked of Fingers, hushed.

'Serc,' the mage whispered.

A scream made everyone jump. One of the ritual mages had leapt to his feet. He pointed at Yath, mouthed something unintelligible. Two of the Avowed, Dim and Reed, stepped in to calm him. He wrenched his arms from their grasp, clasped his hands to his head, all the while howling his own personal horror. The Avowed fought to subdue him but incredibly the skinny fellow pushed them aside. He gouged at his face as if he would tear it open then in two long steps reached the side and threw himself over. His shriek was cut short as he passed beyond the barrier.

'Otataral madness,' Devaleth said to no one in particular.

'Perhaps . . .' Su answered, her black, wrinkled eyes almost narrowed shut. Ho turned to snarl another warning about her damned airs but stopped, realizing that her gaze was fixed upon Yath, and that the man's sharp glittering eyes returned her steady stare.

'I have identified the disturbance,' Su announced, her gaze unwavering upon Yath.

'Yes?' Ho asked.

'It is a general contagion that infects almost all of us to greater and lesser degrees. But which is concentrated mainly in two carriers . . .'

Yath slowly straightened from his cross-legged position. He levelled his staff across his front. A wide, hungry smile crept up his lips.

'Yes?' Ho asked again, vexed. 'Who?'

'Its two main foci are our Seven Cities friend and . . .' she turned her head aside, pointed, '. . . him.'

Across the stern Blues' brows rose. He pointed to himself. 'What? Me?'

'Oh yes . . .'

Yath pointed his staff at Reed; the Avowed looked to Blues, unsure. An aura identical to that of the shifting walls surrounding them lashed out from the staff to strike Reed who shrieked, writhing. Before their eyes the mage-fire consumed him, leaving a blackened smoking corpse.

'. . . And we have made a terrible error,' Su finished quickly.

'*Queen take him!*' Blues was up, his speed incredible to Ho. He was halfway across the deck before Yath could bring his staff to bear. Pink and violet fire arched. Blues raised his Warren in answer and the energy deflected, splashing like water. It recoiled outwards to spread in a fan that sliced into the barrier around them – which burst.

The deck fell out from beneath everyone. Ho clasped his arms around Su and Devaleth, pinning them to the side, grasping handholds. Figures flew off screaming into the infinite nothingness of all directions, though none of the ritual-bound mages shifted at all. Yath had fallen and struggled to reorient himself. An Avowed, Dim, was close. The man was belaying himself by rope toward the Seven City mage.

'Steady us!' Ho shouted aloud to everyone.

'I'm on it!' Fingers answered.

Dim closed on the Seven Cities mage, reaching out. Then Sessin was there, leaping from behind Yath to grapple the Avowed. The men swung wildly together, only Dim's grip holding them to the vessel. They fought, grappling and gouging as they flew – then gone, both spinning away in silence. The deck rose up to brutally knock the breath from Ho.

Yath lashed power again, catching Blues unready, but the stream of raw inchoate energy passed through him leaving him unharmed. Both Blues and Yath straightened, astonished. Blues stared at himself, uncomprehending.

'Get 'im!' Treat urged from the tiller.

Blues lunged. Yath stood now amid the sitting ritual-bound mages, all as still as statues. He swung his staff and a wall of the rippling power cut across the deck. Blues, Treat and Sept all struck it, rebounding. The Seven Cities mage laughed behind his barrier.

At Ho's side Fingers lay prostrate, his face contorted in a grimace of effort. 'Can't keep this up for ever, people,' he ground through bared and clenched teeth.

'Get us out of here!' Ho bellowed to everyone.

'Where?' Devaleth snarled.

'Anywhere!'

'You wish to go?' Yath called, his voice hollow-sounding through the coruscating banner of power. 'I will take us somewhere – though I do not think you will much care for it, my friends!' and he laughed anew, gesturing. The distances became opaque, darkening, taking on a grey-green tinge like an eerie nightfall. The vessel eased gently down on to something, canting to one side. Fingers let out a grateful gasp, his arms and clawed hands unclenching, and he sagged. A roaring, grinding noise like a waterfall swelled to smother all other sounds. A stink assaulted Ho, making his gorge rise. Treat, near the side, flinched away, pointing: 'What in Hood's own dread is *that*?'

Ho stood. They were sliding down a tilted flow of some fluid. It reminded him of a lava flow only clotted, streaked in pus-like yellow and sickly green. Figures writhed within, melting and re-forming, gesturing and beckoning only to fall back into the churning stuff from which they arose. 'The edge of Chaos,' Ho said.

'*Yes!*' Yath answered. 'You invade my lands spreading death and destruction! It is only fitting that I bring a taste of such *chaos* in return!' He opened his arms. 'My lands have been cursed with it . . . Now it is your turn! From here I shall bring such a plague upon your continent that you will never rise again!' He turned his back, raised his arms high, staff clenched over his head.

Forming another portal – this time leading directly to Quon. Ho found himself staring at the Wickan witch. 'What can we do?'

'Nothing. We haven't the power. He commands the might of some twenty mages. We are only a few.'

'Nothing? *Nothing!*'

Su eyed him sidelong. Her wrinkled mouth pulled up in a mocking smile. 'Who am I to say, Ho? Are you not the expert here? Did you not walk these very shores?'

Damn her! How can she know these things? 'Very well.' He raised his voice. 'Blues, Fingers, Devaleth! Join us.'

It was not a ritual; Ho would hardly propose such an effort given its latest employment. Rather, it was a parallel focusing. Each readied themselves to contribute their strength to forestalling the creation of a solid enduring bridge from this place to Yath's intended destination – wherever exactly that may be.

As they worked, the vessel tilted ever more severely to the bow until they resorted to gripping the stern. Treat and Sept roped them to the sides, the tiller and the gunwale. The *Forlorn* picked up speed, sliding, grating, down the flow of unformed chaotic matter. Ho wondered whether the shapes they'd witnessed were its inhabitants, or prisoners. Mage, perhaps, caught attempting to manipulate the potential of the inchoate materia – as he himself had dared so long ago.

Ahead an opening on to darkness tore through the flow, bisecting it. Ho glimpsed stars – a night sky? The vessel canted even more precipitously, almost vertical, then pitched within. Ho had the brief impression of falling into nothingness. He reached out then for what Su, Blues and Devaleth were prepared to offer and almost recoiled. *Such capacity! It approached even his own. Beru, do not let him be seduced! No wonder none were willing to offer themselves to Yath!*

'Hang on!'

Plummeting through a whistling, howling wind. An instant explosion of crashing, splintering timbers. An agonizing blow. Tumbling. Nothing.

Nait was sitting with Urfa and Bowl and a few other saboteur sergeants watching their boys and girls trying to get fires going to cook a hot meal. Heuk's darkness still coursed above their position but it was fraying gently, dissipating. Nait figured it'd be gone by dawn. Heuk himself slept still, curled up nearby, a dopey drooling smile on his face, jug clenched tighter than a pricey hired girl, or boy. Nait was all ready to fall asleep too when Urfa sent a bulging, cross-eyed look his way and motioned aside.

There came the Sword of the Empire himself, bandaged and bloodied, armour clattering all bashed and battered, marching up to the officer's fire followed by his guard of lieutenants and captains. Nait hung his head. *Gods no – please don't fuck us up!*

'Why are we not moving?' the man demanded so loud everyone on the slope could hear. 'I gave the order that we march! The Guard remain on the field. We must attack!'

Faces turned among the assembled saboteurs from where they argued over the best way to start the fires. They'd been comparing tinder boxes and flints, slow-burning coal sticks wrapped in leather, goose-down and lint ember beds, and all the while the fires remained unstruck. *Oh, oh.* Nait pushed himself up and motioned Urfa and Bowl to come. The three ambled over to where captains Tinsmith, Kepp and Blossom all struggled to their feet. Kepp and Blossom helped Tinsmith up with a padded stick that had been fashioned as a crutch.

'Yes, Sword?' Tinsmith offered.

'Why have the orders for the troops to assemble not been conveyed?' Korbolo demanded, enunciating his words with great care.

'Move out – where? Sir?' Tinsmith inquired.

The Napan commander jabbed an arm to the west. 'West! A Guard strongpoint remains! They could attack us at any moment. They must be eradicated. Slain to a man!'

Tinsmith thoughtfully ran a thumb and forefinger along his silver moustache. 'Messages indicate they have effectively withdrawn, Sword,' he said with all reasonableness.

Korbolo stepped right up to the captain. His mouth twisted in a frown of exaggerated disappointment. 'You are not refusing a direct order, are you, Captain?' he asked, his voice now very soft. 'Because I will have you arrested. And then, tomorrow, after we have killed them all, I, Korbolo Dom, Sword of the Empire, will be proclaimed victor over the Crimson Guard. Defeater of Skinner. And I will have you and your entire command crucified. Believe me – I've done it before. Now . . . move out.'

A salute from Tinsmith. 'Hail the Sword.'

Korbolo answered the salute. 'Very good, Captain. Carry on.' He marched off followed by his troop leaving Tinsmith hopping in place and studying his crutch. Nait and Urfa and Bowl ran up together with other sergeants. Everyone spoke at once, complaining, threatening, refusing to move. Many pointed in the direction of the sleeping Heuk. Tinsmith, Kepp and Blossom raised their hands for calm.

'We've no choice,' Tinsmith said, curtly. 'Make a stretcher for the mage. We'll take him with us. I want a column of infantry with skirmishers surrounding. At the first sign of trouble we scoot back here. OK?'

Nait could only shake his head at the awesome, monumental stupidity of it all. *He'd managed it: he'd fucked them up.*

Nait opted to range with the skirmishers, leaving Heuk to be carried within the ranks. This squad didn't march so much as skulk, spread out, crossbows readied, hunched. A faint lightening brushed the eastern horizon; the stars were dimmer there. Nait cast quick glances over his people. They'd been lucky, lost only two: Kal and the lad, Poot. The lad hurt the worst. Not because he was young 'n' all that, but because it had been friendly fire. In all the ruckus of people jumping the trench, climbing in and out, someone's crossbow had been jiggled and it fired right next to his head. No warning at all. That had been a hard one for everyone to take.

Thankfully, this portion of the field was relatively empty. The worst was just south where fires still burned and kites and other bold night-feeders wheeled. They'd crossed most of the field when a contingent of horsemen came pounding out of the dark. 'Hold fire! Hold fire!' Nait heard sergeants bellow among the skirmishers. It was a troop of Wickan lancers. They pulled up, halting.

'Who commands?' one shouted – an old veteran. In fact, they all looked like hard-travelled veterans.

'Sword of the Empire,' came the answering shout. 'Korbolo Dom.'

The Wickans gaped, motionless, then hands went to sheathed long-knives and other weapons. Wickan curses sounded. 'What name was that?' the old spokesman asked again as if unbelieving.

'Mine!' Korbolo came walking up from the column. 'What news?'

The grey-haired old veteran rested his forearms on the pommel of his high saddle and studied the man with something akin to amazement. Finally, after a time, he shook his head and spat aside as if to ease his mouth of a sour taste. 'You are bold and brave, I give you that. How does it feel, murderer, to be in our debt?'

Korbolo appeared supremely untroubled. 'I am in no one's debt. I am the Sword of the Empire – I command *all* Imperial forces.'

'Well for us, then, that according to your own Empress, we are not Imperial forces. Yet you owe your victory to us. I wonder, then, what recompense the Throne might offer to repay such a debt, yes?'

The Sword's smile of self-assurance was almost a smirk. 'Such matters are for the Empress to judge.'

'Indeed. And she and the army all bore witness to what happened this night.' The Wickan sawed his reins around and the troop stormed off.

Nait watched them go. Boy, a lot of history there. Official word was that the Wickans up at Seven Cities had betrayed Imperial interests and Korbolo barely managed to salvage the whole theatre. For himself, Nait didn't believe a word of it; and this confrontation clinched things for him. The Wickans had treated Korbolo as the traitor. He turned to his squad who stood watching the retreating horsemen. 'Move out! Let's go! Got ground to cover.'

Ahead, the plain rose slightly in a series of modest hills. One held the retreat of the remaining Crimson Guard. Some three thousand, he'd heard; who knew how many Avowed. Surrounding the hill was Fist D'Ebbin's command plus all the Talian and Falaran and other elements that had joined up with him through the night. The Wickan cavalry circled as well, appearing ready to charge the hill all on their own. But no arrows or crossbow bolts flew. The Guard had withdrawn to behind their shieldwall; the Imperials merely maintained their encirclement.

Kibb sidled up next to him. The lad puffed beneath the unaccustomed weight of all his new armour plus the burden of his crossbow, shield, munitions shoulder-bag and a whacking great scabbarded Grisan bastard-sword, the bronze-capped tip of which scraped along the ground behind him. 'What're we gonna do?' he asked.

'You're carrying too much gear, soldier.'

'Wasn't plannin' on any marching. We're not gonna attack, are we? I mean, we got lucky once – no point pushin' it.'

Nait laughed. 'Listen to you. You was ready to piss in everyone's eye, now you just want to keep your head low. You're all grown up.'

The lad flinched away, bristling. 'Piss on you!'

Nait continued laughing, walking along. Wasn't it cute the way they got all huffy. The chuckling slowly died in his throat as he peered ahead. The sky was looking all strange over the west. Green, yellow and pink lights blossomed there like the ones that sometimes glowed in the north, but smaller, much more contained. A breeze brushed his face, stirred the trampled, broken stalks of the grass. He raised a fist for a halt, knelt. What was this? Some Avowed mage counter-attack?

The column had halted as well, shields being unslung. Nait spotted Urfa's bunch and waved them over. She ducked down next to him. 'What is it?'

'Oponn's own trouble.'

'No kidding. What're we going to do?'

Nait scanned the empty slope – not enough cover for an emaciated rat. 'Don't know.'

'What about your old boy, the wonder mage?'

'He's sleepin' it off. Wouldn't wake even for Hood.'

'Well . . .' She pointed west. 'I think he's coming.'

The aura brightened, thickening. A wind swelled out of the west. *Something big comin' their way.* Then a flash like sheet lightning blinded him. He glanced aside, wincing, as did everyone. An explosion made him drop to the ground. In the distance something huge slammed into the earth, impacting, shaking, crashing in the cacophony of a huge object dissolving into shards. The ground shook beneath Nait. The juddering continued, closing like the constant reports of a thunderstorm on its way. A shape rolled towards them as a mass of churning dirt and pale things flashing. Then it, slowed, falling, sliding, and the blossoming dust-cloud enveloped it, obscuring everything from view.

An eerie silence followed in which rocks clattered, ground shifted, tumbling and sighing. Nait shaded his eyes, blinking back tears.

The great cloud of dust and thrown earth enveloped them. As it slowly drifted away he saw that a bite had been taken out of the shoulder of the hill the Guard held. The bite extended down in a long gouge that cut a swath through Fist D'Ebbin's lines to carry on, shallowing, in a trail of smashed timber to the wreckage of what appeared to be the tangled remains of an actual sailing ship, here, practically at the very centre of the continent.

He stood and stared, as did his squad one after the other together with nearby skirmishers. 'What do we do?' Urfa asked, wonder filling her voice, her askew eyes fairly goggling out of her skull.

'I don't know.'

Movement: someone walking, staggering, out of the shattered

ruins. Nait and Urfa exchanged looks of awed amazement. *Trake's balls! Who might this be?* The figure returned to the wreckage, and then emerged dragging another. That broke the spell for Nait. 'Let's go,' he yelled. 'Help them out!' The squads and skirmishers jogged for the broken tumble of shattered timber.

It was a broad, heavy-set woman. She was struggling to return to the ruins but was now unable to walk straight. She was obviously in shock. Her face was a mass of torn and bruised flesh; she was practically naked and, bizarrely, her head was unevenly shaved. Nait grasped her shoulders. 'What's your name? What happened?'

She blinked, her mouth worked, mumbling, dribbled bloody spit. 'Stop,' she managed.

'Stop? Stop what? What do you mean?'

'Stop . . . him.' And she sat heavily, her limbs twitching. More survivors appeared, being dragged from the shell, all dressed alike in rags, with hair hacked short or shaved as well. *Too intact – they should've all been shredded like the vessel. Must've been protected by magery.*

Two men came running up, dressed just like the ship's crew. One's arm was a lacerated, tattered thing of red flesh, creamy bone, and hanging sinew, but he appeared to be ignoring what would otherwise be an instantly fatal injury to any other human. The other pressed a hand to his side where a length of slivered wood pierced completely through his torso. Blood soaked his front and that leg. *Avowed! Must be.* 'Find him!' this one bellowed, almost weeping his pain. 'An old man – a Seven Cities native! Find him!'

'Just sit down!' Nait yelled, running up. Behind them a troop of Wickans was closing.

'Find him! Kill him!' and he wept, his face contorted in agony. His companion's eyes rolled up all white and he tottered, fell to his knees, then his side. Nait reached the impaled fellow then stopped – he had absolutely no idea what to do. 'Healer!' he yelled. Then he yelped as the fellow had somehow closed and yanked Nait's own shortsword from his scabbard. Armed, he started limping for the wreck. 'Wait! Kill who? Why?'

From behind the vessel's remains violet fire lashed out to strike the closing Wickans in a swath of incandescent destruction. Horses and men flew, spinning. The ground itself shook with the concussion and Nait staggered.

'*Him,*' the man snarled. Cursing, he stopped, grasped hold of the jagged shard of wood as long as a sword, and, with a scream, drew it out.

'Who *are* you?' Nait breathed.

'Ho. Now, get your men – kill him, now!'

Nait signed to the skirmishers to open fire. They hunched, scuttled forward. Violet fire arced into the sky to carve a bright streak across the night. Everyone watched. It hurtled up and over them, curving down to smash into the column. Its churning energies cut a swath some five men wide through the massed ranks. The unit broke like a shattered cup. Knots of men ran in all directions – most back east. *Keep runnin' lads – seek cover – 'cause that worst has just arrived.*

Ho held out an arm. 'Take me to the others.' Nait took his sword back and helped him walk. May came running up, hunched, hands all wet with blood from treating wounds. 'Dig in!' Nait bellowed over the roar of coursing power. She saluted, ran off.

Nait led the man to where the ship's survivors had been collected. Here lay the resilient heavy-set woman and another woman, an elderly Wickan; the fellow with the savaged arm; a young fellow who was even more battered and twisted; and two other blood-smeared, lacerated and traumatized survivors. Healers from among the Untan volunteer ranks and a few from the Malazan regulars were busy at work on them, stopping bleeding, hands pressed to bruised flesh.

'Is this it?'

Clenching down on his pain, Ho said in a tight voice, 'Yes. And many of these here are of the Guard.'

'We happen to be fighting them,' Nait observed, neutrally.

'We'll need them.'

Nait didn't bother asking what for. 'What about you? You need a healer.'

'No – I'm . . . getting better.'

Nait stepped up to the man, examined his naked side where beneath the drying blood and fluids only a pink scar remained of what had been a gouge worse than a sword thrust. *Who – what – was this fellow?*

Nait helped the man sit in the grass then turned to watch the skirmishers. They'd taken cover around the sides of the wreckage, firing at something a way east ahead of the pile. They popped up from the grass, fired, then dropped back down again. *Damned prairie dogs, is what they are. That's it! The Prairie Dogs.*

He was about to congratulate himself when the ground wavered beneath him and he staggered. A curved wall of the dark-blue fire billowed out towards the vessel, scattering the irregulars, erupting the grasses in flame. Nait dived for cover. Something cast an eerie shadow over everything, climbing higher, and he gaped up at a dark mar or bruise in the night sky, coalescing, darkening, seeming to flow inward.

Nait yelled to the men and women staring, gaping upwards, '*Dig in!*'

* * *

Kyle and the Lost brothers did not relinquish their line. They remained standing, weapons ready, while the Kanese likewise stood ready, spears and halberds standing tall. Each force eyed the other. The mounted officers sat examining the north sky, the invigilator still and intent, the commander sighing his boredom and brushing at his surcoat. Kyle stole quick glances as well, seeing nothing more than strange lights in the sky. After a time, the invigilator, Durmis, sucked a loud breath through his teeth, his face puckering his alarm. Even the commander's face appeared troubled. Kyle risked a look. Some kind of dark aura flickered in the lightening sky. No stars were visible through it. Renewed thunder reached them and the bridge shook ever so slightly.

'Remain here if you wish,' the invigilator called out, 'but we will not take our forces into *that*.' To the commander: 'Order the men back, set up a line of defence on the south shore.'

The commander tapped his gauntlets to his thigh, frowning. 'On your authority?'

'Yes, on my authority!'

An insouciant shrug. 'Very well. If we must.' He raised a hand, signalling. Horns blew from the rear. Among the massed forces on the shore signal flags rose, waving. The commander saluted Lean, tilted his head in acknowledgement of their stand. Lean bobbed her own, her face pained.

After a great deal of trouble and reshuffling, the commander, the invigilator and their guards succeeded in turning their mounts. They bulled their way back across the bridge while the ranks closed behind.

Kyle heard Lean ask, 'Should we go?'

'We'll wait,' K'azz replied.

Coots and Badlands sat, took out stones and began cleaning up the edges of their weapons. Coots even whistled a tune. Kyle examined his: unmarred, the blade a thin curve of some dark yellow material, not metal, almost translucent at its edge. He sheathed it, wrapped the cords around its long grip – he'd have to get a new scabbard damned soon.

Stalker came up, examining his dented domed helmet in his hands. 'A hard fight. Well done.'

'Thanks. Now what?'

The scout motioned to the north. 'That thing – something's got to be done about it.'

Kyle was puzzled. 'You a mage?'

A snort. 'Great Darkness, no. Just have a feel for these things. Runs in my family.'

'So? What do we do?'

'Us?' He shook his head. His long dirty-blond hair hung lank and tangled with sweat. 'Nothing. This is for the mages. But they might need cover.'

The Kanese continued to retreat. The rear ranks backed away, spears levelled, watching them closely as they went. The Avowed, Kyle and the Lost brothers all cast quick glances to K'azz, waiting. Skins of water made the rounds. A pinpoint of light suddenly appeared on the bridge and everyone straightened, hands going to weapons. The pinpoint swelled to a swirling, glowing whirlpool out of which stepped a short, skinny fellow in dirty tattered robes with wild kinky hair. Kyle smiled to see Smoky again.

The mage went to embrace K'azz but stopped short. His broad smile twisted down into anxious puzzlement. K'azz waved the man's concern aside. 'It looks worse than it is.' He squeezed the mage's shoulders. 'Good to see you again.'

'And you.'

'What news?'

'It's ugly. Shimmer's gathered all the remaining mages. Good news is that Blues and Fingers are with us – they're battered but alive.'

K'azz froze, his smile faltering. 'I . . . I didn't know they were missing.'

Smoky cursed himself. 'Sorry—'

'It's all right. I know I have a lot of catching up to do.' He turned to Lean. 'Well done. What do you think? Detail dismissed?'

Lean bowed, grinning. She raised her helmet and very slowly, and with great care, pulled it over her bloodied head. 'Detail stand down!'

Cole scooped up Black in his arms. Amatt gently lifted Turgal. Lean gathered up gear, as did Stalker, Badlands and Coots. Smoky came to Kyle, looked him up and down while nodding his approval. 'We owe you an apology and our gratitude.' He held out a hand. Kyle took it, feeling self-conscious. 'And we owe you more than we could ever repay.'

Kyle winced. 'Don't say that.'

Smoky laughed. 'Ah, yes, right. Very good. All the same, thank you.' He returned to the swirling Warren portal, waved everyone through. Kyle came through last. As he lifted a foot in and leant forward all he had was a fleeting impression of bright blinding light, heated dry air, then he stepped down clumsily on to crackling, dry, trampled grasses. The noise of a crowded camp under siege assaulted him.

Dawn was just a short time away yet darkness clung to the battered and churned slopes around him. It seemed to be concentrated over the far side of the field, clinging to its edges as if reluctant to yield to the gathering light. Another smear or dark cloud occluded the centre. It hovered over ruins that appeared to have been tossed across the entire slope.

Kyle peered around, uncertain where to go or what to do. Everyone seemed to have disappeared. What he wanted to do was sleep, but it looked as if there was little chance of that for anyone. Ogilvy jogged up, a toothy grin twisting his round face. He grasped Kyle's shoulders and shook him. 'Well done, lad! Well done. Glad to see you back with us!'

His old sergeant, Trench, appeared to wave him forward. The man squeezed his shoulder. 'Sorry, lad – had no idea.' Kyle waved it aside. 'Anyway, you've been promoted. K'azz wants you. This way.'

Trench led him across the hill. As they walked a shout went up and the Crimson Guard soldiery hunched, ducking for cover. Kyle looked around, surprised, and saw an arcing blue catapult-like fireball or lance streaking for their position. Trench pulled him down. The assault appeared to have originated from the dark occlusion marring the air in the middle of the field.

The lightning, or whatever it was, hammered down just short of their position. It impacted, searing the ground, throwing up a storm of smoke and dust. It gouged through ranks of the besieging force, throwing bodies, doll-like, into the air, spinning to disappear consumed by its awesome raw energies. Its roaring assaulted Kyle's hearing like a firestorm and waterfall combined. Just as suddenly it snapped away, making Kyle stagger as he'd been bracing himself against it. It left behind a great ragged scar of burnt black ash and scoured dirt. *Great Spirits! What can one do against such an awesome thing? Was this the much vaunted Malazan firepower of which he'd heard so much?* Yet it had struck a Malazan entrenchment. As Kyle stared, another of the lashes arced out to the opposite side, descending to the far edge of the field. Trench touched his elbow, starting him from his trance. The sergeant motioned ahead.

It was a meeting at which Kyle felt completely out of place. Stalker and the Lost brothers were gone – ducked out, probably. The only one he knew even vaguely was Smoky. It was a meeting of mages and commanders. Shimmer presided, K'azz next to her. Mages Kyle barely knew were in evidence. He learned names as they talked: Lor-Sinn, Shell and Opal, all female and hardened-looking veteran battle mages. Gwynn, also, whom Kyle knew as one of Skinner's mages. Bald with a goatee and gold earrings, all in black. Apparently he'd parted ways with his old commander. In all, some six Avowed mages.

Over the course of conversation it became clear that they were just holding their own. Deflecting the assaults was taking all their effort. In fact, Shimmer had made an overture to the Imperials regarding a pooling of resources and was expecting an answer. Seemed last night the Malazans had unveiled a High Mage whom no one had known of, but who had impressed everyone mightily.

A messenger ran up, spoke with Shimmer who nodded. She addressed the group: 'The Malazan representatives.' Room was made in the circle. The contingent was only three: two adolescents, skinny with long gangly limbs, long mussed black hair, almost identical. Twins? They were young, yes, but their lined guarded faces spoke of experiences and a maturity far beyond their years. The third was a broad, thickly-muscled older man with short grey hair bearing the bruising and gashes of many treated wounds. His wide brutal features were set in a savage scowl. K'azz, Shimmer and other Avowed all bowed to the man. 'Commander Urko. Welcome.'

The older man gestured to his companions: 'Nil and Nether. Now, what do you propose?'

'Cooperation. Together we can defend all our people from these attacks. But we must pull together.' Shimmer nodded to the youngsters. 'You have two Wickans with you, what of your mage cadre?'

'They defend the east redoubt and all the soldiers who have taken shelter there.'

'I see. So, just us.'

Urko cracked the knuckles of his large scarred hands. 'I hear talk of defence. What about offence? I understand that thing must be closed. But just what is it?'

'A rent,' Shell answered. 'Sources tell of the remnant of one in south Genabackis. There are others. They are tears in the fabric of the barriers between Realms. No sane theurgist would dare create one. Only the Great Matrons of the K'Chain Che'Malle could master them.'

That odd name, K'Chain Che'Malle, lowered a silence upon the gathered mages. Even Kyle felt within it echoes of the oldest of his people's legends: formless terrors of the night.

Pausing to be certain that point sank in, Shell continued, 'This one appears to open upon Chaos. And it is growing. It may never stop. Yes, it must be closed, and at all cost.'

Urko grunted his understanding. 'What's the plan?'

Shimmer's gaze lingered upon the east. 'We understand a single mage is responsible and is feeding its growth. Right now it is not self-sustaining but time is running out. Killing the mage should cut it off.'

'If he can be,' the dour-looking Gwynn, near Kyle, commented beneath his breath.

The hill shook and everyone ducked as another lash of pulsing blue-black power hammered the grounds amid the Malazan lines. The distant shrieks and screams audible even through its roar made Kyle shiver. Urko's fists snapped up quivering as if he would break something or someone that instant. '*Bastard!*' He pointed to the twins, 'Make the arrangements!' To Shimmer: 'We're comin' up!' and he ran.

'A large party would only attract attention,' the girl, Nether, said.

Helmet under her arm, Shimmer pushed back her long, straight black hair, nodded curt agreement. 'A small party.'

'How to approach?' asked the young male twin, Nil.

'You will need the element of surprise,' said a new voice from nearby. Everyone turned. There stood a slim fellow in dark clothes, a smirk on his narrow, pinched face. Shimmer raised a hand to forestall any action. 'Possum. What word?'

'For such a purpose I am empowered to offer Imperial cooperation.'

'Such as?' Smoky asked, his voice acid.

'Passage through the Imperial Warren.'

'That Warren is a death-trap,' said Gwynn.

The smirk returned: 'Only for those not authorized to access it.'

Heads among the mages turned, eyes narrowing. '*Laseen . . .*' Smoky breathed.

The Claw sketched a courtly bow. 'I am only a humble messenger.'

The Wickan twins, Nil and Nether, volunteered. After much debate among the Avowed mages it was decided that Gwynn and Smoky would go as their contribution. Possum would bring them through.

As the mages prepared themselves, Kyle went to Smoky's side. 'Good luck.'

The mage smiled, showing his small, sharp, rat-like teeth. 'Just like old times, eh? Speaking of that – let's see that new sword.'

Kyle drew it and held it out. Smoky went to take it but jerked his hands away. He stared, obviously amazed, raised his eyes to Kyle. 'This blade is not metal. Wouldn't dare try to mark that. Take my word for it – don't show it to anyone.'

Kyle sheathed it. 'Thank you. I'd come if I could.'

A snort, then the mage wiped a sleeve across his grimed brow. 'Might have to. No one says we'll succeed.' He waved goodbye. Kyle saw that Stalker had come to watch. He went to his side.

'What do you think?'

Stalker was frowning beneath his sandy moustache. 'We should all go. Hit whatever that is with everything we've got. Maybe then we'd stand a chance.'

Kyle stared up at the man as he stood watching the mages' preparations, his frown turning ever more sour. *Surely things could not be that desperate – could they?*

* * *

Nait crawled on his belly from one pit to another. The flesh of his back writhed with the knowledge that energies that could evaporate iron crackled and thrummed just a stone's throw above him. *Ants. Just us ants down here 's all.* Finding the next pit, he flopped down into the hip-deep depression where soldiers on their knees frantically dug with those once maligned but now oh-so-valuable saboteur tools: shovels. He shouted over the avalanche churning of power: 'Anyone here get a look at whoever the Abyss it is?'

The nearest answered: 'Yeah. I seen 'im. It's Hood himself come to get us!' He gestured upwards. 'Brought his gate with him!'

Nait pushed the laughing fellow aside, carried on.

'It's a mage,' one shouted into his ear as he passed. 'Wrapped in flame. None of the bolts reached him – they burned. Even melted!' Nait nodded his understanding.

'Where is he now?' he yelled. The fellow gestured ahead. 'Thanks.' Nait pointed back the way he'd come. 'Dig back, link up!' A nod of acknowledgement. Reaching the end of the pit, Nait edged up to slide out. The chest of his hauberk gouged the dirt as he pulled himself along by the insides of his arms and legs. Through the wind-lashed grass he saw the fellow – or what must be him. It was a swirling squat tornado of power inside which he could just make out a human-like silhouette, arms raised.

He turned his head to peer upward. It was misleading, but the summoning, or whatever it was, seemed to hover exactly above him. Its height was hard to guess – top of a tall tree maybe? Darkness tinged by grey boiled and stirred within. Around him dust and fragments of chaff floated upwards, drawn up on a gathering draught that appeared to lead into the thing. *Abyss! And it might just be so, too.*

Something touched his leg and his heart almost burst. He looked back: it was one of the Avowed, his face all purplish and bruised, one eye swollen shut. Blues, Ho had given his name as. The Avowed gestured him back. Nait waved him away: blasted fool! He'd almost made him jump up and run for it! The fellow gestured again, insistent. Fine! Nait pushed himself backwards.

They met all together in a rear trench. Urfa's and Nait's saboteurs worked around them deepening the earthworks. In attendance were the saboteur sergeants, the survivors of the wreck and two sergeants from stranded heavy infantry elements squatting in the grasses: Pellan, a Falaran, and Tourmaline, a Moranth. Nait was surprised and pleased to see Heuk as well. 'What are you doing here?' he shouted.

The old mage grimaced, scratched his patchy beard. 'Bastards dropped me 'n' ran. Woke me up.'

After introductions, the Malazan heavy infantry sergeant, Pellan, spoke up: 'What can we do? 'Cept get our arses away from here?'

'Can't move,' Ho said. 'Anything that moves gets hit, consumed to ashes.'

'So what can we do?' Pellan gestured angrily to the sky. 'There ain't nothing we can do against *that*!'

Ho opened his mouth but the Gold Moranth spoke up: 'It must be closed.'

Everyone turned to him – or her. 'We know of these . . . *things*. A remnant of one still exists to the south of our lands. They are crimes against existence. They undermine the very ground upon which we live, the air we breathe. It must be destroyed at all cost.'

Pellan blinked, clearly impressed by such passion, but he pointed up again. 'What? Way up there? There's nothin' we can do – unless we jump that mage.'

'No chance,' Ho said. 'Anyone coming close would be incinerated.'

Pellan threw up his hands in exasperation. 'Then you mages come up with something!' and he waved to Heuk.

The grimed mage exchanged glances with Ho, the ones named Blues and Fingers, and the big, thick-armed female mage named Devaleth. The last of them, the old Wickan witch, had yet to recover with the aid of the sketchy healing that could be provided. They all still seemed a little punchy, but they were deadly serious; so much so Nait found himself wondering about their relationship with the source of this thing. If they were such enemies why were they all together on the same ship? And pretty much all of them mages, too. As far as he was concerned, you get that many mages, jammed together and things like this are practically guaranteed to happen.

Ho hunched further as if driven down by the appalling furnace hovering above. 'We may not be able to get close to the summoner, but the rift itself is growing, expanding.'

'So?' said Pellan.

Tourmaline nodded his helmed head. 'It is coming closer into range,' the Moranth said flatly.

Ho and the Gold studied one another wordlessly until Ho lowered his gaze, guiltily, it appeared to Nait.

'You're going to try to disrupt it,' Fingers said from where he sat, grimacing his pain and holding his bandaged bloody head.

'Yes,' said Ho. 'A sufficiently large blast might be enough to upset its flow. Especially while it's just establishing itself.'

Pellan leaned back, crossing his arms. 'Oh, wonderful plan! Who's gonna do that?'

'I will,' said Tourmaline.

No one had anything to add to that.

Someone or something jabbed Nait where he crouched on his haunches. May was on her knees behind him, glaring. He mouthed a *what?* She motioned him savagely to speak. The glare deepened into an evil eye. '*All right, all right!*'

'Yeah, I'll help out,' he told Tourmaline. The Moranth gave a short bow. *I'll hold your rope, or something like that, maybe.* Nait signalled Urfa aside. The two put their heads together to talk low.

'How're going to get the stuff from our boys 'n' girls?' Urfa asked.

'Good question. Tell 'em the Gold have munitions to distribute – that'll bring them runnin'.'

Urfa guffawed showing a mouthful of bent, misaligned teeth. 'Goddamn, you're a sneaky one, Jumpy! OK, we'll spread the word. Have some heavies nearby to corral them.'

'We'll need lots.'

✻

After all the crying and yelling died down, Jawl's begging and pleading, Urfa's veterans threatening murder, the heavies dragged the last of the saboteurs off and Nait and Urfa went through the assembled hoard. They were careful. Some jokers weren't above boobytrapping their packs with small charges such as the rare Moranth 'stick fuses'. Tourmaline arrived with all the Gold had with them. They placed the largest of the munitions all together: eight cussors and four crackers. A terrifying assemblage, as far as Nait was concerned. Like nothing he'd ever dreamed seeing gathered together in his entire lifetime. A hoard fit to level a fortress. But when he studied the moiling gap into nothingness turning ponderously like a whirlpool on its side, the pile seemed laughably inadequate. Yet it was all they had.

Tourmaline began packing it all away into the Moranth wood-framed canvas carryalls. After watching for a time Nait helped. They took two bags each, brought them to the closest edge of the earthworks. Urfa followed, arranged the carrying straps, pulled them tight.

'You'd take Ryllandaras over this any day, hey?' she shouted over the constant thundering roar above.

'Naked with jam on my arse!'

Laughing, she gave a thumbs-up.

A number of the mages came sliding down into the dirt trench, faces averted from the stain hanging over everyone. Heuk came to Nait's side. 'What's this?' Nait asked.

'Some are going to head out with you,' the old mage shouted, his mouth close to Nait's ear.

'What for?'

'In case he spots you – they'll do what they can.'

'Oh, great!'

Tourmaline turned to Nait, signed *move out*. They edged up and out. Nait pushed himself along with the inside of his frayed leather sandals, pulled with handfuls of the sharp tough grass. The swirling dust made him want to sneeze. His munition bags dragged to either side. Through the grass he caught brief glimpses of the mages accompanying them: Ho and Blues, at least. Then their differing paths took them from sight.

As they edged along, on an idle thought, Nait spoke to Tourmaline. 'You Moranth, I was wondering, you have women among you?'

'Of course. All are needed in defence of the homeland.'

'And you? What about you? I mean – Tourmaline – among you . . . is that a woman's or a man's name?'

The helm jerked away as if Tourmaline was offended. 'A woman's, of course! Isn't it obvious?' And she shuffled away, kicking dirt.

Nait paused, stricken with wonder. *Gods above and below! He was surrounded by them! May, Urfa, Bala, Hands, now Tourmaline. Strong women! They were a bane upon his life.*

They passed the scattered, tangled ruins of the ship and Nait caught up with the Moranth, finding that she'd taken out a saboteur's shovel and was hacking out a cut in the thick root-layer of the prairie grass. Nait looked up: the mar, or rift, or whatever it was, appeared to hang edge-on, directly above. Dust raised by Tourmaline's efforts puffed up to rise like smoke, sucked up and up, presumably to waft into the gap. Nait winced at that, imagining himself following. *Into the Abyss, or the Gap of Chaos itself.*

Knowing there was only room for one to work, Nait peeked through the blowing grasses to keep watch. The mage stood far off, a flickering darker shape within the spinning curtain of multi-coloured energies surrounding him like a glaring winding-sheet.

He watched for a time. The slanting rays of the sun punished him, heating his pot helmet. He was sweating and damned thirsty. He figured it was nearing mid-morning. Behind him, Tourmaline excavated a bowl-shaped depression in the thick grey topsoil.

Then sudden movement. Four figures had appeared from nowhere between him and the mage: two Wickans, and two Crimson Guardsmen. Nait gaped, then threw himself as low as possible. *The Imperials and the Guard were making a move!*

Power erupted, slamming Nait backwards and pounding the ground to make it shake. Spot-fires burst to life among the grasses. Nait fumbled, bouncing, to throw himself on top of Tourmaline who lay on top of her excavation. Speech was impossible: the howling rabid ferocity pummelled Nait, making him scream soundlessly. He risked a glance up, eyes slitted, face shaded against the blowing dirt and chaff. The four poured punishing energies into the one mage who responded with his own lashes that flailed each. But they were not alone: Ho and Blues had appeared as well and now they too added their efforts.

It looked to him as if the six were making headway; the attacks from the one seemed to weaken, flickering. *Yes! They're going to do it!* Yet the winding penumbra of energy that surrounded him did not appear to be thinning at all. Argent fire searing from one of the attackers was merely deflected to spin inward, adding its own layer to those enmeshing the mage. *What was going on? Why couldn't they overcome him?*

Crashing noise pulled Nait's attention from the front. He glanced behind and gaped, horrified. Broken timbers, jagged fragments of shattered board and rope-tangled ironmongery were on their way, flying towards him through the air. *Look out!* But of course he couldn't warn anyone; he could only duck, covering his head.

The debris swooped over, whipping and hissing through the air as fierce as crossbow bolts shot from a siege scorpion. He watched enraged and aghast as the spinning wreckage lanced into the six attackers. One was decapitated instantly. All were plucked from their feet like scythed weeds to fly spinning through the air. It looked to him as if one had taken a blow to the head from a bent iron bar, Ho was impaled once more by wood shards, and the others similarly swept away in one masterstroke.

Beside him Tourmaline signed for Nait to go help them. Nait motioned to the pit. She shook her head, waved for him to give her his munitions. Cursing, Nait pulled the straps from over his head, then scuttled off keeping as low to the ground as possible.

As he went he kept an eye on the mage in his ring of protective energies; the man appeared to have turned away from the field, dismissing it once more to concentrate on his efforts with the rift. That suited Nait. Crawling through the whipping, singed grasses he yelped to meet two coming towards him – the Wickans, young, adolescent boy and girl, nearly identical. Each carried appalling wounds, gouges and slices that ran with blood, clothes tattered. Nait grasped an arm of each to help guide them back to the trench.

He handed them over to the reaching arms of Heuk, two Avowed named Treat and Sept, and even the old Wickan witch who had come forward. She took them and immediately began berating them in Wickan; the two flinched, hanging their heads, looking like remorseful schoolchildren. Nait turned back to try to find the others. The two Avowed slipped up and out after him, running hunched.

Movement on the field dropped Nait to his chest – two of the fallen mages – up and closing on the summoner: Blues and Ho. Despite torn bloodied rags revealing gaping wounds, Blues' back wet with blood that ran down darkening his legs, both limped inexorably towards the mage. Blues drew two short blades. They reached the outermost spiralling layer of energy, pushing inward, hands protecting their faces. And it seemed to Nait that, somehow, despite the punishing, scouring conflagration, both were pushing through. The two Avowed threw themselves down next to Nait. 'Blues!' one urged, 'Get 'im!'

Even Nait found his hands clenched in fists. *Yes! Get him! Send him to Hood!*

Shapes appeared from nowhere behind Blues and lunged up from the grass behind Ho. The Avowed cursed, leapt to their feet running, drawing weapons. Blues turned, defending himself only to be thrust from his feet by the power of the churning energy to fall in a tangle with his attackers. The three figures tackling Ho struck Nait as all bizarrely similar, as if they were all members of the same family. The four rolled away in a blur of ferocious kicks and blows that sent up swaths of earth.

Sizzling actinic power slashed out to strike the closing Avowed, Treat and Sept, throwing them tumbling across the slope like tossed balls. Two more figures ran past Nait, bent over, faces averted from the blasting magics – the Wickan youths, heading for the brawl of Ho and his attackers.

Lady, this is seriously not what I signed up for. Not what I signed up for at all.

He was considering heading back for the trench when he froze. Someone was standing right beside him. Nait slowly edged his head up: the man wore loose trousers, sashed, and a long-sleeved pale-blue tunic; his long loose hair blew about his mahogany face, which was wrinkled up in sour disgust. Nait had never seen the man before in his life. 'I allow them their petty squabbles,' the fellow said as if thinking aloud. 'I do not interfere in succession. My forbearance I thought unassailable. But *this*! *This* I cannot allow.'

The man merely raised a hand and a blinding eruption threw Nait aside. He rolled tumbling to lie stunned, gasping in the hot dust-choked air. He didn't know whether he blacked out. He couldn't tell. But when he shook his head, blinking and coughing, eyes watering, he reared up to look: a slash of brilliant light was hammering the mage in his gyre of protective energies. It was pushing the entire tornado of writhing force backwards while this new mage advanced at a steady pace.

Hood's balls! Who was this guy?

More wreckage flew overhead, whipping for the fellow. *No! Not again!* But as it neared it burst into flames, the shattered timbers incinerating instantly into wafting black flakes. The mangled iron glowing, melting and misting into smoke.

Three figures emerged from the churning smoke and dust, Ho supported by the Wickan youths. They were making for the trench. Though he was beaten and bruised the mage's face held an idiotic grin. The Wickan girl spotted Nait and signed *retreat*. He didn't need any more encouragement than that.

They piled into the trench. People reached out, supporting Nait. One was Heuk. 'Who in Hood's mercy is *that*?' Nait said.

'Tayschrenn.' The old mage grinned his blackened rotten teeth. 'Ain't he somethin'?'

'I'll say.'

The aged Wickan witch helped with Ho, who offered a broken-lipped smile. 'You won?' she asked him. He gave a tired nod.

'They acceded to me.'

'Good. I knew they would.' She turned on the two youths. 'And you two – where is the other, Blues? Why did you not come back with him? We still may need him.'

The two exchanged suffering glances, but bowed. 'Yes, Nana,' they said, and scrambled back out on to the field.

'Healers!' the old woman barked, waving them to Ho. 'See to him!'

Nait peered up at the mar still hanging in the clear blue sky like a bruise or ugly wound. It had grown since he last looked. 'It's low,' he said to Heuk.

'Yes, but – look!'

The enemy mage, named Yath apparently, had been plucked off the ground. He flailed now, limbs churning, enmeshed in the argent puissance invoked by Tayschrenn. It looked as though the High Mage intended to force him through his own rift.

'Yes . . .' Heuk murmured appreciatively, 'he may just bridge it . . .' Then the mage stiffened and turned to Nait, his face blanching. He gripped Nait's shoulder. 'Eldest forgive me! *What of Tourmaline? The munitions! Tayschrenn stands almost on top of them!*'

* * *

No one asked Kyle to leave the hilltop and so he remained, arms crossed, watching the fireworks of the mage duel out on the battle plain. With him was the Untan nobleman who'd come as part of the Wickan delegation – Kyle hadn't caught the man's name. He watched and listened just as Kyle did, his face torn between awe and dread. The battle below reminded Kyle of the Spur, only on an even grander scale. So this was what the old hands meant when they spoke about the Warren-clashes of the old campaigns. Fearsome stuff. He understood more clearly now the relationship between the different arms of these armies out of Quon. No wonder the presence of a powerful mage corps could deter any aggression – or the lack invite it. Still, from the reactions around him he understood what they were seeing now to be unprecedented; a deliberate effort at whole-scale destruction.

That duelling appeared to jump to a yet greater confrontation as light like the reflection of the sun from still water blossomed on the plain. The Avowed mages remaining around Kyle, Opal, Lor-sinn and Shell, all cursed and winced, Shell staggering backwards as if pushed by some unseen force.

'I know that!' Opal said through clenched teeth.

'Brethren report it is the High Mage,' said Shimmer, her tone amazed.

'The only time I've ever been glad to see him,' K'azz said.

The old Malazan commander, Urko, grunted appreciatively. 'Couldn't turn a blind eye to something like *this*.'

'Did you witness the confrontation at Pale?' Lor-sinn asked of Shell.

Shell straightened her jerkin, her lined face wrinkled up as though pained. 'I watched from the distance.'

'Challenged Anomander,' Lor-sinn breathed. 'Lord of Moon's Spawn.'

Kyle watched Opal shake her mop of curly auburn hair. 'Hubris. The Ascendant held back.'

'And how do we know that?'

Opal gestured to the field. 'And risk such consequences?'

Lor-sinn, Kyle could tell, remained unconvinced. A glimmering brilliance out of the field made Kyle flinch and look away; he glanced back, a hand shading his eyes. The rumbling of a particularly loud eruption of power rolled over them. The mages winced in empathic pain.

K'azz raised a hand for attention. 'Brethren say a messenger is here for Commander Urko.'

'Well?' asked Urko.

'The messenger claims to be an officer of the assembled Cawnese Provincial Army.'

Kyle looked to the Malazan commanders Urko and Fist D'Ebbin. Urko's greying brows rose like shelves. Fist D'Ebbin, though beaten down by what he had endured through the night, at first appeared pleased, then that pleasure slipped into unease as he glanced to K'azz. These two were all that remained of Imperial command in the field – other than the Sword, who was rumoured to be in charge of the eastern redoubt. Cowl's Veils had taken an awful toll.

Urko motioned to K'azz. 'Send him up.'

A soldier climbed the hillside, his helmet under an arm. He wore mail under a white surcoat bearing the diamond design of Cawn. He saluted Urko. 'Commander.'

'Yes?'

'I bear news from the east.'

'Yes?'

The man glanced about at the Guardsmen. Voice lowered, he said, 'Perhaps a more private talk . . .'

'Here will do. As you can see – we are facing a common enemy.'

'I understand. Very well. The Cawn Provincial Army is marshalling to the east. It was judged prudent to remain a good distance away. We bring five thousand cavalry and thirty thousand mixed infantry. Command is Lords Mal Nayman, J'istenn, and Viehman 'esh Wait. We are also pleased to host the Imperial representative Councillor and Assembly Spokesman, Mallick Rel.'

Urko's brows now clenched in puzzlement. 'Mallick? He's left Unta?' He dismissed the mystery with a shake of his head. 'Fist D'Ebbin, would you accompany the captain here and coordinate the commands?'

A salute. 'Aye, sir.'

'A moment,' K'azz called. 'What of your mage cadre, Captain? We may have need of them.'

The captain faced Urko, saying nothing. The old general's face tightened. 'Well?'

The captain admitted, reluctantly, 'Squad mages, only, sir.' And he added, weighted with significance: 'For generations Cawn has given up its best to the Empire.'

Urko glowered a nod. 'Very good. Dismissed.'

Fist D'Ebbin bowed to K'azz and Shimmer. Kyle thought the last look he gave them one of silent apology. The two officers descended the hillside.

Kyle's gaze was pulled back to the field. Why that look of apology? he wondered. *Ah, yes – numbers. The Imperial force was now twice as large.*

The Avowed mages all let out excited calls then, pointing to the field. One of the duelling figures, the summoner of the rift, Kyle assumed, was airborne, wreathed in an argent conflagration. Kyle was still not all that familiar with these contests, but it looked as though this Tayschrenn had gained the advantage.

And should he win? What then? Kyle's gaze edged over to study K'azz. That Cawnese officer probably hadn't even realized whom he'd stood before. And why should he? K'azz was now just another old man, his white hair tousled. He still wore his sun-faded, tattered old fisherman's canvas trousers and shirt. He hadn't even belted on a sword. The only gesture he seemed to have allowed himself was a silver sigil of the Guard at his breast. Yet he clearly was in command. All the Avowed instinctively arrayed themselves around him. While Kyle watched, the Duke's troubled gaze followed not the coruscating mage duel of the plain but the retreating figure of the Cawnese messenger. *Yes, he too must be wondering . . . Laseen gave her word . . . but that was when the field was more even. Would the temptation to try to finally rid the Imperium of its most enduring enemy lead her to reconsider?*

⁂ ⁂ ⁂

Nait edged his way through the blackened ash of the seared grass, the dust of the dirt and gravel powdered by the incalculable forces competing, thrashing, just above his head. *Ants. Just us ants down here. And me the dumbest of them.* The High Mage was close, manoeuvring to edge the writhing, flailing shape of Yath above into the mar. Close enough to be blown to droplets by Tourmaline's cussors. *What a monumental fuck-up!*

Nait paused – which way? All looked the same: churned-up, flame-scorched, blasted wasteland. Then a glint of gold through the ash-grey and black. He shuffled over. The Moranth was in a bad way. Thrown soil covered her, disguising the worst of her injuries. As it was, Nait winced. Her back was one burnt scar of puckered flesh and the strange chitinous Moranth armour all melted and twisted. She was lying on a mound – the buried charge.

'Tourmaline!' Nait called, his head next to hers.

The helm stirred, turned to him. 'You return, saboteur.'

'Your charms.'

A chuckle. 'You have no idea, little man. But get me out of this and perhaps I shall enlighten you.'

Don't think I won't take you up on that. He studied the mound of pressed earth. His hair stirred to stand and his breath caught as he glimpsed in one of the Moranth's gauntleted fists the tall slim length of an acid fuse. Using both hands he gently prised it loose and only then managed to exhale. *Gods below – my nerves weren't going to take much more of this.*

He studied the thrashing figure above in its cocoon of blinding, virulent energy, the arcs and sizzling connections between him and Tayschrenn below. The enemy, Yath, was close to the yawning, roiling lip of the rift. 'Not much longer now,' he called to Tourmaline. 'Looks like we'll maybe get to keep all our goodies, hey?'

The banners of power quivered then as if struck. Some snapped to lash the air and ground like whips of flame sending up curtains of blasted earth that pattered down across him and Tourmaline. Nait covered his head. *Damn, I should not have said that!*

He peered between his forearms. Through the penumbra of energies surrounding Tayschrenn Nait glimpsed figures at the man's rear enmeshed in an eerie dance of move and counter-move. Three faced one who seemed some kind of a bodyguard, fending them off from the High Mage's back. This one, slim, short and blurringly quick, whirled a stave feinting at the attackers. And since those three were certainly not Claws, that left Crimson Guard Veils, probably Avowed. *Come to take Tayschrenn while they had the chance!*

Other figures came charging in; Nait recognized Blues, Ho and the other Avowed, Treat and Sept. But the bodyguard fell, having absorbed terrible punishment. Ho threw himself upon one attacker and wrenched the man or woman's head around. Blues and another fell together in a storm of knife-thrusts. The third leapt forward, rolling, evading all to strike the High Mage.

A detonation of power blasted everyone tumbling away like weeds uprooted in a cyclone. A wall of dirt and stones thrown up by the shockwave punched into Nait who yelled as all his earlier wounds pounded anew. But that was not the worst – the worst was his effort to hold the acid fuse steady against his chest like a babe. Once the pressure eased, Nait rolled on to his back, wiped his tearing eyes.

Staring upwards it took him a moment to comprehend just what he was seeing. Close to the rift two figures now rotated around each other – one flailing, the other limp – while the raw Warren energies reverberated between them, thrumming and gyring with the release of all that power. As Nait watched, open-mouthed, the wild spinning tumbled both of them into the open maw of the rift and they disappeared within.

* * *

Standing next to K'azz, Shimmer watched in surprise and alarm as all the Avowed mages within sight grunted and stepped back, rocked by an eruption of brilliance like the sun itself. A booming avalanche report washed over all, striking Shimmer full in the chest. Shell whispered low: 'Tayschrenn's been hit. One of ours, I'm sorry to say. Isha, I believe.' She took a breath murmuring a curse. 'He's drifting, rising . . . there's a pull from the . . .' She lurched forward, hands rising. '*No!*'

'*What!*'

Shell faced them, her eyes revealing her utter disbelief and horror. She pushed a shaking hand through her short hair. 'He's gone. Taken by the rift. Both of them.'

'And that thing? The rift?' K'azz demanded.

'Still growing.'

Shimmer caught K'azz's eye and he nodded. 'Commander Urko,' she called gently, but firmly. 'It would appear that we must pull together everything we have left.'

Urko's grimaced nod almost seemed to grind his neck. 'I agree.'

'We have some six, perhaps eight, Avowed mages. I understand there are many witches and warlocks among the Wickans. What of the mage cadre?'

His dark eyes hidden away beneath a great shelf of bone glared their anger then glanced away. 'Crushed. We have some squad mages but no one of great stature, 'cept maybe one.'

'This Tiste Andii mage?'

'No. There ain't no Andii mage – none I know of. There's an ex-High Mage named Bala. Bala Jesselt. She's at the east redoubt.'

'Very well. Perhaps we may use the Imperial Warren to move—'

K'azz had held up a hand. 'Excuse me, Shimmer. The Brethren report we may have one more option. We should wait.'

'Wait?' Urko growled. His gaze searched K'azz's face. 'What's this? More of your old tricks? Wait for what?'

'For it to grow a bit more.'

* * *

Nait could not believe what he'd seen. The big powers were supposed to bail them out of trouble. Not disappear into a great big steaming pile of it. He studied the slim acid fuse clenched in his dirty hand. *Just me 'n' you now, honey.*

'Are you all right?' someone shouted over the roaring, which was so deafening and constant Nait had almost forgotten it.

Flinching, Nait peered around. Ho, on his knees in the dirt, was peering down at him. Nait nodded, completely bemused. He cocked his head, thinking of the puzzle of this man who seemed able to over-come everything thrown at him and he mouthed: 'Who *are* you, anyway?'

The mage smiled crookedly, nodding his understanding. 'I'm just another damn-fool mage, Sergeant Jumpy.' He pointed up. 'Just like this one. I thought I was capable of anything. But all my researches and experiments brought me only misery.' Improbably, he eased him-self down cross-legged, as if they were relaxing on a hillside. He cast one gauging look up to the rift then returned to studying Nait. 'I was inspired by Ryllandaras, believe it or not. He is Soletaken, yes, a man-beast. But few remember now that he is also D'ivers – one who is many. Who is to know how many there are of him? Perhaps this one *is* the last. In any case, I attempted an incalculably ancient and complex ritual. One none dared re-create, since the few times it was invoked were far beyond living memory. And I did succeed. After a grotesque fashion. I am D'ivers, Sergeant. Human D'ivers. There are four of me left alive. The others conspired to have me cast into prison to be rid of me. But I am returned and they have fled.

'Now,' and he gestured to the mound. 'Is this it?'

'Yes.'

Others came jogging up, hunched, wincing in empathic pain from the churning lip of the rift now suspended so low. *So low!* Nait sat up. He waved to these others, Treat, Blues and Sept – *Soliel help us! What a sad collection of street beggars!* Blues' face mottled in bruis-ing, an eye swollen shut. Treat's clothes tattered, his limbs black with crusted blood mixed with dirt. Sept's ear and neck sliced in a gash that had soaked his front in blood. Nait pointed to Tourmaline. 'Take her out of here!'

Ho arched a brow, mouthed, *her?* But he nodded and gestured the others up. Tourmaline signed a weak negative they ignored as they grabbed hold of her and dragged her off. Ho remained, cocked a question to Nait who waved him away: 'Gotta get to work.'

Ho agreed then straightened, stung. '*Her!* Yes!' He got to his feet, bent low. 'There is another one! Tayschrenn's bodyguard! Oponn favour you!'

Already turned away, Nait gave a curt bob of his head. Dust floated up around him, sifting straight up in the gathering current. He felt the flow plucking at his surcoat. He lay on his side, face lowered, and fought to ignore the yammering oblivion just over his shoulder.

From his bag he drew a wood dowelling about the width of his littlest finger. This he pushed into the mounded earth. Quickly at first, then slowing, tapping, tapping, until it struck something firm. Then he carefully withdrew it, leaving a hole. He gathered up a handful of the grey topsoil, spat into it, squeezed and moulded it in his hands into a ball. *Strong adherence. No sand or clay. Thick and slow.* This ball he threw aside, then he gathered up another, smaller, handful. He spat, rolled the dirt loosely around his palm. *Not too tight.* He rolled an elongated ball that he gently eased into the hole. Taking up the dowelling again he pushed the wet ball down the hole, slowly, tapping, until he met resistance.

He took a long breath then, exhaling, watched the twitching of his cut and battered hands. *Easy. Easy. Slow down, Nait my boy.* He glanced up to the rift. Damn close – but close enough? How much longer dare he wait? He watched broken stalks of grass lifting to spin up past his head, sucked into the hissing, roaring gale that hung what seemed just a few man-heights above his head. Experimentally, he threw up a handful of soil – none came back down.

Maybe that's close enough. But they'll only get the one chance. Maybe – no! This is damn slow dirt; who knows how long it'll take? Right. Do it.

He gave the dowelling one last press, eased it out and threw it aside – it spun upwards, whipped from sight. *Shit! Close enough!* Bent over the hole, he thumbed the stopper from the fuse. Slowly, achingly slow, he eased his hand over, tilting. He watched holding his breath as the thick viscous acid mix eased out. One drop swelled on the lip of the tube. *C'mon!* It hung, wobbling – *Oh, for the love of D'rek!* – fell.

Right. One . . . maybe two. Yeah. Two – best be sure. He tilted further. A second drip swelled, fell. He threw the fuse away and ran. But in his rush he mistakenly straightened fully and something grabbed him from behind, pulling him backwards. He threw himself down again. His helmet was torn from his head. He grasped at handholds of the grass, pulled himself along. His feet kicked in the air behind him. A sandal was sucked from one foot. *Leave me be, Hood! Your bony hand ain't quick enough!*

He pulled and pulled, sliced his palms open on the sharp crisp grass blades until he fell again and rolled, came up running. He pelted it, arms pumping, one sandal flapping. As he ran he imagined the heavy acid fluid permeating the saliva, increasing its concentration next to the casing of whichever munition he'd touched. Six per cent, seventeen, twenty-eight, fifty. Until a reaction began, irreversible, that started eating that casing until soon . . . soon . . .

Nait slowed, stopped, turned. The black and grey moiling maw of the rift had touched down – or so it appeared. A reverberating roar ten times louder than that which had been afflicting him struck his chest and face like a mallet blow, knocking him backwards. Enraged, he stood again, waving his arms at it. Dirt like an avalanche in reverse was speeding up into the void of its black mouth. *Shit! It's sucked it up! Fucking arse-wipe cock—*

Light. A blow kicked him into the air and he flew, arms pinwheeling, to tumble, rolling, amid falling earth and clumps of roots and stones. He lay staring at the clear bright-blue sky. *Beauty. A beauty of a blast.*

Something nearby was making an Abyss of a racket – loud enough to penetrate the ringing in his ears. Loud enough to annoy Nait into raising his head. The rift itself was now turning in a great sweep, but bent, irregular. Nait watched as its border region rotated, revealing a great warp or bite that turned itself forming its own spiral within the larger. And that rotating was speeding up.

He tried to stand, failed, sat heavily, arms limp on his lap, gazed at the rift. Blood dripped anew from his nose to pat the back of one hand. Even to his layman's eye the mar was clearly in trouble. It appeared to be diminishing in size overall, yet the smaller inner spiral was growing – it seemed to be feeding on the larger which was thinning, fast eroding. Like a snake eating its own tail. While he watched, the spinning accelerated to a blur and the rift shrank to a fraction of itself. The rotating and contraction continued, each becoming faster and faster, feeding each other perhaps, until the rift appeared to wrap itself out of existence to disappear without a sound.

Hunh. Nait spat out a mouthful of grit. Well, there you go. He tried to stand again, failed. Fine. Maybe he'd just sit here awhile. Enjoy the glow. Yeah, that's it. Job well done and all that shit. He wondered where Tourmaline had gone off to. Maybe it was time to find out how those Moranth got out of their armour.

CHAPTER IV

Mysteries intrigue us. That which we cannot easily understand or
explain away holds our attention; we return to it repeatedly.
Conversely, the simple and easily grasped is quickly consumed and
dismissed. So it is that *she* remains. She defies all explanation, refuses
to conform to our human, craven, self-serving need to explain ourselves. To be liked. To be 'understood'. And so of course we are all
mortally offended and hate her.

Musings on Laseen
Essayist Quillian D'Ebrell, Arath

POSSUM MAINTAINED HIS VEILS OF DISTRACTION AND DEFLECTION
summoned from Mockra, though that Warren was not his
strength. He walked its twisted paths only in as much as they
intersected and complemented the penchant in Meanas for trickery,
illusion and misperception.

He remained hidden because his instincts told him it was not over.
No, not yet. Though soldiers laughed and celebrated in nearby
hastily dug trenches here in the centre of the field of battle; though
Laseen now walked in the open, apparently completely unguarded.
The soldiers paid her hardly any attention at all. They obviously
thought her just another cadre mage, or Claw. She'd even
approached a common Malazan sergeant for a cloth and been given
a dirty rag with which she then wiped her sweaty face and blood-
caked hands. For his part, Possum was troubled. What *was* she up
to?

She walked the blasted and burnt field, untying her wrappings as
she went, throwing its tattered remains aside. Beneath, she wore a
silk short-sleeved shirt soaked to a dark green by sweat. Her
muscular arms revealed the bruising and cuts of her night's hunt –
having slain, what, five, six Avowed? The wraps at her legs came

next, kicked off from silk trousers, tight at the ankle, likewise sweat-soaked. Her short brown hair glistened, pressed flat like an animal's pelt.

She came to the edge of the crater blasted from the plain and there she stopped. Smoke still threaded from the blackened bare dirt after its astounding explosion. She raised her face to peer up for a time into the clear, so deceptively peaceful, pale-blue sky and suddenly Possum understood. Ah, yes. The last. With Tayschrenn now gone. Choss dead, Toc reported dead, Amaron missing, and Urko reported fled before he could be arrested, or, perhaps, pardoned. Leaving Surly/Laseen. The last survivor; single remaining representative of that generation that had built so grandly. And victor. Now un-contested ruler. Empress.

Was she providing the final irresistible bait to end everything now for ever and for good ... herself? Possum now knew he was not alone in his watching. She had told him who also watched. Another, even more carefully hidden presence waited. And had been waiting for some time now. He was poised for the appearance of one man and one only – such was the price of Laseen. *The question was, would that man bite?*

Of course he would.

Possum eased his blades in their wrist-sheaths. Now. It must be now. This would be his last opportunity before the army clasped Laseen to its bloody, battered but victorious breast.

And the man did bite. But not as Possum had assumed.

A sharp blow to his back was Possum's last sensation. He was flung forward stunned by the power and sudden violence of that strike. Vital seconds passed before his eyes fluttered open once more to view through kicked-up dust two figures enmeshed in a dance of exquisite choreography.

It was the one they wanted; the only one who remained a true threat and whom they would always be watching their backs for. Master assassin and High Mage of the Crimson Guard. Dancer's rival all those years ago – Cowl.

He was astonishing to watch. Blades bared, darting, feinting, and Laseen blocking with kicks that lashed out to punish chest and head. A gesture from Cowl and Warren magics wavered the air like heat ripples only to dissipate to nothing upon Laseen. *Of course, the lingering Otataral dust.* That useless effort from Cowl drew him a blow to his head that sent him spinning from his feet. Yet he was up again, unfazed, and closed, leaping. A blurred series of slashes from him, spinning, knives reversed; Laseen slipping each, hands jabbing, and the edge of a foot slamming Cowl back. But her shirt and trousers now hung slashed – blood bloomed upon her front, dripped from her hands.

Possum decided that perhaps he'd watched for long enough. He stood, shook himself. He had been delivered a terrible blow. Mortal had it struck true – deadly still should it not be treated, but he had the minutes he needed. For it had always been his habit when wreathed in Mockra to appear a good hand's width taller than his true height. He drew his wrist-knives and joined the fight.

A flash of surprise from Cowl's slitted dark eyes was Possum's reward as he closed, lead foot sliding up. Cowl stepped edgeways, a blade directed to each of them. But neither Possum nor Laseen pressed their advantage; each crouched, content to guard themselves. The master assassin's head tilted just a fraction as he considered this. Then his eyes widened.

He threw himself sideways but not quickly enough as a new figure appeared, leaping from a Warren to lash out, kicking him in his side, sending him tumbling down into the blast crater. This new figure launched himself after, scarecrow thin, tattered clothes flapping, his long white hair a dirty tangle. He leapt upon Cowl and the two slashed at each other, dirt and dust billowing in a blur of shifting feet, rolls, sweeps, grips attempted and broken, and throws.

A kick from Cowl sent the other flying backwards, but in the air an arm snapped forward and a thin blade slammed into the Guard assassin. He gestured, disappeared into a Warren and the other, landing cat-like on his feet, white hair flying, waved to disappear as well.

And so they are off chasing each other across Realms and Warrens. Cowl and Topper, hated enemies and rivals from their first meeting. Will Topper finally succeed where Dancer failed and ascend to the peak of his calling? Will it always be Dancer and Cowl – never him? Will we ever see either of them again? Myself, I hope not! Possum fell to his knees and a hand, his chest cramped. Gods! He couldn't breathe! Punctured a lung, he was sure of it.

'Bring a healer,' Laseen called to the soldiers who'd run up. She actually sounded winded – a first. Possum smiled, meaning to make a joke of that, but he saw behind Laseen's dirty blood-smeared feet two others: two small girl's feet snug in fine leather slippers.

Oh no! No! Others can wait just as patiently!

He straightened though his chest flamed and his vision blurred. Laseen was staring ahead, a puzzled look in eyes that had otherwise always guarded all expression, all hints. The girl-woman who'd bested Possum twice before backed away, long stilettos bloodied, a wicked sharp-toothed smile, eyes bright with savage glee.

'*Done!*' she gloated, then jumped, blades flashing to parry thrown heavy knives that hissed past Possum. Warren magics blew her backwards in waves of power and she writhed, snarling and flailing amid the blackened dirt of the crater. A Warren opened and she fell within, her form melting, transforming into some *thing* else.

Soldiers and mages ran up. Possum knelt before Laseen, who had eased forward on to her knees. 'Laseen,' he breathed, hardly able to form words. '*Laseen . . .*'

Her eyes held no recognition, no awareness. The face softened. The hard, so long held lines of watchfulness and calculation melted away to reveal a seemingly younger woman – one whom Possum would call far from plain. She fell forward to the burnt, trampled ground. Mages pushed Possum aside, knelt, turned her over. Hands eased him down as well.

I failed. One job to do – just the one. And I failed. What am I to do? What could there possibly be for me now? He felt Denul healing magics stealing upon him, dulling his pain and his senses.

Do not, dear healers, bother to wake me.

* * *

Shimmer watched the ranks upon ranks of Kanese cavalry as they came swelling up out of the south to encircle their position and unease tightened its grip on her chest. Not far behind marched their thousands of infantry. Simple precautions? Once the mar had been sealed the last Malazan officer remaining, Urko, had tilted his head to K'azz in ironic salute and walked off down the hillside all alone – to the west. Another disappearance now that Laseen had overcome all? Very possibly. She glanced to K'azz. 'Shall we too strike out, head west?'

He shook his head, hands clasped at his back. 'No. Not yet. No orders seem to have been given yet regarding us. So long as we do not move, they won't.' He gave her a reassuring smile. 'Sometimes acting in fear of a course of action brings that very course about. Since they are the sea right now – we shall be the mountain.'

Pure K'azz. But she still could not get used to hearing his voice, his words, coming from the mouth of what appeared no more than an elder with thinning hair, grey stubble at his thin cheeks.

A Brethren wavered into presence before Shimmer and she was

still unnerved and saddened to see that it was Smoky. He inclined his head to her and K'azz. 'She's dead,' he announced.

'Who?'

'Laseen.'

Both she and K'azz gave a shocked '*What?*'

'Assassinated.'

'Cowl!' K'azz snarled. 'We'll have to flee.'

'No.'

'No?'

'He failed. Topper ambushed him from the Imperial Warren. Intervened. The two are off. Probably still duelling. Gods know where.'

'Who then?' Shimmer asked.

'An unknown talent. New. But inhuman.'

'*Inhuman?*'

'Of mixed blood descent would be my guess. Human and demon.'

'From *where?*'

'Don't know. Not from Quon Tali. Someone must have brought her in.'

K'azz raised a hand. 'Thank you, Smoky. And . . . I am sorry.'

An insubstantial shrug. 'Had to happen eventually. At least it was quick.' He faded away.

K'azz squeezed his eyes with a thumb and forefinger, sighing. 'Good thing it was an outsider. Things could've gone very badly for us otherwise. As it is, they may still want blood.'

'And Tayschrenn is gone.'

'Yes.' He shook his head in genuine regret. 'His presence kept so many in line. Now, I truly fear what may be unleashed. Still . . .' and he gave her a speculative look, 'I would not count that man gone yet.'

While they watched, yet more cavalry came riding on to the field, this time from the east, up the trader road from Cawn: the provincial Cawnese cavalry. These forces too ranged themselves facing the Guard from the north and east. So many.

'And where were these armies just two days ago?' she murmured, unintentionally giving voice to her thoughts.

'Elsewhere, thankfully,' K'azz grinned, but then he nodded his understanding. 'We are being granted a rare sight, Shimmer. The gathering might of a far-flung Empire in truth. Seems in our absence the Malazans have pulled together a true political and logistical whole . . .' He paused, the crow's-feet at his eyes deepening as he squinted, his mouth drawing down. 'We are the invaders now, Shimmer. Quon does not want us.'

And Shimmer exhaled. Some long-held breath clenched deep within her stomach relaxed after so long. *Thank all the Gods he sees this. There is hope for us yet.*

She glanced around the retreat: yes, all that were left now were Guardsmen and the Untan noble who accompanied the Wickans. The Bael recruits came walking up, Stalker, Badlands and Coots. They joined Kyle. From what K'azz had told her of them she hoped they would ease themselves back into the Guard, but something told her this would probably not happen. The scout, Stalker, raised his chin to the field. 'Damn lot of them. We heard the news. Any idea who's in charge down there now – if anyone?'

'It had better not end up the Sword,' a voice said from nearby. Shimmer turned. It was the Untan nobleman. Rillish?

'Why?' K'azz asked.

The man drew a long breath as if searching for where to start. 'The Wickans told me of his actions up north in Seven Cities. The man's bloodthirsty. Has no mercy. He'll order you all wiped out – the Wickans as well, probably. He has a hatred of them.'

K'azz appeared doubtful. 'Surely enough blood's been spilled . . .'

Shimmer recounted her meeting with the man – only one day ago? Seemed like years, another world. Yes, the Untan's evaluation struck her as true. A man to whom lives meant nothing. 'I met the man with Skinner,' she said. 'At the parley. From what I saw of him I agree with Rillish.'

'I see.' K'azz pursed his thin lips. 'Of course from a military point of view I can understand it . . . I had just hoped we'd moved on to a political solution. But, if not . . .' He motioned to her. 'Have the Brethren summon all mages.'

She nodded.

A Wickan elder came walking up, his thick, greying, unkempt hair blowing in the wind, a hand on his long-knife pommel, his walk bow-legged. He raised a clawed hand to Rillish. 'You're wanted on the field.'

The Untan noble bowed to K'azz. 'Until later, Commander.'

K'azz gave a brief tilt of his head in assent. 'Yes, I hope to hear later on how you came to join the Wickan command – I'm sure it must be quite a story.'

The man's smile was solemn. 'Yours, I think, would interest most here far more. May Burn guard your way.'

Shimmer watched him jog down the hillside. Only the Guard now remained on the hilltop retreat. 'What do you have in mind?' she asked.

A mischievous half-smile pulled at his lips. 'I think we should have a look at the Imperial Warren.'

* * *

Ho remained while Imperial regulars, Malazan, Falaran and Moranth, saw to the treatment of Laseen's corpse. They formed an unofficial guard, held back the gathering crowd, wrapped the body in clean cloth, then appropriated a supply wagon brought down to collect wounded, and carefully placed the body on its empty bed. The woman he'd found on the field, Tayschrenn's bodyguard, they sat up front. She'd given her name as Kiska and seemed shattered – not by her wounds, but by the trauma of having lost Tayschrenn. The other remaining Claw operative, once his wounds had been stabilized, had got up and simply wandered off to become lost among those many milling about the battlefield.

Of the other mages who had come together to attempt to counter Yath, all save one had gone their separate ways. The surviving Crimson Guardsmen, Blues, Treat, Sept, Gwynn and Fingers, had discreetly slipped away to join their brothers and sisters on their hill-top position. Blues and Gwynn had carried Fingers on a stretcher as just another of the wounded, and, Hood knew, there were more than enough of those. The Wickan twins, witch and warlock, had ridden off with a troop of horsemen who'd come leading extra mounts for them. They'd left with Su, who, from what he'd over-heard, was in truth the elder cousin of the twin's grandmother, and very possibly *the* eldest Wickan alive today.

'It's not over,' Su had called to him from where she sat gently cradled by a rider astride a mount, enigmatic and true to form. He'd just waved goodbye.

The saboteurs, including sergeants Jumpy and Urfa, seemed content to sit sprawled in the shade of their trenches, helmets and armour shed, re-dressing wounds and cadging water and food from the many Kanese and Cawn cavalry wandering the battlefield, collecting wounded and souvenirs.

This left him and the priest-mage, Heuk. The impromptu honour guard forming up surrounding the wagon had set out north. Ho invited Heuk to join the wake. 'I'm curious to have a look at this Mallick creature the Cawn officers are so puffed up about.'

Heuk walked with him. He gestured to the wagon. 'I still can't believe it.' He wiped a dirty sleeve across his equally dirty face, winced at the glaring sun.

'Neither can I. It seems impossible.'

Ho saw his feelings echoed in the stunned, numb faces of the regular soldiers all assembling without fanfare, without orders, all gathering together to follow the wagon as it made its slow way north to the trader road. Only now, it seemed to Ho, were they becoming aware of what they had had in their Empress. Unflinching. A presence so solid they need not even have considered it. For all her faults it may be that it was she who held them all together. Now, with her gone, the break with the past was complete. Who was left to take the throne? Who could possibly fill that cold, hard, perilous seat – or would possibly dare? No one that he could think of. But then, he'd been away for a very long time, and even a day can be a lifetime in Imperial politics.

Heuk had been eyeing him edgewise, an unwelcome calculating look in his eyes. 'The Empire has a need of a High Mage . . .'

'I'd rather have my skin flayed from my body. What about you?'

'*Me?* I'm just a squad mage.'

Certainly. A squad mage who terrifies all other mages. But he let it lie – they each had their secrets and preferred anonymity.

The cortège eventually reached the encampment of the Cawn command near the crossroads. Here it stopped and the Cawnese provincial nobles gathered to pay their respects. Also present were many assembled Imperial officers. Beneath his breath Heuk pointed out each to Ho: 'The tall pale one is High Fist Anand. Next to him is Fist D'Ebbin. Don't know the names of the Kanese and Cawn officers and mages here.' A palanquin pushed its way among the gathered officers, a bald, armoured, giant Dal Hon at its head. Ho exchanged knowing glances with Heuk. *Bala.* Quick to sidle up, she was.

Searching among everyone Ho saw no one dominating figure. Rather, it was the way they all stood in an uneasy semicircle slightly apart from one particular figure that directed his gaze to the man: the seemingly harmless short, rotund, figure who must be this Mallick Rel. The man's pale moon face held an expression of deep remorse and sadness, but beneath this Ho read rigidly contained triumph.

'A poignant day for the Empire,' Mallick said softly to High Fist Anand next to him. Though in pain from his wounds, Anand looked down at the man with obvious disgust. 'A day to be remembered.' He clasped his hands across his stomach. 'Yes. And for more than this one compelling reason. For while we mourn the loss of our Empress we must also rejoice in the surmounting of this misguided secessionist movement. And for the crushing of our old enemies, the mercenary Crimson Guard.' The man glanced to the ground as if in humility. 'Such is Laseen's legacy of peace and security to us.'

Gods, he really slathers it on. Ho looked to Heuk, who rolled his eyes to the sky. *Yet what can one do but stand in awe of such breathtaking, bare-faced audaciousness?*

'Mallick!' a great deep voice bellowed. Heads turned. Puffing, battered and limping, Korbolo Dom, Sword of the Empire, pushed his way forward supported by two of his officers. 'What is this, Mallick?' The Sword glared about the assembly. 'What is this delay? Why are we not marshalling for attack? Now is the time!' Panting, he glanced about from face to face. 'We have them surrounded. Outnumbered. We must strike! Behead every last one of them! I will take overall command—'

'Sword,' Mallick interrupted softly, 'we rejoice that you are still with us, but we are pained by reports that have come to us from the engagement with the Talian League.'

Korbolo stared, mouth gaping his utter consternation. '*What?*'

'It has been reported from many sources that when your phalanx broke you withdrew to the rear. Do you deny these reports?'

'To take command of another unit to lead it into battle – yes. Mallick, what is this foolishness? We are losing time—'

But the Falaran native was shaking his head, his thick lips downturned as if forced into an unwilling duty. 'I am sorry, Korbolo, but the Sword – once committed to the field – does not retreat. To do so is to announce capitulation to the entire Imperial force.' Mallick raised his gaze to study the assembled officers. 'And I take it as a powerful testimony to the resilience and temper of these forces that they did not break then and there.

'Therefore, as Imperial Councillor, Spokesman of the Assembly, it is my regretful duty to order you imprisoned until a court of inquiry into these events may be convened.'

'*What!*' The Sword stared, his mouth working, then suddenly he lunged at Mallick. The officers who had formerly been supporting him now restrained him. 'You . . . *creature*! You cannot do this to me! I am the Sword! Victorious! I won this battle!' The man struggled, arms wrenching. He glared with bulging eyes at the assembled officers, his Napan face darkening, foam at his lips. 'I am your commander! I led you to victory!'

'The prisoner will be silenced,' Mallick ordered.

A rag was jammed into Korbolo's mouth. He was led away kicking, fighting, gurgling and screaming behind the rag.

Mallick shook his head in sad regret.

'Your wisdom and forbearance are an inspiration to us all, Councillor,' an old woman called out.

Mallick's gaze sharpened, searched the crowd, settled on one face and narrowed to glittering slits. 'Let that one come forth,' he called.

The Wickan twins advanced, supporting Su between them. Ho tensed to advance but Heuk held him back.

'So, you Wickans. Before me once again. Yet I hear accounts from all sides that your charge smashed the Guard and opened the way to Imperial victory. For that we are all in your debt. And we thank you . . .'

Su bowed shallowly. 'We ask only for what is by rights ours.'

'Ah, yes . . . of course.' Mallick reclasped his hands across his stomach. 'This most recent distressing policy regarding your lands. Ill-conceived and inhumane. I was always against it, of course.'

Now the twins lurched forward, faces twisting, but Su's clawed hands clutching at their shoulders held them back. 'Perhaps these new Imperial holdings could be granted twenty-year leases from us,' Su suggested, 'thereby avoiding further violence and upheaval.'

Mallick's lips pursed. His fingertips tapped one another across his stomach. 'Details to be negotiated in treaty, of course.'

Su inclined her head. 'Of course.'

Mallick waved negligently. 'Very well. We are done. You may withdraw.'

'Your honesty and compassion are a lesson to us all,' Su crooned, bowing. Ho sent the old witch a wink as the twins helped her away.

'M'Lord Councillor,' Bala called from her palanquin.

'Yes, High Mage?'

High Mage. Ho shot Heuk a sharp glance – the old mage looked skyward once more.

'Multiple Warrens have been accessed on the hilltop.'

Nodding thoughtfully, Mallick faced the assembled officers. 'Send word to the Guard that it is our belief that enough of our good honest soldiers have died today. Enough blood has been shed in this useless vendetta. Speaking – unofficially – for the Empire, our leave is given them to withdraw.'

'Convenient, that,' Heuk muttered aside, 'since they're *already* withdrawing.'

Ho bent down to answer, 'It'll look good in the histories.'

Heuk motioned aside. 'C'mon. I've had a bellyful of this. One more pronouncement from him and I'll puke. Let's have a drink with those good honest soldiers.'

'I can just see those history books, too,' Ho said as they walked along. 'Kellanved the Terrible. Laseen the Bloody. And Mallick the Benevolent.'

'Mallick the Just,' Heuk offered.

A voice bellowed after them. 'Cadre mage!'

They turned. Bala's palanquin was following, led by the bald, sweating, giant Dal Hon. 'The High Mage requires your attendance,' he commanded.

'This is enough to drive me to an early retirement,' Heuk murmured.

They waited while the palanquin closed. 'Groten,' Bala called through the flimsy white cloth hangings, 'allow them to approach.'

The guard, Groten, bowed. 'Yes, mistress.' He curtly waved them closer.

Sighing, Heuk stepped up, followed by Ho. 'Yes, Bala.'

'That's High Mage – please remember henceforth.' The High Mage, Bala, lay reclined upon pillows, sheer silks arranged decorously. She was a voluptuous Dal Hon woman; Ho noted her six sturdy bearers were sweating furiously. She slowly fanned her face. 'Since I am now High Mage to all the Empire, I cannot deal with the trivialities of the mage cadre in any one army. Therefore you are now in charge of the cadre for the Fourth. You report to me. And you . . .' the fan pointed to Ho. 'You are not welcome in the cadre. We do not want the likes of you.'

Ho bit down on laughter. He waved his assent.

'Too much a threat, hey, Bala?' Heuk said.

'Do not bore me with your meaningless talk, Heuk. Good day. Our audience is over. Groten!'

The bodyguard loomed over them. 'Out of the way!'

Ho allowed himself to be edged aside. He watched the palanquin lumber away.

'I know a soldier,' Heuk said musingly, 'who, if he'd seen her just now, would've fainted dead away.' Gesturing, he invited Ho on.

'What of Laseen?' Ho asked.

'Mallick will probably spare no expense on her mausoleum in Unta. How it would gall her.'

'All the more reason from his point of view, I suppose.'

'And what of you?' Heuk asked.

'Retirement in Heng. I have a lot of catching up to do there. A lot.'

Heuk eyed him sidelong, scratched at his scraggly stained beard. 'Really . . .'

'Yes, really . . . Yes!'

Heuk straightened the earthenware jug he held under one arm. 'Un-huh.'

671

Kyle and the Lost brothers had waited while the Guard filed through the opened gates to march away through the Imperial Warren. The last to leave were K'azz, Shimmer, Shell and two very battered and bruised Avowed mages named Blues and Fingers.

Throughout the withdrawal, the lines of Malazan infantry and assembled cavalry from Kan and Cawn had watched, shields readied but swords sheathed and lances raised. K'azz approached Kyle who motioned to the surrounding ranks of Imperial soldiery. 'They let you go.'

The old man nodded. 'Yes. This Mallick no doubt intends to blame all this bloodshed on Laseen's policies, so he could hardly add to it. But what of you? You're sure you won't come along? You are very welcome.'

'No, thank you. But if you could move us a touch, though, we'd appreciate it.'

'I see. Where will you go?'

Kyle shrugged. 'Not sure. We have to talk it over.'

'Very well. I'll leave things to Shell here. In any case,' he held Kyle's shoulders, 'I owe you more than I can say. You can always call on the Guard. Yes?'

Embarrassed, Kyle just waved all that aside, but nodded his thanks.

K'azz went to the portal, turned and waved. Kyle and the Lost brothers raised their hands in farewell. Shimmer waved then also, bowing, and stepped through. Blues and Fingers followed and that gate snapped shut with a whoosh of displaced air. Shell waited next to hers. She waved them over. 'I have instructions on where to take you.'

Kyle exchanged looks with Stalker, Badlands and Coots, cocked a brow. Coots stepped up, rubbing his hands together. 'Where're we off to, lass? Darujhistan? Korel? Aren?'

She just smiled, the lines around her mouth tight. 'After you.'

Kyle had only the briefest sensation of disorientation then his moccasins touched down on a dusty dirt floor in an empty, long-abandoned room. He spun, taking in the dusty quarters – what was this? Stalker and the brothers joined him, stepping out of nowhere, to flinch as well, hands going to weapons.

'Where are we?' Stalker breathed the question aloud for all of them.

Badlands crouched at a gaping window. 'Eternal Ice take it! We're still here!'

'*What?*' Everyone joined him.

'There's the battlefield!'

'I see Cawn pennants.'

Stalker stepped away from the window. 'What is this . . .'

'The Sanctuary . . .' Kyle murmured, peering around. 'In the east – the butte. What did Shimmer call it?'

'The Sanctuary of Burn,' Coots supplied.

'So why here?' Stalker asked.

''Cause someone else is here,' said a new voice.

They spun, weapons hissing from sheaths, to see one of the Crimson Guard Brethren. 'Stoop!' Kyle exclaimed.

'Aye, lad.'

'What in the Wind King's name are you doing here?'

The shade walked up, grinning, dressed in his vest, ragged hanging shirt and tattered trousers as he had been in life. 'I'm with you, lad.'

Everyone shoved their weapons away. '*With* me?'

'I'll be taggin' along with you for a time. K'azz's dispensation.'

'Really? Just as those other Brethren come to K'azz?'

'Yeah – for a while. Till the Vow pulls me back, I s'pose.'

'Just like back home,' Badlands said aside to Coots, who glared for silence.

'So, why can we see and hear you then?' Stalker demanded, ever sceptical.

A translucent shrug. 'I guess because you was Guardsmen for a time.'

'So no one else would see or hear you?' Badlands asked.

'I dunno. I ain't no mage. Unless they're priests o' Hood or mages, I s'pose.'

'*Too* much like back home,' Badlands commented behind a raised hand.

'*Shut it*,' Coots answered, and he shook himself, brushing dust from his thick mane of hair.

Kyle went to the window, leaned against the ledge. Out on the plain fires glowed in the gathering twilight. *So many. Where had they all come from?* 'Are we here because you are here?'

Stoop scratched his temple with his shortened arm just as he used to in life. 'Naw. I go wherever you go. There's someone else here. C'mon, I'll take you to him.'

Kyle and the Lost brothers exchanged looks as the shade walked out of the room through one of the open portals. A moment later he reappeared, waved them on. 'C'mon. This way.' Stalker motioned

Kyle to lead. Kyle opened his hands as if to deny any part in this but he went out first.

Stoop led them through a jumbled labyrinth of tumbled, fallen-down rooms and halls. Some were no more than canted walls open to the sky, others as dark as collapsed mines. The dust and litter of years lay thick upon everything.

After a time Kyle smelled wood smoke and cooking animal fat. Pausing, he turned back to the brothers and touched the side of his nose. They nodded, carefully eased weapons from sheaths. Crouched, he slowly advanced through the thick shadows of a nest of small chambers. The crackling and snapping of a wood fire led him on until he saw the glow ahead. He paused, waited for the brothers to catch up. The shade of Stoop had gone on ahead. Once they were all together Stalker signed for Kyle and himself to take the right and the left while Coots and Badlands would cover the centre. Everyone nodded.

On a silent count, they crashed into the room, weapons raised. A big man sat against the wall of a littered chamber, a small cookfire burning.

'Is that you, Kyle?' the man exclaimed, surprised. 'What're you doing here?'

Kyle straightened, his weapon falling. 'Greymane!'

One of his eyes was swollen shut. His upper lip split and swollen. The entire side of his face was blossoming dark purple while his hair was clotted with dried blood. His armour lay piled in a corner. He gestured to Stoop's grinning shade. 'I knew it would be a Guardsman, but I wasn't expecting you.'

Kyle crouched at the fire. 'What're you *doing* hiding here?'

The man looked uncomfortable, lowered his gaze. 'Well . . . the Imperials still have a price on my head, you know.'

And Kyle remembered. *Head worth a barrel of black pearls.* He waved to the brothers. 'Well, we'll help get you out – won't we, Stalker?'

The eldest of the Lost brothers pressed a hand to his brow, sighed. 'Sure. Of course. Seems that's all we do.'

Badlands crouched at the fire. 'What's that you got roasting there?'
'Rabbit.'
'Looks done. C'n I?'

Greymane gestured for the man to help himself.

'We should go south,' Badlands said, pulling off a tear of flesh and licking his fingers. He rested his great hairy arms on his knees.

'North,' Coots immediately said.

'I was kinda thinking west,' Greymane offered, somewhat bewildered.

'I like north,' Stalker said, nodding to himself.

Chewing, Badlands raised a hand for silence. 'But you know – south would really be better.'

Kyle just grinned, sat down next to the fire and started untying his leggings. This could take all night.

* * *

'You're shittin' me, aren't you?' Nait told Heuk.

'No – it's true. I've heard it from all kinds of people.'

'People like who?'

'Like all kinds.'

'Damn.' Nait sat back into the cool of the trench. 'Dammit!'

A cavalry officer bearing Cawn colours rode up next to the trench. He squinted down into the dark of the deepening afternoon shadows. 'I'm looking for a Sergeant Jumpy.'

Urfa stood, goggled up at the man and smiled her uneven teeth. 'Nice horse.'

Jawl, Stubbin and Kibb came walking up carrying broken timbers and slats that they dropped next to a pile. The officer eyed what looked like a large bonfire in the making. 'You're not going to sit out here tonight, are you?'

'Yes, we are,' Nait said, standing. 'What of it?'

'I understand orders are to marshal east along the trader road. This is one broad killing field. It's unhealthy. And dangerous. There'll be jackals.'

'Jackals don't like fire,' Nait said, deadly serious.

The cavalry officer blinked, uncertain. 'So . . . there's no Sergeant Jumpy then?'

'No, sir,' Nait answered. He waved to Least who, passing, raised a hand in salute. 'Lim?' Nait called. Least gave a thumbs-up.

'Try third company,' Urfa suggested.

'What company is this?'

Urfa's eyes crossed as she frowned. 'Don't know, sir.' She turned to the trench. 'Hey, you useless lot! What company are we?'

Voices muttered from the shadows. 'I thought we was first.'

'Fourth.'

'Naw, I think it was first.'

Smiling raggedly, Urfa winked. 'There you are, sir. We're either first or fourth. Sure you won't stay? Got a fire. Got a big ol' fish to fry. We're gonna get drunk and say goodbye to all our friends.'

'Sounds enchanting,' the Cawn officer observed drily. He gave his reins a gentle pull. 'I'll leave you to it then.'

Urfa fell back down into the trench. 'Damn. He was cute. I like cavalry officers.'

'He'll find the cap'n,' May warned from where she lay in the last of the sun next to the trench.

'Eventually,' Nait said. He crouched again next to Heuk, who sat hugging his jug to his chest. 'So – they can't take it off? Really?'

Eyes shut, Heuk gave an exaggerated nod. 'Never. Doesn't come off.'

'Shit.' Nait stood, examined the wood pile. 'Call this fuel for a bonfire? I want twice this! C'mon, another trip to the wreck. Let's go!'

Groaning, his squad slowly climbed to their feet, ambled off.

'I thought that, from what she said . . . that maybe, y'know – it was possible.'

Heuk mouthed a silent 'No.'

'Then how do they do it?'

A lift and drop of the shoulders from Heuk. Cursing, Nait threw down a handful of dirt and stalked off. Heuk cracked open an eye to watch him go and smiled. *Good. Tourmaline – you owe me three kegs of Moranth distilled spirits. And you better come through else ol' Nait will discover that armour does come off after all.*

CHAPTER V

THE SLAUGHTER SPREAD FOR NEARLY A LEAGUE IN ALL DIRECTIONS. Hurl walked her uneasy mount gently around the field of picked-clean Seti dead. Two days and nights old they looked to her; stench beginning to thin; clouds of carrion drifting away but for the odd fat kite or crow too befuddled with food to bother flying from them; jackals and their rival wolves trotting slunk low across the gentle hillsides.

The column was quiet behind her and Rell and Liss. Many rode two to a mount as the journey had proven too hard for the weaker, sicker horses. As every sign pointed to a long pursuit Hurl considered more seriously sending most of them back. After all, she'd seen Ryllandaras, knew what he could do. Why throw these troopers against him when really, in the end, it would come down to Rell and the burden slung on the back of her mount?

And Ryllandaras was not one to challenge such a large column. He was a scavenger, an opportunist, a predator of humans. No doubt he would merely run and run, on and on across this seemingly endless plain dominating the centre of Quon Tali until they gave up the chase. Or became so weakened as to prove a tempting target. If she sent the column back leaving, perhaps, ten . . . that might, as they say, . . . sweeten the offer.

They came upon the main Seti encampment: tattered, abandoned wikiups, trampled cookfires, abandoned equipment, and dead. Many dead. Men, women and infants. A camp massacred and abandoned. Mounted, Liss pointed ahead and Hurl squinted, a hand pressed to her nose and mouth against the flies. A horse and rider waiting ahead. Hurl angled the column towards the man. He was a large fellow, tall and broad, dark bluish-black Napan, wearing an expensive coat of blackened mail. Old as well, his tightly curled hair going grey. Hurl raised a fist in a halt. The men and women of her column dismounted. She heard Sergeant Banath ordering a search for survivors – and food and water.

She stopped in front of the man, who inclined his head in greeting. From his appearance she was afraid he would be who she suspected he might be. His wary, almost resigned expression only supported her suspicions. He directed her attention to a pole stuck into the ground beside a large fire-pit. A grisly object decorated the pole, a man's head gnawed by scavengers, eyes gone, tongue gone from slack jaws.

'Imotan,' the man said, 'Shaman of the Jackal warrior society.'

'Did you have any part in this?'

He shook his head. 'No. I came to do it. But Ryllandaras beat me to it.'

'*Ryllandaras?* Why?'

'Imotan tried to compel him,' Liss said, stopping next to Hurl. She tilted her head in wary greeting. 'Amaron.'

Laugh, Hood! It is him. The man who'd tried to have her killed; who, along with his Old Guard cronies, was responsible for all those dead at Heng. Including Shaky. Hurl turned away, looked to the sky, blinking to clear her eyes.

Rell arrived to stand close to Hurl, watching Amaron warily.

'Why did you come?' Liss asked, tired and rather curt.

'I came to answer a murder.'

High-pitched laughter burst from Hurl. 'What? A murder? One murder?' She opened her arms wide. 'Take a good look around!'

'You're not one to talk, Hurl,' he answered, his voice as unforgiving as iron.

She stopped laughing as if slapped, clutched at her throat.

'In any case,' he continued, 'he was a good friend and a good man. He had befriended the Seti. He should not have died the way he did.'

Liss nodded, accepting that. She pushed back the matted curls of her greasy hair. 'And now . . . ?'

Amaron lowered his gaze, let go a long slow exhalation. 'I *ask* to join your party.'

Hurl laughed anew, either at his staggeringly brazen request, her glaring culpability behind it all, or at both of them. Even she wasn't sure. Liss said nothing, only looking between her and Rell, her face held carefully neutral.

Rell crossed his arms, saying flatly, 'We could use him.'

They camped upwind a short distance from the slaughter. As dusk gathered the barking of jackals and calls of wolves closed. Hurl doubled the perimeter guard.

'You don't expect him this night, do you?' Sergeant Banath asked Hurl as they sat around the fire eating hardtack scavenged from the abandoned Seti camp.

'No. Just being careful.'

'Mightn't he circle around to return to Heng?'

'Not with us after him,' Liss said, then she went on to explain: 'Right now, we're far more attractive.'

Banath's brows rose in such a way that said maybe he didn't really want to know that. Hurl just watched sidelong to where Amaron had thrown down his gear.

Dawn brought a whistle and a call from the perimeter guards. Hurl straightened from a smouldering fire, a cup of tepid tea held in both hands to warm them. Rell jogged up to her side fully armed and armoured, visor lowered. 'What is it?' she called loudly.

'Four riders approaching!'

'Seti?'

'No.'

'Ready arms! Crossbowmen!' Hurl tossed back her tea, sucked her teeth, handed the cup to an aide. Amaron joined her as she walked to meet the horsemen. She could not help but watch him warily.

A modest smile played at his mouth. 'No need for alarm,' he said. 'I know one of them.'

'Friend of yours?'

'Yes.'

Hurl didn't know whether to be reassured or uneasy. The closer the riders came the more impressed she had to admit she was by their cut. A more hard-bitten, intimidating gang you'd be hard pressed to gather anywhere.

Amaron stepped out to greet them. One threw a leg over his mount and the two hugged. The other three dismounted with much groaning, back-straightening and feet-stamping. Hurl now saw that each was also rather long in the tooth as well.

Rell came to her side, arms crossed. Amaron escorted the four to her. 'Urko,' he said, indicating the burly, square-faced one with silver brush-cut hair. *Gods, the old commander himself.* 'Master Sergeant Braven Tooth.' The fellow gave a short bow, his thick gnarled brows nearly hiding his eyes. 'And, ah . . .'

Of the remaining two, the obvious Malazan veteran inclined his balding tanned pate. 'Temp.'

The last, an old burly Seti warrior, gave a peremptory tilt of his head. 'Sweetgrass.'

Hurl introduced herself, Sergeant Banath and Rell. Liss was nowhere to be seen.

The veteran who'd given the name of Temp raised a hand to Rell. 'You the one who stood against Ryllandaras?'

Rell nodded. Temp and the Seti exchanged a long glance.

'So,' Hurl addressed Urko. 'What can we do for you? Everything's been settled down south, I understand. Shouldn't you be making yourself scarce?'

The Old Guard veteran may not have led part of the siege against Heng, but he had abetted it. Now, he rubbed a gouged and scarred hand over his head, grimaced something resembling discomfort. 'We, ah, come to join up.'

'Join?'

'Yes. 'Gainst Ryllandaras. We want his head.'

'Why?'

'We saw the field hospital, lass,' Braven Tooth said.

Urko nodded. 'Word of it came to me after the battle. I went and saw the remains. Hundreds of wounded soldiers massacred. Unarmed men and women. He made a mistake there. No one does that and gets away with it.'

'We're after him, with or without you,' Temp said, matter-of-fact.

They would too – just these four. Oponn forefend! They may have a chance now.

Hurl gave a noncommittal bob of her head. 'We'll see. Welcome, for now.' She waved them into camp.

She found Liss out walking alone on the prairie. The grass caught at her many-layered skirts. The brisk wind pulled at her thick, matted curls of hair. Her arms, bare, showed thick veins, red angry sores, and bulged with fat. Hurl came close to her, found her gazing down at the ground, prodding the dirt with one sandalled foot. 'What is it?'

She took a deep breath, looked away as if studying the horizon, but her gaze was inward. 'Word came last night from Silk. Storo's dead.'

Hurl stared. 'What?'

Liss's dark eyes captured hers. 'A bone infection. Not caught in time. Ryllandaras's wounds are – notoriously virulent. I'm sorry. They want you back, Hurl. To rebuild. Perhaps you should leave this to Urko and his friends. I know who those two are. They may just be up to it.'

But Hurl lurched away. No. It wasn't true. When she'd last seen him he was alive. Weak, yes. But recovering. This wasn't true. She pushed through the thick grass seeing nothing. They wanted her back? To rebuild? That's a joke. She'd destroyed everything. Released a monster that was the greatest mass murderer of men and women known. And what of this curse? True or not? Of those who'd participated in his release who was now left? She, Silk and Rell. Yet, when Liss had met her, she'd called her *builder*. And her attitude to Rell? Looking back now: a kind of reverence? Admiration? She stopped walking. What if Liss really was a seeress, patroness of seers?

She spun and walked straight up to the woman, who turned her face, would not meet her gaze. 'Have you seen us succeed? Will we defeat Ryllandaras?'

Chin pulled in, her puffed pale face rounded, Liss said slowly, 'I have seen *one* way you may succeed.'

'Good enough.' Hurl went to find Sergeant Banath.

Tracking him down she ordered him to return with the cavalry column. She'd only retain a small guard. He objected, of course. Refused to go. But she would not yield and so eventually, later that day, two columns set out. The far larger one south-west, the much smaller one north-west.

Over the next few days Hurl established a kind of an accord with her mount. She came to accept that perhaps the mare wasn't going to do her in for the affront of actually riding her. And for her part, she would admit that perhaps the breed of horse had some claim to worthy service among humanity.

The morning of the third day Liss announced that he'd been close that night; that he'd been watching them. Hurl imagined he was probably trying to figure out whether they were merely appallingly overconfident or might actually pose a threat. Liss believed he would either strike that next night or dismiss them and return to hunting. She said she intended to draw him in.

Liss gave the orders for the preparations that night. She'd been close to the Seti warrior, Sweetgrass, these last few days, talking often and long, and now the man carried a very different expression on his brutal features from the glower he arrived with. He actually appeared thoughtful – if that were possible.

She had them gather wood through the day for a towering bonfire. As evening came she set the few remaining regulars to guarding the horses and motioned Hurl to accompany them.

Hurl just stared, unmoving.

'Go on, Hurl. You're no veteran like these. You have to stand aside.'

'I can fight as well as anyone.'

'No one questions that. Please. It's important to me.'

Hurl waved to the south where they planned to hobble the horses a safe distance away. 'You want me way over there? Fine! I'll go. But as soon as I hear anything I'm coming!'

'Thank you.'

Urko walked up, nodded to Liss. 'Evening's coming.' He tucked his broad spade-like hands up under his armpits. The man's giant arms were as wide as Hurl's thighs. 'Amaron tells me we should give your plan a go.' He cocked a brow. 'So, what is it?'

'You men should lie low in a broad circle around the bonfire. When Ryllandaras comes, encircle him. Keep him close to the fire. If you keep him close he won't escape.'

'Really?' The man's fleshy mouth drew down in disbelief. 'Just like that?'

'Yes. If you do your part and don't let him past you.'

'Oh, we'll do our part – you can count on that.' And he walked off scratching his head.

Hurl listened to all this with a jaded frown. 'What about you? Where will you be?'

'I'll be at the fire, Hurl.'

'The fire?' Hurl glanced out to the gathering dusk. 'With *him*? What kind of a plan is that? Why should he come to the fire? Didn't you say he's an opportunist? Why not attack the regulars at the horses?'

The woman actually gave a shy, modest smile. 'Because I'll summon him.'

Hurl stared, hardly believing what she was hearing. 'You'll summon him? What kind of nonsense is that? He'll tear you to pieces.'

The woman's smile grew. 'Not so long as I dance, Hurl.'

'*Dance?*' Hurl turned to call to the others. 'Rell, talk some sense to her. You know what he can do!'

Scratching his cheek, Sweetgrass rumbled, 'The old Seti legends say—'

'Oh, shut up!'

Liss took her arm. 'It's all right, Hurl. I can do this. You forget who I am . . . seeress and dawn-dancer.'

Were, you mean. Hurl looked her up and down. 'Liss – sorry to say this, but you are no young thing any more.'

The old woman's laugh was coarse and loud. 'The beauty isn't in me, Hurl. It's in the magic of the dance. Now go – see to the horses.'

Blasted horses! What do I care about horses? But she went.

Rell jogged over, following her. 'Do not worry. If the beast shows, we'll all close in on him and bring him down.'

'Thanks. Watch out for her.'

'Yes.'

'And warn Urko and his boys I'm gonna come – and I'll come loaded!'

'Yes, Hurl. We've all seen your pack.'

'Right. Well, OK then. Burn favour you.'

'We Seguleh do not accept the idea of luck or chance, but thank you just the same.' The man jogged away.

Hurl glared at the horses and her men. *Horses. I can't believe I'm guarding Hood-damned horses.*

Night came. Hurl set out a watch order then sat down to pack her shoulder-bag. Sharpers – as many as she could fit. And two – no, three cussors. That should send him on his way to the Abyss. Every noise from the dark yanked her to her feet. She scanned the dark. Liss's bonfire lit an intervening rise in bright silhouette against the night. She sat back down again, checked her weapons for the umpteenth time.

The horses nickered nervously, shifted, pulled at their staked hobblings. The men moved among them, calming, whispering. Hurl strained silent, listening. Had that been something? A noise? Distant rumbling?

A sudden grating snarl made her jump. The horses shrieked, kicking and rearing, entangling in their ropes. 'See to them!' she shouted and, grabbing her shoulder-bag, ran. Puffing, one arm pumping, the other supporting the stuffed shoulder-bag, she made the rise, started down.

Ahead, between her and the roaring bonfire shooting its sparks into the night sky an elemental vision confronted her: men, arms outstretched, shuffling side to side, closing in on a monster rearing some three times their height, slashing, bellowing. Beyond the fire the shape of Liss, dancing, circling the fire, turning, arms above her head twisting, somehow always opposite the monster no matter which way it lurched to reach.

Hurl stood transfixed. She imagined that if this were a troubadour's song at this time Liss would somehow be transformed into her younger lithe self by the magic of the dance. Her beauty would enchant the monster. But this was no courtly romance. Liss still held her familiar ungainly shape. Her arms were still thick, her waist heavy. Yet the dance itself was beautiful, its movements mesmerizing. From where did the woman draw such grace? And it drew the man-eater. This must be old magic. A ritual of some kind – an ancient calling.

So fascinated was Hurl that she'd forgotten the battle. Six men now closed upon the beast. Roaring his outrage, Ryllandaras swept his long muscled arms to throw them aside. But none fell. His blows slid from firm broad shields, met sharp iron. Rearing once again, he hammered Temp down with a swipe of one long arm. He bent down to snatch the stunned man in his maw, larger than a horse's head, but Braven Tooth was there to cover Temp. He wielded a great two-handed blade with which he deflected raking swings from Ryllandaras. Incredibly, Temp stood once more, shook the shattered ruins of the shield from his arm, drawing a second weapon. The Seti warrior, Sweetgrass, charged in next, slicing savagely, bellowing his own challenge. He leapt in against Ryllandaras's leading leg – a hamstring! But the monster kicked him away; Hurl could almost hear the ribs breaking from where she stood.

Remembering herself, Hurl looked down to the sharper in her hand. She almost laughed at its puniness. No! This won't do at all . . . she started down the gentle slope while fishing for a cussor.

Behind Ryllandaras, surrounding the fire, a rippling in the night now grew where Liss danced. Hurl squinted. What was this? The ritual? For what? But her thoughts flew at the sight of Ryllandaras suddenly straightening with Urko on his back. She almost dropped the cussor to leap her triumph – who would have thought it possible, but who else could have achieved such a thing? The old commander had slid one cabled arm under the beast's jaws. The monster bellowed hoarsely, clawed at the man. The others charged in swinging, thrusting. And Ryllandaras gagged. His blazing carmine eyes rolled. He fell to his knees, then one taloned, misshapen hand. Urko's face was contorted black in effort, one fist closed at his opposite elbow, yanking, crushing. Ryllandaras was gasping for breath. Hurl could not believe what she was seeing; was this possible? The man-jackal, Quon's curse, brother to Treach, strangled by a mere man? She'd heard stories of Urko, of course – the man's feats were legendary, yet Ryllandaras seemed a force of nature.

A wide rake from the man-jackal sent the rest of the men staggering backwards. He reached up behind his head, talons tearing, grasped hold and yanked. Urko was thrown flying overhead, spinning, to disappear into the dark. Hurl heard the crunch of his fall.

Howling his own rage, Amaron charged. A massive blow gouged the man-jackal's side, sending him backwards one step, but the beast captured the weapon and slashed talons in a backhanded swipe across the big man's front that threw him spinning in a dance of torn mail and sheeting blood that stained the trampled grass wet.

Hurl continued to close. Now she could hear their laboured gasping breaths, grunts of pain. Though it appeared to her that Ryllandaras would slaughter them all, the beast tried to dash away then, only to meet Rell who fended him back into the circle, blades rippling and flashing in the firelight. Braven Tooth completed the encirclement, aiding Rell. Ryllandaras whirled with his astonishing speed: his jaws slashed the man's shoulder as he ducked, sending him stumbling backwards, bellowing his agony. Sweetgrass was up again; the man limped, hugged his chest, and his chin was dark with coughed-up blood but he closed, a long-knife in each hand.

And Liss emerged from behind the fire, beckoned to Ryllandaras's back. The beast spun – alarmed, it seemed to Hurl. It slashed at Liss but she wavered away, teasing, just beyond reach. She seemed to ripple as if a heat mirage. The glimmering band of light encircling the bonfire now glowed a gold and crimson brighter than the flames. Ryllandaras flinched from the radiance, turned away to face the remaining men. Temp, a longsword in one hand and heavy parrying gauche in the other, held each out wide, hunching low. Rell stretched his arms as well, one of the twin longswords almost touching Temp's blade. Sweetgrass also held his arms out, shuffling side to side.

Rearing back to his full massive height the monster opened its black-lipped jaws and loosed an infuriated eruption of frustrated blood-lust that stunned Hurl where she stood. It leapt upon Sweetgrass, hammering him to the ground, but Temp was there to bull him back like a man holding up a falling tower. A slash from Ryllandaras's black talons raked the mail and banded armour from the man's front and he fell to his knees. Rell lunged in, jabbing, thrusting, and the man-jackal yielded a step howling his agony. Its eyes rolled now, seeking escape, it seemed to Hurl. Rell pressed on, feet shuffling forward, blades dancing like liquid flame in the brilliance now bathing Ryllandaras's back.

The beast glanced behind, its eyes widened white all round. Rell lunged, one blade thrusting deep within the monster's furred stomach. Shrieking, it tottered backwards, sent one last swipe across Rell, ripping the helm from his head and spinning him from his feet. The effort threw the beast back as well and it fell into the circle of rippling light to disappear.

Hurl stared, cussor heavy in her sweaty hand. Not one remained standing. Only Temp on his knees, reeling side to side, head sunk forward. The spinning coruscating ring, or gate, or whatever it was that Liss had invoked, snapped away in an eruption of air that blew a storm of sparks from the low embers of the bonfire.

Hurl staggered forward. 'Liss? Rell? Liss?' Of the shamaness there was no sign in the dim glow of the fire. A figure came lurching out of the dark: Urko, holding himself tightly. Hurl ran to support him. He grasped her shoulder in a grip that shot lances of pain up and down her side. He peered blearily at her from a face gleaming with blood. The face turned to examine the battle. He blinked. 'Coulda used a few more men, hey? Like maybe the Fifth Army.'

'Take it easy now.'

He frowned at her, tilting his head down. 'You take it easy.'

She saw that she carried the cussor tucked under her an arm like a helmet. 'Sorry.' She gently eased the man to the ground and just as gently slipped away the munition. 'Are you OK?' *Gods, what a stupid question!*

But he waved her off. 'Go see to the others.'

The nearest man was Amaron. Dead, torn open across his vitals. Reports of hooves hammering the ground pulled Hurl to her feet. A column of cavalry closing at a frantic pace. Well, nothing she could do about that. Braven Tooth was closest then: he lay with a hand pressed to his wound, blood soaking the ground beneath his shoulder and lacerated arm. Though ghostly pale, his face glistening with sweat, he motioned her on with a curt jerk of his head.

She came to Temp; the man was struggling drunkenly to stand. She helped him up, groaned beneath his solid weight. He still held his weapons but his armour hung from him in lacerated tatters, clattering and swinging loose. 'Gods damn him,' he kept repeating. 'Gods damn that *thing*.' His wild gaze found her and he grinned his pain. 'If you don't mind, lass, I'll have me a sit down. I think I'm gonna retire.'

'Yes, go ahead.' She eased him down.

Next was the Seti, Sweetgrass. He was breathing but shallowly, wetly. His eyes tracked her when she moved. He mouthed something to her. She bent her head close. '. . . She did it . . .' came the faintest whisper.

Hurl nodded, 'Yes. Yes, she did.'

'. . . Maybe she really was . . . really . . .'

Hurl soothed him with a hand on his hot brow. 'Yes – maybe.' *Or maybe she was just a crazy old mage.*

The guards came running down the hillside, gesturing, while the column of Seti horsemen overtook them. The riders threw themselves from their mounts, ran to the wounded. Hurl saw among them many who looked like shamans and shamanesses, but none carried any animal totems that she could see. She left them to it as a number came to Sweetgrass and she crossed to Rell.

For some reason she'd come to him last. The moment she realized this she knew why. Something in the way he'd fallen. So limp. So . . . final. He lay now as he'd struck the earth. She knelt on her knees at his side. He was dead; his throat torn out and scarred face further gashed by the flesh-rending talons of the man-jackal. *Oh, Rell. I am so sorry.* She smoothed his ragged, newly grown hair. *This was not the way it was supposed to happen. Heng had taken you as its new protector. You were to take her place in the city temple. Usher in a long and prosperous future . . . yet here you lie. You gave your life to end the curse. Perhaps that was what they sensed. That somehow you would end it for them. This was just not the way anyone wanted it to happen.*

What will we do? Go on, I suppose. Rebuild. Ha! Build. And only Silk and I are left. We alone survived the curse. If there ever was one. Yet there was, wasn't there? Ryllandaras himself.

She stood, walked the grounds around the dying fire just to be sure but found no sign of Liss. *So she succeeded where all others had failed. She'd delivered the Seti of their curse. And hadn't she given her own? What had it been . . . ?*

Seti shamanesses came and spoke to her but she ignored them, shaking her head. *No, not yet. What had it been? Ah, yes! That they would wander lost until they prayed for her forgiveness! Well, Lissarathel or not, the woman had just assured herself a place in their pantheon, or at least their legends. Certainly their prayers.*

She rubbed her face, glanced around, sighing her exhaustion. Hours till dawn. She waved the corporal of the guard detachment to her. He ran up, saluted smartly, his eyes hugely wide. She motioned to Rell. 'Wrap him up. We'll return him for burial. And bring the swords. They have to be returned. It's time to go home.'

EPILOGUE

A BENT FIGURE DRAPED IN RAGS EMERGED FROM A SAGGING, dilapidated tent of hides and felt blankets. He hobbled down to a broad white sand beach, leaning heavily on a stick of driftwood, pausing occasionally to catch his breath. He came to the surf where a turquoise lagoon washed up weakly in a thin line of spume. An armoured giant of a man lay half-buried in sand at the surf's edge. The bent figure stood looking down for a time then gave the figure a sharp rap with his stick. The man gasped, fumbling awkwardly, pushed himself heavily to his feet. He yanked off his tall helm to let it fall into the wet sand, clutched at his neck just beneath his blond beard. His eyes filled with wonder.

'Yes, you are healed, Skinner.'

The man, Skinner, towered over the bent figure. 'You answered . . .' he rumbled.

'Of course. Have I not been nearby for some time now? I know you sensed my aid here and there, yes? I have had my eye on you, Skinner of the Avowed.' The figure, his shape obscured in the layered hanging rags, gestured to his tent. 'The question is, what can you do . . . for *me*?'

Skinner ignored the invitation, peered up and down the shore. 'Where are my people?'

Turning away, the figure shuffled haltingly back up the strand. 'They are being held in abeyance until we have reached an accord, Skinner.'

'We have an accord, Chained One,' Skinner growled, straightening and wincing. He still touched at his neck.

The figure glanced back, his rag-wrapped head bent almost to the sands. 'Oh? We do?'

'Yes.' Skinner studied the shore, squinted in the dazzling light reflected from the white sands. 'Here are my terms – I deliver to you myself and some forty Avowed and in return I claim the title of King.'

'Oh? You *claim* it?'

Skinner drew off his gauntlets, let them fall on to the sands. He nodded, his gaze hooded, almost sleepy, on the bent-double figure. 'Yes. It is mine.'

'Good.' The figure hobbled off. 'It's about time *somebody* took it.'

'My people!'

A negligent wave of a misshapen hand over his shoulder and the figure ducked within the low sagging tent. Skinner turned to examine the surf. In ones and twos men and women appeared washed up in the lazy waves. He went to help pull them up on to the strand.

*   *   *

It was night, and the battlefield of gouged, naked soil and blackened stubble was empty but for sniffing, hopeful jackals and the odd human scavenger searching for loot. A man in a mail coat under laced leathers stood motionless, his head lowered. His long black hair blew about his scarred dark face.

'Greetings, Dessembrae,' spoke a nearby gnawed skull, once buried but since dug up by scavengers. 'And I say Dessembrae for I see you are here now in that aspect.'

The man let go a long breath, rolled his neck to ease its tension. 'A long time, Hood.'

'Indeed. Dare I say how just like those old times?'

The man's face twisted in loathing. 'No, you may not.'

'Yet here you are – why are you here?'

'I am bearing witness to a death. A soldier's death.'

'How . . . commonplace.'

'He was no common soldier, though he knew it not. Had the Seti remained he would have out-generalled the Imperial forces, and had his bodyguard been a fraction of an instant faster, would have proven victorious over the Guard as well. He would have made High Fist and risen to become one of the greatest commanders ever thrown up by the Empire. But all that potential died here today, unrealized. Known to none.'

'I know, Dessembrae. I took him.'

'Yes. As you take everyone – eventually. And I will not ask what all others ask of you – why? Because what I have come to understand is that there is no *why*. To ask why is to impose expectations on mute

689

existence – expectations it is in no way obliged to meet or even extend. And so I make no more, ask no more.'

The skull was silent for a time – as skulls are. 'So that is the course of your thoughts,' said Hood, and the man believed he detected a note of . . . surprise.

'What of it?'

Silence.

We will speak again, I promise you.

*   *   *

Lurin, Amagin and Shurll were out throwing stones at the Deadhouse. That was what everyone in Malaz city called the old abandoned building in its creepy grounds of trees that never grew leaves in any season. They'd always thrown stones at it, and their mothers and fathers before them had tossed their share as well. This night the streets gleamed from a cold rain that had swept in from the south. Lurin, barefoot, felt the chill so he put an extra effort into his arm to warm himself up.

'Did you see that?' he called to Amagin and Shurll. 'Went right in that window – I swear.'

'Didn't,' Amagin sniffed.

'Did too!' He looked to Shurll for support but the older girl was just hugging herself, staring off down the street where it descended to the waterfront, the wharf and the sea glimmering beyond. She'd been doing that more often these days. 'It did too, Shurll,' he called. She shrugged her bony shoulders.

Amagin held out a stone, grinning, his nose wet and running. 'No way you can hit that window.'

Lurin snatched it from him. 'You'll see.'

He held the stone out before himself to sight on the window – heavier than he'd have chosen – Amagin always picked poor throwing stones which was why he couldn't hit any target to save his life. Tongue tucked firmly between his teeth, he drew back, raised one foot and threw.

The instant he released something changed on the grounds. A man now stood where Lurin couldn't recall ever having seen anyone walk. The man's hand snapped up then held something to his pale face. While they gaped, dumbfounded, he walked up to the wall near them.

Amagin was already sobbing. Shurll stared, immobile. Lurin flinched, tensed to run but unable. The man's clothes hung open in sliced folds. Dark wetness gleamed beneath down his torso and arms. Scars gleamed also at his neck like lines of pearl. He held up Lurin's stone between thumb and forefinger, leaned over the wall.

'Run.'

Blubbering, Amagin ran. Lurin threw himself at Shurll. She had not moved, perhaps not even blinked. He wrapped his arms around her, buried his face in her chest, too terrified to look. They were dead. It was a spirit come to drag them away to the Abyss. He waited for that bony touch that was Hood's beckon.

But after a time, heart in a frenzy, nothing happened. Shurll made quiet soothing sounds while her hands brushed his shoulders.

'Welcome, Topper!' Lurin heard the spirit call, his voice distant.

He dared a glance: the spirit, or man, had moved away and now faced the low front wall.

'Don't be a fool, Cowl,' another voice answered.

Lurin turned completely, pressed his back to Shurll, glanced up to her; she watched, avid, her eyes huge.

Cowl, the one within the grounds of the Deadhouse, gestured an invitation to the other with his blades. 'Come in – let us finish our debate here. Who will have the last word, do you think?'

The other, Topper, stepped into view: long tangled white hair, dark-faced, clothes hanging rags. But his eyes! Angular and bright like lamps. He shrugged. 'By my hand or the House's . . . is of no matter to me.'

Cowl spread his arms wide. 'I choose my own fate, Topper. I remain undefeated. You lack the will to challenge me? So be it – the defeat is yours.'

'Dancer took you.'

Cowl's eyes rolled as he made a show of considering. He pointed a blade to his neck. 'I call this a draw.'

'You are mistaking desperation for defiance. You only fool yourself.'

'And you are a coward.'

Topper motioned to the grounds. 'Time is short. Flee while you can.'

Lurin glanced across the yard and jerked, terrified. The tree branches were moving. Never had he seen those black limbs shiver or bend, even in the strongest of storms. Steam as of freshly turned earth climbed from the heaps that littered the grounds. The heavy mist gathered to carpet the yard.

Cold like a winter morning bit at Lurin. He shivered uncontrollably.

'Fool!' Topper called. 'It will have you! Flee, now!'

Cowl stumbled as if something had yanked upon him. But his smile was fixed, his teeth bright and sharp. 'I choose defiance!' he yelled, wild fever in his voice.

'You choose despair.'

Falling, the one called Cowl went on one knee. He laughed, low at first, but climbing in pitch and volume until it rang so loud it drowned out a comment from Topper. And then Lurin's skin crawled in horror as the one named Cowl appeared to sink – yes, sink straight down into the steaming earth as if pulled. 'Come join me!' he shouted, laughing mockingly.

Topper lunged forward to grip the top of the stone wall. 'Fool! You are Avowed! You will never die!' The man sounded genuinely horrified.

Cowl's answer to that was to burst forth with even greater fevered, ardent laughter – exulting, darkly triumphant – the mirth of a man gone truly mad. Lurin buried his face once more in Shurll's chest. Eventually, the peals choked off, fell to silence. When Lurin looked back the grounds were empty.

His gaze caught the one called Topper staring directly at them. Lurin's breath caught and he froze. The eyes burned in the night as he'd heard some jewels do. Then the man bowed, an arm across his stomach, the other held out. Stepping back he disappeared into darkness.

Eventually, Lurin found he could breathe again. He peered up at Shurll, whispered: 'What happened?'

And she, looking off into the night, her gaze so distant, stroking his head, murmured repeatedly, 'Nothing. It's all right. Nothing happened. It was nothing.'

* * *

In the morning Talia demanded he recite it all again – from the mad ride through the Abyss, to the battle, and Laseen's funeral cortège to Cawn – even the dull journey by coastal merchantman to Unta.

'And the Imperial Funeral?' she asked.

Rillish laughed, sitting up. 'Gods no. We aren't invited to that.'

'But you're a member of the official Wickan delegation to the Throne!'

Rillish leaned back, tucked a rolled blanket behind his back. 'Believe me – I am no more welcome in Unta than the Wickans themselves. We are there on sufferance only.'

'And this Mallick creature is to really succeed Laseen?'

'By unanimous acclaim of the Assembly and all regional governors, Fists and all.'

She shook her head, her brows crimping. 'And I've never even heard of the man.'

'You should get out more, sergeant.'

She made a face. He pushed the sheets off her belly, eased his head on to her stomach. 'Huh. Funny . . . You don't look pregnant.'

'Not *yet*, you fool! Gods, you men.'

'Humph . . . If you say so.' He gently pressed a hand there on her belly. *Son or daughter – you might grow up in a world where all this is but an ugly memory. And perhaps those decades from now if I am still around I will be able to show you all that might be yours by right of your name. And perhaps I will be able to give you more than my love. Though I know that even that is precious enough. And more than some.*

* * *

Proprietor, merchant, innkeeper and ex-Imperial sailor, Aron Hul knew a dangerous man when he saw one and this newcomer sent all his nerves jangling the moment he dismounted from his well-fed and well-shod horse that bore new, well-oiled tack. Aron noted the man's soft leather boots, the studded leather wrappings at his legs, his fitted armour of boiled cuirass, vambraces, the twin ivory-handled sabres worn high under his arms, and his rich travelling cloak. But what fixed his attention was the extraordinary scar running across the man's face from left temple, notching the bridge of his flattened nose, to mar his right cheek. The man stood for a time in front of his trading establishment, stared south to the Idryn flowing so brown and wide on its way to the Bay of Cawn, and the Nap Sea. Then he turned and entered the trading post.

Aron quickly set out his most expensive wine and spirits. The man sat at one of his two tables. 'Yes, sir?' Aron asked from behind his counter.

'A drink.'

'I have Talian winter wine, spirits of juniper berry from Bloor.'

'The Talian.'

'Excellent, sir.' He brought out a glass and the bottle. The man pressed a gold Imperial to the gouged slats of the table. Aron almost tipped the bottle. An Imperial Sun – didn't see too many of those

693

these days. 'You don't have anything smaller, do you, sir? We're just a small river station, you know.'

The man leaned back, smiled in a way that Aron knew was meant to reassure him. 'I know. It's yours for the bottle and a little information.'

Aron allowed his brows to rise as if in dubious surprise. 'Really, sir? Information, you say? Out here? What could we possibly know out here?'

He gestured vaguely to the river. 'Oh, travel. Shipments and cargo. People coming and going. That sort of thing.'

Aron's nerves now reached a screaming pitch; he kept his good-natured smile. 'Really, sir? Such as?'

'I'm looking for someone who may have come through here about a month ago. During the troubles. A young woman. She would have been travelling alone. You'd remember her if you saw her, if you know what I mean,' and he winked.

Aron walked back to his counter. 'A woman, you say . . .' He shook his head. 'What did she look like?'

'Slim, dark hair. A pretty face. As I said, a woman men notice. Hear anything like that? She may have hired a boat to take her upriver.'

That hired hand who came through on his run south to Cawn – what was his name? Jestan? Jeth? Damn it to Hood!

Aron rubbed his stubbled cheeks; his gaze flicked to the gold Sun shining, winking, on the table. 'I may have heard something about a female passenger on one of the riverboats . . .'

The man's hand covered the coin. He lost his smile. Sighing, he pushed himself up from the table.

Jhal! It was Jhal! What had he said? He'd been up at the Falls transferring cargo and he joked about a boatman fawning over some passenger of his—

The man had come to the counter. He pushed the gold Sun across. 'Think harder. Because you can stare all you like but this coin won't multiply itself.'

Aron licked his lips, swallowed. He smiled nervously. 'I'm trying to remember, sir.'

'Good. Take your time.' He returned to his table, came back with the glass and bottle, poured another drink and slid it across.

Nodding his thanks Aron took it and tossed the entire glass back. *He had to open his D'rek blasted mouth! Now there was no going back. This one doesn't care about the money. This is about more than coin. No one sends a man like this out when only money is in question.* And the man was watching him carefully, his eyes lazy, calm . . . patient.

Aron cleared his throat. He pressed a rag to his face. *Who would have been going upriver then? Oddfoot? No, he's south. Cat? No, idiot! It was a man. Old Pick? He won't go past Heng. Tullen! Must've been Tullen. Been gone for ages now.*

'I heard something about a boatman who'd picked up a woman at about that time . . .'

'Yes?'

'That he'd taken up past Heng.'

The man nodded, frowning his appreciation. 'And do you have a name for this boatman?'

Ask, man. Those that don't ask don't get! 'Well, sir. You wouldn't have another of those gold Suns on you somewhere, would you?' and he tried his easiest smile.

Sighing loudly, the man hung his head. Raising it, he peered about the shop for a time then his gaze returned to Aron's. 'Tell me, Factor. When was the last time the Imperial assessors came through here?'

Bastard! Aw, no. Not the assessors . . .

The man gave a slow solemn nod.

'Tullen. Old Tullen. Boats with his boys. A fine, quiet sort, never made any trouble for anyone.'

'Thank you . . .?'

'Aron Hul. And you . . . sir?'

Pausing at the door the man shrugged. 'Moss. Eustan Moss. Good day to you, Factor.'

Aron went to the oiled hide that served as his one window. The man, Moss – as if that was his real name – mounted, gently heeled his mount and rode off upriver. *Oh, Tullen, what have I sent your way? I'm sorry, old fellow.* Then he remembered the coin. He went back to the counter, snatched it up and examined it. Looked authentic. He bit at it, as he'd heard you could tell the purity of the gold by its softness. Problem was he'd only ever bitten one other. He quickly thrust it away in the pouch around his neck. Briefly, his thoughts touched on this woman. Who might she be? A runaway wife or daughter of some noble? Imagine that! Some noblewoman on Tullen's leaky old boat! How unlikely. No, probably just someone who knew something or had heard something she shouldn't have, and so she ran. Some serving girl probably, or governor's mistress. Best he keep his nose out of business like that.

Thinking of serving girls . . . Aron corked the Talian and brought out a bottle of cheap Kanese red, filled the glass. Maybe he could swing one of them now. A young one. Not so bright and easy to intimidate. He drank the wine, smiling. With long hair.

* * *

Hand on the gunwale, feet spread for balance, Jemain made his way to the bow, a cup of steaming tea in one hand. The *Ardent* pitched suddenly in the savage high seas and the boiling liquid seared his hand but he carried on, teeth clamped against pain. He came to crouch next to a man who sat hunched, head in hands, fingers pushed through his dark filthy hair.

'Drink this, Bars!' Jemain shouted over the roar of waves and gusting wind. 'It's hot! Come, you must have *something*!'

But the man still would not look up, would not even drink, let alone eat. Three days and three nights now. How long could one of these Avowed go without food or water? Corlo had speculated perhaps forever.

Jemain lowered his head once more. 'We've entered the Cut, you know! A Westerly has taken us. Corlo says we may meet the demons who live in these waters!'

No response, just slow anguished rocking.

Shaking his head, Jemain set the cup down between the man's bare feet. He retreated to the companionway, went to talk to Corlo. He found him smoking a pipe in a hammock. 'Still won't answer.'

Corlo took the pipe from his mouth. 'No. He won't.'

'You're a mage – why don't you do something? Ease his madness?'

A snort. 'Not without his permission.'

'So we can do nothing for him?'

'We might pray for the Riders to come. That would bring him out of it.'

Jemain couldn't tell if the man was serious or not. 'No, thank you.' He stared upwards for a time at the timbers overhead, listened to the storm batter the *Ardent*. 'I don't understand. What happened?'

'We're too late. Missed what we'd come all this way for. All we'd endured . . .' He frowned, studied his white clay pipe. 'We lost a lot of friends. He thinks he should've been there to help. Blames himself.'

'And you?'

A shrug from Corlo. 'It's different for me. I'm not Avowed. The connection's not so strong.'

'I thought you were – Avowed.'

'No. Next best thing, though. I'm First Investiture. First round of recruiting after the Vow.'

'Oh, I see.' Or thought he did – he wasn't sure, though he suspected that recruitment probably happened far longer ago than this man's seeming forty or so years would imply.

Another of Bars' party, Garren, thumped down the companionway, shouted, 'Ship sighted!'

It was a vessel of a cut and design Jemain had never seen before – which wasn't surprising, given that he'd never sailed these seas before. But he was surprised at the ease with which it rode the high, steep waves here in the Sea of Storms – the Cut, Corlo called it. Long and low, hull tarred black. Square-sailed, single-masted, bearing a brutal ram below the waterline that breasted each wave, sloughing water and foam, as the vessel pitched. And, incredibly, the galley boasted four ranks of oarsmen. Surely it would've keeled over in such a sea.

'Who are they?' he shouted to Corlo.

The mage's face was grim. 'Looks like a ship out of Mare. We have to run.'

Jemain almost laughed, but wouldn't show the despair that vessel struck in his heart. *No chance of outrunning that*. He yelled: 'Hard larboard! Put the stern to them, Watt!'

'Aye, sir.'

'Man the deck! Ready crossbows!'

The crew lurched from side to side, stowing equipment, distributing what few weapons they possessed. Jemain made his way to the stern; Corlo followed. There, he watched through the waves where the vessel appeared in glimpses between the grey waters and the equally grey overcast sky. It was swinging around them, nimble as a gull, while the *Ardent*, a single-banked slave galley, so battered by its long ocean crossing, wallowed like a log.

It was going to ram.

'Brace yourselves!' To Watt: 'Ready to swing to port.'

The old tillerman clamped his toothless gums together, his lips wrinkling. 'We'll give it a go, sir.'

Corlo tapped his shoulder, gestured to the bow. Bars was now standing, his hands clamped on the gunwale, gaze fixed upon the closing vessel. 'Pity the Marese, maybe, hey?' he said.

Pity us first. Jemain, a lifelong seaman, could only stare in awful appreciation of the skill and seamanship as the vessel bore down upon them, cresting the last wave just in time to lurch downward, adding the impetus of its weight to the thrust of the blunt bronze-sheathed ram cutting the water and throwing a curled wake higher than the vessel itself.

Beautiful. 'Port!' Watt threw the arm sideways; the *Ardent* only began to respond before the ship was upon them. *Too slow – no chance. No chance at all.*

The blow drove the *Ardent* sideways. It snatched Jemain from where he stood to throw him against the gunwale and over. The frigid water stung as if it were boiling. It stole what little breath he possessed. Vision and sensations came in glimpses as his head broached the surface. The *Ardent* wallowing, side caved in. Men tumbling overboard. Bars at the canted bow, fists raised in rage. Then frothed grey water as he spun in the waves. Frigid, life-sapping water numbing his arms, face and legs. And he sinking, weakening in the all-embracing cold. The numbness spreading to take his vision and thoughts.

He awoke coughing and spluttering on hard decking. Limp. Limbs useless. Other crewmen from the *Ardent* lay about like gaffed fish. Mare crewmen in dark leather armour were gathered around one particular netted man, truncheons rising and falling, beating and beating. Seeing him awake, one crewman came over, wiped his brow, panting. 'You are of Genabaris, yes?' he asked in a strange mangling of the South Confederacy dialect.

Jemain nodded mutely.

'We usually capture ships – except Malazan – but yours was such an insult we had to sink it.' He smiled as if that somehow made up for it. 'My apology.' He wiped his brow again, taking a deep breath, and gestured his truncheon to the netted, now limp, crewman from the *Ardent*, whose identity Jemain could guess. 'You are all going to the Korelri. Especially that one. He would not go down – good thing the waters had done half our work, hey? We should get a good price for him.' He smiled his white teeth again. 'I think he would do well upon the wall.'

GLOSSARY

Terms and Titles

The Agatii: among the Seguleh, their first thousand ranked warriors

Ascendant: individuals of great power/influence

Baya Gul: Seti Goddess of divination and guide to their sun mysteries

Brethren: term among the Crimson Guard for their fallen comrades

Cadre mages: Malazan organization of mages/warlocks/sorcerers, many of whom serve in the military ranks

Deck of Dragons/the Dragons: deck of cards, their identities unfixed, used in divination

D'ivers: a high order of shape-shifting

Eleint: term for the elder race of dragons

First Investiture: those of the first round of recruitment by the Crimson Guard subsequent to its Vow, with Second and Third following

Fist: Malazan title for commander, military or administrative

High Fist: Malazan title for a regional or campaign commander

Old Guard: those whose Imperial service goes back to Emperor Kellanved

Prevost: old Quon Talian title for a military officer, roughly equivalent to captain

The Seguleh: a fierce isolationist island people off the coast of Genabackis

Shalmanat: protectress of Li Heng

Soldier of Light: a position among the divinatory deck, the Deck of Dragons

Soletaken: shape-shifting

Sword of the Empire/First Sword: Imperial champion, Malazan and Imass title

Talons: an organization of Imperial assassins begun by Dancer, Emperor Kellanved's cohort and bodyguard

Thel Akai: 'First People', first-born of Mother Earth, ancestors of Thelomen, Toblakai and Trell races

Veils: Crimson Guard assassins, begun by Cowl in response to the Imperial Talons

The Warrens

The Elder Warrens

Kurald Galain: the Elder Warren of Darkness

Kurald Emurlahn: the Elder Warren of Shadow

Kurald Liosan: the Elder Warren of Light

Kurald Thyrllan: another name for the Elder Warren of Light

Omtose Phellack: the Elder Jaghut Warren of Ice

Tellann: the Elder Imass Warren of Fire

Starvald Demelain: the Eleint Warren, the first Warren

'The Paths' (those Warrens accessible to humans)

Thyr: the Path of Light

Denul: the Path of Healing

Hood's Path: the Path of Death

Serc: the Path of Sky

Meanas: the Path of Shadow and Illusion

D'riss: the Path of the Earth

Ruse: the Path of the Sea

Rashan: the Path of Darkness

Mockra: the Path of the Mind

Telas: the Path of Fire

The Deck of Dragons

High House Life
King
Queen (Queen of Dreams)
Champion
Priest
Herald

Soldier
Weaver

High House Death
King (Hood)
Queen
Knight (once Dassem Ultor, now Baudin)
Magi
Herald
Soldier
Spinner
Mason
Virgin

High House Light
King
Queen
Champion (Osserc)
Priest
Captain
Soldier (Kyle)
Seamstress
Builder
Maiden

High House Dark
King
Queen
Knight (Anomander Rake)
Magi
Captain
Soldier
Weaver
Mason
Wife

High House Shadow
King (Shadowthrone/Ammanas)
Queen
Assassin (the Rope/Cotillion)
Magi
Hound

High House Chains
The King in Chains (Skinner)
The Consort (Poliel)
Reaver
Knight (Toblakai)
The Seven of the Dead Fires (the Unbound)
Cripple
Leper
Fool

Unaligned
Oponn
Obelisk (Burn)
Crown
Sceptre
Orb
Throne
Chain
Master of the Deck (Ganoes Paran)

Elder Races

Tiste Andii: Children of Darkness
Tiste Edur: Children of Shadow
Tiste Liosan: Children of Light
T'lan Imass: ancient non-human race thought to be extinct
Jaghut: ancient non-human race thought to be extinct
Forkrul Assail: ancient non-human race thought to be extinct
K'Chain Che'Malle: ancient non-human race thought to be extinct
Eres/Eres'al: an ancient race thought legendary
The Eleint: the Elder race of dragons
The Trell: a non-human pastoral nomadic people
The Barghast: a non-human pastoral nomadic people
The Thelomen Toblakai: a non-human pastoral nomadic people
The Teblor: a non-human pastoral nomadic people
The Thel Akai: a forgotten people, progenitors of Thelomen, Toblakai, Teblor and perhaps Barghast